The Goebbels Diaries

The Goebbels Diaries

1939–1941

Goebbels, Joseph

Translated and edited by

FRED TAYLOR

G. P. Putnam's Sons
New York

Library of Congress Cataloging in Publication Data

Goebbels, Joseph, 1897–1945.
  The Goebbels diaries, 1939–1941.

  Translation of a part of Tagebücher 1924–1945
entitled: Tagebücher 1939–1941.
  Includes index.
  1. Goebbels, Joseph, 1897–1945. 2. Statesmen—
Germany—Biography. 3. World War, 1939–1945—
Germany. 4. Propaganda, German. 5. Germany—
Politics and government—1933–1945. I. Taylor,
Fred. II. Title.
DD247.G6A2913 1983   943.086   82-18574
ISBN 0-399-12763-1

Printed in the United States of America

Contents

List of Illustrations   vii

Foreword by John Keegan   ix

Translator's Note   xiii

Map of Europe, showing extent of German Occupation by
December 1941   xiv–xv

PART ONE: 1939   3

PART TWO: 1940   83

PART THREE: 1941   227

Appendix I: Chronology of Goebbels' Life   455

Appendix II: Chronology of The Goebbels Diaries 1939–41   457

Index   461

Illustrations

Between pages 142 and 143

Goebbels (*Barnaby's Picture Library*)

Lida Baarova (*National Film Archive/Stills Library*)

Goebbels and Magda at the Berlin Press Ball, 30 January 1939 (*Popperfoto*)

Goebbels broadcasting a message to Germany's children (*Keystone Press Agency*)

Goebbels and Magda and their eldest children with Hitler (*Bilderdienst Süddeutscher Verlag*)

Goebbels and a daughter greeting the Fuhrer (*Popperfoto*)

The Goebbels family during the war years (*Ullstein Bilderdienst*)

Goebbels at his desk in the Propaganda Ministry (*Popperfoto*)

Goebbels addressing a Party rally (*Keystone*)

Goebbels launching the 1939/40 Winter Aid Fund in the Berlin *Sportpalast* (*Keystone*)

Buglers summoning Berliners to donate clothing for the Winter Aid Fund (*Popperfoto*)

Goebbels at the *Theater des Volkes*, with Robert Ley (*Ullstein*)

With Alessandro Pavolini (*Imperial War Museum*)

Giving an interview to the press, 1939 (*Internationale Bilderagentur*)

Goebbels at the Ufa film studios, May 1939 (*Popperfoto*)

Hitler reviewing SS troops (*Popperfoto*)

Between pages 302 and 303

'Cultural workers' from Alsace being received by Goebbels, November 1940 (*IBA*)

Staff at the Propaganda Ministry packing books for Argentina (*Popperfoto*)

Goebbels and Ley with Käthe Haack, February 1940 (*Ullstein*)

Goebbels in Danzig, with Albert Forster, 1940 (*Ullstein*)

Hitler Youth parade (*Barnaby's Picture Library*)

Hitler and Goebbels at the Berghof (*Barnaby's Picture Library*)

Goebbels with Eva Braun and Albert Speer at the Berghof (*National Archives*)

Goebbels in Paris (*Keystone*)

Goebbels at the Ufa Palace, with General Keitel and Leopold Gutterer, 1940 (*Keystone*)

U-boat commander Günther Prien, with Grand Admiral Raeder (*Imperial War Museum*)

Prien in the conning-tower of his U-47 (*Ullstein*)

Goebbels in Hamburg, 1941 (*Ullstein*)

The Nazi élite: Hess, Göring, Streicher, Goebbels (*Keystone*)

At the Kroll Opera House: Seldte, Kerrl, Rust, Gurtner, Funk, von Neurath, Goebbels, Frick, Ribbentrop, Hess (*BBC Hulton Picture Library*)

Goebbels with Reich Student Leader Scheel and Frau Scholtze-Klink (*Ullstein*)

Goebbels meeting a 'War Reporting Company' of the Waffen-SS, January 1941 (*Keystone*)

Goebbels with Emil Jannings at the première of *Ohm Krüger*, April 1941 (*Keystone*)

Goebbels broadcasting, 22 June 1941 (*IBA*)

Foreword by John Keegan

Joseph Goebbels, Hitler's Minister for Public Enlightenment and Propaganda from the 'Seizure of Power' in 1933 until his suicide in the Reich Chancellery bunker in April 1945, was an unflagging and voluminous diarist. Part of every one of his overfilled days was set aside for the writing – later, when he had found a stenographer who could keep pace with his breakneck delivery, for the dictation – of a long diary entry; and, among the other arrangements he made when he had decided to imitate Hitler's form of exit from life (they included the poisoning of his six children) was a scheme for the safeguarding of the thousands of pages his diaries had by then come to fill. They were copied in miniature on photographic plates, which were buried in woodland outside Berlin; the originals remained in the Reich Chancellery. Both sets of records were later recovered in part, most by the Red Army, and have since had a circuitous passage through the hands of historians. Sections from 1942–3 and 1945 have already been published in the West, together with longer passages from the pre-war period. This series, the authenticity of which has been established by the Wiener Library, forms the largest portion yet to be printed.

For the Anglo-Saxon reader, it offers a fascinating and entirely novel angle of vision on the outbreak and opening years of the Second World War. Albert Speer's memoirs also presented a new look at Nazism; they were very accurately entitled *Inside the Third Reich*. But Goebbels' diaries track the focus closer: they might be called *Inside Hitler's Capital*. For Berlin was, in a variety of senses, Goebbels' home town. It was not his birthplace. He was a small-town boy from the Rhineland, son of a lower middle-class Catholic family, whose traditional piety and simple decency were for him as constricting as the humble streets in which he grew up. Berlin rather was his spiritual home, where he found the room in which his brilliant intelligence and brazen tongue could compensate for his lameness, tiny stature and charity boy's education. He was made Nazi Gauleiter of the city in 1926, elected a Berlin deputy to the Reichstag in 1928 and took an enormous pride in his 'Ten Year Struggle' to transform the capital into a Nazi fief. But, above all, he immersed himself from the start of his party work there in what today we would call its 'media life'. Berlin was the centre of Germany's newspaper, broadcasting, film and publishing industries – and also of the news and gossip which gave media people their raw material. Goebbels thrived on it and eventually dominated it. Hitler had always had the keenest appreciation of the importance of feeding the media with what they and he both wanted: he made news, in every sense of the term. But Goebbels went further. He managed news. Hitler, the self-declared 'artist', who had chosen politics as his means of self-expression, lacked the taste or application for anything more than the occasional sensational display of emotion, in particular the great set-piece speech which mesmerised the mob and left him drained of nervous energy. Goebbels, on the other hand, though a galvanic speaker in his own right, directed his overflowing energy into the day-by-day and minute-by-minute organisation of the means by which news was transmuted into influence and then into power.

His first great days in the management of news were behind him when these diaries open. Those had been during the *Kampfzeit*, the 'era of struggle' as the Nazis called it, when he had founded newspapers, organised the events which filled their columns and written or inspired the devastating attacks on Hitler's enemies within and without the party that unchallengeably ensured his hero's mastership first of it, and then of Germany. This 'heroic' period persisted beyond the Seizure of Power itself, into the months when Hitler was consolidating his hold on the state and extending his grip to secure every institution of public life – the universities and professions as well as the trade unions and youth movements. After this *Gleichschaltung*, the pace and intensity of Goebbels' propaganda work, at least at home, diminished. The need to sell the new régime abroad naturally grew in importance; and the conflict of interest with Ribbentrop's Foreign Ministry that this requirement generated, was to exercise him intensely. But within Germany the brunt of his effort shifted from 'propaganda' to 'enlightenment'.

'*Aufklärung*' (enlightenment) is a word of several connotations. One denotes in particular the intellectual awakening known in France and Britain as the Age of Reason, of which in Germany Goethe was the leader and principal ornament. It was deeply ironic, therefore, that under Goebbels' touch 'enlightenment' should come to stand for an approach to the German mind which was anti-rational and emotive in every regard. But so it did. Like Hitler, Goebbels believed in the primacy of the spoken over the written word as an instrument of thought control. The provision of a radio set to every Grman household and the detailed direction of what it broadcast consequently became for him a major priority. Like Hitler, he was also a passionate devotee of the cinema. But, while the Führer used the medium chiefly as a means of personal relaxation, Goebbels understood and seized on its power to sway the national imagination. The capture of the German film industry was one of his first tasks on becoming minister. But he himself was also captured by it and the resulting symbiosis, in which Goebbels talked, thought and lived films, chose film people as his boon companions and conducted the most notorious of his many amours with a leading star, Lida Baarova, bore fruit in an output of films of the most brilliant technical quality.

Thus, by 1939, Goebbels had become an altogether more expert and many-sided lord of the media than he was when steering German opinion to accept Nazi victory during the *Kampfzeit*. The new Era of Struggle was not one to which he had looked forward. Berlin was for him world enough. But, since the only principle to guide his life was that of unswerving obedience to the Führer's will, he threw himself when war came into manipulating the truths and rumours of strategy with all the relentless dynamism that he brought to making lies the instrument of political victory. There was a difference, of course: even before the Seizure of Power he had had available crude physical means to reinforce his attacks on Hitler's enemies. The Storm Trooper, as much as the cutting editorial, had been his weapon against opponents of all colours and, as Gauleiter of Berlin, he had used his Storm Troopers ruthlessly. He could not use Storm Troopers against Churchill (whom, interestingly, he identified as Hitler's real antagonist months before he became Prime Minister). But that limitation seems to have made the challenge of his mission all the more electric. Indeed, these pages of the diary reveal, as perhaps no other document does, the excitement which the manipulation of news in wartime can stimulate in the mind of a media monomaniac.

The period of the war which these diaries cover provided, of course, material for propaganda with which even the most inept manager of news could make hay. From the blitzkrieg against Poland in September 1939 to the opening days of the invasion of Russia in June 1941, the boots of the Wehrmacht stamped out for Hitler a production-line sequence of victories: over the Poles in 1939, the Norwegians and Danes in April 1940, the Dutch and Belgians in May, the French in June, the Yugoslavs and Greeks in April 1941, together with a succession of humiliations inflicted on the British and the beginnings of an apparent triumph over the Russians. Goebbels might have contented himself with trumpeting the big stories – as Göring contented himself with the easy aerial triumphs, thus initiating the eclipse of the Luftwaffe. But, on the contrary, the Minister for Popular Enlightenment and Propaganda devoted himself daily to every aspect of his responsibilities. On 6 April, for example, the opening day of the 1941 offensive against Yugoslavia and Greece, Goebbels found time to digest the news from all fronts, particularly of air activity, for as Gauleiter of Berlin he was responsible for damage control and relief in the city, to comment on British, Russian and American press reaction, to issue a guideline to the German press on the handling of news from the Balkans, to sample *Sicherheitsdienst* reports on national morale, to 'try out new (radio) fanfares and south-eastern (Balkan front) songs . . . reshuffle the Request Concert again and send planes down for the first Propaganda Company material', receive a winner of the Knight's Cross, work at home on the afternoon news bulletins, issue a warning to American correspondents in Berlin about 'impudence', forbid dancing in Berlin ('not suitable during an offensive') and finally – his unvarying nightly task – view the latest newsreel.

Such meticulous attention to detail paid off when there was bad news rather than good to handle – and there was bad news even during 1939–41. The result of the Battle of Britain could be fudged and the importance of British victories over the Italians in the Western Desert minimised. But the sinking of the *Bismarck*, pride of the German navy, could not be hidden in the small print, while the defection of Rudolf Hess, the Führer's Deputy, presented Germany's enemies with the sort of lead story which at first not even Goebbels could think how to counter. Fortunately, he had learnt at the beginning of the war, over the sinking of the *Graf Spee*, the mechanics of putting the propaganda machine into reverse. He had then too early proclaimed a victory, news which he had had subsequently to retract. Over the sinking of the *Bismarck* he took the precaution of following the operational intelligence very carefully, and so was able to prepare public opinion slowly for the coming of the tragedy. He then played the tragic element for maximum effect, while simultaneously amplifying reports of the fighting in Crete, which fortuitously was swinging Germany's way. By 30 May 1941, only three days after the sinking, he could calculate that there was, in the propaganda scales, 'a gloomy blanace for England'. Thereafter the battleship is not mentioned in his diary. The story was dead. The real strategic consequences did not interest this supreme media man.

The defection of Hess, strategically trivial though it was, bulked far larger and longer in his mind. The newsman in him became obsessed with the propaganda opportunities that Hess's appearance in Britain offered to the 'Ministry of Lies' (the British Ministry of Information), and with the frustrated curiosity in a sensational 'human drama story' that the German public all too clearly felt. 'I instruct the press and radio to devote vigorous attention to other things,' he noted on 15 May 1941, two days after the story had broken, when he had somewhat recovered his nerve. But the British inactivity kept him sleepless. 'If I were the English Propaganda Minister I would know exactly what to do,' he wrote on 14 May; 'London is cunningly letting us wait for an official statement,' (15 May); 'London has not hit on the idea of simply issuing statements in Hess's name without his knowledge' (16 May); 'what I would have made of this case! But England's ruling class is ripe for a fall' (17 May). He seems never to have grasped that London preferred the truth in this weird episode: that Hess was mad, and had been so for some time.

Yet the Hess episode may, nevertheless, have prompted the beginning of a new approach to propaganda which would eventually become Goebbels' most significant contribution to Germany's war effort. For all his gibes, he admired Churchill and his unblinking public honesty. He never himself shrank from the truth. The noted moments of family idyll or communion with the spring which spatter the diary, are nothing more than conventional concessions to the culture of sentimentality in which he was raised. The real Goebbels was a tougher man. When the reality of war turned irreversibly against Germany, he was to be the first to invoke its force and, through it, seek to evoke from the Germans a will to resist to the death. That so many did so resist was to be his supreme triumph as journalist and orator. That he chose to join them was a myth-maker's identification with a story and its end.

Translator's Note

Since Goebbels appears to have written most of the entries early in the morning, I have kept this prefacing word: 'Yesterday . . .' While in some ways it would have been easier to have simply dated the entries according to the events described, there are cases when he deals with several days at a time and hops forward to the day to come. On balance, I decided that the reader would soon accustom himself to the convention, and so I left it as it stood.

Biographical details of individuals mentioned by Goebbels will be found, in most instances, in the Index.

**Europe showing extent
of German Occupation
by December 1941**

Neutral Countries   SPAIN

Limit of German advance
December 1941

To USSR Sept. 1940   ESTONIA

| 0 | 100 | | 400 miles |
| | 300 | 600 km | |

ICELAND

NORWAY

Trondheim

Oslo

BRITISH
ISLES

NORTH
SEA

DENMARK

Copen

Edinburgh

Newcastle

Hamburg

Liverpool

NETHER-
LANDS

BA

Coventry

London

Amsterdam
Rotterdam

Berlin

ATLANTIC OCEAN

Plymouth

Dover

Dunkirk

BELGIUM

GERMANY

Elbe

Buchenwald

Seine

Sedan

Cologne

Pragu

Loire

Paris

Nuremberg

Bohemi

FRANCE

Meuse

Dachau

Rhine

Munich

Vienna

Bordeaux

Vichy

Vichy
Government
June 1940

SWITZ.

AUSTRIA

Rhône

Milan

YU

Turin

PORTUGAL

SPAIN

Madrid

Marseilles

Toulon

Corsica

ITALY

Rome

Naples

Sardinia

MEDITER

Gibraltar

Oran

ALGERIA

Tunis

Sici

Malta

RA

Vichy Government June 1940

N

Vichy Government June 1940

TUNISIA

Tripoli

Part One

1939

These surviving fragments of the Goebbels Diaries *for 1939 – a few dealing with the last months of peace, most with the period of 'phoney war' from October 1939 – cover a very difficult time in Goebbels' life.*

At the beginning of 1939 Goebbels was still in the shadow of the Lida Baarova affair – the passion for a Czech film actress that had threatened his marriage and his political position in 1938. He and Magda Goebbels were living together because Hitler had ordered them to avoid a scandal. However, their relationship was clearly extremely difficult, as the references to Magda Goebbels' unreasonable attitude, as well as the continuing confidential discussions with the Führer, indicate. The private Goebbels of this period is depressive, isolated, and vulnerable.

As for the Minister Goebbels, in peacetime he seemed to have some time on his hands. The years of struggle were over. There were leisurely viewings of films and long talks as well as hard-headed business meetings. From October 1939, however, the picture changed. The propaganda war, in the absence of a real, shooting war, took on a new importance. Goebbels travelled quickly to inspect the conquered territories in Poland. The pace of work stepped up. The self-pitying tone of January 1939 disappears from the diaries. There is an impression of manic activity. Nevertheless, his mistakes, including the affairs of the Ark Royal *and the* Graf Spee, *in which he had reacted over-hastily in sounding the victory fanfare, show through between the lines.*

Goebbels also faced another, major practical problem. A Führer-Order of 8 September 1939 made all propaganda abroad subject to the Foreign Ministry, an intolerable situation so far as Goebbels was concerned. The order was later modified so that only 'consultation' was required, but the result remained a running war between Goebbels and the Foreign Minister, Ribbentrop, which colours almost every entry in the diaries. Goebbels' rich vocabulary of abuse, and his unflagging capacity for intrigue, are exercised to the full.

3

1 January 1939 (Sunday)

Friday: I am still very tired and ill. Worst of all, I can no longer sleep. All my attempts to achieve some sort of peace have failed.

In the afternoon, I dictate my New Year Speech. I find it very hard going. It is almost as if my brain has become a vacuum. Finally, despite everything, I complete it.

I lie awake for long, enervating hours in the evening. Saturday: Hanke comes for a meeting. A frosty occasion. He gives me an account of a disgraceful attack that Speer is planning against Lippert in the newspapers. I don't mince my words when I give my opinion. Wonderful: too cowardly to attack him openly, and so he stabs him in the back. Very nice. No one can get away with that kind of thing where I am concerned.

Funk writes me a very pleasant, affectionate letter from Sicily. He is a decent fellow. One of the few whom one can rely on.

A pile of New Year telegrams. Polite rubbish that sticks in my gullet. Printed scraps of paper sent out to everyone on the address-list, and one is supposed to feel honoured to have been included.

Helldorff comes visiting in the afternoon and keeps me company for an hour. He means well and tries to cheer me up, but at the moment this is impossible.

In the evening I deliver my New Year Address on the radio. It goes fairly well. I am quite satisfied with it. Then to bed. Turn of the year! Horrifying! I would be happy to string myself up.

3 January 1939 (Tuesday)

Sunday: No word from Magda.

I give Demandowski and Waldegg a long lecture on the cinema, etc. They are deeply impressed. Then we watch a few films. Nothing very special among them.

Late in the evening I draft an outline for a new film about the press. The 'Seventh Great Power'. I think it will be really something!

And then some sleep.

Monday: Some work at midday.

The Führer writes me a long and very touching letter. I am very moved by it. I answer him immediately and give him a very frank, confidential summary of my position. It does me some good. Hanke will take the letter with him to the Obersalzberg.*

In the afternoon, a little cinema with Ritter, Hadamovsky, d'Alquen, Fandere, etc. We discuss the film on the press, which begins to take some shape. It is a good idea. It will see the light of day.

* The *Berghof*, Hitler's retreat on the Obersalzberg, near the resort of Berchtesgaden in the Bavarian Alps.

Exchange ideas with the others for a long time. Work into the night. To bed exhausted and run-down. Sleep, sleep!

4 January 1939 (Wednesday)

Yesterday: Spend the entire day mulling things over. Take a drive in the open air. It does me a lot of good. Out to Potsdam. Fresh air, snow, sun.

Work during the afternoon. The Führer invites me to the Obersalzberg. His foreign-policy speech has been postponed for the moment.

In the evening, to the *Merry Widow*. A magnificent production, but the splendour a little cold. Otherwise, very good to look at and colourful. Wait and see.

Talk late into the night. Sleep, sleep!

Today: I accuse Dr Frick of a vulgar slander. He is evasive, just as I would have expected.

Talk things over with Magda. But she starts off with the usual suppositions. This is the pattern. I don't know her any more.

Play for a while with the children in the afternoon. They are so sweet and affectionate. And then to Berlin. Pack. Off to the Obersalzberg!

Hoping for peace at last!

(Entries for 5 January – 18 January missing)

19 January 1939 (Thursday)

Yesterday: A lot of work. Discuss personnel questions with Hanke. Arent's *Merry Widow* comes in for a great deal of criticism, even from the Führer.

Theo Lingen tells me of his private troubles. I am able to help him to some extent.

Thoroughly study a fat report about my propaganda abroad. Much is being achieved in this area.

With the Führer at midday. Dr Dietrich has written me a rather forceful letter regarding our problems with the *Berliner Tageblatt* and the *Wiener Freie Presse*. Only the Führer is competent to decide on these issues.

The Führer talks about military questions. He is very sceptical in his attitude to the Wehrmacht's bureaucracy.

To Schwanenwerder in the afternoon. The dear, sweet children! A long talk with Magda. Perhaps a solution will be found despite everything. I hope so.

To bed, tired and late.

(Entries for 20 January – 23 January missing)

24 January 1939 (Tuesday)

Yesterday: To work very early. The foreign press continues to whip up hatred against me. If only it would end!

Dictate an essay: *The Intellectual.* An uncompromising blast in that direction. Discuss the extensions to the house at Lanke with Hanke. Plans good. A series of adminstrative and personnel questions. Demandowski has some film problems. Discussion with the Sudeten-German writer, Pleyer. He makes a good impression. Describes the bitter racial struggle against the Czechs.

The manager of Father Coughlin, the anti-Semitic radio priest in America, tells us that America is basically more anti-Semitic than we give it credit for. He would like us to take a more positive attitude towards Christianity.

I tell the Führer about this. He intends to touch on the question in his speech to the Reichstag. He intends to put out feelers to the Americans and give an outline of Germany's general position. I believe that this speech will be very important.

At table the Führer makes another strong plea for vegetarianism. I consider his views correct. Meat-eating is a perversion of our human nature. When we reach a higher level of civilisation, we shall doubtless overcome it.

At the office, work. Franco is now making swift progress towards Barcelona. We can only hope that he makes it now. Our newspapers are doling out too many victory laurels in advance.

To Schwanenwerder. Play with the children, who are very loving and sweet.

In the evening, check films. *New Year's Night on the Alexanderplatz* not quite successful, somewhat slow and confused and too vulgar in its handling of the language and the milieu. *Immortal Heart* by Harlan a little overdone in parts, but quite good in others. *In the Name of the People*, a bad crime film immediately recognisable as official in its inspiration.

To bed late and tired.

(Entry for 25 January missing)

26 January 1939 (Thursday)

Yesterday: Dead tired, but work without ceasing. The elimination of Jewish influence in the Reich Chamber of Culture continues. But now considerable financial difficulties are apparent. We shall overcome them.

Film exports have declined further. I must do something decisive in that area.

The people in Salzburg are causing more and more difficulties with the programme for their Festival. I give them an ultimatum.

The takeover of the Admiral's Palace has now been completed. Hentschke is to be in charge. He is an experienced veteran of the theatre.

Discuss problems of the house at Lanke with Dr Lippert. I believe that we are almost there. Talk with Dr Ley about the proposed 'Eighth Chamber'.* We are in full agreement. All that remains is to talk to Hess and Rosenberg. Ley is a good sort.

Breakfast for Farinacci. He is an old Fascist warhorse who goes his own way, never compromising. I give a hearty speech of welcome at Schwanenwerder. I dictate an essay and a speech for the 30th January.** Not quite right yet. Chat with the children.

Franco is advancing fast. He is already in the suburbs of Barcelona.

In the evening, check films. *Humans, Animals, Sensations*, a typical Harry Piel film. Also *Between the River and the Steppe*, a mediocre Hungarian film.

I am so tired, but I cannot sleep.

(Entry for 27 January missing)

28 January 1939 (Saturday)

Yesterday: Leave Schwanenwerder early. A grey winter day. Just suited to my state of mind.

Barcelona has fallen. Franco is already advancing beyond the city. A great triumph for him and his cause. World opinion is gradually moving in his favour.

The rumours and the gossip are never-ending. I suffer greatly. I must try to see things through, but it tears at the nerves.

The expansion of the radio network is moving ahead more quickly. It is now seen as important for war purposes. A concession that marks a great success for us. The re-organisation of the weekly newsreel is also now an accomplished fact.

I believe that we are finding increasing favour with the Führer.

. . . The radio people come to see me. More arguments. I manage to create some peace and order. The programming is re-organised. More good music, less foreign product, and a rationalisation of the model types. This is urgently necessary, because the prevailing mess in this area has become

---

* Later referred to as the 'Seventh Chamber', after one sub-section of the Reich Culture Chamber, that for radio, was abolished in October 1939. The Reich Culture Chamber enabled Goebbels' ministry to exercise total control over all forms of artistic activity and communications media, since no individual or organisation could function in these fields without being granted membership. The individual chambers during the war years were for: literature, music, films, theatre, fine arts, and journalism. Although the question was discussed throughout 1939–41, nothing came of the attempt to add the mass-entertainment division proposed by Ley.

** The anniversary of Hitler's assumption of power on 30 January 1933, one of the key dates in the Nazi calendar.

unbearable. The Führer has signed the document naming Esser as State Secretary. Esser is very pleased about it.

27 January 1939 (Friday)

Yesterday: A day of hard, strenuous work. To Berlin early. Problems and more problems. But I must swallow it all . . .

. . . To the Führer at midday. He talks at length about the Spanish question. Barcelona is about to fall. The question is whether Franco can deliver the *coup de grâce*. A nationalist Spain will guarantee that in any coming conflict the country will at least remain neutral. Also, whether Franco will be able to deal with reactionary and clerical elements.

Discuss Danzig's* problems with Forster. The question of the Munich *Kammerspiele* has also been settled.

In the afternoon, watch the film *Hotel Sacher*. Superbly made, but not quite politically watertight. I shall have it re-edited and a few scenes reshot.

Dictate and attend conference.

Schwanenwerder. Play with the children. They are so infinitely sweet.

Work a lot in the evening. Then to bed, exhausted.

(Entries for 28 January – 2 February missing)

3 February 1939 (Friday)

Yesterday: With the Führer at midday. We discuss a thousand different topics. He has now completed his speech.

Long discussion with Hanke. There is so much to do. Winkler reports to me on the staff re-organisation at the German News Agency.** Once again, Dr Dietrich has behaved like a bull in a china shop. I am forced to glue things back together. But it turns out all right. The issue of the newsreel has also now been settled.

I should like to put an experienced financier in charge of each film company. A man who also has great artistic understanding. But I cannot find such people. They are thin on the ground.

My piece on the 30th January appears in a prominent position in the *Völkischer Beobachter*. I think it works well.

To Schwanenwerder in the evening. Play a little with the children, and then work on into the night.

* Now Gdánsk in Poland. Danzig had been detached from Germany in 1919 by the Peace of Versailles and transformed into a Free State under the League of Nations in order to assure Poland a port on the Baltic. It was, however, effectively controlled by local Nazis even before Hitler seized the city in September 1939 and unleashed the Second World War.

** The *Deutsches Nachrichtenbüro* (DNB). The official German news agency.

4 February 1939 (Saturday)

Yesterday: [. . .] delivers a report on Spain. The military position is good.
Franco hopes to bring the war to an end within a few weeks. I am not yet
prepared to believe it will happen . . .

. . . Work at the ministry. Coffee shortage. Huge queues outside the
shops. I shall write an article roundly condemning it.

Schwanenwerder. Watch the children at their gym lesson. They are
charming and quite delightful. Holde is a sweet little thing . . .

5 February 1939 (Sunday)

Yesterday: My article against political jokers, combined with the appropriate measures, has caused an earthquake. Now those intellectual cowards are
crawling into their holes. They are terrified.

I immediately dictate a new article against the coffee queues, which are a
result of a temporary shortage of coffee and are causing a great deal of bad
feeling. I intend to take vigorous steps against these shortcomings.

Otherwise, a variety of work. Roosevelt has made a speech claiming that
America's frontiers are on the Rhine. The question is whether we should
withdraw American films from circulation. I am not quite clear in my own
mind about this.

Work during midday and into the afternoon. Harald is sitting his school-
leaving examination.

Stojadinovic's government has resigned. Obviously he went too far in his
election frauds. And the opposition was too strong. Typically Balkan. Not a
good thing from our point of view, I believe. We could deal with Stojadinovic . . .

. . . In the evening, Leni Riefenstahl reports to me on her trip to America.
She gives me an exhaustive description, and one that is far from encouraging. We shall get nowhere there. The Jews rule by terror and bribery. But for
how much longer? . . .

6 February 1939 (Monday)

Yesterday: A rest day.

Some work. Lunch in the company of my dear ones.

I write the introduction to my latest book, *The New Society*. I think that it
will be very good.

Watch a film, *An Old Heart Goes Travelling*. Tedious and incomprehensible. Also *Secret*, a very old, nauseating Jewish film. How far we have come
from that kind of thing.

Franco is advancing at a tremendous rate. Azaña has fled over the border
into France. Soon the Reds will be finished. That will be a blessing.

In the evening, continue to work until late. And today another dreadful week begins!

(Entries for 7 February – 3 March missing)

4 March 1939 (Sunday)

Yesterday: I am so tired when I get up. Almost no sleep. I prepare my Leipzig speech, which turns out quite well.

Greven refusing to knuckle under at Ufa.* But he will have to. In any case, he is incompetent and a complete idler.

I give some more thought to constructing new, more powerful radio transmitters.

I am having trouble with the theatre in Vienna. At times the situation down there seems to be one of total chaos . . .

. . . We have now discovered the traitor and writer of anonymous letters in the ministry: Dr Thomalla. We were already hot on his trail, and during the night he gassed himself, along with the secretary he was involved with. His suicide note contains a full admission of guilt. I am happy that we can breathe a little more freely. I arranged immediately for a few more arrests, so as to reveal any possible circle of accomplices. The police will look after the rest.

Midday with the Führer. He is considering whether we should abrogate the Concordat with Rome in light of Pacelli's election as Pope. This will surely happen when Pacelli undertakes his first hostile act.

In afternoon, 'ballet rehearsal' at the Führer's in preparation for today's reception for artists. Good, some excellent achievements on display. Afterwards a little more talk.

To Schwanenwerder. I see my sweet children again. They are all so loving and welcoming. Little Holde, especially, is turning into a proper jewel.

Talk for a long time with Magda. She is totally involved with preparations for a trip to Italy.

I work throughout the evening. Minister Kotzias has arrived in Berlin. An embarrassing mistake: he feels himself a guest of the government, but actually was not invited. I immediately clear things up with the Foreign Ministry and he is now my guest. If anyone deserves it, it is he.

Today, for the first time in an age, I get a proper night's sleep again.

(Entries for 5 March – 16 March missing)

* *Universal-Film-Aktiengesellschaft.* Germany's largest film company, under government control after 1933. Ufa was also responsible for producing the weekly newsreel under Goebbels' close direction.

17 March 1939 (Saturday)

Yesterday: Only three hours' sleep. Get up still dead tired. Six years ago today I was sworn in by Hindenburg. What a road from that day to this! I am happy and satisfied. I have triumphed over all odds. It has cost toil, suffering and sweat, but success has come . . .

. . . The press carries very approving articles about my ministry. It has earned its laurels . . .

. . . At Blomberg's* for the celebration of his forty years of service. He is very pleased, also about my gift, the Propylaen edition of the *History of Art*. Funk is also there. Full of top military brass. Blomberg is intelligent and pleasant, but unfortunately [. . .]

. . . Our note to London regarding the Western Pact has caused a great sensation. Italy acted with us. There is not much in the note itself. Again, the aim is to give us time. Paris and London have become oh-so modest. Belgium wants to preserve her absolute neutrality. Meanwhile, Mussolini has been on a tour of North Africa, paying homage to Islam. Very clever. Paris and London are immediately very suspicious.

Work. Meal with Magda. She is in excellent form, and the baby is making wonderful progress. I hope things continue this way. Magda is so sweet . . .

(Entries for 18 March – 1 May missing)

2 May 1939 (Tuesday)

[First part of the entry missing]

. . . In the Red areas of Spain, they sabotaged non-intervention and the recall of the volunteers by secret naturalisation. Typically Bolshevik.

Hungary wants to re-open negotiations with Prague. The Hungarians are cowards. Mussolini seems to be drawing back a little. He recommends direct negotiations.

In Prague pro-German voices are being raised more frequently. The country will be our best vassal.

London is embroiled with troubles in Palestine. And Chamberlain has to complete his cabinet. Duff Cooper has to be replaced, and Lord Stanley has died. Will he now include the Opposition?

Japan is making sturdy progress in South China. Soon she must be able to show a major success.

Hanke comes to give a report. Nothing important. But I send him to Magda, to talk to her. Every way out is blocked as far as I am concerned.

I get up in the late afternoon, read and write a little. Then back to bed, exhausted. Dreamless sleep. Today I am feeling better again.

* Despite the unsavoury circumstances surrounding his resignation from his post as Minister of Defence in 1938 (*see* biographical note in Index), Blomberg was saved official disgrace. It seems clear that the Nazi leadership was careful to continue to pay its respects to the Army's grey eminence.

11

3 May 1939 (Wednesday)

Yesterday: Slept out here again for the first time. All is filled with sadness and quiet melancholy. But I am peaceful and relaxed. Life is so hard, by its very nature. Why should one create extra suffering for oneself?

The press is full of reports about May Day. The award of the film prize to Frölich meets with general approval. Everyone had feared that Ritter was due for it.

The Polish press is kicking up a fuss. But it will soon have its big mouth shut for it. Just a matter of waiting and keeping patience.

Ribbentrop is complaining about *folie de grandeur* again. This time, though, Dietrich did not act cleverly. He is often too abrupt.

A grey, melancholy day . . . In the evening talk and music. Then read on into the night. First thing today, back to Berlin.

(Entries for 4 May – 18 May missing)

19 May 1939 (Friday)

Yesterday: Long sleep. Work on my speech. Finish my leader-article. The Foreign Ministry still has a few small objections, but now I think it works very well.

In the afternoon a small party to visit me. We swap stories, take a boat ride, walk through the blossoming spring forest, and inspect the new building work, which is progressing very well. In the evening, back to Berlin. Work a little. Today I am off to Cologne and Düsseldorf.

(Entries for 20 May – 26 May missing)

27 May 1939 (Saturday)

Yesterday: I order attacks on the foreign press for their lies about alleged flooding on our West Wall.* Otherwise a myth will establish itself. My essay, *The 'Encirclers'*, is now to be reprinted throughout our press. For the rest, all is rather quiet on the polemical front.

At Ufa the situation has become well-nigh intolerable. I finally send Greven on leave and instal Leichternstern in a commissarial role. He must try to impose his will.

Otherwise, a few things to be dealt with. Then I take a Whitsun break. A very uncertain Whitsun celebration.

In the afternoon to Schwanenwerder. The children are all beside them-

* The 'West Wall' – known colloquially abroad as the 'Siegfried Line' – was begun in 1938 to prevent a French attack across Germany's western borders. Its massive concrete bunkers and defences were designed and built by Todt's organisation.

selves with joy. Helga stays with me and we chat. She is quite grown-up these days. A stroll through the garden and across the island. Helga walks beside me the entire time, prattling away. I tell her my basic ideas about Europe, in quite a primitive and simple fashion, and she is very proud at having learnt so much.

Films in the evening. An art film from Munich, gloriously botched.

Border Power, a quite nice and exciting film from the Bavaria studio.

Mr Deeds Goes to Town. Marvellous stuff from America, with Gary Gooper. Wonderfully made, excellent ideas, beautifully acted. I am delighted.

Then a long, glorious sleep.

28 May 1939 (Sunday)

Yesterday: A little work. Leichtenstern has made a good start at Ufa. I hope he will push things through.

Ley writes me a tough letter on the question of uniforms. This is all I need.

Mother rings up: she has been slightly ill, but now she is feeling better again. I must keep an eye on her. She has earned it.

Draft a short Whitsun message for the Press in consultation with Fritszche. Not much to report. The programme for the Condor Legion's* return is made public.

I devote some time to the children. Helga is so sweet and clever, and Holde is like a little angel.

Long discussion with Magda about our future. She is quite reasonable.

In the afternoon, reading and writing. My piece in the *Völkischer Beobachter* has come out well.

In the evening, watch some films. A good documentary film about Libya. Fascism has achieved a great deal there. Also a series of films from the Weimar time. Speeches by Braun and Severing, marches, the Red Front, etc. How far off, how far!

Another viewing of *If We Were Angels*, Frölich's masterpiece. And his first talking picture, *The Night Is Ours*. Still quite primitive and often too downright childish for today's tastes. But it has something, nevertheless.

Sleep. Dream!

Whit Sunday! The loving festival?

29 May 1939 (Monday)

Yesterday: Weather like October. Spend the entire day talking, playing with the children, walking.

* The force of 'volunteers' from the German Luftwaffe which took part in the Spanish Civil War on Franco's side. Among the Condor Legion's exploits in this dress-rehearsal for World War was the destruction of the Basque city of Guernica in 1937.

In the evening, films: *All Quiet On The Western Front.* A very clever propaganda vehicle. At the time we had to sabotage it. *Eight Girls In One Boat.* A film made in 1933, but skilful and modern. Still a pleasure to see today.

My health is not good. What a Whitsun day.

30 May 1939 (Tuesday)

Yesterday: Read a little in the morning. Curt Goetz, always pleasant and amusing.

Then take a stroll with the children through the Grunewald. They are all so sweet and affectionate.

Long discussion with Magda. The time had come for us to talk things over again. But she continues to view everything in such a false, distorted light.

Harald* arrives. He is with the Labour Service and makes a terrific impression.

In the evening, a boat trip with the children, then read and write and have another long talk with Magda.

Back to work today.

(This is the last peacetime entry. The entries for 31 May – 8 October are missing.)

9 October 1939 (Monday)

Yesterday: Rest day. Sleep my fill and then study the press.

World opinion is loosening up a little. Things no longer look quite so bad. Lloyd George has written an article for Hearst in which he recommends serious consideration of Hitler's proposals.** He would not be able to do this if the right mood did not exist in England. Above all, the neutrals are gradually seeing the light. We must make sure that we press the message home.

* Harald Quandt, Goebbels' stepson.

** On 29 September, after the fall of Warsaw, Germany and the Soviet Union had issued a joint appeal to the world to recognise the new status quo in Poland. Hitler made a formal peace offer to Britain and France in a speech to the Reichstag on 6 October. Lloyd George, who had already pleaded in the House of Commons that Britain 'should not come to a hurried conclusion' if Germany submitted detailed peace proposals, went further in an article that also appeared in Beaverbrook's *Sunday Express* on 8 October. He wrote: 'If we antagonise Russia by our reply to Hitler, we must face the stern prospect that an offensive and defensive alliance between Russia and Germany could not be overthrown by a three years' war. I dare not contemplate all the possibilities of such a tremendous combination of strength against us'. He pleaded for Roosevelt to act as honest broker in the setting up of a peace conference, since 'nothing would be lost, and everything might be gained, by such a conference'.

The children come into town from Schwanenwerder. We walk in the garden and chat and play together a little.

Arent comes at midday. He has a lot of interesting things to say about the Polish campaign. He went through everything, experienced and saw a lot. But everyone would like to see peace.

A nice request programme for the Wehrmacht on the radio. I study a heap of letters to the radio, which provide a good cross-section of German public opinion.

Watch a few children's films with the children. Otherwise work.

A serious railway accident at Gesundbrunnen. Twenty-five dead. This is very regrettable, particularly as most of them were soldiers.

Late to bed, tired.

10 October 1939 (Tuesday)

Yesterday: Lloyd George's article has caused a big sensation. L.G. would be in charge of the London government if he were still young and active.

A very positive anti-Allies article in *Izvestia*, absolutely tailored to our standpoint. The rumour is that Stalin wrote it himself. At the moment he is being extraordinarily helpful, which has been noted with thanks. So far the Russians have kept all their promises.

A slight relaxation of the atmosphere in Paris. They are no longer quite so intransigent. The press is still rabid, but political circles have become a little more cautious. The tone in London is harsher, but then they can afford to talk, since they don't have to pay such a high price in blood. There seems to be a lot of popular pressure on the governments.

There is increasing talk in the USA of a peace mission by Roosevelt. Perhaps sometime he will be more inclined than he is at the moment.

The Italian press is giving very strong support to our position at the moment. A useful aid to us. Moscow, true, is a little clumsy, but nevertheless very useful. The neutrals are gradually waking up to reality. They are against the war, because they will be on the losing side, whatever happens. Poland is finished. No one talks about a restoration of the old Polish state any more.

We test out a projectile-thrower for sending leaflets across in the French sector of the front. We think that the preparations will be sufficiently far advanced by the end of the week for things to get under way.

I am increasing the Party's involvement in state affairs; above all, to ensure that the horrendous blunders in the Economics Ministry are avoided in future.

Dürr and Fink report from Cracow. They have brought the *Illustrated Cracow Courier* back to a respectable level. The newspaper has been cunningly filled by our people with disguised political material. Dürr has become a real disciple of Machiavelli. Fink is also doing excellent work. Our people are learning a great deal.

I discuss the work of the BdM* in Berlin with Fräulein Mündel. It is difficult to get the girls together for regular meetings. I intend, if necessary, to put the cinemas at their disposal on Sunday mornings.

Fischer reports on the position in the Gau of Styria. Things there are excellent. I donate 20,000 Marks for the travelling theatre . . .

With the Führer. He welcomes Lloyd George's article, which was certainly a clever move. The man stands head and shoulders above the present crew of British politicians. He foresees the deep crisis of the Empire. Hence his plain speaking.

The Führer also affirms that the article in *Izvestia* was written by Stalin. Stalin is an old, experienced revolutionary. Nothing happens for nothing. Stalin's control of dialectic during the negotiations** was shown to be outstanding.

The Führer's verdict on the Poles is damning. More like animals than human beings, completely primitive, stupid and amorphous. And a ruling class that is an unsatisfactory result of a mingling between the lower orders and an Aryan master-race. The Poles' dirtiness is unimaginable. Their capacity for intelligent judgement is absolutely nil. Even Lipski believed that we would lose our nerve after a week of war. Poor fool!

The Führer has no intention of assimilating the Poles. They are to be forced into their truncated state and left entirely to their own devices. If Henry the Lion had conquered the East, a task for which he possessed the power at that time, the result would certainly have been a strongly slavicised race of German mongrels. Better the present situation: now we know the laws of racial heredity and can handle things accordingly. The Führer takes a very positive view of the general situation. We can only watch and wait. We dare not lose our nerve or our peace of mind.

Mountains of work at home. But I work gladly when I see such goals set out before me . . .

. . . I study lists of our former domestic enemies. What a picture of misery and corruption! What has become of all these nobodies! And how decently we have treated them. We have carried through the cosiest, least bloody revolution in history.

Put together the weekly newsreel. Turned out very well again. I ask for the Führer's verdict on one thorny point. Now it is ready.

Old film, *The Threepenny Opera*. Typical Jewish humbug. This is the kind of thing that they were allowed to set before the German people with impunity. To our credit that we have got rid of all this rubbish.

Read and write for a long time.

* The *Bund deutscher Mädel* (League of German Girls). The female equivalent of the Hitler Youth.
** The negotiations leading up to the Nazi-Soviet Pact of August 1939.

16

Yesterday: Work on the re-organisation of the field post service. This is our problem child, the thing that causes us most trouble. Our greatest failure!

No change in the military situation. Scarcely any activity in the West, either.

We have captured an English propaganda balloon. A very complicated thing that costs a lot of money to very little effect.

I order the press to be warned once more about illusions and pessimism. We cannot have the German people being pulled in one direction or the other.

Bernard Shaw has published a very sarcastic article directed against the British government, saying that instead of getting rid of 'Hitlerism', they should concentrate on 'Churchillism'. And many other witticisms. Causes a big stir, surely because he is expressing the thoughts of a section of British public opinion.

Suddenly a whole series of rumours are in circulation: the English King and Chamberlain have resigned. Daladier as well. The Prince of Wales* and François-Poncet are to succeed them. This unleashes a veritable storm of joy. Factories, even ministries, begin to celebrate, and people embrace each other in the street. I immediately issue a denial and have it broadcast over the radio. This causes great disappointment. The whole thing was the work of the British Secret Service, to test the mood of the masses in Germany. But I have neutralised its effects instantly . . .

. . . Midday with the Führer. He is gratified that I quashed the rumours from London so promptly. They were spreading right through the country and causing all sorts of harm. Shaw's article pleases the Führer particularly. Shaw is one of the world's most inventive satirists.

The Führer still has no clear idea of what England intends to do. For the moment one can only wait and let things take their course. Everything is in flux. What will come out of it? In any event, it is the English who must decide whether the war is to continue.

Launching of Winter Aid Fund** at the *Sportpalast*. Filled to overflowing, and a highly-charged atmosphere. I deliver a short progress report, and then the Führer speaks: very quiet, precise and self-assured. Peace or war, whichever our enemies care to choose. He is ready for either. The crowd cheers wildly . . .

. . . In the evening, check films to see if they will be of any use for the war

* Presumably the Duke of Windsor, Prince of Wales until George V's death in 1936.
** *Winterhilfswerk*, the main Nazi charity, used to finance the Party's welfare organisations. In his dual role as Gauleiter of Berlin and Minister of Propaganda, Goebbels played an important role both in the publicising of the charity drive and in the distribution of the proceeds.

effort. *The Journey to Tilsit*, a Harlan Production with Söderbaum, Dammann, van Dongen. A well-made, artistic film. But an excessively tormented, tragic view of marriage. Harlan is letting his own experiences show, and not even tastefully.

Daladier makes a speech. A relatively mild tone. Paris wants guarantees. If that were all! Otherwise the speech is not very aggressive. It is hard to glean much from it. We shall have to wait for Chamberlain . . .

12 October 1939 (Thursday)

Yesterday: It has now been confirmed that the unsettling rumours of the previous day were planted by London, to test popular feeling in Germany. I begin a thorough investigation, including old cases of telephone 'mystifications', and intend to have the guilty parties shut up in concentration camps. If one does not stamp on these things in good time, one is defenceless against all manner of rumour-mongering.

As thanks to Lithuania for surrendering its sovereignty, Moscow has ceded Vilna. And the good Lithuanians are hanging out the flags for the occasion . . .

The military situation: our flyers attack English naval detachments in the North Sea. The English Ministry of Lies* answers by claiming that we got ourselves in a mess. But we hold our end up and give them something to think about.

Press conference: I issue instructions that will put an end to rumour-mongering. Shaw's entire article is a masterpiece of irony and political humour. I release it in its entirety for use by the German press.

With the Führer. He is also amused, and laughs until the tears come when I read Shaw's article aloud to him. We can exploit this.

The Führer approves my moves against the English liars. My actions to combat rumour-mongering also cause him satisfaction.

The Führer is gloriously convinced of victory. He shows how different the situation is from that in 1914, declares that our defeat then was a result of treachery alone. Today he does not intend to spare the lives of traitors; he objects to the view that the frontline soldier's life has no value, whereas the civilian's life, even if he commits treason, is sacrosanct. Pacifism leads to war. He has some harsh words for Attolico, who behaved in a pathetic, cowardly way during the crisis.

With the Führer leading us, we shall always be victorious. He unites in his person all the virtues of the great soldier: courage, discretion, flexibility, a capacity for sacrifice and a lordly contempt for his own comfort. It can only be an honour to fight under him. It is one of the great errors of British policy to assume that he is bluffing. He does not bluff; he pursues his goal, by any

---

* The British Ministry of Information.

18

means necessary. Daladier's speech arouses only contempt in him. How can a frontline fighter feel respect for an army that has hitherto sat quietly and waged a 'potato war'? Dr Todt reports on the situation at the Western Front. A proper idyll. Every afternoon, a pre-arranged artillery barrage to show willing, and then tranquillity returns. This is the oddest war that history has ever seen. But we are prepared for worse. The captured matériel from Poland is benefiting us very much now. The quantities are still impossible to judge. London will have its work cut out replacing those losses alone.

Whether it will come to a real world war? No one can say yet.

In afternoon and evening, much work. Look at films. The newsreel is ready. Turned out excellent . . .

13 October 1939 (Friday)

Yesterday: Finland is behaving as if she intends to offer resistance to Moscow. But this is most likely stage-thunder. Massive attacks in the German press against London on account of their supplying mustard-gas to the Poles for use against us. London responds with a barefaced denial. Equally harsh attacks against the Ministry of Lies, the Air Ministry and the Admiralty. From now on, we shan't let the English get away with anything . . . Press conference: guidelines for further attacks on London laid down. Paris to be spared. Departmental chiefs' meeting: I warn them about ever-growing bureacracy and demand more freedom for individual creative work. Otherwise we shall choke slowly on bureaucracy . . .

. . . With the Führer. He is very satisfied with our attacks against England. Gives another account of our military position. Our situation is brilliant, and our enemies scarcely dare attack. What can Chamberlain and Daladier be thinking? Probably very little. As little as Brüning and Schleicher before their falls. If they have taken no action so far, why should they do so in future? Their ridiculous artillery duels in the West are totally unimportant. Their military equipment is antiquated, and they will need a long time to build up new industries. Our chances are, therefore, to be considered good. So long as we do not mess our own nest, we ought to win. And win we shall.

The captured Polish weapons are very useful. We shall use them to equip the forces of occupation. Discuss questions concerning occupied Poland with Dr Frank and Seyss-Inquart.

A visit to the military hospital at Tempelhof. The wounded are just enjoying a concert. Great cheers! I listen along with them, make a short speech, and then go from room to room for two hours. Very seriously wounded men. But the mood everywhere is wonderfully plucky. I am very pleased.

Chamberlain has made a speech. The old phrases with slight hints of conciliation. But still scarcely discernible. This old loud-mouth produces a lot of words, but you don't get wise from listening. A parliamentary windbag! How far superior we are. But now we must do something about it.

Investigation of the rumours completed. They came mainly from the Post Office, from sources in the Stock Exchange and commerce. The trail leads quite clearly to London. That is where the string-pullers sit . . .

. . . The Führer decides to take a sharp line in the press against Chamberlain. It is high time, too. We can no longer put up with his insolence.

14 October 1939 (Saturday)

Yesterday: Chamberlain's speech the big theme. Our uncompromising rejection is seen throughout the world as a very serious development. Now the peacemakers are back at work. The neutrals are stirring themselves. The advantage is with us once again, since now the others have to look for peace. We react very energetically again in the afternoon. With a massive attack on Churchill. Now we await the response.

Great debate about supplies of fat. In hotels, too much meat continues to be given out without ration cards. I take steps against it . . .

. . . The Reichsbahn* has made few preparations. Quite clearly, there has been a general failure in this respect. The Post Office likewise, especially with regard to radio transmitters.

Midday with the Führer. He is glad that we can now hit out at England and has little faith in a peace initiative. The English will have to learn their lesson through suffering.

The military administration in Poland is to be replaced by a civilian administration as quickly as possible. The military is too soft and eager to compromise. And the Poles understand only force. Moreover, they are so stupid that no rational argument has any effect on them. The fact is, quite simply, that Asia starts in Poland. This nation's civilisation is not worth consideration. Only the aristocracy has a thin veneer of culture. It is therefore the driving-force of the resistance against us. For this reason, it must be expropriated. German farmers will take its place.

I give the Führer an account of my visit to the wounded. He is very interested.

His judgment of Hungary is becoming harsher. Even Horthy is part of the clique there: pro-Jew, anti-German, and infinitely egotistical. This is Hungary today! Now, if they could, they would like to make trouble between us and the Italians, poke their noses into our business there. And their most influential men are all corrupt as Turks.

The rumour-mongering was traced largely to the Post Office. Ohnesorge has been summoned by the Führer, given a thorough dressing-down, and ordered to take the most rigorous measures. Some examples must be made, or we shall be defenceless against all manner of rumours. The English

* The German Railways.

attitude has certainly hardened in response to the effect of the rumours in Germany. The irresponsible attitudes to be found in certain departments must be partly to blame for the prolongation of the war. There must be exemplary penalties. Heydrich has been told to name the chief culprits to me by Sunday.

Then it will rain punishments.

At home, work on the campaign of meetings planned for throughout the Reich. Our Party rallies are attracting great approval and enthusiasm.

Diewerge reports on Danzig and West Prussia. The mood there is still very depressed. We are cranking the theatres and cinemas into action. The Poles are being forced out, down to the last one. There can be no mercy. The entire province must become wholly German. The German farmers from the Baltic states are not yet ripe for settlement there. We still have a lot of work to do in that respect.

In the evening, another massive article against Churchill with an emphasis on the *Ark Royal*.* He won't be able to hide that behind his mirror . . .

15 October 1939 (Sunday)

Yesterday: A German U-boat sinks the 20,000-ton English battleship *Royal Oak*. This is a success that we can show off to the world, and the kind of blow that the English cannot ignore. I immediately release my article against Churchill dealing with the *Ark Royal*. London can find no happiness . . .

The order relating to the entertainment of the troops has been issued. The entire planning is centralised in my hands. The KdF** will carry it out . . .

. . . Press conference: the neutral press is starting to scream for peace. London is in an unenviable position. And the serious loss of the battleship on top of everything else. Churchill is clearly beginning to waver. Now we must strike home ruthlessly. And we shall be careful to do so. Our whole cutting-edge is directed against England now.

In the press conference, I attack those so-called officers who make themselves comfortable in commandeered cars and so arouse much resentment . . .

. . . A lot of trouble with the new house in Berlin and the financing of the house at Bogensee. This is all I need at this time. Drive out to Bogensee. The building is now approaching completion. It has turned out magnificently. I am looking forward very much to being able to spend my Sundays here soon.

---

* Goebbels' crowing about the 'sinking' of the British aircraft carrier *Ark Royal* – which had been damaged – was one of his more serious blunders during the early months of the war.

** *Kraft durch Freude* (Strength through Joy). An organisation affiliated to the German Labour Front which controlled all aspects of mass leisure, sport and popular tourism.

Recently I have been very tired and tense. What tranquillity reigns out here. In the deep melancholy of these grey autumn days, for a moment one forgets war and the din of war . . .

. . . Draft a good new effort against Hore-Belisha with Bömer and Berndt. The Führer was particularly pleased with my article against Churchill.

Flak over Berlin. An unknown aircraft passed over Berlin.

16 October 1939 (Monday)

Yesterday: Some rest.

Lloyd George has written another article in the Hearst press containing violent attacks on the British government. Very advantageous for us. I order it to be published without too much fuss, however, so as not to compromise L.G.

I deal with a series of investigations undertaken in co-operation with Heydrich. A small group of defeatists in artistic circles. I have them rounded up straight away.

The children are here. I spend a wounderful hour with the little ones. We gather chestnuts in the garden. A pleasure.

In the afternoon I attend a request concert for the Wehrmacht. I make a profound impression there. Donate 1500 people's wireless receivers* for the front.

Work at home. The torpedoing of the *Royal Oak* is a bare-knuckle blow at England's prestige.

Fandere tells me about a crazy business he has heard of. I get the Gestapo to step in straight away to make an example.

Mother,** Ursel and Axel here. We chat . . .

17 October 1939 (Tuesday)

Yesterday: Renewed savage attacks against Churchill. Propaganda plan against France drafted. A nice little propaganda pamphlet designed for the front. Harsh tone in the press against London. No more talk of peace. The High Command stops issuing reports about Poland. Hippler back from Poland with a lot of material for the Ghetto film.†

English battleship *Repulse* is torpedoed by a German U-boat. England's black day. Poor Churchill.

---

* *Volksempfänger*. Cheap, basic radio sets produced by the Nazi régime for mass-distribution.

** Goebbels' mother, Maria Katherina Goebbels, *née* Odenhausen.

† A 'documentary' later released under the title *Der Ewige Jude* (The Eternal Jew).

Organisational questions with Ley. The problem of what to do with Warsaw. Best put under quarantine.

Kaufmann from the Hitler Youth delivers a report on propaganda, press and film work in the Hitler Youth. He will do his job well . . .

Führer: he is delighted with the magnificent achievements of our U-boats. I show him some examples from my propaganda work. He is very pleased with them. Shaw has let loose a few more *bon mots* against Churchill. The Führer is very much amused.

The Führer describes the fragility of the former Hapsburg Empire. How the German element was neglected. The malevolent and strange character of Emperor Franz-Josef. The tragedy of Mayerling. The beautiful Empress. How he personally became an anti-Semite only in Vienna. How his father was anti-clerical. The great achievements of Lueger. I tell him about my preliminary work on the Jew-film, which interests him greatly. A report to him on our suppression of rumours. I intend to hand the whole business over to the People's Court.

A long meeting of the Reich Defence Council dealing with the food situation. Things do not look too rosy in this area. We shall tighten our belts, and then doubtless we shall get through. A pity that Darré is not at all equal to his task. He talks nothing but rubbish.

The Wehrmacht has had its over-large share reduced. This was necessary. The frontline soldier should get enough, and more, but the soldiers at home should not be so well placed that it causes bad feeling.

15 German bombers carry out an attack on the east coast of England. They all return to their home airfields safely. Result not clear at the moment. London is lying through its teeth again . . .

Film material: the latest newsreel. Good, but no longer as interesting as while the fighting was still in progress. Film of Warsaw. Magnificent. Historical documents of priceless worth. And then footage for the Ghetto film. Never seen anything like it. Scenes so horrific and brutal in their explicitness that one's blood runs cold. One shudders at such barbarism. This Jewry must be eliminated.

18 October 1939 (Wednesday)

Yesterday . . .

. . . Our Stukas' attacks on the English fleet have been very successful. The effect on world opinion has been tremendous. Churchill is continuing to lie his heart out. But now we have him. He will not escape us. We shall not pause or rest until he is a beaten man.

The French have quietly and meekly withdrawn from German territory. It seems they intend to let the English do their fighting for them. We are soft-pedalling the line against them in the press. And going all the harder against England. The London press also seems to have become a little more conciliatory. It is the neutrals, however, who are really doing the work. Our increasing intransigence is causing disarray on the enemy side. And this is, of course, the object of the exercise . . .

. . . Midday with the Führer. We talk about our new tactics. Ceaseless attacks against England. We do not intend to bleed to death on the West Wall, either. At the moment we are hitting the real enemy and giving ourselves a breathing-space. The Führer has nothing but contempt for current English policy. He finds my attacks on Churchill particularly gratifying.

Absolutely nothing is happening on the West Wall. The French withdrawal is more than astonishing; it is completely incomprehensible.

Our Stukas have gone into action against England again. The aim is to keep the enemy on the run.

In the afternoon, to Frankfurt-on-Oder. Test new propaganda weapons. A projectile-thrower that can launch leaflets over 500 metres. Marvellous for our purposes. Its development has reached an advanced stage and it will now be gradually introduced. Then an artificial smoke screen, onto which propaganda films can be projected on a huge scale. That is very useful for the Western Front. But I shall have the somewhat complicated smokescreen replaced by an enormous movie screen. This is more practicable.

Back to Berlin in pitch darkness. Berlin in the blackout has an almost ghostly appearance.

Chamberlain and Churchill have made speeches regarding the grave losses of the English fleet during the past few days. They can come up with nothing but lame excuses and lies. The English people will be none too delighted. And for us there is another pile of material for new attacks.

Brauweiler's plan for anti-English propaganda is polished up. We shall now proceed mostly according to its guidelines . . .

. . . Listen to a superb broadcast reporting the return of our victorious U-boat that sunk the *Royal Oak*. This is good propaganda.

Magda has been in the clinic these past two days. She is unfortunately not especially well. She has problems with her heart again.

I have too little time for work, and too little time for sleep. The days and nights would have to be twice as long for me to get through it all.

19 October 1939 (Thursday)

Yesterday: We launch swingeing attacks against England in the press. I write a furious article aimed against Churchill, packed with crushing facts. That charming gentleman won't be able to hide this behind the mirror.

The French are withdrawing without a fight. In many sectors we no longer have any contact with them.

I study the press. At the moment it is working marvellously.

The crew of the victorious U-boat arrives in Berlin and is received here with tremendous enthusiasm. The radio fails rather to do it justice. I order an urgent inquiry into its thoroughly bureaucratic methods . . .

. . . Dr Fischer reports from Poland. Conditions there are still rather chaotic. The Poles are becoming insolent and rebellious once more. We shall have to take a hard line with them; above all, they must be made to work. Our military authorities are too lackadaisical in their approach. The Party must take this task as its own.

Magda is getting better again. This pleases me very much.

Chamberlain delivers another speech in the House of Commons. He produces the old, lying Churchill denials yet again. From a political point of view, he is a little more conciliatory, but otherwise nothing new.

A brief visit to the Wintergarten to meet the victorious U-boat crew. They tell me the story of their truly courageous and daring break into Scapa Flow.* They thoroughly duped the English. A magnificent achievement. The Commander and his men make a marvellous impression. Real men! It is a pleasure to speak to them. The public goes wild . . .

20 October 1939 (Friday)

Yesterday: Our U-boat men are still the sensation of the world's press. Their appearance in Berlin made the best possible impression. They have performed invaluable service for the Reich.

Comprehensive report concerning operations on the Western Front, which finally deals the deathblow to the lies circulated by the French press. According to the report, the time for bravado is past and harsh reality is taking over. The French have withdrawn to the border. It is impossible to say what they intend to do now. A crazy war. The English accuse us of inflating our successes against them, while the French say we are keeping our successes against them quiet. At the same time, we receive a report from America from a certain [. . .] at just the right time, which finally unveils the secret of *Athenia*.** According to this account, Churchill had holes bored in her bottom. We make a really big splash with it. I revise my leader article again. A comprehensive attack against Churchill. Perhaps this will start him rocking on his pedestal . . .

. . . Penalties for the Scala agitators† decided in consultation with Heyd-

---

* Captain Günther Prien's U-47 penetrated the defences of the British naval base at Scapa Flow on the night of 13/14 1939 and torpedoed the battlecruiser *Royal Oak*. 800 British sailors died.

** The passenger liner *Athenia*, en route from New York to Southampton, was sunk during the first hours of the war by a German U-boat. Goebbels expended a great deal of time and effort 'proving' that she had, in fact, been scuttled on Churchill's orders in order to outrage American public opinion and promote a US entry into the war.

† *See* entry for 16 October 1939.

rich. Most to concentration camps. A foreign woman deported. Defeatism must be eliminated.

Du Pré reports on Poland. Heavy infighting between civilian and military authorities over who is in charge. The Party must take this matter in hand. Some Poles are becoming insolent once more. For the moment they must be deprived of any independent cultural existence. I now intend to travel to Lodz and Warsaw in person to orientate myself. I shall put a stop to all theatre and press activity of a Polish character, or place strict limits on it.

With the Führer. He gives instructions on how to handle the case of Churchill. He also believes that we may succeed in causing his downfall. That would mean more than the sinking of two battleships.

Even the Führer can see no pattern of French intentions from their idiotic tactics on the West Wall. Are they retreating for military, political, or psychological reasons? Is the morale in the army poor, or do they intend to desert the English? All will doubtless become clear during the next few days.

India is filled with murmurings against England. We must try to mobilise the entire world against the cowardly warmongers in London . . .

. . . Big discussion with Leichtenstern and Demandowski, with heavy criticism of present state of cinema. I issue several new directives, above all that fewer films must be produced. I hope that our cinema will lose some of its headlong rush and be able to work in a more artistic vein.

Magda is well . . .

21 October 1939 (Saturday)

Yesterday: Count Ciano is against us. But the Duce has intervened in our favour and given Ciano a sharp rebuke. Mutual Assistance Pact signed between London–Paris–Ankara. Admittedly includes a proviso clause with respect to Moscow. Nevertheless, anything but pleasant for us and everyone else. Turkey is now more or less lost so far as we are concerned, it would seem.

As a result, London has, of course, become correspondingly insolent. The London press is puffed up with arrogance. So long as it lasts! We shall wipe the laughs off their faces. Otherwise, Paris is significantly reticent. Their new propaganda chief, Giradoux, intends to take up cudgels against me. Just wait!

Anderson's statements in New York are still the big sensation. We shall hold back our counter-stroke until we have final confirmation from our embassy in Washington. Then we shall let rip with our broadside against Churchill.

The financial success of our films is altogether amazing. We are becoming real war profiteers. In the theatre as well, though not so pronounced . . .

. . . Shortage of salt in Berlin as a result of transportation difficulties. I quickly ensure relief . . .

26

. . . With the Führer: absolute quiet in the West. Absolutely nothing to report. I tell the Führer about our enormous success with the forces' request concerts, which pleases him greatly.

Duties, work, without a break. I am run-down and nervous.

In the evening, a short visit to Magda in the clinic. She is relatively well again. I am so glad. Nothing must happen to her. We chat about all our worries.

We release the attack against Churchill. It will hit home . . .

22 October 1939 (Sunday)

Yesterday: Wonderful caricatures of me appear in the English newspapers. One could laugh oneself sick at them. International journalists are taken to the French prisoner-of-war camps. I intend to ferret out a few more lies.

Our attack against Churchill hit home. It has been taken up by the entire neutral press. The English lies are being noted in Paris, causing great ill-feeling and indignation. These days in London, all they do is tell lies.

The Ankara–London–Paris treaty is the talk of the world. An article in *Izvestia*, inspired by Stalin, reproves the Turks and confirms German –Russian friendship in very clear terms. Extraordinarily valuable for us.

I read an address by a Professor of Theology named Fabrizius. It is bare-faced treason. And the author boasts the protection of the Wehrmacht. A fellow like that should be strung up. A subversive in priest's clothing . . .

. . . Work at home. It is grey, rainy autumn.

In the evening, with the Führer. A reception for the Reichsleiters and Gauleiters. All the good old comrades. We talk ourselves to a standstill. Best of moods.

The Führer speaks for two hours. Gives a picture of our military and economic superiority and our determination to win victory, by all means and with complete ruthlessness, if it comes to battle – which he now considers almost inevitable. We have no choice. And at the end lies the great, all-embracing German people's Reich. The Führer speaks very clearly and with great determination. And inspires everyone with renewed heart for the fight and belief in victory.

With such a Führer and such a Party leadership, we must and shall succeed . . .

23 October 1939 (Monday)

Yesterday: The children are slightly ill. I would have been glad to have had them in Berlin.

A short visit to Magda, who is feeling better again. I hope that she will soon be out of the clinic.

Churchill answers our charges in the *Athenia* affair with a bare-faced

27

denial. This enrages me so much that I immediately set to dictating a radio speech in reply, which summarises the entire case against him in the most biting form. It is a huge success, comes pouring out like water from a spring.

In the evening at 8 p.m. I deliver the speech on all stations and order it to be transmitted in all the world's languages. It will make a tremendous impression. Now I am working stubbornly to bring about this man's downfall. He is the cause of this war, and of its prolongation . . .

24 October 1939 (Tuesday)

Yesterday: My speech against Churchill arouses enormous interest. It is thoroughly reported all over the world, with comments that are to some extent favourable to us, and even the London press is forced to print extracts. Churchill tries to sidestep the issue by blustering evasions, but one can only smile. His main tack is to declare that my speech was too fantastic to deserve a reply. So, a lame excuse! The reaction in the rest of the world is very strong. And that was the point of the exercise.

Molotov has said to Schulenburg that Halifax told Maisky England would be prepared to make peace under present conditions – perhaps even surrender colonies – if Russia and North America would guarantee twenty-five years' peace. But who knows if this is really true? It could be a rumour that has been planted and become exaggerated. In future, we also intend to use such methods . . .

. . . Dr Ley gives an account of his tour of the West Wall. He found morale excellent. We now agree on a grand scheme for the intellectual and cultural welfare of the troops. Radio, press, books, appeals, etc. We shall put this in hand with the utmost energy.

Meet with eight holders of the Iron Cross from the Propaganda Companies.* They describe the shortcomings that continue to affect the Propaganda Companies' work. These are caused more by personnel problems than any failures of organisation. I shall correct these step by step.

Midday with the Führer. He is annoyed by an interview that Sven Hedin gave to the *News Chronicle* regarding his talks with him. Hedin trumpets Germany as Russia's enemy. An immediate denial. Hedin is also forced to issue a denial. The London newspaper's outbursts have the pure and simple aim of sowing distrust between us and Moscow. The Führer has absolutely no thought of peace any more. He would like to put England to the sword.

---

* *Propaganda-Kompanien* (PK for short). Teams of cameramen and journalists seconded to the armed forces. The PKs, armed and subject to military discipline, were supposed to represent a 'new kind of reporter' who, in Goebbels' words 'Besides a pistol and a hand-grenade . . . carries other weapons: the film camera, the projector, the sketch pad, or a writing-bench . . .' The reality was, as the diaries make clear, somewhat more problematic.

He will not hear anything from the English about Bohemia and Moravia.* They have no business interfering in the East. And the solution of the Polish question is purely a matter between Germany and Russia. We have absolutely no cause to interfere on the side of Finland. We have no interest in the Baltic states. And Finland has been so unpleasant to us during the last year that any aid for her now is quite out of the question. Moreover, we must be absolutely clear that the neutrals are basically against us. Particularly the states that were part of the old German Empire.** Their attitude towards us is like that of emigrés with a bad conscience. Therefore our attitude must be: keep strong, and do not weaken.

My attack against Churchill is approved by the Führer. We shall respond with new material during the next few days. Churchill has named four German passengers on the *Athenia*. But these were Jewish emigrés. The response to my speech in the editorial pages of the German press has been enormous.

We chat with the Führer about the changeableness of our conception of feminine beauty. What was considered beautiful forty years ago is now fat, plump, dumpy. Sport, gymnastics and the fight against sexual cant have changed people's attitudes, probably for the better. We are taking huge, swift strides towards a new classical age. And we are the trail-blazers of this revolution in all respects.

England intends to instal a new German government in London, including Rauschning, Treviranus, Wirth, and Brüning. A ridiculous, stupid, and childish plan. But I can believe anything of these idiots.

In the afternoon: censoring of photos and articles.

Magda is a little better again. I hope she can soon come home. Check the weekly newsreel and lay down guidelines for the text. Turned out well. Further problems with our Jew-film. Synagogue shots extraordinarily powerful. We are working on it at the moment, aiming to create a propaganda masterpiece from the welter of material. Afterwards discuss a further range of film problems with Hippler. Deep into the night.

25 October 1939 (Wednesday)

Yesterday: . . .

. . . I issue another directive to the effect that the peace-mongering by Lloyd-George and Shaw should no longer be mentioned in the German press. The English are drawing the wrong conclusions. The more we talk of peace, the longer the war will last. These days we are showing nothing but intransigence. The so-called alternative government that they are trying to

* The rump of the Czechoslovak Republic, under German 'protection' since March 1939.
** The Holy Roman Empire, which had extended down into Northern Yugoslavia, Hungary, and parts of Rumania, and in the north-west included the Low Countries.

create against us in London is by no means to be written off. If the English do this cleverly, it could be extremely dangerous for us. We shall not, therefore, touch this wound for the present.

The Churchill affair is still being widely discussed, but the man himself is wisely refusing to make a statement. Nevertheless, we shall find ways of forcing him into the open.

Greiser reports on the theatre in Posen,* which I intend to take an interest in again. He also tells me about conditions there. Things are still chaotic. The Party cannot properly intervene while it has the military constantly holding it back. But that will soon be a thing of the past. The Poles are being slowly pushed off into what is left of their truncated state. Very little is left of the intelligentsia.

Midday with the Führer: he is still keeping a sharp eye on the *Athenia* affair. Nothing doing on the Western Front. Great nervousness in Paris and London because of our Gauleiter-Conference. They seem to be reading all sorts of meanings into it. But only the completely wrong ones. How else could it be? They judge us according to democratic customs. And yet in London and Paris they are being forced increasingly to accept our maxims. National Socialism can only be combatted successfully by National Socialist methods. Our finances are in good order. We are in a position to finance the war by completely normal means. This is an enormous advantage. The Führer spares only ridicule for the London alternative government.

I mull over some thoughts on radio, film and theatre. I issue new directives ordering that work be intensified on all these fronts. The people have need of them, now more than ever. Apart from anything else, they must have something to spend their money on at a time when there is not much else to buy with it . . .

. . . The English government is not yet decided whether it should answer my massive attack against Churchill. It intends to try its hand with a documented, printed denial. This would be the best thing from our point of view, since it provides the simplest, most effective grounds for protest on our part . . .

. . . Ribbentrop speaks in Danzig. Yet again, genesis of the conflict. Positive towards Russia, Italy, Japan, allied states. Very hard on England, less so on France. Then some revelations about the diplomatic activity. The speech will doubtless make a big impression. Unfortunately it is stylistically poor. And Ribbentrop has no talent for radio speaking . . .

26 October 1939 (Thursday)

Yesterday: Ribbentrop's speech is a big sensation. Universally ac-

---

* Poznán in Poland.

knowledged as the final break. Now the world really believes there is a war on. A good thing. It clears the air.

The *Athenia* affair takes a new turn every day. The English press is defending itself with all its strength, but Churchill still refuses to make a statement. We shall force him to.

Serious shortcomings in the field post. Bad organisation, which is leading to the gravest unrest among the people. I protest to the High Command.

Discuss questions concerning the Reich Chamber of Culture with Schmidt. The division into regions, with authority concentrated in the provincial cultural administrators, will remain. Otherwise we shall introduce a few changes. The whole organisation must be simplified considerably . . .

. . . The exposé of the English Ministry of Lies revised again. This whole business is enormously difficult. England has serious difficulties in India. And Daladier with his parliament, which is no longer quite so willing to be dragged along and is kicking up a storm against his dictatorial ambitions . . .

. . . A long visit to Magda at the clinic. We exchange many worries and complaints. Life is sometimes such a burden that one loses all pleasure in it. My work is my sole comfort.

At home I find an entire mountain of it. The foreign press reaction not particularly good for Ribbentrop. He spoke without sufficient psychological skill . . .

27 October 1939 (Friday)

Yesterday: Our 'Jerry-Letter' affair* is in magnificent swing. This will certainly be a big sensation. We shall see it through to the end.

The work-plan of the Ministry of Lies is now on its way to America. It will be publicised from over there . . .

. . . Savage attacks against England in the press recently. Churchill is no longer defending himself. I provide for a further pursual of the mustard gas business.

We are also taking a somewhat harder line with France. One cannot be relentless enough there. Daladier is having increasing difficulties with his parliament. Unrest is spreading, but one must not place too many hopes on it.

Absolute quiet in the West, apart from some tiny skirmishes.

In the Protectorate, secret preparations are being made for the Czechs'

---

* During the 'phoney war', a variety of letters and diaries purporting to have been captured from English soldiers in France were circulated by Goebbels' ministry in neutral countries and found their way into the French press. These documents, usually anti-French in tone and often pornographic, were concocted by Goebbels' officials in order to sow discord between the Western Allies.

national day on 28 October. I advise Neurath to make a simple announcement that we have nothing against it. We have made some psychological errors in Prague. Sepp Dietrich told me about them. We are too inconsistent in our methods. Above all, the old-school bureaucrats have a tendency to cause annoyance where none is necessary. The Czechs naturally exploit this with all the means at their disposal.

Establish guidelines for the re-organisation of the Propaganda Companies with Wedel and Wentscher. We shall relax the rather sterile work methods and hope to end up with a fruitful synthesis between military discipline and creative expression. Wedel's attitude is very reasonable, but Wentscher is stupid and conceited . . .

. . . With the Führer. Kinntz talks about his experiences as a prisoner-of-war in Warsaw. Quite a story. He had to sit for hours blindfold while they interrogated him, until they finally had to send him back to his quarters without result. The commandant of Warsaw refused to see him. Poland paid for all that with the destruction of her capital. A high price!

Captain Engel has been on a visit to the West Wall. Everything continues quiet and peaceful. Our soldiers lie in their bunkers, with the radio their sole relaxation and pleasure. Our link between the homeland and the front.

The Führer is getting ready for war. He is very serious and has nothing but work and worries.

The Russians have rejected overtures from English politicians in an extremely harsh diplomatic note. It tears the mask from the English. The note suits us very well. We shall put it to good use.

A Russian delegation has arrived in Berlin for trade talks. We signed a treaty concerning millions of tons of foodstuffs in Moscow. This a great human triumph, but also a very practical one.

. . . The English drop more leaflets. These are rather more cunning than the previous ones.

In the evening, at home, I entertain the German poets who have just returned from Poland. We debate things until midnight, very interesting and stimulating. Most of them, though, are not poets but at best good, plodding writers. Nevertheless, much can be learnt from them. They have seen Poland with open eyes. The picture they give corresponds to my own impressions.

28 October 1939 (Saturday)

. . . We are achieving some sort of halfways tolerable relationship with the Foreign Ministry. But it is very hard to work together with Ribbentrop. Our Jerry-Letter is ready. I am simply waiting for the appropriate moment to set it fluttering out into the world.

Churchill is being attacked again and again. He is in a bad way. His way out now is to declare that our propaganda only makes the English laugh. I set our press and radio on to that. We shall soon stifle his laughter.

Things are becoming very tight in the supply of shoes and leather. The Economics Ministry is not quite on the ball. We create a fuss about it . . .

. . . A short talk to the leaders of the Hitler Youth and the BdM. On education and political propaganda. Choice human material.

To the Bogensee. The house is now ready and has turned out particularly beautifully. To be able to rest here for a week, or even two days. Only a few minor details are lacking. How glad I would be to just stay there now.

Back to Berlin. Russia attacks England because of the blockade. London is in a difficult position. The Pope has made a speech. The old story. In the process, partly very aggressive towards us, though covertly. Pious but non-committal words addressed to Poland.

Darré writes me a positively servile letter. Typical of the little man: one moment he runs around making threats and causing a great noise, and then he is back to the old whining and crawling. Not one of the fellows. No character.

Magda is well. She is delighted that Harald has come back. He is on leave for a few days, looks well, and was in on everything in Poland. Our children are turning into men.

In the evening, look at films. Rushes for our Jew-film. Shocking. This film will be our biggest hit. New version of the Poland film. Now much better than the first . . .

29 October 1939 (Sunday)

Yesterday: Awful, rainy grey autumn weather. Makes me quite melancholy. But all the better for working in my room.

Our film losses as a result of the political change are enormous. Close to 10 million. Mainly because of the suppression of anti-Bolshevist films. The Finance Ministry must take a hand here, since it can call on higher powers . . .

. . . America has lifted its arms embargo, but passed neutrality legislation to make up for it. Roosevelt has made a clever bargain. England is undoubtedly the gainer and is accordingly triumphant.

I order the production of a comprehensive report on England and France for the press. Our present polemical activity is too fragmented . . .

The Foreign Ministry is warding off London in respect of the mustard gas affair. But somewhat feebly. We shall put some backbone into them.

The Jerry-Letter is now revised and ready, agreed with Neurath and the Foreign Ministry. It will be launched on Tuesday . . .

. . . With the Führer. He gives a rather damning picture of the food situation in England. Long discussion on the weapons captured in Poland. Those that stem from the Skoda works are exceptionally good and usable. The Skoda works, in fact, are extremely efficient. The Czechs possess a natural gift for technical matters. Hard work and precision – the basis of success in the technical field. At home, Krupp is reliable: the smaller firms, on the other hand, are naturally more inventive.

No national day holiday in Prague. Minor demonstrations and disturbances. Also involving German police and the Wehrmacht. But not serious or widespread.

I show the battle footage from Poland in the Führer's presence. Everyone is most profoundly moved . . .

. . . The Belgian Prime Minister, Spaak, gives a very decent speech on the subject of neutrality. For the rest, the Belgian press is insolent and arrogant. But perhaps we can use this sometime.

The *Neue Baseler Zeitung**is becoming unbearable as well. I think I shall have to ban it from domestic sale. I instruct Bömer to put the ban into effect immediately . . .

. . . Harald tells me of his experiences. He is already a real man and a soldier. And he has blossomed mightily.

By evening, peace has been restored to the office. The gifts and flowers for my birthday come pouring in, but this year it gives me only a little pleasure.

Magda is home again. How glad we are. The children come from Schwanenwerder. Harald arrives with his girlfriend, the entire house is filled with rejoicing. It makes me very happy.

Two old Party comrades come to offer early congratulations for my birthday on behalf of the Old Guard. We chat briefly, Party gossip.

In the evening, watch films with the entire family. *Alarm At Station 3*. A quite good entertainment movie.

Spend a long time chatting with the family. Harald's girl is unfortunately none too impressive. Magda is also a little sad about it. I continue talking with her late into the night.

And today is my birthday. Forty-two years. How many more? I would rather not know.

30 October 1939 (Monday)

Yesterday: My birthday begins with charming greetings from the children, who recite their poems and are completely captivating. Magda gives me a wonderful gold casket with the children's pictures. Then a film made by them is shown, a little work of art. I am very happy. How wonderful that this time there is no official reception . . .

. . . How wonderful such a Sunday with the children is. We read, write, paint and talk. Mountains of flowers, telegrams and gifts, which surely have more to do with my position than my person.

The demonstrations in Prague were, in fact, quite widespread. Shots were

* A German-language newspaper in Switzerland.

34

fired, one death and a number seriously injured. Things were allowed to go too far. Neurath does not take enough precautions.

In the afternoon, Magda and I are invited to tea with the Führer. Speer and the Arents also there.

The Führer is very nice to us, but it is easy to see that he is weighed down with grave worries. He describes the entire plan of the Polish campaign to us again, with particular emphasis on the critical situations that clearly illustrate the senseless, bone-headed conduct of the Polish army command. The Führer also refuses to acknowledge any shortcomings in the field post service. He blames things on the necessity for secrecy. We also discuss in detail English stupidity and the childish arrogance of the French military bulletins. The other side have no idea what we are intending to do, and they are floundering completely in the dark.

A pleasant afternoon and evening. Short talk with Magda. To bed, tired.

31 October 1939 (Tuesday)

Yesterday: Because of fog, I am unable to fly to Lodz. But there is enough to keep me occupied in Berlin.

We now have witnesses' statements regarding deliveries of poison gas to Poland by the English. They will be released at the next good opportunity. Everything is settled for the Jerry-Letter. Today the press will be full of it.

The English radio broadcasts a low, vulgar piece for my birthday. This kind of thing is exclusively the work of the Jews who emigrated from Germany. But then they lost their idiotic struggle against me once already, in Berlin. Let them try again, this time from London. The polemical material from England and France is becoming more idiotic by the day. The *Daily Telegraph* has published a report that we used clandestine radio transmitters to encourage the Poles to resist, by offering them the bait of English aid. This is so moronic that an answer is scarcely worthwhile.

The *Neue Baseler Zeitung* has now been completely banned. It had become intolerable.

The events in Prague call for new measures on our part. I suggest that if the tram workers go on strike, then we shut down the trams, and if the cinema fans do the same, then we shut down the cinemas. This is the best way of making the rebellious elements eat humble pie. No bloody measures, instead the kind that make life burdensome and painful. That hits home! . . .

. . . Midday with the Führer. We discuss the situation. The Russians are now taking a hard line against English threats of blockade. Unfortunately the Italians have not joined them. They must be tougher. But perhaps Mussolini is merely awaiting his hour. It is a fact that the English always pull back when they are met with force. The blockade against us is anything but effective at the moment.

Our administration in Poland is too German. Our desire is to put the Poles' house in order for them, according to the maxim that the German spirit will restore the world. This is quite wrong. The right thing is to leave the Poles to their own devices and to encourage their weakness and corruption. This is the best way to rule inferior races. Like the English in India. Set up many small centres of authority and play them off against each other. The same method should be used to deal with the situation in the Protectorate. And never compromise. Any retreat is viewed as a sign of weakness. And leads to new demands. In this respect, the immortal wisdom of Machiavelli still holds good . . .

. . . Settle some domestic questions with Magda. The children are now to move permanently to Berlin. I am very glad. It is right and good to have these tiny, sweet creatures continually around oneself.

A great deal of work in the afternoon. Mainly on the press. We are now going full ahead once more. The English will have nothing to laugh about. They are not making things too difficult for us, since they are committing error after error . . .

2 November 1939 (Thursday)

Thursday: Plane leaves early. Arrive in Lodz around 11 a.m. Deal quickly with a lot of work during the trip. Our Jerry-Letter has been given big publicity.

Lodz: Seyss-Inquart meets me and delivers a short report. A thousand questions and problems. Lodz itself is a hideous city.

Discussion with Frank. The situation in Poland is still very difficult. For the present, we cannot encourage a revival of Polish cultural life, since what exists expresses the ideas of resurgent Polish nationalism. On the contrary, the German administration must give more assistance to our own people. I am channelling all available funds for this purpose.

Drive through the Ghetto. We get out and inspect everything thoroughly. It is indescribable. These are no longer human beings, they are animals. For this reason, our task is no longer humanitarian but surgical. Steps must be taken here, and they must be radical ones, make no mistake.

Drive on Polish roads. This is already Asia. We shall have our work cut out to Germanise this region.

Long discussion with my people. We decide on the way to be taken now. Radical against the Poles and strongest support for Germandom.

At Frank's house in the evening. He tells me of his problems. Principally with the Wehrmacht, who are pursuing a milksop-bourgeois policy rather than a racially-aware one. But Frank will get his way.

Talk at length. Touch on a thousand problems. Here there is no end to them. The country is oppressive in its bleakness.

I sleep for only a few hours.

Molotov spoke on Wednesday. Very strongly in our favour. Hard words for Roosevelt. Warning to Finland and Turkey. We can be satisfied with this speech. But it has brought no changes in the situation.

Drive to Warsaw across the battlefields, past totally destroyed villages and towns. A picture of desolation.

Warsaw: this is Hell. A city reduced to ruins. Our bombs and shells have done a thorough job. No house is undamaged. The populace is apathetic, shadowy. The people creep through the streets like insects. It is repulsive and scarcely describable.

Up on the citadel. Here everything has been destroyed. Hardly a stone left standing. Here Polish nationalism went through its years of suffering. We must eliminate it utterly, or one day it will rise again.

A short midday rest at the Branc Palace. I receive reports on the situation in the city, which is near-hopeless. The Polish people has its demagogues to thank for that.

Visit to the Belvedere Castle. Here Poland's Marshal* lived and worked. His death-chamber and the bed in which he died. Here one can learn, if one has forgotten, what the Polish intelligentsia is capable of if given the opportunity. In other respects, however, this visit to the castle is completely pointless.

Another drive through the city. A memorial to suffering.

We are all glad to be able to leave . . . We land in Berlin just as darkness is falling.

Briefly recount my experiences to Magda. She is very happy to see me back, and the children are also very happy.

Then straight to work. A lot has piled up during these two days.

Molotov's speech is the main theme. Finland intends to resist and is threatening to break off negotiations. But it will do the Finns no good. London simply advertises this speech as in its own favour, despite the sharp outbursts against England. But this is typical British hypocrisy. London has just published a White Book on our concentration camps, which has aroused great interest. We shall reply with a White Book on English colonial policy. Never defend, always attack.

Changing of the guard in Rome. Alfieri and Starace resign. Pavolini and Muti take their places.** A series of other changes.

A change of personnel or a change of course? This is claimed in England and France. But I cannot believe it. We shall see, of course. I am sorry about Alfieri. He was very useful to us.

Newsreel completed. Turned out excellently. The Führer is also very

* Marshal Josef Pilsudski, ruler of Poland 1925–35 (*see* biographical note in Index).

** As Minister for Popular Culture – Goebbels' Italian counterpart – and Secretary of the Fascist Party respectively. Alfieri replaced Attolico as Italian Ambassador in Berlin at the beginning of 1940.

pleased with it. Then new rushes from the Jew-film, which are also very effective. Then a propaganda film from Ufa about air defence, which tries a humorous approach, actually with great success. Script of the Poland film checked, and thoroughly revised and corrected.

The work never lets up, and at the moment it gives me huge pleasure.

In the evening, speak with Magda again about Harald. He is causing her some worries.

3 November 1939 (Friday)

Yesterday: All quiet in politics and the war.

The English White Book on our concentration camps is arousing some interest. I shall prepare two White Books to counter it: one on English colonial atrocities, and another about the lies of the English press. In this way, I shall neutralise the effect to a great extent.

Molotov's speech continues to enjoy a mixed reception. This is due to the English, who cannot rid themselves of the illusion that Moscow belongs on their side . . .

. . . Press Conference: new moves against England prepared. All cultural contact with the Poles forbidden. Let them help themselves, and then we shall see how far they get . . .

. . . A view of the current public mood. This is excellent . . .

. . . With the Führer. I deliver a report on my trip to Poland, which he finds very interesting. In particular, my description of the Jewish problem meets with his complete approval. The Jew is a waste product. More a clinical than a social phenomenon. England's hirelings! We must bring this out much more in our propaganda.

The Jerry-Letter meets with the Führer's fullest approval. We consider whether it should be included along with the Zionist Protocols* for our propaganda in France.

Question: should we release pictures of the destruction in Warsaw? Advantages and disadvantages. Advantage that of shock-effect. The Führer wants to see the pictures personally first.

The Führer orders the Pilsudski Museum** to be closed, on my suggestion. Otherwise it could become a focal-point for Polish hopes.

With regard to the government changes in Italy, the Führer believes that Mussolini's real purpose was to reduce the influence of Pavolini, who was not unconditionally loyal to him, and to exchange Attolico, who showed

* A collection of forged documents, probably originating in Czarist Russia in the early 1900s, giving an account of a Jewish 'conspiracy' to destroy Christian civilisation. A specially-edited version was prepared in Goebbels' ministry for use in France, where the Protocols were already known in right-wing, anti-Semitic circles.

** The Belvedere Castle in Warsaw (*see* entry for 2 November).

weakness at critical moments, for Alfieri. In any event, he sees no danger in the changes. Starace was too stupid and vain.

We talk about the resettlement of the South Tyroleans.* The Führer has Burgundy in mind for them. He is already dividing up the French provinces. He hurries ahead, far in advance of developments. Like every genius. In declaring war, France has committed the greatest mistake in her history. This will soon become clear.

We discuss personalities. Hess has made no wise suggestions for new Gauleiters. The coming Senate is to be composed of about 60 people. Not just office-holders but also bearers of honours. Not all Gauleiters, and certainly not all Reichsleiters. A body of old, tried and trusted National Socialists. Frick's suggestion, with its 300 names, is rejected completely. The Führer reckons that he should be happy enough to get into it himself.

We stroll up and down for an hour in the park. The trees are already bare. Everyone is waiting for negotiations. Probably not for much longer! . . .

. . . In the evening, check propaganda films. Some not good. I must be more energetic in my supervision. On the other hand, the Jew-film is very good . . .

4 November 1939 (Saturday)

. . . Decadent art has brought us in a lot of foreign currency. This goes into the war-chest and will be used for art purchases after the war.

At my instigation, the foreign press inspects the 'home front'. With great success!

I speed up the work on the two White Books against England. We shall publish these with a great fanfare. I also order the Zionist Protocols to be edited for use against London and particularly Paris . . .

. . . The High Command is working on a re-organisation of the field post. My constant burrowing has thus finally born fruit. It is high time, too.

Correct my speech for Youth at home.

Watch a French newsreel. Cinematically good, psychologically poor.

Little Night-Music, a glorious Tobias film with glorious music. *Hitler Youth in the War*, a useful propaganda film. Film against venereal disease not psychologically good. Must be discussed again.

Work into the night on these films. Then, tired, seek some sleep.

---

* The German-speaking minority in the *Alto Adige* province of Italy, which had been part of the Austrian Empire until 1919. A recent Italian measure had demanded that the South Tyroleans either take Italian citizenship – in which case they were to be dispersed throughout other provinces of Italy – or emigrate to Germany and take Reich citizenship. Germany finally annexed the *Alto Adige* when it installed Mussolini as head of the puppet 'Italian Social Republic' in 1943.

5 November 1939 (Sunday)

Yesterday: We intend to intensify propaganda against France. The only thing lacking is aeroplanes.

I criticise the latest propaganda films, which are too didactic for me. This schoolmarmish business makes me sick.

Alfieri sends me a very downcast telegram of farewell. I send him a particularly friendly answer.

America has finally raised the arms embargo. Now the trade with death can start. All in the cause of humanity and civilisation . . .

. . . I drive to the forest lodge on the Bogensee. The living quarters are ready now, and have turned out very well. We arrange the rooms to make them comfortable. It is so quiet and pleasant out here. I should like to stay here. But unfortunately I must soon be off back to Berlin.

Dr Dietrich is stirring up some trouble. He badly wants to be Press Minister. A bone-head, without imagination or understanding. I shall soon sort him out. He also intrigues continually against Amann and Reinhardt. But for all that, he will get nowhere. Unfortunately his noble friend, du Pré, has been a failure in Poland, as could have been predicted. He has nothing but little people around him . . .

6 November 1939 (Monday)

Yesterday: Out early. To the *Ufapalast** with Schirach. Hitler Youth film festival throughout the Reich. I make a short speech. The Tobis film *0 III 88* is a roaring success with the young people. One must see films in public now and then, since otherwise one becomes too one-sided in one's judgments. The Film Hours will now be staged twice monthly for the Hitler Youth, to cement their political direction.

A grey, wet Sunday. Absolute peace in the political world. But this is probably the calm before the storm. Impossible even to find particular material of polemical use . . .

7 November 1939 (Tuesday)

Yesterday: The London press carries on lying. Somewhat less so in Paris. England and France have considerable domestic difficulties.

We are also taking a harder line against the USA. Holland will also be cosseted no longer. It has published a weak-as-water Orange Book on England's piratical policy.

I restrict the import of foreign, particularly American films. The public

* The *Ufapalast am Zoo* (Ufa-Palace by the Zoo) was one of Berlin's largest and most prestigious cinemas, habitually used as a première theatre for major films.

does not want to see this stuff any more. In broadcasting, I place further limits on the activities of the smaller outlet stations. We must get round to the 5th Network. At the moment we are wasting too much equipment and personnel. Ohnesorge writes me a nasty letter in response to my complaints about the Post Office's failures in the broadcasting field. But I don't leave him short of an answer.

A memorandum from Bürckel on the evacuation programme. Things have been wrong in this area for some time. Bürckel himself is no exception. He has too many jobs. Mental defectives were sent off unattended, their transport was met, and they then proceeded to eat the flowers they were presented with and then bite the hands of the people they were billeted on. That's not very friendly!

Speak with Darré. He has retracted his letter of complaint, with apologies. I explain the situation to him. Göring has made it clear that he is entirely on my side. In any case, Darré has many worries. He is particularly short of transportation.

With the Führer. He is of the opinion that England must be given a k.o. blow. Quite right, too. England's power is simply a myth these days, no longer a reality. All the more reason why it must be destroyed. Otherwise there will be no peace in the world.

When the soldiers say that we are not ready, you know an army will never be ready. Anyway, this is not the real point. The question is whether we are more ready than the others. And this is clearly so. The Führer extols the virtues of the captured weapons, which he says are good, usable equipment. The attack against the Western Powers cannot wait long. Perhaps the Führer will succeed in annulling the Peace of Westphalia* sooner than we think. It would be the crowning-point of his historical existence. The watchword must be: work and fight. We must not let him down.

Serious worries about the financing of the house at Lanke. A cross to bear.

Talk with Ley. He has been to the West and the East. Morale everywhere is good. Everyone is waiting for the hour of decision. Together we put forward our grand war aims. One shouldn't think of such things . . .

. . . An enormous amount to work on at home. Film questions with Hippler: we agree on 100 German films per year. Fewer, but of higher quality. This means we shall be ending the old-style, purely commercial film industry.

Newsreel: a lack of material. But otherwise good . . .

---

* The treaty that ended the Thirty Years' War in 1648, taking France's boundary further east and furthering the division of Germany into small states which lasted until the latter part of the nineteenth century.

8 November 1939 (Wednesday)

Yesterday: We use the press to take a harder line against Belgium, and in particular Holland, for the spinelessness of their neutrality policy so far as England is concerned. A little difficult to get it off the ground. But it works in the end. It will certainly attract a lot of notice.

The B.Z.* has committed a serious political error for the second time. Editor dismissed.

I instruct that our attacks on France and England should be targeted a little more realistically. The German people must not believe that defeating them is child's play. We must not become defeatist, but we must also resist spreading illusionism. For my part, I am convinced that England's position and her power are both weaker than ever before.

The craziest rumours are circulating throughout the country about what will happen next. At the moment I am in no position to do much about this.

Molotov has given a speech to the Comintern congress. Savage accusations against the capitalist states. Also friendly words for us. Otherwise no clues.

Still quiet in the West. The situation at the front has become rather lax, leading to a certain carelessness. But this will not last for long.

Establish the organisational framework for our Ministry in the General Government.** Along similar lines to that of the Ministry proper. Found the 'German Newspaper for the East Lands'.

Köhn delivers a comprehensive report on the work of his department. Our propaganda abroad is very widespread and very good and skilful. Our radio broadcasts, in particular, make a big contribution to wearing down the enemy front.

Winkelnkemper and a group of other journalists present me with some beautiful gifts that they have brought back for me from Japan.

The SD† report on morale is becoming increasingly unreliable. It consists, for the main part, of vague statements by middlemen, mostly anonymous, which are totally incapable of verification . . .

. . . With the Führer: London's situation fairly desolate. King of the Belgians in the Hague. Idle chit-chat. We use the press to strike home.

The changing of the guard in Rome seems now to have favoured us. Mussolini is stirring himself a little.

Frick reports on the Jewish Question in Poland. He is in favour of slightly softer methods. I protest against this. Ley also. I am also not much

---

* The *Berliner Zeitung*, a popular Berlin daily newspaper.

** The title given to the parts of Poland not directly annexed by Germany or the Soviet Union in October 1939.

† The *Sicherheitsdienst* (Security Service). The Intelligence apparatus of the SS. Regular weekly reports on civilian morale were collated by the SD throughout the war years.

enamoured of the proposal to turn Lodz into a German city. The place is no more than a rubbish-heap, inhabited by the dregs of the Poles and Jews.

At home, tea with doctors and Red Cross nurses from Magda's hospital. I hear a great deal about the public's mood . . .

. . . The King of Belgium and the Queen of Holland make a public appeal for peace to the heads of state of the belligerent powers. But it is too late for that now. A move that could have brought the peace-making process into action a few weeks ago, now looks like a mockery.

Long chat with Magda. Talk about past events, some anything but pleasant. Little sleep. Today I fly to Munich.

9 November 1939 (Thursday)

Yesterday: A beautiful autumn day. Everyone is tense with expectation in view of the Führer's coming decisions. In the meantime, the political situation has become somewhat fluid again. The peace appeal by the Belgian and Dutch monarchs has been contemptuously rejected in Paris and London. This spares us the work of rejecting it ourselves. The German press took little notice of the appeal, and made no comment. Anxiety is growing in Holland and Belgium. We no longer bother to deny all the rumours that are buzzing about. This is also a tactic, and an infamous one at that.

The Comintern has issued an impertinent statement, appealing to the proletarian masses against the 'warmongering bourgeoisie'. The same old tone. Despite everything, this alliance with Moscow can give one a slightly eerie feeling . . .

. . . We prepare the public for the clothing ration cards that will soon be coming, and ensure that there will be no rush on stocks of textile goods, leading to empty shops.

Flight to Munich. On the way, read the script for the film *Jud Süss*. The (. . .) turned out very well. The first genuine anti-Semitic film . . .

In the evening, to the Bürgerbräukeller. The old comrades!* Many are missing, many appear in field-grey uniform. The Führer is greeted with unimaginable enthusiasm. In his speech he delivers a biting attack on England. Searing attacks on the banditry of British policy. We shall never surrender. Vows five years of war. And England will get a taste of our weapons.

Wild enthusiasm rages through the hall. This speech will be a world-sensation.

---

* The annual meeting at the *Bürgerbräu* beer hall in Munich was held to commemorate the anniversary of the attempted putsch by Hitler on the night of 8/9 November 1923. It was attended by many Nazi veterans who had 'marched' with Hitler then.

Travel back to Berlin with the Führer immediately after his speech.

Sit in our compartment and talk. We discuss all conceivable sorts of problems. Particularly the lack of foresight and initiative in the Armaments Ministry. The Führer is also very angry about it. But at the moment he can do little to change it. He intends to wait until the war is over before dealing with the Church clique. And quite rightly so! He sees the general situation in a very optimistic light. England must be forced to her knees.

At Nuremberg comes bad news. There the Führer is handed a telegram, according to which an explosion took place at the Bürgerbräu hall shortly after he left. Eight dead, sixty injured. The whole roof crashed down. At first the Führer thinks this must be a mistake. I check with Berlin, and the entire report is correct. There had been unsuccessful attempts to stop the train. The extent of the damage is enormous. An assassination attempt, doubtless cooked up in London and probably carried out by Bavarian separatists.

The Führer dictates a communiqué, which I issue straight away in Nuremberg. We give thorough consideration to the probable culprits, consequences, and the measures to be taken. We shall restrain the masses until we at least know from where the attempt came. The Führer and the rest of us have escaped death by a miracle. If the meeting had gone according to the programme, as every other year, then we would all no longer be living. In contrast to earlier years, the Führer started half an hour earlier and finished before time. He stands under the protection of the Almighty. He will die only when his mission has been fulfilled.

The police in Munich obviously failed in its task. The necessary precautions were not taken. There will doubtless be consequences. From now on, we telephone Munich from every station on the way. But the picture does not change during the night. When we catch the culprits, the punishment will fit the enormity of the crime.

We stay awake right through the night. I set the entire news apparatus in Berlin in motion. This time, we shall not perish in silence.

An hour of sleep. Then immediately back to my post.

10 November 1939 (Friday)

Yesterday: Arrival in Berlin. Göring and Lammers waiting for the Führer's train at the station. The Führer is very strong and erect.

A few clues have been discovered. But they point in no particular direction. It could not have been prepared without the co-operation of the Bürgerbräu staff. A reward of 100,000 marks has been offered for the culprits' apprehension.

Immediately to the Press Conference: I give the facts of the case and issue precise guidelines for the way the case should be handled. The reporting of the assassination attempt in Paris and London is contemptible. As is their custom, they are trying to push the responsibility on to us. But to counter this, I am mobilising the power of the entire German press. The masses want to assemble on the Wilhelmsplatz, but at the Führer's wish I head off any moves in that respect. The November day is grey and dull.

To work. The Führer's speech has been totally obliterated by the news of the bomb-attack so far as the foreign press is concerned.

With the Führer. We go through the entire assassination attempt once more. The number of clues as to the culprits' identities is mounting. But there are still no clear leads. And so we hold back our address to the people. First we must have the culprits. Then it will be unleashed. Himmler's inquiries are very wide-ranging. We have to believe that we shall catch the culprits.

On the Führer's instructions, I call off the Day of National Solidarity.* In these times, it is too dangerous. We must conserve and protect our strength, for we shall have need of them during these critical hours.

A lot of work at home. The world press huffs and puffs. But we shall soon sort them out.

Chamberlain, who is ill, lets Simon reply to the Dutch-Belgian offer of mediation. A holding action. They have to continue to think about it. They will spend so long thinking that they'll get a smack in the eye.

In the evening, complete work on the weekly newsreel. On the Führer's instructions, we shall re-edit.

Spend a long time talking things over with Magda. We have so many money worries.

11 November 1939 (Saturday)

Yesterday: The Bürgerbräu assassination attempt still the big world-wide sensation. London and Paris are trying to push the blame on to us, as they did with the Reichstag fire. We counter this energetically. The morale in the country is excellent. Still no sign of the culprits. A few small indications are coming to light.

Complete quiet in the West. But Holland is living in fear and anxiety. The same for Belgium. Twilight of the neutrals.

I give the press precise instructions. I speak about propaganda films and their methods. They are all too contrived and complicated. We expect too much of the people, and because of this they frequently find us completely incomprehensible. I urge a more primitive approach in our entire propaganda.

Again ban a number of foreign newspapers. They are ruining my entire mood. Even when they dress themselves up as pro-German . . .

. . . A number of Berlin Party comrades have been beating up harmless

* The day of commemoration of the 1923 putsch.

45

passers-by for absolutely no reason. I send them to a concentration camp . . .

Gregory reports on the situation in the Protectorate. A tough struggle for racial identity. I recommend treatment through penalties that inconvenience the entire population, thus alienating it from the small clique of diehard agitators. Closing-down of cinemas and trams, for instance, when the Czechs make the slightest attempt to strike. This will soon cure them of their urge to strike.

With the Führer: I describe conditions in the Protectorate. He approves my suggestions. Hungary is proving itself once more to be brutal and selfish. She oppresses her racial minorities like no other nation. The Hungarian magnates are a real curse for their country.

The neutrals fear us. They must be treated more harshly, so that they learn to respect the Reich.

Russia's army is not worth much. Badly led and even more poorly armed. We do not need their military aid. Good enough that we do not have to wage a two-front war. This was England's plan. But the Czechs surrendered their weapons to us voluntarily, and we have taken Poland. Now it will be the Western Powers' turn to feel the touch of steel.

The Finns are whining that we offer them no help. But these marginal states have never helped us, in the League of Nations they always voted against us, and today they are doubled-up with fear.

Sepp Dietrich, who has come from Prague, confirms my views on the Protectorate.

Mussolini's telegram to the Führer regarding the Munich assassination attempt is very deeply felt. Likewise the Italian King's.

I work on the Jew-film. The script still needs considerable revision. Discussion with Hippler on the film's future form. I believe it will be very good . . .

12 November 1939 (Sunday)

Yesterday: The Munich assassination attempt still holds the interest of the entire world . . .

. . . The victims are buried in Munich. The Führer takes part in this state ceremony.

I have all statements attesting the moral guilt of the warmongers collected together. This is not difficult, for these statements are legion.

Great anxiety in neutral circles, fear of a German invasion. I issue no denials, but let the pot simmer. In America the press campaign against us is appreciably more strident. In the end, Roosevelt will be driven to war. The Jews are working tirelessly at the task . . .

. . . Magda's birthday. The children recite pretty poems, and it turns into a touching little family party. Our sweet little ladies become droller with every passing day. Helga, though, is already becoming a proper lady.

Work in the afternoon. Give a short speech at a comradeship evening for Wehrmacht and Party. Morale everywhere is outstanding.

Then I drive out to Lanke with Magda. To have a little birthday party. And then catch up on lost sleep.

13 November 1939 (Monday)

Yesterday: A lovely day at our house on the Bogensee. Celebrate Magda's birthday. Quite alone. Grey autumn outside. Some reading, music. View both houses, here and there still things . . . But it will be wonderful. We are looking forward to it very much . . .

. . . Paris and London have given a negative answer to the Belgian–Dutch appeal for peace, as expected. They save us the necessity of a painful answer. War, then.

The watchword is: conserve strength and keep our nerve.

We launch swingeing attacks against London for the Munich assassination attempt. The moral guilt is clearly entirely theirs.

Otherwise nothing of particular importance. Only a little activity in the West . . .

14 November 1939 (Tuesday)

Yesterday: Beautiful autumn days now. Sun, mist, and falling leaves. How glorious the world is, and how little Man in general has done to deserve this glorious world.

London is incorrigibly insolent and pompous. But the noble Lords will soon have their arrogant pride knocked out of them. We bang more and more nails in the coffin of English complicity in the Munich assassination attempt. We have convincing proof of it.

Churchill has made a speech. Sailor's gobbledygook.* Full of lies and distortions, but very skilful. I have the press tell him some home truths. He said not a word about the *Athenia*. So he must be guilty.

The neutrals are becoming more anxious by the hour. Panic is becoming discernible, particularly in Holland and Belgium. We pay no attention to this in our press. Let them stew. The peace appeal by Belgium and Holland has been answered by London and, even more strongly, by Paris, with a series of insolent demands. They have even dragged Austria into it. Totally struck blind, then. Perhaps it is for the best. We are given a freer rein, and it makes our reply all the easier. England must be knocked from her high horse . . .

. . . I order some investigations of astrology. A lot of nonsense is talked

---

* Churchill was First Lord of the Admiralty from September 1939 until he succeeded Chamberlain as Prime Minister in May 1940.

and written in this field. Strangely enough, however, all of it speaks in our favour . . .

. . . Serious railway accident in Silesia with almost 50 killed. There have been rather a lot of such accidents lately. Could sabotage be involved? The background to the Munich assassination attempt is still totally obscure. The clues discovered so far are somewhat vague.

With Hippler, establish a new film statute: at the most 104 films per year. Scripts to be submitted for approval one month before start of shooting. Thus a sort of pre-censorship. Better than censorship after the event.

Dr Draeger and [. . .] report on their trip to Scandinavia. The mood there is one of slight desperation and increasing leaning towards England. London has a powerful attraction for these peoples. Up there one feels as if one is on English soil. We must produce much more propaganda against this. Particularly in the field of culture. I issue appropriate instructions. Only Bengt Berg and Sven Hedin are for us. The latter with reservations. Hedin fears our co-operation with Moscow . . .

. . . With the Führer. He makes more assertions about the catastrophic state of the Russian army. It is scarcely battleworthy. This probably accounts for the Finns' stubbornness. It is probable that the low intelligence level of the average Russian makes the use of modern weapons impossible. In Russia, as everywhere else, centralism is the father of bureaucracy, which in turn is the enemy of all individual development. In Russia there is no private initiative any more. They gave the peasants land, and they sat around doing nothing. Then they had to bring the neglected fields back into a sort of state domain. The process was similar in the case of industry. This evil penetrates throughout the country and makes it incapable of using its strength in the correct way. We have found ourselves fine allies.

In our case, the railways have functioned as a state-socialist institution. But only because they retained strong private-capitalist elements. Our legal administrators would like to abolish those in future. The juristification of an institution is the death of it. Now it cannot be avoided. The Führer has some harsh words for lawyers. I shall remember a few examples for future use. But, despite everything, there have been improvements, and the apparatus of the state is becoming more flexible.

Hess tells us about the Munich assassination attempt. He was at the Bürgerbräu in the immediate aftermath. Not one of us would have left the place alive. He suspects that the culprits are already abroad.

At home, a lot of work. My speech on Sunday was given strong coverage in the press at home and abroad.

Among other things, I study scripts for propaganda films, and reports on morale in France and England, which take up a lot of time.

Leaf through books about and against lawyers with the greatest satisfaction.

Films checked: the newsreel, which is good but still needs a lot of work.

Then a few amusing little fairy-tale films for our children, who are hugely delighted . . .

15 November 1939 (Wednesday)

Yesterday: An enormous row with Amann, who creates a proper scene in my office because of a few stupid trivialities. He is quite unpredictable. To some extent, he has a point. Particularly when some minor official or counsellor in the Ministry thinks he can issue regulations. It takes me a while to calm him down. These crazy people are the cross I have to bear.

. . . Midday with the Führer. Bouhler has now agreed with Hinkel on the document question. How much these eternal demarcation squabbles cost in terms of nerves!

In London a legal wrangle is in progress, Rothermere against the Princess Hohenlohe concerning an allowance that this 'lady' is demanding from his lordship. All kinds of painful revelations, including some to do with Wiedemann. Nevertheless, I don't believe that the Hohenlohe woman has been spying. It is true that she has intervened in our favour on many occasions.

The Führer talks about the Munich assassination attempt. The clues have so far brought no results. The culprits have probably fled abroad long since.

Watch the new weekly newsreel with the Führer. Only a few small changes. Apart from on these occasions, the Führer scarcely has any time to concern himself with the arts. Worries and responsibilities occupy his entire time.

In the afternoon, talk over all Amann's complaints with Reinhardt. They are revealed as nothing but trivial niggles. A lot of fuss about nothing!

Long discussion with Dr Ley. He is a good fellow. He tells me all about his trip through the country. Morale remains unshakeably good, though a little anxious because of the long wait.

Report from London: British destroyer hit a mine and sank. Something, at least, in such times!

Carry on working long into the evening. Möller has talked to Fritzsche and has clarified the Amann affair with him. We can only hope that in future there will be a little more co-operation and loyalty. But who knows!

Late to bed, dead-tired. Another one of those days!

16 November 1939 (Thursday)

Yesterday . . .

. . . Report on morale good. Anger against England is rising. Himmler has now found the first of the Munich assassins. A technician from Württemberg.* But there is still no sign of the puppet-masters. As a result, we shall not yet make anything public.

---

* Johann Georg Elser, a carpenter (executed 1945). All the evidence indicates that Elser acted alone.

Study a series of propaganda works. Some not good, still too school-marmish. But the White Book about English propaganda lies has turned out very well . . .

. . . Defence Council. Attack on wages. Ley defends his standpoint. Night shiftwork of more than ten hours forbidden for women. Workers' leave allowances will be maintained. Bonuses for Sunday and night work will be re-introduced. Effective measures against the growing degeneracy among young people. The attempts of the clergy to worm its way into the Wehrmacht are to be resisted. If need be, we intend to cut their finances. The Polish prisoners-of-war are turning cocky. We intend to keep them on a tighter rein. Otherwise a host of problems with the economy and food supplies . . .

. . . Nothing to report in the West. Our U-boats have chalked up noteworthy successes against the British merchant fleet. Otherwise, all is quiet. But this quiet has something uncanny about it. It gnaws at the nerves of nations, and that is a bad thing.

Still a vast amount of work at home. Towards evening I have spots before my eyes from so much reading.

Magda has gone to the hospital with the children.

Film work in the evening. *Polish Campaign* has turned out very well, fluent, with striking effects. We can now do the final editing. The latest newsreel: another masterpiece. *Slope Arms*: a bad propaganda film produced by the Wehrmacht. Comes close to being banned . . .

17 November 1939 (Friday)

Yesterday . . .

. . . The press in London is, as always, totally beneath contempt. The *Daily Sketch* published a cartoon of the Führer, Göring and myself which marked a new low point. But they won't have long to wait for their come-uppance.

The background to the Munich assassination attempt is now fairly clear. The actual assassin is one of Otto Strasser's creatures. Strasser was in Switzerland during the few days in question. After the assassination attempt, he returned immediately to England – obviously creeping back to his masters, the people who supply his bread-and-butter. The whole thing is the work of the Secret Service. We are still keeping everything quiet, so as to avoid alerting the real culprits.

Once again, we are stepping up our work with leaflets against France. These are still very useful at the moment.

I order the deportation of an American journalist who has been cabling the most blatant lies from Berlin to the world. In these matters, one must make short shrift . . .

. . . With the Führer. Neurath and Frank report on the situation in the

Protectorate. The demonstrations were not very widespread, but all the same, *Principis obstat*. We give the matter some thought. If we proceed too harshly, there is the danger that Hacha and his government will resign. That, at the moment, would do us no good. There is no immediate danger. But it could be closer than we think. Most of the blame for unrest among the Czechs can be laid at the door of foreign radio broadcasts. If necessary, we may have to confiscate radio sets. And introduce other vexing measures that directly affect the ordinary people and alienate them from the agitators. Neurath is too soft. Frank would like to do away with the country's autonomous status altogether. But then we should have nothing left to threaten them with.

The Czechs are a strange people. Like all Slavs, they live in a world of make-believe, filled with illusionary dreams that have no basis in reality. They are good cooks. And their history has taught them how to overthrow their masters.

The Führer speaks of our war aims. Now that we have taken the first step, we must settle all the outstanding questions. He has in mind a thorough liquidation of the Peace of Westphalia, which was signed in Münster and which he intends to see set aside in Münster. That would be our greatest achievement. If we were to succeed in that, then we could quietly close our eyes and go to sleep.

Discuss a few things with Göring. He is also extremely angry about the English press.

We have issued a short reply to Holland and Belgium regarding the latest peace initiative, using diplomatic channels. After the brusque rejection by London and Paris, any further talk is a waste of time.

So this chapter, too, is closed . . .

. . . Spieler arrives back from Lodz and Warsaw and delivers a report. He confirms all my impressions. The situation in Lodz is still topsy-turvy. The Jewish plague is gradually becoming intolerable. The various authorities seem to be exercising power against each other, rather than in co-operation. Why should this rubbish-heap, of all places, be intended to become a German city! Trying to Germanise Lodz is a real labout of Sisyphus. And we could have put the city to such good use as a dumping-ground . . .

18 November 1939 (Saturday)

Yesterday: No news in the West. But everyone is waiting for the first blow to fall.

London and Paris remain notably insolent. But behind this is sheer terror. We are making it increasingly clear to the public that there can be no talk of peace. We are taking scarcely any notice of defeatist sentiments in France and England. We have no intention of feeding illusions. We leave that to our enemies.

51

New Film Regulations signed. Script-censorship introduced . . .

. . . We step up our propaganda to France. The Foreign Ministry is moving far too slowly in this respect. Its hide-bound bureaucracy causes us a lot of work.

I decide not to deport the [. . .] American journalist, but to let him starve for lack of news. This is even worse for him . . .

. . . Our SS has nabbed the European head of the Secret Service on the Dutch border.* Our boys made themselves out to be enemies of the state and so lured this piece of garbage to the border. Now we have the fellow, and he can sweat blood.

With the Führer. Clean-up in the Protectorate. Nine Czech students shot. Universities closed for three years. Ringleaders arrested.

Further measures as required. A reserve SS force from Graz has marched into Prague. In consultation with the Führer, I put together a communiqué for publication in the Protectorate. The effect is striking. Peace immediately returns. I discuss with the Führer the confiscation of radio sets, closing of cinemas and tram services. If needed. The Führer also approves this. All one has to do is to cause the masses inconvenience and, as experience has shown, they will turn against the troublemakers. The arrival of our SS Division created a deep impression. Prague is paralysed, silent with awe. Quite rightly! . . .

. . . The Foreign Ministry is conducting stupid, intellectual propaganda against France. We shall not get far like this. Hess is complaining about it in very strong terms. We shall make representations to the Führer at the first opportunity . . .

. . . Discuss book-collection for the front with Hilgen. Fifteen million books have poured in. We add some National Socialist literature, which has been rather lacking until now . . .

19 November 1939 (Sunday)

Yesterday: I have a host of administrative questions to settle. These things pile up. Himmler issues a very good order regarding the illegitimate children of men fallen in action. This is both psychologically and racially very sound . . .

. . . I have a certain Petermann brought to me, a man who has been distributing leaflets against the régime for years. A piece of filth, whose insolence is even greater than his stupidity. We intend to see if he has connections with middle-men . . .

* In the so-called 'Venlo Incident', Major Stevens, head of MI6 in Western Europe, and his colleague, Captain Best, were lured to the German-Dutch border by the promise of a meeting with a 'disillusioned' SS general and kidnapped by the SD. The incident was a coup for the relatively untried SD and a serious blow to the effectiveness and prestige of the British Secret Service on the continent.

. . . I protest to the Führer about the fact that Jews are treated on equal terms with Germans in the matter of food rations. Immediately abolished.

I tell the Führer about our Jew-film. He makes several suggestions. At the moment, films in general are a very worthwhile means of propaganda for us.

Frank is there from Cracow. He complains bitterly of the Wehrmacht's soft, easy-going methods. The Führer will have to intervene there again.

Bodenschatz reports on the Luftwaffe. Very interesting and instructive.

Three more executions in Prague. Now there is quiet throughout the Protectorate . . .

(20 November 1939 (Monday))

[Nothing of note]

21 November 1939 (Tuesday)

Yesterday . . .

. . . Annual accounts of Cinema industry. My prognoses confirmed. On the whole, all the companies have done excellent business. But also big losses because of projects abandoned.

. . . Brauweiler reports on his trip to the Balkans. A general eagerness to protect their neutrality. Our information policy must be handled better. I take appropriate measures. The Foreign Ministry is a great hindrance to us. Now, yet again, they have rejected a few anti-Semitic leaflets intended for France. This is sick-making! . . .

. . . With the Führer. He has a lot of praise for the radio, which he has been listening to. Otherwise there is nothing new, even from him.

Discuss some food-supply problems with Darré. He is trying to ensure that our old, petty difference is forgotten.

No activity in the West.

The Dutch have lost one of their big ships, the *Simon Bolivar*, to a mine. London immediately attempts to put the blame on to us.

Mussolini has made a speech. In favour of autarky – otherwise absolutely nothing. A little thin for a war, one in which he should, by rights, be fighting shoulder to shoulder with us . . .

. . . Weekly newsreel. Good, but somewhat boring. We have no real subjects any more . . .

. . . News from Prague: things have settled down there. One hard blow, and the intelligentsia crawls off into its hole . . .

22 November 1939 (Wednesday)

Yesterday: A wretched cold causes me difficulty. I have to get through a mass of routine work . . .

. . . Furtwängler comes to me with worries and complaints, some of them quite justified. I help him insofar as I am able. He has done us great service abroad . . .

. . . With the Führer at midday. Keitel has been too lax in giving the Wehrmacht permission to listen in to foreign radio broadcasts. I have this put right.

The Führer now intends to issue an official statement on the individual responsible for the Bürgerbräu atrocity. The man performed his task extremely skilfully. And nothing can be got out of him. The power behind it all is Otto Strasser. He must soon realise that we are on to him. We shall settle his hash. The entire plot can, of course, be traced back to England. The swine had been rehearsing it since August, mostly at night. Only the fact that he came back once more to check it out led to his arrest at the Swiss border. Otto Strasser then immediately fled Zürich for Paris and London.

Discuss press questions with Dietrich. Our newspapers are too monotonous. Even if there is nothing happening on the political or war fronts, we must still try to make something of it. We intend to go to work rigorously. One cannot always wage a war in such a way that the newspapers have something to write about . . .

. . . Discuss intensification of our propaganda abroad with Bömer, Fritzsche and Brauweiler. We still have a lot to do. Particularly in using the press. The English have made up a good deal of ground in this area.

[. . .] reports on Italy. The people very unenthusiastic about war, but Mussolini still adhering to the Axis. The army is by no means sound. The reasons for the changing of the guard were based on purely domestic-political considerations. Alfieri had not proved himself competent in office, and Starace had become arrogant and vain. Above all, the army had failed to come up to standard. Ciano is the strongman, even more so than before. Mussolini told his people nothing of their dismissals. They learned about it through the press . . . Politics is often a dirty business. In other respects, life in Italy goes on quite normally. Italy is holding to her neutrality . . .

. . . Arrive home late. Trivial chat with Magda and the children. This is my only relaxation during the entire day. And as necessary as my daily bread.

Gregory rings up from Prague. Complete quiet there.

26 November 1939 (Sunday)

Yesterday: The Munich assassination attempt is still the big sensation: new material unearthed. England increasingly compromised. We hit home hard.

Holland is desperately trying to talk herself out of trouble. But without success. We shall wait a while yet, but then there will be a bitter reckoning in that quarter, too!

London is cocky and pompous. But it will do no good. The sinking of the

Cruiser *Belfast* is yet another severe loss of prestige for Churchill.

Conflicts about book-censorship drag on. Rosenberg and Bouhler are at complete loggerheads. Let the Devil make peace there.

Köhn's successor still not decided. Six colleagues are fighting over the job. At these times, one can become contemptuous of one's fellow-men . . .

. . . Out to Lanke. Magda is staying behind in Berlin. Deep snow outside. All my cares fall away here. A heavenly peace. If one were clever, one would never go rushing out into the loud, vulgar hurly-burly of the world. All that is so cheap, so distorted by envy, egotism and greed. The only genuine, honest course remains to be what one is. The rest melts away as swiftly as snow in the sunshine . . .

. . . Italy and Japan are putting up a strong resistance against the English blockade on exports. Rome has lodged a formal protest, with an official communiqué. This is something, at least. And the neutrals are yapping along at Italy's heels.

The U-boat war has brought further successes for us.

Hess has come on to my side in the Rosenberg-Bouhler conflict. Book-censorship, then.

Otherwise a very cosy, peaceful evening. Work on documents and then some reading.

27 November 1939 (Monday)

Yesterday: Slept my fill. Does so much good. Snow and rain outside.

At midday, Magda arrives from Berlin. Music, reading: Maugham and Huch's *Pitt and Fox*. A very nice, pleasant change.

Our U-boats are achieving fabulous successes against England. The English are gradually beginning to feel the pinch. Rightly so.

Outside it is really winter. But how cosy is such a Sunday after a stormy, hard week.

In the evening, back to Berlin. Bumpy drive over snow and ice.

And today the harsh weekly routine starts again.

28 November 1939 (Tuesday)

Yesterday: Early to the office. A lot has happened. England has lost another 20,000 tons. Our U-boat war is causing devastation. Public opinion in England is completely beside itself. We shall show the Tommies where they get off.

The French propaganda chief, Giraudoux, has made a speech. Literary rubbish! But high praise for our radio propaganda.

Book censorship introduced in accordance with my suggestions. Hess, Rosenberg and Bouhler under one umbrella. That was hard work!

Chamberlain speaks. The old phrases. But very mild, influenced by our successes. With some impertinences. I ensure that the German press gives him a rough ride.

Moscow–Finland conflict deepens. The Bolsheviks claim that the Finns fired on their territory. Hahaha! But combined with this, an ultimatum containing a number of provisos. Finnish troops to withdraw 15 km. The Finns are resisting.

The Churches are becoming insolent. I intend to make pastoral letters subject to censorship, too. This should put a stop to the clerics' abuse . . .

. . . Alone at midday. Helga comes back from school. She is astonishingly calm and graceful. She reads to me from her school primer. Reading is her great passion. She must have got this from me.

In the afternoon, masses of work at home.

The Irish are carrying out bomb attacks in London.*

Our U-boat successes are weakening England's position with the neutral countries. Italy is taking a stronger line against London's blockade on exports . . .

29 November 1939 (Wednesday)

Yesterday: Worries, nothing but worries. Almost nothing doing on the political and war fronts. Administrative matters can eat one up.

In the afternoon, official establishment of English war guilt in the German press. My speech at the *Theater des Volkes* gets a good write-up.

Finland rejects Moscow's demand for withdrawal of troops. Now Moscow must act, or make a complete fool of itself . . . In Moscow . . . the press and . . . war, but the army is apparently in a very bad state.

A French minister talks of a hundred years' war, if need be. A lawyer-run-amok, who needs a bloody nose . . .

. . . Jannings outlines new film projects to me. A very good *Ohm Krüger*, about the Boer War, and a *Fridericus*, with Krauss. Also not bad . . .

. . . Schaffner** wants the ban on the *Neue Baseler Zeitung* lifted. I reject this categorically. I will not allow the German people's strength to be sapped by enemy poison. In any case, the attitude of the Swiss is not important. If they can do profitable business with us, then they will. Even if relations were good, they would refuse to do unprofitable business. They will not attack us, whichever the case.

Attitudes in Yugoslavia and Turkey are also against us. In Yugoslavia the people are very hostile, in Turkey the government. This, however, was to be expected.

* The Irish Republican Army launched a campaign in Northern Ireland and on the British mainland during 1939–40. Bombs were exploded in Coventry, Blackpool, Liverpool, and London.
** Jacob Schaffner, a Swiss-born Nazi writer prominent in the Literature Chamber.

A mass of work at home. Preparations for the move to Schwanenwerder and my trip to the East.

Prien and his U-boat have sunk a 10,000-ton English heavy cruiser off the Shetland Islands. A proud, uplifting deed. This young officer is becoming world-famous.

The English king opens a new session of Parliament with a completely ridiculous and colourless speech containing absolutely nothing . . .

. . . Strike camp in Berlin. Now we are moving to Schwanenwerder. Today I embark on my trip to the Eastern Territories.

30 November 1939 (Thursday)

Yesterday: Off early in the morning. A rough flight to Danzig. More work on the way. The Moscow–Finland quarrel seems to be taking a turn for the worse.

Danzig. Forster is very pleasant. We talk over a thousand different things. He complains a great deal about the lack of unity in the Party leadership. Then he explains the hair-raising 'organisational' abuses that have occurred during the evacuation of the Baltic Germans. These cry out to high heaven. I shall do something about this in Berlin.

Drive to Gotenhafen* and Osthoft. Across the battlefields. Here the war raged. Today very few traces to be seen. Gotenhafen does not make such a bad impression. And as a harbour it is absolutely outstanding. I inspect everything carefully, particularly the way the evacuation is being organised, which is extraordinarily inefficient. Something must be done about . . .

. . . Evening at the theatre and *Schön ist die Welt*, a mediocre Lehar operetta with none-too-strong a cast. But it is a good thing that this kind of theatre is still available in the provinces. Danzig is fully lit-up. A strange sight for us, who are used to the blackout. Chat for some time yet with Party comrades and artists. Very late to bed.

1 December 1939 (Friday)

Up very early. Drive through the Vistula region in rain, storm and fog. This land is wholly German and must be settled by Germans once more.

Graudenz.** A very Prussian fortress – in the style of the Teutonic Knights.

Thorn.† Here it becomes even more apparent. We visit the town hall, a wonderful old-German building. Distribution of radio sets to ethnic Germans. What suffering is written in these faces. The people tell me of their experiences. Forster has a very good Kreisleiter here. They are making a clean sweep of things.

* Gdynia in Poland.
** Grudziadz in Poland.
† Torún in Poland.

Evening drive to Bromberg.* A beautiful town. Here a bitter racial struggle raged. But our gallant Kreisleiter has finally seen things through to victory.

The ethnic Germans tell me of their suffering. One can scarcely believe it.

That night, speak twice to overflowing halls. With indescribable success. These ethnic Germans are still very strongly influenced by their experiences. It tears at the heart.

Carry on talking with people late into the night. All idealists!

Russia has crossed the Finnish border. Thus the war has broken out. This is useful from our point of view. These days, the more instability, the better!

Late to bed. Almost no sleep at all. Today to Posen.

2 December 1939 (Saturday)

Yesterday: Again very early out from between the sheets. I am so tired.

Short drive through Bromberg. A beautiful town. Visit to the graves of murdered ethnic Germans. Here they lie in their hundreds in long rows. One must see it in order to remain hard and not become sentimental.

Drive to Posen. Over endless, bumpy roads.

Posen is a very beautiful. wholly German city. At the castle, visit to Greiser. The castle is completely in the Wilhelmine style. But can be made usable by a few corrective measures.

Discussions with Greiser about the Reich Propaganda Office. We are in agreement on everything. Greiser is doing his job well. He has great difficulties to overcome.

A look at the theatre. This is very fine and can be brought up to scratch by minor repairs and renovations. I briefly watch part of the dress-rehearsal for *Armer Jonathan*. Well performed, particularly Rudi Godden and the Waldmüller woman.

Amazing what there is to eat in this Gau. Compared with here, we are all poor devils in Berlin.

Flight back to Berlin. Very stormy and turbulent. A hair-raising trip through cloud banks. But despite it all, we get some work done.

Berlin in the rain. It is evening. A solemn, bleak city.

To work at the office. All sorts to do. And a great deal of aggravation. But it does not disturb me. I have seen too much suffering during the past few days. And I am sick and tired.

Russo–Finnish war in full swing. Finnish government has resigned. Moscow has installed a puppet government on the border. Unfortunately includes a Jew. This is a fly in the ointment. London and Paris furious, but nevertheless declare that they can do nothing to help. They are too busy with us.

* Bydgoszcz in Poland.

Late in the evening, work halfways completed. Home to Schwanenwerder. The move completed. From now on, this will be our home. Magda has arranged everything beautifully for me. For all my weariness, I am very happy . . .

3 December 1939 (Sunday)

Yesterday: A mountain of work after the long journey. I plunge into it like a man possessed. The Foreign Ministry is causing more difficulties.

Moscow launches a massive attack against Finland. Bombs on Helsinki. A whole theatre with this Communist puppet government. World opinion is in uproar.

Our press has become very bad recently. Because nothing in particular is happening, it seems to be full of boring material. I take energetic measures. We must have no lax habits here.

The English blockade on exports is encountering growing outrage among neutral countries. We are fanning the flames as hard as we can.

Daladier has made a speech. The old stock of phrases. We take no notice.

Report from Wächter on Italy. Mussolini is said to be very loyal to us. Even the Vatican has expectations of peace.

Tschimmer reports on his visit to Bucharest. They are pro-German out of fear. But they have no belief in our victory. England is working very skilfully there.

In the afternoon, exhausted to the Bogensee. The office building is also ready now. Here one can relax from time to time. And that is what I shall do . . .

4 December 1939 (Monday)

Yesterday: In the political world and at the front, scarcely any news.

Moscow has signed a very cunningly-conceived treaty, valid for fifteen years, with the new Communist government that it has installed in Finland. A good chess-move. Now the official government will have a very hard time. The war continues. But Russia, as expected, is not making especially swift progress. Her army is not much good.

Study a memorandum from Darré on the food-supply situation and its future development. There are all possible sorts of problems to be overcome in this area. And in the near future they can only get worse. Darré's responsibilities are unenviable. The transportation question is particularly difficult. We can expect all sorts on this front . . .

. . . I have the time and the urge to read and study things thoroughly. A little stroll through the grounds, which are suffused with autumn melancholy. I enjoy coming here so much, because it is so quiet and peaceful out here. Here the oppressive din of everyday life drops away.

Back to Berlin in the evening. To Schwanenwerder. The children are still up. A little play.

Well rested. Today back into the china shop.

5 December 1939 (Tuesday)

Yesterday: A day filled with hard, demanding work. I can only repeat parts of it.

Article on England's war guilt dictated. Came out well.

A mountain of paperwork done.

At the press conference, relax restrictions on the press further. We must spread our wings a little.

Finnish reports will also be allowed through. Our people are absolutely pro-Finnish so far as this war is concerned. The Russians are not presenting their case with any psychological skill . . .

Oberst von Hacken has produced a new translation of Nostradamus.* Marvellously useful for our propaganda abroad. I shall take steps immediately.

Discuss the *Jud Süss* film with Harlan and Möller. Harlan, who is to direct, has a host of new ideas. He is re-working the script yet again.

With the Führer. He looks wonderful and is in the best of moods. I tell him about my trip. He listens to everything very carefully and totally shares my opinion on the Jewish and Polish question. We must liquidate the Jewish Danger. But it will return in a few generations. There is no panacea against it. The Polish aristocracy deserves to be destroyed. It has no links with the people, which it regards as existing purely for its own convenience. Frank is also present. He has an enormous amount to do and is framing a series of new plans.

There are rumours that Christmas is to be curtailed. I urgently advise the Führer against this, and he shares my opinion.

Discuss the Bouhler–Rosenberg conflict with Haegert. No way that peace can be enforced. But at least a truce. I am sick and tired of these absurd storms in a teacup.

Work at the office until late evening. One decision after another has to be made. Check the weekly newsreel. Turned out well.

Late when I arrive back at Schwanenwerder. How tranquil and cosy it is here. Peace at home, at least . . .

6 December 1939 (Wednesday)

Yesterday: Leave Schwanenwerder early. The children laugh and wave.

* The mysterious – and largely incomprehensible – sixteenth-century book of prophecies. Despite his avowed contempt for the occult, Goebbels was not averse to using it for his own purposes.

What a glorious early winter's day! And such a mountain of work.

Brauweiler reports on his trip in Scandinavia. There is not much more we can do there. A very anti-German mood, which has only been strengthened by the events in Finland. The German people is also absolutely pro-Finnish. We must not let that get too far out of hand . . .

. . . Simon is involved in a dispute with Terboven. I am forced to make new arrangements for my visit to the West Wall.

Good leaflets for France. They will be very effective. Otherwise all quiet at the front.

Press conference: our attitude to Finland clarified. A number of areas of doubt cleared up as well . . .

. . . Conference of the Department heads and Reich Propaganda Office heads. I characterise the general political position with particular reference to press and propaganda policy. With great success. Everyone understands my views.

Back to work immediately. Gregory reports on the situation in the Protectorate. All quiet there. But signs of glimmerings under the ashes. Question whether we should confiscate all radio sets. For the moment, no, but we shall keep this measure in mind. The students are keeping their heads down now. The Czech people as a whole has no anti-German feelings. It wants to live, and to eat.

Party Comrade Glessging gives an account of the situation in the Czech film industry. The Czechs make good films, but too cheap. We can make particularly good use of them as technicians. Whether we allow their films to be imported into the Reich depends on their good behaviour.

Dr Scheinfuss of the Schiller Foundation thanks me for my support. I donate an extra 100,000 Marks for artists in need as a Christmas present . . .

. . . Du Pré reports on the situation in the General Government. Horrific! There is so much still to be done there. All still unchanged in Warsaw. Typhus epidemic broken out, widespread hunger. In Lublin they are waiting for the Jews deported from other areas. All quiet and orderly in Cracow. True, the German troops and officials are screaming out for entertainments. The lack of anything to do down there must drive them all mad.

By late evening I am dog-tired. Read through a few memoranda.

Then on to the special train to Essen, Godesberg, Aachen, Trier, and to the West Wall.

7 December 1939 (Thursday)

Yesterday: Arrive in the early morning at Essen. Inspect flak batteries. An impression of the German Luftwaffe's truly magnificent defences.

Journey to Godesberg. There discuss the military situation with Colonel-General von Bock. He and his officers make a very good impression.

From Godesberg to Aachen. There, until nightfall, I inspect the second

61

and first line of trenches. Magnificent and imposing. Excellent impression. I am very satisfied.

In the evening, lots of talk. Late to bed in Aachen.

8 December 1939 (Friday)

Yesterday: Very early out of bed and immediately under way.

From Aachen along the Belgian and Luxembourg borders. On the way we view fantastic new fortifications, some still under construction.

During the journey I get out of the car frequently and talk to the soldiers and the construction workers. There are some difficulties everywhere. But the morale is excellent. My mind is set fully at rest.

Short stop in Prüm. Then it's straight on to the French front. Through totally ruined villages, which had been in French possession and were deserted by the civilian population. Only soldiers to be seen. A striking impression.

One becomes totally convinced that no one will break through here.

Drive to the foremost positions. A general and a colonel are waiting for us. We wade through deep muck and dirt. One can see the French lying there on the other side. At this hour there is complete quiet. At other times, there are artillery duels and some patrol activity. The soldiers here have dug themselves deep into the earth and are waiting for the enemy. Most of their time is spent cleaning their weapons and being good boys.

The weather is appalling. Despite this, morale is of the best. I stay for a long time, talking to the men and answering their political questions. There are no serious problems here. All they want is for things to get started, and to have a go at the English. This wish is universal at the front.

Pea soup with ham is served up in one company. It tastes marvellous. I have a chance to hold a long conversation with the men. Our nation is absolutely wonderful. The front line will never fail us. And we shall make sure that the home front does not do so. We owe that to our soldiers.

Back to Trier. Past endless fortifications, which are being built in an atmosphere as tranquil as peacetime. If it were not for the fact that one sees only soldiers and no civilians, one would never think that a war was in progress here.

Arrive in Trier at night. For two days there has been almost no talk of politics, and that is wonderful. No bureaucratic rivalries, simply life, war, the front. Everything has its compensations.

Terboven tells me that General Reichenau has a tendency towards defeatism. I had not expected any different.

In Trier we scrape off the thickly-caked mud with knives.

In the evening, a reception for many of the Party veterans who are serving as enlisted men and officers at the front. They tell me about the situation at the front, at length and in detail. Late, at about midnight, I make a speech outlining the general situation for the men's benefit. With notable success. We intend to repeat this kind of speech more often, in front of larger audiences. For myself, I find it great fun.

Trier is plunged completely into darkness. Good, determined spirit among civilians and soldiers alike. One need not worry.

Work for a long time in the train. Correct my speech, which has turned out very well, and read telegrams from Berlin. Mountains of paperwork have been sent on to me. This damned politics follows one around. Leave Trier by night. This morning Cologne. Straight away to the airport. To Berlin in fine weather conditions.

9 December 1939 (Saturday)

Yesterday: Land in Berlin in glorious weather. Already freezing. Winter has arrived.

Immediately ambushed by heaps of work. But there is nothing fundamentally new.

The Führer intends to visit the West Wall in the near future. If only the weather were better. In the fog and the mud, it is impossible to do anything.

The German press is launching massive attacks against England on account of her use of armed merchantmen.

At last the Foreign Ministry is clarifying its attitude to the Finnish question, after long urging on my part. The neutral states do not come well out of it. Rightly so.

The Führer intends to give Rosenberg wide-ranging responsibilities for ensuring the ideological soundness of the Party, the state and the Wehrmacht. I have no objections. Rosenberg had not deserved to fall so low . . .

10 December 1939 (Sunday)

Yesterday: Early from Schwanenwerder to Berlin. A mass of work.

At the press conference, report on my trip to the front. No pathos in our propaganda from now on. Only realism.

The Grand Fascist Council* has accepted a resolution in favour of the Axis and neutrality. Quite a combination of ideas.

At the moment we are sinking massive numbers of ships. This is magnificent.

Midday with the Führer. He is not completely satisfied with the weekly newsreel, but if nothing is happening, we can film nothing.

The Czechs want to instal a new, more pro-German government. Let them go ahead! . . .

. . . In the evening, Leichtenstern, Demandowski and Hippler. The

---

* The representative body of the Italian Fascist Party.

Poland film. Turned out quite excellent. A bull's-eye! I am very happy about it . . .

. . . A short break at midday. Receive leaders of the BdM. Protest against the often very bad attitude of German youth in the war. This makes a profound impression . . .

12 December 1939 (Tuesday)

Yesterday: Leave Lanke early. Very cold.

Berlin: a lot of work. The Russians have ground to a halt in the fighting against Finland. But the Russians issue a sharp statement against the English blockade.

Heavy losses for the British fleet. Two English ships torpedoed.

Question whether astrological almanacs should be forbidden. Yes!

The young students in the university towns are becoming impudent. We must take tough measures against them . . .

. . . Midday with the Führer. He launches a strong attack on Churchill. The man is living in the sixteenth century and has absolutely no understanding of his compatriots' real needs . . .

The Russians are making no progress in Finland. This is a good thing, for it means that they are busy for the moment. The [. . .] whole series of examples. The Führer [. . .] so far as Moscow is concerned.

The Führer makes some extremely harsh criticisms of the film industry, particularly the weekly newsreel. I do not think this entirely justified. He does all this in front of the officers and adjutants. But he has a right to. He is a genius.

Office. Work. Talk with Halbicht on co-operation with the Foreign Ministry. I believe we shall be able to put up with each other. At least we now have a partner that we can rely on.

Long discussion with Wentscher about the Propaganda Companies. He is an absolute bonehead. Talks about discipline and military correctness, and is obviously covering up shortcomings that must be dealt with at all costs. I shall get my way, using every method I can find . . .

. . . Check the weekly newsreel. In my opinion, turned out magnificently. We shall see what the Führer says about it. Plus a few little propaganda films.

Do not arrive at Schwanenwerder until 11.00 in the evening. Brief chat with Magda. This was a hard day! Work on until 3 a.m. . . .

13 December 1939 (Wednesday)

Yesterday: Work long hours on films and the newsreel. The Poland film, too, has to be re-edited yet again at the Führer's wish.

We are starting up two clandestine radio stations aimed at France. This should cause a fine confusion. I have good expectations of the project.

A lot in preparation for the Christmas season.

The Ministry's new budgetary allocation laid down. The war has made a re-arrangement of funds necessary. On the whole, we get by.

I issue instructions to the press: on no account to allow a weak, pacifistic tone to creep in, particularly in view of the Christmas season. And not to make light of the enemy, particularly the English. Armed struggle is inevitable, and it will be hard. Our people must know this.

Discuss the re-organisation of the Propaganda Companies with Naval Captain Albrecht. This is now my greatest worry . . .

. . . Minister-President Köhler outlines the situation in Baden. Quiet, determined mood, but no hurrah-patriotism. The position of the theatre in Baden is very bad. I shall give some help there.

Mutschmann outlines the situation in Saxony. Big transportation problems. And also organisational questions. But everything is fine so far as the people are concerned. Mutschmann is a real Gauleiter of the old school.

Discuss the question of the Propaganda Companies with Wentscher and the Department heads. A lot looks very bad in that quarter. The men are being suffocated by military drill and have no chance for solid work. Army life is very harmful to creative expression. But we shall deal with this problem. At the moment, the situation in many units is downright grotesque.

Watch a number of war-propaganda films; only good in parts. The Poland film is being reworked again. We shall put some new life into the newsreel. I see some French newsreels, which are very poor.

Home towards midnight. Brief gossip. Then to bed, dog-tired.

What times!

14 December 1939 (Thursday)

Yesterday: I have a small attack of the 'flu. The weather is filthy. Nothing new from the front. But happily our *Bremen* has arrived back in Germany. A great triumph for us, recognised as such by the entire world, and for Churchill a terrible loss of face.

German White Book on war guilt. Beautifully produced and skilfully put together by the Foreign Ministry. It will not fail to make an impression.

Our two new clandestine radio transmitters begin their work against France on Saturday. I establish guidelines for content and direction. This will strike where it hurts . . .

. . . Foreign radio broadcasts continue to attract an audience amongst us. I instruct a few draconian sentences to be passed and publicised. Perhaps that will help. Word has it that the public mood in Bavaria is not especially good.

Our worst problem is transportation. Something must happen in this area, and something radical at that, or we shall find ourselves faced with a grave crisis.

Discuss the founding and distribution of a weekly journal, the *Deutsche Rundschau*, intended primarily for abroad, with Reinhardt. It will cost a lot of money, but will be very effective. Mündler must be the editor. I shall personally co-operate on the project.

Dr Ley tells me about his trip to Italy. He met with a very cool reception at first. People were piqued because they felt that they had been slighted, and completely ignored on the Russian–Finnish question. Ley's talk with Mussolini cleared up many of these problems. Above all, the Russian –Finnish question, also our potential for waging war and our position at the front. Ley gave astonishingly good answers, along the lines laid down by the Führer. Mussolini has to put up with opposition from the Qurinal* and the Vatican. Paris and London are also putting strong pressure on Rome. They have offered shares in the Suez Canal and perhaps even Tunisia. But Mussolini seems to be remaining loyal. We must not cause him too many problems. In general, we must take more trouble with the Italians.

Mussolini is an enemy of England. He believes in our victory. This is worth a lot in itself. The recent changes were not directed against Germany. Starace was squeezed out by Ciano, who is his worst enemy. Ciano is the strongman. Alfieri has not been demoted.

But the overall picture is good and gives cause for satisfaction. Italy is not neutral from choice. She is simply not yet sufficiently well-prepared. But she is working hard at the problem.

Now, at least, we know where we stand.

All the talk in Geneva is against Russia. But Moscow rightly rejects any feeble suggestions for compromise. This is good. Then, at least, she is kept busy in Finland.

New government in Sweden. Sandler pushed out of office. A result of our pressure . . .

15 December 1939 (Friday)

Yesterday: I am still sick with the 'flu, which hinders my work greatly.

Sea battle between *Graf Spee* and three English cruisers in the estuary of La Plata. *Graf Spee* seems to have given a magnificent account of itself. The three English cruisers seriously damaged. No more detailed information yet. Churchill tries yet again to fool the public. But we immediately issue a clear statement.

I receive a rather bleak report on the evacuation of the Baltic Germans. I pass it on to Himmler for further action. Something must be done there.

Berlin 'society' is celebrating as if it were still peacetime. Undignified

---

* The Italian royal residence in Rome.

sucking-up to the foreign diplomatic corps. I shall intervene and put that house in order.

Discuss the report on the secret session of the English House of Commons with Berndt.

Schirmeister writes me a sorrowful letter about the Propaganda Companies. There is a lot wrong in that quarter. Wentscher is completely incapable of presenting our demands in the right way. I shall have him dismissed. I cannot continue like this.

Discuss our differences with the Foreign Ministry with Habicht. He will help me to sort them out. I think he is a partner I can work with. Even Ribbentrop seems to be tired of the constant squabbles.

I have a high fever. If only I could properly recover my health. But the work is piled on my desk, waiting to be dealt with.

Study scripts for the press film and the *Jud Süss* film. Turned out well. The *Jud Süss* film, especially, has been rewritten marvellously well by Harlan. This will be *the* anti-Semitic film . . .

16 December 1939 (Saturday)

Yesterday: A hard day for me, since I am very ill. I drag myself along until lunch, but then I have to spend a few hours in bed.

The action in which the *Graf Spee* was involved was not so favourable for us as was at first thought. And so we tone things down in the press for a short while.* I take measures to mitigate the crazy excesses being perpetrated by our censors. Things that are common knowledge all over the world are being treated as state secrets. The military have always had tendencies in this direction. But our news policy suffers from it.

A whole mountain of paperwork.

Brauweiler reports on his trip to Brussels and Amsterdam. Our position there is none too good. England is making great progress. We are losing ground because of our lack of foreign currency and our failure to work together. I appoint Brauweiler as Köhn's successor, and put him in charge of the Foreign Department and the foreign-language section of the radio. Perhaps he will succeed where [. . .] and Köhn failed. Main task is the co-ordination of all propaganda abroad. The confusion in this area must be halted. Brauweiler has some good ideas, he knows the field, and he has absolutely no illusions. First he must take a look around, and then I shall give him further instructions. He is very happy and grateful for his new job . . .

Russia excluded from Geneva. Will probably get over it.

We have shot down ten English bombers over the North Sea.

Moscow is still making no progress in Finland. This is a good thing.

* The premature celebration of the 'heroism' of the *Graf Spee* was another of Goebbels' mistakes during this period, as he is careful to avoid pointing out.

Otherwise the Soviets would be too full of themselves.

Read new piece by Shaw on 'enemy of the people'. Very witty, but no good for our use . . .

17 December 1939 (Sunday)

Yesterday: I am back at my post, but now Magda is sick.

In Berlin, some slackening-off in work. Despite the war, Christmas is making its presence felt.

Deal with a mountain of paperwork. Some harsh sentences for listening to enemy radio broadcasts. I have them published as a deterrent.

According to totally reliable sources, the English used mustard gas in the battle with the *Graf Spee*. I have them pilloried for that . . .

. . . I give instructions that enemy statesman are no longer to be portrayed as comic figures but rather as cruel, vengeful tyrants. This goes for Chamberlain, in particular.

A host of irritations and worries. But I get through. Wentscher has shown himself to be completely unreliable. I shall have him dismissed.

Assemble the staff. Express thanks for their work in a short address. All of them will receive an appreciable gift of money, which they have thoroughly deserved.

To Lanke. Everywhere wretchedly cold . . .

. . . Count Ciano has made a speech. Positive for us, along the lines of recent Italian statements. A few minor niggles, but none significant. Strong denunciation of Versailles.

Defeatism in the London and Paris press. After the orgy, gradual signs of the hangover there. But we don't make too much of it, so as to lure the fox further out of his lair . . .

18 December 1939 (Monday)

Yesterday: A beautiful day at Lanke. Frost and cold. A stroll through the forest, out to the old house.

Long discussions and telephone conversations with Berlin. Ciano's speech was mentioned only briefly in our press. In many respects it was rather unfriendly and malicious.

Jew-film. Much better, but not yet ready. Another series of changes. We work on it for a long time.

Your Aunt – My Aunt, a harmless Roberts-film.

Criminal Commissar Eyk. The usual old crime rubbish. I shall put a stop to this sort of thing . . .

19 December 1939 (Tuesday)

. . . The *Graf Spee* scuttled herself. A heroic end for this proud ship, which had the admiration of the entire world. Only the English revile us. But we shall pay them back. The *Spee*'s situation had become hopeless. In any case, if the ship had allowed herself to be interned, then Uruguay would have entered the war against us so as to get her hands on it. But nevertheless it tears at the heart. This proud ship!

Strong defeatism in Paris and London. But I do not allow this to be publicised here. The German people must steel itself for the struggle.

Long report on the secret session of the English parliament. I shall have this broadcast by the clandestine radio stations . . .

. . . Growing coal shortage in Berlin. I negotiate with the Wehrmacht for railway waggons to be made available. The whole thing is simply a transportation problem.

The Jews are attempting to infiltrate cultural life again. Particularly half-Jews. When they are serving with the forces, they have some reason on their side. Nevertheless, I reject all requests in this area.

The student excesses at Göttingen were not so bad. Yet again, a lot of fuss about nothing.

I am forced to have a number of church publications seized. The priests are becoming rather too insolent.

We reacted too late to Ciano's speech. Another failure by the Foreign Ministry . . .

. . . Midday with the Führer. He is in marvellous form, except that the fate of the *Spee* has saddened him deeply. One day the English will pay a high price for this . . .

. . . We talk about morale in the country. It is very good. We shall take harsh measures against anything that endangers it. Heavy punishments for listening to enemy radio broadcasts. The Führer intends to have all radio sets in the Protectorate confiscated. He is simply waiting for a favourable opportunity. The Prague intelligentsia must be disarmed. He also approves my moves against the *Pester Lloyd*.* We have nothing to thank the Hungarians for, and can expect nothing from them. In any case, our morale at home is more important than any foreign-policy considerations. The radio is our most effective weapon for the maintenance of morale and the confusing of our enemies.

The Führer is fully determined to go for England's throat. I tell him a few anecdotes about characters in the English Information Ministry. He laughs until the tears flow. These gentlemen are totally inferior to us. As they will soon learn.

My thoughts on the Jewish question in wartime meet with the Führer's

* A German-language newspaper in Budapest.

approval. He intends to clear all half-Jews from the Wehrmacht. Otherwise there will be continual 'incidents'.

Berlin 'society' is still celebrating merrily, as if the war had nothing to do with them. The dregs! To the rubbish-heap with them!

We swop reminiscences from the time of struggle. When we used to mislead and mock our enemies by fake telephone-calls. They will get to know our methods again . . .

. . . A moving letter from the commander of the *Spee* to the German ambassador. Vulgar attacks in the English press . . .

20 December 1939 (Wednesday)

Yesterday: Our wedding anniversary. A rather more jolly celebration than last year's. Then it was dreadful. This time we are all back in merry mood. I give Magda a few little trifles. She is still sick. And the children are as happy as sandboys.

The English press is making a meal of the *Spee*. Impossible to feel completely comfortable about that. The big air victory has come at just the right time. We are putting that to the fore. The English are lying through their teeth. But in the process Churchill makes a few psychological errors, which we seize on. So our position is saved. The lying enemy press has lost all sense of proportion. But, on the other hand, this is a good sign.

I ban all German-language foreign newspapers and tighten up the censorship. This is necessary during these critical times. Better to make a clean sweep than have these newspapers appearing with half their content cut by the censor. The maintenance of our domestic morale is more important than any other of our problems. I issue instructions to the press on how to deal with the *Spee* affair and our victory in the air . . .

. . . Gauleiter Simon reports. He is worried about the theatre in Koblenz.

He also tells me about his difficulties with the Wehrmacht. The army is still heavily infiltrated by ultra-reactionary and clericalist forces. Party members do not get much joy in the Wehrmacht. But Simon is too weak to put up a real fight.

With the Führer. Göring is delighted with the air victory. He recounts details. He is outraged by the scuttling of the *Spee*. Not entirely without reason. He makes no attempt to hide his anger and disappointment. Bormann inveighs against the Wehrmacht, which is causing the Party a lot of trouble. But we shall have to wait until the war is over before we can settle this problem. Our air victory is the Führer's great joy. He is very happy about it. In general, he radiates faith and confidence.

Our most serious problem is that of transportation. Berlin has almost no coal. The Wehrmacht has gone so far as to let us have some empty waggons.

The English press is outdoing itself in feats of humbug. But we shall stick to our course and keep up the pressure.

Churchill makes a speech on the radio. Packed with lies and distortions. He has aged a lot. But he remains a cunning old fox.

Write Christmas letters.

Propaganda films for the home front. They are not especially good. I shall have to replace the entire production team . . .

21 December 1939 (Thursday)

Yesterday: Despite the Christmas season, work and the bitter struggle go on without pause. Early away from Schwanenwerder. The children are so sweet.

The Christmas spirit must not be allowed to go too far. I give appropriate instructions to the press. The Führer has gone off to Munich. He will probably be spending Christmas at the Western Front.

Minor problems with the Foreign Ministry. Berndt has been too eager to exclude the Ministry from the operation of our new clandestine transmitters. I correct this . . .

. . . Schumacher, leader of the squadron responsible for our air victory over the North Sea, has given a very successful talk to the home and foreign press.

Churchill is still lying shamelessly. But here and there we are making it too easy for him. We conceal too much. It is impossible to sweep our losses under the carpet, just like that . . .

. . . Press conference: we must give more emphasis to struggle in our propaganda. Otherwise the people will take the war too lightly. This is causing irritation at the front. I intend to take steps against these bad habits and the public danger they present. For the moment, there will be no more talk of defeatism on the enemy side. This makes our people too sure of themselves. Moreover, I shall ensure a sharper edge in our propaganda after Christmas. The anti-plutocratic aspects of the fight will be singled out for particular attention.

Fritzsche also agrees. He has returned from a short leave and was able to gather some impressions. Our people must learn to understand that this war is concerned with our national existence. I dictate my Christmas speech, in which I place very heavy emphasis on this aspect.

Czech film production is to be considerably restricted. The Czechs are trying to turn it into a patriotic weapon. I shall put a stop to this immediately . . .

. . . The commander of the *Spee*, Captain Langsdorff, has shot himself. A heroic decision. A drama that arouses pride and sadness.

22 December 1939 (Friday)

Yesterday: The *Spee* affair and Langsdorff's suicide are the big themes in the enemy press. The London newspapers are convulsed in a frenzy of wild, contemptible abuse. In Paris and New York, they are little better. A real barrage of hate. Obviously, they are trying to cover up our great air victory. But we refuse to be drawn. We take the offensive and launch massive attacks against London, concentrating on the air war, which is undoubtedly their least-favourite subject. The English are far and away the most contemptible. Particularly Ward Price . . .

. . . The Wehrmacht is still hand-in-glove with the churches. Now they want to go so far as to broadcast a Christmas service on the radio. I reject this.

The box-office receipts of the cinemas and theatres are good beyond our expectations. We are investigating the idea of a wartime tax on theatres and cinemas. We must find some outlet for the money in circulation in the country with nothing for it to buy.

The coal situation in Berlin is approaching catastrophic proportions. I shall make representations to all the authorities responsible. We lack transportation; this is our week point everywhere. Dorpmüller took no precautionary measures of any kind. And the Wehrmacht is refusing to be flexible.

The Führer's new job for Rosenberg has been more clearly defined. It is quite broad in conception. Any responsibilities for the Wehrmacht have, of course, now been removed. And that is precisely the thorny point. But the Führer cannot grasp this nettle in the middle of a war . . .

. . . In spite of the season, mountains of work. A lot of things are coming to a head at the moment. The infernal chorus from London on the subject of Langsdorff is still in full spate. But we fight back strongly.

Stalin celebrates his sixtieth birthday. The Führer congratulates him in a telegram. Short articles in the German press. Dancing on eggshells.

Heavy fighting between the Russians and the Finns. The Russians are making only very slow progress. But it seems that they are getting the upper hand.

Check films. New newsreel turned out well, if somewhat risky in overall conception.

Summer, Sun, Erika, a nice, popular film, which in these hard times will do well, if only because of its totally innocuous quality.

Stay late in the office. At home, chat with the children. This quarter-hour is the best in the day.

23 December 1939 (Saturday)

Yesterday: Christmas weather! Snow! The Führer has gone to the Obersalzberg for two days. He made a few small corrections to my speech. He extended the attacks to include France. War to the knife.

Big railway accident at Genthin. Seventy dead. Dorpmüller's authority has failed totally. I release the news for the press.

Very pessimistic report by Scheel on the attitude of the student population. These kids should have been given a good hiding long since. But we shall take a stronger line against them in future . . .

. . . Press conference: I continue with the theme of the struggle against plutocracy. This is my best weapon against England. Our entire polemical effort must be geared more sharply to war. This will begin after Christmas. My speech is to be the signal. At present, we are not allowing any Christmas sentimentality.

Paris publishes a Blue Book on the year 1939. Including a few unpleasant passages from our point of view. We shall soon brush this aside.

According to reports, Langsdorff's funeral was a very moving occasion. The life and death of this man were surrounded by a deep aura of tragedy.

Helder reports on the mood among the troops. Morale good, everyone waiting for action. No complaints worth mentioning.

Dr Lippert has also been on leave, and reports from the Western Front. There too morale is good, though there is no hurrah-patriotism. There too, everyone is waiting for the attack that was prepared in November, and then called off for reasons we all know. Everyone is aware that this time our national survival is at stake. The German people will strike and gain victory.

Lippert also reports on Berlin. War costs such an insane amount of money. But he still has 800 million in reserve. This had been earmarked for building projects and will only be used for absolute emergencies.

Discuss the finished script for the press film with Möller. It has turned out a little too primitive and naïve. Must be re-worked in all essentials . . .

. . . In the afternoon, Christmas celebration for [. . .] in the *Theatersaal*. Many children present. Magda is also there, with the children. They are very sweet and charming, the public are in good fettle despite all their troubles, my speech is greeted with great applause, and there is great delight when Father Christmas arrives . . .

24 December 1939 (Sunday)

Yesterday: To work early. Not too much. Everyone is celebrating Christmas. The weather is awful. Snow, rain, frost and sheet-ice.

We get to work. London is launching massive attacks on us again. But our assaults on plutocracy are giving the English something to think about. They are starting to defend themselves, rather coyly. They will have a whole lot of trouble from us in this area.

Yet another railway accident, in the mountains of Württemberg. More than thirty dead. The disaster at Genthin cost 130 lives. The railway system is breaking down all over the country at the moment.

Berndt wants to wangle an even higher salary for Voss for his radio work. I reject this. He gets enough!

Tschimmer reports on his trip to Greece. Opinions there divided.

Strongly dependent on England. Especially the king. Not so the Crown Prince, but his wife, significantly, is a Hohenzollern princess.* What a pack! They must be eliminated. The princely parasites of Europe.

To Lanke. An inspection. Now almost everything is finished, and very nicely done. I am very pleased. In Berlin it is already Christmas, and at Schwanenwerder, too. Magda is setting out the gifts. The children are happy. For myself, Christmas is my last concern. I immediately intervene in the radio, which is already coming out with Christmas sentimentality. We can have none of that in this year, of all years. We must make our people hard. My speech has prepared the ground well. It has figured prominently in the press at home and abroad. Hate the only response in London.

Russia has issued an official communiqué, excusing herself for her failure to make progress in Finland. It seems, then, that things are not going so well.

We respond to the French Yellow Book. It offers a few exposed flanks that we can attack.

Work on for a long time at Schwanenwerder. And then sleep! How modest one's expectations of happiness have become!

25 December 1939 (Monday)

Yesterday: A restful day. Sleep and the relaxation I so badly need now.

The children are delightful, and full of Christmas cheer the whole day long.

Prien has returned from a long cruise with his fill of kills. He has the stuff in him to make a real national hero.

The two railway accidents have turned out even more serious than had been thought. In all, over 200 dead. Now something must be done in this quarter, or the public will lose all confidence. And once mistrust is there, it is difficult to eliminate it.

Hess releases an open letter clarifying the status of illegitimate children in wartime. Very frank and without false prudery or bourgeois inhibition. We can only hope that this question will thus be freed from the shackles of convention . . .

. . . The Führer is spending his Christmas at the West Wall.

Short Christmas party with the children. They enjoy themselves hugely and are very happy. So they should. They are too small to be able to understand the gravity of the times we live in.

For myself, I have little urge to celebrate. I long to return to work. All this ritualistic nonsense goes against the grain.

Spend the evening reading.

And so we have it behind us.

---

* Princess Frederike of Brunswick, later Queen of Greece.

74

26 December 1939 (Tuesday)

Yesterday: Outside we have snow, rain, slush. Quite a Christmas.

Harald has come on a visit from Posen. He is a dashing boy these days, and will soon be off to the army. The friend he has brought with him has been a soldier for some months now. So boys turn into men.

Spend the whole day reading. Work over some old papers. Necessary from time to time.

Get to know the inner rottenness of English society by reading Maugham. This society will collapse if it is pushed hard enough. And we shall make sure of that.

Such a day of relaxation and reading does a wonderful amount of good. And these days one needs this more than ever.

27 December 1939 (Wednesday)

Yesterday: Sleep my fill again. This is the real value of Christmas . . .

. . . In the afternoon, with Magda and the children to Lanke. Real winter and snow there. But blessed peace; it does one good.

Looked at films. *Mother-Love* again. A real masterpiece. A really big hit from Ucicky with Käthe Dorsch. Receives the highest recommendations.

Two Worlds by Gründgens. A film set in the present and about helping with the harvest – or at least supposedly so. It has totally missed the point. Too intellectual and almost entirely cerebral in its demands on the audience. Gründgens cannot get out of his own skin.

The Pope has made a Christmas speech. Full of bitter, covert attacks against us, against the Reich and National Socialism. All the forces of internationalism are against us. We must break them.

King George has made a speech to the Empire. Nothing but hollow phrases – sterile and idiotic.

Count Bethlen has been so kind as to inform the world that Hungary will stand easy and only make demands when peace arrives. Typically Hungarian! He is so Hungarian that he has absolutely no qualms, not only about thinking such thoughts but also about voicing them.

In the evening, another film. *Twilight*. A smuggler-film. But well made.

How well I sleep out here!

28 December 1939 (Thursday)

. . . In the press conference, again set out the material for the fight against England. We intend to ransack the whole of English literature and law.

Daladier delivers a hate-filled speech. We react vigorously in the press here. We pay no attention to the speeches by the Pope and the English king.

More railway accidents. The system is collapsing totally.

Dictate my speech for the New Year. A broad review of 1939.

Midday with the Führer. He tells me about his Christmas trip to the West Wall, which impressed him deeply. The mood at the front could not be better. The troops were beside themselves with joy. The Führer's visit came as a complete surprise to them.

The Führer speaks of Count Bethlen's article with contempt; he also reckons it to be typically Hungarian. These Magyars will learn another side of us when we have won our victory.

So far as Russia is concerned, the Führer hopes that she has bitten off more than she can chew in Finland. We have no need of a two-front war. So far as the West alone is concerned, we shall soon settle the issue. The Führer has decided on a great offensive so soon as the weather and circumstances allow. The whole nation awaits it.

The Führer ridicules the Foreign Ministry and its bureaucracy. We shall never be able to rid ourselves of it. It carries on eating into the country's fabric like dry rot, he says. This judgement is not altogether correct. Our diplomatic corps often has a difficult job to cope with. And Ribbentrop is trying hard to strengthen its hand. For the most part, of course, it has no understanding of the new Germany, and outside in the world it is subject to strong temptations. And so far as bureaucracy is concerned, these things cannot be eliminated. It is a fact of life, not a sickness. Like jurisprudence. The jurists have managed to manoeuvre themselves into a position where they have no responsibilities to our state. They leave the ultimate responsibility to the legislators. The jurist is a refugee from responsibility. *Pereat mundis, fiat justitia!*

The Führer also pours scorn on teachers. I have no objection to that. Today they have as little right to be called 'creators of the race' as they had yesterday to be called 'popular educators'. They are and will ever remain arse-whackers.

I put forward my complaints about the church. The Führer shares them completely, but does not believe that the churches will try anything in the middle of a war. But he knows that he will have to get around to dealing with the conflict between church and state. At the moment, however, our own extremists are making things too easy for the churches. They are presenting them with cheap ammunition. The Führer passionately rejects any thought of founding a religion. He has no intention of becoming a priest. His sole, exclusive role is that of a politician. The best way to deal with the churches is to claim to be a 'positive Christian'. So far as these questions are concerned, therefore, the technique must be to hold back for the present and coolly strangle any attempts at impudence or interference in the affairs of the state. And this we shall endeavour to ensure to the best of our ability . . .

. . . Back to the Bogensee with Harald. Everything blanketed in snow. Now the children are all there. The house has come alive. What a glorious feeling! The children fill the entire house with their noise. Only now does the place feel like home . . .

Yesterday: Everyone is still celebrating Christmas in Berlin. We are hard at work. The unpolitical ministries have things better than people think.

The amount of incoming paperwork is not too great. A few theatre and film problems.

Grants for propaganda. Read through English leaflets. Again, downright stupid. We shall not bother to react.

In the press conference, outline our attitude to Russia. We must be reticent. No more pamphlets and books about Russia, either positive or negative.

I press for the introduction of censorship with regard to church publications and pastoral letters. The Ministry of Religion is causing nothing put problems in this respect. The Ministry of the Priests.

More detailed reports on the railway accident at Genthin. The whole thing was rather appalling.

New Year speech completed. I believe that it has turned out excellently.

The Pope is playing games with the Quirinal. Probably to do with peace. But little reaction from either side.

Midday with the Führer. Discuss a number of theatre questions with him. But at the moment neither of us is particularly interested in this area.

Russia interests the Führer greatly. Stalin is a typical Asiatic Russian. Bolshevism has swept aside the old, European élite in Russia. This élite alone was in a position to make this colossus capable of political action. It is fortunate that this is no longer the case. Russia remains Russia, no matter how she is ruled. We should be glad that Moscow is busy. We shall know how to prevent Bolshevism from encroaching on Western Europe.

We come back to religious questions again. The Führer is deeply religious, though completely anti-Christian. He views Christianity as a symptom of decay. Rightly so. It is a branch of the Jewish race. This can be seen in the similarity of religious rites. Both (Judaism and Christianity) have no point of contact to the animal element, and thus, in the end, they will be destroyed. The Führer is a convinced vegetarian, on principle. His arguments cannot be refuted on any serious basis. They are totally unanswerable. He has little regard for homo sapiens. Man should not feel so superior to animals. He has no reason to. Man believes that he alone has intelligence, a soul, and the power of speech. Has not the animal these things? Just because we, with our dull senses, cannot recognise them, it does not prove that they are not there.

A further long discussion with Colonel Schmundt about the re-organisation of the Propaganda Companies. The Wehrmacht must come round to a willingness for reforms to be made. Things cannot continue like this. Keitel has written me a long letter, in which he talks at length and very learnedly about military discipline. But that will not solve the problem. We have to find a middle way between military discipline and creative freedom. So far, we have not succeeded. Schmundt will now tackle the problem . . .

30 December 1939 (Saturday)

Yesterday: A biting cold. −17 C. Deep snow outside. Hard to set off so early for Berlin.

Work has not yet got properly under way. I clarify our cultural aims in Prague for Dr Drewes. We must be superior to the Czechs in all areas, and must not compete in those where we have no hope of becoming so. Thus we have either a first-class German orchestra, or none at all. Drewes views everything too theoretically and provincially.

A number of cinema problems with Reichmeister. The Gründgens film can hardly be saved. The *Jud Süss* film is going ahead. François Rosay is abusing us in the most vulgar fashion on the French radio. The old brute!

An American committee of investigation confirms our position on the *Athenia* affair completely. A feast for us. And a terrible defeat for Churchill. We shall fight this one out to the finish.

Fritzsche is rather tired. I have to perk him up. I relieve him of responsibilities for the foreign-language section of the radio and transfer this to Department A* under Brauweiler. This is where the section belongs, and Fritzsche has too many posts.

Our films are improving. We have won the First Prize at Venice for *Robert Koch* and Special Distinctions for *Rauschende Ballnacht* and cultural films. Way ahead of other nations. This makes me proud and happy . . .

. . . With the Führer. Discuss the Propaganda Companies with Schmundt again. He shares my views completely and will now report to Keitel.

I report to the Führer on the conversion of the Admiral's Palace. He is very interested. He intends to increase the spatial dimensions of our theatres enormously in future, and is making a first attempt with the new building in Munich, which will have 4000 seats. Otherwise the theatre will gradually lose all justification for its existence. Somewhere it must still have roots in the people. Otherwise, the new film techniques will prove too strong a competitor for the theatre. But these are problems of peace, not of war.

The Führer is very satisfied with our propaganda. And, indeed, we are hitting out hard. The last weekly newsreel also met with his approval.

An English battleship torpedoed. Unfortunately, the tub was not sunk. It managed to drag itself back into port. Nevertheless, a grave loss for the English, who were sitting too high on their horses. In all, we have now sunk over a million registered tons. We spell it out very precisely for the English in the press. This irritates them more than anything.

Spain has been protesting energetically to the English about violations of its neutrality. If only these sluggards would set to properly. England will remain a power only so long as this colossus with feet of clay is not attacked.

At the office, all sorts keep me busy until evening.

Then Magda arrives. We are able to talk for a while, and then we drive to

* The Foreign (*Ausland*) Department.

the première of the film *Mother-Love*. A spectacular affair, and, as expected, sensational success for the film. Ucicky and Dorsch are very happy. And Stark as well. The public is deeply moved. I am delighted at this victory for German cinema.

Magda stays with the Hommels. I spend the night at the ministry, for the first time in a long while.

31 December 1939 (Sunday)

Yesterday: Straight to work in Berlin. Deep snow outside.

Big earthquake in Anatolia with more than 30,000 dead. A serious blow for Turkey. Will doubtless paralyse her for the present.

The *Athenia* affair features prominently in our press. We shall keep worrying at this!

London is forced to concede our torpedo's bull's-eye, but insists, as always, that casualties were few.

The film *Mother-Love* has been greeted with the sincerest enthusiasm in the press.

The Führer has approved all of my New Year speech. I am now reworking the military section with Schmundt.

I instruct the press to continue dealing with the *Athenia* affair. Also the line for New Year: Steadfastness, no illusions, clarity and unshakeability of our aims . . .

1 January 1940 (Monday)

Yesterday: Ice and snow outside. The Führer has gone to the Obersalzberg. All quiet on the political and war fronts. I am able to relax.

The Führer issues a New Year Proclamation to the Party and the Wehrmacht. Review of the year. 'They want war, then let them have it!' The world can no longer doubt.

Romp, play, and go tobogganing with the children. Then a sleigh-ride with Magda and the children. Very beautiful in the snow-covered forest . . .

Towards evening, to Berlin. To make my New Year speech on the radio. I think it is very effective.

Back to Bogensee with Ello.*

Quiet turn of the year. We chat and tell stories. At twelve we lift our glasses. 'God punish England!' The moon hangs high over the lake. Far away, the village church bells ring.

A new year begins. May God give us victory! The great victory! For that we shall work and fight.

* Elenore (Ello) Quandt. Magda Goebbels' sister-in-law by her first marriage.

Part Two

1940

The chunks of the diaries available for 1940 are concentrated in the first and last months of Hitler's annus mirabilis. *A few give an idea of the excitement of a time when Germany's armies subjugated Norway, Denmark, France, Belgium and Holland in the space of a few weeks.*

Goebbels had by now become locked into a hardworking routine that does not seem to have been disturbed by victory. He continued to watch developments keenly and sombrely, in particular trying to ensure that no tendency to over-optimism ('illusionism' as he dubbed it) was allowed to develop among the German public. The deviousness and flexibility of his propaganda machine was becoming apparent; his intention was that he would be able to deal with any eventuality.

In his private life, circumstances had improved. Magda Goebbels had become a 'good comrade', and in October 1940 their sixth and last child, Heide, was born. The Goebbelses continued to acquire houses and build and extend energetically. During 1940 the problem of the Minister's finances was solved by the German Film Industry (of which Goebbels had total control) acquiring nominal ownership of his home at Lanke, thus becoming responsible for his expenses and decreasing his tax liability. Magda Goebbels' weak heart seems to have been the main cause of personal concern.

There were also long talks with Hitler which show Goebbels' total – and quite sincere – subservience and devotion to his Führer. The Hitler here is the Hitler of victory, seen through Goebbels' eyes as a ruthless, expansive and intolerant genius able to re-make Europe by an effort of will. The main obstacle, Britain under Churchill, is vilified ceaselessly.

Also attacked were the Jews. In the diaries, there are anti-Semitic film projects mentioned, and also Goebbels' support for measures against Jewish citizens in Berlin, his own Party fiefdom. Victory brought no changes in that respect. Goebbels was on hand, as ever, to provide the justifications and 'soften up' public opinion.

2 January 1940 (Tuesday)

Yesterday: A very peaceful first day of the year. Go for a sleigh-ride in the forest with the children.

In the afternoon, Dr Lippert, Görlitzer, Haegert and Fanderl arrive. We talk over political and war problems and pull everything apart.

Gossip until late in the evening.

Sleep my fill again.

And now the difficult year of 1940 really begins.

3 January 1940 (Wednesday)

Yesterday: Early into Berlin. The entire forest is blanketed with snow and hoar-frost.

Everywhere else in Berlin, the offices are still closed. Funk has written from Salzburg. Those gentlemen have a fine life!

My New Year speech is given a lot of attention in the press both at home and abroad.

Gründgens wants to talk to me about that bad film of his. Distressing business! . . .

. . . Report on the return of the Volhynia Germans.* The Russians are behaving very decently in this affair. But the Ukranians are very unhappy at being handed over to the Bolsheviks.

Letters found on German prisoners-of-war published in the Paris press. Very positive from our point of view.

More rumours of peace initiatives from the Vatican and the neutral powers. We take no notice.

I explain the essentials of propaganda to the press conference yet again. Fritzsche is often too literary for my taste. He fails to properly understand the value of repetition in propaganda. One must constantly be repeating the same thing in different forms. The public is basically very conservative. It must be thoroughly saturated with our views by constant repetition. Until the message sticks. Only then can one be sure of success.

Waldegg has come on leave from his minesweeper. He tells me about his tough service in the North Sea. Morale is good there, but everyone wants an offensive or some kind of clarification. If only the weather were better!

Schirmeister has become quite fat and rotund on leave. He has never had it so good as now. All is quiet on the Upper Rhine. What a war. The French on the other side of the river sing and play the England-song.

The Führer is still on the mountain. And so I can drive back to Lanke in the afternoon. There are all sorts of things to do there.

The French are wracking their brains searching for our clandestine transmitters. We shall conceal them from now on as best we can.

* Ethnic Germans from Russian-occupied Eastern Poland.

84

Titel is to take over responsibility for the Propaganda Companies from Wentscher. Major Martin will then act as liaison with the Wehrmacht High Command.

Mussolini has sent a very personal and also politically far-reaching New Year telegram to the Führer. The telegram from the Italian king is all the more reserved and cool.

Franco has attacked England and the Jews in a radio speech. Something, at least, for our money, our aircraft, and our blood.

First hints of peace between Moscow and Tokyo. Temporary settlement of the fishing rights dispute. It would be a good thing if they were to come to agreement.

80,000 dead in the latest Anatolian earthquake. Turkey is thus checkmated for the present. This sounds very callous, but in war charity begins at home, and better Turkish than German dead . . . Increasing press offensive from London and especially Paris, using the peace rumours. We shall probably have to do something, because they are trying to pin these on us.

Count Teleki, as a typical Hungarian, has demanded more territory in return for Hungary's non-participation in the war. A cowardly, ungrateful gang!

The Russians are stuck fast in Finland. No sign of progress. . .

4 January 1940 (Thursday)

Yesterday: Early to Berlin. The Führer is still on the mountain.

Aggravation with Furtwängler, who has fixed up to use only Czechs and Finns for his next concert. I put a stop to this.

Report from Rumania. Feeling rather pro-Entente. We are getting our way only after the greatest difficulty. The others have more money. We lack foreign currency.

Massen, general manager of the theatre in Frankfurt, visited Bucharest with his troupe. He has more positive aspects to report. Their hearts are in France, but their heads are with us. He was given a friendly welcome, but that says very little. They are waiting to see which way the scales tip. He was also in Barcelona. Spain has become a poverty-stricken, exhausted country. The population is very depressed, and it is extraordinarily hard to make a living. The church is gaining more and more power. Franco is no longer so popular. People are waiting for a miracle. There can be no question of their joining in the war under these circumstances.

The English continue to hurl abuse until they foam at the mouth. But it no longer has any effect. Nevertheless, strong peace rumours coming from London. We do nothing to help or hinder.

The French press is going crazy about our clandestine transmitters. Our camouflage has been completely successful. Now we must use them with great care. . .

85

. . . Long session haggling with Gründgens. He is convinced that his film *Two Worlds* is good, and has Göring on his side. This I cannot understand. He makes new film proposals.

Terboven complains about the lack of German propaganda in Holland and Belgium. I lack the necessary foreign currency. Thyssen* has sent the Führer a treasonable letter and is threatening to publish it. Our corrupt industry! A dirty trick!

Heydrich advises against censorship of pastoral letters. He believes that he can achieve the same goal by less painful methods. I am satisfied with this. . .

5 January 1940 (Friday)

Yesterday: London is lying its heart out about the latest air battles. We take energetic counter-measures.

A report on the *Graf Spee* engagement. This report is by no means a source of unalloyed joy. . .

. . . Brauweiler delivers a comprehensive report on the situation in the

---

* The disillusioned millionaire supporter of Hitler argued that in 1933 he had helped Hitler to power on the understanding that he 'uphold the constitution' and that therefore 'my conscience is clear'. He wrote further:

> In the course of time . . . a disastrous change took place. Already at an early stage I felt it necessary to voice my protest against the persecution of Christianity, against the brutalisation of its priests, against the desecration of its churches.
> When on 8 November 1938 the Jews were robbed and tortured in the most cowardly and brutal manner, and their synagogues destroyed all over Germany, I protested once more. As an outward expression of my repugnance, I resigned my position of State Councillor. All my protests obtained no reply and no remedy . . .
> Now you have concluded a pact with Communism. Your Propaganda Ministry even dares to state that the good Germans who voted for you, the professed opponents of Communism, are, in essence, identical with those beastly anarchists who have plunged Russia into tragedy, and who were described by you yourself as 'bloodstained common criminals' . . . Stop the useless bloodshed and Germany will obtain peace with honour, and will thus preserve her unity.'

Thyssen, ending with an emotional 'Heil Germany!', demanded that the letter 'not be kept from the German people'. It was, in fact, never published. In February 1940, Thyssen was stripped of his nationality and all his large industrial holdings confiscated, and in the summer he was trapped in France by the German advance and arrested. He languished in a concentration camp while his confessions, *I Paid Hitler*, were published in the USA.

Foreign Department. We have lost a lot of ground to the Foreign Ministry. We must make this up again.

Speak with Marian about the *Jud Süss* material. He is still not entirely sure whether he wants to play the Jew. But, with a little help, I manage to persuade him.

Demandowski outlines the *Ohm Krüger* material to me. This has possibilities. Jannings in the main role, direction by Steinhoff. I also have a serious talk with Demandowski and Leichtenstern about Tobis' and Ufa's failures, particularly in production of entertainment films. They have too much on their plates. Perhaps I shall divide Ufa, Tobis and Terra into two main sections each: one for serious, the other for lighter productions. I shall instal new production chiefs to handle the light material. In any case, something must be done in this area to counter the lack of good material.

So far as politics and the war are concerned, everything is quiet as the grave. But Roosevelt has spoken to the House of Representatives. Covert but very malicious jibes against our régime and the Reich. He says he still hopes to keep America out of the war. That sounds anything but hopeful.

To Lanke. Deep winter everywhere. Worked on my report on the Propaganda Companies. This is very important for our future work. . .

. . . The Russians are making absolutely no progress in Finland. The Red Army really does seem to be of very little military worth.

In London there is great outrage about our radio broadcasts in English. Our announcer has been given the nickname 'Lord Haw-Haw'. He is causing talk, and that is already half the battle. The aim in London is to create an equivalent figure for the German service. This would be the best thing that could happen. We should make mincemeat of him.

Check a film. *Red Mill*, a nice entertainment film.

[. . .], a typical Russian-Bolshevik hate-film directed against us, vulgar and contemptible but not without skill. Seems very primitive to the likes of us. . .

6 January 1940 (Saturday)

Yesterday: Almost 20 below zero. No weather for military operations. As the Russians are finding out in Finland at the moment.

Göring has established a General Council for the Economy and taken over the leadership of the entire economy. At least this gives some assurance that shortfalls and inter-departmental rows will be kept to the minimum. . .

. . . Our English radio broadcasts are now being taken with deadly seriousness in England. Lord Haw-Haw's name is on everybody's lips. We do not react, but intensify our broadcasts. Our transmissions to Sweden are also, according to a number of reports, meeting with great approval.

We are making no progress in our attempts to co-ordinate action with the Foreign Ministry. But I shall not give up.

Big international controversy in the press about Finland and the Scandinavian states. London and Paris are openly threatening intervention. We oppose this. Our policy towards Scandinavia is rather passive. We ought to become more closely involved.

Discuss the situation in Berlin with [. . . ?] He is playing at being Defence Commissar here. Coal situation still bad. But gradually improving. Lippert and Görlitzer arguing over control of industry. Görlitzer cannot answer my questions satisfactorily. He is so dogmatic and full of twisted, suppressed ambition. But I must get him together with Lippert again.

Discuss the new work of the Foreign Department with Brauweiler. He intends to revive it. Will he succeed? With the Foreign Ministry under Ribbentrop, we shall never get anywhere. But I give Brauweiler full powers. First the Department must be shocked out of its torpor. Then it will be a matter of putting into action the machinery we already possess. This will not be possible without co-operation with the Foreign Ministry. . .

. . . The Führer is still at the Obersalzberg. I drive out to Lanke in the afternoon and have plenty of work to do there.

Reading *The Victors – Afterwards*, a book about France during and after the World War* by Herbert Kraus. Very well written, based on a broad knowledge of the subject, and more evidence of how near we were to victory at times. A view of post-war France that is very instructive. I devour the book like a novel.

7 January 1940 (Sunday)

Yesterday: I feel slightly ill and stay in Lanke. Short stroll through deep, crunching snow.

The Führer has set off from Munich on the way home to Berlin.

Hore-Belisha and MacMillan have resigned. H.-B. probably because, as a Jew, he is a long-term liability. MacMillan because of his notorious incompetence. There is certainly no connection with a change of political course.

Hot debate about neutrality continues, particularly among the Scandinavian states. The Russians are stuck fast in Finland.

Count Ciano meets Csáky in Venice.

A cheerful letter from Alfieri. He is on top again.

The *Times* publishes two very informative articles about our German propaganda. But at heart the English still do not understand us. . .

. . . Report on the situation in France: no great enthusiasm for war, but no defeatism either. Daladier is very firmly in the saddle. The Commune [?] continues to agitate with success. For the moment, there can be no question of a decline in morale.

Otherwise all is quiet on the political and war fronts. Everyone is waiting for the Führer to act. This will soon be possible and necessary.

* The 1914–18 war. Goebbels uses the phrase in this sense throughout.

The world press concentrates on the English cabinet reshuffle.

Hore-Belisha was toppled by the generals. Sir John Reith, the new Information Minister, is, according to our files, an energetic man, but very pedantic and puritanical. And, moreover, a bureaucrat. On the other hand, he should not be underestimated, because of his ability to get things done.

Study huge quantities of letters about our foreign radio broadcasts. Thoroughly good and positive. We must expand this area of operations. Here is the strongest channel for our propaganda.

Film: *Ben Hur*. Old Jewish hokum. But well made.

Dawn, a U-boat film from the same period. Too much patriotism. But could still be salvaged.

Wonderful Sunday today.

8 January 1940 (Monday)

Yesterday: A peaceful day. Snow and frost.

Short sleigh-ride with the children. What a delight!

Read *The Victors – Afterwards* to the end. A superb book, with a brilliant portrayal of Clemençeau. But not for use today. May well have to be confiscated.

Huge controversy in the press over Hore-Belisha. The Jews are beating the drum. A world-scandal. Can there be something more behind it?

Visitors in the afternoon. Hommels and so on. I can spare them little attention.

A quiet, thoughtful Sunday. Strength for the new week.

Today we move back to Schwanenwerder. Bag and baggage!

9 January 1940 (Tuesday)

Yesterday: Leave Lanke. In the stillness of early morning. Helga comes with me and acts as a sweet, chattering companion throughout the drive.

I let loose the press again on the subject of Hore-Belisha's resignation. Jewry is withdrawing its representatives from the firing-line, because things are beginning to look dicey. And London is trying to protect her vulnerable points. These are the main emphases of our polemical effort.

I set up an expert committee to deal with Nostradamus and Astrology. It will supply the necessary material for my propaganda.

The foreign language service of the radio has now been expanded greatly. We can reach almost the entire world, have first-class announcers and enormous authority. Our clandestine stations to France are also doing superb work. Everything still under heavy camouflage, and the French are groping in the dark.

Unfortunately, large sections of the Wehrmacht are still tuning into foreign radio stations. I must take decisive measures against this. The watchword is: *principii obsta!* To achieve something in the present crisis is a

89

thousand times more difficult. . .

. . . Schulenburg sends a report from Moscow on the power structure in Russia. In practical terms, Stalin is sole ruler there.

Talks between Ciano and Csaky: complete agreement. Quite right. The Italians will have their eyes opened about the Hungarians sooner or later. . .

. . . Furtwängler reports on his trips to Switzerland and Hungary. He met with triumphal success everywhere. We can put him to good use, and at the moment he is very willing. He intends now to keep an eye on the music world in Vienna. And to go to Prague to raise our musical prestige. There it is an urgent necessity.

Gutterer outlines a series of new projects. Will be carried through. Amongst other things, an Anti-England exhibition.

Midday with the Führer. He has arrived back from the Obersalzberg and is in the best of form. He seems to radiate vitality and optimism. I show him pictures of the conversion work on the Admiral's Palace, which interests him greatly.

We drink a cup of the coffee presented to him by the Imam of Yemen. He says that it is outrageous enough that England can simply halt, for instance, coffee imports by a nation of 100 million whenever it feels like it. This tyranny and piracy must now be broken, and forcibly. Our enemies committed their biggest mistake when they declared their war aims against Germany, which clearly amount to a dismemberment of the Reich. This absolves the Führer from any moral qualms in future. The gentlemen in London and Paris will come to rue it bitterly.

Our radio propaganda is highly praised by the Führer. He is particularly interested in Lord Haw-Haw. He is a Mosley man. The Mosley people keeping their heads down at the moment. Their only, but perhaps their big chance. With respect to Hore-Belisha's resignation, the Führer shares my opinion. Jewry withdrawing support from a losing cause.

Talk about monitoring of foreign stations by the Wehrmacht with Colonel Schmundt. We shall take action in that quarter, if necessary through an order from the Führer, whom I treat to a detailed commentary afterwards.

The neutrals are scared to death. Our constant attacks, casting doubts on their neutrality – particularly at Geneva with respect to Finland – are making them very nervous.

A few massive attacks on London on the subject of Hore-Belisha in the afternoon in the press. They will stick.

Check the newsreel. Not turned out particularly well. The Propaganda Companies are a complete failure. I shall now take this matter to the Führer.

Final version of the Jew-film. I think we have done it now. In any case, we have done all we can.

Carry out a coup, promoting Dr Schlösser. He must put some more life into the Berlin theatre scene for me. I have not paid much attention to it, and now it is going to the dogs.

Late back. Fetch Magda from Arents. Then some peace and quiet. I am very tense.

10 January 1940 (Wednesday)

Yesterday: I am ill with my kidneys again. The freezing-cold weather, the old story. Work is the best medicine. The children are so sweet when I leave.

Further attacks on Hore-Belisha. English public opinion is already showing signs of nervousness. So we shall step up our offensive.

Talk with the American writer, Stoddard. I outline the German case with overwhelming conviction. He is very understanding and would like to use my outline in interview form. We shall see what he comes up with. He is syndicated in a hundred of the most influential newspapers.

Confer with Ley. He wants to introduce old-age pensions for the entire German people. This would not be a bad idea. The people have nothing to spend their money on; here it could be usefully deposited.

Berndt makes some series accusations about Glasmaier. But he gets nowhere with me. The pair of them must stay where they are and learn to tolerate each other.

Establish a clear hierarchy in the radio service in consultation with Brauweiler and Dittmar. There is too much confusion in this area. Now Fritzsche and Brauweiler have full powers to give orders. Thus authority is clearly defined.

Midday with the Führer. He takes a hard line against all forms of espionage, at home or abroad. He sees it as a damaging factor, or anyway more harmful than beneficial. Let him tell that to the Gestapo. He also asserts that Otto Strasser was a spy from the beginning. He recounts a mass of examples of damaging security leaks from the Party's past.

Liebel tells me some things from Nuremberg involving Streicher, all of an anything but pleasant nature. I am shocked. We must make peace between these two men. And Liebel, for his own reasons, has doubtless exaggerated a lot. Whatever the case, Streicher has his good as well as his bad side.

Speech to the radio chiefs on programming. I express criticisms and issue guidelines.

Speech to the heads of the Propaganda Companies, who have come to Berlin from the front. I deliver some very sharp reprimands, covering all the shortcomings that have become apparent. I call for a synthesis between creative initiative and military discipline. I hope we shall soon see an improvement.

Chamberlain makes a speech. Rather tough. Broad hints to the neutrals. Aid for Finland. New sacrifices demanded from England. Thus a real programme for war, as might be expected. We shall not let him wait for an answer.

Evening at the Press Club with the heads of the Propaganda Companies. Swop experiences. I think that this discussion has achieved its purpose. . .

11 January 1940 (Thursday)

Yesterday: 25 below zero. Very serious coal situation in Berlin and throughout the Reich. We must be prepared for draconian measures if need be. The present situation is having a bad effect on morale.

Raeder delivers a speech to shipyard workers. Harmless and naïve.

Increasing signs of defeatism in the English press. We shall take no notice of it for the present, so that it can continue to spread.

Report on Yugoslavia. The court strongly pro-English. We enjoy powerful sympathy among the people. We must set to work more determinedly there.

Report from Dittmar on our foreign-language broadcasts. We now broadcast to the entire world. The second clandestine transmitter to France began operation today.

Hippler submits a very outspoken report criticising the Propaganda Companies. I shall now proceed with absolute rigour. First pass on the report to Schmundt. If things do not improve, then I shall approach the Führer. The Führer must also decide soon on our participation in the World Fair in Rome . . . Midday with the Führer. Discuss a number of press problems with Amann. Dietrich also has a few difficulties. Ley is looking for praise for his newspaper articles. Jagow tells us about his missions against England. Otherwise, nothing new. Everyone is waiting for better weather. . .

. . . A number of questions discussed with Göring. Particularly the coal problem. We are now stopping all advertising for personal travel.

Gründgens gets his film certificate.

In the afternoon, down to work again. Magda has gone to visit Harald in Posen.

Frau Leander is worried about her children. She fears that Sweden could be dragged into the war. I calm her somewhat. Women are completely unpolitical.

In the evening, to the Propaganda Company at Potsdam. A pleasant farewell celebration. The Company is now transferring to the front.

Schwanenwerder. Late and tired. Never less than a twenty-hour day now.

12 January 1940 (Friday)

Yesterday: Fiendishly cold. Minus 25. Schwanenwerder is empty. Magda is in Posen. Only the children, romping about.

The coal problem is reaching very serious proportions. We must take drastic steps. If necessary, close schools and theatres. Very distressing to me. The Reichsbahn has let us down completely. I issue an explanatory circular to the Gau authorities. Conference with Lippert and Görlitzer, at which suitable measures are agreed. The cold weather seems set to continue for some time yet.

Growing defeatism in evidence in England. Particularly so far as social questions are concerned. We exploit this weakness.

Magnificent report on Ufa. The film industry is booming.

Interview with Stoddard has turned out very well. I release it for publication with minor amendments. . .

. . . At midday, receive representatives from the girls' section of the Labour Service. Talk about problems of youth education. Good human material.

With the Führer. Schmundt, Keitel and Jodl now intend to take steps against monitoring of foreign broadcasts in the Wehrmacht. Hippler's report has hit them like a bolt of lightning.

I shall have to re-work the Jew-film again.

The Führer reckons with a further hardening of English attitudes. He would prefer a cabinet with some energy. Then, at least, one would know where one stood, and such a cabinet would certainly lay itself more open to attack. The effects of Hore-Belisha's resignation are still being felt. We shall continue to worry at it. It is always an advantage to have a clear target.

Discuss the coal situation with Wagner from Münich. Things in Munich are rather better than in Berlin. But even there they have plenty of worries. And naturally this affects morale. But we shall soon master the situation.

Prince Philipp of Hesse is present. He talks insipid rubbish.

Some clashes in the West.

Give Hippler an encouraging prod. He now says he will make every effort to produce decent newsreels.

Glasmaier writes me a letter that oozes with protestations of loyalty. Berndt would like to see him dismissed. But I shall not allow it.

I have a lot to do. A day such as this flies past. One must be strict with one's time to get anything done at all.

Check the film *White Lilacs*. Unfortunately a failure from Rabenalt. I am a little depressed by the way our directors start with a few successes and then always go off the rails and become intellectual. But I shall do something about it.

Political and military situations absolutely quiet. Only personal worries. . .

13 January 1940 (Saturday)

Yesterday: Barbarously cold. The coal situation is becoming graver with every passing day. I issue an explanatory circular to all Gau authorities.

Punishments for defeatism in England. We take no notice of this in the press. But we use it in foreign broadcasts.

Our press must be more inventive. It is resting too much on its laurels. Waiting for material to turn up. It must go out and get things.

Shocking report from Lvov* on how the Soviet Russians are behaving. These people have no sense of decency. And the Jews are in the vanguard. The troops are ill-trained and poorly-armed. The true face of Bolshevism.

Long discussion with Reinhardt. A host of organisational problems regarding the press. We intend to make printers responsible for content as well. . .

(Photocopy lost)

14 January 1940 (Sunday) [Incomplete text]

. . . I intend to devote more publicity to Party members in public life. Party members have to bear many burdens, and find themselves abused for their pains. The Party has been pushed on to the defensive by the war. It must be forced out again. The scoffers cannot be allowed to continue acting as if the war were just a football match and they were spectators. The Party must give more of a lead to the people.

Our radio work has been granted grudging praise in France. I ensure that the German press takes no notice of this.

There have been complaints about failures of security with regard to state secrets in the Party, government and Wehrmacht. I take suitable measures against this.

At midday, back to Schwanenwerder. Magda has just returned from Posen and has much to tell. Harald is behaving himself magnificently there. He has become a real man, with a pronounced social conscience. Now all that remains is for him to join the Wehrmacht and do his job there.

The children are very happy to see their mother again.

Heydrich complains about a new pastoral letter. We let it through and confine ourselves to seizing the printing works where it was produced. This is the best way of dealing with these cowardly brutes. But in the long term, we shall probably not be able to do without pre-censorship in this area, too.

Otherwise nothing much is happening in the world. All quiet in politics and war.

I have lots to work on, and even manage some reading. Such a relaxed afternoon is very welcome in times like these. I drink my fill thirstily.

The children gambol around. Helga has become quite grown-up. Hilde is very sure of herself, while Holde is a little joker. Helmut is an absolute loner. Hedda is troubled with [. . .]

* In the part of Eastern Poland occupied by the Russians in October 1939. Now in the Soviet Union.

15 January 1940 (Monday)

Yesterday: A slight break in the weather. The frost seems to have gone. This would be a blessing for our coal situation.

Scarcely any news, domestic or foreign. Everywhere the same: the calm before the storm.

I am able to stay at Schwanenwerder, work on some things and read.

Arents come visiting in the afternoon. And then the Führer, who talks and plays with the children and gives them a whole assortment of toys. Hilde and Helga are particularly close to his heart. Holde is a sweet little darling.

We talk until late in the evening. The children play with the puppet theatre that the Führer gave them. A peaceful idyll in the midst of war.

Little said of the war itself. The Führer, after all, must spend the odd afternoon relaxing. It is already late when he sets off home.

Gossip some more. Today another hard week begins.

16 January 1940 (Tuesday)

Yesterday: A thaw! Noticeable relief of the coal shortage. Thank God!

A lot of work. Thrash out the Nostradamus verses in co-operation with the Intelligence Service for use in France and neutral countries. Every little helps. . .

. . . Belgium and Holland have cancelled all leave for their armed forces. With a mysterious explanation. The big world-wide sensation. Someone is trying to make us show our hand. But we do not react. I forbid the press to discuss it. Otherwise, I send Fink to join the High Command's propaganda bureau for Belgium and Sabzmann to the bureau in Luxembourg. The pair of them will doubtless master the situation.

The radio has made some psychological errors. I ensure that this does not occur again. One must be incredibly careful in this area, so as not to give away one's hand before the time comes.

Talk over organisational and educational problems in the Hitler Youth with Lauterbacher. He will make a good replacement for Schirach, who has gone to the Wehrmacht.

Dr Lippert complains about Görlitzer. Only partly justified. He should be grateful to have hung on to his own job. The worst of the coal shortages in Berlin are over. Lippert is now firmly back in the saddle.

With the Führer. He is delighted that the weather has turned milder and complains about the fact that we have not even a half-reliable weather forecasting service. But the meteorologists cannot be blamed. It does not, however, change the fact that we shall need more or less decent weather for an offensive to be successfully mounted.

The Führer speaks in broad, human terms about the crisis we are facing.

One must decide, he says, whether one considers life at all worth living. If the answer is no, then one should take a pistol and end it. If yes, however, then one must approach life with courage and optimism . . . Real bravery only comes when there is no turning back; it is then that one finds the courage for really momentous decisions. So long as there is still a way out, it is easy to lose one's nerve under pressure. Thus our attitude in the present situation. It also applies to our policy in Poland. We simply cannot afford to lose the war. And all our thoughts and actions should be guided by this consideration.

The Führer refers to Bismarck in this context. What decisions he had to make! And Frederick the Great! He towers above every other figure in Prussian and German history. He, and he alone, succeeded in transforming Prussia into a historical entity. We should all grovel in the dirt in the face of his greatness. It is not the dimensions within which a historical genius operates which are the measure of his greatness, but the courage and audacity with which he faces dangers. Our own years of struggle provide examples enough. The Führer was always greater in adversity than in triumph.

A conversation like this gives one new strength and fresh courage. All the clamour of so-called world opinion disappears into insignificance. I return to work like a man reborn.

The Führer expresses great pleasure over our children, especially Hilde. She, along with Helga, is particularly dear to his heart.

Dr Dietrich is involved in another tussle with Ribbentrop. Ribbentrop is downright disloyal. Discover a new poet. Arnold Krüger. Note the name!

Discuss propaganda abroad with Schwarz van Berk. He is now working as a 'neutral' journalist, writing articles aimed at world opinion. I give him clear guidelines. He must not go into detail, but must provide more colour than news. At the moment we must titillate rather than inform.

The Serbs and Croats are supposedly in the throes of reconciliation at Zagreb. Who knows how long this will last? Prince-Regent Paul is playing a dangerous game. . .

17 January 1940 (Wednesday)

Yesterday: New bout of cold weather, with frost and snow. Very unpleasant implications for our precarious coal situation. . .

. . . Our broadcasts to England are having a great effect, according to all reports. We operate in tune with the principle: constant dripping wears away the stone.

Morale in the country has declined owing to the coal shortage. But we shall soon make up the lost ground.

Still a great to-do about Belgium and Holland. Obviously inspired by

London. We do nothing to assuage it. Let the world's parasites indulge their anxiety neuroses as they like.

The reports on our successes in the air are not always completely reliable. We must take care in this area, or we shall undermine our own credibility.

I am under massive attack from London and Paris at the moment. Great honour for me.

Discuss new fencing for Lanke with Speer. Grounds somewhat reduced. Proper and necessary.

Check the new newsreel again. Now it has turned out well.

Midday with the Führer. He is working on the offensive. He checks and thinks everything through down to the last detail. And that is why it will succeed.

Debate on the churches. The churches must be left completely to their own devices. A united protestant church is not at all in our interest. Kerrl is taking completely the wrong tack there. Now he intends to establish a religious Arndt-League in Wittenberg. When something is falling, one should give it a push, Herr Kerrl! The Führer is very sceptical about the possibility of finding a substitute for the churches, and rightly so. That will be the task of some future reformer, which the Führer in no way feels himself to be. The problems he wants to solve are purely political. The battle with the churches is unavoidable, but it will certainly last a long time. Reich Bishop Müller has been of little use to us. But the warring clerics have also done him an injustice. It is best that we keep out of this area for the moment. It is a pity that the Wehrmacht leadership is still very devout. But then what can it do? The soldier must have something to cling to. And, as stated, there is no practicable substitute at the moment.

The English are infiltrating a very effectively-produced pamphlet into the Reich. For ourselves, we have produced a very subtle lecture with slides directed against England. This will not miss its mark.

New cabinet in Tokyo, headed by Yonäi. Seems not to be totally according to our taste. We must watch out in that quarter, therefore.

I work on my speech for Posen. I give an overall picture of the situation in it. I think it will be good.

These days one must weigh every word as carefully as gold on the scales.

Film footage of the sinking of the *Spee* and the *Scharnhorst*. Very tragic and moving. Not to be used at home, but a possibility for abroad. . .

18 January 1940 (Thursday)

Yesterday: More cold weather. Coal situation difficult.

Chamberlain has made a speech. Idiotic burbling. Hore-Belisha is supposed to have resigned 'because of his health'. A cruel irony! We give this a hilarious reception. To cap it all, the Jew* issues a weak-as-water statement

* Hore-Belisha.

97

confirming everything. Nothing really to be gleaned from all this.

Interesting Jewish trial in Switzerland. Result not yet clear.

Nervousness in Holland and Belgium subsided slightly. This was obviously a deliberate attempt to inspire panic.

I dictate the press excerpts to be used from my Posen speech. Turned out well.

With the Führer. Himmler reports on the resettlement of the Volhynia Germans. They make a good impression from the racial standpoint and are extraordinarily prolific child-bearers. He has been encountering great difficulties in Rome, less with the higher than with the lower authorities. But now, fortunately, the South Tyrolean business has been sorted out. Luis Trenker, spineless creature, has chosen Italy. We shall settle his hash. The Führer never thought much of him, and I have also cautioned people against him.

A great deal of work through the afternoon. The whole Wilhelmstrasse has been taking a relaxed attitude towards military and political secrets. I issue serious warnings to all Department heads in question. We show all too little care in these matters.

Film-check for *Casanova*, directed by Kowa. Still somewhat over-played, but much better than his first film.

Last two newsreels. Both turned out very well in the end.

Screen test for Marian in *Jud Süss*. Excellent. . .

19 January 1940 (Friday)

Yesterday: Minus 25 and sheet ice. Apalling weather.

The storm in Holland and Belgium has abated slightly.

The Wehrmacht's treatment of Polish officers is too soft. Radios, films, and so on. The Poles do not understand such things. I ensure corrective measures.

The investigations into security matters carried out by Admiral Canaris have been handled exclusively by members of the Wehrmacht. A typical Wehrmacht affair.

The Russians are stuck quite fast in Finland in this Siberian cold. We need not fear a two-front war in the foreseeable future.

Dr Naumann from Breslau has a few requests regarding cultural expansion in the regained territories, which I shall grant where possible. These concern mainly music and theatre.

Frau Käthe Dorsch is back again with her list of requests. She continues to stand up for her hard-pressed colleagues in the most determined and moving way.

With the Führer. He would like to visit the West Wall again, to carry out an extensive and exhaustive inspection.

Our attacks on the English plutocracy strike a deep chord in him. We shall continue in this direction. Our clandestine transmitters are having a disruptive effect.

The Fascist Party's Secretary, Muti, has spoken strongly in our favour, something for London and Paris to think about. Rome is supposed to be standing ready. We can hope so!

The Foreign Ministry is trying to lure away our best people with fat salaries. I take very energetic steps against this in consultation with Greimer.

Study the film companies' new production schedules. This time, they include a whole series of the best national-political material.

In the evening, back to Schwanenwerder with Magda. All sorts to settle at home.

The children are always such a great joy in the evenings. Short night.

Today, flight to Posen.

20 January 1940 (Saturday)

Yesterday: More Siberian cold. It makes one sick.

Deal with the most urgent work at the office. The hubbub in the press about Holland and Belgium has completely subsided. The English have switched to attacking our methods of waging war at sea. But we counterattack energetically.

Press conference. Guidelines on handling historical examples (Frederick the Great, Bismarck). Inexhaustible material there.

Even the security people have not been able to unmask our Communist clandestine transmitter broadcasting to France. In Paris they believe it is coming from Russia. We leave them in this fond belief.

Excellent verdicts from Sweden on our Swedish-language broadcasts.

At midday, set out for Posen from Staaken airfield. Long wait at Staaken. Then a take-off in the ice. Heavy squalls. Then, luckily, in Posen, to be greeted by impossible cold.

Gossip a little with Greiser. Then speak to 20,000 Germans. Reveal the entire problematic of the war. Unimaginable applause. A real battling meeting, just like the old times. I am very happy about it.

Inspect plans for the rebuilding of the Posen theatre by Bartels. Good, but too grandiose and extensive. We shall content ourselves with freshening the place up and build a big, modern new theatre for the Opera.

At the town hall. An old, fine building, unfortunately largely ruined by the Poles. Inspect plans for the rebuilding of Posen. Very ambitious and quite acceptable. Greiser is working very hard. Unfortunately, however, he is having big problems with Himmler, whose behaviour is very autocratic, particularly with regard to the evacuation question.

Harald is there, too. A nice boy, praised by everyone.

In the evening, a forty-kilometre drive out of the town. Through heavy winds and snow to Schloss Schwarzenau. An old nobleman's castle, rather dilapidated and showing its age. The owners have fled.

Here I get a good night's sleep for once.

21 January 1940 (Sunday)

Yesterday: In the morning, a further drive with Greiser through a beautiful forest in biting cold. He explains many of the problems of the new, young Gau.

At midday, work and reading. My Posen speech has figured prominently in the press at home and abroad. It has been a huge success.

In the afternoon to Posen. The *Deutsches Theater* on tour with *As You Like It*. A magnificent performance. Dahlke, who excels himself, is the hit of the evening. A storm of applause.

Afterwards, a small, modest reception for Party members and artists in our Schloss. Good to see other human beings from time to time.

Little sleep. Today it is back to Berlin.

22 January 1940 (Monday)

Yesterday: Leave Schwarzenau on time. Savagely cold. But the sun is shining. Still a thousand things to discuss with Greiser.

Drive round Posen. To beyond the fortifications. Very interesting impressions!

More delay at the airport. The cold is scarcely bearable.

Flight to Berlin. Work on the way. Very pessimistic reports on the situation in Soviet Russia. Moscow is of very little value as military power.

My speech in Posen has attracted a lot of attention abroad. Particularly in Rome and London. Churchill and Halifax have made speeches. Impudent rag-bags of illusions. But the Herr Plutocrats will soon lose their cockiness.

Berlin towards midday. Straight to Schwanenwerder. It is so wonderful to be back with the family. The children beside themselves with delight.

Work in the afternoon. So much has piled up during my absence. But I can always bring it under control.

The Moscow press is lending us magnificent support against London. It seems as if the Russians are in it up to their necks.

The Führer invites us to him at the apartment for the evening. To Berlin with Magda. A very small party. The Führer has the air of a man who has cleared away his problems.

I talk about Posen, which interests him greatly. Polish nationalism consisted of no more than the right of the Polish aristocracy to rob their own people. There was absolutely no trace of idealism.

The Führer has set his mind on a great war against England. As soon as the weather is good. England must be chased out of Europe, and France destroyed as a great power. Then Germany will have hegemony and Europe will have peace. This is our great, eternal goal. Afterwards, the Führer will remain in office for a few years, carry through social reforms and his building projects, and then retire. Then let the others try their hands. He intends to act only as a benevolent spirit hovering over the political world. And write down everything that he is in the thick of now. A bible of National Socialism, so to speak.

We have a long talk about children. Girls, for the most part, take after their fathers, and the boys their mothers. Thus a genius is unlikely to have a genius for a son. Another argument against hereditary monarchy.

We talk late into the night. The Führer is more inspired than I have seen him to be for a long time now.

23 January 1940 (Tuesday)

Yesterday: Still insanely, savagely cold. To Berlin early and without enough sleep.

Churchill's speech threatening the neutrals has aroused a huge response. The old fox has made another serious mistake.

The English radio is very on the ball at the moment. We must take more care.

Paris is still searching for our clandestine transmitter. Excellent!

Berlin. Receive the Japanese ambassador. A diplomatic nonentity. At the moment we can expect little from Japan. I preferred General Oshima as ambassador.

Count [. . .] is off to Sofia. Comes to say good-bye. Rome is very nervous of Moscow. Otherwise standing firm. It is too much to ask that they should treasure our new direction. The Finnish campaign, and particularly its failure, has done Russia a lot of harm. Especially the stupid business with the Kuusinen government.

With the Führer. Discussion on Poland. The Volhynia Germans are said to be very usable. Himmler is shoving whole peoples around at the moment. Not always successfully.

Dr Dietrich has issued a tough directive aimed at the newspaper editors who are letting themselves be lured away by higher salaries from the Foreign Ministry.

The English have just suffered more heavy shipping losses. Excellent!

Reception for writers at the ministry. Invite them to contribute to our war effort in films, press and radio. Great debate about this. How unworldly these people are. Victims of their own intellects.

Invite Dr Schlösser to take responsibility for an artistic revival of the Berlin theatre world. Great success with the public is making our managers somewhat lazy and careless.

In the evening, check films: new newsreel. This time back to the previous standard of excellence. The only problem is that in this cold weather and with so many transportation problems, we lack up-to-date material. . .

24 January 1940 (Wednesday)

Yesterday: Churchill's threatening speech is still going the rounds and arousing the neutrals' outrage. We ignore it. Have no intention of helping out these tiny dwarf-states. They deserve to disappear.

Detailed talks with Admiral Canaris on espionage and security.

There is an enormous amount still to be done in this area. Treason is still too widespread. Security in my ministry is relatively good. But the military shoot their mouths off. Mostly this is merely *folie de grandeur*. A foreman at Krupp betrayed many weapon designs to the Poles. It is scarcely believable to see what goes on. We intend to take energetic steps to counter this. Through education, reinforced by the most severe penalties.

Winkler reports on the state of film production. Ufa in a very good position, Terra the same, good at Bavaria and Wien-Film, still bad at Tobis. Leichtenstern will probably have to be dismissed. The number of productions at Ufa, Tobis and Terra will be halved. I am looking for a few experienced, able men to handle entertainment film production. Apart from this, we intend to establish a Society for Electro-Acoustic Research to improve the technical aspect of our films. The money for the Party's mobile talking-picture shows will come from Winkler. Better, in any case, than letting the Finance Minister swallow it.

Check through the Ufa schedule again. It is not particularly outstanding. Leichtenstern has no perspective and no initiative. He seems to be rather at a loss when it comes to the big problems.

Deal with a mass of press telegrams. These seem to increase from day to day. I do not even manage to go to the Führer at midday.

Motta dead. He was supposed to be a friend of Germany, but in reality he was just a Swiss bourgeois, a head-porter type. No loss for us.

The Japanese are taking a hard line against the English, who took some twenty Germans off a Japanese ship in Japanese waters. Naturally, we stoke the fires.

Check films: bad, run-of-the-mill products. We have only good films and bad films. We lack the serviceable middle range.

Savagely cold throughout the ministry. We work in overcoats.

Tired and ill. Home! To bed!

25 January 1940 (Thursday)

Yesterday: A slight break in the cold weather. Even a hint of a thaw. A blessing for our coal supplies!

Detailed report from Bömer on our foreign press department. This work is excellent, and can claim great successes. We are far ahead of the English. Bömer has done his job well.

The armoured cruiser *Deutschland* has been re-christened as the *Lützow*. We have sold the half-completed *Lützow* to Russia. Nowadays we are building almost nothing but U-boats. These will give us the best return on our investment.

Discuss the production schedules of the various film companies with Reichmeister. On the whole, serviceable. Entertainment films remain the only real source of worry. There is still a lot to do in that area. The industry's box-office receipts are splendid. Millions in profits.

Midday with the Führer. He has just addressed cadet officers at the *Sportpalast*. We discuss the Russian question. The Russians are showing increasing loyalty to us. They have every reason. They cannot get out of the Finnish business, even though they have made serious tactical mistakes. The Führer believes that, despite everything, they will overwhelm Finland in a few months. England cannot, and also will not, help Finland. London has too much trouble of its own. Mosley is making his presence felt very strongly at the moment. If he proceeds cleverly now, he may have a chance. He has written a few clever articles.

General Reinecke tries to explain away the treatment accorded to the Polish prisoners-of-war. We are faced with great difficulties in that quarter. The Wehrmacht leadership is still not totally committed to the racial struggle. We must constantly prod them along. Now they are even intending to build cinemas for the Polish officers. But I kicked up a fuss and the Major-General responsible was sacked immediately.

Interview with an important Greek journalist, [. . .] He tells me something of neutral feeling. I give him a real dose of my medicine. He will write positively for us.

Speech to representatives of magazine publishers. I am in the best of form and speak with powerful conviction. Something for them to take home with them.

Newsreel ready. Incidental music wrong. Will be re-worked.

Report on Yugoslavia. The neutrals are going through a bleak period, and we do not enjoy too much friendly feeling among them.

Work at the office until the evening. Since the offices are unheated, swathed in blankets. What a picture!

To Cologne by train. Chat at some length with the officers accompanying me. Then a short rest!

26 January 1940 (Friday)

Yesterday: Arrive very early in Cologne. Along the autobahn in the icy cold to Düsseldorf. Long talk with Florian. He describes to me all the joys and woes of a Gauleiter. His whole district is packed with soldiers. All are waiting for the offensive. It had already been fixed, but a Luftwaffe lieutenant defected to Belgium with the plans and made an emergency landing. That was all we needed. Now we must wait again. Otherwise the situation here is very good. Florian does not entirely trust Reichenau.

Reichenau comes for lunch. Puts his best foot forward, and actually I can find no fault with him. No defeatist talk of any kind. Despite the strict security, everyone here talks openly about the coming attack. Reichenau does not hold out great hopes so long as the cold weather lasts. If conditions are halfways good, he believes he can break through in fourteen days. Perhaps this is an over-optimistic view. Boundless anger against Holland everywhere here. The pepper-sacks* are blocking our way through.

In the afternoon, visit to the Propaganda Company at the *Malkasten* in Düsseldorf. I come across excellent human material. Everyone makes a very good, solid impression. The technical arrangements are a model of their kind.

I make a short speech to the people.

Drive to Rheydt.** My beloved old Rheydt! I am in a very melancholy frame of mind. Big meeting of Party members, officers and soldiers in the municipal hall. I speak. About past and future. On best form and with huge success. It really hits home.

Afterwards, sit with the people there until midnight. I learn a lot about the mood of the troops. Everyone is waiting for the order to march. It must start soon. . .

. . . Plans for the rebuilding of Rheydt inspected. And then to bed, exhausted.

28 January 1940 (Sunday) [Covers two days]

Day before yesterday: Get up very early. Still dark when we drive off. People call out and wave to me.

To Rheindahlen. Air base commanded by Obernitz. Big reception. The people are delighted. I inspect all the technical installations at the base. Extensive air-photographs of England, Belgium, France, and also Holland. Everything makes a very workmanlike impression.

We watch the new Messerschmitt aircraft make an attack. They go roaring in at almost 700 km per hour. A fantastic sight! Richthofen and particularly Obernitz, are very proud.

To Hellensbrünn. Training manoeuvres for a newly-reinforced battalion. Reichenau explains everything for me. Very clear and instructive. He is a capable sort, for all his faults. He stutters a few apologies for his political doubts.

* A German slang term for the Dutch.
** Rheydt was Goebbels' birthplace.

The manoeuvres are magnificent and impressive. Poor little buffer states!

Meal at the field-kitchen. With a Saxon company. Morale marvellous. I make a short speech. What delight!

To Florian's construction office in Düsseldorf. Superb plans for the rebuilding of Düsseldorf. But still a little vague. But at least something is being done.

Drive through the snow to Schloss Wupper. Talk there with Party leaders. Then to Wuppertal. Inspect the rebuilding work on the opera house at Barmen. Turned out very well. Discuss cultural questions.

Back to Düsseldorf. Florian tells me yet again about his conflict with Terboven. These days it is defunct. The war overshadows all such trivialities. Florian is a nice fellow. Both he and Terboven have their good points.

Back to Berlin in the late evening. Work on for a long time. Piles of paperwork.

Yesterday: Straight to work. I can scarcely see any end to the work. A mass of documents, but nothing particularly important. However, the coal situation has got worse. We shall now have to close the schools, some of the factories, and soon the cinemas, too.

In the radio, Berndt is preparing for Glasmaier's return. But his suggestions are reasonable and good. He is now off to the front. Hadamovsky his successor. Greiner has a host of questions. I can only arrive at broad decisions.

War Report of the foreign press department. Very satisfying. Bömer is doing excellent work. We are now sending neutral journalists to Posen. The English agitation about the Poles is getting louder all the time. We must go on to the offensive.

Frank is making some serious errors. He is working in too uncontrolled a fashion. He is at daggers-drawn with the Party. Frank feels himself to be something of a handicapped Czar.

The *Times* provides yet another glowing testimonial to my propaganda.

A mass of administrative paperwork.

Mussolini has written a letter to the Führer. Ribbentrop has put his foot in it in Rome. Italy has reservations because of our policy towards Russia. I shall see if I can speak to Pavolini as soon as possible.

Wells is demanding that the English defend London by bombing Berlin. I order a tough response from the German press. Slogan: Poor London!

In the afternoon I pack my paperwork together and drive out to Lanke. Here it is purest winter. Magda travels with me, along with the Arents and the Jugos. I have to spend the entire afternoon working very hard. After only two days away from Berlin, the work piles up into mountains.

Another 20,000 tons sunk today.

I make a short inspection of the two new houses. Almost everything is finished. Some gossip with our guests.

In the evening, check films: *Sheer Love*, by Rühmann with Hertha Feiler.

A little thin, but cleanly-made and atmospheric. And then yet another really bad entertainment film. Talk until long after midnight. . .

29 January 1940 (Monday)

Yesterday: First proper night's sleep for a long time. Outside it is harsh and wintry weather again.

The campaign of lies about Poland is becoming fiercer from day to day. Churchill has spoken and added new fuel to the fire. I now prepare for a counter-strike. I shall have Greiser come from Posen and Frank from Cracow. They must now speak to the foreign press. Thereby we shall be able to correct all sorts of problems. I intend, in any case, to be on my guard from now on.

The princesses [. . .] come to visit. I learn a lot about the diplomatic world in Berlin. I am glad that I no longer have anything to do with it. Our German society people are not behaving in a worthy fashion. But society is, and will remain, society. An International all on its own!

In the afternoon, Prof. Fröhlich and Frau Leander come. Discuss films and a thousand other problems. The old gentleman is very nice.

Row with Cracow. Frank has no idea how important our struggle over the Polish question is. He feels himself to be King of Poland.

To bed in good time.

A hard week begins.

30 January 1940 (Tuesday)

Yesterday: Mountains of work.

The agitation about Poland continues. I instruct Greiser on his speech to the foreign press.

Settle the re-organisation of the radio with Greiner. Berndt has been taking too many liberties.

Re-organisation of the film industry with Hippler. I intend to give the present hierarchy another chance.

Hilgenfeldt reports on the resettlement of the Volhynia Germans. Still a lot of difficulties to be overcome. But things are all right.

Discuss establishment of our new newspaper with Mündler.

Midday with the Führer. We talk about the present situation. He intends to speak at the *Sportpalast* on 30 January. I must prepare this for today in absolute secrecy.

Work on like fury for the whole afternoon. Check the newsreel. Turned out well. A host of meetings.

Otherwise, the political scene absolutely dead. Nothing new in any of the theatres of war.

In the evening to Lanke, late. Talk a little with the ladies.
Then to bed, tired.

31 January 1940 (Wednesday)

Yesterday: Still frost and biting cold. The coal shortages are gradually assuming catastrophic proportions. I drive into Berlin with Frau Jugo. She chatters to me about everything to do with films.

Greiser spoke well to the foreign press. Our position has improved somewhat. I instruct Seyss-Inquart, who is due to speak next week. But the exposition by Frank that he has brought with him is not good. Too formal. We must supply atmosphere and detail. The press wants stories. Even the German press is complaining about lack of material. But, of course, we cannot describe anything when nothing is happening.

Conditions in the General Government are not rosy. Great deprivation among the population, and resurgence of illegal activity among the Poles. Tough measures are the only way to win through there. We intend to stop allowing the *Warschauer Zeitung** into the Reich. Otherwise we shall end up entangled in a discussion that could distract our people's attention from the main subject, which is England.

Work for a long time on preparations for the meeting at the *Sportpalast*. I succeed in keeping it completely secret until 19.00. The Führer intends to give an important speech.

Daladier has spoken. Totally vulgar and abusive. Includes unwitting praise for our propaganda. We let the press loose on this speech. It is easily refuted.

I award Frau von Schröder the Honour Cross for Services to the *Volk*. She has earned it. She tells me about the dreadful fate of Frau von Gustedt.

Midday with the Führer. Discussion on the political situation. He intends to give a big speech this evening. He remains completely unmoved by the caterwauling from London and Paris. In his eyes, Daladier is a jumped-up postal official, a petty-bourgeois run amuck, whose aggression is fuelled principally by alcohol. Churchill is an English Oldenburg-Januschau, barefaced but with no capacity for thought, and Chamberlain's toughness is acquired, not natural. Compared with them, Clemenceau and Lloyd-George were real fellows. But even they were only able to achieve what they did because they encountered no opposition on our side. Who were Bethmann, Michaelis and Hertling? Foch was brutal, but no thinker. Pétain, on the other hand, had a good head on his shoulders. But in dangerous situations, strength counts more than intellect. In military leadership, energy is the main requirement.

* The German-language newspaper published by the military authorities in Warsaw.

What Gamelin will turn out like is not yet clear. At the moment, anyway, he seems to be completely indecisive.

We are building ships like the devil. Destroyers and most importantly U-boats. U-boats. They are the main thing. they will do most of the damage for us.

Our fliers have carried out daring raids on an English convoy. Nine enemy ships destroyed. An act of heroism that inspires the admiration of the whole world.

The Führer praises our radio propaganda, which has recently achieved some magnificent successes abroad. We concentrate completely on news and on objectivity in that area. This brings the most effective results.

The situation is good in the Protectorate. Everything quiet. A blessing that the universities are closed. They were hotbeds of disloyalty.

Study the new production schedule of Wienfilm. Serviceable material!

Check over the memorandum on foreign press work. I shall introduce some new guidelines in that field.

In the evening [. . .] reads excerpts from my new book about the Führer on the radio. Very effective.

With the Führer. He is spoiling for the fray. To the *Sportpalast*. Overflowing. A seething ocean of humanity. Frenetic rejoicing. Fantastic storms of applause even during my introductory speech. Then the Führer speaks. Withering attacks on London and Paris. Resolute will to victory. Most unshakeable confidence. The people respond exultantly. Real *Sportpalast* atmosphere. The England-Song* at the finish. The Führer is very satisfied.

We sit around for a long time afterwards at the Party Chancellery. Himmler tells me of his educational plans. Then he reads out extracts from a letter from 'Empress' Zita and 'Emperor' Otto. Hilarious! Goes on until late. To Schwanenwerder in biting cold.

1 February 1940 (Thursday)

Yesterday: Bitingly cold again. Already we are closing schools and theatres. And this savage cold is predicted to last another two weeks.

The response to the Führer's speech is enormous. Particularly among the neutrals. London and Paris are stuttering embarrassed slogans. The speech contained nothing new, and so on. But we broadcast it to the entire world on all wavebands.

A letter from an English diplomat has fallen into our hands, containing quite frank and brutal descriptions of the enemy's war aim, the destruction of Germany. I intend to play this card at the next opportunity. I also bring it to the Führer's attention.

Archbishop Gröber of Freiburg has given a New Year's speech which is

* The anti-British song *Wir Fahren gegen England* (We Are Moving against England).

108

pure high-treason. We must sort that fellow out later.

I allow the press freedom in its comments on the Führer's speech. I also reduce press reports from abroad. The German people must not take the war too lightly. Our coal shortage is also to be discussed more openly and explained . . .

. . . Discuss new material with the writer Rehberg. I suggest he writes a script on the theme of the Opium War.

Reichle delivers a report on the food situation. Everything good in that area. The machinery is working magnificently. We have corrected some faults.

Berndt says farewell before going off to the front. I give him some good advice, to the effect that he should add the qualities of discretion and flexibility to his energy. Then he will be a marvellous colleague.

With the Führer. He is very satisfied with the response to his speech. We talk about our fliers' most recent attacks on English convoys. They have again been very successful. Overall, our Luftwaffe is magnificent. It is the best weapon for attack and the most reliable defence. The anti-aircraft defences are and will remain no more than a last resort. Our armament programme is being pushed forward with feverish energy, especially in the case of the Luftwaffe. The English will be amazed one of these days.

I make stern representations to Hewel regarding the Foreign Ministry's disloyalty. Ribbentrop is trying to lure away my employees with high salaries. But I am taking energetic steps against this. He will not be allowed to destroy the foundations of my work.

To Schwanenwerder. The children are overjoyed: the Führer has come with me. He stays for a few hours, plays with the children. Helga, Holde, and above all Hilde, are especially sweet. We are also able to talk without being disturbed. I constantly fear attempts on the Führer's life. If one were to succeed, it would be terrible. A few attempts have been discovered in time. His private apartment in Munich is a source of concern. He must have his own house in Munich. Until 9 November, he tells me, he had constant premonitions of death. Now all that remains is a firm sense of absolute security. He must live to complete his work.

We revive old memories. Of our house on the Reichkanzlerplatz. How happy we were in those days!

Now our lives are ruled by serious matters and work. But even this is a kind of harsh happiness.

When the Führer leaves, I get back to work. Every day there is a mass of it to be dealt with.

Late in the evening, gossipped for a while with Magda and Ello.

A biting cold throughout the entire house now. Wartime winter!

Yesterday: Siberian cold continues. Now we are forced to close some theatres, cinemas and studios. Hard times!

Discuss educational questions for the press. Education of the public and above all the broad masses. This leaves much to be desired.

Klitsch delivers a report on Ufa. Situation very good. But Leichternstern is not mastering the problems. There must be a change. Otherwise the whole thing will fall apart. Klitsch understands his job. Unfortunately, he knows nothing about art.

Discuss with Johst how our writers can be involved with current questions. Writers are for the most part too remote from the world. Only a very few understand the times and their problems.

Discuss the Wienfilm schedules with Reichmeister. Too little is contemporary and up-to-the-minute.

Midday with the Führer. We talk about our new weapons, which are absolutely ideal. Particularly our new machine-pistol. A miracle!

Amann and Esser make a lively contribution to the discussion. We are all waiting for better weather. The officers from the Reich Chancellery have been on a visit to the West Wall. Morale excellent, but the continual waiting is doing no one any good. The French are not stirring themselves at all, and there were no English in sight. The roads are buried under deep snow. How long still?

Dr Ley is indulging in excessive self-advertisement. Everyone is complaining about the fact.

Session with Göring in the afternoon on the difficult problem of the demoralisation of our youth. This is now giving us cause for anxiety. We must take all possible counter-measures. I suggest a comprehensive programme of education through radio programmes. Rust has nothing to say. His ministry is a complete shambles. The church question also comes into the discussion. What can one teach the children, when one has no new religion? The present substitute is no more than that: a substitute. The spread of venereal diseases is also a cause for concern.

Kerrl complains that he has no real powers. One's heart bleeds for him.

We decide on very tough youth laws. To nip the trouble in the bud. Rosenberg has been given wide responsibilities for educational work. Frick suggests concerted action by the police. The Hitler Youth is also to be taken in hand. Thus we hope to control these evils.

Discuss film matters with Göring afterwards. He promises me his support for the *Jud Süss* film.

At the office until late in the evening. Back to Schwanenwerder with Magda.

3 February 1940 (Saturday)

Yesterday: Even heavier frost. Coal situation desperate. Now we have shut the theatres, cinemas and studios. This is a natural catastrophe against which one cannot succeed by normal means. The Reichsbahn is powerless.

I ban reporting of court cases in the press. These only serve to encourage crime.

Our measures for the disciplining of youth are introduced immediately. The idea of plutocracy must figure more prominently. Under this slogan we shall triumph. There must be no repetition of the last war's mistakes.

The *Times* publishes a bare-faced, hypocritical article. I set the entire press on to it and supply some withering arguments myself. The Führer, too, makes some very effective points.

Our films are working well. We are intensifying this work. Our propaganda as a whole, in fact, is magnificent. Particularly the material for abroad. I am receiving marvellous reports. From Paris and London. And the *Concordia** transmitter is fantastic. Very cunningly done.

I issue precise guidelines for a campaign explaining the effects of the cold weather.

Speak to the Gau film administrators. On propaganda and the cinema . . .

. . . Pavolini complains about a book on the Duce. Since the book is actually very foolish, I ban it.

With the Führer. Even he is complaining about this barbarically cold weather. Now we are paying for the fact that we allowed too many small power stations to be built by private firms, that we left German hydro-electric potential untapped, and that the dead hand of centralism killed many good projects. The Führer has some harsh words for this centralism, which is particularly strong in the Ministry of the Interior, encouraged mainly by the jurists. The Führer hates jurists. They are incapable of thinking organically, only in formulae. This is a great danger for any state that falls victim to them. The Führer intends to have no more jurists in leading positions. They must always play a purely servicing role.

Paper shortage. We have to reduce the size of newspapers again.

Mother is not well. I send her some of my personal rations. She sacrificed so much for me in the World War, and this time I shall take her part. Whatever happens, she must not suffer.

To Lanke in the afternoon. Magda, Helga and Hilde are there already. It is so wonderful to have dear ones around myself in these testing times.

Work on at full speed. The paperwork never seems to let up. But I don't allow it to get on top of me, and always leave some time for original work.

In the evening, check films: weekly newsreel excellent this time.

---

* A clandestine transmitter broadcasting pacifist propaganda to France.

An appalling 'popular film' from Bavaria. A good dialogue film by Rehberg. *Angelika*.

Early to Berlin today.

4 February 1940 (Sunday)

Yesterday: The barbarically cold weather continues. Coal shortage worse. Sick-making. But this cannot last for ever.

The Führer has issued a secret order relating to measures in the territories that we shall be occupying. Everything must be pursued under conditions of the strictest discipline, since otherwise we shall be faced with dangerous problems. Maintenance of secrecy has a higher priority than speed whenever these measures are put into operation.

Greiner wants to join the Party. Not a good time at the moment.

Major Martin complains about Hippler, claiming that his report on shortcomings in the cinema industry is not objective. I inform Martin of an incident in which Polish officer prisoners-of-war collected money for the German poor, care of the Bishop of Eichstätt. The Party comrade who brought an action over the affair is to be punished. I intend to take all necessary measures to prevent this.

On the Strasbourg front, the French are making propaganda against the English. We make good use of this. Overall morale in France and England does not seem to be of the best. Strong defeatist currents. We must exploit this more for our purposes.

Our press has taken up cudgels against *The Times* with great enthusiasm. A hard propaganda blow against England on the subject of the Boer War. We had need of this in these quiet times.

The Kaiser has sided with the Finns in a letter to an American. Complete with the old war-slogans. An incorrigible fool!

At the moment we are working on a big film about the Volhynia Germans and their resettlement. Reichmeister delivers a report on the most recent events in the film sector. A number of still-unsettled questions about material to be discussed. It all takes such an insane amount of time . . .

. . . I need 4000 radio sets for the Western Front and cannot get them anywhere. We must step up the production programme yet again.

We strengthen our propaganda to France and above all to England. In the long term, our steady work must have effect.

Yet again, I am virtually drowning under paperwork and documents. In the end I pack a whole pile together and clear off to Lanke with it. Magda drives out with me from the city. She has been touchingly active, trying to solve my pressing financial problems, and we hope with success. Helga and Hilde are waiting for us out there.

How much good it does in these cold, hard times.

Work the entire afternoon. But I deal quickly with the less important items, since otherwise it is impossible to make time for essential work.

Churchill has issued some more crazy figures on shipping tonnages. If he is to be believed, the English merchant marine is bigger than it was at the outbreak of war.

Conference of the Balkan League in Belgrade. No sensational developments expected.

Checked films in the evening. *Passion*, a mediocre entertainment film. *From a First Marriage*, good entertainment. Director Verhoeven. These days one must check all films oneself, since so much depends on whether they are psychologically correct.

To bed at a reasonable hour, and for once a good night's sleep.

5 February 1940 (Monday)

Yesterday: The cold continues. When will it end?

The new English Minister for War, Stanley, has made a speech. Tougher than tough. He probably wants to make a strong impression as the Jew Hore-Belisha's successor. But his audience responded with boos and catcalls. And our Luftwaffe with massive and very successful attacks on English convoys. Four merchant steamers sunk in the process.

Moscow is taking on a very aggressive tone against Rome. This remains the one painful gap in our calculations. Italy gets ingratitude and disloyalty for her pains. Grist to the Italian mill.

Otherwise nothing special anywhere. Absolute quiet on all fronts, naturally. No operations are possible in this weather.

A day of relaxation and rest at Lanke. I am happy to have Magda and the children with me.

Read, write, and some music. Into the new week today with renewed strength.

6 February 1940 (Tuesday)

Yesterday: Frost, cold and coal shortage. The old story! When will it end? Our metereologists give no hope at all.

Our articles on the coal problem in the press have been very effective. I have the message reinforced.

Prince Schaumburg begins work at the Ministry . . .

. . . Rosenberg is now establishing his committee for the education of youth. I nominate Gutterer to join it. He will do that job well.

Stanley's speech is still being pulled apart by us. Particularly in the English-language broadcasts. The English are lying through their teeth again. But our Lord Haw-Haw is never short of an answer.

Discuss film questions with Hippler. The film archive must be brought up to date.

Gregory and Burgsdörffer report on work in the Protectorate. We intend first to support the German concert orchestras, so that they are capable of competing with the Czechs. No competition in areas where we cannot hold our own.

Major Martin has sorted out the affair of the Polish collection for our poor people.

Colonel von Schell reports on standardisation work in the German car-making industry. He has done a lot of good work. The main problem is lack of rubber. The transportation services in general have failed to meet the challenges. Dorpmüller is not up to his job. It is like a battle lost.

The poet Gunnar Gunnarsson visits. I give him a lecture on the rights and duties of neutrality. At first he is quite taken aback and tries to make excuses, but then he has to concede the main argument. The neutral states are playing a criminal game with us. They should learn from the tragic fate of other countries. But unfortunately human beings only learn from their own suffering.

With the Führer. I show him photos from the Polish campaign, which delight him greatly. We shall increase our support for this artistic work.

At my suggestion, Klimsch will receive the Eagle Badge rather than the Goethe Medal.

I have been reading all the volumes of *Kladderadatsch** from Bismarck's time, and I tell the Führer about it. He has a clear view of things. *Kladderadatsch* in those days was still very tame, as was political controversy in general at the time, in no way comparable with ours. But the world changes with the times and the personalities. *Kladderadatsch* was Greater-German and only against Bismarck insofar as his solution for Germany was only a partial solution. But Bismarck could not achieve more. The dynasties stood in his way. Even Emperor Wilhelm I had, so to speak, to have the imperial crown thrust upon him. And Friedrich Wilhelm IV would take the imperial crown only from the hands of the princes, and not from the people. The Democrats of '48 were Greater-German idealists, not to be compared with the November Democrats.** They all hated the dynasties and Austria, because it destroyed the Reich. One must grasp this connection in order to make correct judgments in this respect. The old Holy Roman Empire was the greatest political creation of the post-Roman era. It took its European character from the Roman Empire, and we shall assume that mantle now. Because of our organisational brilliance and racial selectivity, world domination will automatically fall to us. Only the church stands in our way now. The church has not abandoned its claim to domination over the secular world; it has merely dressed it up in religious clothing. In the days of the

* *Kladderadatsch* (Clatter). An old-established German political review.
** The founders of the Weimar Republic, so-called by the German Right because of the revolt which overthrew the Kaiser in November 1918 and, according to Nazi mythology, dealt the German army a debilitating 'stab in the back'.

Holy Roman Empire, the church possessed that power, too. The state was the tax-collector, so to speak, while the church ruled the people's lives. This lies at the core of the struggle today, in which we must – and shall – be victorious. The Führer draws these perspectives in broad, sweeping strokes. Whenever he talks political philosophy, he seems to grow beyond his normal stature. One could listen to him for hours.

I talk to the military leaders present about the basic concepts of propaganda, using the coal problem as my example. They show great understanding for my point of view.

Receive the Danish actress, Birgel Ipsen, and the singer, Friess, in my office. Together with Heinrich George. We discuss aspects of cultural exchanges. These little neutrals cannot and will never understand us.

Serious paper shortage. We are forced to reduce the size of our newspapers considerably. But better to limit their size than to shut them down altogether. Once that process has begun, it is hard to reverse. The only alternative is to use up the reserves in the west. But we must keep some there for a crisis.

End of Belgrade conference. Nothing of particular note. Turkey seems to have come off badly.

Check the newsreel. Magnificent shots of the attack on English convoys. Hippler is very sick. We must try to find a replacement for him. He has managed to complete a reorganisation plan for the entire German film industry, which looks very tempting. I shall check through it again.

Ribbentrop has written me another abusive letter, ten pages long. In times like these, he has time to spare! I make no answer. Let him whistle for his reply. A megalomaniac!

Back to Lanke late in the evening. Talk some more. Then to bed, exhausted.

7 February 1940 (Wednesday)

Yesterday: Cold, frost, growing coal shortages. The old story!

To Berlin with Magda.

Study press clippings about Unity Mitford. She has left a trail of rumours in her wake, not all of them pleasant.

Settle new salary levels for film industry. No fundamental changes.

From now on, our press will not mention any shortages in enemy countries that are also present here. This does not create a good impression.

London radio broadcasts a play about our ministry. Very flattering and almost true-to-life. Likewise, it mentions a railway accident near Münster that occurred only a few hours ago. How do they know this? . . .

. . . Discussion with Brauweiler and Bömer. A number of new measures, aiming in particular at better co-ordination. The Foreign Ministry is behaving in an increasingly underhand, disloyal fashion. But we shall win through.

Ribbentrop has thrown down the gauntlet to me. This does not irritate me. His own people no longer take him seriously. Dr Dietrich has composed an appropriate response to his letter. Brauweiler is working well, painstaking and cautious. I hope that he will master his assignment.

Speak to the leaders of the Reich Propaganda Offices and the officials of the SD. Outline the entire political situation. Then to the SD officials on the importance of their work among the people and in drawing up the reports on public mood. Then a speech to the officials of the monitoring service in the radio, the Forschungsamt,* the Foreign Ministry and the Reich post. About moral strength, etc.

A 10,000-ton 'Englishman' sunk.

A lot more work. To Lanke with Magda late in the evening. Those sweet children!

8 February 1940 (Thursday)

Yesterday: Frost, rain, sheet-ice, increasing coal shortages. Some theatres closed, and all the Ufa studios.

The Führer has gone to Munich for a few days.

Bibrach reports on his department's plans. Objective, clear and thoughtful. I hope he will succeed.

Discuss the situation of the *Voksbühne* theatre with Klöpfer. He plays out a whole, marvellous scene for my benefit. A real comedian! But nevertheless, I give him instructions, disguised as advice. I feel a little sorry for him, the great bear.

Discuss press business with Fritzsche. He must place more value on system in his work. Propaganda is repetition, constant repetition! Otherwise, Fritzsche is handling his job very well. He also has difficulties with the Foreign Ministry.

Talk over the question of the Peace of Westphalia with Wanowski from Münster and Dr Schuetze. We are starting work on a big project that has more to do with what is up-to-date and usable than pure science. I want material for the daily battle . . .

. . . The Anglo-French atrocity propaganda about Poland is increasing by the day. We take active steps to counter it. Admittedly, our propaganda against England must deal with the present as well as the past. We must not confine ourselves to grubbing around in English history. In any case, the British are becoming franker about their war aims. This can only be welcomed as far as we are concerned. Our reaction is correspondingly severe. English propaganda under Reith has improved considerably. We

* 'Research Office'. The main Intelligence organisation responsible for monitoring communications. A Party foundation independent of the state and military Intelligence machines.

exploit England's difficulties in India gladly.

Eight Irishmen executed in Birmingham.* We seize on this with all our might. This gives us ammunition for several days. I keep impressing my people with one basic truth: repeat everything until the last, most stupid person has understood.

We are trying to introduce Party speakers into the front line. In this way we shall create a counter-weight to the church propaganda in the Wehrmacht. But the ossified generals are none too willing. Now they are demanding censorship of all circulars sent to the front by business firms and Party branches. But I shall be able to stop that one.

New problems with the Foreign Ministry. It is no longer possible to work with these people in good faith. I shall have to look for support elsewhere.

Back to Lanke in the late afternoon. The dear little children!

Still a mass of work. Then check films. Newsreel: this time, magnificent. Glorious film of bombed-out English ships.

Liebeneiner's *The Good Seven*. Witty and nice. Somewhat overdone and a little snobbish. But on the whole a good achievement.

Bolshevik film. *Peter the Great*. Very Russian, Pan-Slavic and not at all Bolshevist. A little too much ecstasy, but highly interesting as an experiment.

Sit for a long time by the fire, talking. Prince Schaumburg reports on diplomatic high-society.

9 February 1940 (Friday)

Yesterday: A hint of a thaw. Thank God! But the coal shortage remains for the present. I have Walter speak on the radio.

Very anti-German mood in Holland. Our propaganda there, which is under the influence of the Foreign Ministry, is much too one-sidedly provocative. We should be supplying more factual material. Our radio broadcasts are having a good effect. Likewise in Rumania, where they fear a German protectorate. The English are stirring up a mood of panic against us. Reports from England do not paint too rosy a picture. Nevertheless, one can scarcely doubt the English readiness for war.

I ensure that circulars to the front from firms and Party branches are no longer subject to censorship.

The Wehrmacht High Command has announced: tonnage lost by the enemy and the neutrals due to our Navy in the war so far, 1½ million tons. And this is just merchant shipping.

Radio Statute considerably abbreviated, re-defined, and then issued.

Göring wants to cut off our supplies of foreign currency. Despite the

* 'Eight' may be an error in the transcription. Two IRA men, Peter Barnes and James Richards, were executed in Birmingham on 7 February 1940 for their part in the Coventry bombings.

serious shortage, I resist this. Otherwise our entire effort abroad will be brought to a halt . . .

. . . The Polish leader Studnitzki* sends me a memorandum regarding events in the General Government. With detailed information. This could be very dangerous for us. I have him taken into custody, for safety's sake . . .

. . . Paris has made a search at the Russian Trade Delegation. Storm of outrage in Moscow. The Russians make a great deal of noise at the beginning, but nothing happens.

In the evening, première of the Poland-film at the *Ufapalast*. Many representatives from government and the Wehrmacht. The film is a huge success. So my work finds some reward in the outside world. I am very satisfied.

Back to Lanke with Magda, late. Roads and fields covered with snow.

10 February 1940 (Saturday)

Yesterday: More cold weather and heavy snowfalls. Above it all shines a glorious winter sun, cheerful and friendly. It's enough to try one's patience! The coal situation in Berlin is deteriorating by the day. We are closing theatres, cinemas and factories, so as to be able to meet the demand for private heating fuel, at least for the present.

Chamberlain has made a speech. Shot though with lies and hypocrisy. But we give him a suitable answer, and straight away.

The French are searching frantically for our secret transmitter. By mistake, the Post Office linked it up with a Czech transmitter. This is downright treason. I have the Gestapo look into the matter immediately. We must act ruthlessly.

The English Interior Minister expresses his amazement to the House of Commons at how we got details of their secret session. He suspects German spies in high government circles. No, it is only a sign of our gift for piecing things together . . .

. . . Discuss the case of his son-in-law with Ley. Koch has been playing the Czar again in this matter. I shall sort it out.

Discuss Rosenberg's new duties with Lammers. Now the Wehrmacht has been included, too. So: Party, State and Wehrmacht. The job is confined to Rosenberg as an individual. He is not to build up a bureaucracy. But he will, of course. I shall keep a close eye on anything that affects my ministry. We are organising ourselves into chaos. The various empires are in each other's ways.

Work through midday and into the afternoon. Read through foreign magazines dealing with the war, particularly French and English publica-

* Possibly Professor Wladislaw Studnicki, one of a handful of Polish politicians who were reckoned as potential collaborators at this time.

tions. Excellently done. Pictures of the Russian catastrophe in Finland. It beggars all description.

Found a book by Shaw, *On the Peace Conference*, from 1919. Contains a devastating critique of the English mentality. I can put this to excellent use in our work.

In the afternoon, meeting of department chiefs in the Reich Chancellery to discuss Rosenberg's new powers.

All affected ministries represented. Long debates. Kerrl delivers his obligatory lecture on World-View and Religion. He has drifted a long way from us. Rosenberg defends his proclamation with verve. I can at least see to it that his powers are restricted to general matters. Otherwise he would be able to interfere in every ministry's personnel policy. Then we should be in a fine mess. General disagreement. Ley starts a row with Kerrl, Rust attacks Rosenberg, etc. And this in the middle of the war, and every one of them invoking the Führer.

Afterwards, Lammers gives me his private opinion; he believes that the Führer will probably not give Rosenberg the powers at all. Rosenberg is too pernickety. There is no helping him.

I give orders for more articles about the cold weather in the press. We must try to soothe the freezing public a little now.

Late home to Lanke. The dear, sweet children! How good it feels to hear their chatter after a day like this. Children are, at least, absolutely honest. They do not think much. But they say what they think. Why don't we?

11 February 1940 (Sunday)

Yesterday: Sun and hard frost. I do not drive into Berlin.

The English consul's letter from Peking figures prominently in the German press. This gilded youth has done us an enormous service. In the afternoon, the editorials are in full cry. Magnificently done.

Churchill has come up with some more wishful figures regarding tonnage sunk. We go straight into the attack.

Secret session of the parliament in Paris. We must sharpen our ears, and our pens.

Roosevelt is sending Welles to all the belligerent countries. First a peace offensive, for domestic-political reasons. Very late, too late, I believe. The Führer's peace speech would have been the time for that. We must just be careful to handle this skilfully, so that we do not end up in the Devil's kitchen.

We begin a big campaign against the atrocity accusations regarding Poland. This is absolutely essential.

The Wehrmacht High Command now wants to sponsor lectures for the home front. I forbid it. The Wehrmacht should look after its own business.

In any case, its ossified admirals and generals are the worst people to speak to the masses.

Gauleiters alone are responsible for organising political meetings.

All sorts to be dealt with. The Führer is back in Berlin. At midday I receive twelve foreign journalists for a talk at Lanke.

Frank has spoken to the foreign press. Unfortunately only with moderate success. He has too little charm in his manner to be able to chain up these bloodhounds.

The reception at my house turns out to be very stimulating. Our Luftwaffe has sunk five more British ships. Good news. We debate until late in the afternoon. All the issues of the moment come on the agenda, and at times I have to operate very cautiously. But I succeed in turning the occasion into a dazzling triumph. All of them drive back to Berlin well satisfied.

Jagow tells me about the war service of his *Tannenfels*. A very interesting adventure. Jagow is a fine fellow and a gentleman.

A U-boat brings home a rich booty. 38,000 tons sunk.

Film *Woman to Measure*. Nice entertainment, but somewhat too obscene. I have the doubtful parts edited out . . .

12 February 1940 (Monday)

Yesterday: The barbarically cold weather continues. A heavy burden for us all. Unfortunately, the press still refuses to say a word about it. But now the clock is striking thirteen! I fetch Fritzsche for a talk, tell him there is only one way to settle things. He can find no excuses. He is too soft and fair-minded. One must take a firm line with the press. Being mealy-mouthed gets one nowhere. I shall give Fritzsche one more chance. If it doesn't work, then I shall put a strong man alongside him. Berndt was less inhibited in this respect and therefore more successful. The press has also devoted a pathetically small amount of attention to the English diplomat's letter from Shanghai. On the other hand, they give plenty of space to the Foreign Ministry's material about the Polish 'atrocities'. This, too, is very important.

After the secret session of the Chamber of Deputies, Daladier received a large vote of confidence in his continued war leadership.

Frau [. . .] visits me this afternoon. We see the American Disney film *Snow White*, a magnificent artistic achievement. A fairy tale for grown-ups, thought out into the last detail and made with a great love of humanity and nature. An artistic delight! All sorts of gossip.

I read Shaw's *On the Peace Conference* from 1919. Very clever and witty, but in the final analysis Shaw fails. He has only half-grasped the vital problems. The thing is that he has no firm point of view from which to make his judgements on events. Nevertheless, he is still a literary giant!

Today a hard week begins. We are leaving Lanke again.

(12 February – first section of 15 March missing)

120

15 March 1940 (Friday)

. . . the Americans are too impudent and bare-faced.

We support Leichtenstern, who is under heavy fire at Ufa and is being attacked in the meanest way. Under such circumstances, one can never let a tried and trusted employee down.

With the Führer. Colin Ross is present. A very likeable man. He reports on his travels: Japan has bitten off more than it can chew in China. Making no more progress. The distances are too great. Chiang-Kai-Shek is a great and exceptional man. So long as he is in charge, there will be no capitulation. He can afford to wait, which Japan cannot. There can be no question of Japan's intervention in any other conflicts. And she cannot make peace with Chiang-Kai-Shek, because she must keep face. On the whole, this view may be correct. Ross describes Russia as a cheerless land. No laughter, no joy. Despite this, Stalin enjoys popularity. He is the only hope. Heir of Peter the Great. Proponent of Pan-Slavism. It may be that, as a Germanic people, we shall never understand these Slavs. Stalin is a little father to the Russians. And the fact that, like any prudent gardener, he hacks off the excessive growth on his hedges – that is, liquidates generals and journalists – lies in the nature of Bolshevism. He does not want greatness. In this, he stands in diametric opposition to us, who encourage and cultivate great personal qualities. The Germans work in order to make a better life for themselves. The Russians, perhaps, do not possess this urge at all . . .

(The rest of 15 March 1940 to first part of 29 April 1940 missing)

29 April 1940 (Monday)

. . . to all Norwegians completely in our favour. Advises surrender. Hard line against England, which left Norway in the lurch and must be defeated. Talks of the King, who has fled, and his private government. An upright, manly and courageous appeal. It only serves to increase my affection for Hamsun. For the moment, I shall not have it published. Wait until a favourable moment comes and Oslo has released the statement.

I study German and English magazine material about the war. The English are still greatly superior to us in this area. I shall use every means to ensure that we redress their obvious advantage.

Our newspapers are on magnificent form at the moment, due to my efforts. Of necessity, since the public here has still not grasped the significance of the documentary campaign. England must be exposed and completely discredited. Only then shall we be able to negotiate with her. The English plutocrats are now inventing new expressions like 'anti-climax' and so on. Just like our domestic opponents in the old days, who used to prattle about a 'temperature curve'. Now, as then, there will be a rude awakening.

Chat a little with the children and stroll round the grounds. What a joy to see the tiny, knowing, pretty little girls slowly growing up.

In the evening, check the newsreel with Hippler; still a little confused. Has to be re-edited. A lot of work. The anti-English sketch fails completely . . .

(Last part of 29 April 1940 – first part of June 16 1940 missing)

16 June 1940 (Sunday)

. . . Military situation: Heavy fighting on the Maginot Line. The French are resisting very stubbornly. But a large number of fortified positions have fallen to us. Pursuit of the enemy beyond the Seine. Over 200,000 prisoners so far since 5 June. The German flag flies over Versailles. Triumph! One's heart beats faster when one hears of such an event. We spent twenty-one years fighting for this. Gloria, victoria!

At the moment, Italy is confining her operations to the sea and the air, but they are successful.

I am sending Wächter to Paris. With Knothe and Faber. They are to set up a new office for me there. And assert themselves against the Foreign Ministry. I send the gentlemen off with precise instructions.

Gutterer is put in charge of domestic and foreign propaganda. Brauweiler has not completely proved himself capable of leading in a self-motivating fashion.

Du Pré is recalled from Cracow. Schmidt from Hamburg takes his place.

The Lithuanian answer does not satisfy Moscow. Russian troops march into Lithuania. Cabinet falls in Kovno.

A rush of successes in the afternoon: Maginot Line south of Saarbrücken penetrated on a broad front. First two forts stormed at Verdun, then the citadel and the town taken by us. In the World War, we had to sacrifice hundreds of thousands of soldiers for this. To be a witness to these historical victories makes one quite solemn. A revolutionary régime celebrates its great triumph.

In the Baltic area, the rumours continue. It seems as if Moscow intends making a *tabula rasa* there. The wisest thing that she could do now.

Alfieri comes to Schwanenwerder in the evening. He stays for several hours. He tells me about the Pope, with whom he is on very good terms. The Pope wants to have closer relations with us. But he still has reservations. If he waits too long, it will be too late. Alfieri is delighted at our successes. Who wouldn't be!

The Führer calls up: quite delighted and excited. He wants no talk of peace at the moment. First the French must go down on their knees. This will happen in 4–6 weeks' time. Then we shall see what England intends to do. She will not be able to do much, in any case. First strike the sword out of her hand on land. Huge new military successes are round the corner. The Führer

122

describes them to me in detail. He has been studying the ceremony of the Armistice and the Versailles peace very closely. It is to be our model. Quite rightly so. The Führer is wonderful. So clear and relentless. Every conversation with him is a new source of strength.

Roosevelt cables Reynaud: as much material aid as possible. And America will not recognise any theft of French territory. This will scarcely cause us any sleepless nights.

In the evening, Reynaud puts out peace feelers: France wants to accept Germany's conditions, says the Havas agency via America. We state quite coldly that we know nothing about any such conditions. Then, from United Press, follows . . .

(Last part of 16 June 1940 – first part of 25 June 1940 missing)

25 June 1940 (Tuesday)

. . . I am preparing a big programme of celebrations for the radio. The entire German people is to be involved.

Call from the Führer: he is quite boisterously happy. Praises my propaganda work, which contributed so much to the victory. Does not yet know for certain whether he will proceed against England. Believes that the Empire must be preserved if at all possible. For if it collapses, then we shall not inherit it, but foreign and even hostile powers will take it over. But if England will have it no other way, then she must be beaten to her knees. The Führer, however, would be agreeable to peace on the following basis: England out of Europe, colonies and mandates returned. Reparations for what was stolen from us after the World War. Negotiations are already under way on these issues, via Sweden for example. No one knows yet whether they will be successful. We must wait. We must carry on regardless, working in the old style. England must not be allowed to get off easily this time.

The Führer is unreservedly delighted by our newsreel work. This pleases him especially. For the rest, he too wants a general peace as soon as possible.

Check the new newsreel and change the music. This one beats all previous efforts.

From England, particularly through the medium of de Gaulle, new salvoes against . . .

[part of 25 June missing]

. . . To Lanke. It is impossible to stay in Berlin because of the almost tropical heat.

Discuss the situation in the Protectorate with von Gregory.

The Czechs are slowly beginning to see reason. Hacha's last radio speech was very positive. High time, too. I shall try to offer the Czechs a clear delineation of things in the cultural sector. They must keep clear of any stupid nationalism, and in exchange they will be given greater leeway, at least within certain bounds. Gregory will put out feelers in that direction. However, I shall have to take their broadcasting service away from them. This belongs under the authority of the Reich. It is a first-class means of leading the masses, and we cannot do without it in the long term.

Görlitzer has some personnel questions and complaints against Lippert. These two old, incorrigible fighting-cocks cannot be changed. One must let them have their say.

Work the entire afternoon in steaming heat.

At 19.20 telephone call from Alfieri: at 19.10 the truce between France and Italy was signed. A historic moment. Now the guns fall silent throughout France. Gripped by the magnitude of the moment. A victory, such as we could not have imagined in our wildest dreams, is ours.

Thanks to the Führer! . . .

(Last part of 25 June 1940 – first part of 10 August 1940 missing)

10 August 1940 (Saturday)

. . . Work the whole day through at the office. This does the trick. All that old, neglected paperwork dealt with.

The Italians have taken Hargeisa in Somaliland. They are advancing strongly. A valuable contribution to the war against London.

Revise the Rothschild-film.*

Schirmeister and Prince Schaumburg are off to the army. The others will have to work all the harder than before.

With Naumann, deal with a number of personnel and administrative problems.

In the evening, to Lanke with Magda. A joyful scene when the children see their mummy again.

We have a lot to tell each other. And I have to work on late into the night.

Russian film of the Finnish campaign. Pathetic. Dilettantism in its purest form. The handiwork of sub-humans. Then Wagner music. A blasphemy.

Perhaps we shall be forced to take steps against all this, despite everything. And drive this Asiatic spirit back out of Europe and into Asia, where it belongs.

(Last part of 10 August 1940 – first part of 17 August 1940 missing)

17 August 1940 (Saturday)

. . . The asocial elements must not be preserved for a later revolution. They

---

* *The Rothschilds' Shares in Waterloo*. An anti-Semitic film set during the Napoleonic Wars. Released in October 1940.

will always be a threat to the state, particularly in the large cities. Therefore: liquidate them and create a healthy social life for the *Volk*. Authority is, of course, nothing but a fiction. If the asocial elements succeed in devaluing it – or even denting it – then the door is open to anarchy.

The judicial process is quite incapable of dealing with these problems. It is sterile, completely lacking in perspective or sense of responsibility. It is just about sufficient in absolutely peaceful, stable times. In times of war and revolution, it is best to abolish it and judge according to necessities, and not according to formal laws.

Later we intend to pack the Jews off to Madagascar. There they too can establish their own state.

But back to the present. The English communiqués are being met with strong scepticism not only in the world at large, but also in England. Duff Cooper and Churchill have gone too far with their lies. Our attacks on the airfields continue. Soon we shall have bases for our night-fighters. Then we shall have a little more peace on the home front, too.

Lammers has now issued the edict regarding German works of art in the occupied territories. I shall approach this work in the most enthusiastic and thorough fashion.

Agree a number of propaganda measures for the SS with Himmler . . .

(Last part of 17 August 1940 – 30 September inclusive missing)

1 October 1940 (Tuesday)

Yesterday: Weather changeable. More absolutely massive attacks on London. It is possible to see the demoralising effect from the English press. Insignificant incursions into the air space of the Reich. One can no longer discern English intentions with any certainty.

Serious problems of evacuation of children from Berlin. The NSV* has proceeded very clumsily in this area and has created enormous discontent. And I had expressly ordered that the process should be carried out without compulsion. I summon the ten Berlin Kreisleiters and read them the riot act. They are to warn the local Party branches immediately and bring order back into the situation. Unfortunately we cannot clear matters up through the press. But I hope things will work out, even so.

Stalin makes a statement in *Pravda* on the Three-Power Pact.† Very positive. Russia had been informed beforehand, had no objection. So the

* The *Nationalsozialistische Volkswohlfahrt* (National Socialist People's Welfare), the main Nazi Party war-relief organisation.
† The so-called 'Pact of Steel' between Germany and Italy was extended to include Japan on 27 September 1940 and became known as the Three-Power (Tripartite) Pact. Other states joined as they came within the German orbit in 1940–41.

plutocrats, who had been speculating on help from the Bolsheviks, have the wind taken out of their sails.

The Americans are becoming increasingly restless and perplexed, while in London they carry on trying to appear innocent and ingenuous. But there are very serious voices coming out of England, too. Opinion there is completely divided.

The mood here is also volatile. The child-evacuation problem has caused us some setbacks. Mothers are becoming nervous, and that is a bad sign. But I shall soon make up the lost ground. In London, on the other hand, the provision of air-raid shelters is their most pressing problem. Conditions there are apparently appalling.

Enke gives a brilliantly incisive report on the bombing of London, which will provide superb material for propaganda at home and abroad. I order it to be used accordingly. The Berlin air-raid warning system is not working too well. I intervene in this business, too, and sort things out. It is, of course, a difficult task to chase four and a half million people into air-raid shelters and then get them out again. The greatest precision is required.

We must devote more propaganda to the army, or people will forget its existence altogether.

Discussion with Schweikart and Hertell on Bavaria. Wagner spends too much time meddling with our affairs there. I ensure order and a clear chain of command. No one can serve two masters.

Talk with Alfieri. He predicts that the war will last for some time yet. Somewhat downcast. He is not a strong character, and frequently needs cheering up. I oblige. He promises all sorts of benefits from the Three-Power Pact. But we shall have to wait and see for the moment.

Midday with the Führer. He, too, is very angry at the false air-raid alarms. Has intervened in person. He is also very concerned about the evacuation of children and the attendant problems. I tell him what I think, and he approves: no compulsion; only those who want to, and who can go alone, should do it; transport will be provided by the NSV. This is the way to make it work, and the way to make it understood.

Stalin's statement causes the Führer satisfaction. It helps us a little bit further on our way.

So far as London is concerned, the Führer cannot understand their tactics, either. It is impossible to see what they intend. We can only continue to attack and await results. We have caused crippling damage to the English aircraft industry. Things are progressing slowly, but the direction is forward.

The Führer shows me a recent photograph of Kaiser Wilhelm. Taken in Doorn. Wearing the Iron Cross Class I and a straw hat. Grotesque. Like an old Jew. He may well have Jewish blood in his veins. This would explain his character and his carping criticisms.

In the afternoon, some wild rumours reach us from London. Hither and thither. But no one has any hard information.

Fetch Farinacci in the afternoon. I have invited him to Berlin on a three-day visit. Big reception. He is exceptionally pleasant, a real old fascist whom one cannot help but like. We are back on friendly terms immediately.

Brief chat with Alfieri at the Adlon hotel. Then work long and hard on the crisis in morale caused by the evacuee problem. Too many people have been fighting to rule this particular roost, and hence the brouhaha. But now I intend to take the reins and steer the operation to its conclusion: tough instructions to Görlitzer, and a soothing statement for the press. Thus, I hope, peace will be restored.

Circular to the Wehrmacht re. content of welfare provisions for the troops. In it I spell out the basic principles and content of this work.

Reception in the evening at the Adlon for Farinacci. A lot of guests. Farinacci is very charming. We are surprised by an air-raid alert, which lasts until five in the morning. Wait at the Adlon. Hardly any bombs on Berlin. English tactics to tire us out.

Only two hours' sleep.

2 October 1940 (Wednesday)

Yesterday: Relatively quiet. Few air incursions into the Reich. The usual quota of bombs on London. But no clear view through the fog. The English press continues obdurate and cocky.

The Führer intends to meet the Duce on the Brenner soon. To write a full-stop.

My announcement in the press has now clarified the problem of child evacuees in Berlin. Complete peace has been restored. The announcement was absolutely necessary. Saturday's false air-raid alarm has also been investigated. It was due to lack of foresight. I make an enormous fuss and order some major changes.

Military situation: no earth-shattering events. On the whole, unchanged. Things are stagnating a little.

Big entertainments programme for the troops signed and sealed. Hinkel is making himself very useful in that area. Summer time will be maintained for the present.

Administrative questions with Gutterer. Hippler is warned to act rather more peaceably and not to play the smarty-pants. He is too liable to dismiss the official view.

Heiduschke returns to his post. I am glad to have him back. Naumann does not want to return yet, and I agree that he should stay with the army.

Long talk with Farinacci. He is a real fascist and a true supporter of the Axis. A pleasure to speak with him. A chip off the old block. He has met the Führer and was deeply impressed. At midday we are guests of Dr Dietrich, who delivers a pompous speech of welcome.

Much, much to do. Willkie has made a disgraceful speech; but probably only so hostile towards us because he has to cover himself against Roosevelt and public opinion. The same goes for emigré Germans. We punish his speech by contemptuous silence.

70,000 tons sunk. Planes shot down: enemy 68 to our 31.

Izvestia expresses opinions favourable to the Three-Power Pact. Russian policy is moving in a favourable direction at the moment from our point of view.

I have to consult Professor [. . .] Nervous disorders due to overwork and lack of vitamins. This must be remedied as quickly as possible.

Guest of Alfieri in the afternoon. Big tea party, but I am not in the mood. The Führer is concerned that Farinacci's schedule is too busy. I cut it very considerably. The best course, particularly at the moment, when there is little peace at nights. The Führer tells me that we shot down ten English planes during the night.

With Farinacci in the evening to the *Deutsches Opernhaus* to see an act of *Liebestrank*. Beautiful voices. What a pleasure after such a long abstinence from theatre-going!

Drop Farinacci at his hotel.

Then to Lanke. What peace out here!

The American press is playing things rough, while the English are being cunning. But neither impresses me. They are simply trying to hide their weakness.

Work a little more.

Then to bed, dead-tired.

Air-raid alert for an hour. But I sleep on. Scarcely any damage in Berlin. So: more English attempts to tire us out.

3 October 1940 (Tuesday)

Yesterday: The weather here is good. But no use to us, because over England it is bad. Nevertheless, the usual quantities are dropped on London. Only moderate incursions into the Reich.

False optimism in London. They are talking of having won the air battle, about new types of bombers, etc. This may have some effect in the rest of the world, particularly in America. But it does not impress us. For my part, I order a counter-campaign. Using the radio and the press. The main aim is to destroy Londoners' illusions.

New broadcasting system on permanent frequencies agreed with the Luftwaffe. Now we can broadcast for longer again. Very important, particularly with regard to England.

More excellent reactions to my speech in Prague. They want to establish a Czech Chamber of Culture, and especially a Chamber of Films. I am opposed to this. A simple administrative organ would be better. It is quite sufficient and not so risky.

I leave Farinacci to be entertained by the Leys. They are to drive to Dresden in the evening, so as to have a decent night's sleep away from the air raids.

Discuss the re-organisation of the ministry with Gutterer. I shall be establishing five main departments in all. I am not yet entirely clear about personnel. The fur will probably fly. The chief priority will be to cut Hippler down to size. He is too young, and also rather too full of himself. And as a result causes ill-feeling everywhere. I shall put Berndt on his back. Discuss some new material for political films with Hippler. We have quite a quantity of this nowadays.

Save the Request Concert. The bureaucrats wanted to change the concept out of all recognition. I return it to its old form from 1 November.

Party Comrade Friede reports on the situation in Turkey. Government anti-German on the whole. The people quite the opposite. Papen is wholly unco-operative so far as propaganda is concerned. I shall hand this work over to the AO.* The aim in our propaganda is to speak to the people, and not to some hireling government or diplomatic corps. Friede outlines an extensive plan to me, and I place the necessary funds at his disposal.

Discuss the problem of original musical scores in France with Dr Gerigk. Immense quantities of scores, part of Germany's cultural heritage, are lying around there. I reach agreement with Dr Gerigk that they should be shipped back to Germany. Particularly pieces by Gluck and Mozart, but also Schubert and Wagner. The French have let the material go to rack and ruin. It is a real cultural scandal.

Magda comes for a short visit. She has got out of bed for a few hours. Helmut is five years old today. I can only speak to him by telephone. He is such a nice, clever boy. He gives us all such a huge amount of fun.

Work through the afternoon. Philharmonic in the evening. Furtwängler conducts. Wonderful! Concerto for three pianos by Bach, clear and almost mathematical. *Death and Transfiguration*, hammered out with magnificent verve. And then the Fifth Symphony. Ravishing! What a joy for me after such a long time without music. I feel reborn.

German-Italian Society. Fetch Farinacci and take him to the station. A few more friendly words of farewell. He is a fine fellow and a sincere fascist. *Addio*!

Late home to Lanke. Work on for a long time. It never lets up.

The Führer intends to meet Mussolini during the next few days. To discuss the situation. That is necessary from time to time.

Two-hour air-raid alert during the night. An English bomber is shot down

---

* The *Auslands-Organisation* (Foreign Organisation) of the Nazi Party, which embraced all Germans abroad. Bohle headed the AO with the rank of Gauleiter and Secretary of State at the Foreign Ministry. His attachment to the Foreign Ministry led to frequent disputes with Ribbentrop.

in the vicinity of Lanke. It hits the ground with a mighty crash. At last, one brought down by the flak. That is something, at least.

4 October 1940 (Friday)

Yesterday: The Führer has gone south for his talks with the Duce. The meeting is still being kept completely secret.

British government reshuffle. Chamberlain kicked out. With a sentimental exchange of letters. Influence of the Labour Party increased. Churchill still firmly in the saddle. The effects of this change in the government are not yet clear.

The weather is very bad again. The usual quota of bombs on London. Reports from the British capital are totally divided. Some very pessimistic, some very optimistic. Illusions are obviously being fostered by the government. We counter-attack with all the power at our disposal.

Wodarg reports to me on the slight weakening in the morale of Luftwaffe units operating against London. It seems to them as if they are fighting a kind of aerial Verdun. Demands on them are far too heavy. The crews hardly get any rest. It is true that they are inflicting horrendous damage on the enemy, but we are not being let off lightly, either. Something must be done for these boys. The mood in the country at large is ambiguous. People still hope that the war will end soon. It is difficult to convince the public that this may not be so. The consequences of the over-hasty evacuation are still discernible in Berlin. I take action against that yet again. I issue a circular to all Reich authorities, to the effect that in future I shall not stand for any interference in the Berlin Gau. We can see what it led to in this case.

Report on the mood in France: our people are working hard, but attitudes remain frosty and cool. The big propaganda campaign we had planned has not yet got properly under way.

Receive the Iranian ambassador. He complains about our broadcasts to Iran, or at least the radio announcers. I ask him to be more precise. Whatever the case, we cannot allow Iran to interfere in our internal affairs.

German-Italian co-operation in film projects discussed with Orasi. We must be very careful in this area, and not give in too much to the Italians.

Talk over aspects of Vienna with Hitler Youth Leader Kaufmann. He is to take charge of the Reich Propaganda Office there. I outline the tasks he will face. He is very personable and intelligent, but still rather young. He will have a very wide range of duties to fulfil in Vienna. In particular, he will be responsible for clearing up the bad feeling between Berlin and Vienna. He is probably the right man for that. He knows Schirach well and has a quite tolerable acquaintance with me. So let him start.

Work through lunch. Deal with a mass of things that have been neglected previously. I have time for that, now that the Führer is away and Farinacci is no longer taking up my time.

To Lanke. I can work there with less disturbance. The rain is pouring down. Dreary. Praise God that Magda is feeling better. But she must continue to rest and wait.

I take a look at the English aircraft that crashed in the neighbourhood. A pile of old iron and metal, inside it the charred remnants of three corpses. A dreadful sight. But better the English than our boys.

Check films: very good newsreel. Re-edited version of *The Girl from Barnhelm* now good and unobjectionable. And *A Life Long*, with Ucicky, Menzel, Wessely, a really big hit from Wienfilm. Gripping and heart-rending . . .

(Last part of 4 October – first part of 5 October missing)

5 October 1940 (Saturday)

. . . Report from Prague on my latest speech. Was a very big success. I shall be making my first visit to Prague in the near future and intend to expand on it. We can win over the Czechs now.

More rumours in Berlin about gas attacks and evacuation of children. However, I take vigorous counter-measures and have the rumour-mongers locked up.

Gutterer gives me an account of the end of Farinacci's visit. Everything went brilliantly. A number of routine tasks dealt with. Talk with Dr Ley: he intends to revive and reorganise the German fashion industry. This is a laudable project. He renews his plea for the KdF to become the Seventh Chamber in the Reich Chamber of Culture. I have nothing against it and intend to pursue the idea in concert with him. Perhaps this is the best solution to the present difficulties. Ley is in very high spirits. A nice fellow, with whom one can work.

Visit by Furtwängler: he has some worries because of his commitments abroad. I advise him against Switzerland for the moment. Particularly against Winterthur, where emigrés from Germany are still active, even now. He is very helpful and offers to give a concert with the Berlin Philharmonic during my visit to Prague. This visit must be the consummation of our work of reconciliation. I shall give it a skilful build-up.

Visit to Magda in the afternoon. Lord be praised, she is well. We gossip a little. Then I drive to Lanke.

There I manage an hour's rest. Then work calls once more. The talks on the Brenner went well. Very positive communiqué issued.

Report from England, via Lisbon. According to this source, things in London are really gloomy.

Forger, a new film produced by the Gestapo. Bad, because too didactic.

Carry on reading and writing until late. But then sleep nicely into Saturday, which I intend to spend at Lanke.

131

Yesterday: Proper night's sleep for once. Almost no enemy incursions into the Reich. We bomb London and other English cities with the usual quantities of explosives, despite the fog. In London, meanwhile, the illusion-mongering campaign is being continued and showing some success, especially in the USA, where they are willing to accept it at face value. I receive a report from the USA which outlines the unpleasant results of this propaganda. I shall now take strong counter-measures. The press and the radio will be drawn firmly into the service of anti-English propaganda. We shall let it run for a while. I expect great things of it.

The SD report registers a slight weakening in popular morale. We must take rigorous steps to prepare the nation for a second winter at war. I shall introduce a large-scale propaganda campaign in the Reich to this end. It will be pursued using all the tricks of modern propaganda, and I expect it to be very successful. Report on vegetable and fruit supplies in the Reich: vegetables in plentiful supply, the fruit situation very bad. A delayed effect of the harsh winter, and a serious blow. We must see how we can deflect it.

Report on the situation in France: our big propaganda drive is starting to roll. The accent is strongly anti-England and also against the French plutocracy. The mood has already improved somewhat. A decisive change, however, will only be discernible after this big operation.

The Führer has returned to Munich. Outcome of the Brenner talks good, as I am informed by telephone. This is exceptionally gratifying. We shall be able to expect some results in the near future. The Führer is playing his pieces with extraordinary skill. One day Churchill will find himself in check-mate.

Stupid business in Vienna: our spokesman in Vienna has written a very foolish, but very caustic article in one of the local newspapers, attacking Berlin, its way of life, and its people. Without any apparent cause. Schirach calls me up as a result, absolutely furious. I give him full powers to remove the man from his post immediately and take him into custody for a few days. All I need at the moment is for my own employees in Vienna to start attacking the Reich and Berlin in public. It is high time that Vienna was made to behave itself. Schirach is well on the way to that goal.

Final investigation into the case of Hettlage: not much can be proved against him. He can stay with Speer but will not be accepted for membership of the Party. Speer has been charged by the Führer with the job of providing large numbers of air-raid shelters in Berlin. An exceptionally difficult problem for the coming winter, which will now be attacked with vigour.

Things are different in London. There they have been scratching their heads over the problem for weeks now, without coming to any decisions. It is an advantage, after all, to live in an authoritarian state.

The air-raid shelters in Schwanenwerder are totally inadequate. I shall have the children come to Lanke for the holidays. Magda, unfortunately, is not at all well. She is again suffering badly with her heart.

I have a so-called day off. My colleagues have used it to bury me completely under memoranda and documents. It is sick-making. I work my way laboriously through the whole mass of paper. To be a Minister in this Reich today is no easy matter.

The English are cobbling together a tissue of lies about the success of their bombing attacks on German military targets. We issue no denials, but leave them in their fond belief. The targets that they hit were almost all dummy installations. They are making far-reaching changes in the leadership of their Air Force, which does not say much for its strength and success. In London there is great dissatisfaction over the cabinet reshuffle. It does not go far enough. Churchill still has to make up some lost ground.

Otherwise, general quiet. Our bombing attacks continue, but due to the permanent bad weather they are meeting with no more than limited success.

Work furiously until evening. Then a stroll through the forest in the twilight. Everything around me is sad and bare. A mantle of profound melancholy envelops the forest. It makes the heart so heavy.

In the evening, read and write. It helps dispel foolish moods. Rabble-rousing American film, *Pastor Hall*. The supposed fate of Niemöller. A moronic piece of rubbish. Not worth the time spent watching it.

7 October 1940 (Monday)

Yesterday: Dreadful weather. Rain, storms! The war in the air is slowly grinding to a halt. Almost no English incursions into the Reich. On the other hand, heavy attacks on the Channel coast. Rotterdam especially hard-hit. It seems that our English gentlemen believe it has not yet suffered enough. Not quite the usual quota of bombs on London. Fierce fighter battles, however. Result 30:7. The English, of course, make it into another great air victory. They are forced to lie in order to say anything at all. They are indulging in the craziest fantasies; now they are drivelling about an invasion of Germany, among other things. It is scarcely credible, but they can still find idiots who accept all this at face value. I step up our anti-illusion campaign to full power. The press is not quite so keen to co-operate, since continual repetition makes them feel uncomfortable. But it must, it must. From now on I shall keep chewing over the arguments against England *ad nauseam*. Then the world will believe them too. This is the essence of propaganda. And we intend, in old National Socialist style, not to operate defensively but offensively. The English will be amazed. Their cheap tricks will not work with us.

The situation in London continues to be reflected in mixed reports: some more pessimistic, some more optimistic. It is scarcely possible to arrive at a coherent view. Therefore we must continue to attack on all fronts. The

English are withdrawing their essential raw materials from London by sea in huge convoys. Rich pickings for our U-boats. And also an indication of how bad things must look in London.

Great conjecture over the talks on the Brenner. But all wide of the mark. London is behaving as if she knew everything, in fact as if she had been there in an advisory capacity. A world empire with only its façade left intact.

A quiet day at Lanke. The rain pours down, the storm rages. Not sweet music to our air-crews. Magda is slightly better again. She has had a lot to bear during these times. That is the woman's contribution to the war effort. It too is hard, painful, surrounded with anxieties and dangers. But then so is life!

Read, write. A drive through the autumn forest in the rain and the wind. Nature is sunk in deep, heavy melancholy.

Newsreel in the evening. Well thought-out. Then a long time talking.

A very gloomy report from London. If it is correct, then we are in a good position.

8 October 1940 (Tuesday)

Yesterday: Weather changeable. Easing-off in our attacks on England. 56 tons on London. Nevertheless, heavy damage. Almost no incursions into the Reich. Some successes for the English in their attacks on the Channel coast, however.

Gloomy reports from London. Despite all this, Churchill's press continues to sound off about the victories to come. A truly massive fantasy-campaign, which is as impudent as it is mendacious, and therefore typically English. We shall now initiate an anti-illusions campaign that will strike the English deaf and blind. It will go on until we all have it coming out of our ears. Then every last person in the world will have got the message. Now the English are claiming that we, of all people, were responsible for spreading rumours of peace. We are supposed to have mobilised Roosevelt and the Pope. Then again, they have secret hopes of Mussolini. A completely directionless barrage of lies that it is impossible to make sense of.

A letter from Wiegand in America: he describes the prevailing intellectual terror there, exercised by the Jews and the plutocrats, and a country reeking to heaven with corruption and cowardly lies, inhabited by a hotch-potch of races not worthy of the name 'people'. To the devil with it!

Discuss aspects of entertainment for the troops with Hinkel. The salaries have been pushed too high by the KdF. I therefore set the highest at 2000 Marks a month . . .

. . . Ott reports on his trip to Paris: everything is being bought up. A real scene of pillage that makes one's gorge rise.

Reports from Prague: the mood in the Protectorate can be described as something close to excellent after my speech. I find this particularly gratifying.

The children come for a visit: Helga and Hilde. What a joy! We inspect our house in the Göringstrasse. It will soon be ready, and will be very nice. Then we go off together to buy books, visit mummy, who is quite well, and then drive to Lanke. The Führer is still in Munich.

A big gasworks destroyed in London. The air-raid shelter problem is still the most burning issue. London may wreck itself over this.

In the USA they are talking openly of joining in the war, the sooner the better. But they will certainly wait until the elections, unless the Jews lose patience first. Pitiable country!

Busy until evening. The autumn storms rage round the house.

Visitors: Professor Froelich, Frau Leander, Frau Ondra and Ello. Put the finishing touches to the newsreel. Despite the present stagnation, turned out magnificently. And talk and discuss a great deal.

Another late night. Air-raid alert at 10.00. Lasts more than five hours. The heaviest English attack yet. Twenty-five dead and fifty seriously injured. Hospitals, etc. bombed. Almost no military targets hit. But some damage to civilian targets. But we shall pay the English gentlemen back, with interest. Really massive day and night raids on London and other English cities. This time they have earned it.

Only a few hours' sleep.

9 October 1940 (Wednesday)

Yesterday: Glorious weather. The bombing continues. The Luftwaffe wants a relaxation of the regulations pertaining to use of air-raid shelters. I am against this, and the Führer also rejects it firmly.

We take steps to secure our position in Rumania.* Huge outcry in the world press. We divulge nothing.

Farinacci has sent 5000 books for our soldiers. Thoughtfully enough, the content is anti-fascist. A real joke. I quietly get rid of them.

Discuss cultural films with Hippler. Much to do in that area.

Discuss situation of the radio with Glasmaier. We are aiming to resume transmitting until midnight. The stations in Prague, Brussels and the Hague we intend to acquire for the Reich. The Request Concerts will be resumed in the old style. The Reich's dominance in the radio field will be more secure than ever. Particularly with regard to the protectorates and the conquered territories.

Frielitz tells me about the situation in Denmark. Much better than in Norway. But the Danes continue to harbour a few illusions about their future as a nation. I intend to invite a large group to study in Germany.

Continue working at Lanke. The Führer is still in Munich. The two children, Helga and Hilde, are outside in the sunshine.

* German troops invaded Rumania on 7 October 1940 to support the new, crypto-fascist government of General Ion Antonescu.

Very fierce air battles over England. Kill ratios 32:13. But London talks stubbornly of victories in the air. This is becoming downright pathological. London has re-opened the Burma road: a clear challenge to Japan.

Dr Dietrich is working overtime at making trouble for the press department. I deal with that easily.

Ribbentrop is feuding with the AO and has refused Schmidt-Decker a visa for Rome. I become angry. Hess intervenes and Schmidt-Decker sets off on his travels, against Ribbentrop's will. A painful humiliation for him.

Churchill makes a speech. Somewhat subdued. He admits a lot. Talks his way around sensitive areas with a few cynical remarks. Makes a new contribution to English fantasy-policy. But nevertheless he seems to be having a devil of a bad time. We give him a dusty, loud answer. The German press is in excellent tune at the moment. Hitting the English as only it can. Now reading the newspapers is fun again. We have to whip up our journalists from time to time. Otherwise everything goes to rack and ruin.

I have to sleep for an hour in the evening, since I am close to dropping from exhaustion.

Then it's back to work. A thousand problems to deal with. When one is fresh and well-rested, work is a pleasure. Lack of sleep makes one ill.

Write and read a lot into the night. Watch a few good new cultural films. No air-raids.

10 October 1940 (Thursday)

Yesterday: Excellent weather. Heavy air-raids on Bremen. In return, we attack London without pause by day and night. And to considerable effect. The old lamentations yet again. But we have enough weapons to hand to counter them. A whole series of incursions into the Reich by enemy aircraft.

Churchill's speech has not had too great an effect. On the other hand, Willkie is making speeches against us that are, if anything, harsher than Roosevelt's. Electioneering! I keep our anti-illusions campaign against England going relentlessly.

A great deal of rumour-mongering about Romania. We make no comment, so as to keep the enemy in the dark. The detachments of troops that have arrived there are still only tiny. But they are sufficient to set the world in uproar.

Our Luftwaffe's losses have been heavily exaggerated. It goes without saying that the losses among squadrons against England have been considerable. In all, including all those destroyed in accidents during training, we lost fewer than 700 aircraft in September. And we produced 1800. Thus a quite tolerable ratio. Losses have been kept within normal bounds even for air-crew. Against this we must set the English losses and the devastation in their country. Just now there are dramatic reports of this from London. If these are true, all hell must be loose over there . . .

. . . Bohle describes to me his difficulties with Ribbentrop and the situation in the Foreign Ministry. Things are looking rather gloomy there. I shall continue to make use of the AO in my foreign propaganda, by sober hard work and building on my successes. We are well on the way to success.

Dr Grawitz outlines the situation in the Red Cross. He still has some psychological inhibitions to overcome in his attitude to the Party. I shall help him to do this. He is to receive another 25 million marks from the WHW.

Klöpfer tells me his old tale of woe regarding the theatre schedules. He is hot to stage *Fuhrmann Henschel*, which I consider too gloomy for these times. We agree on a middle course; he will stage it for a few days and then drop it.

Work through the day at a roaring pace. London is making the wildest claims about devastation in Germany. We must proceed even more decisively against this propaganda. True, the Luftwaffe believe it helps them in their defensive role, but psychologically it is very damaging for us, in that it gives the English people constant new encouragement and also impresses world opinion in the most undesirable fashion.

10,000-ton auxiliary cruiser sunk. Kill ratios 16:3. Very favourable. London sat in its air-raid shelters for 11½ hours last night.

In the afternoon I inspect the dance troupe established by me at its first appearance at the *Volksbühne*. I can stay only for a few minutes. But the whole thing is rather too forced and intellectual for my taste. Dance must glide, as if on wings; it must express beauty and embody grace, but not make ideology. Modern dance suffers greatly from this tendency.

Short visit to Magda. She has a lot to put up with and is very nervous and irritable. One has to show her consideration. To Lanke in the evening. The two little ones are waiting for me.

Ribbentrop has now embarked on an enormous row with Bohle. On account of my Reich Propaganda Office. Threatening to disband the organisation, etc. Empty words! Bohle behaved well, and Ribbentrop has really shown his true face. We intend to relax and let things happen. Sooner or later, it will be sorted out.

A few cultural films. And Ritter's *Above All in the World*. Absolutely naïve and primitive, but could well be a big hit with the public. Ritter says patriotic things with a lack of inhibition that would have anyone else blushing. A few things still have to be changed.

Then exchange opinions with Hippler and Naumann for a long while. A peaceful night!

11 October 1940 (Friday)

Yesterday: Ideal weather. We attack England and in particular London without pause, by day and night. Wild devastation. But only a few incursions into the Reich. London's psychological situation is deteriorating daily. The

USA is the only place where anyone takes their part. There all the talk is of war, and only a few voices of reason can be heard.

We can now resume issuing denials when London claims bombing successes; so long as the English have not hit dummy installations. This makes the task of our propaganda a lot easier. I also hope that I can gradually win a longer transmission-period for our radio.

Minor acts of sabotage in Belgium. Our authorities there fix penalties that are very psychologically adroit and therefore win over the population. A glimmer of hope . . .

. . . Schlösser has arrived back from Vienna. I put him straight into action against ideological dance. He must take far-reaching steps to eliminate this evil. Dance must speak to the senses, and not to the intellect. Otherwise it is no longer dance, but philosophy. In that case, I would rather read Schopenhauer than go to the theatre.

Schmidtke reports on France. The mood there is improving by leaps and bounds. Our campaign is beginning to have an effect; everyone is delighted by it. Schmidtke wants to protect the Paris fashion industry. I refuse. We must take a leading role in this field and not be troubled by inferiority complexes. Thus *Vogue* will still not be published for the time being . . .

. . . The English radio is launching swingeing attacks on our clandestine transmitters. We say nothing and behave as if it had nothing to do with us.

Midday with the Führer, who is back from Munich. I show him the newest examples of Italian 'art'. His only response is a contemptuous smile. Discussion of the broadcasting situation: we shall embark on yet another investigation, in concert with the Luftwaffe, to see if we can broadcast without restriction after all. Because the English will find Berlin whatever we do. The Führer has returned to share the air raids with the Berliners. Some people continue to hold the view that we shall be able to force England to her knees during the next few weeks. I consider this view to be ill-informed. In any case, one cannot rely on this happening. And we should ensure good protection against air raids. All our energies are being concentrated to this end. The Führer is also issuing quite clear-cut regulations on behaviour. So that the public knows where it stands. We are receiving isolated reports of revolutionary undercurrents in London. But all this is completely unsubstantiated. Moscow has issued a tough, uncompromising snub to London's attempts to carry favour. Good news. As always, the Swiss are impudent.

Question of what war films should be made. Each branch of the Wehrmacht wants to make its own film about France. I put a stop to these ambitions and draw all the relevant plans together.

Talk over the re-organisation of the ministry with Gutterer. We come to a conclusion. Artistic and political departments to be brought together, each making up a group. Under Hinkel and Berndt respectively. Should be workable.

Then work on for a long while at the office. To Lanke in the evening. Our sweet children are waiting for me. I look forward to this the whole day through.

A little baby-talk. Magda is well. Maria,* unfortunately, is very sick. Mother telephones and is very concerned about her.

Check films in the evening. *The Eternal Jew* now ready, at last. Now it can be released. We have worked on it for long enough.

A quite nice Gigli film. Insofar as one places any value on light-opera films.

Good flying weather.

All hell is loose in London. I would not like to be an Englishman at this moment.

12 October 1940 (Saturday)

Yesterday: Massive attacks on London, day and night. But also some strong incursions into the Reich. Weather good on both sides of the Channel. Berlin not affected. Morale slightly lower at home. Our people have to first accustom themselves to the thought of a second winter at war. I am receiving a whole series of complaining letters. We must conduct our propaganda more intensively and with more skill . . .

. . . The Hungarians are victimising the Rumanians in the ceded territories** to their hearts' content. A bunch of filthy swine! Raskin reports from Rumania: the Iron Guard† in the same situation as we were in February 1933. Good leadership material still there. Antonescu is asserting himself well. Most of the Iron Guard want something like a German protectorate. The old corruption still stinks to high heaven.

Brauweiler reports on his department's work. He has restored some order to the outfit. Esser would not like Berndt as head of the Main Department for Foreign Propaganda. I shall think it over again.

Schwarz von Berk comes to me to complain about morale. I have two long talks with him and tell him exactly what I think. He should be getting on with his work instead of running around causing trouble.

I make further representations for an extension of broadcasting time. And ensure a painstakingly precise and correct psychological line in the entire

---

* Goebbels' sister, married to the film producer Max Kimmich.

** Rumania had been forced to cede most of Transylvania to Hungary, and Bessarabia to Russia, under the so-called 'Vienna Award' of August 1940. This national humiliation had led to King Carol II's abdication and the seizure of power by Antonescu.

† The Rumanian fascist organisation, led by Codreanu until his murder in 1939 and thereafter by Horia Sima (*see* biographical notes in Index). In temporary alliance with Antonescu.

German propaganda effort. Especially at this time, when everyone is so nervous.

Our Luftwaffe is moving into its winter quarters. There is no longer much hope of a quick peace. But we shall hold on. This is not a crisis, but more in the nature of a disappointment, which we shall easily shrug off.

Midday with the Führer. He makes detailed enquiries about the position of the theatres. Is glad that the theatre in Saarbrücken remained undamaged and is back in use. The situation in the Berlin nursing homes is bleak: no air-raid shelters at all. We shall rebuild them after the war. They are not worthy of a civilised state. We must do a lot for mothers and children in general, particularly now in view of the air-raids. The fact that the Führer has given shelter to children has again been completely twisted by the rumour-mongers: they are supposedly being used for experiments with gas. The Führer is quite furious about this. The best intentions are distorted by these swine. There are some people who will always oppose us. Our every success is a slap in the face for them. These people are reactionaries, former communists and clericals. The whole pack of them must be eliminated.

I explain to the Führer: wealthy parents are allowed to send their children away from Berlin at their own expense. This is not desertion. On the contrary: the more are out of the way, the better. In Posen, Greiser tells us, they are using rather strict penalties to control the Poles. It is the only way to keep them at bay.

Churchill carries on lying. We catch him doctoring statistics in the most outrageous way. This is given great prominence. The Conservatives have voted unanimously to make him their party leader.* They obviously have no intention of allowing him to evade his responsibilities.

We are preparing a few surprises for him during the next weeks and months. He will be amazed.

The Führer advises me to cut the radio news service slightly. There is nothing much happening any more. And it should not quote so many foreign newspapers.

Horrific reports from London. A metropolis on the slide. An international drama without parallel. But we must see this through. Kill ratios 12:4. The ratio is improving by the day. I have a few more statistical refutations prepared for the press.

In the afternoon, I have Schwarz van Berk fetched to me again. He heads for home afterwards, thoroughly chastened.

Short visit to Magda. She is well so far as her health is concerned, but she

---

* Although Churchill had taken office as Prime Minister of a coalition government in May 1940, Chamberlain remained leader of the Conservative Party and a member of the government, evidence of the mistrust felt by the Conservative party machine for the maverick Churchill. Chamberlain resigned the leadership – and his post as Lord President of the Council – during his last illness.

suffers from depressions. But they will go away. At the moment, we must all keep a grip on ourselves.

To Lanke. In the pitch dark. An hour with the children, who are waiting for me. They are so sweet and affectionate.

SD report: morale among the people is not of the best. We must get to grips with this.

Then work for a long while. I am dog-tired.

A week such as this is one big test of nerve.

13 October 1940 (Sunday)

Yesterday: Usual attacks on London. Incursions into the Reich, but not very deep. We tone down our propaganda re. London slightly. It is impossible to know how long this will last. We also stop issuing summaries of English incursions into the Reich. They reveal too many military secrets.

Churchill's lie about the numbers of English prisoners-of-war is given great prominence in German press and propaganda. A real bull's-eye. In the course of mentioning a new English evacuee convoy taking children to Canada, I make it clear to the public that the wealthy people here are also entitled to send their children away, since the same facilities exist for the children of the poor.

Deal with a mass of work at Lanke. I do not drive into Berlin, so as to be able to take a thorough look at all the material that has piled up. This is always necessary at the weekend, since otherwise much is completely neglected.

The children are romping around the grounds. Magda is also well.

The war takes its usual course. The most important things now are attitudes and the capacity to see the issue through. And this time we shall show the world that we do not lack either quality . . .

. . . Hadamovsky has talked to Göring about the broadcasting situation. We shall soon get some concrete results on this issue. Göring awarded Hadamovsky the Iron Cross First Class, and has invited me to his head-quarters on the Channel coast for a few days. I shall accept this invitation.

Wonderful drive with the horses in the forest. Bracing!

Harald, now a paratrooper, has come home for two days' leave. He has become a real man and makes a marvellous impression. Army life has made all the difference.

Major Martin has mislaid an important secret document. A very sensitive and unpleasant matter. I shall try to sort it out.

The English are bombing Dutch cities relentlessly. Queen Wilhelmine donated the planes for the task. Unheard-of perversity, which we are quick to make full use of in our propaganda.

There is time for Harald to tell me all sorts about the army in the afternoon. One learns a lot by listening. The children are mightily pleased that their older brother has come. A real celebration.

The election campaign between Roosevelt and Willkie is still raging in the USA. We are the only real issue. Willkie has made a massive attack on me. Using a false quotation. We do not react at all.

Our military missions have arrived in Rumania and have been received with great pomp . . .

. . . Gloomy pictures of morale in London. This city is gradually experiencing the fate of Carthage. But Churchill will not have it any other way. And so on with the fight.

Check films. Watch a few middling products. But we must have those, too!

In the evening, time to read, at length and without disturbance. What a relief!

Two-hour air-raid warning. Little damage. Four bombs on the airport at Tempelhof. One dead.

14 October 1940 (Monday)

Yesterday: Few incursions into the Reich. Extensive attacks on England, particularly day and night raids on London. The weather is relatively good. And so the fun goes on.

The presence of the military missions in Rumania is now announced by us, at my instigation. We could not keep quiet about them any longer.

Poor instructions for the press from Fritzsche. I give him a good dressing-down. This is all I need, just at this critical time.

Nothing of importance to report except a speech on press policy by Dr Dietrich.

At midday I drive with Helga and Hilde to Schwanenwerder, where Magda and Harald have arrived, too. A day with all the family, after such a long time. The children are all enchanting. I am so glad to have them all around me again. Also there are Harald's friends, who are already proper men and soldiers. Discuss domestic worries with Magda. This too is necessary at times.

The High Command's report still talks of widespread destruction in London. But Churchill's monster is not yet on the point of collapse. And so we must keep hammering at him and not let ourselves be deflected. Bevin, admittedly, has made a rather pessimistic speech, but this is probably aimed at domestic opinion and the USA. Roosevelt responds with abject, vulgar outbursts against us. We do not react to this electioneering stunt.

Magda returns to the nursing home in the evening, and I drive back to Lanke. Check the newsreel, which contains all sorts. But no war, and in the middle of a war! Unfortunately, we cannot wage it purely for the convenience of the newsreel.

Goebbels

a Baarova. A studio publicity photograph of
he Czech actress whose affair with Goebbels
lmost led to his resignation in the summer of
1938

Goebbels and Magda at the Berlin Press Ball, 30 January 1939, Goebbels' first public appearance for some time

Goebbels broadcasts a message to Germany's children, in which he tells them: 'We see our Reich respected or, at least, feared abroad.'

Goebbels and Magda and their eldest
children with Hitler during the late 1930s.
Hitler's influence was crucial in preventing the
collapse of their marriage at this time

Goebbels and a daughter greet the Führer

The Goebbels family during the war years. Above l. to r.: Goebbels; Hilde (b.1934); Helga (b.1932); his stepson Harald Quandt, now a serving soldier. Below l. to r.: Helmut (b.1935); Holde (b.1937); Magda Goebbels; Heide (b.1940); Hedda (b.1938)

Goebbels at his imposing desk in the Propaganda Ministry

Goebbels the orator addresses a Party rally

Goebbels launches the 1939/40 Winter Aid Fund at a mass meeting in the Berlin *Sportpalast*

Buglers summon Berliners to donate
clothing for the Winter Aid Fund

Goebbels at the *Theater des Volkes* with (to his right) German Labour Front leader Robert Ley, November 1939

with Alessandro Pavolini, the Italian Minister for Popular Culture

Goebbels gives an interview to the press, 1939

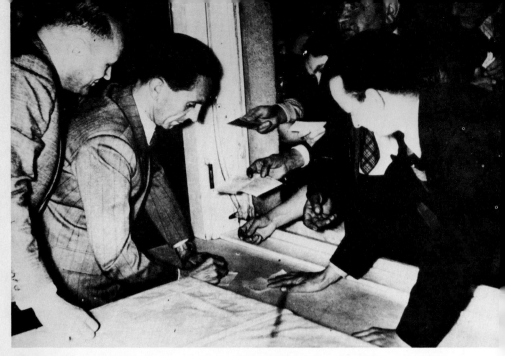

The Minister as a star: Goebbels signs autographs during a 'comradeship evening' at the Ufa film studios, May 1939

The real world: Hitler reviews SS troops a few months before the outbreak of war

Then a long time talking. And waiting for the English.
But they don't turn up!

15 October 1940 (Tuesday)

Yesterday: A headlong, stimulating and hardworking day. Weather good.
Usual attacks on London by day and night. Few incursions into the Reich.
New Air Defence Regulations laid down in Paris under Göring's chair-
manship. All our wishes granted. Now we know where we stand. Again,
experience has proved a good teacher.

According to the latest report, situation in Belgium good. Buvers is
working satisfactorily. Morale at home is on the rise again. I am working
hard at it. On Sunday the Request Concerts resume transmission. I switch
the emphasis of the newspaper comment. More political analysis, rather less
military material, since otherwise people will get tired of it. And less obvious
pathos. Gradually bring the people round to the idea of a second winter at
war. This will be difficult, but it must be possible.

Discuss the affair of the lost documents with Martin. I intend to let him off
unscathed. I consider him too valuable as a colleague.

Discuss re-organisation of the ministry with Gutterer. Berndt is under fire
from all sides. But I shall not be deflected.

Glasmaier reports on his negotiations with Italy about broadcasting
matters. Relations have improved in that area. The Foreign Ministry had
been queering the pitch for us.

Winkler reports on the film industry. We are buying up Paris as far as the
cinema is concerned. In Holland and Belgium we are buying the movie
theatres. The European market must belong to us.

Midday with the Führer. Speak to Hess. He is somewhat concerned about
the situation. But I talk him out of it. He is so honest and decent. Discuss air
defence problems with the Führer. He complains bitterly about the countryside, which is not taking the blackout seriously. He is right. It is why there
have been so many bombs dropped on villages. The peasant does as he
pleases. We shall take rigorous steps in this area. Big air-raid shelters are
under construction in the cities. We are now attacking these problems with
real energy.

The Führer has nothing but contempt for England. Otherwise, however,
he is thinking and mulling a lot over in his mind. He will hatch some plan. He
finds the latest newsreel excellent. He gives me new guidelines for the
coming tasks. All in all, he is so nice to me that I set to working with a
renewed love.

Reception for farmers' delegations in the ministry. Substitute for the
Harvest Festival. I make a speech to the farmers. They are very grateful for
such recognition.

Work at the office until evening. At a furious rate. Scarcely time to draw breath. But to work like this is a joy. Particularly now, when the situation tends to hang heavy and there are signs of a minor crisis of will, one must stand by one's duty and carry on one's way without batting an eye. It is as things were in October–November 1932.* Then, too, we had to keep the right attitude, and because we did, we won through in the end.

Magda is getting the apartment in the Göringstrasse ready. So that I have somewhere to stay in the city during the winter. My only worry is that she is demanding too much of herself in her present state of health. When one is in tune with her, she is such a nice, sweet and good fellow, and a proper comrade.

To Lanke in the evening. Put some finishing touches to the music for the newsreel. It is now quite outstanding. The Führer has given me permission to pay tax-free bonuses to film artists plagued by tax problems. Great relief. Professor Ritter was facing bankruptcy. I shall wipe out his debts.

A few visitors at Lanke. We swop ideas and talk. But today I lack the time, the urge and the desire for even the most modest attempt to be sociable.

Two air raid warnings during the night. Until five in the morning. Civilian casualties, and another hospital. The old story! Blackout not sufficiently effective.

16 October 1940 (Wednesday)

Yesterday: Several incursions into the Reich. Large-scale attacks on London by day and by night with discernible success. Something, at least. Otherwise no important military news.

America is sliding ever more surely into war hysteria. Roosevelt is a posturing blabbermouth, and Willkie is trying to outdo him.

Rumania is still a big sensation. A magnificent coup on our part.

Morale at home unchanged. The air-raids are causing us a lot of work. I shall now ensure that the remains of any hollow pathos are removed from German propaganda.

Deal with a host of film and theatre problems. Vienna has a number of requests, which I am able to agree to, and Posen too.

Discuss more energetic leadership of the cultural departments with Hinkel. These seem to me too anaemic and to have too little contact with life. Particularly music and literature. The sterile chit-chat of the literati, increasingly remote from the people. But now I intend to intervene and bring some order.

* When Hitler refused to serve under Papen as Vice-Chancellor in the summer of 1932, fresh elections were called. In these elections, in November 1932, the Nazis lost votes and seats in the Reichstag. As Goebbels recorded at the time, the leadership suffered a 'crisis of will', and there were rumours of a split in the ranks. By the beginning of January 1933, however, Hitler had kept his nerve, dealt with his opponents inside the Nazi Party, and secured the allies in President Hindenburg's entourage who gave him the Chancellorship on 30 January.

In company with Funk, receive the Italian Economics Minister, Riccardi. A very interesting conversation about the situation. He makes an excellent impression . . .

. . . Auwi* visits me. Blurts out a few minor complaints. To do with speakers and the coal situation. I am able to help him a little. He has aged. He is a good-natured but slightly stupid fellow.

To lunch with Magda at the nursing-home. We are able to hold a nice little domestic conversation. Good from time to time.

35,000 tons sunk. London attacked in the night and again during the day, more heavily than usual. Kill ratio 6:1.

In the afternoon, the Führer receives the farmers' delegations. A solemn moment. The Führer thanks the farmers for their efforts in a quite long speech. Expresses his firm belief in victory. Says that the weather and concern about excessive casualties is restraining him from an attack on England at the present. But that this problem has already been solved militarily since the defeat of France. A very fine, intimate and confidential speech, which moves us all deeply.

The Führer is worried about the state of my health. I get too little sleep. In the long term, something has to give. The Führer orders me to ensure that I get some sleep. I must try to fit it in during the afternoons. At night there are the air-raids, and in the mornings I must work. But a way will be found.

The Führer is also very profoundly affected by the meeting with the farmers. It is wonderful to see a whole segment of our people gathered together in intimate surroundings.

To tea with Hess. We discuss the entire situation. He is back in form. A good, reliable man. The Führer can rely on him blindly. He is unhappy that Epp is to become Minister for the Colonies, a function that he is already exercising in part. Bohle would certainly have been better in that post. But he hopes that we can at least have him made State Secretary. Hess's opinion on Ribbentrop is completely contemptuous. A sick man, childish, vain and puffed-up, and with little substance behind the facade. Hess is vigorously defending himself against Ribbentrop, and so is everyone else. One of these days, he will cut his own throat. An increasingly uninteresting case. Into the files and forget him!

Hess also has one or two small matters to sort out with Funk. But Funk is a regular fellow, and so I advise him to moderate his stance, which he agrees to do.

We are both worried about the coal situation. And so we decide to join forces and try to do something. I hope we succeed in putting some urgency into the issue.

Hess makes an excellent impression on me: he is quiet, objective, frank, and very confident. From now on, I shall meet with him more often.

* Prince August-Wilhelm von Preussen, son of Kaiser Wilhelm II (*see* biographical note).

145

The Führer is off to the Obersalzberg to commune with his muse. In the evening I drive out to Lanke. Some more work. And then to bed in good time.

17 October 1940 (Thursday)

Yesterday: After a two-hour air-raid warning, which brought no attack on Berlin and which, in any case, I slept through, a busy, stimulating day. Heaviest raid yet on London on Tuesday, with hitherto unequalled quantities of bombs dropped. Horrified squeals in the world press. But it makes no difference these days. The plutocrats must pay now.

The military situation has brightened considerably as a result. We are sending troops and particularly tanks to Libya. The attack on Gibraltar has been postponed for the present, since the Spaniards are demanding too much.

Despite all the good news, I continue with the reserved tone that our press has been showing lately. Thus, if we meet with any military setbacks as a result of bad weather, then we shall not need to do a volte-face. In any case, the English are so scared that they are ensuring the widest publicity for our successes all over the world. The mood in the country has become firmer. Our only real worry is the continuing lack of clarity in the air defence question. I have a lengthy conversation on the subject with Colonel-General Weise, who is now in charge of air defence in Berlin. He is in the process of co-ordinating the many installations that are directly or indirectly under his command. Unexploded anti-aircraft shells are the cross that we have to bear. At the moment they are causing more damage than the enemy's bombs.

Moscow has issued an impudent statement on Rumania. They claim they were not consulted at a sufficiently early stage, etc. Window-dressing for American consumption, as one might have expected. There the talk is of Russian troops invading Rumania. But this is rubbish. Moscow would never dare it.

Discuss re-organisation of the ministry with Esser. He has strong reservations about Berndt, who also has opponents elsewhere. Esser intends to produce a new plan for the organisation of the office. I am thrilled. I could find more use for him if he were not so dreadfully lazy.

Bibrach reports on the architectural exhibition in Belgrade, which has been a big success for us. We are world leaders in this area.

Personnel matters with Gutterer. And air defence questions. Gutterer is a good worker, careful and reliable. One day he will be my State Secretary.

At midday, wild stories of devastation in London. The picture that England presents at the moment is unimaginably bleak. But London asked for it. Now they must pay for the war.

The Führer has gone to the Obersalzberg. Göring has invited me to his

146

headquarters for three days. I intend to fly there immediately . . .

. . . Kill ratio 35:7. 36,000 tons sunk by U-boats. Also, the Italians have sunk the English cruiser *Ajax*. So: a quite decent list of statistics for one day. It all adds up.

Horrifying descriptions of the misery in the London underground. No people can keep this up for long.

Stroll through the autumn forest. A wonderful, light-dappled sunny day. Read and write some more in the evening.

And today I am off. To Göring at his command post.

18 October 1940 (Friday)

Yesterday: A crazy, flat-out day.

Leave Tempelhof early in the morning. In Paris just before 13.00. Straight to Göring's headquarters, although he is on an inspection trip to Holland. The headquarters are in a train. Lunch with the General Staff. Jeschonnek outlines the situation, which is viewed very optimistically here. Magnificent attacks on London. How long can Churchill hold out?

To a nearby bomber squadron in the afternoon. The men are marvellous, and morale is superb. We sit together throughout the afternoon. They tell me about their missions against London. Real heroes! And quite cool about it all.

Drink tea at the Palais Rothschild. If I had told myself ten years ago that I would be doing this! I am delighted by the young officers.

Back to Headquarters. Göring has arrived in the meantime. He is very pleasant to me. I take part in the situation conference. Everything very disciplined and correct. The operation here is absolutely watertight.

Talk for a long time with Göring. A thousand questions. Impossible to repeat in detail. His people are wonderful.

To bed only at two in the morning. Dog-tired.

Today we are to go to the coast.

19 October 1940 (Saturday)

Yesterday: Thick fog at headquarters. We are unable to fly to the coast. Despite everything, our Luftwaffe has given London a good pasting. 340 tons of bombs. No incursions into the Reich. I observe the work of the Luftwaffe General Staff: everything is clear, simple, constructive and systematic. Solid work. One can find no fault with it.

To Paris with Göring. First visit an exhibition of Flemish cloths. Simply wonderful. I am thrilled by it.

Then away. During the drive, we discuss the problem of Ribbentrop. Göring is boiling with rage against him. This fellow is ruining all our sense of comradeship. But he has not a single friend left. Göring is completely on my side. In him I have a very important supporter.

147

Paris. The ancient magic of this wonderful city, which is pulsating with life once more. Big military presence. I stroll through the streets with Göring. A huge sensation. Then I do a little shopping.

To the Casino de Paris in the evening. A variety show. Not as good as in Berlin, but a lot of beautiful women and disarming nakedness. We could never stage something like that in Berlin.

Eat at Maxim's. With Göring, who is very good to me. A marvellous way to live. There is no sign of war here. The pilots sit and drink. They have earned it. The army grumbles about it, but they should keep their mouths shut. Göring is fantastic. He really is a good fellow.

Fall into bed, late and dead-tired.

20 October 1940 (Sunday)

Yesterday: Glorious weather over Paris. Work hard at the hotel. Discuss the situation in Paris with Schmidtke. The High Command has still not put the recent Führer Order into effect. This has been going on for two months. I create hell. In an hour the order is operative.

Schmidt, the Württemberg Interior Minister, outlines the economic situation in France to me. In one word: bleak. The price of their frivolous declaration of war.

Knothe complains about the embassy. The place is seething with Francophile activity. Sick-making!

Heavy raids on London again. But no incursions into the Reich.

Eat with Göring. He has spoken with Abetz and, as might have been expected, has a very low opinion of him. A loudmouth!

Flight to Thouville. The English coast opposite us. Glorious weather. Fighters and fighter-bombers buzzing all around us. Sperrle is waiting for us. Big lecture on the situation in the air war. A very complex organisational machine, but operated with German thoroughness. One can only respect it. Göring has everything going great guns. Sperrle is a terrific fellow. And his men, well, they are fantastic.

After a three-hour visit, flight back to Paris. Farewell to Göring. He is particularly pleasant. We part as friends.

Paris. A thousand things still to sort out. And a lot of aggravation from Berlin.

In the evening, to a little bar where French chansons are sung. Very nice and charming. This city is a dangerous place, particularly for unpolitical Germans. Little sleep. Back to Berlin very soon.

21 October 1940 (Monday)

Yesterday: Plane leaves from Paris very early. A glorious day dawns over the metropolis. Deal with mountains of work during the flight.

More heavy raids on London during the night. But no incursions into the Reich. Our U-boats have sunk more than 300,000 tons in two days. Prien is far and away the top scorer and gets oak leaves for his Knight's Cross. The English can no longer make any proper flights into the Reich: danger of icing-up. Very good.

Stop in Cologne to pick up mail. Unfortunately not sent off. A sickening amount of trouble with the administrative people at the ministerial office. This our old German curse.

Berlin. Glorious day. To Magda in the nursing-home. She has not been at all well these last few days. Circulation trouble. I am seriously worried about her. The children are all there, too. They get delightful toys from me, gifts from Paris, and are enchantingly sweet.

Back to work. Labour away at Lanke with the rest of them. The amount of material to be dealt with is inhuman. Ribbentrop is causing me worry again. And so is the re-organisation of the ministry, which is encountering a lot of opposition. Hinkel has made some errors of judgement in this respect that have made the department heads very disaffected. Everyone is against Berndt. I send a cable recalling Naumann from his army service.

The Führer is still at the Obersalzberg.

Horrendous reports from London. The American newspapers give a picture of the inferno raging there. A delicate peace-feeler from London via New York–Helsinki and aimed at our address. We take no notice of it.

I intervene vigorously in press and news policy. No notable errors occurred during my trip. Fritzsche did his job well.

Newsreel in the evening. Again, they have made the best of things. What there was to make. And some fine footage despite everything. Discuss the matter of French film production with Hippler, who is now to take the problem in hand. In this area we must secure ourselves as much influence as possible, for the present and for the future. We consider the best method to realise this aim. We intend to build a camouflaged system, so that the average Frenchman scarcely notices who is really calling the tune. This is the way the English have always done things. One thing is certain: I shall not relax until the entire European film industry belongs to us.

Air-raid alert again in the evening. Late to bed.

22 October 1940 (Tuesday)

Yesterday: The air-raid warning lasted until 6 a.m. Only civilian targets. Fourteen dead in Charlottenburg. I inspect the destruction and take appropriate measures. Two Englishmen shot down over Berlin.

Hitting London hard day and night. The reports from over there are becoming more and more pessimistic. Along with them, though a little hoarse, it is true, the old illusion propaganda. But we have already neutralised that to a considerable extent.

149

Martin reports on the military situation. 10,000-ton auxiliary cruiser sunk. Our U-boat arm is in great form at the moment.

A few small sources of friction with the High Command. Martin, yet again, is able to deal with them. Morale in the country has improved again.

Hinkel has been acting in a tactless manner towards Schlösser and Drewes. I cannot give him any instructions regarding these gentlemen at the moment. Even Esser is demanding so much new power that I think it better to postpone the re-organisation of the ministry again. Hinkel and Berndt are devastated. But Schlösser, with whom I have an exhaustive discussion, is overjoyed. I encourage him to lead his department with more energy.

Hadamovsky has now managed to extend transmissions on the long-wave broadcasts until 2 a.m. A big gain for our propaganda. I instruct the press to switch its day-to-day editorial emphasis towards larger issues. We must not let ourselves be bogged down in mundane number-crunching, but instead ought to be returning the people's attention to wider perspectives.

Ribbentrop has demanded that Bohle shut down his Reich Propaganda Office. I reject this. Bohle agrees. He gives me an account of the truly chaotic state of things at the Foreign Ministry. Ribbentrop understands absolutely nothing about organisation. And his ministry has not a ha'penny's worth of *ésprit de corps*.

The Reich's theatres are prospering well, despite the air-raids. Only the Kammerspiele and the Schiller-Theater not so well. I have this looked into.

Final draft of paper on the stolen works of art. Magnificently put together by Geheimrat Kümmel. I intend to submit it to the Führer.

Visit the house in the Göringstrasse. Everything will soon be ready, and it will be fine and inhabitable. Magda has created another masterpiece . . .

. . . Newsreel in the evening. Turned out very fluent and stylish.

Churchill speaks to France. Crying over spilt milk. Seething with insults against us. A hotch-potch of slogans. Not worth talking about.

A long day comes to an end. Short night's rest.

23 October 1940 (Wednesday)

Yesterday: Weather here good, bad over England. Few incursions into the Reich, but neither do we drop much on London. On the other hand, more on other English cities. Churchill has made an appeal to the French people: impudent, insulting, and oozing with hypocrisy. A repulsive, oily obscenity. I release the speech to the press for them to give it a really rough and ready answer. Otherwise the English will carry on living in illusion. We shall battle on remorselessly to destroy their last hopes.

The military situation has scarcely altered. The navy alone is very active. Otherwise, we are preparing strong contingents of troops for action in Libya, under cover of [. . .]. This will bring considerable difficulties so far as our work is concerned.

The air defence problem is becoming increasingly thorny. The question is: into the shelter, or not. The Führer says yes. Many people, mostly out of laziness, say no. We shall have to see how the air war develops.

I postpone the re-organisation of the ministry for the present. It was causing too much discontent and needlessly irritating the department chiefs. At the moment we cannot afford for this to happen.

Titel has a host of practical and personnel problems in the Propaganda Companies. We are suffering from shortage of staff in that area, too.

Bömer puts in a good word for Schwarz van Berk. But he has to be called to order from time to time. Schirrmeister also, because he is too brusque in his dealings with the departments. I shall send him first to the Wehrmacht. Let him be properly trained as a soldier.

Schmidt-Decker reports on our work in Italy and the Balkans, which is progressing well despite the Foreign Ministry's interference. Ribbentrop, moreover, has been causing himself to be saluted as Bismarck's heir by the press, a move which I step on very quickly in his own interests. In general, we must handle the press very carefully in the present nervous state of public opinion.

Discuss the new Ritter film *Stukas* with Hippler. This is going to be quite good.

I speak on the short-wave radio to German seamen stuck in foreign ports. Not a pleasant fate.

Tschimmer reports on the situation in Hungary: the Nazis are on the ascendant. Way being prepared for the coming government crisis. Anti-German feeling among the intelligentsia. This is our thanks for our help. The Hungarians are a real rabble.

In France, on the other hand, a change in attitude is becoming discernible, albeit slowly. Our propaganda is starting to bite. High time, too.

Work through lunch. Draft speeches for Danzig and Vienna. I intend to say something about the situation. This is very necessary at the moment.

A big Spanish newspaper publishes a marvellous report about me and my work.

Fantastic reports from London. There it is hell on earth. In contrast, we expect pleasant news soon from Vichy. Laval would dearly like to join us against England.

At Schwanenwerder to see the children, who are indescribably sweet. I stay to have coffee with them and am guest at their big children's table on the verandah. They play their little tricks, and we all have a lot of fun . . .

[missing in the manuscript]

. . . Mercedes delivers a new limousine, a beauty of an automobile, but only suited for peacetime.

Visit to Magda in the nursing-home. She has not been at all well for the last few days. Stoeckel talks about this with serious concern and makes me really anxious. A few days yet, and her critical time will come. She awaits it with great courage. All said, she is a sweet, good woman. What I would not do for her.

Late back to Lanke. A lot of work, and then worries about the move. I intend to be living in Berlin again from the beginning of next week. Then our new house will be completely ready. This will make my work a lot easier and save me a lot of time.

To bed late and tired. I have rarely felt so worn out by struggle.

24 October 1940 (Thursday)

Yesterday: No incursions into the Reich. Only a few bombs dropped on London. Some on other English cities. London crows. But the Italians inflict a rather demoralising naval reverse on the British.

The big event is the meeting that has now finally taken place between the Führer and Laval. The ground is being prepared for the big new development. If France is well-advised, she is being offered a real chance. The entire world press is full of the wildest conjecture. People are already talking about France's entry into the war against England. Things have not yet reached that stage. But the situation will change to the great disadvantage of England. We are pulling the strings. Comments from Vichy are very optimistic. Also, Moscow and Tokyo are on the point of agreeing to a Non-Aggression Pact. Things are on the move. All in all, the face of the world is changing.

The mood of the Reich is still not quite settled. I continue to battle against psychological blunders. These days, even the smallest are noticed and criticised. Therefore our watchword must be: take care.

Esser makes a suggestion for re-organisation of the ministry. This has more to do with extending his sphere of operations than with any clear logic. He suggests that the Foreign Department be closed down. In the present situation there can be no question of this.

Deal with a host of personnel and budgetary questions. The film industry continues to prosper and make big profits. I take steps to overhaul the editorial side of the foreign-language broadcasting service. I have ferreted out some weaknesses in that area.

Receive first Bulgarian and then Italian journalists. Outline the situation for them. With some success.

Visit the house in Berlin. The work there is going ahead according to schedule. I am glad to have a place to stay in Berlin again.

Magda is rather better. This makes me very happy.

Kill ratio 3:2. Mölders is credited with these three. This puts him right back at the top.

Big sensation in Spain. The Führer is to meet Franco. His talks with Laval have set a bomb under London. These will not be a pleasant few days for Churchill.

A few people at home in the evening. After newsreel, showing of the Leander film, *Heart of the King*, now re-worked and very serviceable. Now it can be released. Discuss a series of film problems with Professor Frölich. As always, he is amiable and fatherly. The best horse in the stable.

Things go on, and it gets very late. Then an air-raid alert until six in the morning. Some damage inflicted on Berlin. An hour's sleep. To work!

25 October 1940 (Friday)

Yesterday: The Führer has now had his projected meeting with Franco. I am informed by telephone that everything went very smoothly. According to the information, Spain is firmly ours. Churchill is in for a bad time.

Unfortunately, only small quantities of bombs on London. The weather is too awful. This is a great pity, but there is nothing to be done.

Deal quickly with a mass of routine work at the ministry. Whole heaps of papers land on my desk. But I make short shrift.

Issue new guidelines at the press conference. Starting immediately, we must wage a tougher and more interesting polemical war against London. So many important things are happening in the diplomatic field, matters that we must conceal from the people, that this vacuum has to be filled. The answer is to return to the methods that we used last winter. Keep attacking, sharply, wittily, amusingly. Fritzsche does not quite grasp the point, but I finally win him over.

Receive Colonel Pinelli, who is in charge of propaganda amongst the armed forces in Italy. Everything is still in its infancy so far as our allies are concerned. Scarcely worthy of the description. This area shows yet again how far ahead we are of everyone else.

Flight to Danzig. During the flight, sleep like a dead man. Forster puts on a splendid show when he meets me. He has been Gauleiter in Danzig for ten years now. A proud day of celebration for him after the completion of a historical mission. He is a nice fellow, works like a dray-horse, and has a direct, cheering enthusiasm. Heartiest congratulations.

Some work at Zoppot. Then off with the generals and admirals-in-command to the *Bismarck*, which is being refitted at Gotenhafen. What a ship! The biggest, and probably the most beautiful warship in the world. And so fine-looking. I am given a joyous reception. The commander shows us the entire ship, which is a miracle of technology. Magnificently built, huge, a floating laboratory. The only question is whether the sea war can continue in this direction. If it does, then our sailors will have to become technical experts. In any event, we can learn a lot from this ship.

Visit the Reich Propaganda Office. Diewerge has his operation going full steam ahead.

Then a speech to old Party comrades. A storm of welcome. Forster and I

153

speak. I speak in the old style from the years of struggle. A celebration for us all.

Long talk with Forster. He complains strongly about the intrigues in the Party in Berlin, hatched by various Reichsleiters who can never have enough to satisfy them. He is not entirely wrong.

The Führer has now received Pétain. So this series of meetings is concluded. I can glean no further details from here. But from the state of things it seems that we have reached the desired goal. Poor England!

I sleep like a dead man. After so long, a peaceful night at last. A five-hour air-raid warning in Berlin again. Some damage. This obviously has a depressing effect on morale.

26 October 1940 (Saturday)

Yesterday: Stranded in Danzig. Sudden bad weather. We cannot fly.

Some more discussions. Watch shooting for the new U-boat film from Ufa at the pier. It is bitterly cold. In October!

A mass of incursions into the Reich. Considerable damage. We, however, could do little against London. Report on the mood in London: says that the people's morale is holding up.

The Führer's meeting with Pétain has raised speculation to fever-pitch. We are holding our fire. Let them rack their brains in London. The Foreign Ministry has fired another salvo at our ministry. But Gutterer has already defended himself very effectively.

Report on morale in the country from the SD: according to this, things are none too rosy. We absolutely must do more to keep morale high. The continual air-raid alerts are making the people nervous. We must be careful.

Crazy flight to Berlin. Impossible to continue to Vienna. Gutterer gives me a short summary of the situation when I arrive at Tempelhof. Nothing crucial.

Visit the Berlin house. It is almost ready and very fine.

Deal quickly with routine work at the ministry. Agree a new schedule for two days in Vienna with the people there. Magda, thank God, is very well. I hope she will not cause me worry during my trip.

I have so much on my plate that I scarcely find time to draw breath. To Vienna by train in the evening. Work during the journey.

Little sleep.

Arrival in Vienna.

27 October 1940 (Sunday)

Yesterday: Arrive in Vienna early. Very big reception. It is pouring with rain. Talk with Schirach. He is really attacking the problem of Vienna. The complete opposite to Bürckel.

Visit Wienfilm. There they are hard at work. I am very satisfied. Hartl and Hirth are doing their work well. Watch clips from new films, which especially please me. Shooting at the *Theater an der Wien* for Forst's film *Operette*. The theatre has to be renovated from the foundations up.

Eat with Schirach. He is sitting in Metternich's room. The Congress of Vienna took place just by here. Historic rooms. Here in the corner, Dolfuss was shot.

View the House of Fashion. Very tasteful models. I buy something for Magda. She is well, thank God.

Speak to representatives of the various Gaus in the parliament building. With success.

Work at the hotel. Some incursions into the Reich at night. Berlin quiet. London given a bad pasting again during the night. Horrendous neutral reports on it. We sink a 42,000-ton British steamer. That strikes home.

The talks with Pétain are the big talking-point. Good relationship created. Countless rumours buzzing around the world press. But most miss by a whisker. America reacts impudently. Probably out of anger. And London hasn't a clue. They will soon see where the changes are leading.

I speak at the Concert House in the evening. Before 20,000 people. I am in the very best form and reap endless storms of applause. The people of Vienna go wild. I launch a savage attack on yesterday's men. This strikes home. Schirach is very amiable and pleasant.

Then sit with Party comrades. Chat and exchange ideas.

Work into the night. Air-raid warning in Berlin again.

28 October 1940 (Monday)

Yesterday: Two air-raid warnings during the night in Berlin, but few bombs. Also few incursions into the Reich. London bombed as usual.

Kaufmann takes office. Makes a good speech in the process. I announce that the Festival Weeks of the Reich Theatre will take place exclusively in Vienna from now on, which causes the greatest delight.

Concert. Furtwängler with the Vienna Philharmonic. Wonderful 6th Symphony by Tchaikovsky. Furtwängler a genius. Piano concerto by Schuman, played in masterly fashion by old Professor Sauer. Altogether gloriously enjoyable.

To the Schirachs for lunch. Frau von Schirach is very nice. We mull over old memories of our youth and the days of struggle.

Visit Frau Göring, who is living in the same hotel. We have a nice hour's chat. I bring gifts for little Edda.* She is a sweet child, very natural. And very trusting.

Tea for the artists. Talk with Furtwängler, who would like Raabe's post,

* Edda Göring, daughter of Hermann and Emmy Göring.

which is out of the question, and Professor Sauer, who is a worthy old gentleman. I set him up wth an honorary pension.

State Opera. Back to this wonderful building. *Don Giovanni* in a masterly production by Ströhm. Things in Vienna are ship-shape under Schirach. We sketch out great plans for the future. We shall stage the next peacetime Festival Weeks of the Reich Theatre in grandiose style . . .

. . . The farewells. These were two wonderful days.

Deal with a pile of work in the train.

Discuss Luftwaffe subjects with Major Wodarg.

My speech has an excellent reception in both the domestic and the foreign press.

Late to bed.

Little sleep.

We are in Berlin.

The old pressure of work is waiting for me.

29 October 1940 (Tuesday)

Yesterday: Another air-raid alert in Berlin yesterday, this time a short one. Massive attacks on London and particularly on Liverpool. Pessimistic reports on the situation in London. Morale is rising again at home.

Rome issues an ultimatum to Athens. Metaxas rejects it. Italy moves into Greece. Mussolini would not be dissuaded. He too wants what he can get. The Führer meets the Duce in Florence. They discuss the international position. The world reaction to his talks with Pétain is still very strong. Vichy has agreed. France has therefore joined the continental bloc. London is totally isolated. And is becoming increasingly nervous. We shall gradually put her in a trap.

Repair a lot of damage yet again at the press conference. Block a few stupid moves by the High Command. Their propaganda comes straight out of the filing-cabinet. Real bureaucrats! But I simply forbid such idiocies. For the rest, we switch to a solid propaganda effort all along the line. We have got morale under control in just a few days. All one needs is the courage to persist with the right arguments and not to allow oneself to become bogged down.

Fritzsche has also been giving public speeches. With great success. Hinkel has a number of problems regarding the entertainment of the troops. And Hadamovsky more aggravation about transmission times. I shall send him back to the Luftwaffe Command to defend his position with all vigour. We shall get our way in the end.

New house in Berlin ready. I inspect it thoroughly: it has turned out wonderfully, so comfortable, modern and attractive. Scarcely any criticisms. Magda's masterpiece. She understands this kind of thing like no one else. I am very happy here. Straight to the fine, big new writing-desk and to work. How good it is to have a real home again.

Visit Magda in the nursing-home. She is in excellent health, thank God. Her baby could arrive any moment. Nevertheless, we are anxious and concerned.

Newsreel in the evening. Needs a lot of work, since it had not been viewed before. But we get it done.

And then I sleep in the new house for the first time. The work has been done. Into my birthday. My forty-third. How one ages through revolution and war.

One sometimes wants to have something from life. Not always to exist just for other people's sake.

30 October 1940 (Wednesday)

Yesterday: Forty-three years old. A little retrospection and contemplation. A good thing on such days. Then, however, back to work and the hurly-burly.

The children are the first to congratulate me. They stand up straight and pipe up their poems and hand over their gifts and flowers. Wonderfully sweet! Together we all watch the film that Heinz Rühmann made with the children; brings on laughter and tears, it is so beautiful. Then we wander through our new house, which is tremendous fun for the children. They are overjoyed at the sight of their sweet little rooms.

The house is filled with flowers and gifts. And people come to congratulate me, although I thought I had got all that out of the way. Daluege, Görlitzer, the gentlemen from Paris and many others. They all mean well. Funk presents me with a princely gift.

Only a few incursions into the Reich. Our Luftwaffe believes that it has hit the English bombers hard on the ground. Thus the lack of activity. But that remains to be seen. We drop the usual load on London, and a particularly heavy raid on Birmingham.

To Magda with the children. She swamps me with gifts. She is so good to me these days. The new little citizen of the earth may arrive at any moment.

At midday, play host to my closest colleagues. They are all very jolly. I express thanks and recognition for the work they have done.

Then work, work. Mountains of telegrams have arrived. From all quarters, and most very sincere. Many good wishes from ordinary people.

Wild surmises on the political and military fronts. London completely in the dark. Italy publishes its note to Athens and announces its advance into Greek territory. Turkey is still wavering, but more out of fear than patriotism. London excels itself with purely platonic promises of aid. Metaxas will not be able to buy anything with those. To add to this, London has had to admit shipping losses of 180,000 tons during the past week. A healthy little total. Gradually climbing.

Another hour's chatter with the children. The Führer is on his way home to Berlin. I look forward to being able to talk with him again.

A few guests to a party in the evening. Only colleagues and close acquaintances. Then we finally hear the news: Magda has given birth to a daughter. What a delight! I drive over to see her straight away, along with the children. She weeps with the bliss of it, and I too am very moved. A sweet little baby; I am so happy that it is a girl. We name her Heide.

At home we celebrate a double birthday, and everyone is nice and happy along with us. No incursions to Berlin. The party goes on until late, and gives me a few happy hours after all these weary days. I am so happy!

Short sleep. The Führer has arrived back in Berlin.

31 October 1940 (Thursday)

Yesterday: Few incursions into the Reich. But very strong forces against London and Birmingham. Major airfields hit. Our U-boats sink 80,000 tons. One day England must collapse.

I demand that our foreign correspondents provide more material from London for polemical use. The SD report is more positive once again. We are slowly getting morale moving in the right direction. It would have been ridiculous to give in to a momentary depression.

A whole list of promotions at the ministry. Heiduschke becomes a government counsellor. Naumann is back. Discuss re-organisation of the ministry with him. I intend to postpone the whole question for the present.

At the moment the Party is making yet another attempt to get its hands on the radio licence fees. I object vigorously. They are the way we finance our entire cultural life.

The Foreign Department shows me its work in an open day. Very solid and serviceable. And achieved with very few staff. The Foreign Ministry needs 1000 men for the same results. And in the end that leads to water on the collective brain.

Chat for a long while with Sepp Dietrich. He is an amiable, solid fellow. Has all sorts of complaints. Nice to chew the fat with an old Party warhorse like him.

Receive Swedish journalists. Discuss the situation with them.

The *Theater des Volkes* stages a private performance of *Susanne's Secret* by Wolf-Ferrari. Delightful music, and delightfully acted.

The Greek question still the big issue. But no clear picture for the moment. Turkey is still keeping very much out of things.

Visit Magda. She and little Heide are well. I am very glad. We chat for a while. So wonderful after so much worry.

Newsreel ready. Turned out magnificently. Another showpiece.

Play with the children. Read through a big report on the new cultural films in production. A lot is being achieved in this field.

Then poke around in some of the work that has piled up.

The pressure never lets up. No air raid during the night.

1 November 1940 (Friday)

Yesterday: Heavy night raids on London. Also on a whole number of other English cities. Churchill invents a new lie about a massive attack on Berlin that never actually took place. Things must be very bad for him. And no one will let him wriggle out of the responsibility.

The Italians are making very poor progress in Greece. When all's said and done, they don't have the right spirit.

Discuss new rules for the press conference with Fritzsche. He alone will have the right to speak, and the Foreign Ministry will merely supply the material. The press must be given a single, clear lead, and it cannot serve two masters.

A host of film problems with Hippler. Our dramatists' work has not enough sureness of touch. Too many wrong decisions. Must be sorted out . . .

. . . Midday with the Führer. Dr Dietrich tells me the news from the Reich Chancellery. A number of unpleasant intrigues among the aides there. Not good. In contrast, glad to hear from Prien, who has been invited to meet the Führer. He is a marvellous fellow and a real popular hero. Very self-effacing about his own deeds of heroism. Altogether so amiable and likeable, in the most direct and uncomplicated way.

The Führer is very pleasant to me. Has words of the highest praise for Magda. And is genuinely glad that it is another girl.

To the situation: crazy reports from London. But the English are tough. They still holding out, after a fashion. The Führer intends to keep hammering at them until they break. No one knows when that will be. But the goal is clear. They must be driven out of Europe once and for all. They will not find another foothold on the continent now. Russia? Stalin is too wily. And our Wehrmacht too strong. Stalin wants to have peace and quiet to count his winnings. And he will not take any wild risks. He will not try to get his hands on the Rumanian oilfields.

Our bombs on England and our torpedoes will soon wear Churchill down. One must simply have patience and fight on without flinching.

The Führer's opinion of Spain and Franco is not high. A lot of noise, but very little action. No substance. In any case, quite unprepared for war. Grandees of an empire that no longer exists. France, on the other hand, is a quite different matter. Where Franco was very unsure of himself, Pétain was clear and composed. With a realistic view of things. No attempts to gild the lily. France is clear about the fact that she has lost the war and must take the consequences. And she does so with dignity. Pétain retains a clear, cool head. But his dignity and France's dignity are no longer bolstered by real power. The French seduce by dint of their character and charm. Pétain made a profound impression on the Führer. We Germans, who have been the losers, the oppressed, for 300 years, must re-learn this old, sovereign self-assurance in our action and behaviour. This will come with time. Our soldiers in Paris already possess it. I tell the Führer about Göring's and my visit to Paris. He is very interested. Even more so, however, in the report I make on my visit to the *Bismarck*. He says that our shipbuilding experts must achieve a revolutionary transformation. These big tubs are so vulnerable to U-boats and aircraft. But all that will come after the war.

Now we must wage war in such a way that we win victory as soon as possible. All means are justified. Our end is clear: a new world empire of Germans.

New reports from London. So profoundly pessimistic that they are almost unbelievable. The collapse must come sooner or later.

I discuss the entire situation with the Führer. He gives me a host of hints and suggestions. He is very satisfied with my work.

The election campaign rages on in the USA. It is hard to say whether Roosevelt or Willkie is making the running.

Discuss a propaganda campaign for the Luftwaffe with Major Wodarg. A few reactionary officers continue to have doubts about whether Luftwaffe officers should speak to the public. But I quickly dismiss that problem. Wodarg is a valuable aid to me in all this work.

Brief chat with the children at home. Then sort out a lot of neglected paperwork. That lasts until late evening. Read a very pessimistic report on the present situation in Spain. According to this, the whole country is still in a wild, almost anarchic state of disorder. Franco is not at all in control, and the country is restless, wracked by internal spasms. Symptoms of senility in a former world empire. The present system did not develop organically, but has been imposed.

Draft the speech for Prague. Check over some problems with cultural films. And then sleep.

2 November 1940 (Saturday)

Yesterday: No incursions into the Reich. Bad weather for England. We also dropped only a little, forty tons, on London. Nevertheless, waves of pessimism emanating from London. Lord Chatfield has delivered a very worried speech about England's command of the seas. Chamberlain has scuttled off to California.* The reports of morale in London are gloomy in the extreme. Bad days for John Bull.

---

* Chamberlain was, in fact, dying at a borrowed house in Hampshire.

The Italians are making scarcely any progress in Greece. The English have moved their Gibraltar fleet to the west. New attack on Dakar planned?

Report from the USA. According to this, Roosevelt's position is none too secure. But the agitation against us is monstrous. Willkie would keep the USA out of the war.

I instruct the press not to emphasise the pessimism in London too strongly. Otherwise it will cause over-optimism here.

Discuss newsreel problems with Hippler. After the war, we intend to produce three different newsreels again. And bring all state-owned film theatres together in one holding company. This will take some work.

Winkler has visited Göring. He sorted out my problem with Lanke. This causes me enormous relief. Besides this, a host of other personal worries have been dealt with. Winkler is a real jewel from my point of view.

Talk with Berndt about his future. He has all sorts of ideas about himself. But first he must learn how to get on with his colleagues. I give him a proper lecture. He seems to take it to heart.

Midday with the Führer. He returns to the subject of Franco and compares him with [. . .] This may well be accurate. The Italian 'offensive' against Greece does not meet with his whole-hearted approval. It has been badly conceived and does not present an elevating spectacle, at least at present.

I tell him about Vienna. About the city's love of music, about Furtwängler and Professor Sauer, which all interests him very much. He praises the old school's capacity for hard work, its nimbleness, systematic approach and good basic technique. He has a very low opinion of Karajan and his conducting. The city of Vienna is increasingly regaining his sympathy.

A lot of work at the office. In the afternoon, I speak to the chiefs of Party branches in Berlin. I outline the military and political situations quite soberly and without embellishment. I think that the position in Berlin has clarified once more. The Party is the upholder of morale. We must use it during campaigns to raise morale. It knows how best to handle the ordinary people, particularly when the leadership must remain silent for political or military reasons.

Visit in the evening to the air-raid warning centre in Berlin. Here all the threads of the Reich capital's air defence system are drawn together. I have my closest colleagues with me. Colonel-General Weise delivers a lecture. A miracle of system and organisation opens up before our eyes. Better too much care than too little. Just then, an air-raid warning is sounded and lasts for four hours. The English come in in three waves and cause some damage. Twelve dead, among other things. I am able to watch the entire apparatus of air defence in action there. Magnificently conceived and also well-executed. I visit several public air-raid shelters in the west of the city. Morale is in part very good, for the rest only just good. As the night goes on, people naturally get very tired and, probably as a result, rather nervous and hysterical. But on

161

the whole the city takes the strains of this kind of alert in its stride. The general problem has not yet been solved to a satisfactory extent. I intend to make another report about it to the Führer.

Sit in the air-raid shelter with the children at home. They are all sleeping in one big bed and look as sweet as little angels.

It goes on until late into the night. Another air-raid warning comes at five in the morning. The whole of Berlin has to get out of bed and into the shelter. Terrible! One asks oneself whether it would be better just to sit tight and take what comes. In any case, I sleep on despite the heavy flak. I am too tired to get up.

3 November 1940 (Sunday)

Yesterday: Berlin today is a tired town. I work at the apartment in the city.

German bomber scores a big success on a convoy. London and also Birmingham attacked again, in great style. Enormous quantities of high-explosives unloaded. Berlin main target at home. Eighteen dead, ten of them in Berlin. Also some damage to buildings, but nothing of particular importance.

Inönü makes a speech. This and that. With a lot of friendly words for London. In general, however, Turkey would not consider entering the war for England's sake. We had not expected that she would.

Very slow progress in Greece. The *Blitzkrieg* is a German invention, and so far has remained a German patent.

Rather negative reports from Spain. Suñer is very unpopular, Franco too weak, and the Falange* is totally irrelevant. Strong clerical influences. Spain is in no condition to wage war at the moment.

A lot of work, and a heap of aggravation. It is always so at the weekend. The Foreign Ministry, in particular, is putting spokes in our wheel.

Receive film people. All the trappings. They are to get extra payments for especially valuable and successful work.

Winkler gives me a glorious pair of horses for a late birthday present. Trakehn geldings, wonderful black horses, and a fine carriage to go with them. A real delight, particularly for the children.

Visit Magda. She is in excellent health. I am so glad.

Another 47,000 tons sunk. Very pessimistic reports from London. I withhold publication, so as to avoid illusion-mongering among the German people.

Film people visiting, to whom I show the American epic, *Gone with the Wind*, which arouses general admiration. Rightly so, because it deserves it. But some doubtful opinions too.

Late in the night comes the usual air-raid warning. Two aircraft scuttle

* The Spanish fascist movement.

162

over Berlin. And for that, a city of 4½ million people must take to the shelters. I go off and get some sleep.

Later it turns out that the planes concerned were German machines that had lost their way returning from the battle. The pilots survived.

4 November 1940 (Monday)

Yesterday: Few incursions into the Reich. Pretty bad weather. Nevertheless, we drop some 250 tons on the English. Several losses through icing-up, however.

The English are claiming that they have landed in Greece. But details are lacking. The Italians are making a certain amount of progress.

The election campaign is in full swing in the USA. The things being said there are bare-faced lies.

The re-organisation of the press conference by Dr Dietrich has been successfully accomplished. Even the Foreign Ministry has complied and knuckled under. So it must be. Nowhere is clarity of leadership more urgently needed than in the press.

Play with the children. They are suffering greatly from the continual air-raid alerts. Take them for a short visit to Magda, which goes surprisingly well.

During the afternoon, when it pours with rain, I have a few hours spare to read and pay a little attention to myself. So good after all the crazy to-ing and fro-ing.

Liebeneiner's *Bismarck* film ready. A really magnificent achievement. I am very pleased with it. Now it is politically watertight as well. It will be a huge success.

London continues to report landings on the Greek islands without further details. The Italians tell us that their offensive will start in grand style very soon. We shall see!

Bad weather. No incursions. So a peaceful night for once, even for us.

5 November 1940 (Tuesday)

Yesterday: Scarcely any incursions into the Reich. But also little air activity over England. On the other hand, big U-boat successes. Two English auxiliary cruisers sunk. We receive reports that morale in London has reached rock bottom. Some even claim that riots have taken place. I do not place much credence in these. We have to keep on striking the enemy until he breaks, and we must not allow ourselves to be distracted or seduced by illusions, however attractive they may be. Our Luftwaffe is allowing too many English victory claims to go unanswered. 'For military reasons'. I consider this to be the purest bureaucratic nonsense and take appropriate

163

steps to oppose it. English victory claims must be denied except when a dummy installation has been hit. And when they are really lying, we must issue an appropriate denial. At the top of our lungs. An interview given by Göring to the American correspondent Huss is just right for us. Göring gives an outline of the current situation in the air war. Very instructive. I change no more than a few trivial points of style. For the rest, get it on to the news-stands. In time before the presidential elections in the USA.

Morale at home has become a lot better. Our systematic campaign of enlightenment has achieved a lot. But we must work on tirelessly.

Gayda* publishes a tough article pitched against the USA, which the German press repeats parrot-fashion. I forbid this to happen in future. If we cannot, or will not, find anything to write about a particular issue, then we certainly must not let the Italians tell us what to do.

Big report on the war of the airwaves produced for the Führer's benefit. He must be put thoroughly in the picture regarding this very important work.

The updating of old, dusty operas and operettas is proceeding according to plan.

The decline in film production must be reversed. I give my film experts a good dressing-down. Production must continue at the old levels.

Deal with mountains of paperwork. I can scarcely see an end to it. And this all before I leave.

Hinkel has problems in troops' entertainment. The High Command is interfering at every level. Also trouble with film censorship, where everyone wants to have their say. I take vigorous steps to stop this.

Schmidt-Decker has his usual arguments with the Foreign Ministry. I shall soon sort them out.

Gutter reports on the way that the Navy High Command are treating Prien. A downright scandal!

Receive Alsatian artists.** They make a good impression. I speak to them. They present me with a portfolio of their own work.

Land Group Leader Thomsen of the AO in Spain reports on conditions there: simply unbelievable. Franco and Suñer are completely the prisoners of the clerical faction, totally unpopular, no attempt made to deal with social problems, enormous confusion, the Falange totally without influence. All areas of the economy in ruins, a lot of grandiose posturing but nothing behind it. Germany is looked upon with awe as a wonderland. Many people there would like us to come in and restore order. This is a picture of a country after a revolution that cost nearly two million dead. And an ally of ours. Horrifying! How fortunate that we did not rely on playing that card.

With the Führer. Epp has some questions on colonial matters. Koch and

* An Italian journalist. Writer for the *Giornale d'Italia*.
** Alsace-Lorraine was annexed from France in 1940.

Forster argue about the East. The Führer laughs and makes peace between them yet again. All of them would like to offload their rubbish into the General Government. Jews, the sick, slackers, etc. And Frank is resisting. Not entirely wrongly. He wants to create a model country out of Poland. This is going too far. He cannot and should not. So far as we are concerned, the Führer states, Poland will be an enormous reservoir of labour. From there we can get people for the menial jobs, where there is a great shortage. After all, we have to get them from somewhere. Frank is reluctant, but he has no choice. And we shall shove the Jews out as well, later.

I tell the Führer about my experiences in the air-raid shelters, which he finds very interesting. The Italians are none too popular with him at the moment. Mussolini is the only real man they have. England will collapse one day, the Führer says. We must simply have patience, keep up our attacks, and be tougher than she is.

And Greece? The way things are, that could last some time.

Schirach talks to me from Vienna. My speech worked wonders there.

Winkler has now completely settled the Lanke business. He has taken a tremendous weight from my shoulders. I still have a pile of taxes to pay. And scarcely know where the money is to come from. If only I had a fraction of the sums that our enemies accuse me of amassing.

Magda is well. Harald is on leave for a week. He comes to pay his respects: looks fantastic. Military service has done him a lot of good. We dine together in the evening. He tells me all sorts of stories. He is with Ursel Quandt, who has separated from her dreadful husband and now looks quite enchanting.

The children have gone back to Schwanenwerder. The big house is empty.

Quickly check newsreel. Then departure for Prague. Carry on working in the train with my people until late.

Then a short, dreamless sleep.

6 November 1940 (Wednesday)

Yesterday: Arrive in Prague at 10 a.m. Big reception. Local people still very cool. Drive through glorious Prague, which is a wholly German city. All the buildings, bridges and towers are evidence of it.

Visit the district headquarters. Henlein lectures me on the troubles of the embattled Germanic population. The Sudeten Germans see things a little too much in black and white here. Justifiably, they are still full of resentments. I promise to help where I can. The Czech-language press in Prague gives me the warmest of welcomes.

I stay up at the castle:* a glorious building with a wonderful view of old Prague in the sunshine. Visit to Neurath: he also gives me a detailed report on his troubles. The mood here has improved greatly since my speech, but

---

* The Hradschin Castle, traditional seat of the government in Prague.

165

still leaves much to be desired. Neurath also spends a lot of time abusing Ribbentrop, whom he hates and despises, quite justifiably. A fellow with the manners of a pig.

Speech to German cultural workers in Prague at the Czerny Palace, concentrating on their German mission on this hotly-contested soil. I eat with the Neuraths, who are very pleasant and impress one as attractive, presentable people. The right people in the right place.

Situation: no incursions into the Reich at all. We drop 100 tons on London, despite the bad weather. More gloomy voices from London.

Ley is developing a big social programme for after the war. Fantastic, and huge sums mentioned. He says: gigantic. A bit less might do more good.

I speak to the Germans of Prague in an enormous hall. Some 15,000 people. The entire local German population. A big political speech on my best form. To a storm of applause. The Führer changes only a few details from the press release of the speech.

At the castle. A few hours of furious work. Telephone call to Magda: she is well, thank God. But the children are rather sick.

To the *Ständetheater* in the evening, for the last act of *Kabale und Liebe*. The theatre is really delightful. A charming place, straight out of Mozart's time. The acting is excellent, though a mite too loud. But that will be ironed out. Otherwise, Walleck is obviously doing his job very well.

Eat with Frank at the Hotel [. . .] With a hearty speech of welcome. Get to know a lot of people. Spend a long while chatting with German actors who are shooting a film for the Bavaria company here. Late to bed.

7 November 1940 (Thursday)

Yesterday: Rain and mist. Prague shrouded in grey.

Tour the city. What a jewel. St Vitus' Cathedral with all its treasures. The old buildings, streets and squares. The view over the Moldau. An unforgettable sight. I have fallen totally in love with this city. It exudes the German spirit and must become German again one day.

Reception at the city hall. In a very fine room. Long speeches. I also say a few friendly words. The locals here are always re-opening old wounds and battering the Czechs over the head. That is not good propaganda. I try to redress the balance.

Look round the castle. Very impressive. The defenestration of Prague* took place here.

Visit Hacha. With all the solemn ceremony. Hacha is a pleasant, rather tired-looking old gentleman. I am very nice to him. He really would have preferred to have nothing to do with politics. Now realises, however, that his historic decision was wise and correct. He complains about all sorts of trivial

* The *casus belli* of the Thirty Years' War of 1618–48. Imperial emissaries were thrown out of the window of the castle by angry Czech notables.

matters, the many arrests and the closure of the university. I shall help him where I can. But otherwise he seems to be loyal. He shares the views I expressed in my speech to Czech intellectuals, which he knows in detail and approves. I believe that my visit was very fruitful. I get on well with the old gentleman. In any event, I have the impression that he has taken me to his heart.

To the Neuraths for lunch. They too complain about the sledgehammer methods of many extremists. And the senseless arrests carried out by the SS. These must be stopped. I am alone with the Neuraths for lunch, and they are touchingly pleasant to me. Frau von Neurath shows me some wonderful old Gobelins, which I should like to buy. But they are so outrageously expensive.

Work at the castle. Double rations of bombs dropped on London by day and night. Scarcely any incursions into the Reich. Berlin untouched.

Small party to tea. Very pleasant and amusing.

To the Franks in the evening. Frau Frank is a young, charming woman. We talk for a long time about tactics to be used with the Czechs. I express the opinion: tough, where toughness is needed, but leniency where non-essential matters are concerned. And small gifts keep friendship alive.

At the National Opera. A very beautiful but slightly shabby building. *Bartered Bride*. Brilliantly sung and acted. Under a wonderful conductor. The scenery is very crude. Hacha is with me. He takes great pains and nothing is too much for him. The public is very polite and respectful. I am introduced to a host of Czech ministers and dignitaries. Not a single one among them makes a strong impression. Commonplace types, middle-rankers. But this is a very good thing.

Chat with my people for a long time up at the castle. They are all delighted with the visit and its success.

Election day in the USA, Roosevelt re-elected with a big majority. Not that it makes much difference any more. The USA has in any case given London every possible material support. After his statements, Roosevelt will hardly be able to enter the war in an active capacity. All we can do is wait and see!

Churchill has made a speech. Impudent and cynical, as if he already had victory in his pocket. He is seriously deceiving himself if he thinks that he can bluff us. The British press in general has recovered its arrogance and cockiness, doubtless on orders from above. But it will soon go sour. US correspondents are filing more and more stories about the chaotic conditions in London.

Work on far into the night. A mountain of paperwork to be dealt with.

I collapse into bed, dead-tired.

167

8 November 1940 (Friday)

Yesterday: Air-raid alert in Berlin, but scarcely any bombs dropped. We are back in London, dropping 170 tons. Seven million tons sunk so far. Despite this, the English press is still playing it smart, insolent and cocky. But they will soon laugh on the other side of their faces. Their two main hopes are Roosevelt, who has been given a big majority, and Greece.

Listen to the Sudeten-German orchestra in the morning. Has become quite good under Keilberth's direction. The only problem is the string section, which is still somewhat lacking in confidence. But that can be remedied. Keilberth is doing a good job.

Visit to the Barand [. . .] Inspect the film studios. Big, modern and expansively laid out. 51 per cent of them belongs to us. Scenes from the Carl Peters film. With Albers. This will be something. A hundred negro prisoners-of-war are also involved in the work. The poor devils stand around in rows, trembling with fear and the cold.

I see rushes from the Peters film. Selpin is doing good work there.

Meal with the film people. Almost all of them organisation types. Extremely boring.

Short drive through Prague. What an enchanting city.

Work at the castle. Ribbentrop has written me two more insolent letters. I make not the slightest acknowledgment and do not let myself be irritated by them. The man must be ignored.

In the evening, Furtwängler gives a concert with the Berlin Philharmonic. *The Moldau*, *Eulenspiegel*, and Beethoven's Seventh. A solemn occasion with Hacha, the Neuraths, and the entire Czech government. Everybody of rank or name in Prague is there. *Moldau* indescribably beautiful. *Eulenspiegel* interesting. The Seventh a great masterpiece. Ravishingly played. The public goes wild. Hacha very nice.

Shortly afterwards, attend a reception for the German performers. Much talk. To the train late at night. Sleep through until midday. In Eger.

10 November 1940 (Sunday)

Yesterday: A lot of work piled up in Berlin. But I master it.

Few air-raids on the Reich. Munich has had its baptism of fire. The usual quota on London. Grim voices from London. Particularly on account of the shipping losses, which have amounted to over 100,000 tons in the last two days. It must have an effect sooner or later. Kill ratio 17:4. Things are on the way up again from a military point of view. Except for the fact that Italy is making scarcely any progress in Greece. No talk of Blitzkrieg there. De Valera, however, has given Churchill a clear, brusque refusal on the bases question.* Whether the old fox will let that stop him is another problem.

The Führer's speech finds very little support. It was directed exclusively at the domestic population. The Führer's first instinct was that it should not be broadcast at all. But I insisted. Hadamovsky really worked hard at the Führer on this issue. Failure to broadcast it would have caused a scandal abroad.

Raskin has died in an accident while flying to Bucharest. A serious blow for me and my work. In him I have lost one of my most capable foreign propaganda people, and I shall not be able to replace him. Ice on the wings. But what use is an explanation? Raskin was very precious to me from a human point of view, too. I feel as though I have been struck by lightning when I hear the sad news.

And it had to be now, when I needed him so badly.

All sorts to be dealt with. But almost nothing of importance. All routine work.

Home. Magda is at home again. A joyful, touching reunion. The little baby is also there. How wonderful to have everyone together once more.

Work through until the late evening. And then everything is done. Everything behind me. What a satisfying feeling.

Churchill has made a speech. What he doesn't say he will liberate: 'Austria, Czechoslovakia', etc. We shall show him. I order the most savage editorial comment . . .

. . . No air-raid warning, no incursions into the Reich.

Announcement that Molotov is coming to Berlin. A slap in the face for England. Will do Churchill no good.

Chat for a long while with Magda and Ursel Quandt, who is visiting us.

And then sleep, sleep!

11 November 1940 (Monday)

Yesterday: No incursions into the Reich. Day and night-time raids on London with visible success. About 100 tons during the night. The weather in England is very bad. In contrast, we have a sunny autumn day in Berlin.

The press in London is partly impudent, partly subdued. No clear line.

Chamberlain has died. Collapsed morally and physically under the weight of our attacks. He wanted to see Hitler's downfall. We have seen his and his Empire's downfall.

Make preparations for Molotov's visit. But I personally shall remain somewhat in the background. The visit is arousing great interest in the rest of the world.

* The Irish Free State, though part of the British Commonwealth, remained neutral in the war. De Valera repeatedly refused British requests for use of the naval and port facilities on the west coast of Ireland during the Battle of the Atlantic.

Study Dittmar's report on the radio service. Having to close down early is doing us enormous harm. I shall have to make another foray in this area.

Otherwise, all sorts to deal with. An insolent letter from Ribbentrop. I put it with all the others without bothering to answer.

A pleasant and cosy lunch and afternoon. Ursel Quandt is visiting us at the moment with her little kiddy. She is so glad to be back among human beings again.

Wodarg comes to tea. Discuss a number of Luftwaffe issues with him. The Führer has also returned to Berlin. Endless rounds of talks.

Check the newsreel in the evening. Turned out well. Only minor changes.

Three-hour air-raid alert. But no bombs on Berlin. At midnight we celebrate Magda's birthday. I give her all the gifts that she deserves. She is delighted beyond all measure. A fine party for us all. Harald is off back to the army. A short night!

12 November 1940 (Tuesday)

Yesterday: Wodarg introduces his successor, Major Hoffman. A useful colleague. Wodarg is to have an operation.

Few day attacks, but massive night raids on London and other English cities. Incursions into the Reich of the usual extent. Berlin not bombed. London is making a tremendous fuss about the raid on Munich. The Bürgerbräu is supposed to have been destroyed, the entire railway network devastated. All lies, but we were too lax to issue a prompt denial. I raise the roof about it. If one is away for a few days, everything goes to pot. Now we are back in full cry again.

No progress at all in Greece. Rome, placing too much trust in diplomatic pressure, prepared the entire operation very lackadaisically. Italy is already completely on the defensive. The situation must now be viewed as very grave from the military standpoint. A problem of crucial importance for us, too. Shame, shame!

Prepare Molotov's visit. I ensure that there is no SA guard of honour. That would be going too far. Also no deployment of the general public. The Foreign Ministry is sufficiently insensitive to propose this.

We are suppressing too much news. This is absolutely crippling our press policy. The Foreign Ministry is responsible. I intervene vigorously in this area, too. The mood in the country has become rather tense again. The SD report supplies details.

Raskin's death has created a gap which cannot be filled. I am preparing an honourable burial for him. The Führer has awarded him the War Service Cross. The question of who can succeed him is insoluble. Glasmaier is deeply affected.

Discuss the radio transmission situation with Dittmar and Hadamovsky. More representations will be made to the Führer about close-down times.

We must keep burrowing away at this problem, or the English will be left in command of the entire field. Hadamovsky is the number one man . . .

. . . Wonderful birthday with Magda and the children. We are all very happy. A new life is starting for our family. In the afternoon, the Führer comes on a surprise-visit, to congratulate Magda. We show him our new house, which he likes very much. He inspects everything very closely and is delighted with the layout and the execution. We talk away the afternoon, he is in lively mood, nice to the children. I am able to give him a report on Prague and our programmes of entertainments for the troops; he praises Hinkel highly, has some touching words for Raskin, and makes jokes about Churchill's campaign of lies. Altogether, he seems more relaxed than I have seen him to be for a long time. Ecstatic talk about the coming peace.

Very pessimistic reports arrive from London regarding naval matters. They are short of everything over there. We shall soon humble them.

Molotov is already on his way here with a huge entourage. Moscow places great importance on this visit. We shall know how to exploit it.

In the evening, a small party for Magda's birthday. Everything is very pleasant and cosy. Magda dazzlingly beautiful again. The Führer arrives again towards ten in the evening and stays until four in the morning. He is absolutely confident and relaxed, just as in pre-war times. He exudes a sovereign calm. A few side-swipes against England. Harsh words for Chamberlain and particularly Halifax. With regard to France, he repeats firmly that she must pay for the war and will not be let off lightly.

Long talks on vegetarianism, the 'coming religion'. The Führer is totally consistent in this question and has all the arguments at his disposal. Even he longs for peace, for happiness and a chance to enjoy life. We day-dream about all the things we shall do after the war. It will, and should, be wonderful then.

We are very pleased to have the Führer as our guest for such a long time. Here he can be a proper human being again.

Short sleep.

13 November 1940 (Wednesday)

Yesterday: Bad weather. No incursions into Germany. We are also unable to do much against London. A few ships sunk. In Greece, the situation is appalling. Mussolini made no proper preparations. Now they are supposed to be working out a plan for a great, new offensive. That could have been done beforehand.

I instruct the press to take a tougher line and to come up to scratch. Our newspapers have become lazy and boring again. In particular the local publications.

Molotov arrives in Berlin in the pouring rain. Cool reception.

Settle the final honours for Raskin in consultation with Glasmaier . . .

. . . Dr Westrick has arrived back from the USA and delivered a report: on the primitivity of the people, the crudeness of political methods, and the cynicism of the Roosevelt-clique. He believes that Roosevelt will formally declare war. I still doubt it. In any event, that is not a country where I would like to be buried.

Work at home. The Molotov visit is the big theme in the world press. London is finding consolation in lame excuses. The thanks they get is some 70,000 tons sunk. Despite all the propaganda bluffing, things are very bad for England.

All sorts to be dealt with in the afternoon. So much trivial paperwork is building up. I have to deal with every little bit of rubbish myself, because it could be important after all.

In the evening, an hour's time to read and chat. It is nice to have Frau Ursel in the house.

Magda is very sweet and comforting to me.

14 November 1940 (Thursday)

Yesterday: Fifty incursions into the Reich, with little effect. Berlin unscathed. More massive night attacks on London, with 150 tons of bombs. Italy is sitting stuck fast in Greece. 120 Alpini have been flown in. A pathetic business. Also, another air attack by the English on Taranto, in which the *Cavour* is very seriously damaged.

Memorandum concerning the effect of English bombing raids on Reich territory so far. Particularly noticeable that the English have been extensively duped by fake installations. The economy of our denials has been justified, apparently . . .

. . . Fritzsche reports on his visit to Rome. Very positive. He is the kind of man who gets his way wherever he goes, smoothly and easily. A valuable colleague.

SD report on morale in the Reich: noticeably improved since the Führer's speech. Now everyone can clearly see both the end and the means.

Discuss the re-organisation of the newsreels with Hippler. We have established a new company including Ufa, Tobis and Bavaria. I intend to keep personal control of it. After the war there will be three different newsreels again. Now, in the middle of a war, this is not a practical proposition.

Work at home. Study a mass of paperwork and deal with it. A clearing operation.

Magda and Ursel return from Lanke. They have been tidying things up there.

In the evening, check films. First German colour film, *Women are Better Diplomats*. Bad script, but the colour effects good. We have made a lot of progress in this field.

Newsreel also very good. In the meantime, a short air-raid warning without serious consequences.

15 November 1940 (Friday)

Yesterday: Weather here wonderful, awful in England. So only minor air activity over London, by day or night. The English don't get very far here, either. Few incursions. But the English are basking in the glory of Taranto, which cost the Italians serious damage to three of their battleships. The other vessels left the port. Churchill has made a very emotional speech about this engagement in the House of Commons. Rome alternates between bitter silence and lame excuses. I order some, at least, of the material from Rome to be edited for use abroad.

The whole problem is due to the Italians' extraordinary carelessness, as is the mess they have got themselves into in Greece. The Greek campaign was based wholly on bluff. This is the most serious mistake that one can make. Before undertaking such actions, one must reckon on the worst, and not the best. Now the Italians are in the soup and are having to plan, organise and prepare everything anew. Ciano was responsible for the whole affair, against the views of the majority. Another windbag, a companion for Ribbentrop.

Our participation in the Libyan campaign has been called off. On the other hand, the action against Gibraltar will soon escalate, and therefore the question of Portugal will become acute. But we are making preparations: with due thoroughness and attention to the resources required. This business will not be child's play. Our contingents in Rumania are being reinforced. If the Greek campaign drags on, the British could acquire an appetite for the Rumanian oilfields.

I instruct the press: in view of the somewhat unclear military position, more political polemics. Exactly as during last winter. Additionally, more humour in press, radio and film. This is the best thing to see us through difficult times. We are taking everything so dreadfully seriously. It harms morale.

In the Ministerial Conference, I make my views on the Russians and Molotov's visit quite clear. All the gentlemen share my opinion.

Hadamovsky explains the transmission situation to me with the aid of maps and statistics. The early closedown is causing tremendous damage to our propaganda effort. He is now to make a formal report to the Führer.

Terboven reports to me on Norway. Quisling is gradually gaining more support. The old political parties are largely in ruins. Our cultural campaigns, theatrical tours, films, etc. are having a particularly good effect on local feeling. I shall further intensify this work. But first I intend to travel up to Oslo. The Führer is not so satisfied with Terboven's work. But he has probably been misled by the Navy, who are constantly having rows with Terboven. We plan big campaigns for entertaining the troops.

Von Arent shows me the rebuilding plans for the German Theatre in Prague. Very ambitious and expensive, but well done.

Dr Gross reports to me on the Italians' work in the area of racial theory. Everything is still in its infancy there. Bottai has wrested control in this area away from Pavolini. Bottai is generally on the ascendant.

Discuss the question of propaganda abroad with Bohle and Butte from Rome. The Foreign Ministry only tries to influence the top ten thousand, but we must turn to the people. This is the cardinal difference in our view of things. We shall continue on our path and not allow ourselves to be led astray by the Foreign Ministry's dilettantism.

Unfortunately I am unable to go to the Führer at midday, since pressure of work keeps me at my desk. This enables me to catch up to some extent.

It is such a pleasure when the work visibly diminishes.

But it never ends.

Molotov leaves. 'Agreement on all questions of mutual interest'. A cold shower for the 'friends of the Soviet Union' in London. We can be satisfied. Everything else depends on Stalin. We shall have to wait for his decision.

48,000 tons sunk by the Navy and the Luftwaffe. England's shipping losses are becoming more ominous with every passing day.

In the afternoon, receive some 200 armaments workers who had previously been with the Führer. I deliver a short speech, then enjoy many personal conversations with them, from which I am able to learn a great deal. Their morale is very good, despite everything. The people are, and will remain, the rockbed of our work. I get to know a number of magnificent workers, men and women who are very outspoken. A marvellous hour's chat with real people. What is all that intellectual nonsense, compared with this!

Speak with Ley about the Seventh Chamber. It seems to be a project very close to his heart. But Hess and his people are reluctant. Ley gives me a long litany. I shall think everything over again.

Soldiers' welfare problems with Hinkel. He is doing good work and achieving an extraordinary amount in this area. He has a few faults, but otherwise he is a very useful man. Particularly when hard work is required.

Home in the evening, exhausted. Short chat with the ladies. Last look at the Bismarck film, which has turned out magnificently. I am very pleased with our German film production teams' achievements during the past months.

Three hours' air-raid warning in the evening, two more during the night. But the new procedures enable us to shoot down eight Englishmen. This is wonderful. I telephone Colonel-General Weise, who is very happy. Damage in Berlin is more serious than hitherto. Wodarg arrives during the night with items of booty and secret papers taken from a crashed English aircraft. Generally a very exciting and tense night. But almost no sleep.

16 November 1940 (Saturday)

Yesterday: Fairly extensive incursions into the Reich. London only lightly bombed. On the other hand, 420 tons on Coventry. This centre of the armaments industry is virtually destroyed. It should give the English a salutary shock. The interview with Kennedy gives a very pessimistic picture of the situation in England. This is the way things must actually be.

The Italians beat back a Greek attack on Albanian soil. What a humiliation and a disgrace! The Taranto affair continues to loom large in the English victory bulletins. We are still chalking up a lot of sinkings of English ships.

Instructions on putting bite into our editorials at the press conference. The military aspects can also be given more prominence now.

The Führer is now beginning a programme of visits and receptions. Half of Europe will be appearing for roll-call during the next fourteen days.

Hadamovsky has talked to the Führer and explained the transmission situation. The Führer intends to leave the final decision to me and Göring.

Hinkel is working like a beaver on troops' welfare.

Ribbentrop is complaining about Dittmar, who has stepped into Raskin's shoes with a vigour that does not meet with the approval of the gentlemen from the Foreign Ministry. I shall make sure everything is sorted out there.

Receive Greiser and Maul. They want me to make a speech about Germany's cultural mission to the East, which is necessary and which I agree to. Greiser wants more freedom of transmission, which I allow him. Otherwise, a few small things, which we reach agreement on. Greiser has a clear brain, and Maul is doing his job well.

A number of press questions with Reinhardt. Go-ahead for work on *Das Reich*.* I intend to write more for it myself. Mündler will not do in the long term. In the press generally, there is a shortage of new blood.

Hippler delivers a new work-statute for the state-owned film companies. This is necessary, particularly in the face of the Bavaria company's wilfulness.

Breakfast at the Japanese Embassy for the 2600th anniversary.** The Führer is also there. He is in the best of moods. Very happy at our successes in the air, which are, of course, beyond all expectations. Twelve enemy planes downed over Reich territory. Plus the almost complete destruction of Coventry, which has now been conceded even by London. This is no small thing. Another wave of pessimism from London. The Führer tells me a whole series of details which complete the picture of devastation resulting from our work.

---

* A quality political weekly founded by Goebbels in May 1940 to 'present radical arguments in a decent way'. From early 1941 he wrote the weekly leader-article, and with his support *Das Reich* reached a circulation of a million. The last edition was published on 25 April 1945.

** Of the Japanese Empire.

Speak with Hess about Streicher. He has nothing but harsh words for him, and will not hear of mercy. Holz has performed well on active service, but Streicher seems to be a little *mente captus*. Hess is still incorrigibly hostile to Ribbentrop. Lammers, too, is complaining bitterly about him. He also tells me of the gloomy position which Kerrl and Rust find themselves in. Ministers with nothing to do. Dreadful and desperate.

I am able to discuss the transmission situation with Milch again. Göring has gone on leave for six weeks, and Milch is deputising for him. We intend to settle the entire transmission situation in the near future.

Police matters with Himmler. We must give the work of the police more prominence. Particularly, however, the Fire Service and the LsHD.* They are performing a tremendous service. The whole atmosphere of the Japanese party is very pleasant. They make a great effort.

The Greeks are already fighting on Albanian soil. The Italians have got themselves into a terrible jam. A painful humiliation for all of us.

Work at home in the afternoon. Terboven comes visiting. I am able to have a detailed discussion of the Norwegian problem with him. There are all sorts of things to check and think over. We are organising a big shipload of gifts for our troops in Norway at Christmas. Terboven is taking a lot of pains and doing his part magnificently. He is the untrammelled master of Norway. The old parties and government bosses are completely out of the picture.

Then Dr Dietrich and his wife join us. We watch the Bismarck film together, and it meets with the greatest admiration. A success. Liebeneiner is entitled to be proud of it.

No raid on Berlin. Last night, twelve planes downed by flak. These are the first results of our new procedures.

17 November 1940 (Sunday)

Yesterday: Heavy raid on Hamburg with considerable damage. The main English target. Revenge for Coventry. Otherwise, hardly any incursions into the Reich. 340 tons on London again, despite fog. And another mass of bombs on Coventry. The raid on Coventry has had an enormous effect throughout the world. Even newspapers in the USA have been deeply impressed. Total helplessness in London. A great wave of pessimism from there. If only the Italians were not making such a mess of things, our stock would be standing very high at the moment. The Italians have made a very bad start against Greece. They are being given a proper pasting down there.

I sign Hippler's new film statute. This should bring order into the state-owned film companies. Wagner in Munich is interfering too much.

Some idiot in the Ministry of the Interior has made a summary of the old regulations from the nineteenth century dealing with the slaughter of

* *Luftschutz-Hilfdienst* (Auxiliary Air Defence Service).

livestock, including the eating of dog-flesh, etc. This is, of course, just the right moment for such a thing. It has leaked into the press, and the press in the USA is turning it into a famine story, complete with dogs being turned into meat, etc. I kick up a dreadful furore, with Frick, with Fritzsche, with [. . .] etc. But now the harm has been done, and redressing it will be a gradual process. Trivialities are turned into worldwide sensations. A bad business, politics.

Great arguments about Raskin's successor. Still no agreement in sight. And so I postpone the decision and make Glasmaier temporarily responsible for continuing Raskin's work. Berndt has behaved very badly again. He is an intolerable man.

Put some urgency into work on the newsreel. One must constantly keep pushing.

The Führer has started his big tour. First to Munich and then to all the many meetings planned. Suñer's visit has already been announced. Keitel is having discussions with Badoglio at Innsbruck. I hope he does more with Badoglio than utter simple platitudes.

An insolent letter from Ribbentrop. But I keep stubbornly to my method of silence and non-acknowledgement.

Our new horses and carriage have arrived. A magnificent team. Magda is overjoyed.

I do not feel well. A minor infection. I can no longer stand. Two hours in bed, then I can continue.

The reports from Coventry are horrendous. An entire city literally wiped out. The English are no longer pretending; all they can do now is wail. But they asked for it . . .

18 November 1940 (Monday)

Yesterday: I wake up rested and fit once more after ten hours of refreshing sleep. It was badly needed.

The weather is glorious. Wonderful autumn! We had several incursions, mainly affecting Hamburg again. But without serious damage. Because of the miserable flying conditions, we were able to attack England only to a limited extent. Coventry was treated to another load. It is now no more than a heap of ruins. This affair has aroused the greatest attention all over the world. Our stock is on the rise again. The USA is succumbing to gloom, and the usual arrogant tone has disappeared from the London press. All we need is a few weeks of good weather. Then England could be dealt with.

The Italians have nothing to report from any of their theatres of war. We are happy enough: no news is better than bad news. Morale at home is very much on the rise again.

I have to take a little rest for my health's sake. Short stroll through the autumn day. I enjoy the sun and the fresh air like a newborn baby. At midday, Gravenhorst reports on his trip to Paris. He had all sorts of experiences there.

In the afternoon, receive artistes who are entertaining the troops. They have all worked so hard for the cause, and with the greatest idealism. I thank them profoundly and they delight us with a little improvised concert. Glorious voices, wonderful playing. What a joy after such a long time starved of music. Bockelmann, Rudolph, Anders, Cebotari, a colourful hotch-potch of great names.

Afterwards, Gutterer reports to me on Moscow. All my views are confirmed: it is bleakness elevated into a political system. No culture, no civilisation, but only terror, fear and mass-delusion. Awful! Gutterer is glad to be back here.

Newsreel. This time turned out very well. A rare poor film from the Bavaria studios, *Heart Weighs Anchor*, which I should really like to ban.

No raid on Berlin.

Today departure for Nuremberg and then to Munich.

19 November 1940 (Tuesday)

Yesterday: Early departure from Berlin. Mountains of work in the train. Report on morale is completely positive again. We are slowly mastering the situation. Long consultations with Naumann about my closest colleagues' salary levels. I must do something about this, or all my best people will leave me.

The Duce has made a speech. Very firm and manly. Predicts the fate of Carthage for England. The rest balm on the wound of Taranto.

The Führer's new housing programme published. Very strongly socialist in emphasis. 300,000 new homes during the first postwar year alone. And roomy dwellings for big families. Ley Reich Commissar for Home Building. Seldte would never have been up to it. An enormous task, as glorious as it is necessary.

Ciano and Suñer with the Führer on the mountain. Feverish activity on the diplomatic front. Gibraltar is the main topic. One can only hope that some agreement is reached. Herr Churchill will be amazed.

Several incursions into the Reich. Principally against Hamburg, which is suffering the most at the moment. Our aerial activity over England mediocre. Weather conditions over there are very bad.

Arrival in Nuremberg. Grandiose reception. Liebel and Martin in the vanguard. But no Streicher. He is sulking at his country seat. It feels strange to be in Nuremberg without seeing him. But so it must be. The blunders he has made are too big to be ignored. After the war, we shall see. The Führer cannot drop him altogether.

Speech at the *Ufapalast* to the Gau officials. Outline the entire political and military situation. I am on top form and give the people plenty to think about. Storms of applause.

To tea with Liebel. Long negotiations with Professor Gradl, who is painting new pictures for our entrance hall. A fine artist and a real, serious worker. I like him. I intend to give him some more commissions.

The manager of the *Stadttheater*, Hanke, who makes a good impression, has adapted a work by Lortzing, *Hans Sachs*, and we see it at the theatre in the evening. Well directed, and excellently staged and played. Wagner took most of the motifs for his *Meistersinger* from this amiable work. But one can scarcely speak of plagiarism in the case of such a genius, since he raised this primitive, childish material to the highest levels of art. In any case, the performance is great fun. One can see that even the greatest genius can – and must – borrow ideas.

Out to the Faber-Castells' hunting-lodge near Nuremberg for a meal. We spend a pleasant hour chatting. A likeable couple.

Back into the train. Sleep for a short while at the station.

Arrive in Munich early in the morning. Magda and the children are well. The whole family is now to move to Berlin. This will make things cosier and easier.

20 November 1940 (Wednesday)

Yesterday: Little doing over London. Southampton and Coventry heavily bombed, however. Few incursions into the Reich. Berlin untouched.

All manner of routine work. Otte reports on the works of art bought in Holland and Belgium. Some very beautiful things among them.

At midday to the Reich Propaganda Office heads at the City Hall. Sketch a picture of the situation. Frank, open and clear. Great success. Truth is the best propaganda. Discuss artistic questions in Munich with Fiehler. He sheds a few tears to me. And invites my people to eat with him. In the process, he makes a speech praising me and my work. A good-hearted, but somewhat primitive person.

To the Bavaria studios in the afternoon. Inspect building plans and hear the latest news. Uncertain whether Schweikart can handle running the entire operation in the long term. Perhaps it would be better if he did some directing.

We see some of the shooting of the film *Philine*. Dorsch and Krahl. Pabst directing. He has it well in hand.

Rushes from *Philine* and *Girl from Fäno*, which I find exceptionally pleasing. Discuss plans for the re-organisation of Bavaria with [. . .] and Schweikart. Bavaria is now falling into line with our regulations. In fact, it has no choice.

To the hotel to work. We have sunk another 50,000 tons or so. When will

that creature Churchill finally surrender? England cannot hold out for ever!
A lot to be dealt with.
And then I am so tired that I fall into bed like a dead man.
The day is over, and this book is finished.
What shall I write in the new book?
Who knows!
Perhaps the beautiful words: peace has returned!

(Here ends the first book of the diaries. The next book, covering the period from 21 November 1940 to 23 May 1941, is preceded by the motto: 'I hate the false wisdom that avoids danger'.)

21 November 1940 (Thursday)

Yesterday: Thus, with fresh courage and trust in God, we approach this new book. What tales of happiness and unhappiness shall I enter in it?

Sleep through my first night without an air-raid alert for a long time in Munich. The press cables give evidence of new English insolence. They are not allowed even to talk of capitulation.

Several incursions into the Reich. Long air-raid warning in Berlin, too. But very little damage. London attacked only to a limited extent. But 500 tons on Birmingham. This will be a second Coventry. I am eager to hear the reaction in London. One English city after another must suffer. Until Churchill weakens.

The Hungarians have joined the Three-Power Pact in Vienna. Antonescu is coming to Berlin very soon. The Bulgarians and the Slovaks are following in a week. The new Europe is coming into being under our leadership.

Work with Naumann. Milch intends to distribute a poster about air defence which is psychologically ill-judged. I manage to stop it at the last moment. The general public, and particularly the Berliners, are extremely sensitive in such matters. One cannot be too careful.

Nothing new from Berlin. Magda and the children are well. But the long air-raid alerts are very exhausting.

In the afternoon, to the Reich Propaganda Leadership* and the 'German Greatness' exhibition. The new offices of the Reich Propaganda Leadership are very pleasant, but only temporary. The people who work there are, with a very few exceptions, wholly mediocre. The organisational aspect is good. Fischer has not proved equal to his job. On the other hand, he is loyal and faithful. And therefore I shall keep him on.

* The *Reichspropagandaleitung* (RPL for short). The main Nazi Party office for propaganda, with its headquarters in Munich, which Goebbels also controlled. There was considerable overlap between its functions and those of the Ministry of Propaganda – although, as Goebbels makes clear, the RPL tended to be staffed by Party hacks rather than experts.

180

'German Greatness' exhibition staged by Rosenberg's office. Very solidly constructed and put together with a lot of hard work. Survey of how the Reich came into being. A good thing, which ought to be sent round the Reich.

To tea with Wagner.* Talk with Schw[. . .]er** and Siebert. Issues of the moment, particularly regarding the German Academy, on which we reach absolute agreement. Frau Troost is a clever woman, but a bit of a bluestocking.

Some work in the evening. Then back to Berlin.

Just arrived. It is still cold and dark in the early morning.

22 November 1940 (Friday)

Yesterday: Straight to work. Heavy raids on Birmingham again during the night. The English and American press had hardly had time to digest the previous night's mayhem. Now this too. Deeply pessimistic voices. We shall be able to make something out of this.

Hungary has now definitely joined the Three-Power Pact. Not of any great value, but of some psychological significance. The Führer in Vienna for a day. Antonescu on his way to Berlin. The Führer will also be back soon.

Find a lot of work waiting for me. There was no air-raid warning in Berlin. Few incursions into the Reich either. But heavier raids on England. We are now taking on the English provincial cities one by one. In the long term, this will have a more demoralising effect than concentrating on London alone. The press has plenty of material again.

Things are very bad on the Greek front. The Italians may well meet with a painful reverse there. On the other hand, they have downed an English plane over Sicily and captured an English Air Vice-Marshal and a number of generals.

Row in Paris between Schmidtke and Wächter. I make peace between them yet again.

Personnel matters with Gutterer. Brauweiler is not up to his job in the long term. I should like to let Bömer have him back and replace him with Hunke. Then cut down the work of the Publicity Council and give some of its exhibition work to Maiwald in a special section at the ministry. Drewes is too much of a theorist for me. I need a man with some experience of life to take his place. Above all, someone who knows and understands music for the broad masses. I shall then send Drewes back to the theatre. He has tolerated a situation where the popular composers have to give up most of their income to the so-called serious musicians via the *Stagma*. This is a downright absurdity. Those who can do their job feed, at least in part, the 'serious' ones – that is, often, the failures. I intend to abolish this forthwith . . .

* Gauleiter of Munich (*see* biographical note in Index).
** Possibly Hans Schweitzer, the cartoonist (*see* biographical note in Index).

181

. . . Discuss the matter of an international committee of evaluation for German cultural values with Dr Gast. The project is still in the initial stages of research, and will doubtless present many difficulties. Drewes is in the way there, too, picking fights with God and the whole world.

Spieler is also causing me some concern. He is not providing sufficient support for Naumann's work and does not work systematically enough.

Look at beautiful old [. . .] that Bibrach has purchased for the house. Also some designs for tapestries by Eisenmenger from Vienna.

Report from Hungary: there everyone, with Horthy in the lead, is anti-German. A corrupt feudal system that is as far from us as the moon is from the sun. We shall never get anywhere with this Hungary. It must be overthrown one day.

A host of travel plans: to Oslo and a trip on the *Bismarck* for gunnery practice, which I am looking forward to particularly.

England realises the greater implications of the danger of encirclement and blockade. On this level, too, the doom of the Empire draws on.

Work on all kinds of projects in the afternoon. But there is still some semblance of quiet. The Führer is on his way back to Berlin.

I busy myself with checking films. *Roses from Tyrol*, good entertainment. Two good cultural films and a brilliant newsreel.

Ello and the Hommels are visiting. They have been to Italy. Very little evidence of war there. The [. . .] Romans are leaving the fighting to us. More news of withdrawals on the Greek front.

Then a long talk with Magda.

No air-raid warning.

23 November 1940 (Saturday)

Yesterday: Glorious weather. No incursions during the night, probably because of icing-up risk. But neither are we able to do much over England. Flying only possible by dead reckoning. Deeply pessimistic voices from London. Frau Churchill has made a whining speech in which he deals with India. He and the King have spoken to parliament. A bloodless, banal affair. Scarcely any talk of victory any more. Secret reports from London say that Halifax [. . .] The only thing keeping them going is the famous English stubbornness.

The Italians have now evacuated Koritze, as they themselves admit, with significant losses. They are constantly queering our pitch. We have picked fine allies!

We have not much material for propaganda at the moment. The Luftwaffe wants to participate in educating the public about the air war. They have produced a good specimen lecture. Definitive regulations on air defence duties and compensation of those affected by air raids have now been published. We are keeping to the middle way in this area.

[. . .] is suggested to me as Raskin's successor. From the SS. He seems to meet the requirements, halfways at least. Berndt will take over the Radio Department again. Hadamovsky will go back to his old post as head of Reich Broadcasting . . .

. . . Naumann has put my finances and the business with Lanke in order. So I now have that personal burden lifted from my shoulders . . .

. . . Schmidt-Cracow wants Frank to have full powers over his film and radio work. I reject this. The Reich must keep control when it comes to the chief machinery of intellectual leadership of the nation. There can be no compromise on this issue. It is precisely in this area that we must keep a tight hold and a clearly dominant role for the Reich. Frank feels himself to be not so much the representative of the Reich as King of Poland. But that will not get him very far.

Hilgenfeldt has personal worries: he wants to marry a young Bessarabian-German girl and must therefore have a higher salary. I agree to both requests.

I work straight through lunch. I have no time to go to the Führer. Besides which, he is waiting to meet Antonescu.

I am able to work on without interruption and deal with a whole heap of paperwork. Check the war film about the campaign in the West, put together from newsreels. Turned out well. One has to be filled with admiration, even now: what a Triumph!

Draft a speech for the fiftieth Request Concert.* No air-raid alert. And so to sleep!

24 November 1940 (Sunday)

Yesterday: Some peace at last, so that I can work in a relaxed way. A series of incursions into the Ruhr area without serious damage, but some into the occupied territories successful. We can do little over London, but attack Birmingham very severely all through the night. This probably causes the Herr Englishmen the most pain. The Italians' withdrawal from Koritze has had a downright catastrophic psychological effect. Whether it will turn into a military disaster depends on the Italians. Probably not, but then with the Italians one never knows. The Greeks are beside themselves with joy at their victory. Metaxas has made a pompous speech.

The English have collected a large force together at Gibraltar. To what purpose is not yet clear. Are they intending to do something? Or simply bluffing? In Churchill's case it is difficult to predict.

* The *Wünschkonzert für die Wehrmacht* (Request Concert for the Wehrmacht). A programme of musical requests broadcast with a live audience from Berlin to Germany and occupied Europe every Sunday afternoon. It was extraordinarily popular, and Goebbels, realising its propaganda value, took a keen personal interest, at times intervening to secure the services of star performers for the show. It also spawned a film and a book.

The Rumanians have acceded to the Three-Power Pact. [. . .] is on his way to Berlin. Also intends to sign. The Three-Power pact as a protector of small states. Turkey has introduced a state of siege in some areas. But at present this is purely a precautionary measure.

Work at home. A number of film and theatre problems. Plus a few financial problems of my bureau, which cannot be neglected. Drewes has calmed down again and is carrying out my orders promptly. Particularly in the field of popular music, to which we shall pay far more attention than previously. After all, it represents the major part of our musical activity as a whole. And is also the stepping-stone to great music. One must do justice to both. Drewes would like to turn the entire population into Bach enthusiasts. This is, of course, neither possible nor ultimately desirable.

Now the entire family has moved from Schwanenwerder to Berlin. All the children are here, and Holde and Hedda are royally pleased to be back with their brothers and sisters. And no one is more pleased than I.

At midday to the Führer for an official breakfast with Antonescu. A very small party. Antonescu makes a very good, manly impression. One can feel some confidence in him. His Legionaries are still a little lacking in grace, but they are all glowing with idealism. This is worth something. One of them speaks to the Führer, full of profound admiration. They are very reverent about their murdered *capitano*. Antonescu is not quite considered a real fellow, since he is not a Legionary. But there are no serious conflicts. Horia Sima is not present, but from all accounts he is young and energetic. And absolutely honest, which naturally means a lot in Rumania. The Foreign Minister, Sturdza, does not seem particularly impressive. Everything is overshadowed by the ghost of Codreanu, who is revered like a saint. In his testament, he clearly establishes Rumania's political role at Germany's side. I am told how he was murdered. Cut down by a King who was not worthy to lick his boots.* How long can a dead man continue to influence the living? The Jewish question is the key to Rumania's problems. Every eighteenth Rumanian is a Jew. That makes a devil of a lot of work still to be done. But these people are all young. One can still feel sure of them. The Führer says in answer to an enquiry that he feels Rumania has passed the nadir of her political development. This must be right. The Führer looks wonderful and is in the best of moods.

Discuss the Seventh Chamber with Ley. He wants it, while Hess's staff do not. I am not particularly interested in it . . .

. . . Work at home. Small tea party for the people who worked on *Heart of the Queen*. Very interesting. And good for me to see some different faces for once. Frölich, Leander, Birgel, Mackeben, Lotte Koch, Koppenhöfer, etc. Much exchanging of ideas and stimulating talk.

Short air-raid warning. Then print of the new film, *Request Concert*. Well

---

* King Carol II of Rumania (*see* biographical note).

184

produced. Spun out for rather too long. Otherwise, however, very effective . . . a real film for the people.

Then chat for a long while. Grim reports from Coventry and Birmingham. When will Churchill surrender?

25 November 1940 (Monday)

(Yesterday:)

[Entry largely undeciphered]

. . . But Churchill is not yet considering surrender.

Stalin has recalled Schwartzev in Berlin and sent Dekanosov, Deputy Commissar for External Affairs, in his place. They intend to activate the German-Russian relationship.

Read and write in the afternoon. Check films. Newsreel particularly good. An entertainment film, *Head High, Johannes*!. Very bad, and completely ruined under Kowa's direction. Scarcely salvageable.

No air-raid warning. A quiet night.

26 November 1940 (Tuesday)

Yesterday: Grey, misty weather. A few incursions into the Reich. Mainly against Hamburg, with some damage. But we launch heavy attacks on England. London and particularly Bristol. Said to be a similar inferno to Coventry. The Italians cannot even hold on to their new positions in Albania. The Greeks [. . .] Our Allies are turning tail and running. A shameful sight. They made no preparations at all. The English are crowing with triumph. But our air attacks unleash another wave of pessimism in London.

Wild fabrications in London regarding supposed air attacks on Berlin, with not a word of truth in them. I have denials issued through the press, the air attachés and neutral journalists. Big story in the German press. Read an essay on the English: their best weapons are their phlegm and their stupidity. In their position, any other nation would have collapsed long since.

Personnel and organisational questions with Gutterer. Ley wants to bring the KdF into the Reich Chamber of Culture. But demanding too many rights in exchange. Hess against it. I am too, at heart. Ley pushes and pushes. He is a [. . .] grumbler and a stubborn negotiator. But I shall soon deal with him. Gutterer warns me urgently against such a re-organisation.

Have purchased beautiful new tapestries from Holland, Belgium and France. Mainly eighteenth century. A valuable acquisition.

Establish guidelines for the fiftieth Request Concert. The last one was not particularly good. But we intend to score a hit with the next one. I shall speak personally. And General Dietl as representative of the front.

Abetz gives me a talk about France. He makes a very bad, vague impression. Soft and weak. He is totally bound up in the French mentality. Puffed-up and pompous. I would not trust him to cross the road. He does not get on well with Wächter. But they have to work together. I will not have continual conflict. But it goes without saying that Abetz has no independent powers. I will not allow the Foreign Ministry to push me around any more.

Midday with the Führer. Ley tries to push through his Seventh Chamber again, but I take a very reserved stance. He must clear things with Hess first.

The Führer is in the best of moods and in fine fettle. He expresses the highest regard for Antonescu, who defended his national interests in an amiable fashion. Neither the Rumanians nor the Hungarians recognise the Vienna Award. This is no bad thing. A little discord in the Balkans is always good security. But they should keep quiet just at the moment.

For England the Führer feels only pity. The Empire is destroying itself. There is scarcely any chance of salvation for England now.

Discuss flying. From its beginnings to the present. What a proud story! [. . .] talks about flying in Germany during the postwar years. What a proud story from then to now!

Hess is flying back to Munich. He looks very bad and is not in good health. He is such a decent fellow! It is a pity that his capacity for work is constantly sapped by ill-health. He is delighted by the Bismarck film.

An auxiliary cruiser makes 95,000 tons of enemy tonnage sunk.

Dictate speech for the fiftieth Request Concert. Work through the whole day at full stretch. One scarcely comes to draw breath.

Half the children are in bed at home with 'flu. One infects the other. A dreadful situation.

In the evening I receive six cameramen from the Propaganda Companies, who have just returned from active service on all fronts. They have seen and done a lot, and are able to tell the most interesting stories. One cannot hear enough.

We watch the unedited version of the new newsreel together. This is their work, which they are very proud of, and rightly so. And then they report some more about their experiences, from Narvik to the Bay of Biscay. A heroic saga of German war-reportage. I am very pleased. We sit until late at night by the fireside and chat. A wonderful evening. Then talk for a long while with Magda and Ursel.

The Foreign Ministry is causing me trouble again in Paris. But I do not let it disturb my equanimity.

Little sleep. A hard, strenuous day begins.

27 November 1940 (Wednesday)

Yesterday: A grey day. Scarcely any incursions into the Reich. Almost no raids on England. The weather situation is too unfavourable. Despite this, pessimistic voices from London. The rot is gradually spreading over there.

Prophesies of doom are everywhere, including even the USA. In Greece the Italians have slowly recovered. They are no longer in retreat.

Report from Titel on his inspection of the Propaganda Teams. Everything is going well. Our new concept of War Propaganda has met with complete [. . .] everywhere . . .

(The rest of the entry for 27 November is missing or, inasmuch as occasional words and phrases have been deciphered, hardly comprehensible. The very short entry for 28 November is also only partly deciphered and contains indications of a trip by car and ferry to Norway, accompanied by an escort of seven German warships. The narrative resumes in coherent form with part of the entry for 30 November, covering the previous two days.)

30 November 1940 (Saturday)

Thursday: Early . . . arrival. Big reception. Terboven, Falckenhorst [. . .]

[. . .] To the military cemetery high above the city. Here lie our dead soldiers, with the same view of the fjord which they had while they were taking the city. I am astonished at how ugly a city can look surrounded by such a wonderful natural setting.

Colourful hour with the soldiers. Good music. I speak. Greetings from the homeland. Storms of applause.

Midday with Falckenhorst. In the quarters from which he directed the campaign in Norway. He makes a flattering speech on my account. He is a splendid old gentleman, with whom one could go horse-stealing.

Out to Skan [. . .]. Seat of the former crown prince, where Terboven now lives. With great [. . .] and a magnificent view of Oslo in the distance.

We [. . .]: he does not get on well with the Navy, which is giving itself great airs here. The fewer ships, the more Admirals.

Big reception in the evening. Many Norwegian cultural figures. But nothing special.

In Rumania the Iron Guard has shot some of the old corrupt types. One can only say 'bravo' to that.

Heavy raids on England [. . .] Wave of pessimism from London. One can clearly begin to hear the foundations creaking there. A desperate raid by the English on Cologne. Hardly affects us.

Friday: Out early after a short sleep. It is [. . .] Out on board a warship into the fjord where the *Blücher* sank.* General von Engelbrecht gives me a dramatic account of those tragic hours. Tears well in his eyes. What times, what men!

* A German heavy cruiser torpedoed by a British submarine in Oslo fjord during the initial German assault on the Norwegian capital, 9 April 1940.

Anchor at the fortified island. It was here that the fateful torpedoes were launched. Everything is re-enacted to illustrate the events. Tense moments. I talk for a long while with soldiers and officers who were there at the time.

What a wonderful day! This beautiful town. I lay a wreath at the memorial to the *Blücher*.

At the German House. I meet a host of old comrades there. A short visit to the Storthing. An enthusiastic reception. We have two insolent Norwegian students arrested. Stupid boys who tried to stage a demonstration.

Coffee with the entire staff of the Reich Commissariat at Holmenkollen. How wonderful! Short visit to the Luftwaffe and Colonel-General Stumpff. Impression good.

After [. . .] Contact with Berlin. It has been raining bombs over London again. The voices of desperation from there are really becoming stronger. Can this be the end of the story? One dares not think of it. We shall wait calmly and fight on!

A lot of work. Endless conferences. Inspect models of some of our soldiers' hostels in Norway. And then fall into bed, dead tired.

1 December 1940 (Sunday)

Yesterday: Away early. It is cold. Flight in a Junkers 52 above Oslo and the fjords. The sun hovers blood-red over them.

Inspect the big new airfield with Colonel-General Stumpff. Magnificent work, organisation fantastic. I deliver a short but powerful speech to the pilots. Then another to a neighbouring infantry battalion.

Flight back to Oslo. Look round a small Norwegian radio exhibition. SS barracks, which are very practical and attractive. Give a short speech there, too.

To Skange [. . .] Few incursions into the Reich. Mass raid on London with 400 tons. That will have some effect. Pessimism in London growing.

An hour's chat in the block house at Skange sitting round the fire. Then work.

In the evening, a touring company from the Nollendorff Theatre with *Wiener Blut*. A charmingly staged and brilliantly-directed performance. Harald Paulsen has created another masterpiece, from the acting standpoint as well. The audience, particularly the Norwegians, applaud wildly.

I have a short talk with Quisling. He utters platitudes and gives a weary impression [. . .], the [. . .] Minister, is much more impressive. Energetic and intelligent. The best horse in the stables.

Afterwards, farewell party. With the artistes from the Nollendorff Theatre and the German colony. Very jolly. Late home. Then it is straight back to Berlin.

2 December 1940 (Monday)

Yesterday: It is still dark when we leave Skange . . . [. . .] These were a very fine few days.

The sun rises over the fjords. An indescribable sight!

Flight [. . .] Beneath us are German convoys heading northwards. [. . .]

[The next paragraphs undeciphered except for incoherent phrases dealing with a stopover in Copenhagen]

. . . At home. Magda and the children. All of them are pleased to have me back.

It is good to be home.

The situation: very heavy night attacks on England. Plymouth is burning. No incursions into the Reich. Major [. . .] missing, probably killed. A grave loss. He was our best fighter-pilot.

A new row with Ribbentrop. He wants to place his spies in our branch offices. I have them thrown out. He tries to bring in the SS heavyweights. But Himmler gives him a dusty answer. My decision remains in force: his liaison people belong at my central office, not in the subordinate agencies. I inform him of this in a very frosty letter. *Basta*!

Fiftieth Request Concert. A very big affair. I give a short speech. To great applause. Thanks to the radio and its people. General Dietl speaks. Short, folksy and effective. Parade of the [. . .]: [. . .], Leander, [. . .], Karajan and many others. A complete success. And the entire nation, at the front and in the homeland, is glued to its radios. I am very satisfied with this magnificent achievement. The Führer awards Goedecke the War Service Cross.

Long chat with Magda and Ursel. We have so much to tell each other.

Newsreel. Somewhat thin. I perk it up a little. Discuss a number of important film problems with Hippler. Once again, all sorts of things have piled up during my absence.

Sit up with Magda for a long time. These days, the Lord be praised, we have such a good understanding.

3 December 1940 (Tuesday)

Yesterday: Glorious weather in Berlin. We had scarcely any incursions into the Reich during the night. But we attacked London and Southampton, the latter in massive strength. With the greatest success. The pessimistic voices in London and particularly in the USA are growing stronger. Are they beginning to see reason, even there? I cannot believe it yet, and thus keep all such voices, however muted, out of the press.

Things have improved in Greece. At least the Italians have started to defend themselves.

I have settled my argument with Ribbentrop without trouble. I didn't even need to get excited. The man is a fool!

Hinkel reports to me on aspects of entertaining the forces. The KdF is trying to scrape the butter from our bread. I shall put them in their place. Ley's people have every right to be ambitious. But kindly not at the expense of my work.

Our newsreel work is somewhat in a rut. I order a few cameramen from the Propaganda Companies to be placed at my disposal. I shall use them for special tasks.

The Führer is still on the mountain. I thus have a good opportunity to deal with the work that has piled up. Morale among the public is excellent again. I systematically suppress any illusion-mongering, so as to protect us against any more unforeseen setbacks.

The pessimistic mood in London is assuming near-grotesque forms. With every reason. Heavy bombing of English ports. Horrific descriptions in the neutral press. An auxiliary cruiser sunk. 78,000 tons.

Bürckel wants to publish his speech on [. . .] in Lorraine. Inopportune at the moment. Long telephone conversation with Terboven regarding several pardons that the Führer has granted in Norway. We solve the problem.

I put Ribbentrop right about his influence on the radio. He is wrong all along the line.

Check the newsreel in the evening. Now it is much better. One has to be constantly prodding them. New Ufa film *Wedding Night*. A typical Ufa production: mediocre and characterless. Just like Leichtenstern.

Then talk for a long while with the ladies.

4 December 1940 (Wednesday)

Yesterday: Fog over the entire country. We had no incursions into the Reich. But we hit out hard at England. Particularly against Southampton. 160,000 tons of English shipping have fallen victim to our U-boats in one day. We are striking really hard against England now. The pessimistic voices are on the increase again, particularly in the USA. We suppress them by all means available, so as not to feed false hopes. One has to leave so many unpleasant things unsaid, but the same goes for pleasant things.

Our attack on Gibraltar should be going ahead in about three weeks. Large forces are already standing ready in Spain. The Italians, however, are undergoing one débâcle after another at the hands of the Greeks. The whole project is rotten to the core.

I have the achievements of the radio and the film industry highlighted in the press. Bormann has intervened again on the Foreign Ministry's behalf in the broadcasting question. But for the moment, I remain immovable. I shall not allow myself to be [. . .] from that quarter.

Discuss building matters with Bartels.

[. . .] reports from the Hague: mood hardening. Everyone there is still hoping for an English victory. The Mussert movement has a difficult task. And Mussert is making every effort. Whatever the case, he is the only element in the country that we can rely on. I intend to receive him next week.

Discuss the problem of child evacuation with Görlitzer. The parents want their children back. One can understand this, since at the moment there are no air raids. But the bombs will probably return. And so we must remain hard on this issue. We cannot let ourselves be swayed by passing sentimentality. In any case, transporting them all back over Christmas would be impossible because of the transport situation. All in all, this will be a hard nut for us to crack. But we shall sort it out.

Discuss new film projects with Frau Ullrich. She has returned from a big trip round the world and has a lot of interesting things to tell.

Midday with the Führer, who has just returned from the Obersalzberg. He jokes about my row with the Foreign Ministry. It does seem humorous sometimes. Harshest criticism for Italy's military conduct in Albania. It is turning Rome into a laughing-stock, which is a curse. And the Italians had been intending to attack Yugoslavia at the same time. That could well have been a catastrophe. But perhaps it is good from our point of view. It enables us to put the lie to the legend that Italy played anywhere near an equal role in defeating France, which was, of course, far from the case. The Führer asserts that Italy would be given a hiding in North Africa if she were to attack France there. But now there can be no more doubt about who is to lead Europe, Hitler or Mussolini.

I give the Führer a detailed account of my trip to Norway, which interests him very much. He is particularly eager to know about the attitude of the Norwegians. So long as there is still the ghost of a chance, they hope for an English victory. And apart from that they hope for something from Russia – quite wrongly, as will finally become clear. Russia has committed some tactical blunders in Bulgaria, which wants to join the Three-Power Pact. She has tried to mobilise the streets against the King. This one must never do. Now Sofia is in a fix. The Bulgarians should have joined immediately. Moscow is unfurling the Pan-Slavic banner in the Balkans, and that is also a bad move. But she will never do anything against us – from fear.

Watch the newsreel with the Führer, who is very pleased with it. The shots of London burning make a particularly profound impression on him. He also takes careful note of the pessimistic opinions from the USA. Nevertheless, he does not expect the immediate collapse of England, and probably rightly. The ruling class there has now lost so much that it is bringing up its last reserves. By which he means not so much the City of London as the Jews, who if we win will be hurled out of Europe, and Churchill, Eden, etc., who see their personal existences as dependent on the outcome of the war. Perhaps they will end up on the scaffold. We can expect little resistance to them from the masses at the moment. The English proletariat lives under such wretched conditions that a few extra privations will not cause it much discomfort. There will be no revolution, anyway, because the opportunity is lacking. England will thus survive through this winter. The Führer shares my opinion: that one must not allow the German people to harbour any illusions on this issue. And so we must continue to dampen things down. The American aid for England cannot be very great. We shall have to wait and see so far as the new aircraft are concerned. There is no defence against night attacks. And even now, in winter, our position is better than that of the English. This is proved by our continued capacity to attack.

The Führer does not intend to mount any air-raids at Christmas. Churchill, in his madness, will do so, and then the English will be treated to revenge raids that will make their eyes pop.

I give an account to the Führer of the Request Concert and Dietl's speech, which gives him visible pleasure. He intends to visit the Borsig Works during the next few days and make a speech to the Reich's armaments workers. He accepts the suggestions that I make by way of advice. This will be an important affair, under the eyes of the entire nation.

Then a long discussion of technical matters with General Jodl. One can work with him, because he is so reliable.

Lots more to do in the office. Draft a memorandum to the Führer on the German film industry's successful contribution to the war. A number of telephone discussions with Terboven. He intends to complain to the Führer about the Navy in Norway. And he has every reason to do so.

Sit at my desk at home for a long time. By late evening I am so tired. When the war is finally over, I should like to withdraw completely into private life for a few months.

That would be wonderful.

Everyone has his fantasy for after the war.

Mine runs as follows: be lazy, sleep, make music and read good books, lie in the sun, never touch a newspaper, and never hear a thing about the Foreign Ministry.

5 December 1940 (Thursday)

Yesterday: Dreadful, fog-smothered weather. Scarcely any incursions into the Reich. But we are unable to do much over England. The reports of our raid on Bristol dominate the entire world press. As do the successes of our U-boats, which again amounted to 40,000 tons in one day. This is striking at England's heart.

The Italians are withdrawing further on the Greek front. A shameful business. Mussolini's prestige has suffered terribly. The Italians are at rock-bottom so far as world opinion is concerned. Our stock has risen all the higher.

I am taking extensive measures for Christmas. Our main aim, which takes priority over all else, is to avoid any sentimental mood among the general public, and thus there will be little leave from the front and no children returning from their evacuation billets. This is hard, but unavoidable.

The finances of Lanke and my tax affairs have now been settled down to the last detail. At last, then, order in my financial situation. It was high time, too. If I were to die now, my position would be one of plus and minus nil. A reward of sorts for twenty years' service to the fatherland. My family would be amazed.

I make a suggestion to the Foreign Ministry to solve the broadcasting problem: a liaison man in the Foreign Department, who is also involved in broadcasting. If that is not acceptable, then they can take a running jump.

A long session spent coming to an arrangement with Drewes. He must find some more space for popular music in his budget. Serious music is all very well and very important, but particularly at the moment, the people want to relax and be entertained. Drewes is too dry and serious. He will have to hire people who are closer to real life. He promises me his best efforts. I hope that he keeps to this.

Discuss the problem of propaganda abroad with Hunke. He is prepared to take control of the Foreign Department in Brauweiler's place, and to retain the Publicity Council. I would then transfer Brauweiler back to the foreign press. Maiwald would become vice-president of the Publicity Council. Hunke will undoubtedly put some life into our propaganda abroad, which at the moment is our greatest problem. Gutterer will handle further discussions.

Discuss the continuation of the Salzburg Festival for next summer with Rainer. We want to stage it for the frontline soldiers and the workers. Its wartime character will therefore be strongly socialistic. Rainer also outlines a number of useful plans for the rebuilding of Salzburg.

Otte reports to me about the accounts of the 'Thanks to Artists' scheme. An impressive achievement which has done a lot of good.

At home, chat with Magda and the children. The things from Oslo have arrived. It is like a Christmas celebration. The whole house is topsy-turvy. And I am more delighted than anyone.

The Times has published a pretty shameless leader article. Which aims to prove that, despite everything, England is defending democratic freedom. A pathetic confection, which we cut to pieces in the press.

Teleki makes one of his speeches. Pretty insolent about the new order in the Balkans. And kid-gloves so far as the Jewish Question is concerned. These Hungarian aristocrats are a real burden.

Magda and Ursel leave for Vienna in the evening. They are as excited as children. Magda, in particular, has earned a few days' relaxation after all the difficulties of the birth.

Shocking reports on the devastation in Southampton. According to these, that city is one big ruin and life there is hell. So things must continue, until

193

England falls on her knees and begs for peace.

Check films in the evening: one very bad, one good entertainment film by Tourjanski. And then a long, refreshing sleep.

6 December 1940 (Friday)

Yesterday: Dreadful weather. Scarcely any English incursions. We drop only 140 tons altogether. Churchill is alternating deliberate pessimism with deliberate optimism. But that will not be possible for long. The Greeks are driving the Italians even further into retreat. A colossal loss of prestige for Mussolini. The attitude of the German public is one of great indignation. It is hard to dampen down such feelings. Italy can thank Ciano for all this.

We are to step up propaganda in praise of our radio service and the film industry. I am continuing my relentless struggle to ensure that our entire news apparatus stamps hard on public over-optimism about an early end to the war. If such hopes are not fulfilled, then we shall reap a bitter harvest in future.

There have been complaints that the KdF variety shows are too vulgar, and that the compères are too fond of smutty jokes. Also, naked dancing is creeping back into shows, even in the countryside, in completely perverted forms. I intervene with all vigour, not for moral reasons but on grounds of good taste.

The Foreign Ministry has withdrawn from radio headquarters. So Ribbentrop has been forced to surrender in the face of my stubborn resistance. A grave loss of face for him. The Führer was involved. The entire Reich Chancellery took my side. Even Schaub was up in arms.

Gutterer is involved in consultations with Hunke, Maiwald and Brauweiler. I intend to re-organise the entire Foreign Department.

Discuss change of format for *Das Reich* with Reinhardt. It now has a circulation of almost 900,000. The kind of publishing success that one dreams of. I intend to go back to writing the leader-articles myself.

Talk over a host of film problems with Hippler. They seem to pile up all the time. But we can point to plenty of successes. I help Frau Meyerhofer in her search for a good part. Leni Riefenstahl reports on her work on the film *Lowlands*, which is very ambitious and expensive. On the other hand, she shows me some glorious sample footage. She has something, and if she is used properly, then she can produce results.

Deal with a mass of paperwork. Visit artists' studios: Professor Klimsch, who has several superb works in progress. I buy one outright, a wonderful figure of a reclining woman. His sculpture for our summerhouse is fabulously beautiful. Breker's sculpture for our park is also very imposing. He is working on a totally monumental scale. His work for the next ten years is taken up by sculptures for the triumphal arch. Wagner is working on the four figures for the dining room. They are not quite so successful. There is a certain lack of maturity in his work. Has a lot still to learn.

Inspect the air-raid shelter at the ministry. Some 200 children from Berlin are sleeping here every night now. They are rampaging noisily around the washrooms. A refreshing scene.

Home seems quite empty. The children are very hang-dog. We miss mummy in every way.

Great concern in London about shipping losses. They are hitting England where it hurts.

Check films in the evening: both the most recent newsreels, which are magnificently successful. Some rushes from films in progress. Also very promising. Terboven comes by for a short visit. He intends to give the Führer a picture of the situation in Norway and his differences with the Navy. But the Führer does not seem to be very receptive on this issue.

Peace debate moved by the Independents in the English House of Commons, but rejected with only four dissenting votes. The mood in London is hardening slightly once more. This was, of course, to be expected. As experience shows, any crisis has its high and low points until the catastrophe finally arrives.

I read a book by the Englishman MacDonell, *Self-Portrait of a Gentleman**, an unspeakably frivolous and cynical concoction that shows the English plutocrat without his mask. This is the face of the people whom we must overthrow.

7 December 1940 (Saturday)

Yesterday: Dull weather again. No air activity over Germany and only a little over England. About 100 tons in all. I see aerial photographs of the destruction in Coventry, Bristol and Southampton. To judge from those, it must have been quite horrendous. Another thing that they can be grateful to their Lords for. Our allies are retreating still further on the Greek front. But they are pouring in reserves. The events there are slowly taking on the proportions of a politico-military scandal.

The English Ministers are trying to raise the flagging morale of their people by speeches. England's every hope is directed towards the USA. But there is little to be seen or heard from that quarter except encouraging speeches and articles.

The Foreign Ministry is in full retreat all along the line so far as the broadcasting issue is concerned. Accepted all my conditions without exception. That's what I call a victory. Now their liaison people are coming into the ministry. I shall sort them out with no trouble. And so this wretched

---

* Goebbels may have been referring to Archibald Gordon MacDonell's *Autobiography of a Cad*, which was published in 1939, one of a number of satirical works by the Scottish author of *England, Their England*. It seems that Goebbels' understanding of the British sense of humour was extremely limited.

business would seem to be settled.

Complete plans for the radio schedules during Christmas. These will be very fine. *Simplicissimus** is being checked and censored by too many different authorities. I put a stop to this. One must have room for manoeuvre in order to make jokes.

The re-working of old operas and operettas is making solid progress. We shall have our first concrete successes within a few months. I am concerned about filling vacant managerial posts in the theatre. There is a shortage of suitable candidates. I relax book censorship slightly, since there have been some absurdities in this area lately.

Gutterer has some administrative questions. He is settling into his duties with increasing confidence. He will soon be ready to take on State Secretary's job.

Hinkel reports to me on a whole number of measures to entertain the troops. Successes in this area under his leadership are quite exceptional.

Winkler reports on personnel questions in the cinema industry. Films are becoming too expensive. I set maximum budgetary limits. In Paris we are aiming at a controlling interest in the French film industry. We are putting new life into the entire technical side of film production. The Theatre-Park is to be taken away from Ufa and largely de-activated. Hippler is given a dressing-down; work on the newsreels is behind schedule again. He has too much on his plate and so does not take sufficient trouble with projects. Winkler has big new financial plans. We shall realise them little by little. Otherwise, things in the cinema industry are in good shape. Except that money is being spent too generously. But I shall put a stop to that.

Frau Leander reports to me on her work. She enjoys being in our team.

Chat with the children for a while at home. The house is so empty when Magda is not here.

13,300 tons sunk. Air losses 10:7 in our favour. London is twisting this into a great victory. Mussolini has recalled Badoglio. Punishment for Greece. He would do better to sack Ciano, too. He deserves it most.

In the afternoon, première of the Bismark film at the *Ufapalast*. Great crowds. The film's success is absolutely sensational. Another hit. I am very glad. Our film work has real class now. It has cost a lot of trouble and labour, not to mention worry and disappointment. But now we are being repaid with success.

Into the train straight after the première. To Vienna. I am looking forward very much to this short visit.

During the journey, confer with Kaufmann from Vienna. About the Vienna fashion industry, which Ley would like to gobble up.

This must not be. One cannot collectivise everything. Particularly fashion. That is women's business, after all.

Then read for a long while. Vienna!

* A German satirical magazine, similar in many ways to the British *Punch*.

8 December 1940 (Sunday)

Yesterday: Early arrival Vienna. A glorious day. Magda and Ursel meet me. Both pretty as pictures. Schirach is also there. Short talk. Engel: paragraph 175.* Immediately handed over to the police.

Short drive around the Kahlenberg and the Leopoldsberg. Some fresh air during a pleasant stroll. Beneficial after so much stress.

No incursions into the Reich. Some activity over England. Thus return of pessimistic voices.

The Bismarck film is being given an enthusiastic reception everywhere, as expected.

Look round an exhibition of tapestries at the castle. A splendid display, enough to make one die of envy and covetousness.

Clock Museum of the City of Vienna. An unusual collection of clocks from all countries and all ages. Very interesting.

Some work, telephone calls and reading.

To the *Burgtheater* in the evening. *Romeo and Juliet*. With [. . .] and Gusti Huber. And Paul Hörbiger. Directed by Müthel. A quite wonderful performance. Müthel has really brought the *Burgtheater* back into a commanding position. Unfortunately he has problems with the critics and Vienna's troublemakers, which, however, I sort out on his behalf. He is very happy about this.

Carry on chatting for a long while at the hotel.

9 December 1940 (Monday)

Yesterday: We are scarcely able to do anything over England. The English, however, attack Düsseldorf with some success. Eight dead and some damage to buildings. England has more significant shipping losses. Our Italian allies continue to withdraw. This seems to be developing into a real catastrophe.

Concert by the Vienna Philharmonic under Knappertbusch. *Mazappa* by Liszt and a quite ravishing *Moldau*. The Philharmonic shines in the brilliance and mellowness of its string section. It is enchanting. Afterwards we treat ourselves to the *Domestica* by Strauss and then go for a bit of a stroll through Vienna. Such a fresh, wonderful Sunday midday.

Put the manager of the Vienna *Werkl*, a local cabaret, in his place. This establishment flatters itself that it can get away with sly subversion and typically Viennese griping. I draw the gentleman's attention to the dangers of his activities in no uncertain terms. He will be more careful from now on.

In the afternoon, deal with a mass of work that had been sent on from Berlin. But not much of any importance. Then a visit to the Schirachs. It is

* The section of the penal code dealing with homosexual offences.

very pleasant out there. A few others also visiting, people one can chat with very well. Members of the Vienna Philharmonic play Schubert's *Forelle* Quintet, the Emperor Quartet, and a few other musical miracles. A real treat for the ear. We are all delighted.

Theatre in Josefstadt, [. . .] *Eisheilige*. The piece very stimulating and acting quite masterly. Hilpert the guiding light.

And then back to Berlin. Chat on for a long time in the train.

10 December 1940 (Tuesday)

Yesterday: A glorious day in Berlin. We are two hours late.

Very heavy air raid on London. Some 600,000 kilograms. Entire districts of the city engulfed in flames. Only one aircraft lost. A really fine show. London is playing things down, but the American reports are strong and vivid. Nice to hear. The previous day they were talking about a decline in our offensive capability.

A few incursions into the Reich. Düsseldorf and also Mönchengladbach –Rheydt rather hard hit. But losses and damage not too serious. The Italians are still retreating. This affects their prestige, but also has a negative influence on the situation in the Mediterranean and the Balkans. The Führer is very angry and dissatisfied. He had a three-hour interview with Alfieri and told him clearly of all his doubts and worries. He had intended to see the Duce as well, and all the travelling arrangements were in hand, but Mussolini cried off. Said he was too busy. One can sympathise with him for not wanting to face the Führer at the moment. But things cannot go on like this. He is sacking one commanding officer after another. He should fire Ciano, and the Führer should do likewise with Ribbentrop. Both are vain poseurs and dilettantes. This becomes all too clear when they are given a great task to carry out alone and unaided. In any event, the Greek affair has now reached a point where something must be done.

England is still refusing to admit the devastating effects of our night attacks. Reports from New York, on the other hand, are becoming more horrific all the time. Morale over there must be very low. Here, on the contrary, it is rising day by day. It is even a little over-optimistic. I shall put something of a damper on the mood. Otherwise the people will believe that the entire thing will be over by Christmas.

Dr Dietrich reports to me on his trip to France. Everything is going well there so far as our work is concerned. Conflict between Abetz and the military administration. The Foreign Ministry is fomenting discord all over the place. An order from the Führer has granted Abetz special plenipotentiary powers. This he is now playing up for all it is worth. I tell Dietrich how I gave Ribbentrop a black eye. He is very pleased about it. The Führer intends to visit the front at Christmas. The *Bismarck* film now meets with his approval. It is being received with the greatest enthusiasm everywhere.

198

Gutterer reports: he has now sorted things out with the Foreign Ministry. A broadcasting attaché in Bucharest, Mathäi, has been engaged in the most bizarre activities aimed against me. I protest vigorously to the Foreign Ministry. One can only live on a war footing with these people. Gutterer has also made progress with the ministry's personnel problems. Hunke takes up his position on 1 January. Brauweiler is to take charge of the entire range of information services, and Maiwald becomes department head in charge of exhibitions.

Drewes has taken a middle course to solve the problem of payment for serious and popular music. I agree to this.

Film problems with Hippler. Newsreel already checked by the Führer. Question of film-script policy in the ministry. We must be very careful in this area. The gentleman concerned have too little contact with me. Several of the most recent films have been bad. But we must release films, or otherwise we shall have a general shortage.

Terboven calls me: he has reported to the Führer and fired off some heavy salvoes against the Navy. The Führer was all ears. He now wants a written report. I shall help Terboven with this.

Short chat with the children at home. And then deal with a lot of work that has piled up.

Terboven comes in the evening with his memorandum. It amounts to a massive attack on the Navy in Norway and its political experiments. The Navy is trying to play off Quisling against Terboven. This damages our position very seriously. Terboven has also brought into play the story of Böhme's ice-cold attitude towards me in Oslo. I cut out a few slanders which are dear to Terboven's heart but will do his cause no good. Thus the memorandum can go to the Führer.

Schmalz–Hannover arrives in a very excited state: he has been given a vote of thanks and sacked, and Lauterbacher has been named Gauleiter in his place. His whole life's work has been destroyed at a stroke. I comfort him a little and smooth the path for an interview with the Führer.

The film writer Gerhard Menzel is to receive 50,000 marks from me as a bonus for his excellent achievements. He is overjoyed.

Set the newsreel to music: it works very well. Especially impressive footage of the Request Concert and the battleship *Bismarck*.

Rough cut of Axel's film *Irish Tragedy*. Overall effect somewhat banal and cold. No great achievement. Axel must put in a lot more work on it. Then again, we have quite enough of these Irish films. The theme is not conclusive enough.

Then talk with Magda and afterwards with Ursel. Little sleep.

11 December 1940 (Wednesday)

Yesterday: Filthy weather. Hardly any daylight. Few incursions into the

Reich, and we are unable to do anything at all over England. This is a pity, because we would so much have liked to give London another pasting. The reports that are beginning to pour in about the big raid on London are horrendous. Herr Churchill would not have it otherwise.

Warship sunk overseas, more than 100,000 tons. So the edifice begins to crumble. One day England will see the light. The Italians seem to be fighting back on the Greek front to some extent. They will say no more than that. They are probably too ashamed. They have also been attacked in Africa by the English. Our transport aircraft have now arrived in Albania. A small help, at least. Italian losses are reckoned at about 10,000 dead. Now no one wants to be responsible. Ciano is trying to push it on to Badoglio, and Badoglio maintains that he was not consulted: an appalling orgy of dilettantism.

I have a thousand things to deal with. Wagner is resisting the new charter of the Bavaria company. But I cannot help him. We must have order and clarity. Only one person can give the orders, and in this case it must be me.

The Führer addresses the armaments workers at Borsig at midday. I fetch him. He is in the best of moods, takes a very optimistic view of the situation, has some bitterly ironic comments for the Herr Englishmen, and is looking forward to speaking to the workers. We drive out there in the pouring rain. The public greets him with delighted applause. The huge factory is packed with weaponry, while the people, only workers and no guests of honour, are beside themselves with enthusiasm. I give a short introductory speech. Then the Führer speaks: The contrast between plutocracy and our system. Brilliantly-hewn phrases. The applause is deafening. Determination to fight. Belief in the German people. Gratitude to the workers and farmers. We shall triumph. An incomparable speech. The Führer speaks as a man of the people. The scene is a glorious one: the Führer before his workers, flanked by monster weapons. He himself is absolutely thrilled and delighted. He is always at his best when speaking to ordinary people.

Triumphal drive through thronging masses back to the Reich Chancellery. The rain pours down the entire time.

The Führer's speech will put backbone into our entire nation. We shall now be able to make it through a few crucial weeks with some grace. Particularly because the Führer said that he wanted no prestige successes at the expense of human life. That got the loudest applause.

Discuss the Greek campaign with Jodl. His judgements on the military aspects of the affair are pessimistic. Rome has really put a spanner in our works.

The Führer is absolutely full of his speech. He now intends to speak more often. The people are his real audience. He knows them better than anything else. The so-called intelligentsia is not, as you would expect from its name, in the slightest intelligent.

We come round to talking about popular guidance and the problems it presents. The sexual problem worries the Führer greatly. Particularly where it affects the cities. What can a young person do in this respect? The problem solves itself in the countryside. Christianity has infused all our erotic attitudes with dishonesty. The so-called 'morality' of today is mostly nothing but hypocrisy. The erotic urge, next to hunger, is the most vital element in human existence. A fundamental urge that cannot be dismissed with a few banal maxims. We must view this question completely from the standpoint of popular health. That must be our morality. The Führer praises the Spartans in this respect, because they were hard, but also honourable and healthy. And nothing is right for everyone. What is acceptable in the city is not always acceptable in the countryside. One must act according to the intellectual range of the people involved.

The Führer stands for very clear, frank and unprudish views. He is the greatest popular educator that one could imagine. An hour packed with delights, during which I am able to learn a lot. He intends at some time in the future to have his opinions on these issues committed to writing. One important principle: marry young. The main thing for people is to have children. They remain whatever else happens, and help preserve the race.

Receive twenty-six neutral journalists based in Paris. I open myself up to their questions, which impresses them all profoundly. I give them information about the situation of the Reich, discussing any aspect they wish. Some ticklish questions are also asked, but I am able to parry them skilfully.

A lot of work with the Christmas parcels and gifts. I have to distribute them to the 120,000 soldiers and flak gunners in Berlin alone. But I enjoy it. And then the host of personal commitments. These are increasing from year to year.

Deal with masses of paperwork and memoranda. One drives into the office in the morning before first light, and then one comes back in the evening, long after the day is over, still loaded down with work. A real dog's life. That is why a little break to chat with Magda and the children does me so much good.

Churchill has stated in the House of Commons that the Italians are faced with a grave defeat in the Western Desert of Egypt. According to our information, he may well be proved right. And now this! Our fascist allies are turning into a real millstone round our neck! England is, of course, seizing the chance to rekindle hopes that had all but disappeared. Appalling!

Check sample excerpts from films in the evening. A Bavaria-film *In the Shadow of the Mountains*, a melancholy-dreary piece of froth.

And catch up on some sleep.

12 December 1940 (Thursday)

Yesterday: Bad weather. Few incursions into the Reich. None at all over England. Otherwise scarcely any military news. Relative quiet on the Greek front. But very bad situation in Egypt. England claims to have taken 6000 Italians prisoner at Sidi Barrani. Even so, the Italians' strategic situation is not all that bad. All they have to do is to act. But, but . . .

The Führer's speech very effective. Strong negative reaction in the USA. They feel offended, and rightly so. London maintains an embarrassed silence. Very pessimistic voices are being raised there again. I release very little of this for the press. Illusionism is on the increase again among the German people and is giving cause for concern. We must be constantly taking steps against it. We also give a lot of thought to what we can do for Italy in publicistic terms. The popular attitude in Germany towards Rome is very bad. But then the Italians are not making much effort to defend themselves. They seem to be rather shattered by it all. How the Duce must suffer from the incompetence of his entourage!

Discuss personnel matters with Gutterer. Things are now clear re. Brauweiler, Hunke and Maiwald. He is still negotiating with the Foreign Ministry.

Decree on nude shows published. Harsh penalties threatened.

Receive Dr Basch, leader of Germandom in Hungary. He reports on the devious policies of the magnates. A filthy crew! They intend to stab us in the back when they get the chance. Basch makes a good impression.

Speak to Flemish artists at the end of their tour of Germany. I explain our cultural principles to them. This they find very impressive.

Gerl and Bruvers report on the situation in Belgium, which has stabilised to a great extent. Degrelle is involved in some intrigues. Our people are doing excellent work. England is our opponents' last hope. But that will not last for ever, and soon we shall prove those hopes to be misplaced.

General von Haase, the new commander in Berlin, presents his compliments: an outstanding officer who has a very positive attitude towards the Party. We shall be able to work with him.

With the Führer. I give him an account of Basch's report, which causes him great exasperation. His speech is the main topic. He is annoyed by its reception in the USA, although it is no more than we could have expected. Perhaps he will soon allow us to attack America at will; that would be a real pleasure. The Japanese Foreign Minister has issued a statement to the effect that an American declaration of war against us would be followed by an immediate Japanese declaration of war against the USA. This has had a very sobering effect on Washington.

The Führer speaks to the Gauleiters: the war is as good as won from a military point of view. He describes our new weapons, our armaments potential, our U-boat construction programme, all of which are actually astonishing. England is isolated. Will gradually be beaten into the ground. She can no longer set foot in Europe. Just as last year he prophesied France's collapse, now he predicts England's. Nevertheless, he did not want this war and would be prepared to accept peace on any acceptable basis. No invasion planned at present. Command of the air necessary first. He is wary of water. Also, he does not like to try risky experiments if he can do without them. He wants to avoid heavy casualties. This is good and right.

Harsh words against Italy regarding the Greek undertaking. He warned them, was about to warn them again in Florence, but by then it was already too late. Everything badly prepared, in the end a huge loss in prestige. Situation in Egypt also rotten. The Italian military commanders have failed completely.

Russia continues to watch and wait, but we do not fear her. She had hoped to have all manner of things fall into her lap, and so had hoped for a long campaign in the West. But we were naturally ill-disposed to do her such a favour. Now the limits of our interests are clearly defined, particularly in the Balkans. New contingents of troops to Rumania. We shall let no one in there. The Führer states nothing but sober realities. And they tell us that the situation, with the exception of those aspects affected by the Italians, is thoroughly favourable. We have victory in our pocket, so long as we do not throw it away by our own mistakes.

The Führer speaks with a powerful faith that he transmits to his audience. A complete success. Now they will return to their labours with renewed strength.

Meyer from Münster wants money for his theatres. As does Eigruber from Linz, to whom I intend to give special help. Discuss press matters with Amann. The German press is in superb form, better than ever before. A successful result of our systematic work.

Discuss financial questions with Schwarz. He is still the loyal old comrade-in-arms, who has more merits than any of the braggarts. Our Reichleiters and Gauleiters in general are in fine fettle today. There are still a few bad apples among them, but the rest are real men of distinction.

The Italians have conceded the Sidi Barrani fiasco in their latest military communiqué. The English are drunk with victory. One can only comfort oneself with the fact that the Italians always suffer defeats but in the end always end up on the winning side. So it will be this time, too.

My interview with the Paris correspondents has been grotesquely distorted by Unipress. I have a denial rushed out for foreign consumption. Journalists are almost always reptiles. One can hardly ever tell them anything in confidence . . .

. . . Slave away until late in the evening. These days are filled with work and worry. Things will continue like this until Christmas. But then I intend to take things easy for a few days.

Newsreel very good. New Jugo film *Our Fräulein Doktor*. Pleasant, but not as good as the previous Jugo films. Somewhat carelessly made.

Read and write for a long while into the evening.

13 December 1940 (Friday)

Yesterday: Miserable weather. Raid on Mannheim, but without great significance. We attack Birmingham massively. More of the usual caterwauling from the enemy. A U-boat sinks 30,000 tons. That hurts them. Our U-boat programme is making huge strides. Soon we shall be invincible in this area.

A certain stalemate has descended on the Greek front. But in Africa serious losses for the Italians. London is already talking of 20,000 prisoners. That would be a catastrophe. Whatever the case, Italy is now a very worrying factor in our calculations.

The English ministers are now attempting to counteract the effect of the Führer's speech in a series of speeches of their own. Morrison babbles about a future Europe under English leadership. We go straight for the throat on this issue. Our polemical stock is back at a high level. Our enemies are trying to steal our ideas and take them for their own. Papen and Schleicher tried to do the same thing in 1932. The extent of their success is well known.

Our Reich Stattholders want their own budgetary powers, which will extend into the spheres of the individual Reich ministries. I oppose this vigorously so far as my own sphere is concerned.

Broadcasting problems with Glasmaier. He is working like a bee at the moment.

Schmidt–Decker reports on the propaganda effort of the AO. The Foreign Ministry is suffering defeat after defeat in that area as well.

Manage to shake out some substantial funds for theatres. Particularly those in the Eastern Territories, which need extra cultural support during these times.

Discuss the revision of school books with Bouhler. This has now become a problem with very far-reaching implications. I begin by pleading for the abolition of the so-called German Script. These days, our children have to learn eight different alphabets. And our 'German' script is a great barrier to German's becoming a real world language. Then a history book must be created for secondary schools, one of a kind which to all intents and purposes does not yet exist. Three lessons on religion, and not one history lesson: that is Rust's glorious achievement. It is enough to make one weep. This dilettante must be chased out of office. Bouhler has a great and fine task ahead of him. We can only hope that he does not build up a huge bureaucracy in the process. He has a strong tendency in that direction.

Rosita Serano has a few requests, which I am able to meet. She is a real vocal phenomenon. And an enchanting lady.

Choose Christmas gifts! Make Christmas arrangements along with Magda. The children are sweet. Unfortunately, one or the other of them is always ill.

The Führer has left for the Obersalzberg. A few days away from the turmoil. Things will become quieter from my point of view as a result.

Very hostile mood in Holland. Everyone there is placing hopes in England. And now the Herr Italians are supplying grounds for that hope. England is making a big propaganda effort in the USA. Churchill is heaping lie on lie. Lord Lothian has had his swansong and died of a heart attack. Grave loss for the English. There is talk in London of a cabinet crisis. Reasons and implications not specified. Therefore to be ignored for the moment.

Farinacci has launched a massive attack on Badoglio in the *Regime Fascista* on account of Greece. This is a bad way to behave in wartime. But the Italians have become nervous under the pressure of all the blows raining down on them. Mussolini is remaining absolutely silent. He must be going crazy with all these setbacks. The old fascists are horrified. We must do something to buck them up again. I give appropriate orders to the German press and radio.

Spend a long while in the evening with Naumann, catching up on work . . .

. . . The problem of Italy is causing us great worry.

14 December 1940 (Saturday)

Yesterday: No incursions into the Reich. Are the English tired? In contrast, we launch massive raids. 500,000 kilograms against Sheffield. Said to be worse than Coventry, according to our fliers' reports. The effect in London and particularly in the USA is devastating. London continues to press for an American entry into the war, the last hope at which she can clutch.

Italy is in a very depressed state. London claims to have recaptured Sollum. Italian public opinion blames Ciano, quite correctly. A certain degree of stalemate is discernible on the Albanian front. Italy is hoping for the intervention of the German Wehrmacht, and in the end we shall probably have no alternative. Morale at home is once again very good. Unfortunately, still too many illusions. I dampen things down further.

The press has turned my tips on big leader-articles to good account. In this rather difficult time we are working at full steam, bring every ounce of our intelligence to bear . . .

. . . A short speech to the leaders of the BdM.

Furtwängler is complaining about Karajan, who is getting too much fawning coverage in the press. I put a stop to this. In other respects, Furtwängler is behaving very decently. And when all is said, he is our greatest conductor.

At home, the children are all a little sick. Hedda has a severe bronchitis, and Holde is also in bed. Magda and Ursel are full of Christmas.

30,000 tons sunk. How long can the English continue to hold out? More rather pessimistic voices from London. They are trying hard to keep up appearances over there. But how long can it go on?

Draft speech for Blohm and Voss in Hamburg. Geared totally to the needs of workers in a city that is often threatened from the air.

Long talk with Naumann, who is deluged with job offers from all sides. But he does not want to leave me, and at the moment I cannot afford to let him go. He is a marvellous character and an absolutely indispensable colleague. Discuss the situation at the ministry and my personal plans with him. We are proceeding completely within the rules in this area. Talk over the re-organisation of our work with the Foreign Ministry. Even this seems to be falling into place now. And a lot of problems regarding Christmas. This year I am distributing gifts to something like 400,000 people: all the soldiers in Berlin, the flak batteries, and countless children. They are to have a celebration, despite everything.

Watch a Russian film about Lenin. Completely void of talent and ideas. Bolshevism is death to the soul. A German entertainment film provides a refreshing contrast. Christmas chatter with Magda and Ursel. Very late to bed.

15 December 1940 (Sunday)

Yesterday: Gloomy weather. No aerial activity on either side. But heavy sinkings. Reaction to the Sheffield raid is slowly emerging now. Horrendous. England is being dealt some very hard blows. London is drunk with victory because of Egypt. The situation there is still unclear. But the Italians have certainly suffered extremely heavy losses. Likewise on the Albanian front, where the Greeks are attacking relentlessly and in massive force. Our allies are a millstone round our neck! What will come of it all?

Hadamovsky has now managed to arrange reasonable transmission times after a deal of haggling with the Luftwaffe. Now we are superior to the English again. Now we can broadcast at full power. We have already made all the appropriate arrangements . . .

. . . Then at midday I drive out to Lanke with Magda and Ursel. Back there after such a long time. How happy I am!

After lunch, drive through the forest, which is already blanketed with the first snows. What peace, how relaxing! Here I can feel content. I inspect the various building works, which are going ahead at full speed.

Aggravation due to a number of errors that our office has committed. Intellectualism is the worst enemy of propaganda. I am constantly reaffirming this. Give [. . .] a dressing-down because he has allowed the magazines to stray too far from the correct line.

Darré has made a speech dealing with our food situation. We are well-placed in this respect, it seems. Report on morale: very firm following the Führer's speech. Everyone is now becoming used to the idea of a longer war. This is a good thing, and will help to avoid possible disappointments in future.

Check films: an idiotic production from the Bavaria studios, which I cannot watch for long. Schweikart has come up with several failures lately. Great pity!

Make a little music with the ladies. A few hours spent relaxing after such a tough week.

Laval has resigned. It was becoming impossible to keep him on, for domestic-political reasons. Flandin has taken his place. Pétain has declared that there will be no change in the policy of reconciliation with Germany.

But given the balance of power, this is fairly meaningless.

16 December 1940 (Monday)

Yesterday: Snow outside. Sun shining over it. What a glorious day!

Almost no incursions on either side. The weather prohibits any real activity in the air. So hardly any news from the fronts. Except that we have sunk another 70,000 tons. This is becoming a very serious problem for England.

The balloon has gone up in Greece again. The Italians have allowed their flank to be turned yet again. Where will it all lead? Things are not good in Egypt, either. It is true that the English are finding it difficult to advance further because of a shortage of reserves, but the Italians have lost virtually all of their motorised units. A difficult time for fascism, one in which it must prove itself.

Complete chaos in Vichy. Laval has been put under arrest. Flandin has become Foreign Minister in his place. It is probably true that Laval has no support among the people. His courting of Germany has been too blatant in its servility. No nation will put up with that kind of thing for long. Pétain has cabled the Führer to the effect that his policy towards Germany will not change. We shall see.

The Führer has had Napoleon's son, the Duke of Reichstadt, transported from Vienna to Paris. A gesture that will arouse a grateful response.

Midday and afternoon at Lanke. A short drive with the ladies. It feels like peacetime. Relative quiet on all fronts. And then this wonderful weather, this tranquillity and remoteness from the world. Sharp, hard frost. Winter is here. I hope that is does not last too long, beautiful as it is.

To Berlin. The children are back on the road to recovery, all of them sweet and delightful. Helga and Hilde are already wrapping up gifts for soldiers.

War situation: English bombing raid on Naples, quite successful. A fairly large unit hit. Things continue to go badly in Egypt. The worst thing is the psychological consequences. The Italians have really done us a bad turn in that respect. London is seizing on to this victory with all her might. She has nothing else, after all. We are torpedoing one English ship after another. The counter-blockade is beginning to take effect. The butter and meat rations in England are well below our levels. The English Minister of Food does nothing but issue hollow statements. This is the proud British plutocracy, which had intended to win the war from [. . .].

It goes without saying that new lies are being passed on to America every day. Now they would have us believe three unsuccessful German attempts at invasion, with 80,000 German casualties. And Churchill intends to spell out his war aims soon. Openly declared, on the model of Wilson. That is all we need. Let him take a tilt at us; we shall soon shut his mouth for him.

Newsreel in the evening: has not turned out quite so well. Will need some work. Forst's film *Operetta*. A huge hit. Lively and tuneful. But a pity that Forst plays the main role himself. He is not the type for today's tastes.

The [. . . s] are visiting. He has just returned from Italy. The mood there is very bad, feelings high against even Mussolini and particularly the fascist party. Ciano is the object of general hatred. He deserves it. Many people are on Badoglio's side. This is a very serious situation.

Spend a long time listening to [. . .'s] report. In the meantime, a short air-raid warning. Unimportant.

Late to bed. Two more air-raid warnings during the night. With some not altogether insignificant damage. It seems that the English have found their touch again. Two hours' sleep. Then back to the grindstone.

17 December 1940 (Tuesday)

Yesterday: A dazzlingly beautiful winter's day.

Rather heavy incursions into the Reich, including some damage to industry. In return, we drop 150 tons on Sheffield and a few on London. And so the game is under way again. A certain degree of stalemate on the Greek front, but a fairly bad situation in Egypt. There can be no question of a counter-offensive for several months to come. The Italians have suffered fairly significant losses. But we have dealt the English a few more body-blows with our torpedoes. Kretschmer has now sunk 250,000 tons in all.

London continues to lie her heart out in the most appalling fashion. I set the whole German news apparatus to work against this. Italy is already being written off in London. One is outraged and ashamed at the same time.

The problem of the children evacuated from Berlin has solved itself again. Our explanatory work has worked real wonders in this area.

Brauchitsch is trying to give himself a puff, but in the worst possible way. This harms him more than he deserves.

I purchase a number of maestro violins, so as to be able to place them at the disposal of suitable German violinists for life. A good cause.

Otherwise: put the finishing touches to my Hamburg speech. Write a leader article for *Das Reich* unmasking the English Lords. And work on a host of Christmas gifts.

At home, read a memorandum from the South Tyroleans directed against

Italy. The blood rushes to one's head. Reason tells one that nothing can be done, but the heart says otherwise.

Situation report of the Luftwaffe covering the past few weeks: here the achievements are so vast that no words of praise can do them justice.

Italy has begun to defend herself from a propaganda standpoint. The entire Italian press has gone on to the offensive, on orders from above. One positive development, at least. One must speak loud and clear during such times of crisis. *Laissez faire, laissez passer*, is poison. The fascist party has spoken; and it was high time.

Report on the domestic situation in England. According to this account, things look very bad there. But there can be no question of collapse in the immediate future.

Grave crisis in France. Laval's departure has stirred up a hornets' nest. No one knows where it will lead.

Discussion with Jannings. He is working on his Boer film like a man possessed. I see some rushes. By the looks of it, it will be a big success. The latest newsreel is good. 'Request Concert' film. Now it is more relaxed, good to look at and gripping. Another big success.

18 December 1940 (Wednesday)

Yesterday: No aerial activity over England. Incursions into South-West Germany. More than twenty dead in Mannheim and considerable damage. But still easily bearable.

Italy is taking a plucky stand against the English propaganda. We give her cordial support. It is about time.

Train to Hamburg. Work with Naumann during the journey. The broadcasting situation has already improved, both at home and in the occupied territories, as a result of Berndt's assignment. Berndt is extremely useful for these kinds of jobs.

I stipulate sizeable Christmas bonuses for my closest colleagues. They must have some sort of compensation for all their work and their ceaseless dedication.

Hamburg: big reception at the station. Kaufmann gives me an account of the situation. Morale good, despite the many air raids. No significant damage. The city continues on its timeless way. Kaufmann is doing an excellent job.

Drive to Blohm and Voss. Herr Blohm, a fine man and a real big businessman, shows me the shipyards. Everyone is working feverishly. Mainly U-boats. All for the Tommys. I talk with many workers. Their attitude is clearcut, honest, manly. Speech in the high machine-shed to the workers. At first typically Hamburg coolness, then wild applause. I give special attention to the social question. And our plans for after the war. Such simple people are my favourite audience.

Then discuss the situation with the gentlemen from Hamburg at the *Atlantik* hotel. I am able to answer a lot of questions and soothe away many doubts.

Back to Berlin. Dealt with accumulated and incoming work during the return trip.

Crisis continues in Vichy. Still no clear outcome so far as we can see. For this reason we have not yet allowed any mention of it in the press.

To the *Capitol* to watch the final part of the 'Schiller' film. A runaway success. Particularly for Caspar, whom I meet and get to know. A nice, modest young man.

Short chat with Magda at home. At the moment she thinks about nothing except Christmas. And then work on for a long while.

19 December 1940 (Thursday)

Yesterday: Several raids on South-West Germany. Ludwigshafen rather hard-hit. We are unable to do anything at all over England. In Great Britain they jump for joy at the fact. Stalemate on the Albanian front. Things seem to be consolidating. Everything still unclear in Egypt. But the English will not be able to advance much farther. We are lending the Italians powerful support in the press.

The 'Fritz' project (Gibraltar) postponed for the present. Franco is not pulling his weight. He is probably incapable of doing so. No backbone. And the domestic situation in Spain is anything but happy. The fact that we shall not have Gibraltar is a serious blow. Also, America has declared its readiness to help England on a much greater scale than hitherto. Roosevelt says that he will find a way around the payment problem. The English seem to be planning an attack on the Dodecanese. And a cargo-steamer carrying iron ore has been rammed in the Kaiser–Wilhelm Canal.* Big impediment to sea traffic. To put it plainly: a really bad day. But every day cannot be Sunday.

New line of attack against England implemented in the press. My article in *Das Reich* lays down the direction. Give Kurzbein short shrift on the subject of illustrations in the German press, which are very poor. For years now they have been publishing the same old material. Myself speaking in Hamburg, but no hint of an audience, which is the most interesting aspect.

Still musical chairs in Vichy. Laval is making a come-back, due to our pressure. At least he is no longer under arrest.

The report on theatres is again very positive. The theatres are putting on excellent productions, and audiences are as big as in peacetime. The Schiller film is having a wonderful reception from the critics.

The broadcasting situation has undergone a fundamental improvement, from the point of view both of the Reich and the foreign-language service. So

---

* The Kiel Canal, connecting the North Sea with the Baltic.

we succeeded in the end. I issue a statement on the subject. Our public will be delighted.

The Führer has returned to Berlin. I have too many commitments and have not yet seen him.

Major Martin complains bitterly to me about the meretricious and heavy-handed propaganda that Brauchitsch is allowing to be peddled around his own personality. This does indeed grate on the nerves. A conceited dandy!

Personnel matters with Gutterer. A number of points of information. Nothing important.

Lauterbacher pays his respects as new Gauleiter of Hannover. Things are at a pretty pass there. Rust has let everything go to the dogs, ignored his responsibilities, and Schmalz had no authority. Everyone has been ruling against everyone else. Now some order and direction is to be restored. I shall help Lauterbacher to the best of my ability. He deserves it, because he is a nice, steady boy, and he is not short of energy. But what are we going to do about Schmalz? . . .

. . . Rome is giving great prominence to my Hamburg speech. Wherever I said 'Germany', however, they have changed it to 'Axis'. That suits me. We must help the Italians at the moment. They deserve it, even though things are going badly for them.

Roosevelt is justifying his extensive aid for England. He is going to the limit, but he clearly cannot afford to risk open war.

Dictate speeches for the various Christmas celebrations during the afternoon. I am so tired after all the hustle and bustle that I long for rest. And there are all these preparations for Christmas, which take up so much time.

The Italians are fighting desperately in Egypt. Wild rumours in the entire world press. London is trying to turn Italy's setback into a big catastrophe. We counter-attack vigorously. The Italians were surprised by the English tanks at Sidi Barani. Their intelligence-gathering was clearly at fault.

Feeling in Greece: exaggeratedly pro-German. But this is purely tactical.

Feeling in Holland: hardening strongly against us. We shall have to win the war before we can achieve anything there.

England is wilting under the force of the German blockade. Her shipping losses are absolutely irreplaceable.

In the evening, check the new Christmas edition of the newsreel. Good, but not overwhelming. Then a few excerpts from productions in progress.

Work until late.

20 December 1940 (Friday)

Yesterday: Our wedding anniversary. I wake Magda early with flowers and gifts. She is delighted.

Situation: Few incursions into the Reich. More bombs on Ludwigshafen and Mannheim, two cities that are suffering greatly at the moment. We can do nothing over England because of bad weather. But the English have had to face more heavy shipping losses. They complain very loudly about it, but our press does not give them an inch.

I order still stronger support for Italy. We must give more prominence to the Axis, its purpose and goals, and not allow ourselves to be be sidetracked by the problems of the moment. Even Churchill is putting a brake on the euphoria. He is slowly becoming uneasy about the disproportionate effect that the victory in Africa has had on English public opinion. Things have consolidated in Albania. We are flying 1000 Italians over there every day in our transport aircraft. And from 1 January our offensive will start to move. Then the Greeks will start to feel the pinch.

Perhaps they will prefer not to offer resistance at all. In any case, there will soon be no more victory celebrations.

The Bulgarians have urgent designs on Macedonia. And a hatred of Yugoslavia that binds them to us. They are also frightened of Turkey and do not trust themselves to join us openly. Moreover, they are not very well armed, and the deliveries that we have promised are being delayed.

I think we should have things moving again by the first weeks of January.

The coal situation does not seem to give cause for concern at the moment. Everything seems to be going smoothly.

Ban on dancing for three days in the week now lifted at my instigation. A good thing in itself, and also serves to raise morale.

We shall have to cut the religious scenes from the 'Alcazar' film. Otherwise we shall have nothing but trouble.

Imhoff shows me the badges for the next Winter Aid collection.

Dictate speech for New Year. I intend to relax completely for a few days over Christmas and get some real rest.

Discuss a number of matters with Colonel Schmundt. So far as he and [. . .-. . .] are concerned, the Bismarck film is too Prussian. I do not agree and therefore make no changes. The new Wehrmacht film about the Western Campaign is ready except for some editing. Hesse wants to release it straight away. I continue to put a brake on things. Hesse is too hasty, a tendency which is also clear in his propaganda for Brauchitsch, which is doing more harm than good.

I launch a savage attack on *Landesgericht* President Braune, who played a prominent part in the Leipzig Reichswehr Trial* and is now active in the High Command. The Führer, who joins us, takes a very keen interest in the discussion and condemns Braune, who is still employed by Canaris, in the strongest terms. He mocks his [. . .] stupidity and expresses some opinions

* In 1930 three young Reichswehr (army) officers were tried before the Supreme Court of the Weimar Republic at Leipzig on charges of disseminating Nazi propaganda in the armed forces. Hitler appeared personally in their defence and turned the trial into a major political confrontation.

about justice that would make a maiden blush. Justice alone cannot protect a state. One must always have a substitute to hand, as we have in the concentration camps. What games we played with justice when we were still in opposition! Juristic habits lead to a total deformation of thinking. Sound instinct is suppressed in favour of haggling over every little clause. Woe to the state that falls victim to justice.

Now Braune will probably meet his downfall.

Jodl gives me an account of the military situation. Italy is back in a slightly better position. We are giving them a great deal of help. A large number of our Luftwaffe units are waiting in Southern Italy, ready to intervene in North Africa. The danger in Albania is no longer so immediate. And we shall be showing our faces there soon.

Work at home. Make some revisions and read. Things are slackening off slightly.

A little chat session with Magda to mark our anniversary.

Churchill speaks to the House of Commons. A pompous victory fanfare over Egypt. But he will not have that pleasure for long. Otherwise he speaks in very gloomy terms about English shipping losses, which he has every reason to do.

Ryti elected President in Finland. How long will the Finns be able to resist Russian pressure?

Check cultural films. We are far ahead of the rest of the world in this field. Our productions are nothing short of models of their kind. Latest newsreel, although it has taken a while, very good. Schweikart's *Girl from Fanö*. A hugely complicated story about fisherfolk with a psychological background. Just the way I had pictured North Sea fishermen, I must say! These dreadful literary types! The Bavaria studios, and Schweikart, will have to look very smart from now on. Otherwise things will not go well for them.

Then a long chat with Magda. Later, Ello arrives from Paris and has a lot of news to tell us. She is as witty and charming as ever.

(No entry dated 21 December)

22 December 1940 (Sunday)

Friday: Churchill's speech is insolent, but not without talent. I have it torn apart by the press and the radio. Few incursions into the Reich. Absolutely nothing over England. But more important sinkings. Things in Albania still give no cause for rejoicing. Likewise in Africa. The Italians have lost over [. . .] men taken prisoner there alone.

The KdF is charging too high prices. The public is complaining about it. I intervene.

Row between Furtwängler and Karajan. Karajan is getting himself fêted in the press. Furtwängler is right. He is, after all, a world figure. I put a stop to it.

213

Find a new press adviser, Dr Semler. Hellensleben is not up to the job.

With the Führer. He has had more problems with lawyers. They have severe laws for use in wartime, but they do not use them. Hand down prison sentences where death would be appropriate. Without the death penalty things are impossible in wartime. We were only able to deal with the kidnapping problem, for instance, by very severe penalties. Either the criminal fears the state, or the state must fear the criminal. We are in favour of the former alternative.

We discuss issues affecting the theatre. The Führer is very interested. He explains such phenomena as Mahler or Max Reinhardt, whose abilities and achievements he does not deny. The Jew can often be quite successful when it comes to mimicry.

Berlin's anti-aircraft defences are to be strengthened further. Better to spend more on flak than on clearing work. How long will the war last? The Führer hopes that it will end in 1941. But who knows? We intend to be prepared for any eventuality.

In the evening we watch the Wehrmacht's film about the campaign in the West. It has not turned out to be entirely satisfactory. No clear line. And insufficient emphasis on the co-operation between the various branches of the Wehrmacht. I am against its being released straight away. The Führer agrees.

He tells stories about the Western Campaign. About the dramatic break-through at Sedan, on which the outcome of the war depended. Everything depends on having the right start, a thesis that Italy is proving at the moment, if only by default. Italy has made a bad start wherever she has fought: first Abyssinia, then France – not occupying Savoy at the outset – and then Albania and Somaliland. Matchless amateurism. The Führer has some harsh words to say on the subject. The Italians have brought the entire military prestige of the Axis crashing down in ruins. That is why the Balkan states are being so obstinate. The Italians are, after all, a Romance race. Now we shall have to attack. Not to help them, but to chase out the English, who have now established themselves on Crete. They must be thrown out of there. The Führer would prefer to see peace between Rome and Athens. But he can hardly tell them so. Mussolini is now completely stuck fast in this imbroglio. He has serious domestic difficulties to contend with: the priests are stirring up trouble, as are the Jews and the nobility. If only he had occupied Crete at the outset, as the Führer advised him to do. But Rome is [. . .] The Führer is drafting a detailed letter to Mussolini outlining the situation as he sees it.

We talk for a long time about the new weapons which are now being put into production. They will provide a few surprises.

America, the Führer believes, will not enter the war. Fear of Japan. But neither does the Führer have much desire to cross to England. He is shy of water. He will only do it as a last resort.

Air-raid warning. We carry on talking in the air-raid shelter. Niemöller is asking for leniency. No question of it. Let him eat well, get fat, so that no one can mistake him for a martyr. But he won't be let loose on the human race again. He should have thought of that earlier.

We discuss Prussia's mission in the creation of the Reich, which the Führer values very highly. But only a South German and a Catholic could have completed the great work of German racial unity.

We recall the 'Princess' Hohenlohe, who has now been deported from the USA, quite penniless. Wiedemann became quite sexually infatuated with her.

The air-raid warning lasts until 2 a.m. We have used it to discuss the entire situation in rare peace and quiet.

Then a short chat with Magda at home. Then another two air-raid warnings during the night, until 7 a.m. Not pleasant with all the children, some of whom are still sick. Only two hours' sleep. I am so tired.

Yesterday: Some damage in Berlin. Including part of the cathedral, two factories. The theatre in Potsdam. Otherwise few incursions into the Reich. We drop 200 tons on Liverpool. It was high time. Horrendous fires. Low-level precision flying. That always hits them especially hard.

The Italians are having to retreat again in Albania. This will not last much longer. Our transports are already on the move. 30 trains a day. We shall spice the Herr Englishmen's soup. But we cannot do much in Egypt, and things there are not exactly perfect. The Italians have not been able to match the English techniques of motorised warfare. But that was also something that they should have thought of before.

Report from the USA: Roosevelt does not want to take the risk of war. I don't believe that he will, either. And the feelings of the people at the top there are anti-English, at least in part.

The Times publishes a letter from the churches containing peace proposals. Completely vague and not worth discussing. But nevertheless notable as a symptom. I do not believe that this is a peace-feeler, but perhaps an attempt to gauge the lie of the land.

The agreement between myself and the Foreign Ministry is not yet signed and sealed. The Foreign Ministry keeps shifting its ground. But I do not let it get me down. I have time.

Visit Wodarg: he is much better now, and is extremely pleased to see me again. He is a fine fellow!

Some of the children are still sick. I [. . . . . .]. And all the exhausting work for Christmas. It never lets up.

My article in *Das Reich* is widely quoted and commented on in the Italian press. These days, Rome is grabbing at any straw.

A Jew Law has been passed by the Sobranje.* Not a radical measure, but

* The Bulgarian parliament.

nevertheless something. Our ideas are on the march throughout the whole of Europe, even without compulsion.

Our Christmas ships have arrived right up as far as Narvik and have given tremendous pleasure. I worked on that project with genuine pleasure.

Terboven comes for a conference in the afternoon. He complains about the Navy, who are still causing trouble for him. The situation in Norway has, of course, become more tense in the wake of the Italian 'victories'. Terboven has much to put up with from Lutze, as we all do. He is a decent fellow, but too quarrelsome for my taste.

Terboven intends to open a German Theatre, mainly for grand opera and operettas. I shall give him vigorous support. Mainly because of the strong cultural-propaganda effect of such an institution . . .

. . . In the evening, the pace of work slackens. Peace reigns all around me. I am looking forward to a little rest and relaxation. I shall enjoy these as never before. The war has drained us all tremendously.

Now I must spend a little time restoring lost energy.

23 December 1940 (Monday)

Yesterday: Long, refreshing sleep. I feel reborn.

Moderate incursions into the Reich. No serious damage: Berlin is untouched. But we attack Liverpool with 250 bombers. Demoralising results. Sets London whining again. Relative quiet in Albania and Africa. I receive a report on the domestic situation in Italy. It must be totally bleak. Church, aristocracy, the Jews, even part of the working class against Mussolini. Already having serious disciplinary problems in the army. The royal family want a Latin bloc, including France. Of all nations! The aristocrats are stupid, and treacherous into the bargain. But these days the masses' sense of humour, which is merely a disguised form of anger, is not sparing even Mussolini. Things will, of course, improve when we intervene in the Balkans. Mussolini has no easy task in trying to make the Italians into a warlike race. 'They are no Prussians; hardly even Saxons!', as a witty painter from Dresden, Kriegler, told me recently.

I busy myself with reading, and write a leader-article for *Das Reich*, in which I let rip against the British plutocracy and especially Churchill.

Alfieri and his wife visit us in the afternoon. He is very depressed, and I cheer him up a little. There are too many idiots among us who cannot keep their mouths shut. They talk quite openly in front of the Italians to the effect that feeling against Rome here is very bitter, that we would far rather be allied with France, etc. I talk him out of such nonsense. Emphasise the strength of the Axis and our friendship, explain that this is the feeling of the Führer and the people, but make no bones about the fact that a number of things have displeased us. He understands this completely. I cite Farinacci's article attacking Badoglio, which could only have had a harmful effect so far as Mussolini's authority was concerned. He concedes the truth of this. But, he says, the Duce had consulted the generals before embarking on the Greek project, and Badoglio had expressed no objections. The commanders had even talked of a stroll down to Athens. And then when the catastrophe struck, Badoglio went absent, and anyone who was prepared to listen was told that he had been against the undertaking. If this is true, then Badoglio is guilty of infamous behaviour, but Farinacci is guilty of stupidity. History passes verdicts on wars. The people, however, must never so much as suspect that mistakes have been made. Otherwise it loses faith in the cause, and it is the people who must, of course, die for it. Alfieri intends to send a cable detailing all this to the Duce, who is very grateful to me for the attitude of the German press. I shall continue, indeed redouble my efforts, to ensure that no hint of discord creeps into our relations. Alfieri is very grateful to me. He leaves visibly relieved. I believe that this conversation was very valuable.

Carry on dictating and reading for a long while. MacDonell's *Self-Portrait of a Gentleman*. Simply horrifying. One can feel nothing but outrage as one finishes the book.

We launch more attacks on the capitalistic character of the English plutocracy in the press. The London press gives us plenty of ammunition.

The USA intends to impound our ships, on England's behalf. We declare at the press conference that this would be a very grave matter. A great outcry in the American press because of this. Journalists are so corrupt that it stinks to high heaven.

A quiet pre-Christmas evening.

It is only now that I notice how tired and battle-weary I am.

24 December 1940 (Tuesday)

Yesterday: Forty-five dead in Berlin after the last air raid. So considerable losses, after all. As a result, I do not allow an extension of bar opening-hours, even for New Year. Only a few incursions last night. But we launch a massive raid on Manchester with 360 bombers. Also very high figures for shipping sunk. Great howl of pain in the London press.

Halifax is going to Washington as ambassador. Eden succeeds him as Foreign Minister. So now the old warmongers are back where they belong. I have Eden attacked in the press in the strongest terms.

Italy still retreating in Albania. The situation remains serious in Africa, too. Comprehensive report from Graziani to the Duce. Trying to excuse what is scarcely excusable. Nevertheless, I issue fresh instructions for the press to keep out of the affair, particularly in view of my conversation with Alfieri. One day we shall be rewarded.

Göring writes offering me the State Theatre for use in entertaining the troops, a favour which I accept gladly. I must involve myself with the theatre again and organise some tours. Schlösser is working well and proving reliable.

Film returns: box-office situation good, almost all films returning good profits. Except for the Bavaria studios, who have had a number of depressing failures. I shall have to put things right there at some stage.

The coal situation has improved greatly. No cause for concern at present. But, all the same, I forbid the press to gloat or boast. Prudence is the mother of wisdom. In general, the press must operate with more psychological finesse in many areas. It often takes short cuts, and the resultant follies wreak havoc with public morale.

I give my new essay to the *V.B.*, because it must have something from me now and again. It could do with it.

Visit an art exhibition organised by Schweitzer. A very respectable standard. I buy a few pictures. A painting by Padua, 'Mars and Venus', is somewhat daring and also rather clumsy. The Führer had it removed in Munich, and I do the same in Berlin.

Christmas party at the ministry with [. . .] . . .

[The rest of the entry undeciphered]

25 December 1940 (Wednesday)

Yesterday: Churchill makes an appeal to the Italian people to dissociate itself from Mussolini and join the House of Savoy in making peace. The old intriguer and traditional plutocrat. I have the German press give him the answer he deserves. The USA squeezes a drop more drama out of this absurdity.

General Oshima is coming to Berlin as Japanese Ambassador. The right man. Proof that Japan is with us and will stay with us. Few incursions into the Reich. Danger of icing-up too great. But we put up a strong show over England. Manchester attacked again with 200 tons, and London too, though less extensively. The main thing is to give them no respite. A number of heavy shipping losses. And our U-boat programme will only start to bite in February. Churchill will be amazed.

No new alarums from the African and Albanian fronts. Things seem to be settling down slowly in that quarter. Italy has forfeited her entire military prestige in the world's eyes.

Yet again, spend hours processing trivial paperwork. The department chiefs, showing a brilliant sense of timing, have deluged me with memoranda for Christmas. Plus this flood of Christmas mail, at least some of which ought to be dealt with.

Make some decisions on broadcasting problems. The English are planning to invade all our frequencies at a predetermined moment. I take appropriate countermeasures.

All the noise about 'sacred Christmas'. Chance would be a fine thing.

But there are positive aspects: People's Christmas for the children at the *Theatersaal*. I speak to the people over the radio. A quite simple speech. And then distribution of gifts to the children, amid much rejoicing. Magda and the children are busy helping.

Christmas with the police at the Brandenburg Gate. I give a short speech and express my thanks for their service, protection and help.

And in the evening to a flak battery at Teltow, at the gates of Berlin. First I inspect the battery's position with Colonel–General Weise. An imposing sight. Here is our protection. Then a very atmospheric Christmas party in the barracks. Wonderful music. I thank the flak briefly for providing our shield and protection. And then hand out an absolute mountain of gifts.

I feel most at ease among such simple people.

Churchill's speech directed at the Italians has been seized on by the entire American press. One can see, then, what purpose it was serving. The House of Savoy has said not a word about it so far. Monarchy-[. . .] We can be very grateful that we have a popular form of government.* The German press gives Churchill the proper answer. Not to mention our Luftwaffe. The reports from Manchester are horrendous. This is hell. Now we intend to hold our peace until 27 December.

Home late in the evening. Distribution of presents to the staff and the children. Great joy in all quarters. But I am glad that the entire Christmas commotion is over.

Now I hope I shall have at least a few days' rest.

Little chat with Ello. She tells me all the local gossip. Very pleasant and entertaining.

The children have gone to bed, in transports of delight.

I am so tired.

Glorious sleep!

26 December 1940 (Thursday)

Yesterday: First day of Christmas. Military situation absolutely quiet. No air activity on either side. The peace of God, agreed but unspoken.**

Hess has delivered a Christmas Address. Nothing of importance.

We drive out to Lanke at midday. To leave all our cares behind us for

---

* *Volkstaat*: literally 'people's state' but with overtones of the organic, folkish community. Clearly Goebbels, in drawing the contrast, would wish to avoid the hated word 'republic', with its Weimar associations.

** An informal bombing truce, to extend from Christmas Eve to 27 December 1940, was agreed through diplomatic channels in Washington.

once. Two-hour drive during the afternoon with our new horses, a tour through the snow-bedecked landscape. How refreshing!

Then reading, music, and talk until late in the evening. With Magda, Ello and Ursel.

No news from the political world or the war.

I am totally happy out here in tranquillity and solitude. A few days' relaxation, and then the engine will run well again.

27 December 1940 (Friday)

Yesterday: Quiet everywhere. No military activity. As I had expected.

The King of England and Pétain have both made speeches. Nonsense and slogans. Unimportant.

Sleep, rest, relaxation. It is snowing outside. Stroll through the wintry forest. Ello is at home, we are here quite alone, Magda and I, Ursel and Heiduschke.

This is indescribably pleasant and cosy.

Read a lot that I scarcely had a chance to get around to before. No interruptions from cables or telephone calls. How good it feels!

And a hint of longing for peace. But that we shall have to fight for, not dream about. It is the surest way.

28 December 1940 (Saturday)

Yesterday: Long, blissful sleep. It has snowed. Beautiful, white forest!

The Führer was at the front with his troops all over Christmas.

Churchill's hypocritical appeal to the Italian people is still being given a lot of attention in England and the USA. But it will get him nowhere. Rome has issued a very uncompromising reply. The wildest rumours – peace, reduction of tension, etc. – are floating around the world. The Christmas psychosis! I let none of them into the Reich.

No military operations on our part. The English attack cities in Belgium and France. Excellent grounds for retaliation. In any case, we give it a big splash in the press. The English stayed away because of the weather, then, and not because of Christmas. We can exploit this kind of opportunity very well.

Things are still in a state of flux in Albania and Greece. The Italians are making a big effort at the moment. Our transporters are rolling into Rumania. The press in the USA is already making a big noise about it.

At midday, deal with the most urgent matters in consultation with the gentlemen from Berlin. Following on the holiday, there is not much. And I put anything unimportant straight into the pending tray.

A lot of aggravation with the staff. This is all I need, just when I am on leave.

Stroll and a drive through the frost-covered forest. Clear my lungs. And spend a long time discussing and exchanging ideas with my people.

Nothing of importance in the political world. Only that Churchill is trying to intrigue against us, not just in Italy but in all the European countries. The English always try to win their wars in this way. But this time they will not succeed.

Today, back to Berlin for a few hours.

29 December 1940 (Sunday)

Yesterday: Into Berlin early. Snow and frost. The Führer was here for a day and has now gone off to the Obersalzberg.

Few incursions into the Reich. Too much danger of icing-up. But we are able to hit London very hard with around 150 tons. Great gloom in England. They had thought that the Christmas truce would continue. The psychological effect is enormous.

We suppress Brauchitsch's Christmas speech. As a camouflage measure. He had said that the Channel did not present a serious barrier.

My essay attacking Churchill appears in the *V.B.* Works extremely well.

I send the German Opera House company to Holland for propaganda purposes. Slight difficulty over whether Roder should continue to sing the Sachs. I leave things as usual for this time.

Otherwise, some more Christmas reading. This mass orgy of correspondence at Christmas is a nuisance that robs one of one's rest.

To Lutze's fifty-sixth birthday. He has earned the honour. We have a long, cordial talk. I give him a film projector, which we try out straight away with the latest newsreel. A lot of people there, particularly from the SA. Stout fellows from the time of struggle, bursting with the best of intentions and glowing with idealism. The only problem is an occasional lack of intellectual insight and breadth of vision. But all the other things are very important, if not more so.

Back to Lanke with Helga and Hilde, who are overcome with joy. Then there is a reunion with mummy for the little ones. Now, at least, we have them out here with us. Work at all sorts, get rid of paperwork. Then read copiously.

Our troop transports to Rumania are causing a stir in the world press, particularly in the USA. Sensation! We keep quiet about them, as a camouflage measure. The USA is sliding increasingly into war-psychosis. But will Roosevelt actually declare war? I have strong doubts on that score.

Newsreel in the evening. Not exactly overwhelming. But it is Christmas and a slack period. One has to be content with what one can get.

And they call a day such as this 'relaxing'.

30 December 1940 (Monday)

Yesterday: Scarcely any air activity on either side. The weather is too bad.

In Albania the Italians have launched some attacks, but the Greeks are attacking even harder. The English intend to land a division.

Bardia* will be able to hold out for a time, but not for ever. They still have provisions for a month. An entire Italian division is at risk there.

The entire world is full of peace-rumours. But no substance. Great conjecture about Roosevelt's foreign-policy speech. The USA is moving closer to war.

A grey day out here. I do some reading, dictate a leader-article for *Das Reich*. There is always something to do. In it I attack Churchill for his attempt to seduce Italy. That will do the Italians some good.

Fairly extensive sinkings reported. Close on 50,000 tons. The Waldeggs come visiting. With a cute brood of children. He tells me some interesting things about the Navy at war. Räder has a lot of no-hopers in his outfit, and could well be one himself.

Newsreel in the evening. Turned out well, after all. Give Hippler a number of tips, particularly re. the Berlin milieu in our film dramas.

And then a lot of routine jobs.

Already no question of leave or relaxation.

31 December 1940 (Tuesday)

Yesterday: Roosevelt makes a scurrilous speech aimed against us, in which he slanders the Reich and the Movement in the most boorish fashion and calls for the most extensive support for England, in whose victory he firmly believes. A model of democratic distortion. The Führer still has to decide what to do about it. I would be in favour of a really tough campaign, of finally pulling no punches towards the USA. We are not getting far at present. One must defend oneself sometime, after all.

We have very few incursions and no bombs. But our Luftwaffe carries out massive raids on London and Portsmouth. London trembles under our blows. The press in the USA is thunderstruck. The best possible response to the English Christmas raids and Roosevelt's speech. If only we could keep up bombing on this scale for four weeks running. Then things would look different. Apart from this, there are heavy shipping losses, successful attacks on convoys, and so on. London has nothing to smile about at the moment, that is for sure.

No significant change in Albania and Africa.

Report from Paris. Our propaganda there is wearing itself out with trivialities. It is totally lacking in a wider perspective. One has to be born to it, have a brain and great imagination. I am disappointed most of all with

* A port on the North African coast, just inside Italian Libya.

222

Wächter. In the Unoccupied Zone. Pétain is making desperate attempts to build bridges to the people. Now he intends to establish a Propaganda Ministry as well. But for that he will need a Propaganda Minister, a great idea, and a lot of daring. France, in her senility, lacks any of these things.

Fink in the Hague is doing a good job. He is one of our old school. People with that background are irreplaceable. Neumann is on leave. Spieler and Schaumburg have not shown themselves equal to the demands of work in the ministry. I must keep an eye on them, too.

Big fire at the Anhalter Station. Large parts of the station burned to the ground. Cause still unknown. I have this matter rigorously investigated.

To Berlin at midday. Make my New Year speech on to a recording machine. So that I do not have to come back tomorrow. A whole mass of work has piled up for me at the ministry. But I deal with it in no time. Naumann is back. He is a very valuable help to me.

The fire at the Anhalter Station is not traceable to sabotage. Lord be praised!

Horrendous reports of the devastation in London. Does good in view of the impudent arrogance of the English during the past few days.

Vichy has issued a soothing disclaimer to counter lies about Franco–German relations. Almost all the lies stemmed from London.

Roosevelt's speech has been given an ambiguous reception even in the USA. We make no mention of it.

Première of *Request Concert* at the *Ufapalast am Zoo*. A big crowd invited. The film meets with a magnificent reception. I am all the more pleased because the idea for it came from me. Another job well done.

The most pleasing thing is the extraordinary common touch which the film shows. It will kindle a spark throughout the German people.

I stay on for a while to be with the artistes, who are overjoyed at their success. Then back to Lanke through a savage snowstorm.

Sometimes I hate the big city. How beautiful and cosy it is out here.

Sometimes I would like to never have to go back.

The children are waiting for us at the door with hurricane lanterns.

The snowstorm rages outside.

All the better to chat by the fireside.

It troubles my conscience that we have things so good out here.

But then I shall soon have to be back on the treadmill.

(Here the extant text for 1940 ends.)

Part Three

1941

The diaries are extant from the beginning of February to the second week of July 1941, dramatic months of a new Blitzkrieg in the Balkans and preparations for the invasion of Russia that took place in June.

Less is on view of the private Goebbels; he is almost entirely absorbed in his work. Magda Goebbels spends a lot of time travelling, while his children are in Austria, where he grants them one brief visit.

On the other hand, Goebbels is increasingly concerned to note every detail of the war's progress, and there is a great deal to report, whether it be air raids at home, or jockeyings among the Nazi leadership for plum posts in the coming German world-empire, or the seemingly inexorable progress of the Wehrmacht in South-Eastern Europe and North Africa and, at the end, in the Soviet Union.

The depressed, insecure man of January 1939 seems to have been banished; Goebbels revels in his power, his skills, and his cunning. He is moving back to the centre of the stage. With the invasion of Russia, he can finally cast off his inhibitions and return to his old role as anti-communist agitator, calling Germany and Europe to arms against the Red Peril. There is a sense, expressed openly several times, that Nazi Germany has gone too far to return to the normal community of nations and that the battle is for life or death. It was in that struggle after 1941 that Goebbels, the propagandist of total war, found his element.

(1 January – 9 February missing)

10 February 1941 (Monday)

Yesterday: Little air activity. The English attack Stavanger. We shoot down two of them. We attack Malta in several waves. Two aircraft lost. Reuter reports that English ships shelled Genoa in the early morning. Otherwise quiet. No news in the political world, either.

I am having serious problems with the press leadership. Nothing but blue pencil and lacklustre attitudes in that quarter. Fritzsche has no talent for going out and putting fire in people's bellies during slack periods. The picture work is also extremely poor. I receive eleven photos from Hamburg, for instance. I am the only thing in sight on them; the meeting that I was addressing does not feature at all. I shall have to goad the press into action. The journalists' excuse is always: nothing is happening. But when something does actually happen, they cover only the superficial aspects and completely miss the core of the story.

This constant need to be on the alert can drive one to distraction. I hate to think what will happen when the few live wires are gone. The entire journalistic scene will subside back into the old, deadening tedium. No one makes any attempt to encourage the journalists at the press conference. All they hear is: forbidden, classified, undesirable. If things go on like this, the nation will fall asleep in the middle of the war.

I have a lot of bones to pick with the *DAZ*.* The paper behaves as if we were still at peace. I shall sort it out.

Laval has refused to enter Pétain's cabinet as a Minister without Portfolio. The Vichy crisis, this storm in a tea-cup, drags on.

Hess makes a speech in Breslau to mark Hanke's assumption of office as Gauleiter there. His address contains nothing new.

Some visitors in the afternoon, and some talk. Ello, the Jugos and Hommels. I hear a whole lot about the film world and Berlin society. The usual twaddle.

Newsreel: this time rather mediocre.

Clips from *Ohm Krüger* by Jannings. Very good. This will be a hit.

An American film, *Public Opinion*. Excellent. They can do this sort of thing over there, without thinking twice about it.

Then read on until late in the evening. And a hard week begins once more.

11 February 1941 (Tuesday)

Yesterday: No air activity on either side. We attack a few English airfields. The bombardment of Genoa turns out to have been very heavy. The Italians report 72 dead, and the English claim to have fired 300 tons of shells on the port. Rome had prior knowledge of English intentions, and units of the Italian fleet were on their way, but it seems that they arrived too late. The affair is highly mysterious. The Italians seem to exist in a state of complete chaos. Our naval liaison officer is screaming blue murder about it.

The fronts are stable in Albania. But things look very ominous in Africa. The English are 600 kilometres from Tripoli. The Italians want to make their stand there, and no sooner, while we are demanding that they turn and fight much earlier, and are offering aid to that end. But we have not been able to talk reasonably with Rome for a long time now.

The English are advancing from a number of directions in Abyssinia. And

* The *Deutsche Allgemeine Zeitung*. A Berlin daily newspaper.

rebellions are breaking out among the natives 260 kilometres from Addis Ababa, but the Italians still hope to suppress them.

Churchill has made a speech. Insolent and certain of victory. At the height of his illusory triumph. Completely sure of US support. Packed with poison for the Italians. A skilful speech, but one with little substance behind it. We shall answer loud and clear. I issue exact instructions for the way the attack is to be conducted. I hope the press will respond well.

I express the strongest criticism of the press in the Ministerial Conference. It is too lax, lacks fighting qualities, which means that it is constantly on the defensive, and insists on publishing worthless articles about society events in Rome, as if there were no war on. Its photos are poor and mostly miss the point entirely. And my instructions are followed half-heartedly, at best. In short, a general lethargy. I create merry hell. Fritzsche is quite stunned and comes to see me later with Dr Bömer. Then I let rip. Gutterer gives me magnificent support. Fritzsche tries to push most of the blame on to Dr Dietrich and Sündermann: he says that they have been lecturing the press lately instead of inspiring them to fight and attack. This is not my concern. I want an offensive spirit. We must talk to the people, not to a few dozen intellectuals. I hope that my Philippic has done some good. From now on, it must be into step and off to fight the enemy. We shall soon regain the propaganda initiative from the English.

Willkie has issued an appeal: all possible material aid to England, or she will lose the war. Despite this, Bömer insists that Willkie is our friend. A nice friend! Admittedly, his speech does not bode well for England.

Discuss reform of the Request Concert with Glasmaier. It is too philistine, uses too many foreign performers, and the fare it serves up is often mediocre. Besides which, too many official departments are blowing their own trumpets in the breaks between the performances. I shall make Goedecke directly responsible to Glasmaier and take more control myself . . .

. . . Discuss personnel problems with Gutterer. We must put a few Nazis at Schmidtke's elbow, or the whole thing will go to blazes. He is resisting this, of course, but it will do him no good. He must. Because he hardly understands anything about propaganda. At best, he is a good censorship officer.

Gutterer is glad that Rosenberg has protested at the idea of a Seventh Chamber. He had never liked the project, anyway. Now Ley is trying to counter-attack.

By midday I am quite exhausted by the continual in-fighting. We have been through a spring-cleaning operation, so to speak. Now, however, I hope that the change will be noticeable. I am hoarse, tired and tense.

Carry on working at home. Correct articles and press proofs. There seems to be no end to it. If only one had even a few people with whom one was in complete accord, and whom one could rely on unconditionally.

Packing and travel-fever on the part of my wife and children. The entire house is full of it. Off on Wednesday, and then I shall be alone in this enormous house. That will be a difficult time.

25,000 tons destroyed by our bombers. These days, they are doing more than our U-boats. Under Raeder, the Navy is not completely up to its job. It spends too much time in church, and not enough on the water.

The Rumanian Minister of Education, one of Antonescu's generals, has ordered the nation's youth not to concern itself with politics, but to concentrate on written school work. This is their reward for the revolution that brought Antonescu to power. A real tragedy! Politics often corrupts a man's character.

Evening: newsreel with music. Not good, not bad. I complain again. Two marvellous German cultural films. We are world leaders in this field. Demandowski shows further samples from *Ohm Krüger*. Quite outstanding The evening gets very late. Every day has its new troubles and worries.

12 February 1941 (Wednesday)

Yesterday: A day full of worries and aggravation.

Air raid on Hannover. Forty-three dead and great damage to buildings, caused mainly by the English incendiary bombs. I make proposals for more intensive countermeasures.

Thirty-three English aircraft destroyed in all. One near Treuenbrietzen. We do very little over England. But air raid on Malta. 50,000 tons of shipping sunk in joint operations by the Luftwaffe and U-boats. Further successes for the English in Abyssinia. The Italians are also pulling back further in Albania.

Churchill's speech continues to reap high praise in New York. Our press rejects it in the strongest terms. I give Fritzsche another lesson on the value of audacity in political propaganda. Dr Dietrich does not understand this either. He is not trying poke his nose in. Would be preferable if he were to create a better press. Instead he doles out schoolboy essays to the journalists.

Theatre in Lille ready. Supposed to be opening at the end of March.

Personnel and organisational questions with Gutterer . . .

. . . Chat with the children at home. Helga is a little queen. Magda reports on her visit to the People's League for Large Families. There is an enormous amount still to be done there. Harald has marred his military career for the moment by a very stupid business. A really idiotic kid's trick with serious implications. We can only hope he doesn't do anything else, or the fat will really be in the fire. Heiduschke has behaved very decently over the whole affair.

Report from Italy: very pessimistic. Corruption and more corruption. Particularly around the Cianos. And defeatism in influential circles. The

Duce is no longer giving a lead. Rumour has it that Mussolini wants to meet Franco. To discuss the Mediterranean question. No one is sure what will come of it. I would not trust the Italians very far. It is true that a number of unlucky circumstances prevented an effective defence during the shelling of Genoa. But nevertheless!

London has broken off relations with Bucharest. Now the English may well try to attack Ploesti.*

In the afternoon, I speak to the factory leaders and shop stewards of Berlin in a packed *Sportpalast*. The mood is magnificent. Spangenberg speaks first, a little dry, but very effective in this auditorium. Then it is my turn. I attack the meeting straight away with a series of jokes, and then continue in this style, to storms of applause. A real pleasure for me to be talking to Berliners. They are the most rewarding audience of all.

I am buoyed up by the response and speak at my very best. I intend to do this more often, both for the cause's sake and my own pleasure.

Arrive home quite exhausted but very satisfied.

In the meantime, Fritzsche has given the press a good talking-to. We can only hope that it will pull its weight more in future. I have done everything possible. Some more to-ing and fro-ing. Dr Dietrich is muttering dark threats around the place. But that is not to be taken seriously.

In any case, my top-blowing exercise was necessary, and it has achieved its purpose.

Pétain and Franco are now to meet, too. But no one knows details. We shall soon find out.

A few more things to be done in the evening. But I am very tired and tense.

13 February 1941 (Thursday)

Yesterday: A few incursions here. Virtually no effect. Little over England. Malta bombed again. Heavy fighting in Albania. The situation in Abyssinia is becoming more serious for Rome, and in Libya it is quite catastrophic. No good news. Reports from Italy mention profoundest defeatism. These days, the Führer is their only hope. Ciano is absolutely finished, and the Duce's popularity is approaching zero level. Added to this are disorganisation, corruption, in short, a state of affairs verging on chaos. We must soon make a move, or Italy will crumble into nothingness.

Convoy of 50,000 tons sunk in Mid-Atlantic. U-boat sinks 21,000 tons.

Rumours stronger in Bulgaria. We maintain a stubborn silence.

My speech at the *Sportpalast* has been excellently received. This disturbs Dr Dietrich. He issues a malicious order to the press. A soggy individual, mediocrity incarnate. But I shall soon shake him off.

* The main town in the Rumanian oilfields.

231

Personnel questions re. the Reich Propaganda Leadership with Gutterer and Fischer. We shall soon be where we want to be: Wächter, Lapper and Studentkowski have already been won over. Now we have to fill the Cultural Department. Also, the personnel problems in Paris have been sorted out in tune with my wishes. The High Command has given in. All one has to do is remain stubborn . . .

. . . Situation in Belgium: close to famine. Widespread bad feeling against us. England is gaining support. I am damming the tide as best I can. But when people are starving, there is not much one can do.

Report on Rumania from the former Rumanian ambassador here: according to this account, Antonescu is a tool of the freemasons, who have turned him against the Legion. This cannot be the whole truth, but there may be something in it.

Meeting between Franco and Pétain formally announced. We shall see!

Diewerge gives a report on Russia. Coincides on many points with Gutterer's, but a little more positive. I shall ensure that the Führer sees it.

Clarify question of soldiers' hostels with Conti. He intends to postpone propaganda against smoking compartments on the underground railway until after the war. At the moment this will only serve to cause discontent.

Discuss the work of the foreign press in Berlin with the Swedish journalist, Svendström. I shall involve myself more closely in future.

Establish guidelines for the new school of dance in consultation with Kölling. Beauty, grace, physique. No philosophising disguised as dance. New blood for our many theatre ballets and a master-class for one big showpiece ballet. He will prove more than equal to the task.

A lot of aggravation and bad feeling. Talk over the problem of Harald with Magda. The stupid boy has really blotted his copybook. But we shall give him a good talking-to. Our children are sweet and affectionate: my best friends!

Watch a performance of the Elberfeld Puppet Theatre at the ministry. Marvellous from a technical point of view, but quite inadequate and insipid in content.

Work on into the evening at full tilt.

At 10.00 in the evening, Magda leaves with the children. To Göring's house at the Obersalzberg. And then she is going on to Dresden. Sadness mingled with the jollity of farewell. I accompany them to the station. Much crying, laughing and farewells. The children are so lovely. Heide in her little travelling cot. Magda the matriarch. The parting is hard for me.

Adieu! Happy holiday!

Then chat for a little longer with Ursel. To bed, exhausted.

Yesterday: Scarcely any air activity on either side. Malta heavily bombed. Situation in Africa remains serious. Keren is still holding out, but for how long?

We have caused serious damage to the Suez Canal. Widespread flooding on both banks. The *Admiral Hipper* has mined an enemy convoy and destroyed 13 ships in the process. A fat haul!

Study an analysis of working women. I shall campaign for those from better circles to be recruited, and right vigorously.

Still no clear agreement with the Foreign Ministry. They must take us for absolute fools. Dr Dietrich has been extremely rude to Gutterer, and has had the temerity to base his insolence on the Führer's wishes – quite unjustifiably, as I soon determine. He is a man of mediocre talents, swollen with ambition and vanity. Much as it goes against the grain in these difficult times, I may well have to turn to the Führer for support. Because the limits of authority must be clearly defined somehow. The present situation is gradually tearing my nerves to shreds.

Budget conference. We shall have to ask for a lot more money and manpower. But I do not want too much inflation from the staff point of view. Around 1000 people will have to continue to suffice. Any superfluous manpower will have to be shunted off to subordinate offices. But the deficit of close to 40 million is scarcely to be avoided, given the state of our income. We must now work to right the situation with all the energy at our disposal.

Discuss a new film treatment about euthanasia with Liebeneiner. A very difficult and delicate, but also a very important and pressing subject. I give Liebeneiner a few guidelines.

The architect Paul Köhler shows me some plans for theatres. Very thorough, logical and attractive. From now on he will be working with us. He is very pleased.

Bartels shows me rebuilding plans for Schloss Glienicke. Also excellent.

Wild rumours regarding the Balkans. But no one has yet hit the right track. Mussolini had a two-day meeting with Franco. Positive. Otherwise, things in Italy are not good. The Duce is making a host of psychological errors, in his private life as well. To the common people, Ciano is a devil. And he must be incredibly corrupt. The Italians will continue to give us plenty to worry about.

The house is lonely and empty. Magda and the children have gone. The entire huge palace has sunk into heavy silence.

I write a new leader article for *Das Reich*. That will annoy Dr Dietrich. And it turns out particularly well.

Meeting between Pétain and Franco. Great conjecture world-wide. Our troops are standing ready in the Balkans. Nervous, near-hysterical ripples through the entire enemy and neutral press.

Willkie is revealing himself to an increasing extent as a swine and a super-interventionist. He has become a spokesman for Roosevelt's policies, but rather more radical. The Führer was right in his judgement yet again.

Magda has arrived at the Obersalzberg with the children, dead-tired. But has found everything in order up there. Now the children can begin the rest-cure that they so badly need.

Check films in the evening. A whole series of visitors in the meantime. Frölich's *Gas-Man*. Very witty and comical. Excellently made, but for smiles rather than belly-laughs. I am very satisfied with it.

Bertram's *Battle-Squadron Lützow*. An ambitious look at the Luftwaffe's war service. With monumental scenes. Unique accuracy in background descriptions. I am gripped.

Some more film problems to discuss with Hippler. His report on Italy is rather more positive.

The Yugoslavs are on their way to the Obersalzberg. Things are gradually starting to move.

15 February 1941 (Saturday)

Yesterday: Fog, snow and frost again.

No incursions. We carry out very few missions over England. The raid on Hannover was pretty devastating, as it has turned out. Over 400 buildings destroyed and eighty dead. We can expect more of the same when the spring comes.

Raids on Malta and Cyrenaica. No news except rumours from the Balkans. Yugoslavia is the focal point at the moment. Situation in Africa still serious.

The *Admiral Hipper*, we now learn, sunk 52,000 tons in her big coup. Our auxiliary cruisers overseas have now bagged a total of 670,000 tons. An altogether acceptable situation!

Check writings by Lieutenant-Colonel Hesse. No objections.

Study the case of the 'poet' Betzner. A swine, on whose behalf I have no intention of intervening. He deserves his five months' jail.

Professor Auler reports on the state of modern cancer research. An enormous amount is being achieved in this area. Real miracles. Auler is sovereign in the field. I place 100,000 marks at his disposal, since Rust – one has to see it in writing to believe it – managed only 7000 marks.

Bruwers reports on Belgium: real famine conditions there. The party-political situation is stabilising. Degrelle is busy again. We intend to establish a Flemish Theatre in Brussels.

Winkelnkemper reports: he has already settled into the short-wave service and started to get his way. Working outstandingly well. Perhaps he will fill Raskin's place, after all.

After a short break at midday, straight back to work.

Report in the *Vreme* on the bombardment of Genoa. This must have been pretty horrendous. And only civilian targets. Typical of the English.

Antonescu has issued a general report on the rebellion. According to this, Horia Sima must take exclusive blame. Only children and intellectuals will believe that.

Sit down and do some creative writing. It gives me a lot of fun.

Women in the USA demonstrate against Roosevelt and England. Nothing serious, but a symptom.

Matsuoka makes a very pro-Moscow speech. A good thing that this matter is slowly being settled. Now we must concentrate all our energy against England.

The talks with the Yugoslavs at the Obersalzberg dominate the entire world press. But naturally no one has any idea of what is really going on.

Speak with Magda on the telephone. She has sorted everything out up there. The weather is wonderful. She is dining with the Führer this evening.

I spend a long time writing and reading. Then to bed, tired and tense.

16 February 1941 (Sunday)

Yesterday: We can do nothing over England. The English attack Duisburg and Düsseldorf. Fourteen dead outside the shelters. I have this mentioned pointedly in the press. A number of sinkings, particularly by the Luftwaffe. Four Spitfires shot down over South-East England. Otherwise nothing of importance.

I work at home. Deal with all the rubbish that has piled up during the week. A lot of distasteful and unpleasant stuff among it. But that is how things are, and they will never change. One wastes more energy on these demarcation disputes than on the war. Nothing of great moment, but plenty of aggravation and annoyance. Forget it!

Hadamovsky is doing an excellent job. He has suddenly turned into a solid, reliable colleague.

Through to midday. Then straight to the Schiller Theatre for the War Congress of the German Film Chamber. I speak on the subject of the present film situation. Its difficulties, but also its successes. A comprehensive report that is greeted with general applause. The big new film projects deserve every praise. They prove that one can combine artistic merit with profitability. A fine and certainly very useful meeting.

Work at home. In the evening, première of the *Gas-Man* at the *Ufapalast am Zoo*. In the presence of the members of the Reich Film Chamber. Everyone who is anyone is there. The film is a great success. The public screams with laughter. Acting and direction, however, very low-key. Unfortunately drags a little in parts. But otherwise a great artistic achievement.

Then afterwards a reception held by Professor Frölich at the KddK. A little conversation. But home in good time. Magda is very well up on the mountain. She is with the Führer just when I ring. Things are very busy up there.

I feel tired and drained.

Today I am driving out to spend a few days at Lanke. I must have some rest.

17 February 1941 (Monday)

Yesterday: Armed reconnaissance over England by day. A number of ships seriously damaged by Stukas and some sunk. Airfields in England attacked during the night. 158 aircraft in the air. Heavy activity over the Mediterranean also.

The English attack Essen, Düsseldorf and Cologne fairly heavily during the night. Casualty figures 1:13 in our favour. Also raids in Holland, Belgium and France.

Glass reports from the Balkans. Things in Rumania are just as I described them. Antonescu without popular support. But the Foreign Ministry is supporting him. The SS and the SD are taking a tough stand against Ribbentrop for having supplied the Führer with incomplete information. Because personally he is no Nazi. He is a Jeremiah! But I intend to have another meeting with the Führer about this. The freemasons are forcing their way back into their old positions, and even the Jews are coming back. Poor Antonescu! Now he has officially destroyed the legionary character of the state. It is hard to say where things will lead if they continue in this unhappy direction. We only seem to support nationalists when they have no nations behind them. Like Mussert and Quisling. What a disaster!

In Bulgaria, Glass says, an ultra-reactionary clique is at the helm, people of whom we can expect nothing. And in Greece there is actually no feeling against us at all. The Italians alone are the object of general hatred. The Italian prisoners-of-war who have been brought back to Greece are totally in rags and demoralised. This is the result of inadequate fascist education.

Otherwise nothing of importance. I drive to Lanke in the afternoon.

What a blessing: away from the noisy bustle of the city. Back in the forest, under the old familiar trees. In the midst of nature.

Drive out with the new horses. Kaiser's rebuilding work on the house inspected: turning out very well and will be comfortable. My colleagues should be able to put up with this. On through the far forest. The snow has gone. There is a sort of pre-spring feeling in the air.

Listen to the Request Concert. Very good this time. My shot across their bows was effective.

A whole series of sinkings reported. We are gradually hitting England where it hurts. One must simply be patient and stubborn.

Our press has improved greatly. My outburst cleared the air there, too.

The general commanding the German occupying forces has written an unctious letter to Antonescu. A reactionary type. He would have been one of those who damned us when we were still fighting for power.

Newsreel in the evening. Turned out well again. Things are gradually improving in that quarter as well. Then discuss a number of film matters with Hippler. To bed, tired.

18 February 1941 (Tuesday)

Yesterday: Mist over the forest. I stay out here and work in the house.

No air activity on either side during the night. By day we attack English ports and airfields. Also a whole series of sinkings by U-boats and the Luftwaffe. Heavy air activity in the Mediterranean also. Ominous noises in Africa again, particularly in Abyssinia. The mood in London is once more a little gloomier.

Otherwise, Monday passes fairly quietly.

I have some aggravation in my work. The newsreel production work is being hindered from all sides, choked by censors, regulations, etc. I shall now have to write a letter of complaint to the Führer, particularly singling out the Army High Command, which is stealing my best people, cameramen and film cutters. Now I intend to break the vicious circle.

A number of matters regarding entertainment of the troops, the cinema and the theatre. But these are dealt with quickly.

The report on morale in France is rather gloomy. Collaboration is non-existent. Now the treaty of truce will be put into force. This is the best course in the present situation. France would soon be faced with social revolution if it were not for the threat of German arms. How quickly the face of the world changes in these dramatic times.

Tug-of-war with Forster in Danzig over Diewerge. He wants to keep him, but I must have him to replace Berndt, who intends to go on active service in Africa. And so I insist on my rights.

Speak on the telephone with Magda in Dresden. She is just beginning her course of treatment and is still feeling well. The first reaction will come during the next few days.

She tells me about her visit to the Führer: all very nice and pleasant.

In the afternoon a drive through the forest to Wandlitz. The fresh air does one so much good. It cleans out the lungs.

Hess rings up: he has a number of objections to *Gas-Man*. Quite humourless. The best thing we could do would be to tie ourselves up in straitjackets and stick ourselves in jail. The Seventh Chamber has been torpedoed by Rosenberg. And Hess is looking for a compromise, which in turn makes Dr Ley very sad. I act in accordance with mother's motto: 'Keep out of it!.' This is the best course at the moment.

Discuss his new film, *Battle-Squadron Lützow*, with Bertram. We still have a minor disagreement about the ending, but this will soon be sorted out.

A few people visiting in the evening. Albert Hehn and Brennecke from the film world. Plus Frau von Frowein. Put the finishing touches on the newsreel and music. Not outstanding, but what else can one do in these quiet times?

Gossip for a while afterwards. Herr Brennecke and Fräulein von Möllendorf tell stories about the film world.

And then read for a long time.

I do not fall asleep until morning.

19 February 1941 (Wednesday)

Yesterday: Few air attacks on either side. We attack ports. No activity in the Mediterranean. A few sinkings. Nothing new in Albania and Africa. The weather is dreadful so far as military operations are concerned. But now the sun is coming through. The Führer is still on the mountain, waiting for better weather.

Non-Aggression Pact signed between Bulgaria and Turkey. A serious blow for London.

Some sun out here. I work through the day at full tilt with Hadamovsky. Until the sparks fly. A mass of accumulated material from all quarters. More or less aggravating.

The English are shooting a line again. Fantastic lies. Plus the usual social promises for after the war. I have our people flay them alive. Our press is doing its job well now.

The Führer was very satisfied with the latest newsreel.

Arrangements made for Kriebel's state funeral. It is to be held in Munich.

I am at full stretch all day. There can be no question of relaxing.

A little drive through the forest in glorious sunshine during the afternoon. The snow is completely gone now, and everything smells of spring. I hope it comes soon. We have need of it. For ourselves personally, but particularly for the war's sake.

Off along the country road, passing fields and villages. It does one good, refreshes body and spirit.

In the evening at Lanke, write an article for *Das Reich*. On total war. Very successful.

Chat for a while on the telephone with Magda. She is well. Watch a few rushes from films in progress. And then to bed at a reasonable hour.

20 February 1941 (Thursday)

Yesterday: No incursions on either side. Only patrol activity in the Mediterranean. But a whole series of sinkings by the Luftwaffe and U-boats . . .

. . . Balkans still in ferment. Lively activity in Africa. The English withdraw from [E . . .], probably because of the effectiveness of our Stukas.

Dictate leader-article. Draft speech for the Leipzig Fair.

The Führer has now issued a definitive order on Wehrmacht propaganda, which is to be taken out of the hands of the various branches and centred in the High Command. A great easing of my burden.

A number of issues affecting the cinema and theatre. Theatres in Berlin continue playing to packed houses. Hess's objections to *Gas-Man* are totally unworthy of discussion.

The SD report contains great praise for our film work. Particularly the newsreel. Otherwise, the mood in the country is quietly expectant.

I am faced with a mass of demands for personal appearances and interviews. Sometimes I feel like a block of wood being shoved from one place to another.

Deal with routine work with Hadamovsky. A mountain of it. Heiduschke reports on Harald, whom he has visited. Things are all right again.

Long letters from Magda in Dresden and from the children at the Obersalzberg, which give me great pleasure. It is so wonderful to have a family!

I am reading and writing the whole day. The work never lets up. No question of resting. Speak to the children on the telephone. They are all very amusing and jolly. It is Holde's birthday, and I have sent her a few gifts on the courier-plane. What a joy!

Lord Alexander has spoken on the war situation: very pessimistic. Woolton likewise. The English have no clear sense of direction at the moment.

Things in Rumania are developing just as I had feared. Antonescu is ruling with the aid of the freemasons and the enemies of Germany; our minorities are being oppressed and the Reich has gone to all this trouble for nothing. Another brilliant coup by the Foreign Ministry.

Speak with Magda. She is well. She is very sweet to me.

Visit by the Hommels and Ursel. We gossip a lot. Early to bed. Today up very early. Flight to Munich and Kriebel's funeral.

21 February 1941 (Friday)

Yesterday: Up very early. To Staaken. Still dark when we take off. A rather hair-raising flight with the plane in constant danger of icing up.

Schirmeister is back at work. Rosy-cheeked and healthy.

Work during the flight: the Führer has now given permission for us to attack America. It was high time. Now we shall let rip. Tough comment in the press.

Transgressions against the ban on foreign stations are still widespread in the Wehrmacht. I shall take vigorous measures now.

I write the Führer a letter about the newsreel's difficulties with military departments. This should cause something of a shake-up.

The State Opera is off to Rome. Big tour that I arranged.

A host of film and theatre matters. Problems with the press leadership. Trouble with the General Government, which is making itself out to be a 'neutral state'. They are trying to put my branch offices under the control of their bureaucracy. But I resist vigorously.

English speeches and articles very cocksure again. But not for much longer.

Time passes in a flash. Munich. State ceremony for the late Party Comrade Kriebel in the *Feldherrnhalle*.* Very dignified and solemn. The Führer and Göring also present. Hess makes an excellent funeral oration, which moves us all deeply. Adieu!

I talk over a few things with Göring: he is waiting for better weather, and then he intends to send in the Luftwaffe on a grand scale. That would be desirable. He has had some trouble with Brauchitsch about his idiotic propaganda. The Führer is also very annoyed about it. Brauchitsch is being egged on by Hesse. The Führer has a very poor opinion of him.

I come to an agreement with Göring about the Propaganda Companies. He is willing to put camera operators at my disposal, but not at the High Command's. He is completely dismissive about Brauchitsch's film on the Western Campaign. He laughed himself sick at the *Gas-Man*. He is a frank, open man. One can talk with him, and work with him.

The children gave him great pleasure up on the mountains. They are very well.

Discuss a few matters with Amann. Dr Müller reports to me on Munich. Everything is going well these days, even at the Bavaria studios. All they have to do is to make better films.

Straight back to Berlin. Dictate my speech for the Leipzig Fair during the flight. Hard to do in an aeroplane. Revise leader-article and read through paperwork. The plane rocking like mad the entire time. Appalling!

Back in Berlin around 14.00. Into the office again. Quickly deal with a number of things.

Much talk about an attempt by Tokyo to mediate. But mere empty chatter. We want victory.

No incursions into the Reich. Little over England. But Swansea and London more heavily bombed. A number of sinkings, mainly by the

* The Nazi shrine in Munich, where those who fell in the attempted coup of November 1923 were commemorated.

Luftwaffe . . . The English are still looking for the *Admiral Hipper*, which reached port long since. Quiet in the Mediterranean. The Italians are holding on in Albania, and they are also giving a good account of themselves in Libya and Abyssinia . . .

. . . Warmongering continues in the USA. Now quite openly. Mrs Roosevelt is shooting her mouth off around the country. If she were my wife, it would be a different story.

Chiang-Kai-Shek has made a bold speech attacking Japan. There can be no question of peace in that quarter for the present.

The short-wave service is having cables from the USA about our programmes sent via lines paid for by us. A delicate matter which I shall probably put a stop to soon.

General nervousness. The weather is becoming fine, and spring is on its way. Things will soon be on the move.

In the afternoon I drive out to Lanke. The Hommels are with me, and Ursel is there as well. We stroll through the forest, breathe fresh air and talk.

Music and reading in the evening. Magda rings up: she is well. But a slight attack. Reaction!

I feel very much at ease in the forest and would like to never leave here, if only that were possible.

22 February 1941 (Saturday)

Yesterday: No incursions here. We do a few things over England. Particularly Swansea and London. And a number of sinkings. Little in the Mediterranean.

General Rommel has arrived in Tripoli. He has been granted full powers by Mussolini. Along with three Panzer divisions. His goal is the reconquest of Benghazi. Because of the air base. Graziani has already been relieved of his command. And so some sort of order should be restored there. Bitter trench warfare in Albania.

I have a lot to do. Reorganisational work on the Reich Culture Chamber. Likewise on the Request Concert, where there has been too much interference by other departments recently. I shall free Goedecke of his overlords. Too many cooks spoil the broth. Film and theatre matters. We get our way with the *Gas-Man*. Otherwise, day-to-day routine, but it takes up my entire day.

Bulgaria is kicking over the traces a little. But nothing serious. In any case, it is too late for that.

The mood in the USA is moving ever more radically towards war. Now it is being spoken of openly, even in the highest circles.

In England they are bragging their heads off. They are dreaming up the wildest deeds of daring against us. The fact that they can do this at all is due to Italy's failures. I receive a report from there, which is very gloomy again. Above all, there is increasing doubt about Mussolini's capacity for leadership. That is the worst thing imaginable. High time that the spring came. Another wartime winter would be hard for us all.

Short outing in the car with my visitors, the Hommels, Ursel and Hadamovsky. I am able to settle a host of important problems with him. Far easier in the fresh forest air than in the office.

Spend the evening talking and reading. The last days of winter are crawling by like years. The entire nation's nerves are stretched to breaking-point.

Come, sweet May!

23 February 1941 (Sunday)

Yesterday: Everything covered in snow outside. Winter has returned.

The English take to the air over North and West Germany. No damage of note.

In general, no great air activity on our part. We attack Swansea and London. Visible successes. Also a number of sinkings. Raids on Malta and particularly heavily on Benghazi. We are really giving the English a pasting there. Otherwise nothing of importance.

Rumours in and about Bulgaria. The world is gradually pricking up its ears.

Report on Degrelle: a rather tardy attempt to justify his activities. He is critical of our propaganda. He would be better advised to improve his own.

We are having to release 30,000 workers from the printing trade for work in the armaments industry. A serious blow, but it will enable us to rid ourselves of a lot of superfluous and wholly harmful printed matter. Especially religious tracts . . .

. . . Dr Dietrich has been singing a hymn of praise to the Propaganda Companies in Paris. I have this toned down somewhat. An excess of praise harms the Propaganda Companies in the eyes of other branches of the forces. Thus the psychological benefits are outweighed by the negative effects.

Colonel von Wild is putting out a literary concoction for 30 marks whose production cost only three marks: a shocking scandal. I intervene and create merry hell. A serious embarrassment for the Army High Command.

The cables from the USA to the German short-wave service are, on the whole, very positive after all. Only 25 per cent, mostly from Jews, are negative. Now, following the scheme's complete success, I am having it wound up.

Work through a mass of paperwork left over from the week. If only one could have a weekend free once in a while.

Short drive through the snow in the afternoon. Nature shrouded in silence. Magda rings up: she is well. She has made a good recovery from her heart attack.

Visitors in the evening: Martin, Hinkel, Hippler, Fritzsche and his wife. A lot of talk and music.

24 February 1941 (Monday)

Yesterday: No incursions here. We launch middling raids on England. Increased activity in the Mediterranean. Pretty massive attacks by our aircraft on the English positions in North Africa. On the other hand, things do not look very good in Abyssinia. Keren is still holding on, but the English have crossed the Juba and beyond it they are encountering no obstacles of note. There is already talk of a collapse of the Italian front there.

A whole series of sinkings by the Luftwaffe.

Otherwise nothing new in the political world or the war.

Wonderful weather. Sun on the snow again. One can breathe deeply. I shall soon no longer have opportunities such as this.

Farewell mood at Lanke. I leave here so unwillingly. A last, long drive between the fields in the afternoon. Snow and sun. So beautiful.

Then back to Berlin. This huge, empty house! Dreadful!

Debate on war aims renewed in London. Nothing to be gleaned from it.

Mussolini makes a speech. I listen to his address on the radio. He speaks with great firmness, though understandably not quite so confidently as hitherto. The audience's reaction is good. Perhaps a little muted. He describes Italy's very difficult position. All the arguments that have been in the air lately. At last, at last! Italy, he says, has been at war since 1922.* He rejects the criticisms of his diehard opponents. He spares some friendly words for Germany, particularly for the Führer. Tough line against the defeatists in Italy. Evidence that England must lose. Unqualified admission of Italian defeats. An extraordinarily skilful speech, which must be a light on the horizon even for the Italians.

Straight to work in Berlin. Newsreel: very rich in content and varied. They have made good use of their material. Film, *Rides for Germany*. With Birgel, direction by Rebenalt. A little clichéd, and the dialogue is too wooden. At the end, very good and gripping.

Speak to the Children on the telephone: they are all a little sick, but otherwise jolly and full of fun. I often feel a great longing for them.

Ring up Magda. She is well.

To bed late and exhausted. And today another hard week begins.

25 February 1941 (Tuesday)

Yesterday: No incursions into the Reich. We attack Hull and London in middling strength. The devastation in Swansea is quite considerable, according to the neutral press. Some air activity in the Mediterranean. Signs that English forces in North Africa are avoiding combat. After initial encounters with our armoured patrols. They will soon have a chance to show

---

* The year of Mussolini's seizure of power in Italy.

243

their mettle. The Italians are holding the predetermined line in northern Abyssinia. In the south, however, the English have achieved some important successes. On the whole, the Italians have been putting up a better show lately. They are in the process of occupying [. . .]. Mussolini's speech has been marvellously effective. Big mass-rallies in Italy, some with German troops participating. Italy seems to be overcoming her crisis to some extent. Mussolini's speech was very cleverly thought out. He knows his people. The only thing is that it came very late in the day. Italy would have been spared a lot if he had spoken earlier.

A number of sinkings. The English are still searching for the *Admiral Hipper*. Wild rumours about the Balkans. We maintain a steely silence.

Preparations for the Führer's speech on Party Foundation Day in Munich . . .

. . . Problem of the illegitimate children of soldiers billeted on families. I suggest several measures to the Army High Command which will help girls who have been left in the lurch.

Brauchitsch is up to his conceited tricks again. Pictures of him with his pushy wife in fashion magazines. Appalling! Colonel Wild, under pressure from me, immediately yielded in the affair regarding the picture-book about the Field Marshal which he published. He had fallen into the hands of a crooked enterpreneur.

In Vienna they now want to put Müthel in charge of the Opera. I refuse permission. They should appoint a real opera expert. I give Keppler appropriate instructions.

Magnificent box-office returns for our cinema industry. Fifty-six million in profits last year. This year it is looking even better. And all the films originated by me have notched up record audiences.

I reorganise the film export effort. From now on it will be based on political rather than financial criteria. This is a propaganda question rather than a money matter. Particularly where friendly powers are concerned. But Italy must make some concessions to us. Better dubbing of German films. I take more steps to hold down spiralling film salaries.

Artistic matters with Bibrach. Particularly architecture and sculpture in the Balkans. And degenerate art, which is already on the increase again in many places.

Schirach wants twenty-one million from the Winter Aid Fund, but I have reduced the sum to fifteen million. So it will stay. And Vienna will then receive a special grant for its summer budget. Now I shall be able to support the other needy Gau authorities with a total sum of fifty million. Hilgenfeldt is to show me the new budgetary estimates in the near future.

My new dining room in the ministry is ready. Has turned out very nicely. It has now been transformed into a very tastefully furnished suite of rooms.

Home is empty and bleak.

I feel almost swamped in the big house.

I work like a machine.

A whole series of very impressive sinkings. A convoy sent to the bottom of the sea. Our U-boat campaign is getting under way. The Führer makes more play of it in his Munich speech in the afternoon. He is in excellent form. Going straight to the heart, specially for the old Party comrades. Uncompromising towards England. Wreaks destruction on the British campaign of lies. Words of solidarity for Italy. A thrilling appeal to the nation, which will understand and respond. The broadcasting quality of the speech is magnificent. A quite strange feeling to hear the Führer on the radio for once.

Magda is well, as are the children. Schirach sends me a letter of apology for his aggressive tone during our conversation in the morning.

A defensive statement by the Turkish Foreign Minister denying any pro-Axis tendency in the Turkish-Bulgarian pact. We had been pushing that element too hard.

Cables from the USA to the short-wave service are generally very positive. My work is also greatly respected there. America does not consist entirely of Jews and plutocrats. It is just that they can shout the loudest.

In the evening, I am host to the thirty bearers of the gold honour-badge.* Here are the old, brave and true warhorses of the Party, who marched at my side from the beginning. I feel particularly happy in their company. What memories! All the old faces! A wonderful mood of comradeship. First we watch the latest newsreel with music, all very alert and attentive. Then we swop stories and report on our doings. Covering all the matters of the day, in every Gau and from all fronts. I learn so much. Morale is good everywhere. We can look confidently to the future.

It gets very late, but it has been worth it.

26 February 1941 (Wednesday)

Yesterday: No incursions on either side. Some activity in the Mediterranean. In Cyrenaica the English are starting to dig in, which means they are going on to the defensive. They are now slowly coming into contact with our Panzer forces.

Our U-boats have sunk 250,000 tons. First results of the intensified campaign. London is simply issuing bare-faced denials. But we shall not let up. We shall make them eat their lying words.

The Führer's speech makes a big impression throughout the world. Particularly his announcement of intensified U-boat warfare. We launch swingeing attacks on London, which pretends exaggerated indifference. Warmongering continues unabated in the USA. A few lonely voices of reason.

I put some more life into the Request Concert. The personalities are not good enough. Bring on the stars! The radio schedules in general must be

* The decoration awarded by Hitler for meritorious services in the Nazi Party.

made more flexible. Fewer reports from the front when there is nothing to report.

Discuss a tighter control of the Reich Culture Chamber with Gutterer. Main object a unified management which confines itself exclusively to organisational matters. I have Hinkel in mind for this.

The Führer has gone back to the Obersalzberg once more.

A lot of film and theatre problems. Tours abroad. We are forced to restrict them somewhat because of transport difficulties. Still the vexing question of the theatre in the Behrenstrasse. But I shall not give in.

Give Paltzo guidelines for his work in Paris. I demand active work. And in accordance with the old methods. With a dash of rabble-rousing. He must not let Schmidtke bully him. Paltzo will soon master the situation, in his quiet way. It is by no means impossible to win over Paris to our side. I should like to spend a few months there myself, to work that miracle.

Strongly recommend to Hentschke that he should not only stage his own works at the *Metropoltheater*. He should let others have a word in. I am thinking of Mackeben, among others. Otherwise the *Metropol* will turn into a *Monopol*.* Hentschke grumbles, but he has no choice.

Discuss the new situation in the paper and printing industries. We are having to release 30,000 workers for war work. Thus the superfluous publications, such as the German Labour Front's tame journals, will disappear, and the useful material will remain untouched. *Das Reich* will soon have reached a circulation of a million. A rare publishing success, which which I have not been entirely uninvolved. Our newspapers in the occupied territories actually carry more news than our papers here in the Reich. This must be stopped or we shall be faced with a breach in our information policy. I intend to wait out developments for the moment. Reinhardt has delivered a discussion document proposing the expansion and establishing of serious German magazines for foreign consumption. A far-sighted plan which I shall support.

The situation in Bulgaria is reaching boiling-point. The wildest rumours. But all wide of the mark. The American Ambassador in Sofia stages a drunken incident in a bar. We succeed in minimising the damage.

London is claiming that it knows nothing about abnormal shipping losses. We shall soon make them eat their words.

Magda writes me a very loving letter from Dresden. She is sweet and good to me these days. And I can do with it.

Work the entire afternoon. We are issuing an official announcement in the press, recalling troops on leave from Norway. A little stratagem to deceive the enemy.

Some small demonstrations against us in Amsterdam and the Hague, plus a few strikes. Seyss is too hesitant in his reaction. The old story. He is no real Nazi!

* A pun on the name of the theatre and *Monopol*, the German word meaning monopoly.

The U-boat campaign is being taken very seriously in London. People are very anxious after the Führer's speech. And rightly so. The figures of tonnage lost are being ignored or falsified. Typical of Churchill! But such methods will not get him far.

Woolton has announced further shortening of rations. The strain is telling, it would seem. This, and not Churchill's propaganda-figures, is the real truth.

Legal judgment: not only are we not duty-bound to feed the populations of the occupied territories, but we can even requisition provisions there. An important argument in the controversy over the blockade.

A little peace and quiet in the evening. Speak to Magda on the telephone. She is making a good recovery.

Film: *Swedish Nightingale*. With Ilse Werner, Gottschalk and Diehl. The film is not a success. The dramatic conflict creaks, the entire thing has no atmosphere and is often quite banal. I am very disappointed. Direction by Brauer. Another achievement of this nature, and things could become rather bad for him.

Alfieri has had to have an operation in Milan. He writes me a very amiable letter to tell me that he is recovering well. A good fellow!

Continue working until late.

27 February 1941 (Thursday)

Yesterday: We carry out several raids on English cities. The English attack the Ruhr area. Middling casualties. Five dead. Nothing of note in Albania. Considerable air activity in the Mediterranean. We bomb Benghazi again. The English bomb Tripoli. Considerable damage. One of our transporters seriously damaged. Has to be beached. The Italians lose a cruiser and 500 crewmen. British destroyer sunk. The Italians are holding their line again in Abyssinia.

Speeches by ministers in London have taken a gloomy turn again. The threat of an intensified U-boat campaign is causing the English particular worry.

Complications in Amsterdam. Martial law declared. I give Seyss a few pieces of advice. One must hit the Dutch in their wallets and in their comforts. I suggest a penalty of fifty million Gulder. That would soon do the trick. But has Seyss the temperament for it? When all is said and done, the fellow is only an Austrian.

Morale here remains good. The Führer's speech was marvellously effective. Good news about the Request Concert. Goedecke is now free of his watchdogs.

I agree to substantial financial grants for theatre and propaganda purposes. Particularly for work among the ethnic Germans.

Bureaucracy is on the spread. Even in our ministry. Like dry rot.

Film matters with Hippler. Independent production facilities in Warsaw refused. Sharp criticism of the *Swedish Nightingale*.

A long heart-to-heart with Lutze. He has a lot of bones to pick with the Party and with Bormann. I intend to highlight the SA rather more. He is active on Brauchitsch's behalf. I would also like to be able to support Brauchitsch. But Hesse and Brauchitsch's extremely ambitious wife are making too many gaffes. Nevertheless, we intend to get together at the Lutzes' house. Viktor is an honest fellow and a real old Nazi.

Agree grants for the poor Gaus with Hilgenfeldt. Fifty million in all. This will be a pleasure. New budget of the Winter Aid Fund agreed. Will probably end up by totalling 830 million. A gigantic sum, which arouses not only admiration but also envy. We shall have to set aside a reserve of 150 million for extraordinary expenditure. Who knows what may happen this summer? Hilgenfeldt and Janowski are doing marvellous work. One can rely on their integrity absolutely. I shall defend them against Conti's ambitions.

There are moves afoot to place the propaganda leadership in the General Government under the authority of the administration. I am taking steps to prevent this. Propaganda is not a function of administration but of guidance. The gentlemen concerned will act accordingly. I deal with a number of tendencies which may lead to a lesser or greater degree in the direction of increased autonomy for the General Government – its own film production facilities, radio stations, press authority, etc. This is not on. At this rate, Poland will be a separate state again, under German guidance. Neutralism. That is all we need. It will not be tolerated, at least in my sphere. So far as the rest goes, Schmidt is getting on well in Cracow.

Preparations for the big visit of the State Opera to Rome.

Eden in Ankara. An attempt to save what can still be saved in the Balkans. They are terrified of the springtime, and particularly of our German U-boats. The entire London press is full of them again. We leave it all to run its course. The sensational report about Norway is serving its purpose, and moreover it has a genuine basis in fact, for actually the Baltic is rather clogged with traffic, and the men from Norway, instead of being recalled, are having an extra week's leave.

My new piece in *Das Reich* is again marvellously effective.

The balloon has gone up in Holland, after all. Strikes and demonstrations. In Amsterdam we are forced to shoot to kill. Seventy-eight dead. Schmidt, who is forced to see the affair through in Seyss's place, introduces all the measures that I had suggested. Unfortunately rather late in the day, and so even harsher measures are necessary. The Jews are at the head of the opposition. I would like to get my hands on them. But it is the old story: if prompt action is taken, then one can succeed with minor measures. If too late, then there is blood and casualties and lasting hatred . . .

. . . Amazing neutral report on the destruction in London. I ban it, since it

248

would tend to arouse false hopes in the German public.

Our High Command's Bulletin has reported the first clashes between German and English armoured forces in Libya. Big sensation.

Speak to Magda on the telephone. She is well.

Ursel visits me in the evening.

We chat a little.

She is so nice and naïve.

And so uncomplicated.

Refreshing, when one is tired and overworked.

28 February 1941 (Friday)

Yesterday: We attack London and Cardiff. English raid on the Ruhr area. Middling force. Massive raids on Malta. Stalemate in Libya. English successes in Italian Somaliland. Mogadishu has fallen into their hands. Considerable sinkings again. A U-boat hunt in progress against a convoy, but they have not yet caught up with it.

Report from Italy: fairly negative. But written before the Duce's speech. Wait and see.

Peace restored in Amsterdam. The measures that I suggested have succeeded. Big English convoy destroyed by our Luftwaffe.

Growing anxiety in London. At last they are beginning to see the realities of the situation.

Increased tension in the Balkans. Eden is up to no good in Ankara.

Despite his promises, Antonescu is proceeding merrily with his wave of arrests. A complete betrayal!

Some slight increase in domestic opposition to Roosevelt. He is modifying his Aid to England Bill a little. But makes no practical difference . . .

. . . With Tiessler. Discuss the new pamphlet on the Führer intended for the occupied territories. This needs major changes.

Rust has been doling out English army communiqués from the present war as a language teaching aid in schools. Insane! I kick up a tremendous stink! Heads will have to roll in Rust's and Bouhler's ministries.

Address editors of fashion magazines. Fashion as an expression of our national life. I am greeted with applause all round.

Discuss changes in the format of the Request Concert with Goedecke. Everything has now been settled. He is to get his own office and have suitable staff placed at his disposal. And I shall free him from the attentions of all those supervisory authorities . . .

. . . The Führer is to be in Vienna on Saturday. Solution of the Balkan Problem. About time.

Write leader-article: 'When Spring Comes over the Mountains.' Nicely-judged.

At my desk all day. By evening I am dog-tired.

The Foreign Ministry has started a totally absurd rumour that the English Queen Mother has fled to the USA. I forbid the German press to report this piece of amateurish nonsense.

Magda is well. She is looking forward to my visit. The children are also well. I speak to them on the telephone. What twittering and singing!

Check films for the rest of the evening. And then to bed, tired. The film was good: *Men's Business*. An engaging film aimed at farmers and common folk. Something decent from Ufa at last.

1 March 1941 (Saturday)

Yesterday: Snow and rain. No incursions on either side. But we attack English airfields by day, because they are few and therefore packed with aircraft. Some activity in the Mediterranean. In particular, our aircraft attack the English positions in North Africa. Once again, enormous quantities of shipping sunk by the Luftwaffe and the U-boat fleet. We are gradually doing London damage where it hurts most.

Bulgaria has now decided to join the Three-Power Pact. Signing ceremony today in Vienna. The Führer is on his way there. That was a difficult birth.

Opinion still divided in the USA. The opposition is hard at work stirring things up. Roosevelt makes a cocksure speech attacking us. About freedom and so on. And [. . .] against Moscow. A real *enfant terrible*. We make good use of it.

Turkey is sneaking oh-so-slowly over on to our side. We are leaving her completely in peace and maintaining the utmost reserve in the press and radio.

Absolute quiet restored in Holland. Schmidt got his way with the aid of the measures suggested by me. I advise him urgently to keep them in force, which he does. The Jew-pack must be shown the size of our teeth.

We acquire a priests' seminary in Trier as a propaganda training school. In a very beautiful setting and laid out very practically. Simon thought it was very funny . . .

. . . Negotiate with serious composers. Richard Strauss is unreasonable, senile and stubborn. Werner Egk is the most reasonable. Graener is only interested in money. I stick to my view. Popular music will get what it is due, while serious music will be supported by the state. In the end, they all accept this. I whisper a few sweet nothings in Strauss's ear on the subject of his insolent letters. He seems unable to stop writing letters, and this has already caused him a lot of trouble. But next time I shall give him something to think about.

Fräulein Riefenstahl is causing me a deal of worry with her *Lowlands* film. A hysterical person, who has a new project every day. Hesse is now demanding the highest certificate of approval of his *Victory in the West*, the same honour awarded to *Battle-Squadron Lützow*. I refuse. The High Command is furious about it, but I can do no other.

Luftwaffe sank 58,000 tons the day before yesterday. 32,000 yesterday. This is delightful news.

King Alfonso of Spain has died. No loss for humanity. A weak king, who outlived his time.

In the afternoon, première of *Battle-Squadron Lützow* at the *Ufapalast*. Big attendance. The film is an enormous success. And it is well made; clear, realistic, with a wonderful plot and great scenes. A genuine war film for the people.

All sorts piled up at home. Peace negotiations between Thailand and Indochina meeting problems. Tokyo is taking an aggressive line against Vichy. Not without cause.

Speak to Magda on the telephone. She is well. We are looking forward to our reunion.

Things go on until late again. After such a hard week one really longs for a freer day.

2 March 1941 (Sunday)

Yesterday: No night raids on either side. Bad weather for war operations. Hardly any activity in the Mediterranean, either. A few sinkings. Quiet in Albania and Libya. The Italian retreat in Italian Somaliland was, at least, orderly.

Things are getting hot in the Balkans. Bulgaria is under the wing of the Three-Power Pact. The Turks have no real idea what to do.

Weekly clean-out. There is still so much to be dealt with. The Führer is in Vienna for Bulgaria's accession to the Three-Power Pact.

Mood in the country: Our film, radio and press work is highly praised. We are making the best of the thin material available. The Führer's speech in Munich has, as expected, been wonderfully effective.

Conflict in France between supporters and opponents of Collaboration. Laval is merely compromising our cause. He is a crook. But this seems to be a characteristic of all modern Foreign Ministers.

Report, including figures, on what we got out of France after the surrender. No cause for anyone to complain on that score. We took a good swig from the bottle. France certainly had cause to notice that she had lost the war.

Still absolute peace in Holland. Our crack of the whip there has been effective, it would seem.

Minor disputes in the Ministerial Bureau. Between Frowein on the one hand and Schaumburg and Spieler on the other. The last two work too little and blab too much. But I shall soon put things right.

Such beautiful spring weather outside. But I must remain at my desk.

The hysteria about Bulgaria has reached its climax. London is threatening war if Sofia joins the Three-Power Pact. Meanwhile, however, the Führer is already at work in Vienna. Filov completes the signing. Ciano is also there. Bounced back up from the depths again.

They are throwing blue fits in London. Proof that this coup of German diplomacy has hit them hard. And there will be others in the near future. England will get what she has always wanted: war!

The opposition in the USA is becoming very active. But there seems to be little hope of the Aid for England Bill's being sabotaged. Roosevelt will have his way. If the war ends this year, then the damage will not be too great. If it goes on into next year, then naturally the situation will be somewhat more serious.

In February, it has now been made known, we sunk 740,000 tons. That is a blow to England's merchant tonnage that she will be hard-pressed to make good in wartime.

Work on the newsreel. This time there is a certain lack of good, gripping material. Another area in which it was time the war began again.

Work on this problem in the evening, writing and revising. But I cannot make much of nothing. A new Ufa film, *Boys*. Not a masterpiece. But it will do.

Very high financial penalties have been imposed on the Dutch cities of Amsterdam and Hilversum. That will soon cool their ardour. If one wants to hurt the pepper-sacks, one must aim for their wallets. At last, at last, long-overdue action is being taken.

The anxiety in London is on the increase. They now deny having given Bulgaria an ultimatum, and are pretending total lack of interest. Those old poker-players! Eden's preaching in Ankara seems to be falling on deaf ears. Our position in the Balkans is excellent.

Magda rings up from Dresden. She is looking forward so much to our reunion. I read Tore Hamsun's book about his father.* A whimsical old man, a real original, who becomes even more sympathetic from a human viewpoint at close quarters. This man Hamsun is a hunk of nature, or better still, of earth. The greatest of living poets, because he is so close to Mother Earth.

Then a long discussion with Hippler on film matters in the evening.

Late to bed. Away early today. To Leipzig. Opening of the Spring Fair.

3 March 1941 (Monday)

Yesterday: To Leipzig. During the trip, work with Bömer, Maiwald, and Hunke. Foreign Policy.

Bulgaria has joined the Three-Power Pact. Big sensation. Now things are

---

* Knut Hamsun (*see* biographical note in Index).

252

ready to roll in the Balkans. Turkey is keeping clear. Eden's trip to Ankara was unsuccessful.

Heavy bombing raid on Cologne. Thirty dead. Quite considerable damage. We Shall have to sit and take it now.

Another 30,000 tons sunk. Discuss current problems with Mutschmann. He is a good soul. Freyberg and Fichte have now reached agreement.

Exchange ideas with Colonel-General von Schobert. He is watching our back against Russia. Useful job.

Fair opens. Solemn declaration. Glorious music from the orchestra of the *Gewandhaus. Prelude* by Strauss. Thrilling!

My speech is very effective. Leipzig as the sole Reich Fairs City.

Meal with the guests of honour. A lot of ministers from the Balkans. How small they are! I explain the European situation to them.

On to Dresden by train. Arrival there around 16.00. Magda at the station. What a joy to see each other again! The Hommels and Ursel are there, too. Out to [. . .].

A little tea party. We chat. Stroll in the spring air. Magda tells me all her little news. Everything is very nice and harmonious.

More news. Serious damage in Cologne. Some fifty dead in the Gau as a whole.

Italy is sounding off in the *Popolo d'Italia*, and has announced the occupation of Bulgaria by our troops. Another provocative leak. We immediately issue a special announcement: inviolability of Bulgarian neutrality, Sofia's full consent, protection of her national sovereignty. The Italians are beyond all shame. They are trying to steal our thunder.

Filov has stated the basis of the entire business to his parliament. Big celebrations in Sofia. Belgrade will not be able to wait much longer now.

London is making great play of Eden's 'success' in Turkey: they claim that this completely compensates for our triumph in Bulgaria. And then they get the cold-shoulder of an icy denial from Ankara for their pains. Poor Churchill! Now let him look to his head. The time is coming.

Then an hour at Bellevue in Dresden. Affectionate farewell. In Berlin at 2 a.m.

4 March 1941 (Tuesday)

Yesterday: No incursions on either side. A number of sinkings. Malta attacked. Likewise Tobruk. Keren encircled. [K . . .] taken by de Gaulle troops. In Italian Somaliland, our Axis friends have taken to their heels.

Occupation of Bulgaria goes smoothly, with some slight delays because of a bridge collapse. We advance as far as an agreed line, but not up to the Turkish border. The Bulgarian people welcomes our soldiers in a very friendly fashion.

Contrary to all agreements, the *Popolo d'Italia* blurted out all the details of the operation in advance. Very damaging. We demand they be prosecuted for treason. Time we laid our cards on the table. Great relief among the public here. Boundless rage and gloom in England. They are pretending lack of interest. But that fools no one. The Americans are also very depressed. A great success for the Führer. Turkey is striving to remain neutral. London's vainglorious declarations about far-reaching agreements with Turkey, etc., are coolly but categorically denied.

Report from the SD on Rumania. Exactly as I had thought. The Legion has been toppled from power and decimated, partly, at least, with the aid of our diplomats. Antonescu is a tool of our enemies. An appalling situation. In tune with the whole affair, Antonescu received 99.9 per cent of the votes in the elections, which naturally were by open ballot. The biggest Balkan swindle that one could possibly conceive.

Our diplomats are guilty of many sins against Rumania. One day there will be a bitter reckoning.

The English radio spokesman, Priestley, has been spouting the most outrageous nonsense against us on the radio. I have him dealt with accordingly.

Moscow has been proving very popular in Leipzig, to some extent demonstratively so. I have the SD investigate this more closely.

Film problems with Hippler. Hesse has written a letter, in which he tries to blackmail us into giving his film a better certificate. I summon Wedel and Martin immediately and renounce any further co-operation between myself or my ministry and Hesse.

Personnel and organisational matters with Gutterer. The German Academy, led by Siebert, is in a sticky situation between the various ministries. Siebert doubtless thought that things would be much easier. And the Foreign Ministry is breathing down his neck. This is what happens when one does not make a definite decision. I warned Siebert at the time.

Spieler's work is very unreliable. He has no staying-power and also no real enthusiasm. I tell him the harsh truth. Likewise with Schaumburg, who is totally lacking in concentration and is very forgetful.

Study a mass of memoranda and accumulated paperwork during the afternoon. Speak to Magda on the telephone. She is well. As are the children, who I ring up on the mountain.

Newsreel in the evening. A host of new and very impressive pictures from Bulgaria included. By dint of single-minded work, we are able to get it ready for this week. Hard going, when there is such a dearth of material.

5 March 1941 (Wednesday)

Yesterday: Few incursions on either side. Malta attacked. Heavy air raids on our part in Africa. Our Axis friends retreat further in Italian Somaliland. Occupation of Bulgaria completed without problems. London trying harassing manoeuvres. Moscow issues a blustering communiqué: to the effect that the occupation increases the danger of war and that Russia can no longer support Bulgaria's policy. A paper threat in my view. We make absolutely no reaction. But London inflates it into a massive setback for us. The matter will be soon forgotten. Realities, and not communiqués, are the decisive factor. Nevertheless, we shall keep a watchful eye on Moscow.

Eden in Athens, begging for fair weather. He obviously left Ankara with a flea in his ear. And even Greece is showing considerably more reluctance to fall in line.

New reports from Rumania: my view confirmed once more. But Antonescu has only one no-vote for every thousand yeses. Like hell!

In the USA they are waiting on events. All we have to do is to be careful, make no false moves. If we do, the entire pack will fall on us. Belgrade is still thinking things over. But that cannot last much longer.

The Hesse Affair is fast turning into the Brauchitsch Affair. Keitel is for sacking Hesse. Brauchitsch is hanging on to him. I have closed the press and radio to Hesse. We shall see what happens. Whatever the case, I shall not give in. I am now handing all the material over to Göring for his information.

A number of administrative matters with Gutterer.

Forster wants aid for his theatres. He shall have it. He tells me about a bizarre case of a leak involving the SD. He will have to be on the alert in that quarter. This snooping is nauseating. Denunciation turned into an industry. Let them just cross my path. Forster is very depressed. I cheer him up a little.

Johst gives me a report on the literary situation. Somewhat confused. He has written a good film script, 'Thomas Paine'.

Speech to writers for young people. We must have better children's books. The material on offer in this field at the moment is complete trash. I find an understanding attitude.

Lovely letters from Helga and Hilde.

Professor Ziegler delivers a report on the Chamber of Art. A few specialist problems, but nothing of importance. Ziegler is so boring that he literally sends me to sleep.

A crazy pace right through the day. And glorious spring weather outside all the while.

In the afternoon I drive out to inspect the film studios and films in progress. First to Johannisthal. Things look very bleak there. The studios are quite inadequate and will have to disappear after the war. Neither do the staff make a very good impression. All so lax and lifeless. I shall sort this place out.

At the Grunewald studios to see Jannings, who is filming *Ohm Krüger*. The big studio is one enormous camp. Jannings is working on a wonderful scene. Then we see rushes from the film, which put all previous material in the shade. We spend a long time deliberating whether we should bring the film out in one part or two. I think one part, because this will make for greater impact.

Great enthusiasm for our soldiers in Bulgaria. A flurry of shots from London, but none of them hit home. The wildest rumours are flitting around the Balkans. Our denials-machine is at work round the clock.

Papen has delivered a note from the Führer to the Turkish President. Soothing words and guarantees of the country's borders. Accepted in a very friendly fashion. Turkey and Portugal will soon fall in with our line. England is totally isolated in Europe.

Work until late. Magda is a little unwell. But the children are in good spirits. I send them a pompous telegram, which amuses them hugely.

It is very lonely at home. Work is the only cure.

6 March 1941 (Thursday)

Yesterday: Few incursions into the Reich. We bomb Cardiff and London very heavily. In the Mediterranean, raid on Malta. Big raid on the Suez Canal. A few sinkings. The English 'conquer' one of the Lofoten Islands, but withdraw again immediately.

Everything is going according to plan in Bulgaria. Great conjecture about Greece and Turkey. Both have cold feet about the English. We can expect a few more sensational developments in that quarter. In any case, our best course is to keep absolutely clear of there. The wildest rumours are in circulation, involving everything from an armed invasion to a peace-offer. We leave everything to take its course.

New reports from Rumania. Antonescu's 'election result' completely rigged. The Jews are becoming arrogant again. The generals and the freemasons rule. Quiet as a graveyard. The ideal state so far as our diplomats are concerned, for they have always preferred political sterility. One day it will kill them.

Hesse tries to play the innocent and submits plans for new films. I have him shown the door. The battle between Keitel and Brauchitsch is intensifying. I am a mere observer at the moment.

A few reforms of the broadcasting service. Particularly, more of the common touch in the programmes.

Problems of the day with Gutterer. Reinhardt has a mass of questions concerning the press. Paper shortage, exclusion of Kern from *Das Reich* on the Führer's orders, new magazines, funds for the Propaganda Company staff, which Lammers also rings me about. A whole mass of problems, but we soon agree on them.

Kube tells me of the atrocious events in the Bavarian Eastern Marches Gau. [. . .], who I, of course, always disapproved of, has become absolutely impossible. He is a pocket tyrant and for this reason universally disliked.

The *Uschla** already has him in its grip. So his days are numbered.

Schaumburg and Spieler tell me their personal troubles. Partly a matter of pride, partly bad conscience. I really give them a rocket and warn them to take more care in their work. They lack drive and initiative. They promise to improve.

Schmidt-Cracow does not emerge from the trouble there totally without blemish. I recall three of my people from Cracow. The people in the General Government all develop a sort of tropical frenzy in the end.

Relations between London and Sofia broken off. This changes nothing.

The rumours about Turkey are assuming downright grotesque forms. They are now being nurtured by London and Washington. One more proof of how badly things are going for the enemy. In Rome they are already drivelling about peace with Greece. The Italian press is showing a grave lack of discipline, particularly over Bulgaria. We shall pay back the Italians back in their own coin. One cannot play games with these people. They have no conception of loyalty.

Carol has fled from Spain to Portugal. With a forged passport, the Spaniards say. Supposed to imply that he did so with our covert support. The Spaniards are playing a dirty game. Franco is no more than a jumped-up sergeant-major.

Speak with the children on the telephone. Their sweet chatter! How much better I feel afterwards. I am really happy. Magda is still suffering from her bronchitis. An unpleasant business.

Finish reading Tore Hamsun's book, *My Father*. Old Knut Hamsun is a knotty, sometimes downright strange character. But impressive. Such a healthy contempt for the world and society is totally refreshing.

Catte's *Conversations with Frederick the Great*. What a giant! What a universal spirit, but also what a sensitive artistic soul. My admiration increases with each page. I read deep into the night.

7 March 1941 (Friday)

Yesterday: No incursions on either side. Malta heavily attacked. A few sinkings. Ineffectual assaults by the Greeks in Albania. No news from Africa. The occupation of Bulgaria is proceeding according to plan. Wild conjecture in London. They are issuing optimistic statements about the negotiations with the Greeks. The reports from Athens sound considerably more reserved. This is the beginning of the sea change.

A brazen article in the magazine *Daheim* attacking the Führer's strategic abilities. I should like to bet that Hesse is behind this yet again. I have it investigated. Keitel shares my view of the Hesse case. He has written to Brauchitsch in this vein. The latter has not yet expressed an opinion. But he must do so soon.

* *Untersuchungs- und Schlichtungsausschuss* (Committee for Investigation and Adjustment). The internal disciplinary court of the Nazi Party.

Strong opposition to the Aid for England Bill in the USA. But it will be passed, despite everything. For this reason we make little mention of the opposition.

Lord Alexander makes a speech with a strong undertone of pessimism. Has every reason to do so. We cut it, and him, to pieces.

I take steps against the fashion world, which is plugging clothes that need a lot of material, now of all times. This is all we need in the middle of a war.

Discuss reform of the Reich Culture Chamber with Gutterer. We must do something in that quarter. Hinkel is to carry out the operation.

Consultations with Stephan about welfare provisions for the Propaganda Company people. I establish a fund of a million marks for after the war. Otherwise the publishers will gobble up all the money.

Reich Culture Chamber and KdF matters with Ley. He comes back to his Seventh Chamber. I remain non-committal. In everything else, one can get on well with Ley. If it were not for his wife!

Musical matters with Raabe. I let him have the money for his Liszt Museum, explain my position on the question of serious and popular music. He approves my view and has some very harsh words to say on the subject of Richard Strauss. He is a real moneygrubber. But he can write music.

Write leader-article for *Das Reich*. This gives me more pleasure every time. It also strikes a loud chord with the public. New title: 'The Old Cynics'. A showdown with the Lords.

Peace between Thailand and Indochina imminent. Tokyo has turned the screw.

Quiet in Bulgaria [. . .]. Still the big theme of the moment.

The Pope and his cardinals are praying for peace. Too late. The game must be played to its conclusion.

Aircraft losses in one week 23:15 in our favour. England has lost 370,000 tons of shipping in this period, of which she will admit only 60,000. The main thing, however, is that the ships are at the bottom of the sea. The English lie on principle. One is powerless against it.

Great conjecture about Yugoslavia. London has already given her up for lost.

Magda and the children are well.

Read *Conversations with Frederick the Great* deep into the night.

8 March 1941 (Saturday)

Yesterday: No air incursions on either side. Attacks on La Valetta.* The English attack on our Lofoten Islands was more serious than at first thought: we lost 15,000 tons of shipping in the process. Espionage by the Norwegians was involved. Terboven has gone straight there and is clearing things up. There have also been a mass of death sentences in Amsterdam. I argue in

* The main port of Malta.

favour of the rope for Jews. Those fellows must learn their lesson.

Everything in the Balkans according to plan. In Africa, our Stukas have attacked English camps and military concentrations near Benghazi. Otherwise nothing of note.

Hesse has been sent on leave. Bravo! One nuisance fewer! Now, however, we must do something for the army in our propaganda. I immediately open discussions with Bertram for a new war film dealing with the army: 'The Road to Abbéville'. I explain the basic approach and direction to him. Bertram is delighted and sets to work straightaway. The war film *Assault Group Hallgarten* has been something of a failure, as I predicted. Another glorious achievement of Hesse's. I now intend to get rid of all this amateurism.

Discuss reorganisation of the Reich Culture Chamber with Gutterer. It will be totally separated from the ministry, for it must be a movement rather than an administrative machine. Hinkel will become chief manager and, if need be, Under-Secretary of State. I shall give him wide powers. He is to build the entire thing anew. Deal with the most important matters at the centre, but for the rest, decentralise.

Lauterbacher has announced a ban on all dances in Hannover. Wants to extend it to the entire Gau. I consider this to be premature. Hitler Youth methods!

Discuss a mass of new film material with Hippler. He is doing an outstanding job.

Winkler reports. The film industry's earnings are magnificent. Sixty million in one year. We shall raise the hire charges. [. . .]-yearly another thirty million. With this money I shall build new film theatres in the East and the West. Winkler wants to release *Ohm Krüger* in two parts. I shall have to see it first. The new Riefenstahl film is causing us worry. Crazy sums of money are being poured into it. Winkler brings reports of the reception given to *Jud Süss* abroad. Quite magnificent. It caused street-demonstrations in Hungary. This film is as good as a new political programme. Proof that films can exert influence and provide inspiration completely in line with our ideals.

I have so much to do that my head is literally buzzing.

12,000 tons sunk by U-boats.

Weygand in Vichy. But probably also on a secret mission. He is not to be trusted.

Peace between Thailand and Indochina almost in sight. Tokyo has exerted pressure.

Much conjecture about Yugoslavia. It will soon be answered. In London founded more in fear than in curiosity. Churchill has leaked something like a set of war aims via the USA, as a feeler. Everything exactly as in 1919. Learned nothing, forgotten nothing.

We demand the return of our people from the French Foreign Legion.

They will be formed into units for Africa. They can rehabilitate themselves there.

The cables from the USA to our short-wave service were mostly positive. Now they are being answered by negative ones every evening. The Jews are inadvertently giving us cheap publicity.

Visit to the AO in the afternoon. The younger Hess, Bohle and Schmidt-Decker are very pleasant and affable. I am now able to use the AO for my purposes. It is completely at my disposal. I speak on 'Propaganda and "Propaganda"', am in my best form and enjoy a very good reception. Little sarcastic asides aimed at the Foreign Ministry.

Bohle shows me his organisation. An imposing achievement which is worth seeing. The main thing is that Bohle has good people working for him.

At the Foreign Club. Ursula van Diemen sings. Blissful folk songs. Then I hold a question-and-answer session with the foreign journalists. A few delicate subjects are touched on, but I get through by fast talking. I settle those boys' hash in any case. I have the outgoing reports subjected to censorship.

Terboven rings up. He has established a punitive court of the harshest kind on the Lofoten island which aided the English and betrayed Germans and Quisling's people to them. He has ordered saboteurs' farms to be put to the torch, hostages to be taken, etc. This Terboven fellow is all right. One does not need to pussyfoot with him; he knows himself what he must do. The opposite of Seyss-Inquart, who is so busy weighing everything up that he never makes a decision. But I do not intend to have the affair taken up by the German press again. We have had enough of it, and the German people has already forgotten it.

The Balkans are in ferment. Bizarre tales are being peddled there, each more fantastic than the one before. Particularly regarding Turkey and Yugoslavia, the two pressure-points of the South-East.

Antonescu receives the press and praises his election result. Wretched hypocrisy!

It gets so late. And I am so tired.

9 March 1941 (Sunday)

Yesterday: No incursions here. We attack eight English airfields with great success. Some 50,000 tons sunk in all. This is the most painful, and the most important, area as far as England is concerned. All quiet in the Balkans, except for the rumours. Bulgaria has been occupied without any problems. We are already in position along the predetermined line. Athens is still making up its mind.

Nothing of importance in Africa.

The English raid on the Lofoten Islands is still the big theme in the London press. We make no further mention of it. Terboven has taken punitive measures that the pro-English Norwegians will not forget in a hurry.

Still a lot of activity in the USA. But Roosevelt will soon have his Aid for England Bill under his belt.

More trouble about Hesse. I inform Brauchitsch via Lutze that I see no possibility of keeping Hesse in his post. Now Brauchitsch must decide. And the Führer has placed all Wehrmacht propaganda under the authority of the Wehrmacht High Command. A great advance!

The mood of the country is still good, but tense. Cities that are being subjected to heavy air raids (Cologne, Hannover) are rather depressed. Complaints are being made about the jazzing-up of popular music. The radio in general is universally praised.

I now have the piece by Forbes, *The Sixth Wife*, taken off. It is causing nothing but trouble and is a feast for the enemies of the state.

At midday, work on my speeches for Linz and Vienna. And outside there is such wonderful spring weather. One would like to be able to cast everything aside and go for a walk.

Magda is well, as are the children. They are very happy up on the mountain.

A short stroll in our park, where the spirit of spring is already abroad. Then back to my desk.

A total of 62,600 tons sunk in one day. Plus two English destroyers.

Rumours of a pact with Belgrade and Ankara. The English will have something coming to them. They are in for a few nasty surprises. Matsuoka's trip to Berlin is made public and arouses the greatest interest in all quarters. Roosevelt will be anything but delighted by it. But one can hope that he is now clear that our co-operation with Japan is a serious business.

A few people from the ministry and the film world to visit in the evening. In these surroundings, one can discuss a thousand things that would be taboo at the office. Such people provide much-needed personal contact and stimulation.

Showing of an American film, *Romeo and Julia*. Theatre transferred to the big screen, but well done. Shearer and Howard thrilling.

Long talk with the arts people.

It gets very late.

Little sleep.

A wonderful Sunday!

10 March 1941 (Monday)

Yesterday: Our motor-torpedo boats have increased their tonnage sunk by 45,000 since Friday. Plus another 20,000 yesterday by U-boats and Luftwaffe. This hits England at her weakest point. The first of the big new raids on London, with 125 aircraft. 130 tons dropped. Pretty devastating effect. Impression of gloom in London and the USA.

Malta attacked with twenty-five aircraft again. Thus a successful day.

Turkey and Yugoslavia are already [. . .] [. . .] London. Belgrade will make a statement first. Even Greece is showing signs of a conciliatory mood. England's situation is bad. Indochina has accepted Tokyo's suggestion. Likewise Thailand. Another failure for London. On the other hand, the American Senate has accepted the Lend-Lease Bill by 60:1. Without doubt a great success for England, which had been expected and provided for. Roosevelt wants to encourage England to a prolonged resistance, so that afterwards he will be all the better placed to inherit her power. Now they will be able to forget all the defeats and fiascos and celebrate the events in Washington. But how long will it last?

Antonescu has spoken to the press again. What a bad conscience he must have!

For the first time in a long while, I go for a short pleasure-drive at midday, to get a little fresh air. In war one turns into a real indoor fixture.

My drive takes me to the west. Potsdam and a small detour to Schwanenwerder.

Dictate my speech for the opening of the rebuilt Posen theatre.

In Turkey a newspaper has been banned for doubting the sincerity of German assurances. A sign of the times that speaks volumes! The fermentation process in the Balkans continues. Our wine will soon be drinkable.

The raid on London, it is now becoming clear, was very damaging. There were large numbers of fatalities. There will be more.

Magda is well, as are the children. I miss all of them.

In the evening, continue reading *Frederick the Great* for a long time.

11 March 1941 (Tuesday)

Yesterday: No incursions. More punishing attacks on London. Very depressing reports from there. But there will be worse to come. Portsmouth also subjected to heavy raids. Malta bombed again. Giarabub attacked, but the Italians hold on. Things continue according to plan in Bulgaria. Turkey is behaving quite civilly. Even banning anti-German newspapers. Greece is making soundings and trying to talk to us. Yugoslavia is ready. London is weeping.

A few satisfying sinkings. We calculated too high a tonnage during our motor-torpedo boats' last foray. A statistical error that has now been corrected.

Italy wants to start the offensive in Albania now. Well, we shall wait a while.

Again a lot of complaints about Forbe's *The Sixth Wife*. The press is still plugging it in some places. The ghost will be laid on Saturday. Likewise people are complaining about the increasingly unrestrained quality of our dance music. I take immediate countermeasures.

The Führer has permitted marriages between Danish, Dutch, Norwegian, etc. women and officers. This is correct and also politically expedient.

Halifax considers food deliveries to Belgium to be 'fake humanitarianism'. We give him one in the eye. Cowardly, hypocritical swine!

My address at the Foreign Club has had a marvellous response from the neutral press. Perhaps a little too good. I ban mention of it in the Reich. Bömer is given a dressing-down for having failed to put the censors on to it.

We play a few games with England regarding the invasion. The English are to be kept at their defensive preparations and given plenty of cause for anxiety . . .

. . . Feeling in Paris still bad. Likewise in Belgium. I forbid a guest appearance by the Berlin Philharmonic before the public in Paris. They should play for our soldiers. Vichy is threatening escorts of warships for French merchant steamers if England continues to seize them. That is the kind of news I like to hear.

The opposition has given up the struggle in the USA. London is crowing fit to burst about all the war material that it will now receive from America.

Görlitzer has complaints about Meinshausen. Justified. M. is an old troublemaker. Reich Coal Commissar Walter has been replaced by Pleiger. He will give industry preference over private consumption. We shall have to keep a sharper watch than before.

Discuss a number of troop-entertainment questions with Hinkel. He is doing good work.

Brauchitsch comes to see me. Subject: Hesse. I tell him my opinion quite frankly and openly, even concerning the propaganda centred around his personal position. He is quite taken aback. There can be no question of Hesse's being restored to his post, which is clearly what he had intended to urge on me. I also enumerate the mass of tactless acts of which Hesse has been guilty, even towards the Führer. He is doing the army more harm than good. Brauchitsch now intends to put him in some quiet job at the Army High Command. The conversation ends in complete agreement, inasmuch as I succeed totally in enforcing my point of view.

Ever-wider reverberations of the Lend-Lease Law in the USA. London, of course, is seizing it eagerly, like a drowning man clutching at a straw. We must now pull out all the stops to avoid a third winter of war.

Complete my speeches for Posen in the afternoon. They turn out well.

Work on the newsreel until late in the evening. Also successful.

Magda is well, as are the children. A hard day draws to an end. Let it go! Ufa film, *U-Boats Westwards*. Good in parts, but without real pace or much atmosphere. Will need a lot of changes.

Deep sleep!

12 March 1941 (Wednesday)

Yesterday: Cologne bombed. A few dead, some damage. The Cardinal of Cologne dies of a heart attack in the course of the raid.

We carry out a massive raid on Portsmouth with 200 aircraft. Excellent results expected. Also bombs on Malta. Our Panzers encounter the English in Libya. The English are put to flight. Our transports to Africa have arrived without loss so far. This is cause for satisfaction.

Belgrade has still not made up its mind. Turkey very cautious. In the USA the final phase of the battle for Roosevelt's Bill. There will be no more amendments. Triumph in London. Perhaps too early and too loud.

We have finally got rid of Hesse. No one is more pleased than Martin and Wedel.

Organise entertainments for foreign workers. Something must be done for them.

Schmidt-Cracow can hardly be kept on. He fights and boozes too much.

Maraun expelled from the Literature Chamber. This swine had managed to hang on and on. Admittedly only with Hess's protection.

Draft new guidelines for fire-fighting during air raids. We must discard the old methods in this area: sitting in the shelter and letting one's house burn down. Too easy, when all's said.

Deal with a host of trivialities. Gutterer has been in Vienna. Ley gave a dreadful speech at the exhibition there.

Dr Draeger reports on the Nordic Affiliation Bureau. A good and successful organisation. I raise his aid grant to 100,000 marks.

Hentschke has declared himself in agreement with my suggestions for his two theatres. This will bring fresh blood into the Berlin opera scene.

Dr Kriegk has requested an interview on 'intellectual warfare' for the *Woche*.

Clarify a number of matters with Hess. He considers Ribbentrop to be seriously ill. Motto: don't rouse him! A surefire method of knocking the other fellow for six, he claims. But I do not intend to get involved in this kind of thing. There is to be a campaign to encourage women to work, on a voluntary basis for the moment. We are going to organise a big rally at which Hess will speak on the subject.

Peace at last between Thailand and Indochina.

Matsuoka's visit to Berlin is attracting enormous publicity.

New summaries of shipping losses published in London. Very high. They are closer to the truth these days. Profound gloom.

Draft speeches all afternoon, then write an article attacking Halifax. Very successful . . .

. . . Magda is well. Hedda rather ill. Otherwise the children are very cheery on the telephone. Speaking to them is always such a delight.

Sit at my desk until midnight. Then tumble into bed.

13 March 1941 (Thursday)

Yesterday: Early into the office. Raid on Kiel and Hamburg, but no serious damage. We attack Birmingham and London with 200 aircraft. At least we are on the offensive again. London is pretty badly hit. Gloom deepened by the shipping losses, which were admitted to be extensive. This is England's most vulnerable point. We chalk up more sinkings.

We are off to a flying start with our military aid to Libya. All our transport ships have arrived safely. There can be no upsets now. An entire motorised division is in position . . .

. . . Flight to Linz. In glorious weather. For the celebrations marking the third anniversary of the *Anschluss*.* A thousand things dealt with during the flight. Martin is now worried that I shall give in to Brauchitsch. Out of the question. I reassure him.

Check the statute of the International Film Chamber. Well drafted. We must concentrate the whole thing in Berlin, even if the Italians protest. We are the great power in the European cinema.

SD report: morale good throughout the country. Everyone is waiting for the blows to fall. Study paperwork, revise material, discuss things in the plane. Time really does fly. In Linz towards midday. The city is a sea of flags. And this glorious spring sky. Eigruber there to meet me, along with the entire Gau leadership. Big procession into the city. Just like peacetime. One notices very little of the war here. Children evacuated from Berlin lining the entrance to the hotel. They are all chubby-faced and healthy and have absolutely no desire to go back to Berlin. The Burgomaster gives a good speech.

In the town hall, Professor Fink shows me the plans for the rebuilding of Linz. A project on a vast scale, in which one can see the hand of the Führer. Linz must create a cultural counterweight to the increasing industrialisation of the city. A favourite project of the Führer, who cares a great deal about his home town.

Göring Works:** magnificent plan. Plus a comprehensive programme of home-building, which Eigruber is pursuing with vigour. In general he gives an impression of energy and vitality. Will get on top of the job.

To Leonding. Lay a wreath on the grave of the Führer's parents. A-tremble! At the house where the Führer spent his youth. Much has been changed. Not to the advantage of this place. It has been prettied up. Nevertheless I am most deeply moved yet again. The people of Leonding are very enthusiastic.

Drive to St Florian. To the monastery where Bruckner used to create.

* The Nazi annexation of Austria on 12 March 1938.
** A massive steel works planned for Linz as part of the *Reichswerke Hermann Göring* (Herman Göring National Works), the state corporation created by Hitler to control the German steel industry.

What a wonderful baroque building. We intend to turn the priests out of here and found a music college and a home for the Bruckner Society. A marvellous plan.

A superb marble hall. Spectacular hand-carved work in the sacristy, plus this unusual church. Bruckner's organ. His last surviving pupil is playing it. A time for recharging one's inner strength. Then I stand for a while below by his tomb in the crypt, which is placed precisely beneath the organ that he played for so many years. A farm boy who conquered the world with his music. How rich this district is in culture, history, and artistic power, even today. As we see when the Gau cultural prize is awarded at the District House. Names such as Richard Billinger are read out. I am very pleased. Even say a few words myself about the future cultural mission of Linz.

We continue to drive between endless lines of spectators. Marvellous enthusiasm. And the people do not even know that the Führer intends to come this evening.

Short rest and a break at the hotel, a rather primitive concrete construction.

To the meeting in the evening. Between huge crowds. The cheering never stops. Meeting overflowing. Fantastic atmosphere. I speak on the war situation. Each sentence is punctuated by storms of applause. I am on good form. Then the Gauleiter makes a short speech. And now, completely unexpected so far as the meeting is concerned, the Führer arrives. The storm of applause is quite indescribable. The Führer is lively and buoyant. He speaks for thirty minutes with the greatest élan. Total confidence in victory. The crowd goes wild.

Drive between endless crowds. At the hotel. Then I stand with the Führer on the balcony of his hotel room, and we look out over his home town. He loves this city very much, and this is understandable. He intends to establish a new centre of culture here. As a counterweight to Vienna, which will have to be gradually phased out of the picture. He does not like Vienna, basically for political reasons. I tell him a few things that I know about Vienna, aspects downright hostile to the Reich, which annoy him greatly. But Linz is his darling. I give him an account of my impressions, which he is very pleased with. He intends to make alterations to St Florian at his own expense. He is also increasingly satisfied with Eigruber. A wonderful evening with the Führer. He expounds his views on the situation to me: everything is going well, both militarily and diplomatically. We can be very satisfied.

Then we spend a long time chatting with people from Linz. Real German men. Not like those Viennese mongrels. It gets very late. Three hours' sleep.

14 March 1941 (Friday)

Yesterday: A minister for eight years. What a time, how many joys and how much work! But what a path to the top! I am very grateful to fate.

The Führer leaves very early to inspect the city of Linz. Hearty farewell!

Heavy air raid on Berlin. Some 30 dead and widespread damage. A six-hour air-raid warning. Plus heavy raids on Hamburg and Bremen. But we attack Liverpool with 400 aircraft in good visibility. Devastating results. London in despair. And there is more on the way! We shall soon force them to their knees. Summary: in the past months, two million tons sunk. That was supposedly a 'pause'. London denies this violently.

Unfortunately, only a few sinkings by the U-boat fleet. And the Italians are not so keen to go on to the offensive, after all. An idle, cowardly crew!

Turkey continues to reserve her position. Anxious guessing-game in Greece.

Roosevelt is about to sign the Lease Bill. Trumpets his infamous opinions in a detailed letter to Congress. Nothing but a brutal urge to prolong the war. In the press he is threatening us with war if we sink his arms convoys. He will soon come to see what we can do. In London, there is, of course, jubilation. Churchill makes a spirited speech of thanks to the USA. But it will do him no good.

Leave Linz by plane. I receive yet more gifts. The Party Comrades here are very amiable. Real types from the Upper Danube. The Führer's home Gau.

Work at a cracking pace during the flight. The snow-decked peaks glisten in the distance. Big reception at Wiener Neustadt. And a fantastic drive into the city. Cheering crowds. Vienna is celebrating its national day.

Discuss a few things with Schirach. We reach agreement about Caspar. Each of us will have him for six months. And Müthel can take over the State Opera as well as the *Burgtheater* so far as I am concerned. Perhaps this is the best solution.

Schirach is involved in a furious row with Ribbentrop. Who isn't?

Rally on the Heldenplatz. 200,000 people. Vienna is overflowing. Wild enthusiasm. I speak on my best form. Attacking the carpers, who are given the title of 'Bobby', while I portray myself as 'Piefke'. I think that a breakthrough has been made in this area, even in Vienna. When I leave the Heldenplatz, I find myself trapped by the enthusiastic crowd. It takes three-quarters of an hour for me to get out. I have rarely seen anything like it. There is your 'oppositional' Vienna!

Flight from Wiener Neustadt. A lot of work on the way. A mountain of paperwork to deal with. Grant a heap of money for a host of causes.

Arrive in Berlin in darkness. Gutterer reports on the air raid. It seems that Berlin suffered heavily. I immediately order a number of measures to alleviate the worst effects.

Two correspondents from our *Transozean** agency have been arrested in the USA. I consider retaliatory action against US journalists in Berlin. Churchill is forced to give chapter and verse about the shipping losses in a secret session of the House of Commons. He would rather have kept quiet about those. He will not have had it so easy there as on the radio. And we shall make every effort to cause him a few more worries.

In Istanbul a bomb has exploded in the luggage of the English Ambassador to Sofia. They are trying to put the blame on to us. The probable truth is that an employee of the Secret Service was a little careless.

Funk has made an excellent speech about our financial position.

Continue reading, studying papers and revising material until late in the evening. How tired I am!

15 March 1941 (Saturday)

Yesterday: A high-pressure, crazy day. I am at full stretch the entire day.

No attack on Berlin. The one the previous night turns out to have been very heavy. Twenty-six dead. The city's morale has not suffered. This time, raid on Hamburg. Fairly heavy. And a number of industrial and military targets hit. In response, we attack Liverpool again, then Glasgow with 250 aircraft. Striking at industry and ship repair facilities. Hull gets a pasting besides. US reports on our raids are sensational. Our fliers are talking of two new Coventrys. We shall see how long England can put up with this.

More bombs on the Suez Canal. Slight activity in North Africa. In Albania, the Italians are still waiting for us to pull their chestnuts out of the fire.

We have exposed Willkie as a turncoat. The US press has given this big coverage. A corrupt type, a white Jew, and it is well-known that they are worse than the genuine article. In the USA they are visibly putting a damper on English optimism. London, however, is still claiming that the Balkans are turning against us. One more sign that things are going badly for the English. Tension is growing everywhere. Rumours race around the globe, but none of them have any substance. Once again, we alone have the key to the situation . . .

. . . At midday I am host to all the department chiefs on the ministry's anniversary. A very pleasant gathering, all good brains and real men.

And then work and more work the whole day through. It never lets up. At times one can feel quite crushed by it. And so through to the evening without pausing.

Speak with Magda on the telephone. Hedda had to have an operation. This is sad news. But everything went well. One worries twice as much when the children are away from one. They are now to go to the Salzburg area.

* The Propaganda Ministry's overseas news agency.

Watch the Bavaria Studios' *Carl Peters* film. With Albers. The film is not outstanding. Too much editorialising and too little action. The message is too crudely expressed, and the parts attacking the government of the time do not hit their target. I am very dissatisfied with it.

Reach agreement with Frau Bernau regarding her engagement at the National Theatre in Weimar. She will be a valuable addition to the ensemble there.

The English have not arrived by one in the morning. So off to bed!

16 March 1941 (Sunday)

Yesterday: Devastating raids on Glasgow and Sheffield. Give them what for! A few sinkings. Only middling raids in the West here.

A lot of work to do. Scarcely time to breathe. The entire Saturday is booked up from beginning to end. Help Frau Margit Symo a little in her career.

In the afternoon, watch *Ohm Krüger* with Jannings and Demandowski. A really great, thrilling work of art. The supreme achievement of the entire war. This is a film to go crazy about. Jannings is very happy. The film can only be released in one part.

Magda rings up from the Obersalzberg in the evening: Hedda is feeling better. The poor little dear. I should so love to see the children again. I talk to them all on the telephone. The sweet things!

The Führer is back in Berlin, but I have had no chance to speak to him yet because of the pressure of work. In the evening, to the Lutzes, where I am together with Brauchitsch. We sniff each other warily. He is quite pleasant, but his wife makes a dreadful impression: so loud and uneducated. She will do him a lot of harm.

So late, and so tired, to bed.

17 March 1941 (Monday)

Yesterday: Roosevelt has made a blustering, shameless speech attacking us. A lacky of the Jews! I have him attacked unmercifully by the press and radio. There is no point in holding back any longer. It only makes the Americans more insolent. In exchange for the temporary imprisonment of our *Transozean* correspondents in the USA, I have the representative of United Press in Berlin arrested on suspicion of spying. So that the Yankees realise that they cannot do as they like with us. I am also taking steps against the brazen US radio reporters who are making disgraceful broadcasts from Berlin. The USA will have to be shown that our patience and forbearance are now exhausted.

Little air activity over England. Only some unimportant trouble in the West here. The weather was too bad. Good to be able to get a proper night's sleep.

Heroes' Commemoration Day.* A glorious spring day. Ceremony at the Zeughaus. The Führer makes a wonderful speech. Absolutely confident of victory, even against the USA. That will cause a big sensation. Admittedly he is no longer absolutely clear that this will be the last year of the war. This is better from the psychological standpoint. One can never know how things will develop, and it is always a bad thing to give precise dates.

A smart march-past. Our Wehrmacht is in better form than ever, both at home and at the front.

Discuss the problem of the church press with Kerrl. He would like to save it, but I shall seize this favourable moment and do away with it. And I shall never let it appear again. It has behaved wretchedly, particularly during the war. Ley comes back to the subject of the Seventh Chamber. A stubborn fellow!

Reach agreement with Jodl on the Hesse case. This is now settled. Lutze also has some disparaging things to say about Frau von Brauchitsch.

Interview for the *Woche* on 'intellectual warfare' completed. Turned out well.

Ursel comes to lunch. She has been to the Obersalzberg for two weeks and is able to give me a lot of news about the children. We stroll around the park. What a beautiful day! And what a pleasant afternoon! We listen to the Request Concert, which is magnificent this time. And then some more music. Ursel looks marvellous. She tells us all kinds of things about the Obersalzberg.

Speak to Magda on the telephone in the evening. Hedda is well, and a new place for the children to stay has already been arranged. This is good news.

Newsreel re-edited, but seems to turn out all right.

Bad news from Bremen: the steamer *Bremen* is on fire in several places. It is anchored at the mouth of the Weser. Arson and sabotage are suspected. A great misfortune if, as is thought at present, she cannot be salvaged. Certainly a dirty trick by the Secret Service. But we shall survive this blow, like all the others.

To bed late and tired. Every day has its worries and its burdens.

18 March 1941 (Tuesday)

Yesterday: Such a glorious day! And brings nothing but suffering and woe.

No incursions into the Reich. We launch pretty heavy raids on Bristol, Bournemouth and Portsmouth. 4000 tons sunk. Our U-boats are out of luck at the moment. Torpedo aircraft attack three English warships in the Mediterranean with some success.

---

* Known as the National Day of Mourning before 1933; renamed by the Nazis to give it a more bombastic ring. On 16 March, Germany's war dead were remembered and money collected for the upkeep of military cemeteries.

At my suggestion, the Führer allows Roosevelt's speech to be released to the press for comment. We take a very hard line against it. England is making a big sensation out of the US aid. 'Turning-point of the war'. We must spare no effort to counter this claim. But what else has England to cling to? One has to have some kind of a support when one intends to continue such a harsh struggle. The Führer's speech at the Zeughaus has resounded round the world. His phrase 'England will fall' sets the tone for the international debate. Very useful!

The *Bremen* has been completely destroyed by fire. The ship is unsalvageable. English sabotage, perhaps even by parachutists, is suspected. This version seems highly fantastic to me. All the same, this catastrophe is a national misfortune. We give a lot of thought to how the German people should be informed. We agree finally on a colourless, neutral report, which first reports on the serious fire. London has good reason to be pleased.

Have not yet made any progress in attempts to co-operate with the Foreign Ministry. I do not intend to give it any more thought. Let the individual officials fight it out amongst themselves. I have now tried hard enough to reach a modus vivendi.

I shall now raise the contributions from publishing houses, film and radio for the Propaganda Companies to five million. The Führer has expressed no objection to this, despite Dr Dietrich's trouble-making.

The staff changes at the reich Propaganda Leadership are now complete. We are recruiting some good people. Fischer may well be somewhat outclassed, but I must keep him and support him, because he is such an old and faithful colleague.

Hinkel will now assume the central management of the Reich Culture Chamber. I have granted him wide plenipotentiary powers to this end. I hope that he will restore order to this pretty chaotic outfit. It is high time.

A whole series of new film problems. There are new ones every day. But the work they cause is worthwhile. The German film industry is currently at a level higher than ever before.

Get rid of a mass of degenerate art. This rubbish continues to appear on the market.

Discuss a number of office problems with Gutterer. These days he is a quite indispensable colleague.

Count Helldorff reports to me on a number of unpleasant personnel matters. I take appropriate measures. Discussion about air defence in Berlin. The police are very sceptical in this area. If really heavy air raids occur, things in Berlin will look pretty nasty. Our new shelters are nowhere near sufficient. But we have done, and will continue to do, what we can. And what London can put up with, Berlin will also have to bear, if the worst happens. I am not so despairing as Helldorff. He was always a pessimist.

Report from Müller in Oslo. Situation hardening. Sabotage and opposition everywhere. This will certainly last until we win the war. Until then we must be content if we can at least neutralise the people.

Party Comrade Salzmann from Shanghai reports on the situation in the Far East. He sees things in very clear, simple terms. Japan has got herself stuck, she cannot hold down the huge areas she has already occupied. China is avoiding set-piece battles. Chiang-Kai-Shek is the man so far as all Chinese are concerned. Time and human beings are unimportant when measured against these huge expanses of territory. Both the nations involved would probably like to make peace, but neither wants to lose face. Japan is in no position to take large-scale action anywhere else. This view seems to me correct. I am presented with it in written form, and I intend to make it available to the Führer as well.

With the Führer. He is in the best of moods and very pleasant to me. Enquires in interested fashion about my rally in Vienna, but seems to know almost all the details already. In his view, Vienna will still have a large role to play in future. But Linz is closer to his heart. The Ostmark* as a whole is his particular concern. He intends to do a lot more for it, and to spend a lot more on its behalf. He is very amused by my new creation, the political Bobby. This is how we must reach the carpers. Vienna will soon be entirely Jew-free. And now it is to be Berlin's turn. I am already discussing the question with the Führer and Dr Frank. He puts the Jews to work, and they are indeed obedient. Later they will have to get out of Europe altogether. Everything is in order in the General Government at the moment. Frank does not rule, he commands. This is probably the right method there. He can no longer put up with Schmidt. We shall likely have to send Ohlenbusch from Warsaw to Cracow.

The Führer defines the concept of authority. It cannot tolerate any so-called freedom of the press. In a democracy the ruled criticise their rulers, while in an authoritarian state it is the other way around. If those with ability do not rise, then in the long term there will be a revolution. But even a revolution must be creative, and gradually it will broaden out into conservatism. The final goal of any revolution must be to restore authority. Otherwise it will lead to chaos in the last analysis.

The Führer praises the hard work and inventiveness of the Czechs. The Skoda works have served us extremely well in this war, and particularly at the moment with the invention of the new, double-barrelled flak gun. Skoda will remain in existence. Competiton is a good thing. Krupp, Rheinmetall and Skoda are our three big arsenals. The Führer would like to remove Brünn from the Protectorate and give it to [. . .] as Gau capital. After the war. Then, too, the rebuilding of Berlin and its transformation into a monumental imperial capital will be begun on an ambitious scale.

The Führer sees the situation in very optimistic terms. We are slowly

* 'Eastern March'. The name given to Austria after its incorporation into Germany.

choking England to death. One day she will lie gasping on the ground.

Discuss the Hesse case with Schmundt. Keitel and his people are in total agreement with my approach.

Bormann wants to promote Stennes' people in the Labour Service. I shall have to have a decision from the Führer on this. I make a complaint about Schultze-Strathaus, on his staff, who is pursuing a very un-Nazi cultural policy. Bormann will keep a watch on this. It was he who burdened us with Maraun.

Professor Kreis shows me designs for a war memorial on the French coast facing England. Very monumental. The Führer has given him a special commission for the design of war memorials and cemeteries for our heroes. The right man for the job.

Gandhi's brother-in-law has been taken prisoner on a captured English ship and wants to speak to me. Wants to make anti-English propaganda aimed at India. I shall think about it. Perhaps it has possibilities.

More death sentences carried out in the Hague. Right! It is the only way to keep the peace in an occupied country. The Führer gives us another reminder of the Zabern Incident.* A textbook example of how authority first abdicates its right to rule and is then destroyed.

Have to work all afternoon at full stretch. I have so much to deal with before I leave for Posen.

Berbera retaken by the English. By a trick. The Italians were caught napping yet again.

Lloyds have issued figures for shipping losses that are far higher than the official English ones. We use this as the basis for a hard-hitting attack on Churchill.

Newsreel in the evening. Excellent. Plus a mass of film matters.

Magda rings up: she has found lodgings for the children in Bischofswiesen. Thank God! And Hedda is still improving. One thing less to worry about.

19 March 1941 (Wednesday)

Yesterday: Early flight to Posen. A good flight with a tailwind. Work on the way. Few attacks on England. Bombs on Wilhelmshaven and Oldenburg. Little damage. *Bremen* completely lost . . .

. . . Big reception in Posen. Discuss current issues with Greiser. He has things well in hand. Maul also. Greiser cannot get on with Forster. Forster rather jealous. I shall try to mediate between the two of them.

* In the winter of 1913–14, a German officer arrested some citizens and closed down the local newspaper in the small Alsatian town of Zabern (Saverne), then part of Germany. Subsequent protests by Liberals and Socialists in Germany – including an unheard-of vote of censure against the Chancellor, Bethmann-Hollweg, in the Reichstag – were claimed by the Right to have undermined the authority of the army and the authorities on the eve of the European War.

A big clearing-out operation everywhere here. Particularly Jewish rubbish. This is necessary. I explain the situation to Greiser.

New theatre. Rebuilding by Baumgarten and Bartels has been a great success. A feast for the eyes. Glorious colours and proportion.

Fine opening ceremony. Maul speaks well. Greiser very well. I outline the situation in the East and am greeted with the greatest applause.

Out to Schloss Johannesbach. A rather run-down manor house, formerly belonging to a Polish landowner. But one has peace and quiet. Talk and work.

Back to Posen in the evening. Inspect the small auditorium of the theatre, which Bartels has refurbished. Quite delightful. A real theatre as they used to be in Mozart's time. I am happy that this project of Bartels' has been so successful.

In the large auditorium, *Prinz von Homburg*. A respectable production. The cast are already well-versed in the play. The audience roars its approval. What a fellow that Kleist was!

Reception at the home of the head of the administration, Jäger. Field Marshal von Bock tells me a lot about the offensive in the West. He has a clear mind and is a real gentleman.

At Johannesbach, sit by the fire talking until deep into the night. Sleep very badly. The place is too noisy. And too dirty. Still a bit of Poland!

20 March 1941 (Thursday)

Yesterday: Heavy raids on Kiel and Bremen. Some damage, including military installations. A few ships also seriously hit in Kiel. In response, we attack Hull with 420 aircraft. Mainly incendiary bombs. A quite outstanding success. Raids on Malta. Two English warships struck by air-launched torpedoes. 40,000 tons sunk. The English are now admitting to five million tons, but the real figure is closer to nine million. This is their most vulnerable point. And this is also where the caterwauling sets in. In his latest speech, Churchill has adopted a very gloomy tone. In a very minor key. And he continues to kow-tow to the USA. Proud England! How far she has fallen!

The English continue to advance into Abyssinia. Not that it will do them any good.

All sorts to be done at Johannesbach. Work pursues me everywhere. The Americans have re-arrested our correspondents. We shall take retaliatory measures. Moreover, it seems probable that the American correspondent whom we arrested really is a spy.

A look at the countryside around Posen. How beautiful it is in the first sunshine of spring. I am reluctant to leave. To Posen. The High Burgomaster welcomes me and presents me with two fine lamps as gifts.

Speech to the people from the Reich Propaganda Offices. A survey of the general situation. I am on top form. Very successful. Now all my colleagues are recharged.

To lunch with them. I learn a great variety of things from every Gau. About the Ostmark, in particular. A righteous anger against Vienna down there. This city does not enjoy much affection in the rest of what used to be Austria.

My speech on culture in Posen has been widely and well received.

Plane from Posen. Affectionate farewell from Greiser. He is doing an outstanding job. Schmalz is now his Deputy Gauleiter. Good that he now has something, at least. He is still full of complaints about the way he has been treated. He has some justice on his side.

Heaps of paperwork during the flight. At the airport, I am immediately deluged with demands and questions. Icy cold. At my desk until late in the evening.

Speak to Magda on the telephone. She is coming back at the end of the week. I am looking forward to this very much.

The four new landscapes by Gradl have arrived. Wonderful! They will be a superb ornament to our entrance hall.

It is so late, and I am so tired. Sleep.

21 March 1941 (Friday)

Yesterday: Few incursions into the Reich. We attack London with 450 aircraft. 430 tons of explosives and 11,000 incendiaries dropped . . .

. . . Good monthly report from the Berlin theatres. Full houses everywhere. Hilpert is the only one who seems to have had a streak of bad luck in his theatre. He will have to be cheered up a little . . .

. . . Renzetti comes to say goodbye. He has been torpedoed by Ciano. He complains bitterly about the fact, about the entire clique surrounding the Duce, about the failings of Italian policy and military leadership, about the lack of courage and honesty in the ruling circle. I just listen. But he is right. He has always been a good friend to Germany.

Receive two influential Italian journalists and explain the situation to them. These days they are all so humble and modest. But for how long?

With the Führer. General Rommel is awarded the Oak Leaves.* A magnificent officer. He talks about the difficulties of desert warfare. Our machine is functioning wonderfully. The Italians are causing him nothing but trouble. Not a warlike people. They should be grateful that we are there. The Führer certainly is, and he is also very happy that we have brought our motorised units over there safely. The Führer will not give up Africa under any circumstances. Giarabub is still holding out. The problem is that they

---

* The second ascending grade of the Knight's Cross, the Third Reich's highest award for military gallantry.

have no food. The Italians want to surrender, but Rommel insists that he will raise the siege.

Discuss film matters with Rosenberg and Hess. Neither of them understands much about the subject. But the Führer judges all film problems with instinctive correctness. I tell him about Jannings' *Ohm Krüger*, which he is very interested in and would like to see.

I am able to place fifteen million from the Winter Aid Fund and five million from film profits at the Führer's disposal for social and cultural purposes. He is delighted. I tell him about Posen, about the beautiful theatre, politics in the Warthegau, etc. All this arouses his warmest interest. I gain his permission to have a limited number of musicians declared unfit for army service, to help preserve our orchestras.

He now intends to make the appeal for women workers personally, in place of Hess. Combining it, at my suggestion, with the Red Cross Fund appeal. After Matsuoka's visit at the *Sportpalast*. A good idea. The easiest way of dealing with the problem.

Hess cracks jokes about Ribbentrop. None of us are answering his letters these days. My example has set a fashion. Ribbentrop is an insufferable fellow.

Yugoslavia has still not taken the decisive step. On the contrary, her attitude has hardened slightly. And even more so in the case of Turkey. Scaracoglu has met Eden on Cyprus. Not pleasant news. Eden is a well-known trouble-stirrer. Greece is now boasting that she will resist. How long can this go on?

Dictate a leader-article attacking the faked English statistics. Works well. My pieces in *Das Reich* meet with everyone's wholehearted approval. The English are allowing more and more details of the damage caused by the German Luftwaffe to be leaked through the neutral press. Evidence that things must be really appalling so far as everyday life in England is concerned.

Stojadinovic exiled to Greece by the Belgrade government for continuing pro-German sentiments. A real Balkan affair!

Speak to Magda on the telephone. Everything is going well.

A cheerful Rühmann film, *Main Thing: Happy*. Not exactly a brilliant achievement!

I am planning a new certificate for big films like *Ohm Krüger*. Something along the lines of 'National-Film'. Combined with the award of a ring of honour to its creator. This will act as a further incentive to our film makers in the pursuit of excellence. Our film industry is on the march.

22 March 1941 (Saturday)

Yesterday: No incursions into the Reich. Horrifying accounts of our raids on London. We attack Plymouth with 155 in perfect visibility. Again, devastating results, as even London concedes in part. Plus some sinkings.

The situation in Africa is stabilising to some extent under our influence. Things are, it must be admitted, bad in Abyssinia. The English are advancing on Harrar. Our General Staff has given up most of the country for lost.

Mood in London very low. Air-raid damage and shipping losses give every ground for their gloom. And more voices of reason in the USA now . . .

. . . Thomas Mann has appealed to the German people. Senile windbag! In London they have started using the phrase 'Huns' again. So things must be bad for England.

I am giving close attention to the cultural welfare of the foreign workers in the Reich. There are several hundred thousand of them. Also, the tough line against prisoners-of-war has been relaxed slightly. We are dependent on their hard work. And the Jews, it turns out, cannot be evacuated from Berlin, because 30,000 of them are working in armaments factories. Who would have thought it possible in the old days?

Bormann is making trouble about the Red Cross Appeal. Mere jealousy. In fact, he has been a general thorn in my side. He has also been criticising Ritter's film, *Over All in the World*. But I have managed to force through its release by an appeal to the Führer, who has now gone off to Munich. None of the members of that clique do any work; all they do is to intrigue. But I shall not allow myself to be deflected from my goals.

Now there is a Party Edict in preparation which will open the door for state authorities to be denounced to the Party. I have no intention of putting up with this constant defamation any longer. It must be stamped out.

Discuss personnel and organisational questions with Gutterer. He is doing a good job.

Receive representatives of Japanese youth. Sympathy for Germany. Hatred for America and contempt for England. So far as the rest goes, very tough kids.

Talk with the Norwegian propaganda chief, State Counsellor Lunde. A very clever man, for a Norwegian. Quisling's movement is growing. But in general Norway is still very pro-English. This will change after our victory. Minor acts of sabotage, hardening of mood, listening-in to English radio broadcasts, etc. The Quisling people are in a very difficult position. I give Lunde a few pieces of advice. They must try at the moment to neutralise the people for the duration. Everything will fall into place once the war is over. Lunde is with me for a meal, along with his entourage, who are not up to much. We discuss a thousand different problems. Müller tells me about Terboven's summary court on the Lofoten island after the English withdrawal. Our losses were serious, and Terboven found things in a critical state up there, but as an old Nazi he was able to master the situation without difficulty. We should have more of such people.

Bardóssy, the Hungarian Foreign Minister, in Munich. Nothing of particular significance.

277

I am up to my eyes in work for the entire day. Work would be a pleasure for me, if it were not for the few intriguers who are always souring things.

Polish up my new leader-article. Has turned out excellently.

Magda is well. She is coming home today. I look forward to it very much. Speak to the children on the telephone. Those sweet, gorgeous little voices! I am quite moved. Hedda is a little better. I was very worried about her.

Discussions are still going on in Belgrade. A few ministers have handed in their resignations. Prince-Regent Paul has accepted them and has post-poned any further pro-Axis moves until after the crisis. We shall see.

Check another Moser film. Very funny. And then to bed, tired.

23 March 1941 (Sunday)

Yesterday: No incursions into the Reich. We carry out a devastating raid on Plymouth with 160 aircraft. Plus the U-boats sink 60,000 tons, the surface fleet 120,000. Another very black day for England.

Giarabub has fallen. Raises London's spirits a little. But it is no more than a drop in the ocean. Otherwise the mood in London is very subdued.

A mass of work and aggravation. Constant problems with the Ritter film. The strongest men wilt, but I don't give in. Finally I win through. The film will be released with minor changes. Hippler is very despondent about it. But what does it matter? This is wartime, and we must wait until after the war before we can have our desires.

I ban the entire church press. Because of the paper shortage. The daily press also has to accept very considerable cutbacks. But I ensure that they affect the advertising sections to exactly the same extent as the editorial content. The publishers naturally have no intention of losing good business.

Report on morale very good. Everyone is waiting for the new blows to fall. We can only hope that they will come in quick succession.

For the rest, Saturday passes rather more quietly. I have time to work on old projects. A glorious spring day. The only pity is that one has to watch it from one's desk. Once the war is over, we shall make up for everything that we are missing now.

My interview appears in the *Woche* and makes a good impression.

Roosevelt is stirring up more war-fever. But gradually even he will lose his taste for it. We can now report 200,000 tons sunk in one day. 116,000 tons by warships, 77,000 by U-boats, and 31,000 by the Luftwaffe. This is good news. For both the past two days, planes downed 6:2 in our favour. And the English had been shooting their mouths off about having air superiority and suchlike. We shall soon teach them otherwise.

Weygand has declared for Pétain and against de Gaulle in an interview. This is very useful from our point of view.

Tonnage, tonnage, is the cry in England. Everywhere, even in the USA, there is the profoundest scepticism on this issue. They are not even optimistic about Africa any more. The war's first harbingers of spring have arrived.

Things seem to be falling into place in Belgrade. And it was high time that the situation was clarified. In the meantime, Stojadinović has arrived to begin his exile in Athens.

He should still be Prime Minister in Belgrade. We would have reached agreement with him a long time ago.

Magda arrives back from Dresden in the evening. She looks rested and seems to be flourishing. I am very glad that she is back.

The only thing missing now is the children. And along with them, a victorious peace.

24 March 1941 (Monday)

Yesterday: Stormy weather. Harbinger of spring.

No air activity on either side. Minor sinkings. Air battles in North Africa, in which our Messerschmitts shoot down seven Hurricanes. Otherwise nothing of importance.

Our successes in the Atlantic are making a profound impression in the USA. Roosevelt has had seven billion in credits for England granted. London is using every means to foment intrigue and false rumours in Belgrade. Will do no good.

At midday I drive with Magda and Ursel to Schwanenwerder, our second home, which we now rent and which is prepared and ready for inspection. There are only a few small things to be done there now. Then we shall be able to live on in Schwanenwerder undisturbed.

A few hours spent chatting with the ladies at midday and during the afternoon. A little holiday for myself. Outstanding Request Concert. At last, after a lot of pressure.

Our successes at sea and in the air are arousing great respect throughout the world. All they can do in London is to stutter lame excuses.

In the USA, the Rabbis are praying for Roosevelt. He has earned it. The USA is returning two escaped German prisoners-of-war to Canada. Scum!

Newsreel in the evening. Some additional material needed, which we edit in successfully.

Discuss a host of film matters with Hippler.

Late to bed. Six-hour air-raid warning. Sleep in the air-raid shelter. Tolerable enough.

25 March 1941 (Tuesday)

Yesterday: Raid on Berlin with only slight damage. Mostly fires from incendiary bombs. Four dead. Plus raids on North Germany. We are unable to reach England because of the bad weather conditions. The reports now coming in about Plymouth are horrifying. Worse even than Coventry. But Churchill is standing his ground.

27,500 tons sunk in the Atlantic. I have the big English shipping losses put over to the public by use of concrete examples. Otherwise the people cannot grasp their significance. Actual examples make a deeper impression.

The situation is bad in Abyssinia. The English are advancing closer to Harrar. If only the rains would come.

The Italian commander in Albania has been changed again. But this does no good if the organisation itself is at fault. La Valetta has been bombed very heavily and with greater success.

Matsuoka given a very friendly reception in Moscow. Almost pointedly so. But I do not trust the Bolsheviks.

Yugoslavia is now ready. Nothing stands in the way of her signing any more. London pulled out all the stops. In vain!

Endless paperwork. Film receipts very good. Despite the war, we are doing excellent business. My personal film projects are the most successful of all.

I write a very tough letter to Bormann about the Ritter film. One cannot do whatever one likes in wartime.

Lay down guidelines for the reception for Matsouka with Gutterer. It will be a splendid affair. Will cost a lot of money and lost working hours, but this time it will be worth it.

Gossip a little with the ladies at home. Everyone is tired because of the air-raid warning. Spend the entire afternoon at my desk, in this glorious spring weather.

In the evening, special performance of the *Merry Widow* at the Admiral's Palace with the entire ministry. A festive mood. My people have earned themselves a pleasant evening by their tireless work all through the war. I make a short speech to them, thanking them for their loyal work. They are all good men, so loyal and true. Then a brilliant performance to loud applause.

Work and meetings await me at home. The Yugoslavs have finally got their cabinet crisis out of the way and are coming to the bar. On their way to Vienna to sign. Now the Balkans are ripe.

At last. It was high time.

Newsreel. Marvellous new film of Africa. Those are our boys!

Very good new colour-film shots. We have now caught up with the Americans in this field, thank God. Filmically we are on the march.

26 March 1941 (Wednesday)

Yesterday: No incursions on either side. Weather too bad. Some sinkings. We are working our way forward in Libya. Our equipment continues to arrive safely.

Again I have the matter of shipping tonnage sunk explained to the public with the aid of examples. London claims to have lost only 72,000 tons in the past week. Miserable liars!

Wiegand has given an interesting account of the war in the Atlantic in the US press. He gives us every chance of success.

Matsuoka received by Stalin. Moscow/Tokyo situation beginning to clear. Moscow states publicly that she will not stab Turkey in the back in the event of military activity on her territory. Paper promises! Time will tell.

The Führer in Vienna. Likewise the Yugoslavs. Signing at 12.00. So we have done it. A difficult birth. And what didn't London predict with regard to Yugoslavia! I have it all summarised for our propaganda use. Works very effectively. The English have had no luck with their predictions in this war.

The balance between prices and wages cannot be maintained in some areas, for example in textiles. I forbid any big debates on this issue. We must settle it by word-of-mouth explanation.

A few strong letters to Bormann. He is crossing my path too often . . .

. . . Address propagandists of the AO from all European countries. I clarify their propaganda tasks in the world. Great applause.

Receive twelve editors of influential Swiss newspapers. I give them a clear, unadorned picture of the role that Switzerland has to play in the new Europe. At first they are somewhat bemused, but they swallow it after a while.

The London press is furious about Belgrade. Pure frustration!

Graziani has resigned. Was probably time. Has cancer. Was not up to his job.

I forbid any great discussion of the problem of children evacuated from Berlin. Ufa wants to propagandise about the thousandth evacuee train. That would only be welcomed by London.

Tea for the propagandists of the AO. Bohle tells me stories about the Foreign Ministry. Ribbentrop is very miffed that no one is answering his letters any more. I started the trend. And it is the best way to deal with him.

Our AO people tell me a lot. Still great discontent in Italy. Ciano is the main target. But even feeling against the Duce. The German troops there are behaving magnificently. Our best propagandists. Fascist corruption stinks to high heaven. Ciano has corrupted the entire crew.

Real starvation in Spain. The aristocracy and the priests are running the country. Some feeling against us. The Falange completely finished.

Quiet, determined mood in Bulgaria. Our troops given a hearty welcome in the countryside. Some pro-English feeling in Sofia. And a strong inclination towards Russia. But not a serious danger.

Still strong pro-English tendencies in Yugoslavia. But now, after the signing of the pact, this is to be expected.

Everything in Rumania as I had predicted. Antonescu is completely isolated, his election was a complete farce, he has no credibility among the people, who hold firm to the Legion in the countryside. Horia Sima still in hiding. Freemasons and Jews in charge. But the Legion is not capable of ruling at the moment. Too badly decimated. Antonescu has, at least, the machinery of the state in his hands. But for how much longer?

An interesting afternoon. I hear a great deal, and learn a great deal. Our Party members abroad are better observers than our diplomats.

What a mountain of work awaits me! Sometimes I am downright sick of it.

Intense reaction to the signing of the pact in Belgrade. London is quite taken aback. The intrigues are over. Very pessimistic report from London. Morale seems to have slumped strongly there. They are cobbling together some lies about successes by the RAF, but they are not shouting them too loudly.

The Turks are slowly changing horses. We can expect developments there, too.

Check films in the evening. With Demandowski, look at three possible endings for *Ohm Krüger*. The one put together by me is the best and is accepted. Edit the *Gas-Man*. It can be released now.

It is so late, and I am so tired.

27 March 1941 (Thursday)

Yesterday: Minor counter-demonstrations in Belgrade. But of no importance. Inspired by the English. We guarantee inviolability of Yugoslavia's borders and give an assurance that we will not march through their territory. All we want is the right to use Yugoslav airfields.

Anger and gloom in England. USA somewhat sobered and Turkey very reserved. We shall have them, too.

Halifax explains English war aims. Sheer publicity-seeking. I deal with him in a tough leader-article.

No incursions on either side. We sink 40,000 tons. El Agheila taken by our Panzers. This remains secret for the moment. But it will hit London hard . . .

. . . Wodarg reports. Luftwaffe is furious at the Wehrmacht High Command for having taken propaganda completely out of its hands. Wodarg is now to be attached to my ministry again. I complain forcefully about the fact that the Luftwaffe gave me so little support in the Hesse Affair.

Discuss casting problems for his *Night Without Good-Bye* with Max Kimmich. He is completely incorrigible in many respects. But he must take responsibility for his own films.

Inspect a few purchases of pictures at home. Some gorgeous items among them. Write leader-article and deal with other business.

Berlin welcomes Matsuoka. Hundreds of thousands of people on the streets. My instructions have been followed to the letter. Matsuoka, whom I help receive at the station, gives an impression of great intelligence. The people's welcome is very enthusiastic. The Berliners are well aware of all that depends on the success of this visit.

I discuss the Hesse Affair with Keitel. He concedes the correctness of my view and is very grateful to me.

London is still trying to queer our pitch by fomenting street disturbances in Belgrade. But the scheme will not work. And then they have the gall to declare that Yugoslavia's accession to the pact had been predicted, and that the situation is therefore not too serious. John Bull is a master of double-talk. But we shall soon shut his mouth for him.

28 March 1941 (Friday)

Yesterday: Matsuoka's visit takes the limelight. London slightly depressed. A coup d'état takes place in Belgrade. Prince-Regent Paul and Cvetcović deposed. New military government formed under the seventeen-year-old King. Great confusion, impossible to judge the situation yet. Churchill has welcomed the coup in a delighted speech. But no one knows the details as yet. So wait and see!

No air activity on either side. 40,000 tons sunk. El Agheila in our hands. We make the news public. But the Italians lose Keren and Harrar. A black day. But we shall soon put this behind us.

Quickly got some of my paperwork done, going at full stretch. A thousand trivial details which seem totally irrelevant in the heat of these dramatic days.

By plane to Wilhelmshaven. Dreadful flight with ice on the wings. We are glad to arrive. The city has been pretty badly hit by the recent air raids. I have never seen such serious damage in the Reich before. But morale is good.

I take a look at the rebuilding plans for the city. Very ambitious. Then speak to 15,000 dockyard workers. I get a fantastic response. These people will see things through, even if the situation becomes a lot stickier.

Flight to Hamburg. No planes landing in Berlin. Short stopover in Hamburg. Everything is all right there, too. In contrast to Wilhelmshaven, the city has a completely peacetime look to it.

By train to Berlin. Frowein comes by car to join us and reports: big demonstrations against us in Belgrade. London and Washington have declared their solidarity. Churchill has made a second pompous speech. The old liar is, of course, on his high horse. Moscow, too, seems to have a hand in the imbroglio in Belgrade. The explanation in Belgrade is that the affair is of purely domestic importance, but this is, of course, rubbish. We have no contact with our Mission there. Telephones and cables have been cut. So we have to sleep on it for a night.

Deal with a few outstanding items of work. Berlin. It is one in the morning.

First a few hours' rest. Then we shall see.

29 March 1941 (Saturday)

Yesterday: No raids on England. Middling raid on Düsseldorf. Twelve dead. A few sinkings. Things are bad in Abyssinia. Keren and Harrar have fallen.

Churchill has made a speech, crowing about Yugoslavia. The Führer is outraged. In Belgrade, they are trying to defuse the situation. Would like to keep a foot in both camps. No one is mentioning the Three-Power Pact any more. Want peace with everybody. Wait! We are already working on leaflets aimed at the Croats. Things will have to move, one way or the other. Moscow is already showing signs of cold feet. And they are shitting themselves in Belgrade, too. Prince-Regent Paul has been arrested. A real Balkan affair! Things should become clearer during the next few days.

The USA is being very reticent. And predictions of war are being viewed with much more scepticism there.

Personnel questions with Gutterer. Schmidt is to go from Cracow to Oslo, Müller-Oslo will go to his military service, and Ohlenbusch will go to Cracow. The wireless service will be restructured with clearly-defined spheres of authority.

I shall put all my diaries in the vault of the Reichsbank. To protect them against fire and air raids. They will be safe there.

Current problems discussed with Terboven. He took the right course of action, in contrast to Seyss-Inquart, who is always held up as an example to him. Big propaganda campaign in preparation in Norway. We have some 300,000 troops there now. Moscow will have nothing to smile about if the balloon goes up. A good thing, too. People should know what to expect when they provoke us.

Receive the new staff of the Reich Propaganda Leadership. Many old Party comrades among them. I explain their field of work. Particular emphasis on the distinctions between the Party and the State. And how necessary the RPL's work is in the area of propaganda.

Winkler delivers a report. The film industry is in an excellent position. Seventy million net earnings in the past year. And even more fantastic profits to be expected. We are to create a special fund for building new cinemas. So we shall outwit the Finance Minister. We are now firmly in the saddle in France, Belgium and Holland. And everything in Prague belongs to us.

With the Führer. Lunch for Matsuoka. Almost the entire party Field Marshals. The Japanese are ready to join us. They are still having a few difficulties with their old men. These people want a conservative foreign

284

policy. But we shall see the benefits later. In Japan, England has lost her best friend. The fact of Matsuoka's trip alone is something extraordinary for Japan. Oshima has been preparing the way for the alliance. He is absolutely fanatical in his commitment. We have a lot to thank him for. Japan hopes to impose her will in China in time. If only she could get to grips with USA.

Leeb tells me some interesting details about the Boxer Rebellion. Reichenau talks about his work on field newspapers. He is a very modern general. Discuss the Hesse affair with Göring. He is delighted at the way I forced the issue. He is sending Wodarg to me as liaison man. He has all sorts of complaints about the Wehrmacht High Command. We are in agreement on all issues. One can work with him. He has great admiration for Lord Haw-Haw's work. And indeed, he is the best horse in my stables.

Discuss the problems of Wilhelmshaven with Raeder.

The Führer looks rather harassed. The Yugoslav situation is causing him a great deal of worry. Matsuoka seems very intelligent. We shall be able to work with him. But Oshima is the best of them all. We can expect a few things from him in future.

Still considerable confusion in Belgrade. Prince-Regent Paul has disappeared off to Athens. Cvetcović under arrest. Big demonstrations against us. This is very convenient from our point of view, and we make good use of it in our press. The government in Belgrade is trying its best to keep the situation under control. But once one has summoned up the spirits . . . We may be able to do something with the Croats. We intend to take more of an interest in that quarter from now on.

Visitors in the afternoon: Alfieri, Schlajapin's daughter, Jugo, Ursel Quandt. All sorts discussed. Alfieri is very worried about Yugoslavia. But then he is always worried. Mussolini has been constantly ringing him up. Italy wants war. But whether she will be prepared to actually fight it, he does not say. Alfieri talks too much and acts too little. Marina Schljapin tells me some interesting things about Italy. She is an excellent observer.

Things have become quieter in Belgrade. But not for us. Our people have been advised to leave the country immediately. The Führer does not allow himself to be trifled with in these matters. The Croats are already starting to cause trouble. This questionable patchwork of states will probably be faced with a very unpleasant reckoning. It has now been officially admitted in the USA that Roosevelt gave a little extra help to the operetta revolution in Belgrade. Much good it will do the Serbs. Heaven is high and the USA is a long way away. The rest will follow in the near future.

The long-prepared operation against Greece is due to start on 7 April. But now it is just a small beginning. We shall push forward to Salonica, then Leeb's Army Group will right-wheel and Yugoslavia will be attacked from all sides. Until then, everything is to be kept under strictest security. The problem of Yugoslavia will not cost us too much time. Her army is brave but has few modern weapons. This provocation will be avenged. And they probably realise the fact. They are being so mild and co-operative that it has the ring of panic in it.

The big project comes later: against R.* It is being very carefully camouflaged, and only a very few people know about it. It will begin with extensive movements of troops to the West. We shall divert suspicion to all sorts of places, anywhere but the East. A mock invasion of England is in preparation, but when the time is ripe everything will be switched back in a flash and then the attack will commence.

The Ukraine is a good grain-store. Once we are entrenched there, then we can hold out for a long time. With this, the Eastern and Balkan questions will finally be settled.

The project as a whole presents some problems from the psychological point of view. Parallels with Napoleon, etc. But we shall quickly overcome these by anti-Bolshevism. And the question of the Baltic states and Finland will also be settled. The first targets for our propaganda will be the Cossacks, and then the Russian peasants. We shall create our masterpiece there. The main thing is that we take the crucial step. We stand on the threshold of great victories. The watchword must be: keep one's nerve and a cool head. And prepare everything down to the last detail.

Continue working long into the evening. Chat a while with our visitors.

These days of preparation are dramatic and nerve-wracking.

But it is wonderful to be a part of it all.

30 March 1941 (Sunday)

Yesterday: No incursions on either side. A few sinkings by the Luftwaffe. Big sea battle off Crete between Italian and English ships. Both sides seem to have suffered some damage. Further details not yet available. Two of our transporters have been torpedoed. One has been towed into port, the other sunk. Not a good day!

Anti-German demonstrations flare up again in Belgrade. Our ambassador is booed by the mob. Very good. We are releasing this material little by little. The Croats' attitude towards the new government seems to be completely passive; and the government itself already has cold feet and is continually assuring us of its good will. But London's premature chorus of triumph is forcing it further into a corner, which suits us perfectly. Our troop movements are almost complete. No one out there has any idea of what the Führer intends to do. When he strikes, the blows will be all the more devastating. Our camouflage has been completely successful.

Matsuoka's visit is running according to plan. Today we arranged one more huge farewell procession, although it is no easy task to get such big crowds together on a Sunday. But it must be done, in the interests of German–Japanese friendship.

* Russia. The first, cautious reference to the planned invasion of the Soviet Union.

286

A mass of film and theatre problems. The radio, too, is causing me a lot of work. The renting of our second house in Schwanenwerder has cost me a small battle with a fat capitalist. But that too has been sorted out.

I have my diaries, twenty fat volumes, deposited in the underground vault of the Reichsbank. They are too valuable to be allowed to fall victim to some air raid. They provide a picture of my entire life and our times. If fate allows me a few years for the task, I intend to edit them for the sake of future generations. They may well be of some interest to the world at large.

SD report: morale good. Slight tension among the public regarding Russia. People sense that something is on the cards there. The problem will, of course, be resolved during the course of the summer. Some justified criticisms of the radio.

Some serious excesses by our police at a factory-camp housing Danish women. Very bad from a psychological point of view. This is not the way to make friends. I intervene immediately with some rigorous measures.

A short visit to the Dresden painter, Kriegel, the Dürer of our time so far as flower and animal paintings are concerned. He is a magician with colour. But his wife is dreadful. A real dragon.

They are celebrating the Belgrade events in London. Belgrade, however, is desperately attempting to curry favour with us. Too late. The machinery is already in motion. This fair-weather nation will have to pay for its provocations against the Reich with its life. And its government will now realise that the spirits which it summoned up cannot be conjured back out of existence.

Huge demonstrations in favour of Yugoslavia in Marseilles. A good thing that all these elements are showing their true faces just before the action really begins. Then all of us will know where we stand. It is pathetic to see London rejoicing so prematurely. It can only be good from our point of view. We are noting every little outburst. We shall be able to use them very well to mock the English in future. And so we are not angry. We work away!

Belgrade has sent some senior officers to apologise to von Heeren. Cold shoulder! The withdrawal of our civilians from Yugoslavia has impressed them deeply . . .

. . . The air is heavy with tension and expectation. Soon the first blow will fall.

31 March 1941 (Monday)

Yesterday: No incursions. We attack Bristol with fifty aircraft. Very effective. An English aircraft-carrier badly damaged by bombers off Crete. A few sinkings. Otherwise no military activity. Everyone is waiting for the Führer to press the button.

Some cooling-down in evidence in Belgrade. Now no one will admit responsibility for what has happened. But we ignore them, continue to evacuate the German colony, and publish the anti-German material little by little in our press, with cumulative effect. This sends the chauvinists in

287

Belgrade wild with anger and fear. Now we are in control of the situation . . .

. . . There is still talk of active help in the USA, but also an increase in doubters. Roosevelt makes a speech in which he again abuses us like a back-alley kid. I have him given one in the eye. A task our press fulfils gladly.

In London they are trying to pretend to their people that the air war is an equal affair, and are producing the most ludicrous distortions to back this up. *The Times* is pulling out all the stops, and London radio is quoting the craziest figures: such as 1000 dead in one air raid on Bremen. I order a suitable denial and a new offensive on our part. If we can succeed in persuading the English people of the hopelessness of their situation, then we shall have won half the battle.

On Sunday I have a few hours free for reading. Music and reading are the best relaxations for me in these frantic times.

Draft speech for the Führer's birthday. Very warm and affectionate.

Matsuoka leaves for Rome in the afternoon. Huge crowds of Berliners line the route. As they did when he arrived. Successfully organised. It cost a lot of trouble.

Renzetti to tea for his farewell visit. His wife is appallingly un-Aryan, but he is clever, energetic, and a real fascist. We mull over a few old memories. He has been involved so much in our Party and the creation of our state that he almost counts as an old Nazi. He is being badly treated in Rome. Partly, perhaps, because of envy on the part of the [. . .] diplomats, and partly because of his un-Aryan wife. In any case, I find him very likeable. He spends a lot of time cursing diplomatic bureaucracy.

In Belgrade, every effort is being made to calm the situation and give no cause for offence. No one wants to pick a fight with us. But we want actions, not words. In consequence there is little chance of salvation for this multi-nation state. The Croats are being kept in reserve. We shall take them out of the closet and dust them down when the need arises. When we begin to dangle the distant prospect of autonomy similar to Slovakia's, we may well reap rewards in that quarter. It is being claimed that Italians acted as agitators during the demonstrations. This by no means completely stupid or improbable. Rome would very much like us to conquer the country, so that we can hand half of it over to Italy. A realy dirty trick, of course, and a total betrayal on the part of the Italians. Their appetite for territory is nowhere near equalled by their capacity for battle.

We seem to have burdened ourselves with some peculiar allies.

The sea battle off Crete does not seem to have been too earth-shaking, after all. In any event, both sides are keeping very quiet about it.

Newsreel in the evening. Still a little too long and slightly confused. But I soon knock it into shape. Discuss a few new treatments with Hippler.

A hard day's work on a Sunday. By late in the evening I am absolutely exhausted.

288

1 April 1941 (Tuesday)

Yesterday: No air activity. A few sinkings. Troop movements against Greece and Yugoslavia more or less complete. The enemy suspects something, but knows nothing for certain. Italians lose three heavy cruisers in the aftermath of the sea battle off Crete. A very painful loss. The English are overjoyed. Bad road conditions and communications will cause problems, in Yugoslavia and particularly in Greece. I am already having material prepared to put our people in the picture when the time comes, so that it will realise that these campaigns will be no picnics. The Greek desire for a fight with us is just about zero. Things are coming to a head in Yugoslavia. Our nationals have left. This has made a profound impression. The Croats are still quiet. We are already preparing leaflets and clandestine transmitters. We shall tickle their fancy with a promise of autonomy. The anti-German rallies in Yugoslavia are continuing. We publish everything in the German press without comment. And add a little drop of poison. Our people are already showing signs of coming to the boil.

The situation in Abyssinia is very bad. Italy is becoming our weak point. But there is hardly anything we can do about it. We shall have to try to cancel out her defeats by our victories.

The French coastal batteries are firing on English warships that stop French convoys. This is a real gift for our propaganda in France. We lose no time in exploiting it.

Emotional debates about secrecy. Bömer and Fritzsche want to be able to tell the press more than the Wehrmacht High Command's bulletin reveals. This has to be so. Martin, on the other hand, fears a breach of secrecy. In fact, nothing has been leaked from our ministry. I have the military report at the Ministerial Conference divided into two categories: strictly secret material, and material also intended for close colleagues' use. Even then, I shall still be able to intervene and order things according to individual circumstances. Our High Command's bulletins must be more precise in their reports on bombing damage. Otherwise they will lose their credibility and in the long term become a laughing-stock.

Dressler-Andres in Lublin has committed another extraordinary blunder: published an account of my discussions with the propaganda people of the General Government in a report freely available to the public. I shall transfer him immediately to Cracow, put him under Ohlenbusch's control, and give him one last chance. Any more trouble, and he will definitely be out on his ear.

A host of personnel and administrative problems with Gutterer. My one worry is that he will crack up under the pressure of work and be lost to me. He is doing a very good job.

Discuss new art purchases with Bibrach. Dictate a leader-article:

Talk about his field of work with Todt. He is building on a huge scale along the French coast. No Englishman will get through there. In Lorient our new U-boat base. They are pressing ahead at a tremendous pace. Underground pens for our U-boats. A race against time and the English Air Force to complete them. Once they are finished, however, we shall be secure. Our U-boats are achieving exemplary results. We can rely on them.

With the Führer. The problem of Yugoslavia. He is simply waiting his hour, which will soon arrive. Then he will act. Harsh words for Italy. The Italians made absolutely no preparations for this war, merely shot their mouths off. Marvellous. 'Eight million bayonets'. An idea that has in any case no value in the age of the tank. Plus massive mismanagement, and a deal of corruption. The chief culprit in this respect is Ciano. I tell the Führer a few facts about Ciano, which disturb him deeply. Ciano is a social climber who has lost all respect in Italy. He is also stupid, without manners, tactless and insolent. The Führer is sharply critical of nepotism. In Spain and Rumania, too. It is something that the ordinary people cannot bear. Mussolini should send Ciano out into the wilderness. But who would take his place? Grandi would be even worse, because he has secret pro-English tendencies. But the business with Ciano will end badly. Now we are seeing the results of the constant reshuffles. The Duce has now not a single man who commands a degree of popularity or authority in the country. And there is nothing to be gained by the crucial figures going to the front. Our front is the office where we serve the people. To carry the burden of responsibility here is just as difficult as commanding a unit at the front. In any case, Ciano is finished so far as the Führer is concerned. I tell him about the way Polverelli received Schlösser. This amuses him hugely. The Duce's prestige has already taken some hard knocks. And now, on top of everything else, the lost sea battle. Pray it doesn't lead to a bad end!

I give an account of the air raid on Wilhelmshaven, which interests the Führer greatly. He is glad that the English air raids have hit the most racially select parts of our people. These will show the best attitude. For the rest, the psychological effect of the air raids should not be given too much weight. They serve only to make people more stubborn. We have lost a certain amount of plant and equipment, and that is the only concrete success that the raids have achieved.

The Führer has no time at all for Franco. A vain, brainless peacock. There is no question of his ranking among the great statesmen of the age.

The Führer's only response to the activities of Ribbentrop and the Foreign Ministry is one of amusement. Now that Schirach has dropped out, they have not a single friend left. They interfere in everything, are constantly contesting others' authority, are building a state within a state, and create their own bureaucracy for any task that they are involved in, however remotely. It will do them no good in the end. At the moment, with the war on, things can continue like this, but after the war there will be a big shake-up. Whatever the case, I intend to defend myself against the Foreign Ministry's presumptuousness, wherever it occurs, and the Führer will look on benevolently. Ribbentrop has his merits, but his weaknesses and mistakes outweigh these by a long way. He is a typical political *arriviste*.

I report to the Führer on the achievements of the German film industry, including the seventy millions in profits. Five million of these will go to the Führer's cultural fund, fifteen million to the social fund of the Winter Aid Fund. This pleases him greatly. Our U-boat film met with his full approval.

A mountain of work at home. I am scarcely able to see over it. And then there is the nerve-tearing tension of these days.

Things are running their course in Belgrade. London is trying to get the Croats to behave themselves, but they have no intention of falling into line. Now it will not be long before our Croat and Slovene transmitters, some of them disguised and secret, go into action. These will be effective. I feel that I am back in my element.

Read through endless paperwork and revisions. I am so tired that I can hardly keep my eyes open.

Direaua taken by the English. They are crowing over the victorious sea battle in the Eastern Mediterranean, which was indeed a depressing setback for the Italians. Black days for our Axis friend. We shall have to take action soon, if only to repair the damage.

The pro-Yugoslav rallies in Marseilles are continuing and seem to be quite extensive. The English and the Jews are behind them. The Herr Frenchmen will have to watch their step.

Eden back in Athens. The travelling warmonger. But his activities are no longer a problem so far as our plans are concerned.

The USA intends to use our merchant ships interned there for transporting war materials to England. A scandalous plan, which would create a very grave situation if it were carried out.

Newsreel in the evening. Now good and very tight. Especially good film of Bulgaria and North Africa. And of the havoc wreaked by our warships in the Atlantic. This will have a very convincing effect on the public.

Then work on for a long time, reworking other material. After an eighteen-hour day, one is ready to drop from exhaustion.

2 April 1941 (Wednesday)

Yesterday: Raids with some damage and approx. thirty dead in North-West Germany. We carry out heavy raids on Hull and Great Yarmouth. In North Africa, air attacks on English positions and first Panzer battles. No details yet. Things are even worse in Abyssinia.

They are in two minds in Belgrade. Playing things down but stirring trouble at the same time. Official quarters are afraid, but the mob is on the rampage. We simply report things in the press, but a little more aggressively than hitherto. The USA is more insolent than ever. We continue to hold our fire, on the Führer's orders. Confusion in England over what to do about Belgrade. Eden is in Belgrade. He wants war. He can have it. Our propaganda campaign is gradually beginning to move. We shall concentrate most strongly on the Croats. Stefani* exaggerates. It makes really bad propaganda. But our people are producing real masterpieces.

Report from Spain: 20 per cent at the most behind Franco, starvation, on the brink of chaos. A really miserable situation. After a revolution like that, the people look back nostalgically to the monarchy.

Matsuoka given a very big reception in Rome. But there is something forced about it all.

Discuss personnel, salary and organisational questions with Gutterer. Debate about the reorganisation of the Reich Culture Chamber with him and Hinkel. Hinkel wants to do everything himself. I reject this. He is not to take over the administration, but is only to give instructions and guidelines. Otherwise the central office will rule, the organisation will become top-heavy, and the presidents of the individual chambers will lose their work-satisfaction. Hinkel is to be given the title, 'General Secretary of the Reich Culture Chamber'. This makes him very proud. When all is said and done, he is a vain fellow.

Dr Dietrich has been intriguing with the Führer again. The results arrive in the form of a letter from Lammers to me. I have had enough of these continual backstairs machinations. If there were no war, I would make an almighty fuss. But the way things are! In the face of such great decisions, one would appear ridiculous even to oneself.

Alfieri comes visiting. He is sceptical about Japan. Of course, Matsuoka cannot allow himself to be tied down on the question of the USA. He was very cautious in that respect. Japanese foreign policy is far too conservative for swift decisions. And certainly Japan would be taking all kinds of risks. Alfieri is slightly despondent. It would be better if he were despondent about Italy's attitude. The Greeks are talking about the recent sea battle as a 'shameful, ridiculous defeat'. What a disgrace! Now Alfieri is pushing for the start on the shooting of the 'Prince Eugene' film, with 30,000 soldiers as extras. A downright crazy idea! I reject it out of hand. Everything is naturally conducted on a very amicable basis. But Alfieri is not a solid worker. One cannot rely on him.

With regard to Belgrade, he pushes for action. When we go to war, the Italians are always very much in favour. Sometimes one is almost over-whelmed by nausea.

A host of film and theatre problems. Plus an incredible amount of

* The official Italian government news agency.

aggravation and difficulties from the puffed-up incompetents who are responsible for souring my life. It is probably also due to the tension of waiting, which makes people nervous.

Irkowski from Linz has offered me a nice holiday home for the children. This could well be the best solution for the duration. Magda is also in favour. So off with the children to the Upper Danube Gau. They can go to the village school there. That will do them a lot of good. They will be with ordinary people all the time.

A whole mess of paperwork dealt with at home. Dictate speech for the launching of the Red Cross Appeal at the *Sportpalast*. If only one could work without interruption once in a while!

Belgrade is denying Eden's presence, adding that he has not been invited and would not be received, even if he came privately. Strong words, and dramatic evidence of the Jew-boy funk that the slogan-shouters of last week are now feeling. And now they are frantically trying to mend fences, using every trick they can find. But it will do no good. We want to see deeds. We will not sit idly by and be provoked. And the neutrals have already given up Yugoslavia for lost. So it goes when one acts brave at street demonstrations and shouts one's mouth off. It must always be paid for, and dearly.

Our position is brilliant. So brilliant that London and Washington can only reply with embarrassed silence. This is excellent. Our press campaign is growing by the hour. Not a pretty sight for those affected.

I receive the administrative committee of the newly-founded Radio Union. This is an international front organisation which we are using to establish and build up broadcasting stations abroad with the aid of big industry and banking circles. Exclusively for 'economic propaganda', of course. One must have many instruments at one's disposal if one wants to stage a polyphonic concert. Business circles are glad to co-operate.

News from Budapest. The Serbs are clearing the border areas facing Bulgaria and are beginning to lay mines there. Excellent. Balkan incompetence!

In the evening, first showing of the completed *Ohm Krüger* in front of a quite large gathering at my home. Great excitement. The film is unique. A really big hit. Everyone is thrilled by it. Jannings has excelled himself. An anti-England film beyond one's wildest dreams. Gauleiter Eigruber is also present and very enthusiastic.

We talk deep into the night. On the subject of Yugoslavia.

3 April 1941 (Thursday)

Yesterday: No air activity. Except for an attack on a large English airfield, which destroys twenty-seven aircraft. 77,000 tons sunk by U-boats and the Luftwaffe.

The situation is good in Africa. We have beaten the English in a tank engagement and driven them back still farther. It is hard to understand how the Italians could have been beaten so thoroughly by these people.

Admittedly, the convoys to England are still proceeding undisturbed in most cases. I receive a summary of daily averages from Martin which illustrates this quite clearly. We must therefore not overestimate the effects of our sinkings, though of course we must not underestimate them either.

The operations again Yugoslavia and Greece will now be carried out simultaneously, and not in succession. This is a great advantage. The Führer has ordered it. Date not yet confirmed. It could be any day, and depends chiefly on when the army has completed its order of battle. The mood in Belgrade is one of total Jew-boy funk. They are trying to hold off the evil hour, but mobilising at the same time. We are energetically stoking the flames. Now we have switched to a real tone and a half. My only move is to damp down the most improbable elements. These have been introduced into the campaign by the Italians, who have become hysterical. The Croats remain in reserve. But they too are going to be brought in by our radio transmitters. And everything is ready for a big propaganda effort. Once it is unleashed, heaven help the Serbs. Our Luftwaffe is also ready. Weather is good. And so things can get going.

I receive reports from Italy: morale slightly improved. Mussolini is taking the reins back into his hands. They are placing their hopes in our victory. This is, of course, an impossible situation for a nationalistic régime to find itself in. I would not like to be a fascist at the moment.

Report from the Russian-Rumanian border. Now the Russians are beginning to get the wind up. This is pleasant news. The spring, and our unshakeable will, have wrought this miracle.

Everyone is very tense. I warn my colleagues to keep quiet and not to spread rumours. Everything will fall into place. We are preparing the *Sportpalast* meeting. It is still uncertain, however, whether the Führer will speak.

The radio is continually presenting me with problems. The present time, when we are switching our attention to the South-East, is particularly difficult. Diewerge shows me a statistical summary which details the participation of the various departments in the work of the foreign-language service. According to this, the Foreign Ministry plays hardly any part at all, while we take the lion's share. One can see, therefore, how much credence should be given to their bombastic claims.

Problems of restrictions on the press with Reinhardt. The entire church press is being swept away. Plus a host of useless magazines, but unfortunately also a number of valuable newspapers. Advertisement sections considerably curtailed. But we shall battle through.

Helldorff comes to say goodbye. He is off to the front. Lucky man! Himmler has hived off all his authority in Berlin. After the war he intends to resign. Dear God, so many want to do that. We never seem to come off the treadmill.

Drewes reports to me on a number of musical matters. He is a fanatic, often rather unpleasant, but nevertheless he is in command of his subject.

Daily routine with Gutterer. In these tense times, he is forced to take on a lot of my work.

Feige reports on budgetary matters, particularly regarding Lanke. The Lord be praised that I am free of those worries, at least.

Sefton Delmer is the most abusive of our opponents on English radio. He was another of Hanfstängel's acquisitions.

Following the USA, the South Americans are now starting to intern our ships. These people are real footpads and brigands. But they will have their come-uppance after the war.

An English magazine publishes an article about me: despite their every effort, the highest praise for me and my work.

I am stuck at my desk all day. And outside it is glorious springtime. If only things would get under way. The tension has become unbearable. We are publishing alert after alert regarding Yugoslavia. They are gradually running out of wind in Belgrade. A quote from a Serbian general: 'I shall be in Vienna with my Northern Army in three days'. Just as the Poles were going to cut us to pieces at the gates of Berlin. We have seen all this before. And the outcome will be the same as it was with the Poles.

But it is the best thing. Then, at least, we can have *tabula rasa* in the Balkans. There is no other way we can quieten this witches' cauldron.

On my suggestion, the Führer has cancelled his speech at the *Sportpalast*. This is necessary. If he is due to appear, then the world will expect a sensation. But then he can hardly talk about the Red Cross and working women. I work until long after midnight. To the point of collapse!

4 April 1941 (Friday)

Yesterday: No incursions. 20,000 tons sunk. Shipping shortages now being conceded openly and with the greatest gloom in England and the USA. We have lodged a protest against the seizure of our ships in Washington. Threatening the most comprehensive retaliatory measures. Agedabia taken by our North Africa Corps. Deepest depression in London. General Rommel is doing a magnificent job. The word in London is: if we want a big battle, just let us try it. Well, we shall see. We are making mincemeat of their soldiers, just as they did of the Italians. It is indeed a pleasure, and a dreadful embarrassment for Italy. I would not like to be an Italian at the moment. Things in Abyssinia continue to deteriorate.

Belgrade is still trying to wriggle out of its plight. They are bribing local ethnic Germans to sound off on the radio, in an effort to discredit our propaganda. We notch our propaganda campaign down a gear. The order of battle has not yet been completed, and one must have time to draw breath. The road conditions down there are indescribable. In Greece, too. That will

295

be a hard nut to crack. The English are leaving Piraeus in huge transports. No one knows why. As reinforcements to North Africa? Or to Salonica? Or because they fear a new Dunkirk? We shall see. Down there everything seems at sixes and sevens. Our clandestine transmitters are ready for action, but cannot yet be activated, on the Führer's orders. Calm before the storm! Matschek has declared that he has entered the Belgrade cabinet as Deputy Premier. The Serbs will pay dearly for this. Matschek will try to find a middle way. But it is probably too late for that.

Teleki has died through suicide. Wild rumours. But no one has any details. The opposition claims that he did it for fear of us. This is, of course, rubbish. Instructions to the press to write respectful obituaries.

Problems of the day with Gutterer. The coal situation in Berlin is rapidly taking on the proportions of a catastrophe, even for key factories. I order immediate action. Walter has failed in many areas, and Pleiger still has no idea whether he is coming or going. Petzke, Görlitzer and Steeg describe the catastrophic situation in the footwear industry. We are almost completely out of shoes. The food supply position in Berlin is also causing great concern. C'est la guerre! Hitherto, we had only hearsay to rely on. Now the problems are becoming all too clearly manifest.

Frau Scholtze-Klink reports on the problems of employing women. And there are all sorts. Who is to discipline the women? Female labour must become compulsory. Otherwise we shall never settle the issue. And fine ladies will not carry the Führer's gospel into the factories. And camp life throws up so many problems for women. Frau Scholtze-Klink is quite despondent about everything. I chivvy her up a little. And then, of course, there are the sexual aspects of separating millions of men and women. War means regression to a primitive state for human beings. We must seize victory as soon as possible, and then restore order and discipline . . .

. . . Sign an agreement with Vichy regarding the French newsreel. We gain 40 per cent of it and great influence on production. I would have liked 60 per cent but the Foreign Office gave in too easily.

I am working on a reform of the wireless service. Too many departments are meddling in my business at the moment. I must clarify the position. Dr Dietrich is constantly causing trouble to me. He is a man of exceedingly mediocre talents. A scandal that one has to defer to him at all.

Discuss 'Narvik' film with Harlan. He intends to start shooting in the autumn. The film must be a real blockbuster. Harlan's involvement is a certain assurance in that respect.

Receive graduates of the Leaders' School for the Reich Labour Service. Quite fantastic human material. Kretschmann, my old Ortsgruppenleiter, presents the boys to me. They have come from the front and are off back there.

Morale in the country still good, if very excited and tense. The SD report is too flat for my taste. It makes too little effort to investigate the fundamental, typical elements. I draw the attention of those responsible to this lack. The report must be a real barometer of popular morale. Then it will be fulfilling its purpose and one will be able to work with it.

I instruct the foreign-language service to attack London and Washington tirelessly for their lack of any war aims. This is very unwelcome so far as Churchill is concerned. He cannot answer it. If he demands too little, then he will stiffen German resistance, but if he demands too much, then he will weaken his own people's will to fight. He is therefore stuck between two stools, and we do not intend to make things easy for him.

I do not even have a chance to eat during the day. The pressure of work is threatening to get on top of me. But better to have a lot to do than to sit by and watch things happening.

Budapest has officially announced that Teleki committed suicide. As a sensitive human being in robust times, he succumbed to the burden of his duties. Should we believe this? At first they tried to play down the dramatic aspects, but this did not work. We shall soon hear more details.

The campaign against Yugoslavia has been stepped up again. We have sufficient material at our disposal. If only this nerve-tearing tension would end! In Belgrade itself, they are treading ever more softly. Frightened at their own audacity. Matschek has declared that he has only entered the cabinet to preserve peace. They need him as a front-man and are trying to assuage us by his inclusion. But we want to see deeds.

Belgrade is declared an open city. So they suspect something. Bardossy Teleki's successor. Passable!

The USA keeps up the campaign of provocation. Our sailors led off to prison in handcuffs. Hull is trying to have our Military Attaché recalled. Gangsters in the pay of the Jews. But we shall soon respond with retaliatory measures.

Check new Leander film, *Way to the Open*. A good effort. Effective and tastefully made.

Magda's father is dying. I scarcely know him and his passing will be no loss.

5 April 1941 (Saturday)

Yesterday: No incursions into the Reich. We mount a massive raid on Bristol with 100 aircraft. Some 80,000 tons sunk. Bleak situation in Abyssinia. The Italians are deserting in the face of English bombing. Are getting ready for a terrified defence of Addis Ababa.

The English evacuate Benghazi. And issue a pompous announcement into the bargain. Justifying it by claiming that they are looking for a suitable battle-ground. We make no great play of it, since there is always the danger that they are trying to lure us into a trap. They are still occupying the heights beyond Benghazi. We shall probably avoid entering the city. But neverthe-

297

less things are moving forward in North Africa in a very satisfactory fashion. Wherever we appear, the sparks fly.

The attack on Yugoslavia and Greece is now set for very early on Saturday. In Greece we shall attempt to reach Salonica as quickly as possible. Yugoslavia will be attacked simultaneously by Bulgaria and Hungary. We hope that the operation will not last too long. The state will be dissolved. Italy will get the coastline, Bulgaria Macedonia, and our Ostmark Gau the former Austrian provinces. The rest will be under a military governor. Belgrade is still trying frantically to wriggle off the hook, and the declarations of loyalty are coming thick and fast. But now it is too late. They should have thought of that before. Our campaign of demoralisation is continuing, and the pressure is being stepped up. Our clandestine transmitters are coming into action. Particularly emphasising appeals to Croatia, which is to become an autonomous state. A painful reckoning for Herr Simovic. This is what happens when bombastic generals try to make a big impression on the world stage.

The USA is acting in its usual snotty, impudent fashion. Our people there are being clapped in irons and humiliated. But this will not last long. And first we must creat order in the South-East. I pass on a good slogan for use in England: 'The USA will fight to the last Englishman'. A very serious controversy has already broken out between England and America on this issue. Very useful from our point of view. So stoke the fires!

The hours pass in nerve-tearing suspense. Real feeling of a major offensive!

Gutterer reports on some striking successes in curing cancer by Professor Auler. It would be wonderful to think that I had been of help in this area . . .

. . . In conference with General Jodl: the army is ready. Weather good. And so there are no more impediments to invasion. I speak to the Führer, and he is very relaxed and calm. As always during great events. Yugoslavia will soon no longer exist. The Bulgarians and the Hungarians are a little anxious. But this will pass once things are properly under way. Bulgaria fears that the Turks will attack her. But I consider this to be out of the question. They are happy enough to be left alive.

Great jubilation about Benghazi. The English are squirming and wriggling. Suddenly Benghazi is completely worthless. We, however, are able to give the news a big splash, since our forces have secured their positions. So we don't let the English get away with a thing. The only reason the Führer is halting the advance now is because the supply-lines have become stretched.

Discussion on Spain: things are bleak there. Typhus and starvation. Nothing done since the Civil War. Franco régime.

Talk over a few matters concerning the theatre in Munich with Wagner. We sort things out. Munich must be given equal salary levels with Berlin.

Discuss the problem of the Stennes people with Hess. They are not to be allowed to occupy leading positions in the army.

Divided opinions regarding *Ohm Krüger*. Some find it too horrific. But that is what it must be to work effectively on the public. And that is its purpose.

USA more outrageous by the moment. Italian Naval Attaché declared persona non grata. Our protest rejected. One scandal after another. I consider it quite wrong for the Foreign Ministry to insist on our continued silence. We must shout, create hell, defend ourselves. Damned diplomacy!

In the afternoon, big première for *Ohm Krüger* at the *Ufapalast*. A very imposing cinematic event. Everyone who is any one is there. Glorious music, conducted by Knappertsbusch, *Les Préludes*. Then the film is shown, to the breathless excitement of the public. Devastating effect. It is a success without equal. The audience reacts magnificently. This is not the usual première audience, because I have invited Party people, and now, in this large auditorium, it is possible to see exactly how good the film is.

I sit for an hour afterwards, talking to the artistes. Jannings is proud and happy. He has every reason to be.

No news at home.

The entire nation is trembling with suppressed tension.

In Yugoslavia they do not know whether they are coming or going. They are clutching at last, desperate straws. Nothing will save them.

Magda has left for Duisburg to be with her dying father.

I have a hard and exhausting evening of work.

6 April 1941 (Sunday)

Yesterday: Few incursions in West Germany, rather more on Brest. We bomb Avonmouth very heavily. More sinkings. Summaries of their activity during March by the Luftwaffe and the U-boat fleet give the world an imposing picture. England's shortage of shipping is worsening. Lloyd George has been the first to mention the prospect of starvation, in a speech to the House of Commons. A bad omen.

In London they are trying to minimise the importance of Benghazi. But without success. The shock-effect, particularly in the USA, is enormous. We make no concessions to the English. We repeat back to them everything they said when they captured Benghazi. Our troops have now entered the city, after some fighting. Back on the advance once more. The Italians are covering our flanks, though with German forces to stiffen them. The miracle of North Africa. A dreadful humiliation for England, and even more so for Italy.

Things are very bad in Abyssinia. The Italians have now scuttled four of their own destroyers. We should probably give up Abyssinia for lost, at least for the present.

Attack on Yugoslavia and Greece postponed for another day. Now to start early on Sunday. We are absolutely ready. Belgrade has mobilised. We are already printing leaflets for the Croats. Our clandestine transmitters are in operation. Everyone is dizzy with tension. Night duty roster established in the minstry.

New propaganda idea: each evening in the domestic and foreign service, we quote what an influential English figure said on the same day a year ago. The effects are absolutely astonishing. Today it is Ironside's turn with the 'young German generals'. This is extremely effective.

Discuss problems of daily news commentary with Wildener and Splett-stösser. I shall make more time for our people. They are forced to work too quickly, at the expense of quality. I demand precision in their arguments and stylistic brilliance.

Discuss a few sporting matters with Tschammer.

Ohm Krüger has set feelings ablaze. The critics' comments in the press are fantastic. A few ossified bureaucrats at the Foreign Ministry have taken offence. Otherwise the enthusiasm is universal. I award Jannings the newly-created 'Film Ring of Honour'. For his great services to our German film-making art. He is overjoyed.

A few film and theatre problems. These must still be dealt with, even in these tense times. But one's work must go on, even if one is only half-concentrating on it.

Bouhler is stirring up trouble for me with the Führer on the book-banning issue. But I defend myself vigorously. These little nonentities think that one Reichsleiter is equal to another. But it is not the title that counts, it is the quality.

Magda rings. Her father died shortly after her arrival. She is rather upset. I comfort her as best I can.

Carry on slaving away at home. Impossible to clear the decks completely. When will it all end?

Mobilisation completed in Yugoslavia. It will not do them much good. All in vain and too late. We got up a little too early for them. Pessimism is spreading in London. Particularly, presumably, because of Benghazi, which had been thought securely in English hands. The press and radio are taking on a very subdued tone. Benghazi had been given too great a prominence as a symbol of the English offensive spirit. This sort of thing reaps a bitter harvest. Our propaganda is operating at full speed and is in the best of form. If we have any material at all, we always know how to use it. If the English, however, have no material, they are completely helpless.

During the course of the day, Belgrade has made another attempt to talk to us, via Matschek and Rome. This might have served some purpose a week ago; now it is too late.

We are already working out radio fanfares for the South-Eastern campaign. Overture to *Prinz Eugen*.* We are looking for snappy soldiers' songs

---

* The Austrian general who defeated the Turks and occupied Belgrade in 1718.

for the South-Eastern and North Africa campaigns. Now we are back to the frantic life of a Germany on the offensive.

I speak to the children on the telephone. They are all so sweet. I miss them enormously. How attached one can become to such tiny, insignificant beings! How happy I am to have them.

Speak with Magda. She is rather sad. But things have turned out for the best.

Newsreel in the evening. Rather vague and confused at first viewing, as always. But we shall make something of it. Plus a few test shots for new films.

The evening passes in an atmosphere of heightening tension. I too am infected by it towards the end. I decide to grant myself a few hours' sleep. But at 1 a.m. I am summoned to the Führer.

He gives me another detailed summary of the situation. Things will get under way at 5.20 a.m. He reckons on two months for the entire project. I reckon less. At 7.20 precisely, Belgrade will be bombed by 300 aircraft. The following night, another massive raid with high-explosive bombs and incendiaries. We shall smoke the Serbian plotters out of their lair. The Balkans are a powder-keg. We must pre-empt any possibility of England's being able to light the fuse at her pleasure and convenience. The entire Serbian conspirator-clique must be toppled. The Führer does not fear Russia. He has taken sufficient precautions. And if she attacks, then the sooner the better. Russia has already announced a Treaty of Friendship with Belgrade. If we were not to act now, then the entire Balkans, including Turkey, could slip away. This must be prevented. Hungary and Bulgaria will march shoulder to shoulder with us. Not much, but something. The war against the Serbian fire-raisers will be waged without quarter. The Führer expects guerrilla warfare, with fairly heavy loss of life. But this, and the difficulties of the terrain, will soom be overcome. And then the race will be on, particularly in Greece. Our tactics so far as Greece is concerned are still fairly restrained. The Führer has dictated two appeals, to the German people and to the soldiers on the South-Eastern Front. I revise them in consultation with him. I am to read them over the radio at 6 a.m. I make all the necessary technical preparations. Our machinery is working fantastically well. New fanfare: overture to *Prinz Eugen*. The Führer considers this a brilliant idea.

The Foreign Ministry tries a little intrigue to steal a march on us. I dismiss this without difficulty. Dr Dietrich is very downcast.

The hours pass with painful slowness. I drink tea with the Führer and we chat about other things. I tell him about *Ohm Krüger*, which he values highly. He tells me of the deep impression which the Boer War made on him as a boy. The characters in the film please him enormously. He has some very flattering things to say about our theatre and film work. He is particularly impressed by the films. He wants the profits from films and radio to be used exclusively for the good of the rest of the arts. My old demand. He would like some film studios in Linz. It is to challenge the cultural dominance of Vienna. Graz is too cut-off for that. And Vienna must not be the Mecca for Austrian provincials. The Hapsburgs systematically encouraged this. Rightly, from their point of view. We intend to have Berlin as the political centre, and a series of other cities as cultural centres. I shall do my best to aid cultural expansion in Linz.

4.30. Another hour. Then 5.20. The Führer's thoughts are with his soldiers. He cherishes them with every good wish. As if he were thinking of each individually. It is quite moving. Then he retires.

To the office. Everyone is feverishly at work. I have to sort out a few doubters from other departments. Moscow declares: treaty with Belgrade is now ready. Benevolent neutrality for five years. Let it be more. Tolerable.

Dozens of German and foreign journalists are standing around in the ante-rooms. Everyone looks very bleary-eyed. I feel quite fresh.

I read the Führer's two appeals over all transmitters. Our troops in particular will devour them eagerly. I put everything I can into them.

Then an hour's sleep.

7 April 1941 (Monday)

Yesterday: Offensive started according to plan. Bombing of Belgrade devastating. A large part of the city is in flames. Railway station and castle and many other official buildings. Russia is publicly declaring her desire for peace. Gratifying. USA confining itself to grumblings. London full of gloomy anger. Greece declares that she intends to resist. We shall see how long that lasts. Hungary and Bulgaria are marching with us. The entire plan of campaign is based on their participation. Only as far as Salonica at first in Greece. Report from Turkey: trembling at the knees. All she wants is to stay out of things.

No air activity during the night so far as the English are concerned. We attacked English airfields during the previous day with considerable success. We continue to advance in North Africa. London despondent. Situation in Abyssinia hopeless. The Italians have evacuated Addis Ababa. We have been forced to scuttle four steamers in the harbour of Massawa.

Horrifying reports of the air raid on Belgrade. This is the punishment they have earned. 40 Serbian aircraft already destroyed. Our losses are very small.

Guideline for the press: emphasise the great difficulties. This affair is no picnic. No illusions so far as the public is concerned. Hard struggles lie ahead. The mistakes of Norway not to be repeated.

Morale in the country is magnificent. As always when the action starts. Guideline for propaganda: hard line against the clique of Serbian generals. No attacks on the people. Croats: stroke them! Stand for autonomy. Cutting edge directed at Serbia. Sloveness: somewhere between Serbs and Croats. Step up the clandestine transmissions. Particularly those aimed at the

'Cultural workers' from occupied Alsace are received by Goebbels, November 1940

Staff at the Propaganda Ministry pack books desed for neutral Argentina

Goebbels and Ley congratulate actress Käthe Haack at the presentation of the first 'Strength through Joy' mobile theatre, February 1940

Goebbels visits the conquered territories in the East, 1940. He is greeted on his arrival in Danzig by Reich Governor and Gauleiter Albert Forster (on his right)

Hitler Youth parade

Confidants: Hitler and Goebbels by the fireside at the Berghof

bels in clowning mood with
) Eva Braun and (far right)
Albert Speer at the Berghof

Goebbels in a restaurant in conquered Paris

Goebbels at an official showing of the Wehr-macht film *Victory in the West*, Ufa Palace 1940. To his right is General Keitel, to his left Ministerial Director Leopold Gutterer

U-boat commander Günther Prien, one of Goebbels' propaganda heroes during the early part of the war, is congratulated by the Navy commander Grand Admiral Raeder

Prien in the conning-tower of his U-47. He was later captured by the British, a severe blow to German prestige

Goebbels addresses shipyard workers in Hamburg, 1941. In his diary he complained that press photographs such as this one completely ignored his audience

The Nazi élite: l. to r.: Hess, Göring, Streicher, Goebbels

At the Kroll Opera House. Back row l. to r.: Seldte, Kerrl, Rust, Gurtner, Funk. Front row l. to r.: von Neurath, Goebbels, Frick, Ribbentrop, Hess

Goebbels with
Reich Student Leader
Scheel and Frau Scholtze-
Klink, head of the Nazi
Women's Movement

Goebbels meets a 'War Re-
porting Company' of the
Waffen-SS and is presented
with an album of war photographs, January 1941

Goebbels with the actor
Emil Jannings at the pre-
mière of Jannings' anti-
British film, *Ohm Krüger*,
April 1941

Goebbels broadcasts the Führer's proclamation justifying the German attack on the Soviet Union, 5.30 a.m., 22 June 1941. Directly behind him stands Gutterer, now his State Secretary, and (third from the left) Reich Broadcasting Leader Eugen Hadamovsky

Croats. Stoke up hatred against the Serbs. We want a free state like Slovakia. So far as the Greeks are concerned, we shall take a gentle, cautious line. Until they turn insolent. I put two more clandestine transmitters into operation against Yugoslavia.

Try out new fanfares and south-eastern songs with Glasmaier. Fanfares good, the others not so. I reshuffle the Request Concert again. Send planes down to fetch the first Propaganda Company material.

Private Brinkforth, who was recently the first from the other ranks to be awarded the Knight's Cross, comes to present his compliments. He tells me, in a very amiable way, how he destroyed ten enemy tanks on the Aisne. A marvellous fellow!

The first news comes in. Everything is going smoothly so far. No setbacks as yet.

Lammers rings up: he is also angry at Bouhler and Dietrich and will use my letter as evidence when he makes a complaint to the Führer. High time, too, that a stop was put to those intrigues.

I work at home in the afternoon. The latest news bulletins flutter into the house like doves returning to their coop.

Minor air raids on Graz and Klagenfurt. In return, we bomb Belgrade again with crushing effect. The Belgrade radio transmitter has been silent since then. So far we have had no losses at all in the air. Belgrade has already lost some 80 aircraft. London is making only the vaguest promises of aid. The old story. For the rest, they confine themselves to claiming that our over-extended fronts will lead to our downfall. Italy also makes a statement in the afternoon. About time!

The English reach Addis Ababa. Pity! A drop of wormwood! But we sink another 40,000 tons, to keep the English on their toes.

The American radio reporters in Berlin are showing signs of impudence. I have them given a serious warning and intend to throw them out if they do not mend their ways.

Notes to the government in Belgrade and Athens including documentary justifications for our military action.

Dancing forbidden. Dancing is not suitable during an offensive.

Check newsreel with music. Not exactly up-to-the-moment, naturally. But we shall receive more material about the invasion by air.

Magda is well. I am able to catch up on an hour's sleep.

Then, however, more news comes rattling in. A tense, dramatic, but glorious day!

8 April 1941 (Tuesday)

Yesterday: Belgrade bombed twice, with devastating effect. The radio station is silent. Not a sound from this city. Eerie. We are advancing slowly in Yugoslavia, as in Greece. The mountainous terrain is well-suited to defence. And the Serbs, like the Greeks, are brave fighters. Worthy of the greatest respect. The Panzer thrust to Belgrade will wait a while. Let the Serbs concentrate their forces, so that they can be dealt one great blow. The Greeks are exploiting the ideal defensive terrain well. The captured dugouts are filled with nothing but corpses.

London is wallowing in fantasies. The hacks are in charge. A new twist: they have given up Benghazi so as to save Greece. Not bad, but probably a little short in its life-expectancy. London is publicly admitting her long-prepared infiltration of Greece. A very good starting-point for our propaganda.

No air activity on either side. Air losses in the South-East 90:12. A very acceptable ratio. The Luftwaffe sinks 30,000 tons. In North Africa, our Panzers are already advancing far beyond Benghazi. It takes one's breath away.

Klagenfurt and Graz bombed. Without much success. But the radio station in Ljubljana is a nuisance. The Luftwaffe is trying to put it out of action.

Bad news: the *Gneisenau* hit by an air-launched torpedo. She has survived. But will have to go back into dry dock. An unpleasant marginal note to our successes.

London is still trumpeting big aid for Greece. We do not gainsay them. Our victory will be all the more impressive later. They have some 30,000 men down there. USA is being very cautious so far as concrete promises are concerned. Turkey and Russia remain completely determined to await events. They will speak up after we have won. I toss off a leader-article on British methods of seduction: 'The Old Story'. This time, because of its topicality, for the *Völkischer Beobachter*.

A mass of trivial worries. But Gutterer takes a lot of it from my shoulders. I must have a clear head at the moment.

With the Führer. He also admires the courage of the Greeks in particular. Perhaps there is still a touch of the old Hellenic strain in them. The Serbs are fighting desperately. But once the first resistance has been broken, then the great retreat will begin. More detailed information on the progress of operations is not yet available. Things must be given time to develop. Piraeus has been mined. The Führer forbids the bombing of Athens. This is right and noble of him. Rome and Athens are his Meccas. He greatly regrets having to fight the Greeks. If the English had not established themselves there, he would never have gone to the Italians' aid. It was their affair, and they should have been able to settle it alone.

The Führer is a man totally attuned to antiquity. He hates Christianity, because it has crippled all that is noble in humanity. According to Schopenhauer, Christianity and syphilis have made humanity unhappy and unfree. What a difference between the benevolent, smiling Zeus and the pain-wracked, crucified Christ. The ancient peoples' view of God was also much nobler and more humane than the Christians'. What a difference between a gloomy cathedral and a light, airy ancient temple. He describes life in ancient Rome: clarity, greatness, monumentality. The most wonderful republic in history. We would feel no disappointment, he believes, if we were now suddenly to be transported to this old, eternal city.

The Führer cannot relate to the Gothic mind. He hates gloom and brooding mysticism. He wants clarity, light, beauty. And these are the ideals of life in our time. In this respect, the Führer is a totally modern man.

To him, the Augustinian period is the high-point of history. And so far as the slaves are concerned, the people who were supposedly freed by Christianity: they were far less free and far more oppressed than in ancient Rome. What do we mean by slavery? Is a member of today's industrial proletariat perhaps freer than a slave before the Americans brought 'freedom' to their southern states? It is all a question of preconceptions.

I broach the subject of Serbia again. I have just read an interesting book on the Obrenovics and the Karageorgevics. A wild bunch of brigands. The Führer knows the story in detail. The entire Balkans, with all its puzzles, is an open book to him. He tells me crazy stories about old Nikita, who married his own daughters. He was an embezzler raised to the throne, and he gave old Vienna a bad time. But the Serbs were always the troublemakers. We shall have to deal with them now. The Balkans must no longer be Europe's powder-keg. And Russia must not be allowed to interfere there, as she did before the World War. Vienna dealt with these problems by good, old diplomatic methods. We must impose order by force. This what is happening now. Old Vienna was a cosmopolitan city. It never had overseas possessions, but to all intents and purposes ruled the whole of South-East Europe. Compared with it, Berlin and particularly Munich were provincial cities against a metropolis.

I describe a few bloomers by the English propaganda people. Laughter is the only fitting response.

But back to the war. How wonderful it would be if all this were over.

Even the Führer secretly longs for it.

The afternoon passes with hardly any news. All the operations are still in their initial stages. It is possible to work almost as if were peacetime. But no one can shake off the continual tension.

I read a lot of material about Serbia, the country, its people, its history. A fantastic country! And an even more amazing people. But we shall settle their hash.

Magda is well, as are the children.

Yet again, it gets very late.

9 April 1941 (Wednesday)

Yesterday: A day of furious work. And so just the most important things here in telegram style:

Kiel heavily attacked. Widespread damage. Raids on Glasgow, Bristol, and Liverpool with 400 aircraft. Devastating effect. Belgrade bombed again several times. No sign of life there. Greek fortified line broken. Road to Salonica open. Greeks fight very bravely. I fobid the press to disparage them.

Yugoslavs forced to retreat. Large forces trapped. Panzer Group Kleist ready. March! Will hit them for six. Aircraft losses 63:4.

Rommel takes Derna. Wonderful! English cut off. Stunning blow for London.

Hard fighting everywhere. But the advance continues. London lies in the most obvious way. It will cost dear. Supplies excellent material for our propaganda. We are on top of the world. The USA is completely in the dark.

Relations between London and Budapest broken off. England's shipping losses enormous. They concede 160,000 in one week. Despite everything, we continue to emphasise the difficulties of the Balkan campaign. No illusions at any price. London is making the most idiotic propaganda. Totally short-sighted. My *V.B.* article very effective. Dr Ley copies it wholesale for *Der Angriff.** Except packed with insults. Amateur!

Collaboration propaganda by our Paris embassy too shrill. I put a brake on it. This is not the way. Schmidtke and Paltzo report on France: things are slightly improved. French more friendly, since they fear Italian occupation. Food-supply situation appalling. Lively cultural life. Laval impossible. Admiral Darlan better for our purposes. Abetz is too willing to compromise.

Talk with Oshima. He is a passionate proponent of German-Japanese friendship. But the old men and the Liberals have still not been won over. Will take a while yet. Tokyo also intends to wait and see who wins. Oshima is a fiery character. Wants to underpin our co-operation on a cultural level. I shall help him with this.

Receive Görlitzer, Steeg and Petzke: serious coal situation in Berlin. We have to find coal or close down essential factories. So get to it! Food situation also very precarious. No solution to transport problem. I order immediate action. Lucky that spring is coming.

People are already busy writing the peace-treaty. Particularly the jurists. But we have to win the war first. So into the waste-paper basket!

Clear chain of command created for the radio. All leading back to me. This is necessary at this stage of the war.

With the Führer: he pokes fun at English propaganda. And it is laughable.

* 'The Attack'. A muck-raking newspaper founded in Berlin by Goebbels in 1927 as a vehicle for his views.

He admires the Greeks' courage. Regrets having to fight against them. Great anger at the Serbs. Only contempt for the Italians. He hopes that they won't run away from the retreating Serbs. With them, anything is possible.

Hard words for Serbia's total bankruptcy. Some 60,000 English in Greece. Marvellous that they have left North Africa exposed and are now running straight into our open arms. The London press is beginning to admit this mistake.

Russia is waging war with bits of paper. And Turkey still very tame. Will become even more pliable after our imminent victories. The Swiss press continues very insolent. Have them given one where it hurts most.

We talk about the Bürgerbräu assassination attempt. Ultimate culprits still not found. Assasin stubbornly silent. Führer says Otto Strasser. He tips Torgler as the most likely candidate for the Reichstag fire. I consider this out of the question. He is much too bourgeois for that. The Führer has a few words of friendly respect for our police and judiciary and their powers of detection.

A hurricane of work swirls around me at the office and at home. I am at my desk for 16–18 hours a day at the moment. So tired I could collapse. But it is worth it.

Rome wants to take over the frequency occupied by the Belgrade transmitter, which is still silent. I stop this. Have no interest in chaos on the radio waves at the moment. We are so superior to our enemies that we do not need to fear them. One only takes to others' frequencies for deceptive purposes, when the enemy is approaching collapse. This is not the case here. In any case, the Italians should forcibly silence a transmitter themselves if they want to use its frequency.

The controversy about English shipping losses is assuming quite grotesque forms. In London they must be cringing with embarrassment. This three-front war has brought England no advantages, not on a single front. We hammer home this point to the English amateur propagandists.

In the evening, special edition of the newsreel on the offensive. Arrived quickly and on time, and highly successful.

This is the way we must work.

Magda and the children are well.

Magda's father buried. She is coming straight back to Berlin.

I often have a deep longing for the children.

10 April 1941 (Thursday)

Yesterday: Again in telegram style. There is no time to write more.

Kiel heavily attacked again. Significant damage. 200 dead in two nights. We attack Coventry with 300 aircraft, plus a heavy raid on Portsmouth. Salonica in our hands. The Greek Army of Macedonia surrenders after stubborn resistance. Breakthrough on the Mctaxas Line completely successful. An unimaginable success. What a magnificent army we have. We had a few sleepless nights on this score.

Panzer Group Kleist pushes forward. 100 km into Yugoslavia, deep into the Skopje basin. Wedge successfully driven between the Greek and Serbian forces. 20,000 Serbian prisoners, including six generals. Huge quantities of captured equipment. A great day. And so the fanfares can be sounded on the radio, as I wrote in *Das Reich*, and which amused London so much.

Belgrade has started transmitting again. The station declares that the city is a heap of ruins. Ljubljana station very insolent. The Führer orders it to be attacked by the Luftwaffe.

The advance continues in North Africa. Only now do we report the fall of Derna. Rommel will have to call a halt to replenish his stocks of ammunition, fuel and food.

Then wonderful news follows wonderful news: we reach the Aegean, Nis and Maribor are in our hands.

A very bitter drop of wormwood: Kretschmer in English captivity. Prien and Schepke probably lost. Our three best U-boat commanders in one day. This is dreadful. We publish nothing about it for the moment. The people will be very sad. Particularly in the case of Prien, who is very popular.

The English press has undergone a noticeable change of tack. No more crowing about victories. There is hardly any mention of the British troops' involvement in the fighting. A new, grandiose piece of treachery is in preparation. Extremely pessimistic mood in the USA. The stock exchange has taken a plunge. The best indication of our success. Now London's mistake in handing out premature victory laurels is rebounding on her. In this respect, and despite our better prospects, we have been more careful. We are reaping our reward now. And in the USA this has been noted and greeted with respect. A warning for the future. We are conducting a brilliant war of words in the domestic and foreign services. Now the material that we had to scrape around for only three weeks ago is pouring in by the kilo. A glorious time! We give the English no quarter. Order of the Day: Let them have it! And then there are the huge English shipping losses. All the better for us.

I check new radio songs. A song for the South-Eastern Campaign by Annacker and Niels. Quite good, but not the last word. Needs more work.

Newsreel will be switched back on to a war footing. From now on will cover only military operations.

Splettstösser will have to be replaced as the radio's main commentator. His polemical pieces are not precise or conclusive enough. And these things are especially important at the moment.

Discuss reorganisation of the news and propaganda services of the radio. We are now to subdivide it into domestic, foreign and propaganda services. Thus the news service pure and simple will be separated from the foreign service, which we shall now combine into one unit. A clearcut and easily-supervised organisation. The attempts of other departments, particularly the Foreign Ministry, to interfere will be resisted at all times. Orders will come from me.

With the Führer. He was very worried that the breakthrough would not succeed immediately, and did not sleep all night. Now, however, he is beaming with joy. And he has every reason. This breakthrough is one of the most brilliant feats of arms in the history of warfare. The Führer's only care for the English is to make jokes about their stupidity. He is furious at the Serbs, while he has respect, and perhaps some sympathy, for the Greeks. As a people they have not deserved such suffering. We no longer have much respect for the USA. The only thing that impresses the Jews there is a show of power. Turkey is acting very meek and mild. She will certainly think long and hard before she enters the war. Moscow, too, is exercising great caution at the moment. No one wants to stray into our field of fire. And this is no bad thing.

Japan can do nothing yet, though Konoye and Matsuoka would like to. The old men are still opposed to action. They must first convince themselves that our victory is absolutely certain. Japan thinks and feels in a quite different way to the European continent. But it is very good that we have her on our side.

Matschek has broadcast a speech from Zagreb. Neither hot nor cold. War is terrible, but he trusts in the unity of the Peasants' Party. A programme of sorts, if none too clear. Weighed and found wanting! The Croat leader, Pavelic, who is for separation from Belgrade, is completely stealing Matschek's thunder. In such times one must seize fortune by the scruff of the neck.

Somewhat depressed mood in Kiel. We send Ley up there. I personally cannot leave Berlin at the moment, but I give Ley a few good pieces of advice. At critical moments one must always show the people that one is with them.

The mood in London is one of increasing despondency. The government is trying to instil some courage into the population. Claiming that they have lost only what they expected to lose. And that we have not gained as much as we had hoped. This is not the kind of thing one can argue with. It is pure idiocy. And the world regards it with contempt. We are in the limelight. Our prestige is growing almost by the hour. London is experiencing what must be its darkest hour since Dunkirk. And on top of this comes the loss of 2,000 men and huge amounts of equipment in North Africa. Nothing can be done to help the Greeks, as London already recognises. The noisy fanfares have died away. Belgrade has now announced officially that the city is now nothing but ruins. Herr Simovic and his people are paying dearly.

Magda returns from Duisburg in the evening. We have a lot to talk about.

The stream of news from everywhere does not stop until late into the night. A happy day!

309

Large-scale English attack on Berlin just before 1 a.m. In the air-raid shelter until 4 a.m.

11 April 1941 (Friday)

Yesterday: Serious damage on Unter den Linden in Berlin. State Opera completely destroyed by fire. Only the outer walls left standing. A tragic loss. The University and the State Library also hard hit. We announce it publicly to the world under the headline: Attack on Berlin's cultural quarter. Mainly as a counterweight to the atrocity reports about Belgrade. The State Opera fell victim to incendiary bombs, which set fire to the seats in the auditorium. I order an increase in fire-watching crews for buildings of cultural value, especially the Propaganda Ministry.

A number of other cities in the Reich, particularly in North Germany, also attacked. We concentrate our night raids on English ports. 300 aircraft involved in all. In excellent visibility. Devastating effect. What it must look like over there. The incendiary bombs are much more dangerous than had at first been thought.

Our offensives against Yugoslavia and Greece are now in full swing. The movements of our armies are beginning to assume coherent shape. Monastir is in our possession. No more can be said at the moment. With the fall of Yugoslavia, we shall also take possession of enormous potential sources of raw materials. Particularly copper, which we could do with.

The advance continues unabated in North Africa. So long as Rommel does not venture too far ahead of his lines of communication. Our men have already had no rations for four days. The English are talking about the loss of Tobruk. But this has not yet been confirmed.

The Luftwaffe sinks a number of ships. Our U-boats have nothing to report.

Churchill addresses the House of Commons. A profoundly pessimistic speech. True, he tries to play things down, but it is hard work. His appraisal of the Battle of the Atlantic is couched in the gloomiest terms. The London press in general is also very subdued. They present the lamest possible excuses, which we deal with easily. The mood in the USA is totally pessimistic. Roosevelt had been intending to send his son, Jimmy, to Yugoslavia, but this idea, it has now been announced officially, has been abandoned. A good subject for our cartoonists. The press and radio in the USA has already given up the Balkans for lost. Our prestige is growing by the hour. We are in superb polemical form. Now work is fun again.

In Belgrade they are producing atrocity propaganda with regard to the bombing of the city. But the attack on Berlin gives us some good counter-arguments in that respect.

A mass of stuff to be dealt with. Particularly in the non-political areas. But I cannot give it too much attention. Gutterer takes it from my shoulders.

New radio studios go into operation. Built to the latest technical specifications.

Since the destruction of the State Opera I live in fear that our beautiful ministry could fall victim to the flames. I inspect the damage to the State Opera. It is lost. The entire interior completely destroyed by fire. Hardly anything salvageable. Tietjen is absolutely shattered. I give orders that the State Opera company should be able to use the stage of the German Opera House on an equal basis. Each for a month. The big guest performance by the Italians will also take place at the German Opera House. I cheer up the people from the State Opera a little, even though the sight of these smoking ruins pierces me to the heart. How many happy hours I have passed in this building. And now these ruins. England will be forced to pay dearly for this.

US indictment against *Transozean* released. A cowardly, paper-thin concoction. We shall do exactly the same to UP or AP.

What a glorious spring! Once we have peace again, we shall spend some time devoting ourselves to the beautiful things of life.

Pessimism is on the increase in London. We have to go so far as to play it down in our reports to the German people, for fear of arousing too many illusions. Athens and Belgrade are calling desperately for British assistance in the air. The response from London is a cold-blooded 'business as usual'. We expected no different . . .

. . . A short chat in the evening with Magda and with Ursel, who is visiting us for Easter.

Fräulein Schaljapin also arrives, from Paris. She has a lot to report. She is very interesting.

Zagreb in our hands. Big special announcement.

A storm of pessimism in London.

This is so wonderful and does me so much good.

12 April 1941 (Saturday)

Yesterday: Minor incursions into the Reich. Probably due to the fact that 14 English aircraft were shot down the previous night. Heavy air raids on Birmingham. Good visibility. London concedes great success.

In Greece, mopping-up operations in the conquered areas are proceeding according to plan. We are taking many prisoners and huge amounts of matériel. In Yugoslavia we are sweeping down from the north. Several Divisions smashed. 10,000 prisoners. Enemy forces in South Serbia destroyed. Boundless rejoicing on the part of the Croats in Zagreb. Autonomy proclaimed. We stoke the fires. A Croat Legion is established in Vienna. Horthy releases a call to his people: Hungary will take back her old provinces by force. We press on deeper into Serbia. Belgrade not yet in our hands. Will come soon, however. Everything is proceeding as desired. Further advances in North Africa. Almost too fast and too far.

In London they are devastated. At the same time, the old English cynicism is putting in an appearance. Sappers are busy behind the Greek fighting front. Typically English! Looting, destroying, blowing up, burning. The whole world is asking when the English are going to fight. London says nothing. We give the Tommies no quarter. We beat them round the ears with it, hour after hour. The mood in the USA is very troubled. Churchill's speech, with its pessimistic gloom, has finished the Yankees. We shall have to play down the positive opinions from abroad so far as domestic consumption is concerned, or illusions will be encouraged.

I reiterate the procedures for special announcements on the radio. A few mistakes have been made in that quarter.

Himmler has banned the sale of contraceptive devices. This is very important at the moment. Let people make provision for children. On the other hand, child benefits will do more to increase our population than bureaucratic edicts.

Martin is to keep a tighter rein on military secrets in the Ministerial Conference. Dr Dietrich is jealous because he doesn't get to hear them. A small-minded troublemaker. Idle, incompetent, so gets in others' ways. I shall light a fire under Jodl.

Deal with daily routine with Gutterer and Hadamovsky. Despite these stirring times, there is so much trivial stuff, which serves only to provide aggravation and irritation. I work gladly and passionately, but I am powerless against these intrigues.

The weather is wonderful. A real Good Friday. I drive to Lanke with my colleagues, to work out there and to get at least some fresh air. The forest is beginning to come into bud. Everywhere there is the scent of spring. But I scarcely get the chance to enjoy it.

Magda and Ursel arrive in the afternoon. Schaljapin follows. A little stroll to the log cabins and some talk. But all in the shadow of these dramatic times. One is almost ashamed to take time to draw breath.

London is fantasising about 3000 dead in the last air raid on Berlin. The real figure was eleven. We protest strongly about this.

Great celebrations in Croatia. Horthy blows the trumpet for battle, and so the Hungarians march victoriously along behind our troops.

Newsreel in the evening. Still very incomplete. Needs a lot more work.

Then some chat around the fire.

13 April 1941 (Sunday)

Yesterday: To Berlin early.

No incursions into the Reich. But raid on Brest. The *Gneisenau* unfortunately seriously hit. Seventy-five dead. A palpable loss for our naval capacity. In return, we carry out massive attacks on English ports with 500 aircraft. Good visibility, extremely effective.

The Hungarians are advancing cautiously. Our operations in Serbia are continuing according to plan and with the expected success. Germans and Italians have joined hands. Rome slightly displeased that we do not place enough importance in her help. We are doing a little more in this area now, and the Führer has sent a friendly telegram to the Duce. The *Leibstandarte* Division* may well be brought in against the English, though this is not yet absolutely certain. Growing indications that the English are preparing to take to their heels. We give these great prominence in our propaganda, so as to make this morally impossible. The Führer would rather face them in Greece than in North Africa. On the other hand, this propaganda has the disadvantage that our people sees the battle as already won. We are steering a middle course in this respect. Whatever the case, we must continue to emphasise the grave difficulties of the campaign as a whole.

Great jubilation everywhere in Croatia. Our troops greeted in Zagreb like conquering heroes. Autonomy declared. We intend to move a Propaganda Unit into Zagreb, though the Foreign Ministry continues to oppose this. It will do them no good.

Further advances in North Africa. Our Luftwaffe is wreaking havoc with the entire English defensive line.

Profoundest pessimism in London. We exploit this to the full. The neutrals' belief in England's power and prestige is melting away by the hour. Anti-German feeling in the occupied countries weakening to a discernible extent. A more sober attitude apparent. London is fabricating glorious victories by its air force. Roughly on the level of '3000 dead in Berlin'. In reality the figure is fifteen. I have our press attack without mercy. The English people must be stripped of all hope.

The USA has also become very sceptical. A Jewish newspaper in New York has called the Führer 'the greatest military genius of all time'. A noteworthy symptom of the present change of mood. We use it to the full.

Soon, however, Churchill's tactics become clear: London begins to take a more optimistic line. The English troops have not yet seen battle. We seize on this, too. The gentlemen from Canada and Australia will be astonished to hear such statements.

Meanwhile, our embassy in Paris is staging ballet evenings with the young performers from the Paris Opera. I have all the photographs of this impounded, send them to the Führer, and create merry hell. Paris has turned into a real den of iniquity. And the worst offender is our Major Schmidtke. A complete nincompoop!

Discuss our High Command's practices re. officers' divorces. The system is thoroughly rigid and outmoded. Something must be done about it. I have everything summarised for me in writing so that I can submit a report to the Führer at a later stage.

In conference with Gutterer for a long time. Absolutely no indication that it is Easter. And in any case the weather is too dull and wet.

* The élite 'Bodyguard' Division of the SS, commanded by Sepp Dietrich.

313

Back to Lanke in the afternoon. I still have whole piles of work to deal with. But in such wild, eventful times I enjoy it.

Get a little fresh air with a short stroll. Magda's heart is giving her trouble. I suffer with her.

Total rout in Serbia. No longer any contact between the individual units. Intercepted radio messages herald the beginning of the end. [. . .] [. . .] the King. Reports from air force commands indicate that they have no combat-worthy aircraft left, etc. The Serbs have now been cut off completely from the Greeks and the English. Now we can deal with them piecemeal. The great retreat will soon be under way. Churchill makes a short speech in Birmingham. Sentimental and pitched towards social issues. He goes straight for the tear-ducts, the old crook. But it will do him no good now. The Balkan catastrophe is reaching its climax.

Roosevelt has had the Danish Ambassador in Washington sign over control of Danish ships at anchor in US ports, without the knowledge of the Danish government. A typical piece of gangsterism. Write it down in our little book!

More news from all over the world pours in during the course of the evening. Almost all good. Another amazing day! May we live to see many more such as this!

14 April 1941 (Monday)

Yesterday: Easter Sunday! A day of glorious victories. The fanfares on the radio never seem to stop.

Kleist's Panzers enter Belgrade. Twenty-two generals and 12,000 men taken prisoner in Zagreb. Hungary is advancing according to plan. We are making great progress in South Serbia. A total of seventeen Serbian divisions destroyed to date.

Tobruk surrounded, Bardia in our hands. Black day for England. In addition, a single U-boat sinks 75,000 tons. Aircraft losses 46:2. No raids on either side.

Reports from Coventry: this is hell. Gloomy mood in England. USA very sober. A wonderful Easter for the German people. I give the radio detailed instructions. They are giving our victories magnificent coverage.

We have already sent our people to Zagreb. The Foreign Ministry has a mind to move in on our pitch. No chance of this, it goes without saying.

A turbulent Easter at home out at Lanke. But wonderful.

It is Hilde's birthday. A pity that the children are not with us.

Marina Schaljapin talks about the Bolshevik Revolution, which she witnessed personally. It must have been hell.

Moscow and Tokyo have signed a Treaty of Friendship. Just the right thing at the moment!

Grab some fresh air in the afternoon. And do a little reading. But the

314

hours fly by so quickly. Only now does one notice how tired one is. Speak with the children on the telephone. Sweet chatter. Helga wise and precocious as ever.

Big sensation: Russo-Japanese Treaty of Friendship and Non-Aggression. Mutual guarantees of Manchuria and Mongolia. Stalin and Molotov escort Matsuoka to his train. Stalin embraces the German Military Attaché and declares that Russia and Germany will march together to their goal. This is marvellous and for the moment extremely useful. We shall bring it to the notice of the English with all appropriate force. It is a fine thing to have power. It seems that Stalin has no desire to make the acquaintance of our German Panzers. Today is a grave day for England. One which sees her last illusions crumble. It will gradually prey on her nerves.

I spend the entire day in a daze of feverish happiness.

What an Easter! What a reawakening after the long night of winter!

15 April 1941 (Tuesday)

Yesterday: Into the ministry early.

No incursions on either side. We take Edessa. The German forces in Greece change the direction of their advance. All completely according to plan. Serbia will soon be crushed. The news from there shows all the signs of a rout.

Some 40,000 tons sunk. The Battle of the Atlantic continues.

Stocks of explosives found at the English Consulate in Zagreb. Arsonists! We make something of it.

For the rest, everything is coming to a head in the South-East. We can reckon with crucial developments in the near future.

The Moscow-Tokyo treaty has been given no more than marginal attention here, and has not been dramatised in any way. In view of the well-known and extensive plans being made, this does not suit the Führer's ends at all. The scene with the Military Attaché has been passed over completely. In other respects, however, the affair is very beneficial from a psychological standpoint. Shock-effect in the USA.

Morale among the people quite wonderful. Delighted but without illusions. Exactly as we wanted it. The SD report contains praise for my work.

Continued depression in London. I dictate a leader-article for the *Völkischer Beobachter*, in which I again belabour the English with their history of failures.

Report from Switzerland: the usual anti-German feeling in ruling circles. The freemasons are in control. My statements are given ironical treatment and made light of. One day there will be a rude awakening.

Look at a number of new film treatments. A very good one among them: 'Scharnhorst'.

Film export drive strongly intensified. Without regard for profitability.

315

Films shown abroad make for one of our most effective propaganda weapons. They do not need to make money, and they may even cost money.

News of General Rommel: he has taken Sollum. His headlong advance is almost enough to make one anxious. But Rommel is not only bold; he is also thoughtful, and a stubborn Swabian into the bargain.

Not back to Lanke until the afternoon. Easter Monday. I notice little of it. I am tired and battle-weary and my mind is full of worries. Some visitors out here: the Hommels and Major Martin are our house-guests. A lot of political talk, but I cannot join in, since I must work.

Our High Command Bulletin is already reporting: enemy forces in Yugoslavia destroyed. Those surviving have retreated into the mountains. London is boasting that the real battle has not yet begun, either in the Balkans or in North Africa. Then it is time that it did. Simović makes a pompous speech about resistance and honour and no surrender and thanks to Churchill. Probably for his well-filled bank account. Sickening!

The Moscow-Tokyo pact is still the big sensation. A pity that we cannot make more of it.

Newsreel in the evening. From the theatre of operations. Magnificent footage. Will really hit home. These pictures will go out to the entire world.

Then long session talking. I am very tired but cannot sleep.

An effect of the continual tension. Settle a few film problems with Hippler. I want fewer, but good films, and not a lot of mediocre productions.

Report from the Führer Headquarters: the English are already embarking to leave Greece. A pity, because we would so much have liked to give them a dose of our medicine. Our Stukas sink 30,000 tons and damage another 80,000 in Piraeus harbour. We intend to make the Tommies' farewell as painful as possible.

Great disappointment at the Moscow-Tokyo pact in Washington. We don't know whether to laugh or cry. The treaty is a cuckoo's egg laid in our nest by Stalin. But we shall not let it hatch.

16 April 1941 (Wednesday)

Yesterday: No incursions on either side. The Serbs are making a last stand at Sarajevo. But they are being badly harried by us and are putting up little resistance. Their morale has been broken. Likewise the Greeks: our troops are already on Mount Olympus. The Italians are advancing well. Road conditions appalling. But are the English embarking? They deny it, if none too vigorously. In any case, we are attacking in massive strength, to help them make up their minds. It would, of course, be a good deal better for us if we could keep them in Greece, rather than see them run off to somewhere else.

Piraeus has been bombed again, with considerable success. The other operations in the Balkans are in a state of constant flux, and we expect concrete results to be announced in the near future.

In North Africa the supply-lines are being strengthened. The English are still holding Tobruk, have even made an attempt to break out, but lost six out of seventeen tanks in the process. Berndt and Haegert are there, right in the front line, and have written me moving letters. We have Panzer divisions in North Africa now. These will enable us to do all sorts. Unfortunately, one of our fuel ships has been destroyed by incendiary torpedoes.

Only a few sinkings. Our U-boat fleet has had little to report lately.

Guidelines for propaganda: hard against England for her attempted escape from Greece. We are seeking to discredit her in the most comprehensive fashion. And succeeding. The Turkish press, for instance, has turned very cool towards England. And the proximity of German troops probably also has something to do with this.

In London they are being forced to watch one illusion after another crumble to nothing. All they can do is to stutter lame excuses. We hit home relentlessly.

Pact between Moscow and Tokyo continues to be regarded as the big sensation. Pity that we cannot spend more time on it. Wiegand writes that Hitler has outwitted Churchill yet again. May God grant it! Great rejoicing in Tokyo. Matsuoka's position has certainly been greatly strengthened.

Report on the shortcomings of the Propaganda Companies in the West. The main problems are lack of communication with higher authorities and shortage of viewing equipment. I shall help out in these respects.

Question of whom we should send to Croatia. I shall not choose someone who knows the country, but instead intend to have a good propagandist there. People with local knowledge are usually much too susceptible to influence.

Yet again, the day is filled with enormous tension. I receive a few visitors between times: Jordan from Dessau. He has worries about his theatre, with which I am able to help him. And I am supposed to be making a speech in Dessau. But I cannot at the moment. I am completely tied to Berlin.

Horia Sima has written to Antonescu offering reconciliation. Antonescu has brusquely rejected it and is sitting firmly on his high horse. I suspect that he will rue this one day. And Rumania will probably be caused much suffering thereby.

It has been reported from Cairo that General Wavell intends to give up Sidi el Barani without a fight. It is scarcely believable. But with God – and at the moment also with the English – everything is possible. The Empire is now facing its greatest test. We shall make every effort to ensure that it does not survive it.

Yugoslavia asks for a truce during the course of the morning. Through two separate channels simultaneously. Given the position, this was to be expected. A new situation. The Führer leaves things in the air. It has been reported from Athens that England has ordered the Greek fleet to provide cover for the Tommies' withdrawal. This is really the height of cynicism. A régime cannot sink any lower.

And then news follows news: Rommel has already pressed on beyond Sidi el Barani. London is even claiming that he is at Mersa el Matruh. One almost shrinks from such good fortune; one is tempted to throw a ring into the water to appease the Gods, like Polycrates of old.

Yugoslavia's truce demand has been left unanswered for the moment. We intend first to ensure a number of guarantees, take prisoners, etc. Possession is nine points of the law. And so first we demand compliance with a few formalities. This will take a few days. Even the Swiss newspapers are showing their admiration now. We put them aside and take no notice.

A full-scale transformation in public opinion is under way in the USA. Roosevelt comes off worst. We are on the ascendant again to some extent. Our advance in North Africa has made a particularly deep impression. All eyes are on the road from Mersa Matruh to Alexandria. England is completely discredited. Particularly by her flight from Greece, which is now gathering momentum and which we declare to the world in headlines and hard-hitting editorials. We shall strip the Lords of their fine feathers.

Croatia requests the Führer to recognise her independence, and he grants this with some friendly words of encouragement. End of the Yugoslav fair-weather state!

More happens in a day now than used to happen in years.

This is a great, exciting, but also exhausting time.

17 April 1941 (Thursday)

Yesterday: Night raid on Kiel. No damage of note, because of bad weather. A few other ports affected by it. We send in 450 aircraft against England. Mainly on Belfast. Devastating effect. Even London admits it. Huge fires visible from the air.

No sinkings. Our U-boats are out of luck. And the Navy is being badly led. Raeder is a complete idiot. His obsession with secrecy is also absurd.

The Serbs are still putting up some resistance around Sarajevo. Elsewhere there are only isolated pockets of resistance. A guerrilla war, as even Reuter admits, with the observation that the situation is bad. No more talk of a truce. There is no such thing as a government on the enemy side any more. General Simović is said to have fled. And it is better that we do not negotiate with the rump of Serbia but create a fait accompli. This gives us a free hand for the future.

The English are showing their mettle now. They are fighting alongside the Greeks. Our headlines probably had something to do with it. Their resistance is very stubborn, with the result that our progress in Greece has become slow. We switch the emphasis of our campaign without warning, and there is no more talk of the Tommies trying to dodge a fight. We have, of course, realised our aim of keeping them in Greece. Our losses are not as serious as we had feared at first. 400 killed at the Rupel Pass.

Very gloomy mood in London. Influenced more by North Africa, where we are holding our positions and fortifying them, than by the situation in the South-East. They can already see Egypt and the Suez Canal in our hands. Things have, of course, not yet reached that stage, and I forbid the newspapers to make any such predictions. Our radio transmitters are stirring up the Arabs. We intend to play Colonel Lawrence. Clandestine transmitter put into operation against Greece. Taking a line of the most extreme kind. A pity that there are only 37,000 radios in the whole of Greece. But at such times, rumours spread like wildfire.

Morale has reached rock-bottom in the USA. An earthquake. Now we must follow up our advantage. My leader-article in the *Völkischer Beobachter* has been extremely well received. A tough attack on the English.

We have to wait for the really big news. But I spend some time with Glasmaier, establishing an outline of procedure for all the coming events, so that we shall not be surprised by anything.

Marrenbach reports on Ley's visit to Kiel. Not much cause for satisfaction. The city has been very hard hit. Inhabitants' morale very depressed. Particularly the women. Come evening, thousands head for the woods surrounding the city. Ley is in favour of building barracks there. I am against it. They would be easy targets for the English. I arrange the evacuation of children and some women and the building of shelters. Lohse should have paid more attention to these things. I set a really large-scale aid programme in motion. It is impossible to do too much. We must even get the people furniture. Gutterer is taking over the operation.

A number of film and theatre matters. Hinkel reports on the great successes of his entertainment projects for the troops. Everything is running smoothly.

A two-way broadcast between home and headquarters is being prepared for the Führer's birthday. Hess and Göring are to speak. I shall give an address on the eve of the birthday.

Purchase a few glorious van Dycks from Holland.

Stalin and Matsuoka are exchanging telegrams like old friends. Things change fast in politics, for good or ill.

Ankara is engaged in a volte-face. These days they take their news almost exclusively from the German News Agency. What a victory like this can do!

I have a correspondent from Stockholm deported. He told bare-faced lies about the bomb damage in Berlin. We do not need to put up with this kind of thing any more.

Sarajevo has fallen, and with it huge quantities of equipment and countless prisoners. A battle is raging on Mount Olympus between our men and the allied Greek and English forces. The English, who made a foray towards Sollum, have been repulsed with a bloody nose.

Halifax makes a speech. Palpably low-key and perplexed. We shall soon shut these plutocrats' mouths for them.

North Africa is giving cause for despair in London. The press has gone into open opposition against the government. This may be seriously meant, but on the other hand Churchill may be opening a safety-valve for growing public anger. At any rate, neutral journalists are reporting discontent among the English people. This has been unheard-of until now. Once the inevitable defeat in Greece has been added to his troubles, Churchill will be facing a very grave situation. We shall certainly not make things any easier for him. I have the press warned again about premature references to the Suez Canal.

Everything is hanging in the balance. The enemy has only a few trumps left in his hand.

And so we shall continue to hammer him until he collapses.

18 April 1941 (Friday)

Yesterday: Middling raid on Bremen. We carry out our biggest raid yet on London with 650 bombers. 1050 tons of high-explosive and 50,000 incendiary bombs. In retaliation for the attack on Berlin's cultural quarter. The effect is shattering. Reports so far arriving from London reflect the truly devastating nature of the raid. Right and proper. England must be kept on the run.

Only sporadic, isolated fighting in Yugoslavia now. More in the nature of a police action. A coherent, unified command is no longer in existence. Individuals are waging war on their own initiative. The armies are broken. We are now mopping up. In Greece, on the other hand, extremely stiff resistance. The English are putting up a hard fight. Attempt to outflank Mount Olympus. We shall soon hear details.

Unfortunately, six transports for North Africa sunk by the English. Including 1000 men. There are hopes that some will be saved. And a mass of equipment gone down with them. A heavy blow. The air reconnaissance units were put out of action by bad weather. Bitter fighting for Tobruk. The English attack with their fleet. Our men hold their ground. In Sollum, too, the Tommies are defending like lions. But it will do them no good. They are already withdrawing troops from East Africa, which we must give up for lost, and transferring them to Egypt. Butterflies in their stomach about the Suez Canal.

No sinkings. The Navy will soon have to explain itself.

Report by von Werra on English prisoner-of-war camps. A cleverly worked-out system of interrogation and persuasion. Werra's escape is a fantastic story of adventure. These are our heroes of today . . .

. . . Work on morale in Kiel. Said to be not quite so bad as Marrenbach painted it. Lohse has been a failure there. I initiate a big aid programme. In particular, the Finance Minister must place a special fund at the disposal of the Gaus threatened by air raids.

Discuss film treatments with Hippler. I want to see fewer conflicts about illegitimate children in our films. The legitimate child must remain at least the norm. And then we need new material for the big stars like Leander, etc. We are building new studios in Linz according to the Führer's wish. A special productions studio is to be completed there. With a huge outdoor sound-stage.

Organisational problems discussed with Gutterer. We are sending Maurer-Stuttgart to Zagreb.

We cannot make much propaganda capital out of the English taxation system. The taxes there are not too unfair, particularly for the lower classes. England is, after all, a very rich country.

Purchase a very fine painting, Venus of Sorrento, for the Führer's birthday. He will undoubtedly be very pleased with it. He intends to be back in Berlin at the beginning of next week. His headquarters are near Wiener Neustadt at the moment . . .

. . . Debates about protection of convoys in the USA. But the Isolationists are on the ascendant again. Roosevelt can no longer do what he likes. The US press is trying to push him further, but he has rejected armed protection of convoys for the present. He may have been influenced by England's desperate situation. The consequences of the last air raid are indescribable. Churchill's tame press is frantically trying to keep up appearances. The Wehrmacht High Command's Bulletin has declared that attacks on German residential districts will be answered in kind from now on. I have this announcement conveyed forcefully to the English. It should have a sobering effect. Lord [. . .] was one of the victims of the most recent air raid.

Churchill will have gained little joy from that. Plus another 30,000 tons sunk by the Luftwaffe. A steady drip wears away the stone.

In the end England will collapse. Then we shall have our hour.

In the late evening we hear the news: the remnants of the Yugoslav Army have surrendered unconditionally. So, at last! A proud victory in eleven days. We had thought that it would take so much longer. Our Wehrmacht constantly puts us to shame. We release the news in grand style, even though it is after midnight.

Air-raid warning immediately afterwards. Middling raid on Berlin. Six English are shot down. No damage worthy of the name. But Berlin is forced to spend four hours in its air-raid shelters.

19 April 1941 (Saturday)

Yesterday: A few incursions into the Reich. Damage insignificant. England has lost her punch these days. We hit Portsmouth again with more than 300 aircraft. Excellent visibility. Enormous damage. We must hound the enemy without mercy.

Total collapse in Serbia. Surrender complete. No resistance of any importance now. Thus we have this campaign behind us. Not a trace is left of the Serbian Army's legendary reputation. London and the USA discard this foolish country and its criminal government with a few cold-blooded phrases.

In Greece, the enemy front, even the English-held parts, is slowly beginning to give way. But the fighting is still hard and bitter. The English are putting up a good show. Nevertheless, statements in Athens have a strongly defeatist character.

In North Africa, bitter fighting around Tobruk and Sollum. The advance had come to something of a halt there. As always when we have won great victories, London is claiming that we have suffered enormous losses. But we know how to counter that.

850 men from the convoy sunk on the way to Africa have, thank God, been saved. Operations are still in flux everywhere. We shall not have details or definitive news for a few days yet.

Growing pessimism in London. Public criticism of the government. The US reports of our latest air raids are truly horrific. It is a real inferno over there. Churchill has had his press threaten Berlin. But let him attack. Our Luftwaffe will not be slow to answer.

Public opinion in the USA is beginning to waver. The Isolationists are very active. Colonel Lindbergh is sticking stubbornly and with great courage to his old opinions. A man of honour!

Report from Hungary: differing accounts of Teleki's motives for suicide. One thing is clear: Budapest would like to keep a foot in both camps, using us to gain territory but not queering its pitch with London. Horthy is a real Magyar, i.e. an intriguer and a hypocrite. One must always keep an eye on the Hungarians. They are masters of betrayal.

Report from Shanghai. The Sino-Japanese conflict is in stalemate. Japan is incapable of action, either militarily or in the foreign policy sphere. This may be true, which would account for Matsuoka's reserve. But then even a Japan in reserve is of value to us. She represents a constant threat to the USA, and is perhaps stronger as a neutral than as a combatant.

Push through a host of measures for Kiel. They had become stuck in a mass of red tape here in Berlin. I have put some fire behind them. Now everyone is behaving themselves. One must go hard at such an issue and not be pernickety about who does what. The people of Kiel are very pleased with our aid . . .

. . . Personnel matters with Gutterer. I intend to have him promoted to State Secretary, and a number of others to directorial and managerial positions. We need people in such positions, if only for external reasons.

Technical problems with Hippler. Particularly regarding films for young people, which must be urgently encouraged. Axel is off to Stockholm to persuade Frau Leander to star in his next film.

Franco has made a speech: peace, he says, is merely a preparation for war, and the latter the normal condition of humanity. Then let him create normal conditions and fight alongside us. He is a totally conceited loud-mouth.

With mother for her birthday. She is seventy-two years old. I am so happy that I still have her. She is very healthy and robust. We chat for an hour. She tells me the latest from Rheydt and a lot more besides. To me, with her simple nature and peasant cunning, she is the voice of the people. I worship her.

Aunt Anna died a few weeks ago at the age of ninety-six and a half. The news fills me with profound sadness. How many happy hours I spent with her in Hüls!

I spend the entire afternoon with mother. Her chatter moves my heart and does me so much good.

17,000 prisoners and masses of captured equipment in Northern Greece so far. The big breakthrough is approaching.

Rome has denied that the Duke of Aosta has offered to surrender in East Africa. He is a brave man, but his position seems hardly retrievable.

What a glorious spring day outside. The sun is shining down, very warm and benevolent. How wonderful it would be if we were to win victory and make peace soon. But that is probably still a long way off.

The Führer is absolutely thrilled by the latest newsreel. And it is a real work of art in terms of film content, composition, editing and music. When we have the material, our achievements in this field are unsurpassable.

They are still fantasising in London, wildly exaggerating the air raid on Berlin, talking of mountains of corpses in Yugoslavia and Northern Greece, praising the British tanks, which, among other things, 'cut through the Germans like knives through cheese'. But they are shortening their lines in Greece, and they are having officially to concede defeat after defeat. In North Africa, they declare, England is on the offensive again. This will cause bitter disappointments for the English people, as did our last air raid on London, of which the Swedish press has provided quite horrendous descriptions. And Churchill had given the English people to believe that the danger from the air was past. The English plutocracy is really ripe for its fall. It has outlived its time, is operating with outdated methods, and is in no way the equal of an opponent such as the Führer. We must keep pushing until it collapses. This pack of pirates, money-grubbers and fortune-hunters will be no loss to the world.

Savage attacks on Eden in London. So far as we are concerned, let this pimp stay in office for as long as possible. We could not wish ourselves a better British Foreign Minister.

The Swiss press is being infuriatingly insolent again. I hope we shall soon be able to speak plain German to them.

Favourable news arrives from Greece late in the evening. It seems that we shall soon be through there, too. That would be a real miracle!

Mother here for a chat. With Maria. A wonderful birthday.

20 April 1941 (Sunday)

Yesterday: No incursions on either side. The English dropped a rather terrifying bomb on Berlin last time. No good omen for the future. But only ten of the sixty aircraft that were heading for Berlin got through. The reason is still unclear.

Serbia finished. Only mopping-up operations remain now. The advance in Greece is gathering momentum. Our flag flies on Olympus. Larissa in our possession.

This means that we have broken through. Now the road lies open before us. Now there is no turning back. And the Greek Prime Minister, Koryzis, has died suddenly – whether he died naturally or did away with himself is unclear – and his successor is our friend Kotzias. The King intends to take the government of the country into his own hands. This could mean a compromise course. But no precise details are yet known. In any case, Kotzias is on our side, as I have gauged often enough. We shall wait and see. Greece, it seems, is slowly beginning to waver. English embarkations at Piraeus have now been confirmed. The British are clearing off. We play up Koryzis' death as assassination by the English. It is probably true, anyway.

It is being declared in London that the English people accepts each new blow with indifference. And it is astonishing how little reaction there has been to our latest air raid there. The English are a people of rare tenacity. But sometime they must break. Churchill has stated that he intends to bomb Rome if we bomb Athens and Cairo. Cairo – that is [. . .]. For the rest, London continues to live in a world of illusion: we have suffered indescribable casualties, our Stukas are being shot down by the thousand, and so on. We are not slow to respond. Morale here is good. Slight anger at the Italians for trying to steal our thunder. I shall also have to take steps against the excesses of Italian fashion, which our people have little understanding for. In general the Italians tend to live as if there were no war on.

Franco's speech appeared in our press after all, due to an error. I kick up a fuss about it. Franco should be waging war, not preaching radical military philosophy. He is a conceited, empty-headed peacock.

A *Transozean* report from Moscow: it contains our most precious military and diplomatic secrets. I have it destroyed immediately. Our entire camouflage operation is, it seems, of little value. Stalin must have known everything long since. We shall only be able to conceal our motives through extensive counter-measures.

Diewerge has been at Headquarters. He has a thousand things to report. The Führer is very pleased with our work. As is the entire public. Everything is going like clockwork. A brilliantly-tuned machine.

Wächter has given the Führer 100 original French cartoons of himself for his birthday. A scream! I too am in them, brilliantly caricatured. When such things are done with wit and intelligence, one cannot help but appreciate them.

Tiessler, our liaison man with the Party, has been granted greater plenipotentiary powers by me.

I have instructed Glasmaier to come up with proposals for a redistribution of radio stations after the war. Otherwise we shall have every Gau laying claim to its own broadcasting system.

My tax situation is causing me some drudgery. I believe that the state ought really to remove such worries from one who has already suffered so much drudgery for the public good. But one must pay up, just like Mister Average, and more, because it is not in one's nature to shirk one's duties.

Vichy has left the League of Nations. Astonishing that such a thing still exists! But they are not treating our press representatives well in Vichy. If necessary, we shall have to recall them. I shall have the situation throughly investigated.

Our breakthrough in Greece is looking more decisive by the hour. The entire business there cannot last much longer.

Magda has gone to Dessau. To visit Harald. He will be off soon. Heiduschke has already left for the front.

A lot of work in the afternoon. Short talk with Marina Schljapin.

In the evening, speech on the radio for the Führer's birthday. Combined with a very fine programme of music. I think it is successful. The second programme, from Headquarters, has been carefully prepared by Diewerge. I am unable to prevent a big speech by Lutze. Viktor is a good fellow, but no sparkling intellect.

Kotzias is trying to put together a government. He has made an emotional appeal, saluting the fighting Greek and British troops. This is his first mistake. If he continues in his vein, he will soon find himself in a very sticky situation.

Bulgaria is moving into the territories that she has been allocated. This is very pleasing. The Bulgars are a decent and courageous people. One does not begrudge them their success, unlike the Hungarians.

The USA is now heaping blame on Churchill because of Greece. It is claimed that he forced through his adventurist policy against the opposition of the generals. Now England must pay the price. The opposition to Churchill within the plutocratic camp is on the ascendant, but unfortunately it is a long time since it was a concrete formative influence. Meanwhile, he fantasises on, and has already raised the number of our fatal casualties in Greece to 60,000. Our casualty figures are, in fact, astonishingly small, thank God. But Churchill has to have something to toss to the angry mob. The techniques that he is using are long-established in English history.

British troops have invaded Iraq. Probably to overthrow the anti-British government that recently took power there. Churchill's interpretation of democracy. He makes our job easy for us.

I speak with the children on the telephone in the evening. I hear those sweet little voices which are the things I love most in the world. What a treasure, what a possession! May God preserve them for me!

21 April 1941 (Monday)

Yesterday: Führer's birthday. The city is a sea of banners. Speeches by Hess and Göring on the radio and a broadcast from the Führer's Headquarters. Very impressive.

May God preserve our Führer for a long time yet. Then we can be certain of victory.

No incursions. We attack London again, this time with almost 800 aircraft. A massive raid. Mostly with good visibility. Very depressing reports from there. Morale in England is said to be slipping. Popular saying: we shall lose the war, even if we win it. Even Churchill is said to be showing strongly defeatist tendencies. But nothing can yet be guaranteed. I cannot yet entirely believe it. I think we shall have to deal them a few more hard knocks.

Serbia is being liquidated. More than 250,000 prisoners so far, and huge quantities of equipment. The prisoners will be good labour for our agriculture. The breakthrough in Greece is now complete. The enemy is pouring back in disorder. We are snapping at his heels. Our Stukas are doing magnificent work, particularly so far as the British columns are concerned. Greece's situation is hopeless. Kotzias has resigned his position. Probably got cold feet. It is better this way. He should keep himself ready for the final collapse. We shall put him to good use then. I forbid the press to attack him.

Bitter fighting in North Africa. The English are putting up a stubborn defence in Tobruk and are making repeated thrusts towards Sollum. They do not intend to give up the Suez Canal under any circumstances. This would also be too grave a loss of prestige for Churchill. We shall therefore continue to have our work cut out there.

USA's attitude increasingly cautious. Harsh public criticism of Roosevelt.

Vichy is showing impudence towards our press representatives. We have now been put below Sweden in the order of precedence. But now I play my trump. I have an ultimatum given to the Information Minister. If he does not accept it, then he will regret it . . .

. . . To the Kaiserdamm, where the heavy English bomb fell during the last air raid. The effect was devastating; roofs stripped and windows shattered far and wide. But no really serious damage. I use the opportunity to inspect the short-wave station as well. It is housed in miserable barracks that are totally unworthy. We must build anew there straight after the war. The present quarters are downright dangerous.

Use the afternoon to deal with work that has piled up. How wonderful it would be if one could go back to having Sunday free. The way things are, one is never free of the treadmill.

[. . .] debates with Marina Schljapin. She is a very clever woman.

First Night of the guest season by the Teatro Reale from Rome at the German Opera House. *A Masked Ball* by Gigli, [. . .], [. . .] under Serafini. A feast of the human voice. The public goes wild. At an opera for the first time in some months. What a wonderful and rare pleasure!

Newsreel magnificent. A dramatic display. Though needs to be a little tighter. This is the true face of war.

Magda comes back from Dessau and tells me a lot of good things about Harald.

Weird and wonderful mood in London. Illusions and caterwauling. Outspoken attacks on Eden and even veiled ones against Churchill. Otherwise, big words mixed with pessimism. The last air raid had a demoralising effect. The opposition to Roosevelt in the USA is growing. They blame him for the collapse of the South-East. Not unjustly. The thermometer is at zero in the plutocratic camp.

In Rumania they are screaming for the return of Transylvania. Even Antonescu has added his voice. Borders are being re-drawn again in the Balkans. The big Balkan Conference is being prepared in Vienna at the moment. It is there that the booty is to be distributed. A difficult task for the Führer. The Balkans are, and will remain, a powder-keg.

This was quite a Sunday. By late in the evening I am dog-tired.

22 April 1941 (Tuesday)

Yesterday: The English raid Western Germany. Slight damage. No air activity on our part over England.

Breakthrough successful in Greece. We are already driving beyond the Thermopylae. The Anglo-Greek enemy forces in disordered retreat in some areas. The SS is forced to come to the aid of the Italians, who have some trouble breaking through in their sector.

In North Africa, hard fighting around Tobruk, which the English intend to hold by force of arms. Also serious forays against Sollum. Churchill is desperately trying to prevent an advance into Egypt. English come ashore at Bardia. Captured. Details not yet known.

The Greek King has appealed to his people to fight on. A lacky of the English. I have him given a savaging in the foreign-language service. Already big demonstrations against the war in Athens. We are putting out a very subtle form of anti-English propaganda. In London itself, the atmosphere is one of deepest depression. We exploit it to the full. Slogan: The

USA will fight to the last Englishman. Even American newspapers are accusing Roosevelt of having the prolongation of the war on his conscience, since he encouraged Churchill and goaded Yugoslavia on with false promises. His real object is to weaken the Empire by a long war, so that he can take over its areas of influence. This is a good hinge for propaganda in England.

Very gentle peace-feelers via Tokyo, spread by Wiegand and INS.* Probably originating from the anti-Churchill clique in London. The same reports from New York. They want to put an end to the senseless slaughter. We are well aware of the fact. But we make no reaction. London also is silent.

Article in *Pravda*: They have nothing against Germany, Moscow wants peace, etc. Stalin has caught a whiff of what is cooking, then, and is waving the olive-branch. This is a measure of our strength now. The Russian card is no longer trumps.

I have an American radio reporter silenced. He had been sending back scurrilous reports under the protection of our own censorship. That is all we need. The censors will get their due from me.

Now we have lost a football match against Switzerland. No incidents, unfortunately. I forbid such risky matches in future . . .

. . . I issue orders that Jews in Berlin must wear a distinctive badge. Otherwise they are constantly mixing with our people, pretending to be harmless, and making trouble.

New statute for the Wireless Service and the Radio signed. This means that the chain of authority is clearly defined.

Long talk with Prince Borghese, the Governor of Rome. A very impressive-looking, clever man. He has great admiration for our propaganda, the opposite for Italian efforts. Otherwise we discuss the war situation. The Italian people's attitude has become firmer. Influenced by recent successes. It was high time.

King Boris was with the Führer. He deserves to get something.

I dictate a tough article attacking British propaganda. In the process I make it the object of ridicule. This is not difficult. At the moment it is burbling about mountains of German corpses in Greece. This is the excuse for retreat. A gang, a lying gang!

In the evening, put the finishing touches to the newsreel. It now flows beautifully. A documentary and propagandistic work of art.

23 April 1941 (Wednesday)

Yesterday: No incursions into the Reich. We attack Plymouth with [. . .] aircraft, in good visibility and with great success. The enemy front in Greece is collapsing completely. Our *Leibstandarte* is advancing near Jannina and

* International News Service, a Hearst agency.

cutting off the retreat of the Greek forces in Albania. The last road through is now in our hands. The Italians are very angry about our latest advance. General Jodl has had to fly to Rome to calm them down. Impossible. The Italians should be grateful that we are helping them at all. Otherwise the enemy forces in Greece are in full retreat. The English are embarking in large numbers. The débâcle is said to be even worse than Dunkirk, according to US sources. A report from Ankara talks of a catastrophe. But King George and his Prime Minister are still boasting of glorious resistance. It all makes very little sense.

The situation in Africa is unchanged. The English are still attempting to break out of Tobruk. But unsuccessfully. Likewise with their attacks on Sollum. They have quite a lot of artillery power in Tobruk. And the guns of their ships at sea are also involved. But in vain. Our Stukas [. . .] [. . .] The Italians in East Africa are showing a few signs of life.

I have the victory reports from the Balkans played down a little, so as not to pre-empt the High Command's expected announcement. Big campaign at home and abroad to counter the English reports of our 'huge losses', which in reality are surprisingly slight. Now Churchill is even being attacked in the London press. A few scratches are starting to show. Morale in England has sunk to zero. Duff Cooper is worsening it by making the gravest psychological errors. He speaks like a conquering hero. This will not last long.

Report from Emden on the recent air raid there. Our people have also made some serious mistakes, and morale is not of the best. I have appropriate measures taken and instruct the other Gaus as well. Under such circumstances, the Party must go into action.

I have 500 tickets for the Italian guest season distributed to the general public. Such a thing must not be allowed to become a privilege of the plutocracy.

Routine work with Gutterer. Hilgenfeldt reports on the Winter Aid Fund and its work in Belgrade. Things must look awful there. We are giving first priority to aiding our ethnic Germans. The Red Cross Appeal is going well . . .

. . . Pessimism in London is growing from day to day. Letters from there intercepted en route to Brazil show the fearsome destructive power of our air raids and the psychological consequences. Cries of help to the USA, completely bereft of dignity. The Balkans have been given up for lost, but now there are fears for Egypt, worries about a future loss of Gibraltar. In short, widespread public despair. After all Mr Churchill's loud trumpetings, there is silence. The old man has withdrawn into silence under the heavy pressure of events. At the moment, the best thing he could do.

The Swiss Embassy intends to leave London 'because of the air raids, which have become intolerable'. Rebellion in Australia against the ruthless squandering of Australian troops in Greece. Parliament recalled. New difficulties for Churchill.

329

The Greek Army of Epirus, which was finally cut off by our thrust at Jannina, wants to surrender. The Führer has given instructions for the conditions of surrender to be honourable, as is fitting for brave soldiers. Negotiations are already under way. The collapse of Greece will not be long in coming now. Athens is the next target.

Tension between Portugal and Spain. Developments can be expected there. We must now go all out, never allowing the enemy a respite, until he crumbles.

Vichy now intends to return to a policy of Collaboration. It was high time. Meanwhile, however, the intrigues against our press representatives there continue. They are politely and obligingly received, promised everything, and then the promises are not kept. I shall now have the heavy artillery wheeled up.

The Führer is very pleased with the rough cut of our latest newsreel. But we are to alter a few details at the editing stage.

Churchill speaks – or, rather, dodges questions – in the House of Commons. He refuses to give details, hides behind military secrecy, brags about the bombardment of Tripoli, and says he knows nothing about popular discontent. He is a shameless, bare-faced liar, but one with some style. None of the questioners who press him can get him to speak. And what could he say? English public opinion is expecting collapse. The sole comfort: our supposedly appalling losses. But I shall knock that argument, too, out of their Lordships' hands.

And the surrender will come soon. And with it the end of the Balkan adventure.

24 April 1941 (Thursday)

Yesterday: No incursions into the Reich. We carry out massive raids on Plymouth and Portsmouth. London admits serious losses.

Armies of Epirus and Macedonia have now surrendered. Their situation had been made hopeless by our thrust to Jannina. Minor squabbles with the Italians, who want precedence over us in the reports – since they are, at last, about victories. The fall of Athens cannot be far off. The Greeks and the English are in headlong retreat. King George has cleared off to Crete. He says that he intends to carry on the heroic struggle from there. We shall soon settle his hash. Rome wants the High Command's Bulletin to announce that the war in Greece is now at an end, a step that we manage to prevent.

The Luftwaffe sinks 40,000 tons of enemy shipping, mainly in Greek waters. More fighting around Tobruk and Sollum in North Africa. It seems that the English intend to hold Tobruk, come what may.

Our losses are unbelievably slight. The operations as a whole are a model of modern precision-warfare. Another masterpiece by the Führer. Our motorised units broke straight through the enemy armies and prevented any co-ordinated strategy right from the outset.

Opposition to English policy growing in Australia. Particularly because of the heavy losses in Greece. We are now really twisting the knife regarding the casualty figures.

Werra has escaped from the USA. We need his knowledge and experience. Feigned outrage in official circles there. The opposition to Roosevelt is growing. Senator Wheeler is very busy. I receive the former US Ambassador in Brussels, Cudahy. He is one of Roosevelt's main opponents, firmly convinced of our victory. He sees the future of his country in very black terms, even perhaps Bolshevism. He would like the Führer to grant him an audience, and perhaps to make a declaration of what would happen after the war was over. This will be very difficult, but I shall try to see what the Führer's reaction is.

The Japanese report on the meeting between Matsuoka and Stalin. This seems to have been a real case of Asiatic brotherhood. Tokyo, anyway, is very pleased. But we do not allow this to deflect us from our measures against the East.

Vichy now intends to return to Collaboration. And in the press affair they have become meek and mild. This was to be expected.

The feeling against Italy among the German public has increased. I shall have to do something about it again. But the Italians have themselves to blame to a large extent, since they will make such foolish statements.

The German press's attacks on the casualty figures issued by London lack sufficient precision. I have everything repeated once more, since it is of great psychological importance.

Receive the new Rumanian Ambassador, B[. . .]. A real oily Levantine. This is what Antonescu exchanged for the Legion. It is enough to make one cry, even though it is no affair of ours. B[. . .] is terrified of Russia. Antonescu intends to deal with the Legion after the war. If things do not turn out the other way round. He says that he wants no parties, only the fatherland. We know the phrase only too well. All enemies of the fatherland take refuge behind it.

Kasche named as Ambassador in Zagreb. We can work well with him.

News of Churchill. He is said to be in a very depressed state, spending the entire day smoking and drinking. This is the kind of enemy we need.

I initiate a campaign against the widespread saying that 'the English are more stubborn than we are'. This must be eradicated.

New figures for box-office receipts. Another 30 millions in profits. We are awash with money. Every film is a box-office hit.

A few shortages in Berlin, particularly tobacco and beer. I arrange for them to be alleviated. The public must be kept happy at the moment.

Otherwise, morale is good. Everyone is waiting for the general surrender of the Greeks. Then a short breathing-space. And then the big blow will come.

The English have essayed a few daytime flights into Westphalia, using the

331

cloud cover. A demonstration. Completely ineffective.

I write a leader-article, *The Stubborn English*. In it I deal comprehensively with the honest burghers' admiration for England and Churchill.

It is high time something was done in that quarter.

The newsreel is ready. A fine documentary and a work of art. Shots of Stalin and Matsuoka bear witness to extremely amicable atmosphere.

Simović has installed a new Yugoslav government in Palestine. Recognised by London. Wax figures!

25 April 1941 (Friday)

Yesterday: No incursions into the Reich. Heavy raid on Plymouth. According to UP, panic broke out in the city. The effect is devastating. Secret reports from London tell of a collapse of morale, principally caused by our air raids. We have now reached the other side of Thermopylae in Greece. Athens is at our feet. The English are in full flight. Catastrophic effect on world opinion. Strongest scepticism in the USA. Lindbergh and Wheeler are really busy. The mood there is performing something of a volte-face. Our victories have made a big impression. The Balkan adventure has given us a big psychological boost. The Greeks are sounding off from the safety of Crete. About honour and suchlike. Enough to make one vomit! London, on the other hand, is still very subdued.

Situation unchanged in North Africa. We have been attacking Tobruk very heavily with Stukas.

Again no sinkings. The call is resounding round the entire country: Where are our U-boats? Raeder's prestige has suffered somewhat.

Report from Italy: they are trying to filch our successes and turn our victories into Italian ones. This was to be expected. But the world has nothing but contempt for Italy. Even Mussolini cannot change that. He has issued a pompous declaration to his Army of Albania. At Headquarters! The sound of it!

The Vatican continues to attack us. Through the radio. I have now sent Alfieri to the Nuntius with some material. We shall see what he manages to achieve.

Complete change of mood in France. Our victories carry a lot of conviction. Individuals and nations have to be reminded continually of the bloody lessons of the past.

We have now carried out a great variety of measures in Kiel. Previously no one had done anything for the city. I drummed them into action. It was necessary, too.

Deal with a mass of trivia. Speak to Hannes Cremer, the new head of the Cultural Department of the Reich Propaganda Leadership. He will have to pull himself together. I forbid him to dabble in mystical and hysterical areas. Our promotion of culture through the Party must remain founded in realities. No adolescent romanticism! Practical cultural work!

With Speer. Inspect his new models for the rebuilding of Berlin. They are really very ambitious. Incomparably monumental. The Führer will be raising a memorial to himself in stone. I press particularly hard, at the same time, for mass housing in Berlin. This Speer will include. The model for the great dome is indescribable.

At home, complete essay against 'the stubborn English'. It will cause a furore. But it has to be said. We Germans are always far too fair-minded towards our enemies.

Churchill is stirring up trouble, claiming that we intend to occupy Portugal. Our press counter-attacks strongly. Otherwise today brings no sensational news. Except that morale in London has reached an all-time low. The wildest rumours are flying around, particularly concerning Spain. The London press is trying to get Churchill off the hook, but even the anti-German press in Switzerland is protesting against such activities. The man himself has spoken in the House of Commons. His speech is totally without content. One big evasion. He begs humbly for more time. So things have reached that stage! Australia is the strongest of his critics.

The Duke of Aosta is still putting up a fight in Abyssinia. A brave fellow.

Reception at home in the evening for the Roman Opera. A lot of guests. Close to 150. The Italians sing, mainly Gigli. Tirelessly and wonderfully. A rare, wonderful pleasure. I am very happy.

Horthy has been to visit the Führer: Hungary is unfortunately to receive more territory yet again, but the Führer also made clear his opinion about the persecution of Germans there. The Hungarians are behaving like swine. Constantly at the trough. And they allow no one any peace.

In the seas around Greece, 40,000 tons of transport shipping has been sunk by the Luftwaffe, and another 50,000 damaged. Fighting is continuing on the routes out of Thermopylae.

The Pope is praying for peace. Not that it will be of much help. This contest must be fought to the finish if it is not to be repeated in ten years' time.

26 April 1941 (Saturday)

Yesterday: Kiel attacked with middling success. I immediately order the aid effort to be stepped up. We carry out a raid in strength against Portsmouth. Good success rate in fine visibility.

Still very heavy fighting in Greece. No progress worthy of mention. The terrain is too inhospitable. Lieutenant-Colonel B [. . .] of the Panzer Group Kleist reports on the breakthrough to Belgrade. Very difficult terrain. A miracle that we managed to cross it at all. Serbs defended very stubbornly. Our Panzers wrought miracles. Completely new tactic: they pressed on regardless of what was happening on their flanks. And so also bitter clashes with the rearguards. Belgrade devastation worse than Warsaw. A pile of ruins, filled with stinking corpses. The King's palace completely destroyed, palace belonging to Prince-Regent Paul likewise. He had been arrested during the night before the coup. General Mirković handled the negotiations for the surrender. His legitimation, written in pencil on a scrap of paper, read: 'You have full powers. Simović.' This was the end of the Yugoslavian multi-nation state. A tragicomedy written in blood. The people in the countryside took absolutely no interest in it. It was the concern only of the generals and the politicians. King Peter was still a child, and all they found in his palace were toys. Finis! Nations must pay for their statesmen's mistakes.

The Hungarians are behaving like animals. Our ethnic Germans would rather have stayed with the Serbs than become part of Hungary. This is a complete scandal. The Führer hauled Horthy over the coals on this issue. Horthy promised to do something about this disgraceful situation. He intends to appeal to the Hungarian public in the form of an official announcement. But then the ordinary folk have nothing against our people; it is only the Magyar upper class.

Heavy sinkings of troop transports. To and fro in North Africa. Rommel is settling down and digging himself firmly into the sand. The English are defending stubbornly. They know what is at stake.

The collapse of morale in England continues. I switch the emphasis of our propaganda for England to one of absolute objectivity. We are relying now on argument and irony. Likewise with regard to the USA, where a strong element of disenchantment is now apparent. Roosevelt would like to send convoys, but at the moment he dare not. His Minister for the Navy, Knox, is agitating quite publicly and impudently in favour of such a move. We give him the answer he deserves. So far as the USA itself is concerned, however, our broadcasts are sticking exclusively to the facts.

Sefton Delmer has appeared on the radio, bragging about the terrible damage wrought on Berlin. I have him answered by an American radio reporter.

Hippler reports from Munich. The people down there now seem to be more satisfied with our film leadership in Berlin. *Ohm Krüger* has been a huge success. The Bavaria studios now intend to pull themselves together. Their record is the worst of any of our companies. Deal with the question of centralisation of cinema-theatre management. This must not be effected through Ufa but through a state-owned, neutral firm.

I help out Gutterer with a substantial sum of money. His financial situation is very bad.

Parbel, the new head of the Reich Propaganda Office in Hannover, comes to introduce himself. A deserving veteran of Narvik. Makes a fantastic impression. I give him precise guidelines for his work. . . .

. . . At midday, Ambassador Cudahy is our guest. We exchange ideas through into the late afternoon, and I succeed in clarifying the main problems for him. The USA fears our domination of the world. Then she should not force us into new conquests. She fears our autarky. Then she should open the doors of world trade to us. Cudahy would like very much to speak with the Führer, and then he intends to speak to the American public. He could be very helpful to us, because he has enormous influence over there. He tells me that in London last August they simply refused to believe him. These plutocrats are blinkered. And they will pay a high price for their blindness.

Afterwards, Cudahy is very much on our side. The struggle lasted for some hours, but it was worth it. He put forward all the interventionist arguments, and I believe that I refuted them all. He thinks that I should speak in the USA one day. At the moment I would probably be murdered. But who knows, later? Cudahy is Irish. Our soldiers in Belgium gradually brought him over to our side.

I rewrite the article attacking the 'honest burghers'. So as to avoid providing ammunition for the English, I direct my attack against the US press rather than German citizens.

What a glorious spring day outside! How beautiful the world can be! And we have no chance to enjoy it. Human beings are so stupid. Life is so short, and they then go and make it so hard for themselves.

Our advance into Greece is continuing through the pass at Thermopylae.

Another 44,000 tons sunk. So far 1,900,000 tons brought in as prizes. The High Command Bulletin reports: Kretschmer taken prisoner and Schepke dead. This will move the public greatly.

In London they are still fantasising about the destruction of Berlin. I have us protest in the harshest, most vigorous terms. The English need a shot in the arm in order to keep up morale. Knox's speech is revealed as an attempt by Roosevelt to gauge the public mood. Lindbergh has had more success than we thought.

Everything is in limbo once more. Only our victories will bring things back in motion.

Another unimportant British air raid on Berlin during the night. Almost no damage. An hour's air-raid warning. Otherwise nothing of note.

27 April 1941 (Sunday)

Yesterday: Kiel came off worse than Berlin. This hard-pressed city has a lot to bear. Massive German raid on Sunderland in good visibility. Widespread devastation. The Luftwaffe sinks more transport ships in the Aegean. Our Navy has nothing of interest to report. One of our troop transports sunk off the Norwegian coast. 100 dead. Sabotage suspected.

Massive air attacks on Fort Capuzzo in North Africa. The English are digging themselves in there. Tobruk is also being defended with great vigour. Significant sorties. They are probing the surrounding terrain. But Rommel asserts his control. Bringing up supplies very difficult. Some being transported along the coast by motor-boat. Our latest convoy from Sicily has been recalled yet again. Too much English naval activity. Sollum is still in our hands. No prospect of a further advance into Egypt in the foreseeable future.

In Greece: Thermopylae was not taken by direct assault, but outflanked. Heroic effort by our mountain troops. Advance continuing. Thebes in our hands. No resistance worth mentioning to be expected there. Road to Athens open.

Consolidation everywhere in Yugoslavia. But enormous new tasks for us.

Halifax continues, as ever, to talk complete rubbish. Roosevelt is still pushing for intervention. But he dare not go further for fear of public opinion. Hearst has launched a swingeing attack on Churchill as a warmonger. Things are still seesawing in the USA. But we are not inactive in this respect.

The Jews are leaving Palestine. There is something downright tragi-comic about this.

The Swiss press is very insolent. The theologian, Barth, has made a speech attacking us in Switzerland, which is too much even for *La Suisse*. I have it attacked in the strongest terms by Megerle of the *BBZ*,* including a totally unveiled threat. Erhardt has talked with the Swiss Ambassador here. Fairly strongly defeatist. I have learnt this from a secret report that was leaked to us. The Führer must read it. Erhardt is a conceited type, totally without character. A ridiculous [. . .]

My article on the 'stubbornness' of the English is highly regarded by all who know the situation. I hand it over to *Das Reich* for publication . . .

. . . The USA stands poised between peace and war. The road to either is equally long. Which will she take? Roosevelt wants war, the people want peace. We are doing everything possible to strengthen the position of the people. Who knows whether we shall succeed?

Work through papers at home. Again, a lot has piled up.

In England they are now declaring that England won a moral victory in the South-East. The Tommies can have such moral victories. The main thing is that we win the military victory. For the rest, London has started up the old, illusionary story. Churchill is regaining support. He intends to speak on the radio today.

Strong indications of panic in Athens. We are advancing remorselessly. German paratroops have taken Corinth, Euboea is in our possession. From there we shall move back on to the mainland. Lemnos is also ours.

I devote some time to correcting our daily radio commentaries. Our people theorise too much and provide too little exact information. The

* *Berliner Börsen-Zeitung* (Berlin Stock Exchange Newspaper). The leading Berlin financial daily.

public wants details and loves a clear-cut, popularly-phrased argument. Slogans and generalisations achieve little.

Von Arent visits in the evening. He has now finished his convalescence and intends to take up his artistic work again. As a personality he is very difficult and has many enemies.

When one talks with such people, suddenly one notices that life outside is continuing almost completely undisturbed. The rest of the time one sits wound up in work, the weeks, months, and years fly by, and one slowly grows old.

28 April 1941 (Monday)

Yesterday: Raids on Kiel and Bremen. No great damage. We attack Liverpool. Visibility unfortunately poor, and therefore with questionable success. More heavy sinkings. Our troops are at the gates of Athens. We wait for a while for the leading Italian motorised unit to catch up, but it takes too long. We enter Athens shortly before 9.30 a.m. Our flag is flying above the Acropolis. Proud feeling of triumph. The English are fleeing. Corinth taken by paratroopers. Isthmus secured. *Leibstandarte* thrusts towards Patras. Advance into the Peleponnes. Very slight casualties. Scarcely any resistance worthy of the name.

Bitter fighting in North Africa. Particularly around Fort Capuzzo. English breakout from Tobruk, attack on Sollum. Both unsuccessful. Rommel defends our positions heroically. Our Luftwaffe attacks English transport ships in all the seas around Greece and North Africa, with the greatest success.

The battle over intervention or non-intervention continues to rage in the USA. Result by no means clear at this stage. We are active to the best of our ability, but we can scarcely make ourselves heard against the deafening Jew-chorus. In London they are placing all their last hopes in the USA. If something does not happen soon, then London is faced with annihilation. We are pursuing a purely news-based propaganda line with regard to London and the USA. This will get us farthest at the moment.

The Hungarians came down the Danube to Belgrade, but were taken prisoner. It was believed that they were Serbian deserters. The excruciatingly embarrassing misunderstanding was not cleared up until they arrived at the prisoner-of-war camp.

Dr Dietrich is showing off again. Now he is protesting against my new chain of command in the wireless service and radio. But I give him the complete brush-off. All I need is for him to mess up the radio as well. He is a stupid amateur, who has not the slightest idea about how to influence the masses.

Discuss her new film with Frau Leander. She tells me about Sweden. Opinion has swung in our favour there. This is the result of our great victories, which are being greeted with the most enormous admiration all over the world.

This rainy Sunday brings one special announcement after another. A most happy day. We have waited long enough for it.

I read a series of essays by Dr Hippler on dramatic technique in the cinema. Very wittily and intelligently written. He has a good brain, but he is a little overbearing.

Our military successes are impressing the world in the profoundest fashion. Another 30,000 tons of British troop transports sunk, 80,000 seriously damaged. The English must be sweating blood. They have not got away unscathed this time.

Heated arguments about Turkey and Portugal. This question will have to be settled soon. London announces further withdrawals by the English in Greece. They have no choice now. Our capture of Athens is the big sensation in all the world's press.

First reports of the collection for the Red Cross. Almost 100 per cent increase over last year. We can be very proud of our people.

Uncut version of the newsreel in the evening. Works magnificently again. There were never war reports like these. Our Propaganda Companies' achievements are a model of their kind. They are the trail-blazers of a completely modern type of war reportage. Plus a number of test shots. A lot of work on these.

Italian guest season ends with *Falstaff*. Magda went to see it. She is absolutely enchanted. The performances have proved very popular. At least in this field the Italians have achieved something. Alfieri has lost a lot of his reputation. He moves in somewhat suspect circles, prefers slightly anti-government characters as friends, avoids Nazis and cuts the fascists in his staff dead. A typical misfit! Besides which he is unreliable in his work, absent-minded, fickle, and without capacity for hard work. Things will surely not go well for him. A pity, because he had such excellent opportunities.

Late in the evening we hear more news of British transport ships sunk, among them a cruiser. Bad days for London. Let us have more of them! We shall soon bring John Bull to his knees.

Churchill speaks on the radio. Probably because he is frightened of parliament. A mixture of pretended love of truth, bare-faced distortions, and outright lies. A few valuable admissions. I issue precise instructions on how the speech is to be handled on the Radio, and in the press and foreign language service. We shall not let the old crook get away with anything. He will be trapped in his own web of lies.

Yesterday: Weak English daylight raid on Sunday against [. . .] Exploiting cloud cover. Little success. Nothing of importance during the night. We carry out a middling raid on Portsmouth, with great success. 40,000 tons sunk in Greek waters. Greece, particularly the Peleponnes, is being cleared of enemy forces according to plan. Hardly any resistance. The Italians occupy Corfu.

Furious attempts by the English to break out of Tobruk. We attack Mersa Matruh with Stukas. Otherwise, Rommel is pressing on once more. We have our hands full trying to hold him back. For this reason we release no news of him, so as to avoid arousing false hopes. But our position in North Africa can now be regarded as fairly secure.

Churchill's speech has met with an enthusiastic reception in the USA. This was to be expected. The USA is preparing to make the leap into war. If Roosevelt were not so chary of public opinion, he would have declared war on us long ago. And so he is trying to provoke us in indirect ways. The Isolationists are putting up a desperate fight against the war policy. But the way things are, it is open to doubt whether they will be successful. Our propaganda aimed at England and the USA is objective. Our reliable news service is respected even in the USA.

The Italians are behaving in a brazen, arrogant and downright objectionable fashion. Mussolini has published a telegram to General Cavallero in which he claims the victory in Greece as his own. The Italian forces have refused to recognise surrender negotiations until the Greek Army has officially [. . .] Our people feel something close to hatred for the Italians. Where will it all end? We shall do all that we can to keep morale here buoyant. Now the Italians are claiming the whole of Greece for themselves. I fear a very bad reaction so far as public opinion in Germany is concerned.

[. . .] reports from Zagreb. Maurer has asserted himself well. He is attached to the embassy. Virulent hatred for the Italians in Zagreb. Where are the Italians actually loved?

Brouvers reports from Belgium. Mood is much better. Food situation catastrophic. English propaganda very active. King is keeping out of public life. Degrelle is on his last legs. Chaos among the parties in the Flemish camp.

Lippert reports on the Serbian campaign. He was there. Is now to be sent to Serbia as leader of our Propaganda Squad. I give him precise instructions.

Countless administrative problems with Gutterer. I am having to give the poor fellow some help so that he can find a decent apartment and bring some order into his private life. Otherwise he will die on me under the weight of his troubles. I had been intending to appoint Hinkel as State Secretary. But Gutterer opposes this. Perhaps rightly. Hinkel is so ambitious that he would probably disrupt the smooth running of the ministry.

Discuss casting problems with Symo and Dittmar.

The Führer is back from the combat zone. He has me fetched immediately; dazzlingly good mood due to the victory won. The business in Greece will only last a few more days. The expected two months have become a mere three weeks. Our soldiers have put us to shame yet again.

The Führer is furious with the Italians. They have started playing games, now of all times. Jodl tells me about the joint surrender negotiations. Truly grotesque. I inform the Führer in the strongest terms of the reaction which can be expected from our people if we hand Greece over to the Italians. But he says that it is the only way. We intend to instal a new Greek government. Headed by the general who conducted the surrender negotiations. He is very anti-English and surrendered earlier than he had to, out of anger against Churchill.

The Führer intends to make a major speech. Probably to the Reichstag. Outline the entire situation. I also consider that this would be very useful, particularly with regard to America.

Russia is keeping her head down. But only because she feels encircled.

At the moment we have no reason to fear her. We watch a Soviet film about the Finnish campaign together. Sheer amateurism. We soon cut the showing short. Watch the latest and the previous week's newsreel with the Führer. He is very satisfied with both of them.

Afterwards, long discussions about the Vatican and Christianity. The Führer is a fierce opponent of all that humbug, but he forbids me to leave the church. For tactical reasons. And so for a decade now I have paid my church taxes to support such rubbish. That is what hurts most.

The Führer has a lot of work to do. He is hatching a thousand new plans. Mr Churchill will be amazed. Naumann fought very bravely, so Himmler tells me.

At home I launch myself at a mountain of paperwork and memoranda. It never lets up.

Great applause for Churchill's speech in London. But somewhat forced. Their great fear is of a knock-out blow during the next weeks and months. We shall do our best to justify these fears. Our press and radio campaign against Churchill is brilliant at the moment. We are stripping away his virtuous mask. He cannot fool us any more.

Lindbergh has resigned from the US Airforce. He is a courageous fighter for his rights, and today is Roosevelt's strongest opponent, since Willkie's shameful surrender.

In the evening, put the finishing touches to newsreel with music. It will be a very good one.

The days and weeks rush by in feverish tension. Which round are we fighting at the moment? And when will the devastating knock-out punch come?

Yesterday: No incursions. We attack Plymouth with very strong forces and great success. In Greece we advance beyond Tripolis and deep into the Peleponnes. 18,600 tons destroyed by the Luftwaffe in Greek waters. Bitter and bloody see-saw in North Africa. Berndt writes me a very informative letter from there. He is sitting right in the thick of it.

Once again, our U-boats report no successes. They are unable to do anything without Luftwaffe help. The English are now using a different route to cross the Atlantic. We shall first have to find it. For the moment we are unable to do anything about the wild rumours that are speading among the people regarding the U-boat fleet.

Lindbergh has written a really spirited letter to Roosevelt. He is the president's toughest opponent. He has asked us not to give him too much prominence, since this could harm him. We have proceeded accordingly.

Mood in London still one of despair. The shipping losses are the worst thing. They are the English public's nightmare. Morale at home here is still excellent, as the SD reports show . . .

. . . With the Führer. Discussion of the situation. He is sad to have had to attack Greece in the first place. The Greeks have done nothing to deserve it. He intends to treat them as humanely as possible. The Italians are doing the opposite. By their behaviour they are earning nothing but hatred, and increasing our popularity. Mussolini, for that matter, is anything but loyal to us. But we must remain silent at the moment. Breker, who is also present, is very sad. His wife is Greek. Our entry into Athens was welcomed by a section of the Greek population. If the Italians replace us, then there will be serious disaffection. The Italians are also behaving in an extremely arrogant fashion towards us. Alfieri is stupid and without judgement. A typical nincompoop. Ciano arrogant, bumptious, and because of our victories on the ascendant once more.

The Führer tells us about his visit to Styria and Carinthia. He has great plans for the rebuilding of Graz. The Styrians are proud, upright, somewhat pig-headed, and completely anti-pacifist. The same goes for the Carinthians. We cannot take their weapons away from these people, particularly in the Tyrol, as Frick wanted to do. A centralist policy would be the worst thing possible there. These proud Gaus must be left to run their own affairs. Frick does not understand this. He is a centralist bureaucrat. Styria was once the sword-point of the Reich. One cannot simply ignore the fact just like that.

I outline my film plans for Linz to the Führer, and he approves them immediately.

Heated arguments about Churchill and England's present situation. This could be worse than we know. The English cries for help directed at the USA are becoming frantic. And everyone despises the cynicism with which the British have ignored the fate of the nations that they led astray. It would be hard to beat.

We watch our entry into Athens on the newsreel. The Führer finds it hard to enjoy it, so moved is he by Greece's fate. All the fault of our Herr Allies.

Professor Breker shows us designs for sculptures that will form part of the Triumphal Arch. Indescribably beautiful, and yet monumental. He has given the Führer a sculpture of a woman, which I do not like so much as does the Führer. Breker's men are better than his women.

Deal with a number of unresolved problems concerning the Foreign Ministry during a talk with Hewel. If only all Ribbentrop's people were as reasonable as he is.

The Führer will probably address the Reichstag on 1 May. He is already at work on his speech. A wide-ranging gaze over the horizon. It is a good thing, now that the din of battle has subsided, that a word of reason can be spoken.

Vichy launches a massive attack on Churchill for the Dunkirk fiasco, and in the process provides us with material which we shall be able to make excellent use of in our campaign against England. According to what they say, the catastrophe of Dunkirk was even more devastating than we had thought. The London press is putting growing pressure on Churchill to face the House of Commons. This would be very embarrassing for him, We would have no objections. He has already stated in the House that he intends to allow a debate during the next few days.

The U-boat war is England's worry, but also ours. We await greater success daily. Whether it will come depends on a host of factors, mainly the luck of individual vessels. This is England's most vulnerable point.

London's ambassador to Belgrade, Campbell, has been captured by an Italian torpedo-boat. And so we have the man who goaded the generals into war under lock and key.

What a superb spring day. It is still light at nine in the evening.

Then, however, the oppressive night and the blackout come to the metropolis.

How wonderful it will be when this is all over.

1 May 1941 (Thursday)

Yesterday: Raids on South-West Germany. Heidelberg and Mannheim. Damage insignificant. Massive raid on Plymouth. Even London speaks of appalling destruction. The city has to be evacuated. Very heavy long-distance shelling of Dover with considerable success. Camouflage! Malta attacked again with some success. Mopping-up operations continue in Greece. Southern tip of the Peleponnes reached. 5000 English troops taken prisoner. Most seem to have escaped, despite everything. Meanwhile, the new government has been established. We are reserving official comment for the moment. 35,000 tons sunk by U-boats. Good news in that quarter, at last. Bitter fighting in North Africa. Berndt has written a very dramatic letter from there. But he is keeping his chin up, despite the dangers and the hardships.

Tass has issued a statement regarding the German troops who have landed in Finland. We ignore it. They have seen through our plan and all attempts at deception have, as I feared, proved useless. A big sensation in the world press. But it is not so bad. Things will soon have reached the point of no return. World opinion is becoming increasingly uneasy. There is much conjecture even among our own people. In London they have not the slightest idea of what is to come. The Führer has fixed his Reichstag speech for Sunday. I argue for six in the afternoon, which he agrees to. In this way we shall be best placed to reach American opinion.

Backe gives me a report on the food situation. Meat is going to have to be cut by 100 grams per week from 2 June. The Wehrmacht is too well off and is using up too much of the available ration. Per head, three times that allowed to the civilian population. We can hope to get by so far as bread is concerned, as long as there are no problems with the harvest. Fat is still in reasonable supply. If we have go through a third year at war, then we shall consume the last reserves of bread. But nevertheless we are better off than England in many respects. But our situation is by no means rosy. I now face the question of how I am to put this over to the public. I shall wait for the most favourable moment possible and then make the announcement. The arguments that I can make for it are convincing. Backe's control of his department is masterly. If anything is possible, then he will do it.

Speak with Boselli, editor of the *Corriere della Sera*. A clever Italian. They all have such inferiority complexes these days. I speak to him in a very friendly fashion. One must make an effort to keep one's friends.

With the Norwegian state counsellor, Hagelin. He makes a good impression, even if he seems slightly senile. The situation in Norway has improved slightly. This is the result of our victories. . . .

. . . With the Führer. I give him *Leda with the Swan* as a late birthday present. By Padua. He is very pleased. And a collection of 100 original French cartoons of himself. These he finds killingly funny. We leaf through them with great pleasure.

Koch of East Prussia brings news from the eastern border. Things are starting to whiff a little there. But once we have got going, we shall certainly gain an incomparable victory. The entire fabric of Bolshevism will collapse like a house of cards. And perhaps we shall find that our soldiers will be welcome there as they have been nowhere else. Still impossible to find a good word for Rome. Prince Philipp of Hesse has news from there. He is now our spy down there, or their spy up here.* I do not trust the princely gang so far as I can throw them. . . .

. . . Himmler is in the Balkans, looking to his *Leibstandarte*. He wants

* Philipp of Hesse was married to the King of Italy's daughter.

them back, because they are in urgent need of rest and re-equipment. They have achieved miracles.

Reports from Plymouth: the image of horror.

Choose some pictures with Magda. Discuss and settle a few more things. She and Ursel are intending to set off to visit the children this evening. They are looking forward to mummy's visit very much. I talk with them on the telephone: they go wild with joy. All are well.

Peace terms are being leaked through Tokyo. Some acceptable, some quite abstruse. London has printed them in *The Times*, without comment for the present. Can this be a preliminary 'feeler'? I find it hard to believe, for things have not yet reached that stage. In any event, we make no reaction.

Churchill and Eden are being forced to face parliament again. Again, their explanations amount to no more than an attempt to turn the retreat into a feat of heroism. They sent 30,000 men to Greece – at first it was said to be 300,000. 3000 dead, and a heroic retreat. I have the declarations cut to pieces in the press and the foreign-language service in no uncertain terms. For the rest, pessimism is visibly on the increase both in England and the USA.

They are suffering from a wave of defeatism. After the booze-up comes the hangover. The food situation is causing them particular concern over there. It is a pity that we have to cut our meat ration now of all times. The Duke of Windsor has given an interview to a magazine in the USA in which he pretty frankly disclaims all chance of an English victory. We decide not to use it for the present, so as to avoid suffocating this tender seedling of reason. . . .

. . . Then we have a two-hour air-raid warning during the night. But no damage. Only another disturbed night for the people of Berlin. But better than bombs.

2 May 1941 (Friday)

Yesterday: Few incursions into the Reich. Principally Hamburg and Wilhelmshaven. Damage slight. The English do not seem to be getting through in any strength. Could this be a significant indication? Impossible to know. But it seems that England is in a worse situation than we think. The results of our latest raids are showing now.

Malta bombed again. Our U-boats and planes are reporting big quantities of tonnage sunk. We can only hope that this continues, particularly in the case of the U-boat fleet.

Little left in Greece but mopping-up operations. The new government is beginning to establish itself. In North Africa, bitter fighting. Our fatal casualties for the entire South-Eastern Campaign probably total no more than 800. The announcement of this figure during the Führer's speech will be a sensation. London is admitting heavier and heavier losses so far as its own

344

troops are concerned, particularly in heavy equipment. But Churchill claims that we have an excess of this, in any case. He keeps quiet about the fact that the material is lost to him.

Public opinion in the USA is still in a state of ferment. The Isolationists are very active. Their success depends on what happens in the immediate future. The interview with the Duke of Windsor has, of course, been reprinted in a completely distorted form in the *Popolo d'Italia*. But then even in its original form, it had strongly defeatist undertones. We shall not use it, so as to avoid discrediting him.

Food supply problems increasing in England. I give the press instructions on how they are to comment on our lowering of the meat ration. They are to lay particular emphasis on the fact that we ate much less meat during peace time before the World War.

The latest newsreel is quite magnificent. I order that copies be sent to the troops who appear in it. This is the least our soldiers are entitled to expect.

Hinkel reports on Hamburg and Kiel. We must do a lot more for Kiel especially. The city must not feel that it has been deserted.

To Lanke in the afternoon. What peace out here! I take a deep breath. The dust of Berlin is shaken from me. Here one is a human being. In the freedom of nature. Spring is keeping us waiting out here. It is cold, and the trees are grey and bare.

Speak with Magda on the telephone: she and Ursel have arrived safely in Bischofswiesen. All the children are well. I really long for them. A drive through the forest. A whole lungful of fresh air.

Wild rumours from Russia. They are slowly coming on to our trail. But there so much lying going on that it is hard to distinguish fact from fiction. And at the moment that is the best thing so far as we are concerned. Turkey is on the point of changing sides. We are leaving this gentle process to continue undisturbed.

Reuter reports: we have broken through the defences of Tobruk. No further details yet. No such news on our side yet.

Iraq has protested against the English invasion. Fairly vocally. A storm is brewing there. We can only hope that something positive comes out of it.

A slightly earlier night out here. At least one is in bed by midnight.

3 May 1941 (Saturday)

Yesterday: No incursions. We carry out a middling raid on Liverpool. Fighting at an end in Greece. Crete is to be taken by parachute troops. Otherwise the issue has been settled.

Heavy pessimism in London. The newspapers describe it as worse than after Dunkirk. In North Africa, final battles for Tobruk. We are now almost into the city. The English cannot hold on any longer. Insurrection in Iraq continues. London issues a lame statement. Indian troops are deserting to the Iraqi units.

Cabinet reshuffle in London. Beaverbrook and Cross get a nasty surprise. Churchill makes them scapegoats. Evidence of how bad the situation in England really is. Worse than we expected.

1 May a holiday in France. Pétain makes a speech. Colourless and uninteresting.

Amann, Ohnesorge and Messerschmitt named 'Pioneers of Work'.

The latest newsreels have earned nothing but praise throughout the Reich. The Führer is also very satisfied with this work. I award the War Service Medal to the thirty-two people from the newsreel team.

Argue with Alfieri for an hour and a half. First general skirmishing. Then he complains about the fact that we have not instantly presented Italy with a gift of Dalmatia and Greece. This is really too much. Let them argue about Dalmatia with the Croats. And Greece? Who conquered it? Italian public opinion? As if we had no public opinion here! He maintains that Italy's pro-German stance has suffered a setback. But they are demanding too much from us. They can keep anything they conquer. But first they must conquer something. We have gone to the limits of what is tolerable, and even beyond. But too much is too much. I have difficulty in keeping my temper. Alfieri is scatter-brained and stupid. It is hard to make him understand anything. The Italians are quite unloved everywhere. And would like to pass the buck for their unpopularity on to us. This is not on. I tell him the brutal truth, in the most polite form. At all events, we go beyond the usual diplomatic reserve. We shall have our work cut out with them in future.

With the Führer. I tell him about my conversation with Alfieri. He is very annoyed about it. Naturally, he wants to keep the Italians happy, but they must at least come to an arrangement with the Croats. He complains bitterly about the Italian press's lack of discipline. It is incapable of keeping secrets. It has already blurted out details of the Crete Affair.

The Führer says that the Balkans have now been cleared. The English have lost a lot of heavy equipment. This is extraordinarily bad from their point of view.

A book on Churchill reports that he drinks too much and wears pink silk underwear. He dictates messages in the bath or in his underpants; a startling image which the Führer finds hugely amusing. He sees the English Empire as slowly disintegrating. Not much will be salvageable. The events in Iraq are an example. And India is in ferment. The Führer is giving serious thought to the question of whether he should establish an Indian National Government in Berlin. In any event, the present situation is quite different to that during the World War.

I show the Führer some very clever soldiers' poems about Kirkenes, in the style of Wilhelm Busch, which make him cry laughing. And they are quite priceless. A model example of magnificent soldier's humour.

346

A letter from Berndt from North Africa dealing with the danger from English air activity causes the Führer to press for more anti-aircraft weapons for North Africa. They are urgently needed there.

Discuss the question of Holland with Schmidt from The Hague. Mussert is beginning to make inroads. Our victories have given us a boost there. Heavy fines are slowly reducing sabotage. Reports from influential Dutch circles in London portray the situation in England in very gloomy terms. Particularly bad food situation. I give Schmidt a few pieces of good advice to take back with him. The main thing: to stay hard and not tolerate sabotage. He should take the harshest possible measures against this.

Visit Professor Klimsch. View his new sculptures, *Morning*, *Evening*, and *Anadyomene*. They are intended for our garden. Quite wonderful. Klimsch is the most mature of our sculptors. A genius. The way he handles marble. It is a joy to watch him. We can only hope this old man still has a long life in front of him!

A thousand things still to be dealt with at the office. Organisational problems regarding the Propaganda Companies. The most important thing is that the channels to us must be considerably simplified. The Wehrmacht High Command's methods are too bureaucratic.

To Lanke. It is already evening, and, despite the fact that May has arrived, as cold as winter. What a world. Speak to Magda on the telephone. They are all well. But she does not like Bavaria. With any luck, they will soon be moving to the Upper Danube.

Spend the evening working and writing. What divine peace out here!

4 May 1941 (Sunday)

Yesterday: We carry out a successful raid on Liverpool, while the English attack Hamburg with modest success. 1.1 million tons sunk in April. A good total, and higher than we had all thought. The war in Greece is over. Scarcely any feelings of hatred towards us on the Greeks' part, but all the worse so far as the Italians are concerned. Heavy fighting around Tobruk, which is still being held by the English.

The Italians are becoming increasingly brazen in their demands. The whole of Dalmatia, suzerainty over Greece and Croatia and also Montenegro. Their behaviour is really beneath contempt. And they are already teaching in their schools that Italy defeated France. Despite all this, however, the régime's prestige is still very shaky. The Croatians hate the Italians as deeply as it is possible to hate. We, on the other hand, are high in the popularity stakes. Italy would like to instal an Italian Prince to rule Croatia. Typical! Reaction in the wake of fascism. It is pathetic.

Hearst has written a cutting article against Churchill. Hard fighting in Iraq. Iraq has cut off the English oil pipeline to Haifa. Huge rallies in favour of Iraq throughout the Arab world, particularly in Egypt. The Empire is coming apart at the seams. Once the war is over, the English people will have a few things to thank Churchill for.

Hunke reports on Helsinki. Everyone there is on our side, with a sideways glance at the Russians. Rumour-mongering about Moscow is flourishing everywhere. There is not a single variation, between idyllic peace and bloody war, that is not being peddled there.

Discuss the 'Scharnhorst' material with Hippler. It is still not ready, and so I forbid filming to start for the moment. The film must be a classic.

Daily routine with Gutterer. Organisation of the Reichstag session. Discuss how the Führer's speech is to be broadcast all over the world. We shall be riding high again. The radio in general is providing an exemplary service. The press is lagging far behind. Recently, for instance, it published pieces about the latest newsreels which could not be surpassed for their coolness, lack of commitment and interest. The old newshounds are getting tired. There must be new blood.

Discussion with the Berlin City Commander's Office about whether semi-nude dancing should be allowed at the *Frasquita*. They are rather prudish there. On the other hand, one has to be careful in wartime. People's instincts are under strain, and if you give them free rein, then there can be catastrophic results.

To Lanke. The weather is cold, and it is snowing. What a crazy May! Well, at the moment the weather is not much of a hindrance to our plans.

Tension in Iraq is growing. The entire Arab world is in a state of ferment. We stoke the fires by our Arabic-language transmissions. London can only come up with pathetic excuses. This could be a very serious business from England's point of view. A pity that we have no Colonel Lawrence at our disposal. But I think that we shall gain some advantage, even the way things are.

The 1 May has brought military parades in Russia, with fiery speeches and resounding praise for the great Stalin. But a sensitive ear can easily detect fear of things to come. They are trying to impress us by fantastic statistics. Poor fools!

London is gradually conceding more and more serious losses in Greek waters. Now two destroyers lost to our Stukas with every man on board. So what was once so passionately denied, is possible after all.

Tension in Iraq is spreading to Syria and Palestine. Like wildfire. London is keeping very quiet about it.

I receive an infuriating report about Hungarian persecution of our ethnic Germans. This is the kind of thing we have to swallow. But the reckoning will come. And when it does, it will be thorough.

Outside, the countryside is covered by deep snow. And it is supposed to be almost summer!

5 May 1941 (Monday)

Yesterday: Middling English raids on Cologne, Aachen and Düsseldorf. Not particularly successful. We attack Liverpool with 400 aircraft. Devastating effect. This is the third heavy raid on this city. Soon it will be as useless as Plymouth. It is all over in Greece. The new generals' government promises well. Kotzias now intends to make a come-back.

Heavy attacks against Tobruk. We continue to make progress, but the British are holding on. Malta heavily bombed. There cannot be much left there, either.

Things in Iraq are taking a very satisfactory turn. London very disturbed. Holy War declared. Now the broken British promises are being avenged. The Iraqi government is going to the limit. Disturbances have also broken out in the Transjordan and in Palestine. We stoke the flames assiduously. The Arabic-language transmitters are working at full capacity.

Churchill appeals to the Poles. With a torrent of abuse directed against us. That man lives on the moon. Everything is complete fantasy. Typical of the English insular mentality!

Smuts is a faithful lacky. Has released South African troops for North Africa. But one day there will be a terrible reckoning. God's mills grind slow . . .

. . . Otherwise, this entire Sunday is overshadowed by the Führer's speech. It is announced at seven in the morning and the world holds its breath. We have ensured that translations are ready in time, so that it can be broadcast simultaneously all over the world.

In the afternoon, I have an hour for some reading. D'Annunzio. But one cannot enjoy reading him these days. A tactless, vain, puffed-up loud-mouth!

Drive into Berlin. It is raining buckets. A damp, unpleasant cold is in the air. The melancholy feeling of this grey day oppresses the soul.

Despite everything, there are masses of people lining the streets in the government district. The Berliners' enthusiasm is really admirable.

Reichstag: big day. The Führer speaks. Great summing-up of the South-Eastern Campaign, its brilliant strategic concept and execution. Highest praise for the Wehrmacht. Tough against Churchill and his incompetence. Generous references to our Axis partner; the Italians are given a large part of the credit for our victory. Even if this is not historically correct, it is tactically expedient. The Greeks come off very well. Not a word about the USA. Moscow not mentioned at all. Praise for Hungary and especially for Bulgaria.

Appeal to women to work. In the process he makes his first reference to next year, which naturally affects the audience very deeply. This is the key point: will things end this year? The public harks back to the Führer's words in his New Year Message, and believes that it is entitled to something of that nature. Anyway, there are certain psychological problems in this quarter, with which we shall have to concern ourselves more intensively in the near future. Thanks and confidence of victory at the end. The speech makes a great impression . . .

. . . In Vichy they are still playing musical chairs. How long can this go on! Shall we really have to settle for that filthy fellow, Laval?

The conflict in Iraq continues. No outcome yet discernible. In London they seem to think us capable of the wildest military escapades and are indulging in bizarre fantasies. Russia in the firing-line, too. In general, they are very worried in London. The extraordinarily small number of fatal casualties during the South-Eastern Campaign, which the Führer mentioned in his speech – less than 2000 – must give them pause for thought after all the feverish propaganda in this area . . .

. . . To Lanke. Speak to Magda on the telephone. She has been to the Upper Danube Gau. The children will move there next week. They will have a good life there, and it is where they will remain until the war is over. Who knows how long that may be?

Work on late into the night. Outside it is as still and peaceful as the last place on earth. But often just as lonely.

6 May 1941 (Tuesday)

Yesterday: No incursions into the Reich. We carry out a very heavy raid on Belfast. The damage in Liverpool is enormous. 452 aircraft in action during the night. Situation in North Africa unchanged.

The Führer's speech is the big sensation. The reference to next year is, as expected, the general talking-point both here and abroad. A certain amount of gloom has become perceptible here, because people had reckoned that the war would end this year. We shall have to overcome certain psychological difficulties, Abroad, a veritable chorus of triumph. But we shall soon deal with that.

The Führer is away from Berlin for a few days.

Gauleiters' conference: rather flat and apathetic. Amann explains the restrictions on the press. With sound arguments. Todt outlines the state of the armaments industry. This is better than good. With the exceptions of flak and flak ammunition. But we shall soon make up the shortfall. Our new U-boats are also taking shape. Aircraft manufacturing in great form. Munitions as such are available in superfluity. No danger in that area. Todt has a new commission dealing with the co-ordination of energy. There remains much to be done in that area.

Backe describes the food situation. Along the same lines as his report to me a few days ago. A few extra details, which give reasons for optimism. All we need is a good harvest this year. And then, of course, we intend to be firmly established in the East.

Ley chairs the conference. Very urbane, but without any real vigour. I miss the afternoon session, since I have such a lot of important things to do.

Discuss colonial matters with Epp. He is already easing himself into his coming duties as Colonial Minister.

Ohm Krüger finds nothing but approval from the Gauleiters. I am very glad, since I had placed such high hopes in the project.

All sorts to do in the office. Discuss the situation of the press with Fritzsche. We must now make every effort to help the people through this momentary depression. Another year of war is not a pleasant thing to look forward to. Added to which we are cutting the meat ration. Now we propagandists must show what we can do.

To Lanke in the afternoon. One can work better, in peace and with more concentration, in the deep stillness of the forest. Talk over some new plans with Esser. He emerges from the undergrowth every now and again, kicks up some dust, and then disappears again. A typical wind-bag!

Things in Iraq are getting very tough. The fighting there is costing London a great deal of prestige. We shall turn up the volume on our Arabic transmissions. We must do whatever we can. Making trouble for England is our delight.

I put up two main points from the Führer's speech for discussion, as a possible means of avoiding burdensome debate about a third year at war: our probably very low losses, which the British lie-propaganda throws into particularly sharp relief; and the accusation from the other side that the Führer has thought of nothing new. Our enemies could be trying to force the Führer to betray his plans. Churchill speaks, but he achieves nothing. The Führer acts, and then gives an account of himself afterwards.

Speak with Magda: all is well with the family. Set some music to the newsreel. Turned out magnificently well. Small party in the evening: Jahn, Demandowski, Hippler, and then a few people from the film world. The discussion is mainly about professional matters. But at least it gets me away from politics. Goedecke talks about the Request Concert, which is still enormously popular, and deservedly so.

Things go on until very late, but at least it is a small relaxation.

7 May 1941 (Wednesday)

Yesterday: Night raids on Heidelberg and Mannheim. Little damage. We attack English coastal towns with 460 aircraft. Widespread damage in Glasgow. Bitter fighting for Tobruk. The English have received further reinforcements. Our people are holding their own well. The duel could last some time yet.

Russia becoming more and more the central issue. Stalin and his people seem to be doing absolutely nothing. Like a rabbit with a snake. The same seems to be true of foreign opinion in general so far as we are concerned. It will be a matter of survival of the fittest. If the blow succeeds, then we shall be secure for the present. And it will succeed. What plausible reason could England have for fighting us after that?

Strong criticism of the Führer's speech in enemy countries. Arguments: the war will go on into 1942, serious losses in the Balkans, the Führer has said nothing new. I have our people take a strong line against all this, and order massive attacks on Churchill. The only way to treat that lying old swine is toughly and brutally.

For the rest, I say absolutely nothing for internal consumption on the question of whether the war will continue into 1942. The Führer has spoken on the subject. One cannot take all the people's worries from its shoulders . . .

. . . Belgrade must look horrific. Everyone at the front is talking about the Eastern Campaign now. The young soldiers want to get to grips with the enemy. The veterans, on the other hand, would sometimes like to be back with mother. This is natural and understandable.

Kaufmann here from Vienna. He shows me plans for a massive new conference hall in Vienna. They will do! Things seem to be going well in Vienna in other respects. The Gau authority there wants to establish a Centre for South-Eastern Questions. I reject the idea. Vienna is a Gau, and no more than that. The Reich's policy is made in Berlin. This must be so, and must remain so, if only for the sake of Reich unity.

Back to Lanke late in the afternoon, tired and overworked. The Führer is still in Danzig. I can thus deal with my routine tasks in peace. It is necessary to have the chance from time to time.

Haile Selassie has re-entered Addis Ababa.

Strong feelings of pessimism are spreading again in London. Particularly regarding the shipping losses, which hit England's most vulnerable point. Eden has made a speech in his government's defence to the House of Commons. Banal nonsense, without substance. Nothing but lame excuses.

Matsuoka has given an interview: if the USA enters the war, then so will Japan. I shall believe it when I see it. But a good thing that he is prepared to say it, at least.

Plenty of shooting going on in Iraq. Excellent.

Luftwaffe visitors in the evening. Colonel Schmidt, Major W [. . .] macher, and Captain von Werra, just back from Canada and the USA. He spends until 2 a.m. telling us about his thrilling escape from England, Canada and the USA. A really amazing story that one would need to write a book about to do justice. An exciting, gripping evening. This boy of twenty-six is a genuine hero. One can only admire him.

What sons our nation possesses these days. They are worthy of these great times.

8 May 1941 (Thursday)

Yesterday: Middling air raids on North-West Germany. Kiel is also hit. Slight damage. We attack the Clyde ports with 400 aircraft. Good results. England's production centres are gradually being pounded to pieces. The full effects will be felt only later. A weak England will be better for us in the future than an intact one. The Navy has nothing to report. The English methods of counteracting our U-boats have been greatly refined. Bitter, bloody fighting around Tobruk. We are holding what we have.

Molotov has resigned as President of the Council of People's Commissars. Stalin has taken his place. Still no clarification of the motives. Molotov remains Foreign Minister. I believe that the move is to strengthen authority generally in view of the grave crisis that the Soviet Régime faces. But it will do no good. In London and New York, they do not know whether to laugh or cry. Crying would probably be the correct course of action. At least in the long-term view.

Eden's speech in the House of Commons was a very feeble effort. The opinion seems to be shared in London. We have cut it to pieces. Stimson has spoken on Roosevelt's behalf. A blustering speech, oozing with lies and abuse. We make reply, and at full volume. One should not talk to the USA too often. But when one does, one's words should be plain and with nothing held back. This is the way that they understand over there.

Stephan gives a very vivid account of his journey in the Balkans. It confirms all our previous impressions. Greek attitudes towards us very good, worst possible towards the Italians. Still clear evidence of the fighting there. The English left huge quantities of material behind. Athens is completely undamaged, Piraeus is in ruins.

Report on morale from the SD. Generally good. But extensive sections of the population are longing for peace, more so than before. They view every new undertaking as an extension, and therefore a prolongation, of the war. We shall have to supply the appropriate arguments and constantly keep pointing to the world-wide significance of this war. Also gradually eliminate the fears which are based on experience of the World War. Our propaganda leadership in general meets with high approval.

I forbid the press to publish statistics of the Italians working in Germany. This only serves to feed resentment against Italy, which is very considerable at the moment.

Herr Abetz has now managed to persuade the Führer to allow the State Opera to perform for a week in Paris, including some appearances before the French public. I believe that this kind of attempt to curry favour will do us little good with the French and will harm the morale of German soldiers greatly.

Long conversation with Spanish Trade Syndicate leader, Meri [. . .] I raise the question of film exchanges, which now seems to be nearing a solution, while he draws my attention to certain mistakes in propaganda, particularly those perpetrated by our embassy down there. He is a clever and likeable man, one of the few Spaniards that I have any time for.

Speak to Gauleiter Simon about Luxembourg. There are still a mass of problems to be solved there. Morale rises and falls with our victories and periods of inactivity. We shall only be able to consider these provinces secure when England has been finally beaten.

Discussion paper by Hannes Cremer on the Party's cultural work in the Reich Propaganda Leadership. Clear and convincing. I shall commission him to start the work on this basis.

I study Churchill's new book, *Step by Step*. Speeches from 1936–39, and essays. This man is a strange mixture of heroism and cunning. If he had come to power in 1933, we would not be where we are today. And I believe that he will give us a few more problems yet. But we can and will solve them. Nevertheless, he is not to be taken as lightly as we usually take him.

What appalling weather. Grey, rainy, one has to have the light on during the day in order to be able to see at all. A blight on one's spirits. One turns quite melancholy. High time that the sun finally broke through and the great action began.

Particularly out in Lanke, one's heart is as cold as if one were at the North Pole. Cold and stormy. The devil take it!

Lloyd George has made a tough speech containing accusations against the conduct of the war, and including fairly strong attacks on Churchill. The latter has given an angry answer, making a call for national discipline, the most basic and primitive means of silencing any opposition. Churchill received a vote of confidence with only three votes against. But this, as such, means nothing at all.

Our sailors are being interned in the USA, and the *Transozean* correspondents have been arrested again. But Roosevelt does not trust himself to go the whole way. He is probably waiting to see what the immediate future brings.

Wild conjecture about Stalin and Molotov. Ranging from their joining the war on our side to our attacking them. Nobody has any real idea. I believe that my prognosis is correct.

Check films in the evening. A mass of rushes and test shots. And a good entertainment film, *Three Times Marriage*, from Vienna. A long day comes to an end.

9 May 1941 (Friday)

Yesterday: No incursions worthy of the name. We carry out successful raids on English targets. Successful, but we lose sixteen planes in the process. Liverpool is again heavily attacked during the night. Bitter fighting around Tobruk, with considerable losses on both sides. Our Stukas attacked the water supply with success. We are making some progress at Sollum.

Otherwise, offensive operations have been called off until further notice.

Churchill's speech to the House of Commons: excuses and very little information. But no sign of weakness. Eden's position somewhat damaged. His plea was really too pathetic. Lloyd George's criticisms were harsh but will not meet with general approval. England's will to resist is still intact. We shall therefore have to continue attacking and chipping away at her power-position. Still no victory in sight in Iraq. The English are making slight progress. I have Churchill cut to pieces in the press.

Discuss the new fanfares with Glasmaier. One especially for the Luftwaffe and another for Russia. One must make preparations in this area, too. The radio transmission times will have to be curtailed once again. Because of the daylight raids.

Daily routine with Gutterer. Precise guidelines for comment on the meat ration reductions hammered out. Now the case in unanswerable. Nevertheless, a somewhat embarrassing business.

Treatments and casting questions with Hippler. Winkler wants more films. I am also in favour of this, but not at the expense of quality. I will not have more junk. We decide that the time has come to buy out all the private production companies. They no longer act as a stimulus, but simply rake in money as a result of our work and our successes. They will all disappear by 1 September. Otherwise, I am buying up cinemas in all the countries where it is possible. We must dominate the European cinema industry completely after the war.

Discuss matters concerning *Das Reich* with Dr Mündler. The paper has been a brilliant success. My essays have helped a great deal. A circulation of one million. I suggest: more contributions, but shorter ones. A snappier treatment of contemporary questions. The modern reader has too little time to plough through long articles.

Rechenberg returns from the front. With an Iron Cross First Class. He was at Corinth as a paratrooper. Tells me tales of our boys' real deeds of heroism. Our Propaganda Companies were particularly prominent in the fighting. He does not think much of the English soldiers' fighting abilities. He has to report back immediately. For a new assignment.

Receive a delegation of Flemish publishers and open their eyes for them.

The Führer is back from Danzig. With him at midday. Discuss the situation. Churchill's speech is the product of desperation. He is out on his feet. But what can England do? The Empire will be ruined when all this is over. Roosevelt's only interest is to prolong the war. He and his people intend to profit by it, he is committed to it from the moral standpoint and for prestige reasons, and he wants to inherit England's power. He will never be able to produce as much as we, who have the entire economic capacity of Europe at our disposal. And no enemy will be able to break into Europe. Unfortunately, Italy has done us a lot of damage by her constant defeats. Without those, Pétain would have stayed at our side, and Franco would possibly have opened the way, and Gibraltar would now be in our hands. Turkey would have been winnable, too. It does not bear thinking about what all that would have meant. We would have been able to enforce our will effortlessly in the Middle East, Suez would have fallen into our lap like an over-ripe fruit, England would have already surrendered or would be at her last gasp. The fact that this is all wishful thinking is something we have to thank our allies for. The Führer reserves his harshest judgement for Franco and his lack of intelligence and courage. Even after hours of talk he had been unable to force him to an audacious decision. A clown! Conceited, arrogant and stupid. And that Serano Suñer of his is nothing but a Jesuit. Franco only rose to power on our backs. And that sort of thing never lasts. One must win power by one's own strength. And Italy? Well, let us say nothing about that!

The Führer compares our armaments capacity to that of the Anglo-Americans. We come out of it very well, even by the most pessimistic calculations. Papen reports on Turkey: there everything is in the balance. It is possible that we shall be able to turn them our way, despite everything. The Führer does not think much of the Arabs' fighting capacity, and rightly so. They are not attuned to modern weaponry; they have neither the nerves nor the intelligence to use it. The Führer has great praise for the work the Czechs have been doing in the armaments field. Not a single case of sabotage to date. And what they produce is good, serviceable, and solid. The Czechs have proved themselves. They are hard-working and reliable. A valuable acquisition for us. The quantities of equipment that they brought to us were also very useful. And they are still producing them today. What can the USA do faced with our armaments capability? They can do us no harm. Their talk is mostly beer-hall bragging. One should not take it too seriously.

The background to the government changes in Russia is still not clear. It is being said that Stalin is looking for an opening to us. One hopes not. Rosenberg has been assigned by the Führer to a post dealing with Eastern questions. Nothing special will come of that. He can only theorise, not organise.

The Führer has great praise for the latest newsreel. He considers it to be the best yet from the technical point of view.

The Führer looks well, he is in excellent form. He fears no threat from across the water. England lost the war last May, he asserts. If we do nothing to change things, then London can do nothing. We must work hard and be brave from now on, keep our nerve and our patience. And we shall not be found wanting in any of these qualities.

Then work for a long while at the office. Study English newspapers, some of which are quite extraordinarily stupid. Then back to Lanke in the evening. The weather has brightened up a little. Will spring finally come?

Tass has issued a firm denial that Russia is massing troops on her western border.

Stalin is obviously afraid, it seems. What a difference from the Tass

356

denials of a few months ago, in which we were openly or covertly insulted. So times change, when the open cannon-mouths stand waiting and ready.

Churchill has undoubtedly achieved a success by his speech to the House of Commons. His prestige is undented. England has a thick skin. But we shall pierce through it.

I write an essay for *Das Reich* on the Propaganda Companies. They have earned the right to be praised in public.

Check films in the evening. Change all sorts of details. But in this field everything is flourishing.

Magda rings up: she has now arrived in Aussee with the children. Welcomed by the entire village with banners and songs. Now the family is happy and in good hands.

What a long day! I am so tired that I am almost falling on my feet. How much rest and sleep I shall have to make up after the war!

10 May 1941 (Saturday)

Yesterday: very heavy raids on Hamburg and Bremen with a fair amount of devastation. Approx. 100 dead in Hamburg alone. We shall have our hands full dealing with it. In return, we attack English supply centres with about 400 aircraft. They won't have much to laugh about, either.

20,000 tons sunk by U-boats. Situation in North Africa unchanged.

Tass's denial is the big sensation. We are the beneficiaries for once. We do not publish it at all in the German press.

Assopress reckons the monthly replacement need of the British Merchant Marine at 500,000 tons. In any event, London has already admitted that April was an extremely unfavourable month for them.

I attack the publication of court judgements, which are very ham-handed from a psychological point of view. Educational work can and must be done, even in this area.

Problems of the day with Gutterer. Discuss propaganda for female labour with Tiessler. I do not expect too much from it. The time for volunteers is long since past. Now we must work with duty and service as our mainsprings.

Dittmar wants to go to the front. Everyone wants to go to the front, but who is going to do the work here?

Discuss new propaganda for the USA on the short-wave service with an American woman, Jane Anderson, and Herr von Bülow. I intend to take a greater personal interest in this area from now on. We must grab America by the horns now. There is no point in treading gently any more. So straight to it. A half an hour every day, pitched at the average American. Perhaps we shall achieve something with it.

My leader-article on the Propaganda Companies has turned out well. It clears up a lot of misunderstandings. Which was necessary.

Full discussion of the work of the Foreign Department with Hunkel. He has asserted himself well, particularly against the Foreign Ministry. The co-operation between the various departments in the ministry is exemplary.

Moscow has declared that she no longer recognises Belgium and Norway as sovereign states. Handed their ambassadors their marching-orders. So things have reached that stage. O Nightingale, I hear you twitter. But it will not do Stalin much good now.

Appalling havoc wreaked by our latest air raids on England. Particularly in Hull. Even Reuter has issued some very gloomy reports.

Première of *U-Boats Westwards* at the *Ufapalast*. A naval affair. The film tends towards simple-minded heroics, but it contains some glorious sea footage and wonderful technical props and is a great success. The latest newsreel is gripping, and is given an enthusiastic reception by the public. The Navy is a queer outfit.

Sit around with the artistes for a half-hour afterwards.

To Lanke. Speak with Magda. All is well with my numerous family.

After the session of the House of Commons, strong press criticism of Churchill is reported. But one should not place too much trust in this. Doubtless he remains firmly in the saddle.

How good that a difficult week ends today. I am tired and battle-weary.

One can never escape from the din of it all.

Meanwhile, the weather has turned gloriously fine.

Full moon!

Ideal for air raids.

11 May 1941 (Sunday)

Yesterday: Anniversary of the start of the offensive in the West. What a change in twelve months! And where shall we be a year from now?

Heavy air raid on Mannheim with considerable damage and casualties. Berlin had to put up with a light night attack. We cannot do much in England because of bad weather. The English drop leaflets over Berlin containing the times of their German Hour. As a consequence, I publish a few severe penalties for illegal listening. A lot of talk about Prien. We shall have to announce his loss now, or we shall lose credibility. I press for this to be done.

Heavy fighting in North Africa. Berndt has written a marvellous letter from there. He is now serving directly under Rommel himself.

A big English propaganda effort. She is now forced to admit to 500,000 tons of shipping lost in April. The highest monthly total so far. This is why she fantasises about the huge German aircraft losses and the destruction in our cities. It is the sugar on the bitter pill that the British and the American public has to swallow. We put up a strong show against all this, and attack Churchill personally in the most forceful terms. I pull out all the stops to ensure that our military successes are not transformed into propaganda disasters.

Moscow is ceasing to recognise the sovereignty of an increasing number of defeated nations. Now it is the turn of Yugoslavia, with whom she signed a non-aggression pact just a few weeks ago. Anxiety neurosis! We make no acknowledgment in any branch of our news service.

Our broadcasting effort aimed at Iraq has been stepped up. As a result, I have closed down our service to South Africa, because we are short of staff and equipment. As a general principle, the radio should be declared of decisive importance for the war effort. The Wehrmacht High Command is now helping actively in this area. The entire broadcasting problem is now being tackled with a new vigour.

SD report: morale satisfactory. People are somewhat uneasy re. the duration of the war. The Führer's statement about 1942 is still in the forefront of discussion. Our propaganda work meets with general approval.

Talk over improvements in the management of the Reich Culture Chamber with Hinkel. He is setting to with a will. Very necessary, too.

Discuss the problem of Greiner with Gutterer. Greiner is no great help to me in the long term. He is an old man, makes a lot of trouble and does little work. He wants promotion to State Secretary. But I think I can get rid of him without having to go that far. He is about as necessary as a goitre.

A thousand things to be dealt with over the weekend. Mountains of paperwork to be processed.

Twenty-fifth edition of *Beacon*, a programme for seamen in far-off countries and their wives. A pleasant, artistic programme. I make a short speech and extend a greeting and our thanks to the seamen, some of whom have been stuck away from home for two years now. Thirty wives also speak to their absent husbands over the short-wave link. It is moving!

A very fine, artistic programme.

To Lanke. I have some aggravation with the press, particularly the *Börsenzeitung*, which is making all kinds of psychological errors.

Magda and the children are well.

Visitors in the evening. A few people from the film world. We watch a recent English newsreel: very bad and in no way comparable with ours. Then a German and an American colour film. We are almost level with the Americans. But we must overtake them. I shall do everything I can.

Talk for a long time. About film problems. It goes on until very late. An air-raid warning in between. But no bombs on Berlin. Our defences, especially the night-fighters, are too strong. But Hamburg suffers another fairly heavy attack during the night, with considerable damage to buildings and some fatalities. This city has seen a lot of suffering recently. Something special must be done for it. I shall make every effort to that end.

12 May 1941 (Monday)

Yesterday: We attack London during the night with 400 aircraft. Tremendous destruction. And London had announced that the air-raid danger was largely a thing of the past. Big argument here about whether the air raid on London should be classified officially as retaliation for Berlin. I oppose this, because even if this may be plausible so far as the effect abroad is concerned, at home it will only tend to provoke cities like Hamburg, which have had to put up with a lot more than Berlin. I have already heard this suggestion from several sources, and therefore put forward my viewpoint with all the power at my disposal. Göring takes the opposite view. I get my way, however, and the result is that other cities will be named along with Berlin. In this way we shall avoid the worst risks of disaffection. Things must look horrific in London. Bombed all night in perfect visibility. Anything but pleasant . . .

. . . 30,000 tons sunk by U-boats in the Atlantic. In North Africa, heavy fighting around Tobruk and Sollum, but no significant change in the situation. Iraq is fighting on bravely. They are taking the right political line there, too. The government has declared that the Americans offered them arms and Syria if they would enter on England's side. The politics of gangsterdom!

Heated debates on the shipping problem in London. The admission of 500,000 tons lost has had a demoralising effect in England and in the USA. And so they are manufacturing excuses in London. But to no great purpose. Churchill is in a cleft stick: so far as we are concerned, he would like to admit as little as possible, but to the USA as much as he can. Trapped in his own web of lies. Opinion in the USA always gets cold feet after such news. But it is questionable whether it will affect developments. Everything depends on Roosevelt and his Jewish advisers. And we know only too well what we can expect from them.

Moscow is making every effort to behave herself. London is going at Stalin like a thing possessed. We do not expect that situation to last for long. So wait and see! A pity that we cannot prepare our own people for the coming events to some extent. Everything will come very suddenly. But we must master that problem, too.

An appalling mining accident in Neurode, with 189 dead. Traceable to poisonous gas. A serious blow!

I work at Lanke. The weather is as grey as November again. I study a treatment for a Jannings film, *The Red Stripes*. A film about the General Staff. The opening has turned out very well. We can build on that.

Otherwise, spend the whole day on reading, writing, and take a short walk. At least manage to get a little fresh air. It will have to do for the entire week.

In the evening, reports arrive from London about the latest air raid.

London radio itself declares: it was an inferno! Nevertheless, no indication of weakness or readiness to give in. As there is none here, either, even though the air raids are far more extensive. I telephone Kaufmann: during the past two nights, 200 dead, many public buildings razed to the ground or seriously damaged, including the fine city hall. The people are standing up to things magnificently. Kaufmann asks that the lowering of the meat ration should not be put into effect in Hamburg. I shall see what I can do. It is Darré's decision.

Check the newsreel: not quite as good as the last three, but something can be made of it. English and Russian newsreels that we seized in Belgrade. Absolutely no competition for us. Incomparably poor and amateurish. I am downright proud of our work in this field. We have nothing to fear, either militarily or in the propaganda field, particularly from the Russians. The English films are indescribably naïve. But I think that they are good enough for the English, who are themselves enormously stupid, unenlightened and primitive. We should take this more into account in our propaganda aimed at England.

Otherwise the day is quiet and without great sensations.

This will probably not last much longer!

13 May 1941 (Tuesday)

Yesterday: The devastation in London is, according to all reports on the spot, horrific. But no sign of weakening. English airfields bombed during the night by 300 aircraft, in excellent visibility and with every success. The English raid Hamburg and Bremen again, causing some damage to buildings but little in the way of human casualties. A few sinkings. Attack on Benghazi by English naval units, which is, however, seen off by our Luftwaffe.

The shipping losses are the big talking-point in London and Washington. There is open discussion of the fact that the English figures do not add up. They are merely a compromise between what they want to admit to us and what they want to tell the Americans. We make grateful use of this satisfying theme. The foreign correspondents are filing sensational stories about coming invasions, etc. I have them called vigorously to order.

Stalin is still trying to gain our goodwill, issuing statements filled with simple peasant cunning. Too late!

I have noticed a slight element of cynicism creeping into our reporting of the war, particularly the war in the air, which originates at the front. There they are talking about air raids as 'piecework', among other things. I put a stop to this. Our people, which has had to suffer so much in this war, would not understand it. I also tone down the grotesque exaggerations – 'London a sea of flames', etc. – which have been putting in an appearance again lately. They can only harm us in the future. We must not arouse hopes if they cannot be fulfilled immediately. Our style for this war must be hard, manly, unsentimental, sober, but without smart-Alec cleverness. Sarcasm can only harm things. I also put a stop to the current practice of calling all war products 'German' (German tea, German coffee, etc.). At this rate, every kind of junk will end up labelled 'German'. This is not good advertising.

The Foreign Ministry is against Arabic-language clandestine transmitters. I am now establishing them in co-operation with the High Command. They must be created. It is high time. The war is continuing in Iraq. When will the Foreign Ministry finally wake up!

The problem of female labour has been shelved yet again by the Führer. I make a vigorous plea for conscription. We shall not get anywhere with fine words. Everything must be subject to clear orders and instructions. Then the German will gladly obey. Our fine ladies will not come voluntarily. The Führer has gone off to the Obersalzberg. Calm before the storm. It will not last much longer.

Lay down the law to Greiner regarding his impossible attitude towards work-discipline. He had been looking for an under-secretaryship as his reward. He will wait a long time for that. Not much can be done with such an old, washed-up official.

Short conversation with Alfieri. Through our car windows. I must visit him again sometime.

Our building work is making good progress now. The walls of the new wing of the ministry are already rising. A short visit to Schwanenwerder. The new office there is ready. Now it has only to be furnished.

At Lanke. A little sunshine at last. Is spring on the way now? I have brought work with me. Out here I can deal with the most urgent work in complete quiet. The afternoon newspapers play up the air raid on London in a way that seems to me too heavy and smart-Alecky. I intervene immediately. This can only do harm. The public will start harbouring illusionary hopes, and if they are not fulfilled, then we shall be back to the English being tough and able to take punishment, and all that. We must pursue a consistent line in our propaganda. Not too high, not too low. This is the best way to make it through the war. They comfort themselves with illusions in London. They will have more disappointments there. The US press has announced for the first time that the inhabitants of London are profoundly demoralised. They will have more cause to be as time goes by.

A short stroll through the forest and the meadows. The birches are coming into leaf. The sun is so warm. I feel a great longing for peace, rest, relaxation and a little happiness. But we must only begin to think of these things when the war is over.

Put the finishing touches to the newsreel in the evening. It has turned out well after all, after being complemented by a snappy musical score. Look at a few more English and Russian newsreels for comparison purposes. Absolutely no competition for us.

It is now that one notices how far ahead of the others we really are.

Appalling news comes in the evening: Hess, against the Führer's orders, has taken off in a plane and has been missing since Saturday. We must presume him dead. His adjutants, who were the only ones aware of his intentions, have been arrested on the Führer's orders. The Führer's statement gives delusions as the reason for his action, some madness to do with illusionary peace-feelers. The entire affair is thoroughly confused at the moment. We are forced to issue the statement immediately. A hard, almost unbearable blow. At the moment it is impossible to see where the affair will lead.

I receive a telephone call from the Berghof. The Führer is quite shattered. What a sight for the world's eyes: the Führer's deputy a mentally disturbed man. Dreadful and unthinkable. Now we shall have to grit our teeth.

And above all we shall have to try to shed some light on this totally mysterious affair. At the moment I can think of no way out. But one will be found. I instruct the press and radio to merely report it, without comment. And then wait for the reaction. London will soon have her say. And we shall not be short of a reply.

Hess toyed with the idea of a possible peace. It seems that he had become too remote from the day-to-day struggle and had turned soft. This business is going to be hard to see through. I immediately have shots of him removed from the latest newsreel. Reuter is still quiet. But the storm will, of course, break during the next few hours. I am besieged by telephone calls from all sides, Gauleiters, Reichsleiters, etc. No one wants to believe this madness. It sounds so absurd that it is hard not to dismiss it as a fabrication. The Führer orders that Hess's work in the Party Chancellery be continued as normal. I must go to the Obersalzberg. There I shall hear more details. Nothing can be said on the telephone.

A dreadful evening follows. The reports of the inferno in London seem meaningless. I am totally occupied by this matter. Nothing is being spared us.

But we shall get through this, too. Perhaps more quickly than we can conceive at the moment.

14 May 1941 (Wednesday)

Yesterday: Another crazy day. The wild alarums and rumours start at first thing in the morning. Total chaos. Everything from high treason to peace-offers. Meanwhile, clarity at last: Hess has landed by parachute in Scotland. Let his plane crash and sprained his ankle in the fall. Then he was found by a farmer and later arrested by the Home Guard. A tragi-comedy. One doesn't know whether to laugh or cry.

Into the office. Give instructions to Fritzsche and Bömer. Urge self-control and discipline at the Ministerial Conference. Absolute silence for the present. Ignore all rumours.

Military situation: 22,000 tons sunk by U-boats. War in the air continues back and forth. Not so important at the moment. I order that it be given great prominence. Otherwise keep a tight rein. The public's morale is rock-bottom.

To Ainring by plane. From there by car to the Obersalzberg. Work at full stretch during the journey. The Führer is waiting for me. I read the letters that Hess left behind for the Führer: totally confused, schoolboy amateurism, saying that he intended to go to England, make the hopelessness of their position clear to them, bring down Churchill's government with the aid of Lord Hamilton in Scotland, and then make a peace which would save London's face. Unfortunately, he failed to realise that Churchill would immediately have him arrested. It is all just too stupid. A fool like this was the Führer's deputy. It is scarcely conceivable. His letters are littered with ill-digested occult theory. Professor Haushofer and Hess's wife were the evil geniuses in this affair. They pushed their 'great man' into this role. He is supposed to have had visions, had horoscopes drawn up, and so on. Rubbish. And this is one of Germany's rulers. The whole thing can be traced to his mystic obsession with healthy living and all that nonsense about eating grass. Totally lunatic. I would like to give a good thrashing to that wife of his, his adjutants and his doctors.

Yesterday evening's statement was necessary. The affair had to be blamed on delusions. How else could one explain it? Particularly to our Axis partners, who otherwise will start to doubt our loyalty to the alliance. No one will believe that it just a personal aberration of Hess's. It shows an insane lack of discipline on his part. He is finished so far as the Führer is concerned. The Führer is absolutely shattered. He has been spared nothing. He condemns Hess in the harshest terms, but grants him a degree of idealism. We release a new statement which clarifies some of the background. The public is extremely restless. People are asking, rightly, how a fool like this could have been next in line to the Führer. A Herostratus* and a failed Messiah. Obviously he lost his nerve. The business is so squalid and ridiculous that one can hardly credit it. And it had to happen now, when the Führer has received Admiral Darlan and is about to carry out his coup in the East.

Meanwhile, the enemy's propaganda machine has scaled new heights of hysteria. A veritable flood. But Churchill has little to say about the real motives. He also has little use for talk of peace. And Duff Cooper has exposed himself yet again as a total amateur. If I were the English Propaganda Minister, I would know exactly what to do.

Ribbentrop is flying to Rome to put Mussolini in the picture. I have a long discussion about the case with Göring. His verdict is damning. The Führer does away with the post of Deputy Führer and establishes a Party Chancel-

---

* An Ephesian who, according to Greek legend, set fire to the famous temple there on the night of Alexander the Great's birth, thereby 'immortalising' himself in the most drastic and horrifying way.

lery that will be headed by Bormann. Then he speaks to a meeting of Gauleiters and Reichsleiters. After the initial astonishment, the reaction is one of extreme anger. Göring summarises the feelings of loyalty. Everyone is now firmly determined to stand with the Führer. The watchword now is: stand together and keep calm.

I have a long talk with the Führer. He is very bitter. He had never expected anything like this. One can be prepared for anything except the aberrations of a lunatic. I have great sympathy for the Führer. He, and all of us, will have to tread a rocky path to the heights.

Then I have to get back. Affectionate farewell. I regret very much that I must leave the Führer. But the bustle of Berlin awaits me. Hess's adjutants have been arrested. They knew everything and carry the heaviest burden of guilt.

To Ainring with Lutze. Feverish conversation. One can only shake one's head. Flight back to Berlin. Brief my colleagues on the way. Work. Tempelhof. The department chiefs are waiting for me. And our good Wodarg. I give a short explanation. Everyone shakes their heads.

London and New York are going wild. The storm is breaking. Now we have to keep our head. Churchill has made a speech in the House of Commons. He has given notice of an official English report on the case. That will give us an indication of England's intentions. Therefore wait and see. It is late in the evening. There is no more to be done now. The brew must thicken. According to the SD report, the people's mood is anything but gratifying. But we shall soon settle that. The main thing is to gain time. In a few weeks the whole thing will be forgotten.

I drive out to Lanke and get a good night's sleep in preparation.

15 May 1941 (Thursday)

Yesterday: The Hess Affair has caused appalling damage. At home, according to the SD report and other inquiries, the situation is one of complete débâcle. The public simply cannot understand what has happened. Some gratification among the reactionaries and in the Wehrmacht. The old, good-hearted Party comrades suffer most. The effect abroad is indescribable. It is the universal, almost the sole, talking-point. If Hess's senseless action was calculated to put him in the public eye, then it has succeeded brilliantly. Every possible kind of horror-story is being peddled. London is cunningly letting us wait for an official statement, and thus allowing free rein to the lies. But there is no indication of an underlying grand strategy at this stage. I would be making more of it if I were the English Propaganda Minister. Churchill is being very reticent. The story is that he wants to talk to Hess personally. One piece of good news: official circles in London have said that Hess wanted peace, but on the basis of German strength. The main danger is that they will use him to give authenticity to faked atrocity-reports.

But this has not yet happened. He completely dominates the press in the USA. Child's play!

I outline the affair to the Ministerial Conference. Boundless amazement. Watchwords: at home, keep our nerve and say nothing for the moment; abroad, deny the lies and sketch out the background to the case.

Then I talk to the Berlin Kreisleiters about the case. They must attempt to counteract the wildest rumours by appropriate word-of-mouth propaganda.

Discuss air defence problems with the officers of the Berlin flak. We are in agreement on everything. But even they are shattered by the news.

Lieutenant-Colonel Soldmann reports to me on North Africa. About our troops' role in the fighting, the problems of supply, their homesickness, the boundless cowardice of the Italians and the arrogance of their officers. It is unimaginable. But our soldiers are marvellous. Fighting ceases over there in June because of the heat. I intend to start a massive programme of troop-entertainment then. Soldmann will work with Hinkel on planning the project.

Discuss the financial position of the Red Cross with Hilgenfeldt. Everything is fine. He is also totally devasted by Hess's action. Describes him as an indecisive type and a pathological case. One might have expected something bizarre from him.

Military situation: no incursions on either side. The English carry out a daylight raid on Helgoland with some success. We hit a few ships. Malta bombed. Heavy fighting in North Africa.

Vichy has accepted the Führer's conditions, without a dissenting voice. And so we can start.

I am suffering acutely from the shame of the Hess Affair. One feels as if one has been dealt a personal blow, and one would prefer not to show one's face on the street. All this has been caused by the second-most important man in the Party after the Führer. It is like a bad dream. The Party will feel the effect of this for a long time to come. But we shall get through it. I instruct the press and the radio to devote vigorous attention to other things and act as if nothing had happened. This is the best remedy.

To Lanke. Look over Naumann's study paper on cartoon-film production in Germany. I shall support this, since it is a good and useful thing.

Otherwise, work, study, read and mull over things in my mind. Work is always the best cure. We can only hope that every one will forgotten the affair in a few weeks. One big military victory, and the entire schoolboy prank will be consigned to oblivion.

Speak with Magda. She is also very downcast. I am planning to visit her and the children on Friday and even relax for a couple of days down there myself.

Stroll through the forest in the rain. The old trees are already adorned with fresh green leaves. They have seen a lot of human woe and will see a lot more. So why worry about today? Everything passes, even our torments.

I can already take a more objective view as I read the sensation-mongering reports from London. These are a hideous hotch-potch of lies, scandal and truth. The good Hess is being used in a way that beggars all description. His childish naïvety is causing us incalculable harm. The English are gradually coming to the realisation that they can ascribe the wildest distortions to him. He is, of course, totally helpless in the face of such actions – something he might have thought of beforehand. He will never even be aware of most of them. It is a tragedy.

I spend all my time framing denials. But if things continue like this, we shall have to come up with something more substantial. Bömer is already working on these lines so far as abroad is concerned. As are our foreign-language services. But I am awaiting developments.

On the Führer's orders, the lowering of the meat ration is announced without great emphasis and described as a temporary measure for the summer. We hope to control a considerably-enlarged base for food production by the autumn. Thus it is better to announce it in this fashion.

Talk with Tabody. Description of the situation in Italy and Hungary.

The rumours and alarums continue deep into the night.

Huge mountains of press-cuttings.

Hess has the world's ear.

But not in the way he had imagined.

It is terrible, unimaginably terrible!

16 May 1941 (Friday)

The Hess Affair is still the big talking-point, but is slowly losing its dramatic character. Horror-propaganda very extensive. But little substance. No clear line in its construction. The rumours are cancelling each other out. I am beginning to relax a little. It seems that London has not hit upon the idea of simply issuing statements in Hess's name without his knowledge. This is the big, most alarming danger so far as we are concerned. The thought of it makes me shiver. But it seems as if we have a guardian angel watching over us. We are dealing with dumb amateurs over there. What we would do if the situation were reversed! The impact of the affair is also diminishing at home. The public pities the Führer. This is a very positive change. The affair is by no means over, but the danger is less immediate and dramatic. The rumours are dying away. A slight feeling of hangover everywhere. I put a bar on all news at home and have the real facts discussed abroad. This tactic has proved to be the correct one.

I issue a firm order against occultism, clairvoyancy, etc. This obscure rubbish will now be eliminated once and for all. The miracle-men, Hess's darlings, will now be put under lock and key. Instructions to the Party to explain the facts. Then at least we shall be on firm ground.

Military situation: Little of note. No activity in the air. 30,000 tons sunk.

Malta bombed again. Somewhat delicate situation in North Africa, since the port of Benghazi has been totally destroyed and no supplies at all are getting through. Tripoli is also only partly usable, and so the supply situation is dangerous. But one can hope that we shall soon be on top of the situation. No acute danger, anyway. Blomberg's són, a Luftwaffe pilot, has been killed in action.

Helldorff has been blurting out secrets in my name. I shall sort him out in no uncertain terms.

Things are due to roll in the East on 22 May. But this is still rather dependent on the weather. German aircraft have been sent into action in Iraq. London has declared that it will bomb the Syrian airfields, since we have been using them. A row between England and France would suit us very well . . .

. . . Fink reports on Holland. A thousand interesting details. The important thing is that the mood there has changed very much to our advantage. We are slowly getting our way. I reproach Fink for the policy shortcomings which became apparent when they were faced with rebellious elements in Amsterdam. He intends to be more careful in future.

Work at Lanke. The telephone never stops ringing. Always this damned Hess Affair. But we are gradually getting on top of the situation. A pity that we had to announce the lowering of the meat ration just at this moment. We are limiting it to the summer months. I hope we can keep this promise. Our Wehrmacht will do its best. Fritzsche is nagging me unmercifully to release more details of the Hess Affair at home. I refuse. This business must be killed by silence, not talked to death. And it is quite false, anyway, to swop methods in mid-course, so that one day one is talking, the next day, refusing to speak. Once we open our mouths, no one can know where it will end. And all the dirt will be stirred up again. In the evening, Churchill speaks about the case in the House of Commons. His speech contains nothing new. He intends to report fully, but at a more suitable time. So he has nothing worth saying. It seems the entire furore is dying down to some extent. While in the morning the Hess Affair took up five-sixths of enemy propaganda output, by the evening this has slumped to one-sixth. And now Iraq is coming to the fore. Bevin describes Hess as a murderer and a madman, to whom they have nothing to say. That is, of course, precisely what we wanted to hear. Eden has put in a word, too. I think that we have the worst behind us. Even London is having to concede the brilliant way in which our propaganda has mastered the situation. And it has indeed been a masterpiece of vision, psychological skill and caution. Let us have more of the same. Cairo has declared officially that German aircraft have landed in Iraq. Eden has stated that England will bomb the Syrian airfields. Strong attacks on France. That is enough for me. Now I shall stir the bloodhounds of the international press into cry. They will soon have something other then Hess to write about, and this affair will soon be buried.

The affair is slowly ebbing. One more massive collection of material arrives in the evening. Still all manner of speculation. But now there are many voices counselling caution. I give these some support in the foreign-language service. And in particular make a big noise about Iraq and Syria. One must cover one's tracks. Even in the USA and England, Hess is now considered slightly mad. Otherwise, of course, the whole business is totally inexplicable. Who can see into the depths of a human soul? Or penetrate the brain of a man consumed by ambition but unequal to the great and unexpected tasks thrust upon him? The rest is silence and astonishment.

Pétain has made a speech. Request to the French to follow him and to understand his policy of compromise with us. He has need of it. For the most part, the French are doing us great service at the moment.

Film *Friedemann Bach*, with Gründgens. Good from a cultural-historical point of view, musically excellent, but, as with all Gründgens films, the acting is rather stilted.

It gets very late.

But then we have the worst behind us.

Bright stars are breaking through in the sky once again.

How long will it be until the sun shines?

17 May 1941 (Saturday)

Yesterday: The Hess Affair is running out of steam. London and Washington have other worries. A few rearguard actions. But influential circles over there are urging people not to overestimate the incident. Hamilton, who spoke with Hess, describes him as crazy. London is deeply disappointed that the affair has been such a damp squib. We are still maintaining absolute silence on the case at home. The public is slowly calming down and already jokes about it are doing the rounds. So far as abroad is concerned, we are issuing denials and dark hints that the enemy will have cause to be astonished at what comes. This works beautifully. Increasing perplexity in London regarding the case. Duff Cooper is worth his weight in gold from our point of view. He is really uniquely stupid. What I would have made of this case! But England's ruling class is ripe for a fall.

Hess planned the whole thing quite magnificently. Thus, for example, his adjutant instructed the Saarbrücken radio station to keep broadcasting all through Saturday evening. Hess, he said, wanted to listen in. In fact, of course, he intended to use it for direction-finding purposes. A fool, but a meticulous one. But away with him! I believe that he will suffer a dreadful fate: to be forgotten in no time!

I explain the affair to Alfieri. He seems very satisfied, and his behaviour throughout has been impeccable.

Middling air raids on Hannover. Air-raid warning in Berlin, but no bombs. We do nothing during the night. The dance has begun in Iraq and

Syria. This gives us some new material for the press and allows us to recover quickly from the painful Hess Affair.

A lot to deal with at the Office. I get what I can out of the way quickly, then fly to Linz. After an angry telephone call from Frick, who wishes to protest about Naumann's promotion. I tell him where to get off . . .

. . . Some time for reading during the flight. About the Czar's court during the World War. The whole thing was ripe for a fall. Princes, Emperors and Czars are not in tune with the times. But then we have our Italians setting up a royal prince, the Duke of Spoletto, as King in Croatia.* Poor Croats! At least they are getting a port in Dalmatia in exchange. Lord knows where the Duce's monarchy will get him!

In Linz. Dine with Eigruber. Everything is primitive and simple. We discuss the Hess Affair. He is furious. The people are beginning to feel the same way. A few matters regarding theatre, cultural and film work in Linz. Linz is costing us a lot of money. But the Führer considers it very important. And it may well be correct to support Linz as a competitor for Vienna in the cultural field.

By car through the Salzkammergut to Aussee. What glorious scenery. Irkowski tells me his troubles on the way. The people are very touching. By the time we arrive at the Villa Roth, we are sitting in a car covered with flowers.

And now the children! Their joy is indescribable. They hang on to me like limpets. And they have all grown so much, and look so fit and sun-tanned. Helga and Hilde are already proper little ladies, Holde and Heddda are indescribably sweet. Helmut is still the plump, phlegmatic little chap, and Heide is already laughing and playing. By the wonderful Grundelsee. A beautiful, big summer house. The children will do very well here. I am boundlessly happy here, surrounded by the entire family. We chat and play until late in the evening. Worries seem so far away.

To Aussee with Magda and Ursel. We talk a lot. Particularly about the Hess Affair, which no one can believe or understand. It is so ridiculous that people are saying that it is a crude fabrication on our part.

News from Berlin: the English have entered Sollum. Unpleasant, particularly at this precise moment. The English are already attacking with their air force in Syria. So it has come to this.

Hadamovsky reports that the children sent to East Prussia will now have to be evacuated to the Lower Danube. It will be difficult to inform the parents without betraying secrets or giving indication of what is to come. But we shall find a way round the problem.

Talk with Magda late into the night. She is very clever and understands things better than many high-ranking politicians.

---

* Reigned as King Tomoslav of Croatia. Deposed in 1943.

18 May 1941 (Sunday)

Yesterday: A restless night. The village is such a noisy place. The peasants still have no reason to be nervous, and thank God for that. But I have. I scarcely manage to sleep a wink.

The Hess Affair is now at an end. I allow another little postscript for foreign consumption. Then close the case. Uninteresting! This is how quickly things happen these days. Easy come, easy go. Hess should have realised that before he set out. What will become of him now?

Roosevelt is interning French ships. And is protesting against the fact that we have declared the Red Sea a war zone. He is talking as if he intended to come to blows with us at any moment. Knox has made another insolent statement. Developments in the USA are becoming grave. We shall wait and see for the present.

Big anti-English demonstrations in Syria. General Dentz is doing his duty. Vichy is working well in our interests. I hope that Pétain will stay loyal.

A National Socialist organisation has been uncovered in Glasgow. Not very big, but nevertheless interesting as a symptom. Priestley has launched a strong attack on the plutocrats. There are still visions and miracles to be seen!

Thirty English aircraft over West Germany. Middling raid on Düsseldorf. We attack key war targets in Southern and Central England with several hundred aircraft.

Some work. Telephone calls with Fritzsche and Hadamovsky. Everything is taking its course.

To the lake with the children at midday. We spend a happy afternoon in the open air in glorious sunshine. How sweet the children are! I am able to spend hours with them and am very happy and jolly. We build castles and waterfalls. Helmut is busy being architect. He is a real character. The people of Aussee serenade us. It is like peacetime. But, despite everything, one senses the shadow of war looming behind all this short-lived contentment.

Back to Aussee in the evening. Sollum and Fort Capuzzo, which we had lost, are back in German hands. After bitter fighting.

Sit with the villagers until late, telling them about the Führer. We all idolise him. So long as he is there, no serious misfortune can befall us.

Late to bed. A proper night's sleep.

19 May 1941 (Monday)

Yesterday: Mother's Day! I provide gifts for Magda, mama, and Ursel. Great joy on all sides.

Long telephone conversations with Fritzsche and Hadamovsky. Establish clear course. Hess Affair is laid to rest. Abroad it is being counted as a German victory and a tremendous defeat for English propaganda. And that is exactly what it is.

371

Mass raid on Cologne. Damage not too serious. We carry out more raids on English ports. Some 40,000 tons sunk.

Roosevelt is in a rage. Because France is moving over to our side. German aircraft are using Syria as a stopover point on the way to Iraq. The campaign is continuing. Great anxiety in London. Vichy has kept to the agreed course quite faithfully so far. Pétain obviously wishes to emerge from his isolation. Fighting has already started in Syria and Iraq. The English will have their hands full there.

More work. The German newspapers from Norway and the Netherlands are to be banned from Reich territory. In defiance of our instructions, they have been splashing the Hess Affair all over their headlines. We do not want this in the Reich. The affair seems played-out so far as the German public is concerned. London has missed a big chance.

At midday the children come to say good-bye. We play and chat for another hour. Then farewell! My heart is very sad. How long will it be before I see the sweet little things again? They are all in tears. The dear little things!

So away. To Ainring by car. Magda and Ursel come with me. The weather is none too attractive. But the sun soon breaks through, and then it is wonderful. Past the Wolfgangsee, through Fuschl, and then glorious Salzburg in the light of the sun. Ainring!

Two hours to Berlin. The mountains of paperwork are waiting for me. Nothing of note in the world press. Hess is already scrap-iron so far as London is concerned. It was a one-day wonder, no more than that. The London newspapers are already abusing him; he failed to be of use to them. World opinion is unanimous in agreeing that we won the propaganda battle over Hess. I had never doubted that we would, but I never suspected that it would be over so quickly.

A few pleasant messages from Lammers, acting in the Führer's name, which extend my authority. A lot of money must be granted for all kinds of projects. And then I have half an hour free to think about the children. They were so touching when we said good-bye. Helga tried hard to keep up appearances. She is already a very grown-up person and mothers her sisters all the time. I am so glad that the children are shielded from any contact with the harsh business of war. All the more reason for me to work for the great victory that will end it.

Berlin! Magda is off to Schwanenwerder, to begin preparing things there during the next few weeks, while I drive out to Lanke. Everything is fresh and green out here. A sight that makes the heart leap! The March of Brandenburg can be very beautiful.

A few more political and military discussions. The Duke of Spoletto has been proclaimed King of Croatia in Rome. Poor Croats! In exchange, however, they receive a piece of the Dalmation coast, but are not allowed to have a war fleet. That should not affect them too much. What a reactionary Mussolini can be at times.

Newsreel. Quite good, but not yet a wartime newsreel. We shall not have to wait too long for that, however. Discuss a few film problems with Hippler. And then a blessed night in the divine peace of spring.

20 May 1941 (Tuesday)

Yesterday: The Hess Affair is really over. Only a few remaining stray shots from the enemy propagandists. We refuse to react.

Fighting continues in Iraq and Syria. Vichy is holding her ground so far. Pétain has a big chance here. We give the Americans a mouthful for interfering in France's affairs. Hull has made another brazen speech. I have him given an appropriate answer. I personally dictate a very long leader-article attacking the Roosevelt dynasty. It will cause quite a stir.

Kiel and Hamburg subjected to some weak bombing. We confine ourselves to attacking shipping. Bloody fighting in North Africa. Berndt has written another dramatic report from there. Real trench warfare raging round Tobruk. The drama is coming to an end in Abyssinia. Final battle for Aladshi. The Duke of Aosta is forced to surrender. Meanwhile, his brother, the Duke of Spoleto, is made King of Croatia. A report from Maurer in Zagreb describes the deep disappointment of the Croats. They had wanted a republic, not a monarchy courtesy of Rome. The Italians are completely unloved. Where is it any different? The Croat National Socialists are deeply disappointed. There is still gun-fire after nightfall.

A few sinkings. I forbid the press to publish death notices referring to the campaign in France. These are mostly group advertisements, and they provide the radio in London with material that casts doubts on our official casualty figures.

The SD report illustrates the deep disappointment felt by the German people over the Hess Affair. Another report, from Vienna, shows the catastrophic effects, and makes it clear that the public takes the harshest possible view of Hess himself. For the most part, however, morale is on the rise again, if slowly. The Führer's authority has actually been reinforced.

Discussions about the tobacco shortage. This must be dealt with some-how. The long queues outside the shops are breeding-grounds for disaffection. Anyone who is at work all day has little chance to ensure his supply. So we must take steps to remedy the situation. The Red Cross Collection has declined slightly in comparison with last year. But then 1940 was the time of the offensive in the West. And the Hess Affair may have had an effect.

Schmidt-Decker reports on Spain. Bleak situation. Franco very unpopular. The Führer respected as the ultimate authority. Süner the real fly in the ointment. Public has hopes of us. The entire country is rotten with corruption. An appalling and offensive situation. The AO is working well with Stohrer. Bohle is glad that with Hess gone he still has a supporter in us.

Film problems discussed with Hippler. Central management of film theatres. They must be removed from Ufa. But not at the price of raising taxes. Gutterer is to deal with the problem. Radio issues with Glasmaier. Relaxation of programming schedules during the summer. Request concerts to be replaced by concerts from the front for the homeland. More rhythmic dance music. The boys at the front want it. Particularly on the military radio stations, then. Presentation of a broadcasting plan for after the war. A few showpiece major stations covering the entire Reich. Plus a number of regional stations which will fulfil local needs. Try out the new fanfares for the coming campaign. Some very good ones among them.

Discuss the work of the Radio Department with Diewerge. He is administering the inheritance left to him by Berndt very well. Is hard-working and gets things done. Wächter reports on matters concerning the Reich Propaganda Leadership.

A mass of the day's problems with Gutterer. We must not allow our propaganda effort to be dissipated. The department chiefs are releasing too many small contributions for unimportant publications. It all ends up being glanced at over breakfast, whatever the intention. We must concentrate on producing fewer, but more telling pieces.

Bormann has issued a circular to the Party, in which he introduces himself. His position is under the strongest possible attack from all sides. He is, I believe, neither honest nor clear-minded. He has intrigued rather than worked his way into this job. The Party leadership senses this instinctively, and hence its rejection of him. He will have a lot of difficulty in getting his way. Even the Führer is beginning to see through him. Bormann's dealings with Hess were disloyal. Hess was short-sighted but decent. What, however, can we expect from Bormann?

Work at full stretch right through the afternoon. By the evening, my brain is buzzing with all the problems I have attended to. Sometimes it is too much for one man's capacities.

Magda is at work in Schwanenwerder, so as to have everything arranged by Whitsun.

Newsreel with music in the evening. Now better. Order a few changes. Discuss film and script problems with Hippler. General questions of popular education.

Vichy and Washington are at daggers drawn. Marshal Pétain is determined not to stand for anything and has sent the French press into action against Roosevelt. The language they are using is refreshingly unambiguous. Very good from our point of view.

Look at a pile of English newspapers. I come off very well in them. And all of them are more strongly pessimistic than one had expected.

Check an anti-cancer film. Strong attack against miracle cures. Now that Hess and his crazy ideas are no longer with us, we can gladly release it.

At my desk until deep into the night. A very mild night.

Yesterday: No air raids on either side. We attack only shipping targets. 33,000 tons of tankers sunk. This hits England hard. No change in North Africa. Surrender in Abyssinia. We attack Crete with airborne troops. A dangerous project. But it has been meticulously prepared. We hope to God that it succeeds. In this initial stage, however, everything is still secret. But London will soon make an announcement.

War-fever in the USA. The panic-mongers are stirring and stoking the fires. One war speech after another. Strong exchanges between Washington and Vichy. But Pétain knows where his bread is buttered. Where is the USA going? My article for *Das Reich* will cause something of a stir in this respect. An Egyptian steamer has been sunk with a lot of US passengers and, of course, matériel of war on board. The Americans are trying to make a huge sensation out of it; it is already being called 'another Lusitania'. But all the passengers were saved. They cannot be used as martyrs.

Tiessler and Fischer warn me against constructing a Seventh Chamber out of the KdF in co-operation with Ley. They claim that the Party would be pushed into the background. Bormann also says this. I believe the opposite. The KdF must be looked after. It has millions of members, after all. Ley cannot do it alone. And I do not intend to allow my people to be excluded. So we should have no fear. We shall bring the intelligentsia to this marriage, and Ley will bring the masses. A good match. And the fact that Bormann is against it does not prove me wrong. To the contrary!

Martin brings up a number of delicate military matters. One concerns the fact that the Hess Affair is still affecting the Wehrmacht. But we do not intend to mention the business again, since it will soon die the death of its own accord.

Gutterer has some organisational problems. He is working hard and intelligently.

D'Alquen reports on the South-Eastern Campaign. He went through a great deal and has some amazing stories to tell. He is furious at the Italians, who behaved in an impossible fashion during the surrender negotiations. But Sepp Dietrich, whose conduct has been marvellous, was not slow to express his opinion of them. Naumann was always in the front line and fought boldly and bravely. Just as I have always expected of him.

I give a speech to the Gau Propaganda Leaders in which I outline the situation and the Hess affair. Long talk with Ley about Hess. Like the rest of us, he is still suffering from the shock of it all. He asserts quite firmly that Hess was a morphine addict, which would explain a great deal. His professional and personal judgement is very harsh. He has more respect for Bormann than I would have expected. Bormann is, of course, a good worker. If he shows himself to be honest and loyal, he may well provide an effective bridge between the Party and the Führer. If . . .

Ello Quandt visits me and gives me a rather confused account of her activities and of her experiences in Paris. I end up really none the wiser. She now intends to launch herself enthusiastically into the National Socialist Movement. God save us!

Reception for the Air Defence League people from all over the Reich. I convey my thanks to the men. I am told a lot about the truly heroic actions of these men in Kiel, Bremen and Hamburg. The public's attitude is exemplary everywhere. Heavier raids only make people harder. This is, it seems, also true of the English, at least at the moment. But sometime it has to reach its limit.

Churchill addresses the House of Commons. About Crete, naturally. But the information he gives is still quite vague. He refers to several prisoners taken. But he is unable to report any victories.

We have not yet published anything about this enterprise.

But by the evening all seems well and has gone according to plan so far. We can only hope that things continue to go as well. Heiduschke will be there, and perhaps Harald as well. I am rather worried about the fact.

Back to Lanke very late and very tired. Read for a while.

22 May 1941 (Thursday)

Yesterday: No air activity on either side. The weather is too misty. English propaganda claims that they have Crete firmly in their hands. But that is what the propaganda says. The reality is that we have landed four regiments there, they have conducted themselves brilliantly so far, and there can be no question of a failure to establish ourselves. This has now become a prestige matter for both sides. If the invasion of Crete succeeds, the US press maintains, then one against Britain would also be possible. We have not yet announced anything. The Führer intended to at the beginning, but then decided to wait, since success is not yet assured and we intend to give the English time to show their true face. We are only moving on to the offensive abroad, particularly against Churchill's lying statement that our people have been dressing up in New Zealand uniforms. Otherwise we are letting things run their course for the moment. Towards midday, the English reports begin to turn a little more subdued. So we were right to say nothing.

40,000 tons sunk from a single convoy. Another good, cheering statistic.

Heavy fighting continues in North Africa, with no change in the situation. To and fro in Syria and Iraq. We must try to take a closer look.

As a whole, Churchill's speech was little more than an attempt to gain time, without real substance. We do not react to it. The Crete Affair has totally obscured the Hess Affair. The world's press talks of nothing else. It is a prestige issue of the first order for both sides.

I make 140 million cigarettes from the NSV stocks available for Berlin. We are also raising production slightly. We cannot let this calamity continue completely unchallenged. There are also great problems with clothing. It is impossible to buy the amounts specified on the ration card, and there are no shoes at all. But we cannot do much about it. C'est la guerre! I shall have the matter investigated again.

Bormann is burrowing away at the Church question again. But in trivial ways, a sort of old-fashioned iconoclasm. I inform him via Tiessler that I can see little constructive advantage in such activities.

Relaxation of radio scheduling to take effect immediately. Our people and our soldiers want light music. Otherwise they will listen to English stations. I do not intend to listen to the killjoys any more. Better light music than foreign propaganda. Circular to the Party, in which this is explained in detail.

Fischer from Graz describes the situation in the newly-annexed district of Styria. Population almost exclusively Slovene. 100,000 have been expelled, mostly intelligentsia, and the rest will be Germanised. This will be a difficult task. I instruct him to formulate a propaganda plan to this end. I shall put large funds at his disposal for the job . . .

. . . Discuss the Hess Affair again with Bohle. He came close to flying with Hess, in the belief that everything had been ordered by the Führer. He also translated the documents that Hess took on his mission, in complete ignorance of the real intent. He believed that the Führer was intending to bypass Ribbentrop and make peace with England through Hess. A naïve assumption. Hess's brother has gone completely to pieces. He faces complete ruin.

I address *Landesgruppe* leaders of the AO from all over the world. Give them an outline of the situation. I think the speech is very successful. In any case, things are made absolutely clear.

Film statistics: our financial success is enormous. Top of the league are *Request Concert* and *Ohm Krüger*. A total of thirty-six millions in profits again.

Lanke. Work! Deal with a mass of trivia.

Magda and Ello arrive late in the afternoon, and then d'Alqen. He takes us through to the end of the story of the South-Eastern Campaign. He has a deal of respect for the fighting spirit of the individual Englishman. The achievements of the SS include some real swashbuckling touches. The SS fought magnificently.

It is a good thing that we have such a Party army.

Talk about the Hess Affair. The soldiers' judgement is pretty clear.

De Gaulle has announced that his troops have advanced into Syria. He now intends to take the country from Vichy. No further details are available.

London has announced that she intends to court-martial our paratroops who were taken prisoner on Crete and perhaps have them shot. This would cost the English dear: ten to one. But we shall wait and see. In any event, we spend a lot of time denying that our people were wearing fake uniforms. And in fact this was not the case.

The *News Chronicle* prints a desperate cry of help to the USA. It would hardly be possible to imagine a more dramatic picture of England's situation. This is how bad things have become over there. We give a lot of attention to this item, which was, of course, inspired by Churchill.

I am in the process of trying out light music for the radio. It is very hard to decide how far one can, or should, go. It must be real popular music, but not obvious rubbish. I choose a middle way . . .

23 May 1941 (Friday)

Yesterday: No air activity on either side. The weather over England is still too cloudy. Hard fighting for Crete. We seem to have gained a firm foothold. Despite all the English counter-attacks, we are holding our ground and making continued progress. We have not been lucky at sea. Two transporters with 700 men on board and heavy equipment, on their way from Patras, struck mines. With heavy losses.

We attack an English naval squadron in the Mediterranean with Stukas. A number of satisfactory hits. This takes some of the pressure from Crete. The mood in London is very pessimistic. We spread invasion rumours via Switzerland. A diversionary tactic. The enemy will certainly swallow it.

During the last three days, the USA has taken a more cautious line. There is less talk of, and enthusiasm for, war. Roosevelt is strongly influenced by public opinion. The loud cries for help from London, particularly that in the *News Chronicle*, have had a sobering effect. Perhaps, despite everything, we shall be able to avoid the worst by clever delaying tactics.

We are still saying absolutely nothing about the Crete business. We do not intend to turn the invasion into a prestige issue under any circumstances. At the moment this is very unpleasant so far as our news people are concerned, But on the whole it is right and expedient.

I demand a clear attitude in our propaganda on the tobacco issue. Either we have no cigarette advertisements or we have no propaganda about the dangers of smoking. Otherwise the entire business is too unconvincing. After all, we can hardly present a split personality to the public.

The Führer has rejected compulsory female labour for the moment. And so we shall have to launch a big propaganda campaign for volunteers. I have no great hopes of it. It has been a day of lunacies. Ohnesorge wants to print a manual for his post people at the front which is packed with infelicities and idiocies. I stop it. This is the kind of thing I am forced to concern myself with, even during a war . . .

. . . Party issues with Tiessler. He is still making trouble, influenced by Bormann. But I shall wean him away from this.

Koch from East Prussia reports on the Eastern Question. He is to go to

M., Schickedanz to the U., Lohse to the B.* I am nervous of Rosenberg and Schickedanz. They are doctrinaire types. Otherwise, however, everything is going very well. R. will splinter like touchwood. And our propaganda will produce a masterpiece. Things are gradually moving into gear. Transports are moving back and forth, private travel has been severely curtailed. Now comes the big invasion deception. I am letting Koch have Paltzo from Paris. I shall send Maurer from Zagreb to take his place.

Schmidtke reports on the situation in France. The mood has improved considerably. We are staging some more cultural events. I intend to send the German Opera House company first. Otherwise, Schmidtke has little new to report. He has noticed that I no longer trust him completely. He is still sounding me out, but he is quite right. I had Paltzo come with him as a cover. Once he has gone, Maurer will know how to get his way.

Reinhardt reports: a row between Schirach/Kaufmann and Amann. And I am being asked to sack Kaufmann. I shall not do it. Amann will have to do that deed himself . . .

. . . Crete is the big talking-point. But we are unable to publish anything yet. Churchill is turning it into a real prestige issue. This is stupid and unwise to a degree. His address to the House of Commons was very firm. Meanwhile the London newspapers are screaming: 'We shall defend Crete to our last breath'. Well, we shall see what is behind it.

Dr Dietrich rings up: Bömer has been shooting his mouth off in an absolutely crazy fashion. I fear that I shall have to discipline him severely. It is all due to boozing.

To Lanke in the evening. A fine, mild May evening. What a beautiful world! But for people, wicked people! Nevertheless, one has to find a way of dealing with them, too.

(A new volume of the diaries begins here. Prefaced by the motto: 'Victory is with our Banners!')

24 May 1941 (Saturday)
Yesterday: Bad weather over England. No air activity on either side. The situation in Crete is already much improved. The English have had to withdraw their fighter squadrons. We have been bombing their airfields continually. We now have 15,000 men over there, some with heavy armaments. Bitter fighting. One of our convoys has been badly hit. Two ships sunk. Most of the crewmen saved. The English will have to pull out their fleet for the duration of the action. Our Luftwaffe has sunk four of their cruisers. On the whole, one can hope that things will have stablised to some extent in a few days' time.

* It seems probable that Goebbels is referring to Moscow, the Ukraine and the *Baltikum* (Baltic states). Moscow was, of course, never captured; Koch became Nazi governor of the Ukraine, while Lohse ruled the Baltic states, renamed the *Ostland*.

Contrary to previous reports, it seems that the Italians are still resisting in East Africa, and heroically at that. Their fleet has also made a brave contribution to the Crete project. They have plenty to make up for, of course. London is clearly playing for time over Crete. The effect of our action there has been enormous. Especially in the USA. Peace rumours are being bandied about there, said to originate not from us but from London. We are hard at work spreading rumours of an invasion of England. Making particular use of the neutral press. I hope the English swallow them. Darlan has made a tough speech rejecting English accusations. Germany, he says, will defeat England without France's help.

Public opinion in the USA is undergoing a perceptible change. Roosevelt will have to pay heed to this. He cannot do exactly as he likes. Our power-position in Europe can no longer be ignored.

Bömer has got himself into a very unpleasant situation by some drunken talk about Russia. I do not know whether I shall be able to help him. He has named Professor Hommel's wife as a favourable witness, but she has been unable to help him much by her statement.

Discussion with Jagow. He is soon off to Budapest as ambassador. A good thing that our diplomatic corps is to be perked up by an infusion from the SA.

Hinkel is doing great things so far as entertainment for the troops is concerned, but from now on he will have to devote more time to his duties in Berlin.

Gutterer has been promoted to State Secretary. I am very glad for his sake. In him I shall always have a faithful retainer. The whole ministry has welcomed his promotion. Discuss the question of R. with him. I am sending Taubert as liaison man with Rosenberg. R. will be divided into her constituent parts. Each republic will get a fine dose of freedom. The line is that we shall no longer tolerate a huge monolith in the East. The question is: will Rosenberg be able to master the situation? We shall help him as best we can. Thirteen Propaganda Companies will be put into the field. Saturation tactics. Not just to come up with news material but also to make propaganda among the natives. A unique assignment. We shall soon be able to reach agreement with Rosenberg. He has Gauleiter Meyer of Münster as his deputy. One can deal with him. Bolshevism will be a thing of the past. Thus we shall have fulfilled our one great duty to History.

The relaxation of radio scheduling has now been announced. Millions will welcome it . . .

. . . Out to Lanke at a reasonable hour and continue to work there. Clarify the Bömer case with Frau von Kalckreuth. It seems that he behaved in a less harmful way than the Foreign Ministry's creatures have, for obvious reasons, claimed.

110,000 tons sunk by U-boats. This hits England hardest of all. We take the opportunity to release the news of Prien's loss. Three English destroyers and five motor-torpedo boats sunk in the Mediterranean off Crete. The affair is becoming a naval graveyard for the English, just like Narvik. I believe, for this reason, that they will soon withdraw.

The weather here is so glorious. But one has no chance to enjoy it. All one can do is answer the telephone, which never stops ringing, and act on the news. An exciting, tension-filled life. I shall miss it, in a way, when it is gone.

Short drive through the forest. The new Norwegian log-cabin is just being built. It has a quite idyllic situation.

Look at some of the new colour films. We have come a long way in this field.

A long talk with Dr Bömer and Dr Dietrich in the evening. The whole affair seems to be have been blown up deliberately by the Foreign Ministry. But I try to put a little of the fear of God into Bömer.

It seems that Harald really is involved in Crete. Everything is going well down there.

25 May 1941 (Sunday)

Yesterday: Minor enemy air raids on West Germany. Very little activity on our side. Crete is the focus of public attention. News of it is scarce, both from our side and from the English. So far as we are concerned, things are going according to plan. But we cannot release any news, since success is not yet absolutely assured. The battle between the fleet and the Luftwaffe is still raging in the eastern Mediterranean. Unfortunately, we have had to modify our report that the Luftwaffe sunk four enemy cruisers. It was only two. The phrasing of the relevant statement was distinctly maladroit.

Lindbergh and Wheeler have made strong speeches opposing intervention. At big mass-meetings in New York. Roosevelt will not be able to ignore this. We give it no more than moderate attention, so as not to harm Lindbergh. But he is a brave lad! A change of mood is becoming increasingly apparent in the USA. Roosevelt is, to an extent, trapped. He can no longer go his own sweet way, but must take public opinion into account. The Führer has now received Cudahy, former American Ambassador in Brussels. His line during the interview: invasion of the USA = an invasion of the moon. Protection of convoys by the USA will lead to war. The Führer is still considering the timing of the interview's publication. But it will do us great good. Cudahy is invaluable from our point of view. I make the introduction of a weekly hour's programme for the USA on the short wave, to be named after me, dependent on developments there. The specialists are convinced that it will be very effective. I am still not so certain. Vichy would like to have back their radio station at Alouis, currently being used by us. This, however, is out of the question. I place a station at the French government's disposal, but it is one that they will first have to rebuild and repair.

Discuss preparatory measures against R. with Gutterer and Taubert.

Taubert has made quite a lot of progress in this area. Thirteen Propaganda Companies will be involved. A Propaganda unit will be left behind in each major city where its task will be to make propaganda aimed at the local population. A very ambitious and difficult task. But we are making every preparation . . .

. . . I have a lot to do and work on at Lanke.

We issue an initial, fairly optimistic report about Crete. The effect on the public is really sensational. Profound pessimism about the position in Crete so far as London is concerned. Since the British air force was withdrawn, they have given up all hope. The chorus of woe is starting up in the USA as well. Moscow admires the audacity of the assault – a friend indeed! Now, at last, we are beginning to put our propaganda into gear. The Herr Englishmen will be spared nothing. Harald and Heiduschke are certainly involved down there, so I am informed by Athens.

A German squadron led by the *Bismarck* has encountered strong English naval forces. An English battleship, probably the *Hood*, has been destroyed in the course of the action. Off Iceland. Three British destroyers sunk in the Eastern Mediterranean, three seriously damaged. This is a black day for London. More peace rumours are being peddled all over the world, and reports are beginning to appear in the press. We maintain a determined silence.

Colonel-General Grauert has been shot down over France. An officer with an excellent record in the Luftwaffe.

A Saturday that is packed to overflowing with news. I am busy the entire afternoon making sure that it is properly directed. The British Admiralty has admitted the loss of the *Hood*. A shell in the magazine, blown to bits with all hands. This is a real disaster for the enemy. Plus the serious blows in the Mediterranean.

The invasion rumours spread by us have been effective. England is very nervous. So far as Russia is concerned, we have successfully perpetrated a massive news fraud. So many canards and false reports are in the air that abroad they no longer have any idea of what is false and what is correct. This is the way it has to be. It is just the atmosphere that we need.

Magda visits in the evening. She is very worried about Harald, but I talk her out of it.

We talk for a long time. A week can bring a lot of news.

26 May 1941 (Monday)

Yesterday: More troops landed on Crete. We have inflicted huge losses on the English fleet there. Churchill is being forced to pay dearly for his decision to resist. The operations are progressing as expected. The English are trying to make out that we are behind schedule, or are ascribing fantastic losses to our forces, but we have no trouble shrugging them off.

More bitter fighting around Tobruk. Very little air activity on either side. The weather is too bad. The public seems to believe that the lack of air activity has something to do with readiness for peace. This is, of course, pure nonsense.

The *Hood* was dealt with in five minutes, and a second warship was seriously damaged. Reaction in London and also in the USA devastating. The English continue to make urgent pleas to the USA for convoy protection. But they are getting the cold shoulder.

We now have some real material for our news service once again, and we are giving it everything we have. The Crete business, in particular, is being exploited to the hilt. We are able to lash out to our heart's content again. It is sheer bliss.

The Führer has taken a rather serious view of the Bömer case and has handed it over to the Gestapo for investigation. Things could turn very unpleasant for Bömer. All down to that damned alcohol. I have done all I can for Bömer. If, despite everything, he ends up in trouble, then he has only himself to blame.

Another little strike in Brussels. The people are starving there. All they want is food, but we cannot give them any. Let them complain to the English about their blockade. Not that one can expect starving people to understand such things.

Visitors for lunch and in the afternoon: our new State Secretary, Gutterer, Hinkel, Schlösser, the Hommels, the Kimmichs, and both the Quandt ladies. I am able to discuss a host of issues with the men. Gutterer is doing a good job. He is very popular in all quarters. The Bömer case is making more and more waves. The Foreign Ministry is deliberately inflating the affair. Now Bömer has been taken into custody by the Gestapo for interrogation. Dr Dietrich rings me up, outraged. But we intend to wait for the moment and see what happens.

21,000 tons sunk in the Atlantic. The *Hood* and Crete have made the world hold its breath. We are banging our drum for all we are worth. All the accumulated dross of years is being taken out of store and thrown into the fray. We are drawing out the English lies *ad absurdum*.

Newsreel in the evening. A good selection. But not a war newsreel. Things will soon be very different. We are all looking forward to that.

A lot of talk in the evening. This was a good, profitable Sunday.

27 May 1941 (Tuesday)

Yesterday: No incursions on either side. Battle for Crete continues. We have landed more reinforcements. The Greek King has fled to Cairo. Leaving behind a pompous declaration which we methodically cut to pieces.

Our Luftwaffe is wreaking fearful havoc on the English naval units off Crete. The area is turning into a real ships' graveyard for London. For all that, the English continue to lie their hearts out. English defeats turn into victories, German victories are defeats. This is more or less the line they are taking.

The sinking of the *Hood* is a devastating blow for England. In particular, the effect in the USA can hardly be overestimated. A real coup for us.

The English treatment of our paratroops on Crete is a scandal. But I do not allow it to be published for fear of unsettling our public. General rule: the English must not be dismissed as cowards. By doing this, we discredit the bravery of our own people. Berndt has also written to me in this vein from America . . .

. . . The Bömer case is occupying a lot of my time. The Foreign Ministry wove a clever web of intrigue against him, but he gave them plenty of ammunition. I am doing all I can to keep the worst from him. Ribbentrop is not a fair opponent. He is mixing politics with the world of the champagne salesman,* where, of course, it is a question of clobbering one's competitors by any means available. But just let him try it with me!

London is spreading the wildest rumours about Iraq: the Prime Minister is said to have fled, his cause is lost, etc. However, this is all bluff, and we are losing no time in saying so. Otherwise, the press war is enjoying a lull. Everyone is waiting for Roosevelt's 'Fireside Chat'. People are expecting a lot from it, but I am not so sure. Raeder has given an interview to the Japanese about the USA: protection of convoys will mean a shooting war! The effect on the USA is explosive. It will further affect Roosevelt's attitude. He cannot by any means do as he wishes, but must take proper notice of popular opinion.

Put the finishing touches to the newsreel in the evening. Has turned out to be excellent. Look at the material from Crete: a dramatic and thrilling piece of reporting. A pity that we cannot release it for the moment. We must first await further progress there. All the indications are very good at the moment. Hippler shows me a film about cultural life in America: unspeakable! The place is not a country, it is a cultural desert. And they say they want to civilise us. A good thing that they do not have the power to do so. Our great cultural act was to defeat democracy.

28 May 1941 (Wednesday)

Yesterday: A black day: the *Bismarck* encounters vastly superior forces, defends herself desperately, is hit by a few air-launched torpedoes, and sinks. A fearful blow which will be felt by the entire nation. London is crowing with triumph, and is careful to admit the worst of the English casualties from Crete at the same time: at least two cruisers and four destroyers. A stroke of luck for Churchill. We shall recover from this blow,

* Ribbentrop's former profession.

384

but nevertheless it is a very painful one. And today every German will feel what I feel.

But the situation on Crete is good. We had a few setbacks to cope with, but now we have recovered. The fortunes of war have not been with us this past week, but this is about to change. And misfortune hardens a man. Pretty heavy English shipping losses reported from the USA. Experience tells us that they only admit what it suits them to admit. Heavy fighting continues around Tobruk. No air activity on either side.

I halt the entire propaganda effort relating to the *Hood* and the *Bismarck* in time to save embarrassment, and switch the focus to the Mediterranean. In the USA they are waiting for Roosevelt's speech. De Valera has made a tough speech attacking England for introducing conscription in Northern Ireland.

Work on the draft plan for a postwar radio network. I am not yet completely clear on this issue. All the Gauleiters want their own radio stations. This is, of course, impossible.

Hunke delivers a report on the work of the Foreign Department. He hâs coped magnificently with the job.

Circular re. salary freeze in the theatre. This has become an urgent necessity. And then a series of film and theatre problems, for which I can summon little interest on this black day.

Mull over the Bömer business again. Judging from the statements so far, things do not look quite so bad for him. Studentkowski is now to join the ministry. He will take over the Evening Review on the radio, working alongside Fritzsche, who to add to my troubles is still very ill. Worries and more worries!

Admiral Pomsel reports on the work of the Society for Defence Science, which has been doing a good job. Then I address the Gau administrators on propaganda in wartime and the war situation. They are all good patriots.

Lay down basic guidelines for military censorship with Colonel Weichhold. We manage to arrive at a quite acceptable working agreement.

Discuss a few unpleasant issues affecting the Wehrmacht with Martin. Some things stink there, too, but one tends not to smell them so easily.

Maurer reports on Zagreb and the incompetence and disloyalty of the Foreign Ministry. One cannot work with these fellows. They are too unfair. I shall now send Maurer, who is a fantastic worker, to Gutterer, so that later we can use him in the East. Problems of the day with Gutterer. He is my faithful henchman, on to whose broad shoulders I can lay any burden.

Address the Berlin flak forces at the Admiral's Palace in the afternoon. Thanks and recognition for their services. Watch part of the performance there along with the flak people. But I have little time to spare.

Ley now wants to have the Seventh Chamber signed and sealed. I share his aim. So let us get going!

Back to Lanke late in the evening, exhausted. Magda has been to the doctor about her heart condition. But, thank God, it is nothing serious.

Churchill has made a speech. But not a triumphant one. The British naval losses off Crete, which he used the favourable opportunity to announce along with the sinking of the *Bismarck*, have greatly marred the English joy. And the situation on Crete has started to look serious for the English. They have already admitted some withdrawals and declared that they cannot make much use of their fleet. Thus they have little cause for celebration. The naval graveyard in the Mediterranean is having a depressive effect on English morale. They are marching to muffled drums.

Late in the evening I work on a new book, a collection of my speeches and essays from 1939–41, which is to be published at Christmas. Fräulein Honig is working very hard with me on it.

To bed late, tired, and very sad.

29 May 1941 (Thursday)

Yesterday: Roosevelt has made his speech. Very demagogic and aggressive. With the most reckless accusations against us. Proclaimed a national state of emergency. But gone no further. We must wait and see what he does next. In any event, there is no talk of war for the moment. He dare not. Officially, London is delighted, but Reuter makes no attempt to hide its deep disappointment. They had expected more.

The Führer intends to answer Roosevelt personally. I write a leader-article attacking him, but have to publish it under a pseudonym to avoid pre-empting the Führer's statement.

Roosevelt's speech overshadows all other issues, even the war at sea. We are the only people pushing the question of England's losses in the Mediterranean. But we are pushing it very hard. We are making a big noise and refusing to be diverted by the loss of the *Bismarck*. No details are yet known regarding her sinking. The English admit they had to marshal almost the entire Home Fleet to trap her. A German U-boat that was in the area heard gunfire being exchanged right to the end. A Spanish auxiliary cruiser saved what men she could. Unfortunately, our report of yesterday, including the last messages from Admiral Luetjens, gave away our code key. We were rather over-hasty in that matter and now we must pay for it. A very unpleasant business, which Dr Dietrich will suffer for. We can only hope that the *Prinz Eugen** will not come to any harm as a result. The damage inflicted on the English Mediterranean Fleet is enormous. And they have lost a further 72,000 tons to German U-boats. This is wonderful to hear.

Things are developing favourably on Crete. We now have secure positions which can be used as a base for operations. The English fleet is moving into the area again; to look for a few victories or to cover the evacuation? We shall soon see.

* A powerful new cruiser and the *Bismarck*'s companion in the first part of her cruise.

A few incursions here over West Germany. We do hardly anything over England.

Tiessler reports to me on Party work. I am getting on quite well with Bormann. He is fulfilling my every wish. But we do have problems with the Foreign Ministry. The question of propaganda in the USA, yet again. The Foreign Ministry would far prefer to do nothing. But in the long term that will get us nowhere.

Now I have Frick sticking his nose into purely propaganda matters. Urged on by the Foreign Ministry. But I defend myself vigorously. What a cross I have to bear!

I am fighting a desperate battle against lack of security in all the Berlin ministries. I shall now have to ask the Gestapo for their assistance, not for the first time.

My article appears in the *Völkischer Beobachter* in a prominent position, without a name, under the byline 'V.B.'. The real author will, of course, be easily recognisable from the style.

Work on at Lanke in the afternoon. It is quiet and tranquil here, a place where one can gather one's strength and at least do some coherent thinking.

We have now settled the business of the Seventh Chamber and the KdF. The Party agrees.

Report from Estonia: The Bolsheviks' mismanagement there cries out to high heaven. We shall be welcomed like demi-gods when we march in. And then we shall have wiped this blemish from our shield of honour.

Reports from Italy refer to continued poor morale. But then morale in England is said to be deteriorating, too. Churchill has nothing to smile about, and the Bolsheviks are rapidly gathering support. But it is better not to depend on such things. If they happen, then that is a bonus.

Things progressing well on Crete. Chania is in our hands. The English reports are black on black. To make up for them, London has the *Bismarck* story, which is now being exploited for all it is worth. Likewise in the USA. But this will not last long. The speech by Roosevelt dominates the scene, but it has had a frosty reception in London. They had obviously expected more.

Moscow still buzzing with rumours. Stalin seems to be gradually seeing the light. But the rest of the time he stares like a rabbit with a snake.

Antonescu intends to replace his generals with a civilian government. They will be out of the same mould.

Glorious summer! Mild, fine evenings! But one can enjoy none of it.

30 May 1941 (Friday)

Yesterday: Roosevelt's speech has had a very mixed reception. London is anything but satisfied. The New York Jew-press is trying to goad him on. But he has refused any further comment. Our German propaganda has reacted very forcefully. Along the lines of my article in the *V.B.*, which appears without a name. The polemical battle continues. Japan has declared that war will bring war in its wake. But for the moment Roosevelt seems to be confining himself to his usual activity, which is to chip away at neutrality until there is nothing left. And he will be very successful at that.

In London they seem to have no idea what to do. The King has made another speech.

A few English incursions into North-West Germany with the aim of mining our harbours. We attack English coastal towns. But in only middling force.

60,000 tons sunk by our submarine fleet. The *Bismarck* business is still a talking-point. Attempts to save her crewmen rather unsuccessful. Only five recovered in all. *Bismarck* defended herself to the last shell and took a destroyer and five aircraft with her.

The advance continues on Crete. The English have withdrawn to positions further to the rear. No serious danger at the moment. United Press has reported Schmeling shot while trying to escape from an English POW cage. But still unconfirmed. The loss of such a decent, brave boy would be regrettable.

We have had some partial successes in North Africa. I am currently organising a big programme of entertainments for our boys down there in the Afrika Korps. Berndt has written another instructive report.

All manner of administrative junk. Investigation into Bömer now completed. He is not guilty of high treason, but behaved negligently. The Führer will have to make the decision about him.

Receive the SS commander in Berlin. Address the Press and Propaganda Leaders of the Female Labour Service. Discuss the postwar radio situation with the appropriate departments. Basic principles: let the cable service expand organically, likewise the television, and re-establish the old Reich Stations on a looser basis, if possible. Then vigorously expand the capacity of the *Deutschlandsender* and the Reich Station Berlin on long wave, so that they can be heard far beyond the Reich borders. This is the initial programme. Once it has been carried through, then we shall proceed according to the existing state of technical development.

I watch new film footage of Crete: very good and at times extraordinarily dramatic. Only part of it can be used for public showing, since it contains many military secrets.

Look at a few English newsreels. Interesting, but no match for us.

Hunke delivers a report on our economic capacity to wage war. Very gratifying!

English pamphlet on the air battle over England. Highly exaggerated and boastful, but nevertheless extraordinarily skilfully done.

Work at Lanke in the afternoon.

The Italians are landing a regiment on Crete. Things look very bad there for the English. They are already talking about their own courage and our serious losses, a sure indication that they have lost the game. They are finding it hard to conceal their gloom. They are forced to admit the loss of the cruiser *York*, a big auxiliary cruiser and a submarine. These are all painful wounds on the corpus of the Empire. The War in the air brought a total of fifty-two losses for England, thirty-five for us during the past six days. Thus on the whole a gloomy balance for England. We have only one weak point: the loss of the *Bismarck*.

Reuter has now confirmed that Schmeling was shot while trying to escape. This is particularly regrettable, because he was such a nice fellow. His wife will be inconsolable. I am convinced that the English killed him out of sheer pique.

Speak to the children on the telephone. They are all well. How they twitter down the telephone. What a treasure they are! But they are a great worry to me as well. Every morsel of happiness is dearly bought.

Carry on reading for a long while. Warm rain is falling evenly outside. It is quiet and empty in my room. How hard life is!

31 May 1941 (Saturday)

Yesterday: No incursions. England's situation on Crete is hopeless. Their resistance has collapsed. Flight! Our other forces have linked up with the paratroops at Rethymos. Heraklion is now completely in our hands. The Italians are advancing from the East. The English are beginning to run from combat. The island's fall cannot be far off. Our propaganda is operating at full power. We concentrate on Churchill, who said he would defend the island to the last drop of blood. He is spared nothing. The English have been guilty of appalling atrocities towards our men who were taken prisoner. We announce the severest possible retaliation. Our Luftwaffe has fought magnificently. Schmeling is still alive, after all, and is in a hospital in Athens. I inform Anny Ondra by telephone, and she is overjoyed. After so much suffering. I intend to deal with that loudmouth from United Press. On the other hand, United Press has also been reporting the English atrocities on Crete. We are putting the main blame for these on Churchill personally.

Hard fighting near Tobruk, but no change in the situation.

London is totally confused by the imminent loss of Crete. They are simply disclaiming any precise knowledge and preparing the English public for the worst. We are making a lot of noise on our English-language service. But I forbid them to use the 'Siegfried Line'* song. This will only serve to stiffen resistance.

So far as the rest is concerned, the English are devastated. We have come out on top again.

---

* *We'll Hang Out Our Washing on the Siegfried Line.* A British popular song of the phoney war period.

Situation in the USA unclear. Roosevelt's speech has had a mixed reception. Lindbergh has made a very good, spirited reply, but we ignore it so as not to harm it. The entire world is waiting anxiously for further developments. In response to more rumours in the USA, Tokyo has re-affirmed her loyalty to the Axis.

The Wehrmacht High Command is complaining that we are laying on the propaganda for the SS too thickly. It has a demoralising effect on the army. This is not entirely unjustified, and I shall therefore restrict it a little. But the High Command must also improve the channels of communication with Berlin, or our best material will not reach us in time. I complain about Brauchitsch. He too is beating the drum for himself rather too loudly.

Try out the new England-fanfares. Well conceived. Fritzsche suggests that we should give more voice training to our news announcers on the radio. The people in London are far more sure of themselves. From now on I shall have instructions issued on the intonation to be used during important announcements. This is important if they are to be effective. One is always learning something . . .

. . . The Führer has decided: Bömer will face the People's Court. I am very sorry, but I can do nothing about it. The Foreign Ministry has played a very dirty trick on us. But Bömer's own loud-mouthed behaviour was also to blame.

Hinkel reports on issues affecting the Reich Culture Chamber. He is also chary of a Seventh Chamber. I, however, am not. I have procedural documents drawn up. If possible, we want agreement with Rosenberg, who has, of course, lodged a protest.

Frick and Lammers lodge a protest against Dr Naumann. I insist on his promotion.

A long session with Martin: Operation Barbarossa* is on the move. We shall now be launching the first big deception. The entire state and military machine is being mobilised. Only a few people know the real reason. I am forced to lead the entire ministry along a false trail, running the personal risk that in the end, when everything rolls in the opposite direction, I shall suffer a loss of prestige. So begin! Fourteen divisions will be transported westwards. The England invasion theme will be slowly brought to the forefront. I am having an invasion of England theme written, new fanfares composed, English-speakers brought in, setting up Propaganda Companies for England, etc. The whole thing is set to start in two weeks. It will all cost a lot of time, effort, labour resources, and money, but it is worth it. The only men still to be let into the secret at the ministry are Hadamovsky and Titel. If everyone keeps quiet, and with such a small circle involved one can assume that they will, then the deception will succeed. So off we march!

The coming weeks will be very nerve-wracking. But they will provide

* The official designation of the invasion of Russia.

further proof of the supreme skill of our propaganda. The other civilian ministers have no idea what is going on. They are working towards the apparent goal of England. I am eager to see how long it will be until things really take off.

To Schwanenwerder at midday. Magda is having a lot of trouble with her heart. She has been under great strain, worrying about Harald. She shows me the newly-furnished house. Everything will soon be ready and looks wonderful. If only the plumbing system would stop breaking down. I would like to move in as soon as possible. An hour's chat with Magda. I am so very sorry for her. We shall do everything we can to get her back to par as soon as possible.

To Lanke. Report from Italy: the monarchy in a stronger position. The *Re* is the real imperialist. The Duce has his hands full trying to restrain him. Fascism has lost heavily in terms of prestige. Starace has been put out to grass. A real blessing!

Reports from Croatia: deep gloom, Pavelic dissatisfied because of the treaty with Italy, anger against the Italians and strong pro-German feeling.

Report from Latvia: a message from the hell that is Russia. They are almost praying: 'May Hitler come!' There will be an awakening. And the collapse of Bolshevism will be without parallel.

Our propaganda is working at full steam against England.

We are busily boxing Churchill's ears with the Crete fiasco.

Now we have ammunition again.

The British cruiser *York* was destroyed by our Luftwaffe a week ago in Suda Bay. The English had been issuing denials, but they have admitted it now that Suda is in our hands. We are tarring Churchill with this one nice and thick.

Things are not particularly good in Iraq. London has officially announced that Rashid Ali has fled to Iran. This may, however, be untrue. In any event, we do not react. The English are already close to Bagdad.

The former Kaiser is dying. This should provide some interest for a day at the most.

Magda is very worried about Harald. Particularly after the reports of German prisoners being mutilated. I comfort her and cheer her up a little.

New York has also given up Crete for lost. A serious loss of prestige for Churchill, especially as he had taken such a firm stand on the issue. In London they are also beginning to doubt the effectiveness of the blockade. The gaps have become too large.

Everything is in flux once more. One can scarcely predict a day ahead. But soon a cleansing storm will clear the air and enable us to see.

1 June 1941 (Sunday)

Yesterday: No English incursions. We do very little in the air against England. 44,000 tons sunk. Favourable developments on Crete. It will soon be over. The atrocities committed on our prisoners have been barbaric. We are still holding back the reports in the interests of the men's relatives. The English are trying to escape to the south. Yet again, the Italians are not living up to their promise. We have had to help them out. The old story!

Pessimism is growing in London. The USA is following suit. They have also admitted enormous shipping losses. Our U-boat fleet is on the ascendant again. We are giving the Crete issue everything we can. All the newspapers are pulling their weight, except the *Börsenzeitung*, which is completely failing to rise to the occasion. I have it given a final warning.

The Foreign Ministry has bought up the Belgrade radio station from right under our noses. I do not intend to tolerate this. Protest to the Führer.

Bömer case settled. The line: he has had a row with Dietrich and for this reason has been sent on leave. His wife is in a desperate state, but I cannot help her at the moment.

SD report: public mood ambiguous. Deep longing for peace. This is understandable. But they want a decent, victorious peace.

I have a comprehensive news service set up, despite the Whitsun holiday.

Discussion with my people on the subject of the invasion. I lead them all on to a false trail. Against England. And I set the appropriate preparations in motion. Their secretiveness and general attitude will ensure that it filters through slowly. And that is of course the point of the exercise. I think that in a few days we shall start to notice concrete results.

The Kaiser is dying. Ceremony agreed. He will be buried at Doorn. The press comments will be such that neither republicans nor monarchists will be able to feel offended.

I discipline the correspondent of the *Neue Zürcher*,* who has filed a disgraceful report from Berlin. These press reptiles are quite nauseating.

A few worries about Magda, who is very uneasy about Harald's fate. I use a little ruse to calm her.

To Lanke. Sun, fresh air, forest, and peace. Everything I need most at the moment.

The situation is hopeless in Iraq. The nationalist resistance forces have opened negotiations for surrender. This is not at all to our liking. It rather mars the effect of Crete. There the English are finished. All they can do now is to mumble excuses. It is downright distasteful. But they will still be able to cause some trouble before they collapse. The fact is that they have a world empire, which gives them great resilience.

Moscow has suddenly begun to talk of the 'new ethic' of Bolshevism, which is founded in the defence of the fatherland. This is, of course, quite

* The *Neue Zürcher Zeitung*. A German-language newspaper in Switzerland.

new. But nevertheless it confirms the fact that the Bolsheviks are in a real fix. Otherwise they would not be forced to come up with such phoney slogans.

Dublin has suffered a few bombs. We do not yet know whether they were ours or a provocation by the English. I am almost inclined to think the latter.

What a summer out here! In the afternoon I am able to read, go for a walk, lie in the sun, and it is almost like peacetime. But how far away that is, how far!

Newsreel in the evening. Very good again. Crete, North Africa. Real war.

The Great King, by Harlan. Fails completely. Lacks any atmosphere. Exactly the opposite of what I wanted and expected. A Frederick the Great straight from the streets. I am very disappointed.

Then long consultations with Hippler and Demandowski.

Whit Sunday today!

2 June 1941 (Monday)

Yesterday: Darlan has made a very tough speech attacking England. France is beginning to defend herself. The wisest thing that she could do.

Operations are almost complete on Crete. The Italians have finally linked up with our troops. 3000 Englishmen and 6000 Greeks have been taken prisoner. A destroyer and several transport ships, among them a troop ship, destroyed off Sidi Barani. We carry out heavy air raids on Liverpool and the Mersey area. No enemy incursions into the Reich.

Study discussion paper on stepping up of German film production by Hippler. An extremely complicated problem. We need more films especially for export. On the other hand, I would like better, though perhaps fewer films. This, however, is probably not feasible. I shall have to give a great deal of careful thought to this problem, which is of decisive importance.

Gutterer's mother has died. She was incurable. And so it is for the best.

Nothing of importance. Sun, wind, a sky of deepest blue. What a beautiful day!

Some visitors in the afternoon: Schaumburg, Tabody, Hippler, and others. Smalltalk.

Pleasant drive through the green forest. Glorious solitude!

London has officially announced that the English are withdrawing from Crete with heavy losses. And so this too is over. A proud, great victory for us, and a crippling loss of prestige and a catastrophic defeat for England.

Newsreel with music in the evening: magnificent.

New Ritter film, *Stukas*. Quite good, with some wonderful air footage, but a typical Ritter production. He cannot lead people. Rather too noisy.

I feel rested and have a deep tan. All I need is one day. I am glad that my health remains so stable.

3 June 1941 (Tuesday)

Yesterday: A wonderful day: Crete completely cleared of the enemy. Glorious news. We announce it ceremoniously on the radio. Deeply impressive. So far as Crete is concerned, all the English can do is talk stupid nonsense. A thousand evasions and lame excuses. We give no quarter. The press and the radio belabour them mercilessly. I write a cutting leader-article, *The Glorification of Retreat*. Good stuff! A number of sinkings off Crete, including a destroyer. An auxiliary cruiser sunk. Tobruk bombed by our Luftwaffe. Manchester attacked with 100 aircraft. Extremely effective. No enemy incursions into the Reich. The end is approaching in Iraq.

What a beautiful day! What magnificent victories! One is totally happy and glad to be alive. I dash off my leader-article in no time.

Glorious sunshine outside. A captivating second day of Whitsun.

Visitors in the afternoon: Magda with the Hommels, Ursel, Martin and Wodarg. A lot of chat, and most of all we talk about the war. The victory on Crete has made all our hearts and spirits soar. Nothing is impossible for the German soldier.

The Führer is having talks with the Duce on the Brenner. Current issues. Further discussions about Crete. Pessimism in England. Our *Prinz Eugen* has, thank God, safely reached port. We were very worried about that ship.

Talk and some work into the evening.

A pleasant Whitsun festival!

4 June 1941 (Wednesday)

Yesterday: A number of incursions into the incursions into the Reich. Also a raid on Berlin. Fifteen dead, some damage to buildings, fifteen killed in a flak battery. We confine ourselves to naval targets. Great victories at sea are imminent. The U-boat war is on the ascendant again. The period of stagnation is completely behind us. When the full moon comes, the air war against England is to be resumed on a much larger scale.

The end has come on Crete. Our casualty figures are normal. The operation has lived up to all our expectations. We shall not need to change anything when similar projects arise in future. Theory and practice have meshed perfectly.

We are having leaflets dropped over England. To aid the deception. The invasion is already beginning to haunt the public prints. Crete has had a very depressive effect in London. The most absurd excuses are being used there. We are attacking strongly in the press, but in the foreign-language broadcasts to England our tone is mild and admonitory, to avoid any hardening of attitude among the British public. The USA is veering between peace rumours and active intervention. Roosevelt is also wavering. He would like war, but the people do not want it. US reports on Crete are devastating from the English point of view. And in this case they could not be otherwise. My essay on Crete will be another master-stroke.

Otherwise there is little to report so far as world opinion is concerned. I can therefore devote more time to technical questions. Hunke's foreign department must be considerably enlarged. Otherwise he will not be able to make headway against the Foreign Ministry. I accept his plan. Also study a mass of film scripts, deal with theatre problems, radio problems, choose new radio announcers, etc. The end result is not much, but it is necessary and takes up a lot of one's time.

And this wonderful June. One would like to go and lie in the sun by the sea somewhere and forget everything, everything. Well, perhaps some other time.

The Labour Party has passed a bloody-minded resolution: victory without compromise. We are acquainted with this kind of thing from our period of struggle. The SPD* was always just as big and brave. Otherwise there is general astonishment in London at the revolution in modern warfare which we gave proof of on Crete. Criticisms of Churchill are also being made; covert ones, but nevertheless. They cannot be very cheering. We sank 746,000 tons in May. This will not improve England's situation, either. I have been studying a secret document outlining the economic and general war potential of the two power blocs. It has been compiled with complete objectivity, and the implications for England are demoralising. We are immensely superior in almost all areas, even if one adds the USA to England's strength. The Empire is in the grip of a slow but irreversible decline.

Bömer's last work: a report on the activities of him and his department since the beginning of the war, an excellent summary which makes one regret his sad fate all the more. The whole issue is very painful.

Criticism of the régime and even of Churchill is growing in London. It does not appear to be really serious, but nevertheless.

Our operations on Crete have been greeted enthusiastically all over the world. Deservedly so. We are keeping this subject on the boil.

I speak with the children on the telephone in the evening.

They twitter with joy and are royally delighted.

5 June 1941 (Thursday)

Yesterday: No incursions here. Few in England. Some sinkings. We attack Hull with middling forces. Everyone is waiting for the full moon. The end on Crete. 8000 Englishmen and 4000 Greeks taken prisoner, plus enormous quantities of equipment. Rechenberg has written a very pompous letter: he complains about Schmeling, who did nothing at all, says the Propaganda Company reports were concocted at Headquarters and that the English fought more bravely than we will acknowledge. I use some of it. A

* The German Social-Democratic Party.

395

sandstorm in North Africa, which makes all offensive operations impossible. Tough press battle over Syria. The English would like to move in there. Fighting is still going on in Baghdad.

Our quality newspapers are not exploiting the Crete victory sufficiently. The DAZ and the BBS are particularly conscpicuous by their lack of flair in this respect. Popular press brilliant. I make a strong complaint to Fritzsche. The Crete affair is turning into a *cause célèbre* in London. Harsh and disparaging criticism of Churchill. He will find the going hard in the House of Commons in the near future. The Labour Party has called for an uncompromising conduct of the war. What will those corrupt betrayers of the workers have received in exchange for that?

Wilhelm II is dead. Comment here rather cool. No one loved him or hated him. He deserved a far worse end. But nevertheless, he is dead. He had far outlived his time.

Feder has turned to me for help. The Führer continues to reject him. And it is all he deserves. He once betrayed the Führer in his hour of need.

As an experiment, I have one of Dr Ley's speeches played to me on record. Appalling. His amateurism is painfully apparent. Idealism alone is not enough.

Lippert, as leader of the Propaganda Squad in Belgrade, describes the situation there: life is taking its usual course. Minor trouble. But otherwise nothing but respect for the German soldier. A few newspapers are appearing again. German films are top in the popularity stakes. Unfortunately, the Foreign Ministry has bought up the Belgrade radio station from under my nose. I complain to Lippert about this. He says that he will try to do something about it. He is still the old, spineless Lippert. People scarcely ever change. A weak man will remain weak, and when the hammer strikes, all he can do is to fall apart.

Guidelines for propaganda aimed at R.: no anti-socialism; no return to Czarism; no open admission that the country will be divided up, or we shall lose all chance with the army, which is great-Russian in feeling; against Stalin and his Jewish masters; land for the peasants, but the collectives to be maintained for the present so that the harvest can be saved; strong indictment of Bolshevism, attacking its failure in all fields. And otherwise do what the situation demands. I let Gutterer in on the next stages of the campaign. He will now carry out the necessary organisational measures. We are all atremble with excitement. I can hardly wait for the moment when the storm is unleashed.

Inspect the Göringstrasse. In our park there, work is in full swing on a huge underground bunker. Otherwise, all is peaceful and idyllic. The house is huge and empty.

Move to Schwanenwerder, where everything is brilliance and full bloom. Chat with Magda and Ursel, who is out there visiting. What a fine show summer puts on here!

Work right through the afternoon.

Considerable criticism of Churchill. But probably only for show. Our campaign re. the imminent invasion is beginning to have an effect. The echoes will become louder. And then, in the general confusion, we shall be able to act.

Newsreel completed in the evening. Magnificent!

I stay at Schwanenwerder. An evening heavy with the scent of flowers. How beautiful the world can be!

6 June 1941 (Friday)

Yesterday: No incursions on either side. We suffer a number of heavy sinkings. Nothing serious, but embarrassing. But England will pay. Crete is still the big talking-point. Growing criticism of Churchill, some of it probably orchestrated by Churchill himself. But he is being attacked personally, and hard. There are demands for a public reckoning of account. But accompanied by extreme war slogans. Stronger peace rumours from the USA. On the basis of agreed terms. But they are unsubstantiated. I forbid any reaction on our part. It is not in our interests at the moment.

Fighting continues in North Africa without noticeable change. The logistical situation there is particularly difficult from our standpoint.

Report from Moscow: a mixture of crippling passivity, attempts to ingratiate themselves with us, but some defensive preparations also discernible. Stalin has taken charge of the situation. If war breaks out, the government intends to withdraw to Sverdlovsk. They are slowly making attempts to make the masses aware of the gravity of the situation. But it is impossible to see a clear line. No one believes that there will be serious resistance. It is also likely that they fear extensive internal trouble. They are not yet aware of the scale of the coming events, but they are slowly catching on.

Some official business to discuss with Terboven. He tries to sound me out about future developments. But I cold-bloodedly lead him up the wrong track.

Report from Rumania: Antonescu without popular support, as I had foreseen. His foreign policy is rejected, because no one bothers to defend it. The Legion continues to attempt a revival. The generals have failed. Anti-German feeling on the increase. Everything as one had to expect, given the situation.

Another espionage case in the ministry. A former Latvian diplomat, now an ethnic German by profession, talked his way into the ministry. We shall have to see whether he is reliable. The Wehrmacht High Command doubts his loyalty.

Discuss cultural work of the Reich Propaganda Leadership with Tiessler and Fischer. The KdF is trying to dispute its controlling role. But we shall soon get our way.

Bormann has received his reward: he has been raised to the rank of Reich Minister and becomes a member of the Defence Council.

A mass of theatre and film problems. Discuss the reworking of *The Great King* with Hippler. Harlan is incorrigible, as I expected. If necessary I shall give the job to a new director. The Chamber of the German Cinema is showing foreign films, with the result that every troublemaker in Berlin is turning up to watch them. I put a stop to it.

A number of artistic questions with Bibrach. He is slowly forging ahead . . .

. . . To Lanke in the afternoon. Work on my new book, the collection of my wartime essays. It will be a very fine and effective compilation. Probable title: *Between Yesterday and Tomorrow*. What a huge amount of work this book will symbolise! One writes and says quite a bit in two whole years.

The international debate is focused on Syria. England would like to take the country over, but is wary of conflict with Vichy, or at least open war. The entire controversy is very useful from our point of view. We can carry on quietly, hiding behind such a smokescreen.

Our deception campaign is functioning perfectly. The whole world is talking about the coming military pact between Berlin and Moscow. They will be amazed when they see the real outcome.

Heavy air raid on Alexandria with 100 dead. We are coming to grips with the Tommies, even there.

Otherwise nothing of importance. A quiet day's work. Sit out in the mild June night for a while in the evening.

7 June 1941 (Saturday)

Yesterday: The whole world is full of peace rumours. It is claimed that the USA will not be able to give England any real help for four years yet. England, however, will have to surrender this autumn. The story crops up in a thousand variations. [. . .] visit to Washington started them off. The catastrophic situation in England is becoming increasingly obvious. But otherwise these rumours have little substance. I ban any mention of them at home or abroad. If one is marching through the desert for days on end, one should not talk of water, and for the same reason one does not discuss peace in the middle of a war. If one allows such matters to be discussed, then things can rapidly begin to slide.

The Führer's interview has appeared in *Life*. Through Cudahy's efforts. Content as indicated. It has been eagerly awaited. A few perspectives on the Europe of the future. People had been expecting a peace offer, and now they are very disappointed. We are pushing the invasion idea very hard, but no real success is discernible yet. Everyone is keeping too quiet. I would like to write a slightly more pointed piece for *Das Reich*, and then have most of the printing seized. A rather cheeky trick, but it would work.

Report on reaction to the Hess Affair abroad. The impact has been totally dissipated. Now one can see only the tragi-comic aspects of the case. Idealism and big ideas are not enough, it would seem. One must also have a few brains.

Rommel is complaining about the vulgarity of the propaganda being produced about him. I put a stop to it. He deserves the best presentation that we can give him.

Few incursions on either side. 15,000 tons sunk. Alexandria heavily bombed. Crete still in the forefront. The English press has forced Churchill to concede that his assertions about our troops wearing fake uniforms on Crete were lies. And some of the atrocities against our troops were committed by English and New Zealand soldiers. We make a big splash with this, since the English are trying to play it down. Harald has written a cheerful, jolly letter from Crete. He behaved well.

Captain von Hohmeyer reports from Africa: the Italians are worthless. So far as most of their troops are concerned, Rommel has already become a legendary figure. Tobruk is being stoutly defended. With the aid of the Italian forts which they forgot to destroy when they withdrew. Despite all the difficulties, I intend to push through a big entertainments programme for North Africa, and I cable Rommel to this effect. Berndt is bearing up very well. Long discussion with Hohmeyer about *Transozean*, which he is head of. *Transozean* has done sterling service during the war and will be kept in existence when it is over.

SD report: morale continues to be satisfactory. No serious dangers anywhere.

Discuss the Party's production of films with Hippler and Fischer. The Party should concentrate on propaganda, cultural and documentary films. Fischer, of course, wants to make feature films, but his people are not capable of it.

Report on the state of film technique: things are progressing well in this field, and we hope to overtake the Americans soon.

The Stritzky Case – is he a spy or a simple Balt? – is causing me some worry. So [. . . itsch] has offered me his services. I cannot use him at the moment, but I assuredly shall in the near future.

To Schwanenwerder. The new official residence is ready and has turned out magnificently. Magda has worked wonders in a very short time, and she is very pleased. Now I shall be able to work properly out here. And I fully intend to.

Growing criticism of Churchill in London. But some of it contrived. Hore-Belisha has launched a harsh attack on the government. The *Daily Herald* has said for the first time that England could lose the war. There is, indeed, a certain admiration for our Wehrmacht. Its victories are inconceivable so far as the British are concerned. They will see more in the near future.

Otherwise: increase in peace rumours. But this too is the work of the two democracies, who are trying to sound us out. But we give absolutely no indication.

Rumours of an imminent attack on the Ukraine. Fairly substantial. We shall have to step up our deception effort.

I intend to spend a lot more time on the problem.

8 June 1941 (Sunday)

Yesterday: Nothing of importance at the fronts. 30,000 tons sunk by the Luftwaffe.

Roosevelt has denied the peace rumours in a thoroughly insulting fashion. He claims that England has no thought of surrender and that we are the authors of these rumours. His impertinence is breathtaking. We give him a dusty answer in the foreign service, making it absolutely clear where and when these rumours originated, and at home we pass over the speech in contemptuous silence. It is, however, clear that opposition is growing in London, some, perhaps, engineered by Churchill to absorb the popular anger, but some genuine. In any event, we do not dramatise it. The public here must not be encouraged in vain hopes. Our propaganda will continue to follow the middle way. This is the best way.

Crete is still the big talking-point so far as international opinion is concerned. A rumour, still unconfirmed, is circulating to the effect that Heiduschke was killed there. That would be dreadful! I am devastated and cannot believe it. Neither am I succesful in getting a confirmation one way or the other. Thus all I have left is hope, which I cling to fervently. Reports about Schmeling are not exactly gratifying. He has given a pretty stupid and childish interview to an American journalist: a boxer making politics. He would be better off fighting than sitting in Athens and sounding off.

I have Gutterer give Bodenschatz my grave, considered opinion about his garrulousness in respect of military secrets. He will watch himself from now on.

The Stritzky case is less damaging than I had feared. But I have dismissed him nevertheless. [S . . . itsch] has offered his services against Moscow. The Gestapo believes him to be an *agent provocateur*. I have him put under observation.

Receive the complete schedules for the territorial division of R. The scheme will require a very extensive official apparatus. Asiatic R. is not dealt with. We are concerned only with the European parts. Stalin recently told Matsuoka that he was himself an Asiatic. Then he is welcome to it!

Life has published the Cudahy interview with the Führer along with a carping editorial comment. These American Jews want war. And when the time comes they will choke on it. Read a brilliant letter from Lindbergh to all

Americans. It really tells the Interventionists where to get off. Stylistically magnificent. The man has something.

Receive Alfieri. He reports to me on the meeting between the Führer and the Duce. It is a good thing that the two men have such trust in each other. We make preparations for a visit to Berlin by Pavolini. Plus a few current issues.

Study a memorandum about renewed production of German fairy tales on film. We are not yet ready. This question still needs a lot of work.

Have purchased a wonderful Goya from a private collection in France. A masterpiece!

Otherwise, nothing but work and more work. Pavelic has visited the Führer. His country has only half-succeeded in asserting its right to independence. The Croats are to be pitied.

No good news from Rumania. Antonescu wants to get rid of his generals, but he can find no competent civilians. The Legion is finished, and he is putting its leaders on trial instead of allowing them into his government. And the people has nothing but dumb insolence and contempt for him. Everything is just as I predicted.

The peace rumours are still in circulation, despite Roosevelt's denial and our strong press attacks. It seems probable that Churchill is responsible, trying to smoke us out or compromise us. He will burn his fingers. England is making an attempt to appear stronger than she is. But the ruse is obvious. Talk of peace is everywhere. There must be something in it.

Alfieri comes to visit in the evening. A small party. We are able to relax and chat socially for a change. Colour film with special effects, *Gulliver*. An American production. Very good, very witty, very well made. I intend for us to equal this kind of production, and shall make every effort in this field, despite the war. People who can do this are available here. All one has to do is to find them.

Things go on until very late again. Alfieri makes a good impression on me.

9 June 1941 (Monday)

Yesterday: No air activity on either side. A few sinkings by the Luftwaffe.

The English move into Syria and Lebanon along with the de Gaulle troops. Vichy has declared its intention to fight. General Dentz has orders to this effect. This is a favourable development which could be very much to our advantage.

Peace rumours are still circulating. In London they are trying to claim that we are responsible. We defend ourselves against this charge with all vigour. Roosevelt is the inventor of these bare-faced lies. He personally has a lot of criticism to deal with in the USA.

Otherwise, a quiet Sunday. It rains all day. Very good for our fields.

News of Harald: he fought well and has been put forward for a decoration.

We are all very pleased. No definite news of Heiduschke yet.

In the afternoon, I have some time for reading and writing. A little quiet is very beneficial. The peace rumours continue. We leave them undisturbed. It is realities which are decisive, not little tricks of that sort.

Syria is the big talking-point. London is making a great deal of it. Churchill needs a success. Vichy has declared that she will fight with everything at her disposal. Wait and see!

Newsreel in the evening. Rich in content and also well made.

Afterwards, long talk with Magda.

10 June 1941 (Tuesday)

Yesterday: A few incursions into West Germany, with ten dead and some damage to buildings. We attack English airfields and mine ports. The fighting at the gates of Tobruk continues. Berndt has written me another dramatic letter from North Africa, which illustrates how hard the fighting there is. Our reporting from there is often somewhat unwise. I put a stop to these tendencies.

The English have invaded Syria. Some initial successes. The Vichy position there is none too satisfactory. Pétain has addressed an uncompromising appeal to the French troops in Syria. Much depends on whether they remain loyal to Vichy. London is making every effort to ensure that they do not. We granted the French military concessions to make their situation in Syria easier. We are also bringing all possible propaganda help to bear, without making it into a prestige issue for us. But the English, with their brutal lack of scruples, are profiting by this move.

London is using Syria to raise morale at home. For this reason, we are acting the interested spectator so far as the rest of the world is concerned. The USA is taking a very reticent attitude. An American journalist who has just returned to Berlin has stated that he will happily stay here. Washington, he says, sees intervention as too risky. The Americans want to help England, but they do not want war. This must, on the whole, be correct.

I have now had news from several sources that Heiduschke was killed by a bullet through the head near Chania. I cannot, and will not, believe it. The uncertainty is making me quite ill. I send Wodarg to Athens to make sure. If the reports are correct, it will be a terrible blow, for me personally as well. He is my most loyal and reliable colleague.

Under the circumstances I am most unwilling to lift the ban on dancing now. But it is necessary, to give the best possible camouflage for our next project. The world must believe that we have had our fill of victories and have no interest in anything but relaxing and dancing.

The Führer has issued a new order regarding secrecy. Even the communication of conclusions that an individual believes he can make on the basis of certain indications now count as breach of security . . .

. . . Discuss new measures against Jews in Berlin with Gutterer. In particular, the rule that they may not sub-let to foreigners. This was all we needed. State-recognised centres for atrocity propaganda.

Talk over the problem of fairy tales on film with Hippler. We shall only consider good, old German tales for material, and not insubstantial, modern confections. And only cartoons, not feature films.

Work with Gutterer, making preparations for Pavolini's visit. He will get to see a thing or two.

I work as if in a dream. The question of whether Heiduschke is dead or alive will not leave me in peace. I cannot imagine that such a model of strength and manhood could have drawn his last breath. A horrifying thought!

It is with me the entire day. I cannot forget it.

I work on at Schwanenwerder. I cannot stay at the ministry, I am so disturbed.

Heavy air raid on Alexandria. Panic among the population. A U-boat sinks 32,000 tons.

Syria is the great question-mark. The Americans are applauding the British for all they are worth. All of a sudden, there is no more nonsense about humanitarian values. We intend to note this for future use. London maintains that she has captured 140 German paratroops. An attempt to prove the German 'penetration' of Syria. A crude trick! In Iraq, a semblance of peace for the outside world's benefit. So far as the peace agreement there is concerned, London is playing the kindly uncle. These English are the most mendacious crew imaginable. But they have had some success so far. We shall put an end to their tricks.

We issue a firm denial that we had troops stationed in Syria. Vichy is talking of heavy fighting and claiming that the French are outgunned: a bad omen. In any event, we are not taking a clear line. London is crowing loudly.

Newsreel: after some work, turned out very well.

Inspect new mobile laboratory for film and stills, to be used by our Propaganda Companies. A technical miracle. We are unbeatable in this area.

But a lot more can, and will, be done.

Dictate leader-article: *Radio in the War*. Justifies our radio schedules' heavy emphasis on entertainment.

I spend the whole day thinking about Heiduschke.

What a loss, what a loss!

The good ones go, the bad remain! How cruel and unjust war is!

11 June 1941 (Wednesday)

[First part missing]

. . . Oechsner returns from the USA and reports to an agent of ours: A declaration of war out of the question at present, they are not yet ready, perhaps in a year, if necessary England will continue the war from Canada. Totally bizarre conceptions of what is to come. They will all be amazed.

In consultation with the Wehrmacht High Command and with the Führer's agreement, I draft my 'invasion' article. Title: *Crete as an Example.* Pretty clear. It is to appear in the *Völkischer Beobachter* and then to be seized. London will learn of this fact within twenty-four hours from the US Embassy. This is the point of the exercise. All of it will be calculated to cover up the activity in the East. We have reached a stage when we must use more drastic methods. Otherwise, the entire operation might be so subtle that no one notices it. I finish the article in the afternoon. It turns out magnificently well. A masterpiece of pretence!

The case of the sinking of the US freighter *Robin More* has begun to make larger ripples. The assertion in America is, of course, that she was sunk by a German U-boat. But the ship had war material on board and probably sunk in a storm. Wait and see!

The Duce has spoken in the Chamber on the anniversary of Italy's entry into the war. We have to cut some things from the speech for our internal consumption. He is rather generous in claiming our feats of arms for his own. Claims the USA is already at war *de facto*. This is also very ill-judged. Otherwise nothing but morale-raising stuff for home consumption.

And Churchill speaks in the House of Commons. Something of a confession of sins in the face of considerable opposition and criticism. But his position does not seem endangered in any way. No one knows who would succeed him. He is forced to admit that our paratroops on Crete did not wear fake uniforms. He says that he was wrongly informed. And a few other embarrassing admissions. Things are not going well for him. But in the Empire's present situation he can get away with a lot. This is England's strength, but could one day turn out to be an ominous weakness.

Work on for a long while. Documentary film from China. Nothing but war, war! When will this tormented humanity have peace once more?

12 June 1941 (Thursday)

Yesterday: No incursions on either side. Our Luftwaffe reports several sinkings. Heavy air raid on Haifa. We use the radio to stir up more panic in Alexandria. Artillery duels around Tobruk. The French in Syria are putting up more of a resistance than we had expected. Nevertheless, we are not making Syria into a prestige issue. We intend to be careful, and I remain sceptical about the French will to fight. According to Vichy, there have been no desertions to the Gaullists. But they could be telling us that so as to save face.

Churchill's speech was very weak. He was totally on the defensive and was forced to hit back against a storm of criticism. We attack him good and hard. His position seems to be somewhat weakened. Even *The Times* admits it. Darlan has also made a speech. A plea for Collaboration, to which we devote considerable attention. The Duce's speech is a highly-coloured statement of account. We dress it up a little. In particular, we leave out the reference to the fact that the Italians will now occupy the whole of Greece.

Report from Bessarabia and the Ukraine: the Russians are staring over the border at us as if hypnotised, and are terrified. They are not doing very much. They will be taken by surprise to an extent unique in history. And the Bolshevik ghost will quickly be laid.

Letter from Naumann, who is in the Balkans: the whole region is very anti-Italian. I believe that today the Italians are the most hated people in the whole of Europe.

My article, *Crete as an Example*, is approved by the Führer with some minor alterations. I consult with Martin, Gutterer, Brauweiler, Fritzsche and Hada from the *Völkischer Beobachter* to see how we can best launch it. As few Germans and as many foreigners as possible should read it. In particular, the US Embassy must have a copy. In that way it will reach London and the world press most quickly. We shall carry it on Friday in the Berlin edition of the *V.B.* and have it seized that same morning at 3 a.m. By then it will have done its work. The farce will be played through to the end with absolute thoroughness. The article is very cunningly written. It says a lot between the lines. The enemy will be able to infer all the things that he wishes to believe at the moment. Admittedly we shall need to set a large-scale operation in motion, and I shall lose a certain amount of prestige as a result, but it is worthwhile. We are all enthusiastically in favour of the plan. Everything will run quite normally. There is hardly any chance that the enemy will become suspicious.

Go over preparatory measures for the East with Taubert and Titel. Everything is running smoothly at the moment. The England Squad is slowly being disbanded. I now have [. . .], Maurer, and particularly Paltzo for R. Titel is doing a good job. Test new machines for dropping leaflets. Now they seem to be working well. Thirty million leaflets in all have already been printed. At the Reich Printing Works. The packing is being done by seventy-five soldiers who will not be allowed out until the action has begun. There is no chance that the secret can be betrayed. A huge project is in operation, and no one has the slightest inkling of it.

Work out a new radio schedule with Glasmaier. Now totally biased towards entertainment. Ban on dancing also lifted. All for camouflage purposes. On Saturday the radio is to broadcast light but good quality material. Because of his Saxon accent, Studentkowski is unfortunately not suited to be a radio announcer. We shall therefore have to look for yet another replacement.

Press problems with Reinhardt. At the moment we are buying up many foreign newspapers through Amann. They will be run by an advisory council, on which the Foreign Ministry will also be represented . . .

. . . SD report: morale good. But the public are waiting for something to happen. They will, of course, not have to wait much longer. Opinion in the USA reported as more pessimistic regarding the situation in England. I do not pass such expressions of opinion for release at home, do not place too much reliance on them myself, but things are certainly none too rosy in England. Churchill can expect some more bitter moments.

I try out new fanfares for our special announcements. The choice is so great that it is very difficult to make a selection.

It rains the entire day. For once, one can really work straight through.

In the evening, I hear definite news by telephone from Athens: Heiduschke fell in the fighting for Chania. A head-wound. My heart is filled with a deep sadness. In him I lose not only my best adjutant, but a good, loyal and selfless friend, who was almost part of the family. I shall miss him so very, very often in the future.

He was such a good, decent man, and I could rely on him completely. Why does death always choose the best?

There are so many men hanging around and living their lives. But the ones who are still alive are the ones who are totally useless and will never achieve anything.

A young, fresh life has been extinguished. We owe so much to him that we can never repay!

13 June 1941 (Friday)

Yesterday: English raids on the Rhineland and the Ruhr. Considerable damage and around forty dead. We attack English ports with some 100 aircraft. Also considerable damage. The war in the air is at a tentative stage. Neither trusts the other. This the best thing at the moment from our point of view. 23,000 tons sunk by U-boats. Fifteen enemy aircraft shot down. Major report from the Wehrmacht High Command detailing losses and successes. A truly magnificent reckoning in our favour.

The subject of Russia is coming more into the foreground again. *The Times* has published an article expressing the greatest possible suspicion. And, in fact, fairly accurate. But this can no longer do much harm. In the face of it, we issue reports to the effect that we have found a good basis for negotiations with Moscow. This will restore the situation. My article is handed over to the *V.B.* with due solemnity. Its seizure will follow in the course of the night. For the moment, I shall suffer a severe loss of prestige. But it is worth it. The *V.B.* wants to recall its correspondent from Moscow. I forbid it, at least for the moment. We must keep up appearances at all costs. Things are still going well. But we shall not be able to keep up the whole deception for long.

Bömer has been handed over to the People's Court. He is a victim of his inability to keep his mouth shut.

Increasingly pessimistic view of the war in the USA. They are not ready and have no inclination to run any serious risks. Churchill can expect little from that quarter. I read the book on him by his secretary: he is a vain dandy who wears pink underpants, but also a bulldog who may still give us some problems.

Party problems discussed with Tiessler. Rosenberg continues to make difficulties regarding the Seventh Chamber. Ley visits me and tries to put on some pressure. But I cannot help him.

Now the Navy, too, is trying its hand at producing films. On a quite amateur basis under a naval lieutenant. I stick my oar in and sort things out by creating merry hell.

Discuss the budget with Gutterer. We have had our way in most areas.

Film questions with Gutterer. New problems are constantly arising in this field, mostly due to the war. Knothe reports on his film marketing work in the Balkans. We are busily buying up cinemas and trying to ensure ourselves as much influence as possible. Knothe is doing an excellent job. Hungary is very difficult, and the Italians are getting in our way all over the area. But we shall win through. All we must do now is to produce more films.

Long talk with Görlitzer: Berlin parents want their evacuee children back. This is absolutely impossible at the moment. Particularly since we possess only modest anti-aircraft defences. The parents must be informed of the transportation difficulties, and if they do not understand those, then I can do no more for them.

Things are still very uncertain in Syria. The French seem to be putting up a stubborn resistance, and London is emphasising that there can be no question of a *Blitzkrieg*. Pétain has issued an appeal to the Army of the Levant. Nevertheless, I fear that the resistance will not last much longer.

Make arrangements regarding Heiduschke. Gravenhorst has gone to his parents, taking a letter from me. I intend to help these poor people. At the Ministerial Conference I make an obituary statement in his honour. Everyone who knew him is profoundly sad at the loss.

Harald has written: he has come through everything and is very well. He says that he will be in Berlin on leave in two weeks' time. We all look forward to that very much. Thus, in war, pain and happiness go hand in hand.

Mother says good-bye. She is off to stay in Rheydt for a few weeks. What a good woman!

Inspect my pictures. We have now collected a wonderful treasure-house of art. The ministry is gradually turning into one big art gallery. And this is right and proper, since it is here that the world of the arts is administered.

With Hippler, receive the Italian film actress, [P . . .]. They all want to make films in Germany, because they can see no more room for development in Italy. And we shall have to broaden our range of types and characters, since after the war we shall have to provide many more nations with films. We could make good use of this type.

All astrologers, magnetopaths, anthroposophists, etc. have been arrested and their entire activities halted. Thus we have finally put an end to these fraudulent operations. Oddly enough, not a single clairvoyant predicted that he would be arrested. A poor advertisement for their profession!

It has now been confirmed that Winant was responsible for spreading the pessimistic reports about England's position that appeared in the US press. Roosevelt will now hold us responsible, so as to conceal the facts. And indeed, England's position is extraordinarily bad. The most important and serious American newspapers now admit this. So our watchword must be: keep hitting hard!

Short visit to the Göringstrasse with Magda. A few minor alterations are being made there. And a huge air-raid shelter is being built. It is already half-finished and will be absolutely enormous.

Schwanenwerder. Work mechanically. Impossible to shake off thoughts of Heiduschke. I cannot believe that he will never come back.

The question of Russia is turning into the big international puzzle, hour by hour. We can only hope that it will not be deciphered too quickly. We are doing all we can to disguise our intentions. But as for how long our ruse will work, that is in the lap of the gods.

My days are filled with feverish work, from morning until midnight.

But blessed release will come soon!

14 June 1941 (Saturday)

Yesterday: My piece appears in the *V.B.* and works like a bombshell. The *V.B.* is seized during the night. And now the telephone never stops ringing. The project moves ahead at home and abroad. Everything goes without a hitch. I am very happy about it. The big sensation is under way. English broadcasts are already claiming that our troop movements against Russia are sheer bluff, to conceal our plans for an invasion of England. This was the point of the exercise. Otherwise, the foreign news scene is in complete confusion. Even we hardly know what is going on.

The Russians seem to suspect absolutely nothing. We are massing on a vast scale: thickly concentrated, a sitting target. It is true that the High Command will not be able to sustain the pretence for much longer, since certain military measures are unmistakable. Gutterer wants to recall our press attaché from Moscow to help Taubert. I forbid it. We cannot go too far. I give Winkelkempner secret instructions to begin to describe an English statement about an invasion in the English-language service of the radio, and then to suddenly break off in the middle. As if the censor had suddenly intervened. This will also contribute to the alarm in England.

Churchill has made a speech in London to his governments-in-exile. The entire crew together under one roof. A speech packed with abuse and malevolence towards us. A sign that things are going very badly for him. He is beginning to lose some of his nerve.

Our fine ship, the *Lützow*, hit by an air-launched torpedo. We still hope to get it safely to port in Norway. It is clear that we have underestimated these aerial torpedoes. The English are achieving success after success with them.

Benghazi bombed. A troop-transporter hit. Flak material and other equipment lost. Supplying North Africa is becoming increasingly difficult, despite our efforts.

More air raids on the Ruhr district. Considerable damage and some 40 dead. Our troops are now concentrated so densely in East Prussia that the Russians could inflict the gravest damage by pre-emptive air attacks. But they will not do it. They lack the courage. One must be audacious if one intends to win a war.

Spend some time exchanging ideas with Gutterer, Fritzsche, Martin and Hada. We are playing the little comedy re. the withdrawn copies of the *V.B.* through to the end. The whole ministry is very sad that I have been guilty of such a grave 'mistake'. I do not attend the press conference. This is very pointed. Instead I try out new fanfares for the special announcements. Continue to work on the big entertainment programme for the radio. This fits our scenario very well . . .

. . . Frau Scholtze-Klink had been asking for an appointment with me. She has now suddenly cancelled, because after the article she believes me to be in disgrace. Such is human nature.

Award the Service Cross to cameraman Fuchs, who had both legs severed during a Stuka attack. Heroes of the newsreel!

Address the Reich Circle for National Socialist Enlightenment. Outline the nature and purpose of propaganda. Enthusiastically received.

Letter from Heiduschke's battalion commander. He died very bravely. Bullet through the head! Buried in the battalion's war cemetery on Crete. Poor boy! What would I not give to have him back again. Harald fought very well. He has been recommended for an Iron Cross First Class. Magda and I are very pleased. The boy has lived up to our expectations, after all.

The Führer is back in Berlin. But I cannot speak with him, since I am almost suffocating under the weight of meetings, speeches, paperwork and decisions to be made. Do a little work on my book, so that it can soon be delivered to the printer. These days, everything takes so much time, because we are so short of staff.

Cripps has flown from Moscow to London. A torrent of rumours is pouring out of London to the world. All to do with Russia. And, in fact, fairly accurate. But on the whole, the world continues to believe in bluff or blackmail. We do not react at all. Moscow has issued a formal denial: it claims it knows nothing of any aggressive intent on the part of the Reich. Our troop movements have a quite different purpose. In any event, Moscow seems to be doing nothing to counter any aggression. Marvellous! My article is the big sensation in Berlin. Telegrams are flitting off to every capital. The ruse has been completely successful. The Führer is very satisfied, and Jodl is delighted. One correspondent from Ankara has tried to sound us out by presenting a particularly strong telegram. But we do not fall into the trap. We keep up the pretence.

General [. . .] speaks about Crete on the radio. I 'correct' his speech and slip in a few little tricks. Everything is in full flow. Martin is working like a Trojan.

Long talk with Dr Dietrich; he is very pleasant. It seems that nothing more can be done for Bömer. The Führer has let him fall. I, however, intend to make every effort to ensure that nothing really bad happens to him. That is, after all, possible. We are agreed that Brauweiler cannot succeed him. He is too indolent and not sharp enough. Dietrich is very bitter about Ribbentrop. The Bömer case seems to have affected him deeply. He tells me about life at the Obersalzberg. Bormann is now in a position of total control. A man of the shadows! But another man would do no better. Ribbentrop behaved like a complete swine in the Bömer case. But then that was to be expected. Dietrich had been intending to complain to the Führer about the seizure of the *V.B.* I give him a rough idea of the true situation. In general, the conversation is very positive.

Haifa very heavily bombed again.

Home late. Magda is overjoyed at Harald's decoration, which is now as good as assured. I am also very proud of the boy. A good thing that he did not go off the rails.

It rains the entire day. But I scarcely notice it, since I am inundated with work. I have wild rumours spread in Berlin: that Stalin is on his way to Berlin and the red flags are already being produced, etc. Dr Ley rings up. He has been fooled completely. I leave him in ignorance. It all serves our purpose at the moment.

Finally get to talk with Oechsner, who has just returned from the USA. He says that we need not expect a declaration of war by the USA for another six months. Roosevelt is not yet convinced of England's imminent bankruptcy. They still have to work on public opinion. And, unfortunately for them, Germany is refusing to indulge in provocative acts. Thus we must continue to be careful. The *Robin More* affair is being played up dramtically over there. It is now beyond doubt that it was a German U-boat, but that the U-boat was perfectly justified in sinking the vessel, which was carrying material of war. We are refusing to make any comment for the moment. Wait and see!

A busy, exciting day. I am dead-tired by the time I finally get to bed.

410

15 June 1941 (Sunday)

Yesterday: My article about Crete is the big sensation, here and abroad. At home, people regret my apparent *faux pas*, pity me or try to show their friendship despite everything, while abroad there is feverish conjecture. We stage-managed it perfectly. Only one cable got through to the USA, but that is enough to bring the affair to the attention of the entire world. We know from tapped telephone conversations between foreign journalists working in Berlin that all of them fell for the decoy. The imminent invasion is the talk of London now. Fritzsche reports to me on his efforts to keep the deception going. Schmidt from the Foreign Ministry has come close to seeing through them. Brauweiler is working hard and conscientiously according to instructions. Everything has been a complete success.

The denial by Tass is even more strongly-worded than initial reports indicated. Explanation: Stalin obviously intends to establish clear war guilt by strong talk of peace and the assertion that nothing untoward is happening. We know from radio interceptions that Moscow has put the Russian fleet on alert. It therefore seems that they are not quite so ingenuous as they try to appear. But the preparations are extremely amateurish. Not to be taken seriously when it comes to a real war.

The High Command is very pleased by the success of my article. It helps them very considerably.

A few incursions in the West, with some damage and loss of life. We attack English ports. Heavy raid on Haifa.

The English are giving out the names of German prisoners-of-war over the radio. To attract more listeners. We take the names and broadcast them immediately on our own radio. So we have parried the blow.

I read the English propaganda pamphlet, *Battle for the Atlantic*: complete lies, but excellently done. Recent English leaflets dropped over Germany also indicate that English propaganda in general has greatly improved lately.

Rumours are circulating that are distinctly uncomfortable. One moment we are going to attack in the East, the next against England. A maze in which only the person who knows can find his way. I therefore warn my colleagues against becoming too deeply involved in this irresponsible gossip. Silence is golden.

Reach agreement with Rosenberg re. work in the East. We arrive at a full understanding. If one handles him the right way, one can work with him.

Prince Biesterfeld has given an interview in the USA which amounts to the last word in High Treason. I have him given another lambasting in our press and then close the file on him. A prince, and he is more devious and contemptible than any worker could ever be. One only has to compare him with a man like Heiduschke. Gravenhorst visited his mother. She was deeply affected by the loss of her son. But she comforts herself with the thought that he died honourably for his country. Totally unimportant, modest people,

411

who will sacrifice anything for their fatherland. And now they face ruin. I shall help them as much as I can. Poor Heiduschke! He deserved to return.

More trouble with the Foreign Ministry. On account of the radio stations abroad, which the Foreign Ministry is buying up in large quantities. I write a sharp letter to Lammers, for the Führer's attention. The Foreign Ministry is a state within the state. Or rather: a swelling cancer.

Prepare Pavolini's visit in consultation with Gutterer. Talk with Schwarz van Berk about the foreward to my new book, which he is to write.

The SD report contains nothing of note. Public expectant. Wild rumours. Particularly regarding Russia. London has declared that Cripps will not return to his post in Moscow. They have had enough of the Russian farce. But then they, of course, do not know what is coming.

Schwanenwerder. We talk for a long while about Heiduschke, whose memory is always with us. Ursel is visiting us. She too was very fond of that nice boy.

Jannings, Demandowski and Hippler visit. Jannings talks about his trip to Rome, where his *Ohm Krüger* was shown with sensational success. The Duce received him and was also delighted by the film. Mussolini wants more German–Italian co-operation in the cinema. I also intend to exercise some more pressure in this direction. *Alcazar* is now being released with great publicity in Berlin. The Duce, however, is trying to force us to include the church scenes. I am very sceptical on this issue and shall ask the Führer again. Otherwise the mood in Rome was very favourable from our point of view. Particularly among the general public. All the people who know what is going on, even those from the film world, have inferiority complexes. Jannings talks to me about his new film treatment: *The Decision*,* Bismarck from 1885 until his dismissal. A good project, and one that I shall give every support. Jannings will do some reworking of Harlan's *Great King*. He also finds it impossible in its present form.

Work calls: Rumania is making her preparations a little too conspicuously. Pity! The subject of Russia is still being discussed passionately and eagerly in London. But really they are simply awash with rumours, none of them substantiated. And even when someone says the truth, it disappears in the welter of deceptions. Vichy has announced that the French fleet has set sail from Toulon. But it is probably a storm in a tea cup.

Roosevelt has frozen German and Italian assets in the USA. This is not a devastating blow, and we have opportunities for retaliation.

In the evening, my statement regarding the new programmes is read out on all stations. Well argued. And then an excellent entertainment programme follows until 2 a.m. This will give pleasure to our soldiers and our working people.

I am busy until late at night. This hard week ends in exhaustion.

* The title was later changed to *The Dismissal*.

Yesterday: Russia–Germany the big talking-point. No one believes the Tass denial. Great conjecture about what my article in the *V.B.* really means. London is the source of all the rumours. They are obviously trying to lure us out into the open, but with no success. We maintain an icy silence. The enemy thus has no means of confirmation. Meanwhile, however, the military preparations continue unabated.

The freezing of our assets in the USA is of no importance. We have the capability to do twenty-five times as much damage in return. The experts have already worked it out. It is clear, therefore, that Roosevelt is merely trying to provoke us. He is slowly losing his nerve, it seems.

The *Robin More* affair has been given more dramatic attention in the USA than we at first realised. Sumner Welles has issued a lying statement on the subject. Our naval experts are busy drafting a peppery counter-statement. I believe that the Americans are only making such a noise so that they can appear to be doing something. There is no serious danger of a declaration of war at the moment.

Croatia has signed the Three-Power Pact in Venice.

Slight English air activity in West Germany. We launch some not very extensive raids on the English southern and eastern coasts. It is odd that the English are not attacking us more at the moment, while we are labouring under a handicap. A U-boat has sunk 30,000 tons. Heavy air battles over Tobruk. But the dump seems to be holding on stubbornly. We are having to fight very hard there. An English cruiser seriously damaged in the Mediterranean.

Ley has announced the outline of a new old-age pension scheme for after the war. This is psychologically rather maladroit at the moment. We are promising too much, cannot carry it out at the moment, therefore succeed only in stirring up controversy and whetting appetites. The rule should be to confine oneself to basics and keep quiet about the details.

It rains the entire day. On this Sunday, therefore, it is possible to shut oneself in between four walls and work wonderfully well. Ursel is visiting, and so Magda has something to do. I receive news of Harald: he conducted himself quite fantastically well and everyone has nothing but praise for him. We are all very pleased.

The Führer summons me to the Reich Chancellery in the afternoon. I have to enter by the back door, so that no one notices. The Wilhelmstrasse is under constant observation by foreign journalists. And so caution is needed. The Führer looks marvellous and receives me very warmly. My article amused him hugely. It bought us a small extra breathing-space while our feverish preparations continued. And it was just what we needed. The Führer gives me a comprehensive explanation of the situation: the attack on Russia will begin as soon as all our troops are in position. This will be sometime in the course of next week. The campaign in Greece cost us dear in matériel, and this is why it is taking somewhat longer than anticipated. They have about 180–200 Divisions at their disposal, perhaps rather fewer, in any case about the same as we. And so far as personnel and equipment are concerned, there is no comparison with our forces. The first thrust will be executed at various points. The enemy will be driven back in one, smooth movement. The Führer estimates that the operation will take four months, I reckon on fewer. Bolshevism will collapse like a house of cards. We face victories unequalled in human history.

We must act. Moscow intends to keep out of the war until Europe is exhausted and bled white. Then Stalin will move to bolshevise Europe and impose his own rule. We shall upset his calculations with one stroke. Our operation has been prepared as thoroughly as is humanly possible. So many contingency factors have been built into the plans that failure is totally out of the question. No geographical limits have been set to operations. We shall fight until Russia's military power no longer exists. Japan is with us. The operation is also necessary from her point of view. Tokyo would never become involved with the USA with Russia still intact to her rear. Another reason why Russia must be destroyed. England would like to maintain Russia as a surety for the future of Europe. That was the reason for Cripps' mission to Moscow. It failed. But Russia would attack us if we were weak, and then we should face a two-front war, which we are avoiding by this pre-emptive strike. Only then shall we have our rear protected. I estimate the fighting capacity of the Russians even lower than does the Führer.

Another reason for attacking Russia is the need to free men for other purposes. An undefeated Russia forces us to keep 250 divisions permanently under arms, manpower that we need urgently for our economy. War work must be greatly intensified, to carry through our weapon, U-boat and aircraft production programmes, so that even the USA will not be able to touch us. The materials, the minerals and the machines are there for full production, but we lack the human resources. Once Russia has been brought to her knees, then we shall be able to demobilise whole sections of the armed forces and build, arm, and prepare. Only then shall we be able to begin the attack on England, using the Luftwaffe on a massive scale. An invasion is a very difficult prospect, whatever the circumstances. And so we must try to win victory by other means.

The procedure is to be as follows: we intend to act in a completely different way to the usual. And this time we have come up with a new twist: there will be no press campaign; we shall keep absolutely silent and then on X-Day simply attack. I urgently advise the Führer against calling the Reichstag together on the day. It will destroy the entire system of deception. He accepts my suggestion that we have a declaration read out over the radio. We are already printing leaflets on a massive scale. The printers and packers are living in total isolation until the operation begins, thus ensuring absolute secrecy. The direction of the entire campaign is clear: Bolshevism must be destroyed, and with it England will lose her last possible ally on the European mainland. The Bolshevik poison must be eliminated from Europe. It will be difficult for Churchill or Roosevelt to say anything against that. And if circumstances warrant it we shall also approach the bishops of both Christian persuasions to bless this war as one divinely approved. There will be no restoration of Czarism in Russia, but a true socialism will replace Jewish Bolshevism. Every old Nazi will be deeply gratified to see this hour. The alliance with Russia was always a blemish on our honour. Now it will be washed away. We shall now destroy what we have fought against for our entire lives. I say so to the Führer and he completely agrees with me. I also put in a good word for Rosenberg, whose life's work has been justified by this operation.

The Führer says: right or wrong, we must win. It is the only way. And victory is right, moral and necessary. And once we have won, who is going to question our methods? In any case, we have so much to answer for already that we must win, because otherwise our entire nation – with us at its head – and all we hold dear, will be eradicated. So to work!

The Führer asks me what the public is thinking. It believes that we are negotiating with Russia, but will behave with courage when we call on it to fight. Russian radio stations will be largely destroyed, and our soldiers will have the first opportunity to make a personal acquaintance with the fatherland of the peasants and workers. They will all return as fervent anti-Bolsheviks. This plague will be driven out of Europe. The time is ripe for it.

The Tass denial, in the Führer's opinion, is little more than a product of fear. Stalin is trembling at what is to come. We shall put an end to his double-game. We shall now organise the raw materials of this rich country. And England's hope of destroying us by her blockade will be extinguished once and for all. And then the U-boat war will start in earnest. England will sink to the bottom.

Italy and Japan will now be informed that we intend to present certain demands to Russia, in the form of an ultimatum, at the beginning of July. The news will soon get round. This will buy us a few more days' time. So far as the rest goes, the Duce has not yet been informed of the extent of the planned operation. Antonescu knows a little more. Rumania and Finland are marching with us. So let us begin. The rich lands of the Ukraine beckon. Our military leaders, who were with the Führer on Saturday, have prepared everything as well as is possible. Our propaganda machine is ready and waiting. We shall all combine to produce a master-stroke.

The Führer gives me a detailed account of the Crete operation. I tell him of Harald's brave conduct, which pleases him greatly. He is still very fond of the boy. Crete had to be taken in order to prevent the British from having a base for aircraft against Italy. Because the Italians are not so resilient as our people. And perhaps we shall crush Turkey after all, to get better access to

Egypt. In any event we now have the island of Crete, and the grave sacrifices have been justified. But naturally we cannot repeat this cruel experiment when it comes to England.

Then I inform the Führer of Jannings' success in Rome. He intends to give some more thought to whether we ought to release the *Alcazar* film in an uncut version. The Führer intends to postpone the appeal for cotton fabrics for the moment. Now is not the time to fuel possible discontent. Everything must be concentrated on the single great task.

Now I must continue to prepare everything with extreme care. We must continue to invent rumours: peace with Moscow, Stalin coming to Berlin, an invasion of England is imminent, so as to conceal the real situation. I hope that we can keep it up for a while yet. I shall do my best. The Führer lives under an indescribable strain. It is always the same before operations begin. But he says that when the battle begins he becomes totally calm. And I have seen this happen countless times.

The most recent newsreels have given the Führer particular pleasure. He describes them as the best means of popular education and leadership. And indeed they are.

I discuss a number of other current issues with the Führer, including private matters, and then, in the late afternoon, I disappear back through the rear door in total secrecy. It is raining hard. The Führer is very emotional as we say farewell. This is a great moment for me. I drive through the park, out through the back gate, and then race through the city, where people are innocently walking in the rain. Happy people, who know nothing of all our worries and just live from day to day. It is for them that we are working and fighting, taking all manner of risks upon ourselves. So that our people may live!

Schwanenwerder! I solemnly enjoin everybody to say nothing of my secret visit to the Führer. It would only cause anxiety.

And then I go back to work.

Outside, the rain beats against the window-pane. Dreadful June this year! . . .

(17 June and part of 18 June missing)

18 June 1941 (Wednesday)

. . . Morale bad, no more will to fight, profoundest depression in the face of the many catastrophic defeats. Some of it may well be true, but the English are a tough bunch.

I am reading the book on Churchill by his Private Secretary, Phyllis Muir. The man has something. In any event, he will give us a few more hard nuts to crack. But for him, the war would have been over long ago. As things are, however, there will still be some hard fighting to do. But the fact is that we shall win, because we have more resources and, in the final analysis, we are more thorough.

The book is brilliantly written, quite intimate, a good advertisement for Churchill.

Some expressions of discontent in England. But I have no high expectations in this quarter.

The world is slowly beginning to smell a rat regarding our Russian deception. It has been seen through. High time. The Führer rings me up late in the evening: wants to know when we can start printing and how long it will take to produce thirty million leaflets. If we start immediately, a night. We are starting today.

The Iraqi Prime Minister has given an interview to the DNB on the run. He was forced to yield to superior force, he says, but believes in our victory. We do, too, but we shall not yield.

This evening I have still so much to do. The work is unending.

The days are creeping by.

I wait, longing for the end of the week.

It gnaws at one's nerves.

Once things are under way, then the weight will fall from my heart, as ever.

19 June 1941 (Thursday)

Yesterday: English incursions into the Rhine and Ruhr districts. No serious damage. London has turned the raids into a huge sensation. Making out that our entire armaments industry is in ruins. I have evidence to the contrary supplied through neutral witnesses. Now we must try to do something to bridge the short time left. Twenty-one English aircraft were shot down over the Channel in the course of an attempted incursion. The overall kill ratio is 37:13. A serious setback for England. Likewise, the English attack in North Africa has been beaten off, and heavy losses have been inflicted on the enemy. He lost some 200 tanks. Our troops' conduct was above all praise. General Dentz has gone over to the offensive in Syria. The English have had to retreat. Black days for London. We shall ensure that they never end.

We are still refusing to give Syria any prominence. We have no intention of making it a prestige issue.

Provocations by the USA continue. We have taken appropriate countermeasures. One cannot take everything lying down. Otherwise, we are not dramatising the situation there. To do so would be to grant Roosevelt a favour, because a response is what he wants. Out of the question!

The first thing to be done is to print 800,000 leaflets for our soldiers. I have this undertaken in conditions of the strictest security. The printing works has been surrounded with Gestapo guards, the workers will not be allowed out until X-Day, and food and beds have been provided for them. The leaflets, ready-packed, will be handed over to the Wehrmacht, which will transport them to the front in the care of officers. They will be distributed to each company on the morning of the operation. The entire procedure is very intricate, but this is the only guarantee of complete secrecy. I draw the whole Ministerial Bureau's attention to the need for security. It is the foundation of a great victory.

New SD report: the country is very tense. An atmosphere that almost screams for some kind of release. But that will not be long coming.

Gutterer has hammered things out with Lammers: he shares our views regarding Bouhler and his bizarre censorship commission. It is not be allowed independent power to ban books. Lammers has also been primed against the Foreign Ministry. Ribbentrop is poking his nose into all sorts of things that do not concern him. I shall now take the offensive against him. People like him are only impressed by bare-faced impudence. Lammers has now expressed his approval of Dr Naumann's promotion.

Discuss a number of current issues with Gutterer.

Then to Lanke. I have some preparations to make out there for Pavolini's visit and am also able to work on one or two things in peace. After the bitingly cold weather, it is now high summer again. And it is so beautiful out there. Such quiet, such peace! I am completely content for a few hours.

Inspect the new log cabin. It is growing and will soon be finished.

Otherwise, nothing but work and this tension. Suspicion is now rampant in London. The enemy is slowly realising the situation. This was unavoidable. In Russia itself, they are making preparations for their great Navy Day. A real fiasco that will turn out to be.

32,000 tons sunk by U-boats. The French are advancing further in Syria. The English are saying nothing about their defeats in North Africa. We claim that maps indicating Derna as the target of their attack were found in their positions. Very effective.

Black days for London. There will be no shortage of them in times to come.

We publish documents proving the double-game played in Belgrade. It is a good thing that we smoked out that political hornets' nest.

Absurd claims in London regarding English air raids on the Ruhr district. But the English will soon lose their taste for bravado.

German–Turkish treaty published. The first bombshell. Others will follow.

Newsreel ready. Turned out well, despite lack of direct war coverage. I check a few test shots, which are not good enough.

Such a mild night! I sit up for a long while and read.

Yesterday: an insane amount to do. All in a tearing hurry. So no more than the main points.

English night raids on Hamburg and Bremen. Middling force. We have a few sinkings. Things still good in Syria. English demand for the surrender of Damascus rejected. French are fighting well. Our great victory near Sollum is complete. 200 English tanks destroyed. London claims that it was all a bluff. We give them something to think about. Wavell is having a bad time. Our press attacks are sharp and aggressive.

German–Turkish Treaty of Friendship is the big sensation. Guarantee of borders, economic co-operation, radio and press truce. London says that we had expected more, and so the treaty is a failure. We give them a proper answer. Further documents re. Belgrade published. To pass the time. Finland calls up her reservists, and announces the fact publicly. Moscow is slowly beginning to become more insolent.

I quash rumours that the Reichstag is about to be convened. This was all we needed just at the moment. General Bodenschatz has been talking too much. A real blabbermouth!

The Führer's declaration to the soldiers of the Army of the East printed, packed and despatched. Has to be reset once, however, since the quality is bad. Contents: explanation of the Russo–German quarrel. Up and at them! A brilliant analysis of the situation. We supervise the packing and have them despatched to the front under the strictest security. It all involves enormous difficulties. In the meantime, I quash a few more wild rumours that have been circulating among sections of the Party leadership.

Test new fanfares with Glasmaier. We have still not found the right one. Select films for the Biennale. Discipline Ludwig Schmitz, the perverse swine. He can thank the Führer that nothing worse happens to him. In consultation with Gutterer and Tiessler, prod the anti-tobacco propaganda on to more reasonable lines. Gutterer will arrange things at a lower level.

Discuss German–Italian radio co-operation with leading officials of the Italian broadcasting service. We are ahead in this field too.

Berndt and Carstensen report on North Africa. The Italians are cowards, and their officers are corrupt. We have the worst allies imaginable. Rommel is a legendary figure down there. The Führer has promoted him to General Commanding. I make further arrangements for troop entertainment, where possible.

With the Führer: the Russia business is now ready. The machine is gradually coming into motion. Everything is running smoothly. The Führer praises the superiority of our system when compared with liberal ones. We educate our people according to a common world-view. With the aid of films, radio and the press, which the Führer sees as the most important tools of popular leadership. The state must never let them out of her hands. The Führer also has a good word for the way our journalists have behaved. The

Propaganda Companies have made an essential contribution to this. Our work is in high repute at the moment.

Dr Frank talks about the General Government. There they are already looking forward to being able to push the Jews out. Jewry in Poland is gradually going to the dogs. A just punishment for the way it has caused disruption among nations and has intrigued to unleash this war. The Führer, of course, prophesied this fate for the Jews.

The Führer knows exactly what is going on in Africa. He is also aware of the Italians' cowardly withdrawals, major as well as minor. Nevertheless, he intends to talk to Berndt.

Funk reports on economic questions. A little confused. But he is a good fellow!

Bormann talks to me about Hess. He was a mixture of megalomania and inferiority complexes. And, as has now been proved, impotent. The poor man fell into the hands of astrologers. The results are a matter of record. His wife is still feigning injured innocence. She must bear a lot of the blame for her husband's fall. One can only pity him. He will never be able to appear in public life again . . .

(The rest of 20 June missing)

21 June 1941 (Saturday)

. . . The business of Russia is becoming more dramatic by the hour. Molotov has asked for permission to visit Berlin, but has been fobbed off. A naïve request. Should have been made six months ago. Our enemies are falling apart. I read a comprehensive report on Russian-Bolshevik radio propaganda. It will give us some real problems, because it is not so stupid as the English material. Probably written by Jews. As a precautionary measure, I have jamming stations established on the widest possible basis. Mobilisation in Finland. Moscow must realise the threat to Bolshevism now.

Try out new fanfares. I have now found the right one.

More problems with the Foreign Ministry, which is trying to interfere in all sorts of areas. A bumptious letter from Weizsäcker, which Gutterer answers in equally offensive terms.

Schwarz van Berk talks to me about a new system of word-of-mouth propaganda. The Party, he says, should spread not only unpleasant but pleasant things by means of whispering-campaigns. Particularly in higher circles. A good idea, which I seize on immediately.

Tiessler and Fischer have made another attack on the Seventh Chamber. But this comes from a sense of inferiority on both their parts. I take countermeasures. They would be better off doing their own work than trying to hinder other people's. Things remain as I decided . . .

. . . The Führer has exchanged sincere telegrams of friendship with Inönü. The treaty with Turkey has been of great help to us in the diplomatic sphere. After the initial astonishment, the only reaction London can manage is embarrassed bluster.

Meanwhile, the crisis is developing. An oppressively hot day, during which one waits for the storm that will clear the air, literally as well as metaphorically. There are signs of rising tension among the public, who have been completely calm so far. The operation is now being ushered in with magnificent skill. We shall have a good start.

Work at Schwanenwerder in the afternoon. There I have some quiet and a chance to collect myself.

US consulates here and in Italy closed. This is the kind of language that Roosevelt understands.

Heavy fighting around Damascus. The French are defending bravely.

Berndt and Carstensen from North Africa, Rechenberg from Crete, to report on the situation there. They tell me lot of interesting details, and a lot that is new to me. On the whole, confirmation of previous impressions. The Italians have been revealed in their true colours. On Crete and particularly in North Africa. My people are fighting very bravely. The war in North Africa is harder than any before, and the difficulties involved are almost overwhelming. But Rommel and his men will do their job. They deserve the highest praise and a fame that will go down in history.

Between times, a lot of routine work. Pavolini's train was derailed near Bologna. He and his people were uninjured and have continued their journey by car.

In the evening, a visit from John Knittel, the great Swiss writer, and Frau Springer, whom we are trying to help through the pain of her husband's loss. She has suffered greatly.

I discuss the situation with John Knittel. He firmly believes in our victory, despises the English and smiles at his own compatriots. Egypt is his great dream. He thinks we ought to organise that as soon as possible. We have better things to do.

London has the Russia business completely right now. They expect war daily. Only a few left who say the whole thing is a bluff.

Roosevelt has used the *Robin More* case as an excuse for an address to Congress, which slanders us in the strongest terms. He is hysterical. Ignore him!

The Führer is very pleased with our fanfares. He is having a few more written. Based on the Horst Wessel Song.

New Liebeneiner film, *I Accuse*. In favour of euthanasia. A film that will really arouse discussion. Magnificently made and absolutely National Socialist. It will stir up tremendous controversy. And that is its purpose. Hippler and Demandowski are very proud of their achievement.

To bed very late.

22 June 1941 (Sunday)

Yesterday: middling raids on the North-West. The Kiel airport at Holtenau hit quite badly. Our losses in North Africa have turned out to be relatively small. The first reports are always exaggerated.

London has admitted 500,000 tons sunk in May. And in the process has tried to knock 100,000 tons from April. And now another 56,000 tons from a single convoy. Things are in motion again, it seems. Our U-boats are back in action in the kind of quantities that make them a decision factor. And by the end of July this will be even more clearly the case.

Martin reports on the final preparations. The attack will begin at 3.30 a.m. I am still not clear whether the Führer's proclamation is to be read out on the radio immediately or not until 7.00 a.m. We intend to issue a warning about sabotage squads of Russian parachutists on the first day. A secret report from one of our agents has given urgent warning of enemy plans along these lines.

The issue of Russia overshadows all other political developments. But world opinion is still in the dark. We shall soon open their eyes for them. Roosevelt's slanderous statement against us has been completely lost in the general brouhaha. Not a well-chosen moment from his point of view.

Discuss the radio offensive during the night with Glasmaier and Diewerge. They have to be put in the picture now. The radio stations will stay in operation until further notice. Try out the new fanfares. Including those based on the Horst Wessel Song. But the Liszt fanfare is still the best. The Führer will decide.

Hunke reports on his trip to Italy. The picture that he paints is fairly bleak. There is a complete lack of organisation and system. No rationing, no decent food, but plenty of appetite for conquest. If possible, they intend to leave the fighting to us and then inherit what we win. Very nice. Fascism has still not overcome its internal crisis. It is sick in body and mind. Too badly eaten away by corruption.

Pavolini fetched from Tempelhof. A very friendly welcome. He is a good-natured, likeable fellow, probably loyal, but not exactly a great pillar of the church. We immediately launch ourselves into a long discussion, with Alfieri, about co-operation in cultural matters, propaganda and films. We outline the operation to come. He and his colleagues will soon have the details made clear to them. All of our colleagues at the ministry are to be told now.

Brief discussion with Frau Leander about her new war film.

The day is oppressively hot and close. Dietrich gives a breakfast party for Pavolini at the Adlon. Alfieri tells me during the course of it about the problems that Ribbentrop is causing him. Together with Ciano. These two 'statesmen' are making all our lives a misery. But, thank God, we do not need to take it lying down.

The Italians come out to Schwanenwerder in the afternoon. At home it is so close as to be almost intolerable. But the entire world is waiting for the cleansing storm.

Reception for our guests. A good atmosphere. Alfieri tells me that Rome also intends to make a pact with Turkey. Let her! Pavolini is here. From the personal point of view, he seems extraordinarily pleasant. At his request, the guests watch the American film, *Gone with the Wind*, which they all find very impressive. Meanwhile, I make a few telephone calls. The storm is slowly gathering.

A very pleasant party, but I cannot relax sufficiently to give it my full attention. Talk with Pavolini. About our work. I make some very pointed criticisms of Italian press policy. He admits the mistakes that have been made, particularly the Italians' easy-going attitude towards military secrets. We have big plans for cultural co-operation. Except that the Foreign Ministry is constantly interfering. Ribbentrop has written me a letter telling me that I am not allowed to sign any agreements with Pavolini. Waste-paper basket!

Hadamovsky arrives back from seeing the Führer. The fanfares will have to be altered slightly. The time for the proclamation is to be agreed between the Führer and myself.

The guests watch the film to its conclusion. I have already summoned my colleagues out to Schwanenwerder so that I have them close at hand. Telephone call from the Führer. I go absent from the party and drive to the Reich Chancellery. Galland has just downed his sixty-ninth plane, jumped from his own burning fighter. Oak leaves with swords.* A fantastic fellow. We shot down another twenty Englishmen today.

The Führer is off for a short drive. He looks completely exhausted when he returns. But we go straight into the situation report.

He has dictated a new proclamation to the people, which also gives more consideration to the soldiers. I suggest a few minor alterations. The piece is magnificent and explains the entire case.

The attack will begin at 3.30 a.m. 160 full Divisions along a 3000 kilometre-long battlefront. Everything is well prepared. The biggest concentration of forces in the history of the world. The Führer seems to lose his fear as the decision comes nearer. It is always the same with him. He relaxes visibly. All the exhaustion seems to drop away. We pace up and down in his salon for three hours. I am granted more insights into his most secret thoughts. We have no choice but to attack. This cancerous sore must be cauterised. Stalin will fall. Dekanasov in Berlin has already made representations about our reconnaissance flights over the border. Evasive answer! The Duce will be fully informed on Sunday. He was given an outline during the last talks at the Brenner. We establish guidelines for the struggle.

* Of the Knight's Cross.

423

Clear and unambiguous. We shall lay particular emphasis on the argument that Russia's two-faced policy has prevented a decisive settlement of the English question. The Führer has high hopes of the peace party in England. Otherwise, he claims, the Hess Affair would not have been so systematically killed by silence. The Führer has only contempt when he talks about Hess. If the man were not mad, he would deserve to be shot. He has done the Party tremendous damage, particularly in its relations with the Wehrmacht. He can never return to public life. The effect of his action on our soldiers was very negative. In this connection, I tell the Führer about Berndt's impressions of North Africa. The Führer is completely in the picture. After some discussion, the time for the reading of the proclamation on the radio is fixed for 5.30 a.m. By then, the enemy will know what is happening, and it will be time that the nation and world were informed as well.

The Führer also has a low opinion of Alfieri's intellectual gifts. But the man is a firm friend of Germany, and so he must remain in his post. I support him in this view.

He has me clarify things regarding Pavolini. I tell him about my initiative in press matters, which he approves completely.

Try out new fanfares. For a whole hour. And then we end up sticking with my original suggestion, a short phrase from the Horst Wessel Song. The Führer is very impressed with our work in this area. Then our preparations are at an end. He has been working on this since July of last year, and now the moment has come. Everything has been done that could humanly have been done. Now the fortunes of war must decide.

I then tell the Führer about Professor Auler's cancer research and its results. He is extraordinarily interested in it.

And then farewell. It is 2.30 a.m. The Führer's mood is very solemn. He intends to sleep for a few hours. And this is the best thing that he could do.

I go over to the ministry. It is still pitch-dark. I put my colleagues in the picture. Total amazement in all quarters. Most had guessed half, or even the whole truth. Everyone sets to work immediately. Radio, press and newsreel are mobilised. Everything runs like clockwork.

I study the final telegrams: all rubbish. Our guns will issue the last denial. I shall not say a word. Study the radio situation in Russia. We shall have our work cut out.

3.30. Now the guns will be thundering. May God bless our weapons!

Outside on the Wilhelmplatz, it is quiet and deserted. Berlin and the entire Reich are asleep. I have half an hour to spare, but I cannot sleep. I pace up and down restlessly in my room. One can hear the breath of history.

A glorious, wonderful hour has struck, when a new empire is born. Our nation is making her way up into the light.

The new fanfare sounds. Filled with power, booming and majestic. I read the Führer's proclamation to the German people over all stations. A solemn moment for me.

The burden of many weeks and months falls away.

I feel totally free.

Still a few urgent matters to settle.

Then I drive out to Schwanenwerder. The sun is already standing full and beautiful in the sky.

Outside in the garden, the birds are singing.

I tumble into bed. And sleep two hours of deep, healing sleep.

23 June 1941 (Monday)

Yesterday: An oppressively hot day. Our soldiers will not find the fighting easy.

Molotov speaks: wild abuse, mingled with an appeal to patriotism, tearful accusation, and between a glimpse of fear: 'We shall be victorious,' he says. The wretch! England's attitude is still ambiguous. Caught too much by surprise. No clear line. Nothing but amazement in the USA at present. Antonescu has issued a poetic proclamation to his people and army. Finland has not yet made her move. Hungary making strong anti-Bolshevist statements in support of us. Italy has declared war on Russia. Very decent. A wave of anti-Bolshevism is sweeping across Europe. The Führer's decision is the biggest sensation imaginable.

Our air offensive has begun in the grand style. With 900 Stukas and fighters. Against Russian cities, including Kiev, and against airfields. Battle has been joined along the 3000-kilometre front. The first, minor river barriers have already been crossed at all points.

We carry out a heavy raid on Southampton. English air attacks on the Rhine and Ruhr disticts, but without visible success.

With Alfieri at midday. [. . .] has been summoned to Ribbentrop, who has told him that Pavolini's visit is undesirable. This is outrageous. I shall have to talk to the Führer about it at the earliest possible opportunity.

Discuss film problems with Pavolini: particularly regular exchanges of newsreel material and feature films. We reach complete accord. We also intend to organise reciprocal visits by journalists on a large scale.

The psychological situation becomes clearer in the course of the afternoon. The Führer's proclamation has been reprinted word for word all over the world. London's initial response is to claim that Hitler is mad, and in the process to cite the example of Napoleon, a parallel already suggested by Molotov. We shall have to deal with this. A few English voices call for a reasonable approach and indicate what England will lose if we conquer the Ukraine. The USA has turned to abuse. But words, as is well known, never hurt anyone. If we win, we shall have right on our side. No statement yet from Japan.

The Russians have already suffered extremely serious aircraft losses.

During one attack on Tilsit they lost twenty-two out of forty-three aircraft. Operations are proceeding according to plan.

Report from a neutral eye-witness in London: heavy damage in almost all the cities bombed. Morale, however, completely intact. Strong socially-aware and anti-plutocratic feeling. Churchill still very popular. His position is still very strong at the moment.

I work through the afternoon at full stretch. After my reading of the Führer's proclamation, Ribbentrop added his pennyworth. The needs of vanity!

Russian movements are similar to those of the French in 1870. And her armies will suffer the same catastrophe. During the initial stages, the Russians are defending only moderately well. But their air force has suffered appalling losses at the outset: 200 planes shot down, 200 destroyed on the ground, and 200 damaged. A considerable deficit, whichever way one looks at it. We shall win. We must win, and quickly. The public mood is one of slight depression. The nation wants peace, though not at the price of defeat, but every new theatre of operations brings worry and concern.

The Spanish press is setting to with a will. As are the Swedish newspapers. Europe is filled with a crusading spirit of a kind. Very useful from our point of view. But we shall not place too much emphasis on fighting 'for Christianity'. That would, after all, be just too hypocritical.

Antonescu has appointed his brother as his deputy. This is not exactly wonderful, but it is no concern of ours. Still no clear line in London. The shock has been too great.

During the early evening, a small reception for Pavolini at Lanke. A number of pleasant guests. But I have no leisure to play host. More news is arriving with every passing minute. Mostly very satisfying. 1000 Russian aircraft destroyed so far. This is a real body-blow. Brest-Litovsk taken. All the day's objectives reached. No problems so far. We are entitled to be very pleased. The Soviet régime will crumble like touchwood.

Churchill has made a speech. A hysterical tirade against the Führer. Otherwise, his speech is nothing but confirmation that London and Moscow have been working together against us.

Pavolini's visit passes very pleasantly. We spend an enjoyable, stimulating evening together. Work on the newsreel with him present. He and his people are quite overcome with wonder.

To bed very late again. Sleep has become a luxury for us recently.

24 June 1941 (Tuesday)

Yesterday: Military developments in the East are excellent beyond all our expectations. Our new weapons are carrying all before them. The Russians are emerging from their bunkers trembling, unfit for interrogation for a day afterwards. We are advancing along two huge fronts. 1500 Russian aircraft destroyed so far. They are falling like flies. Their fighters are slower than our Junkers 88. Everything is going to plan, and better.

Insignificant English air raids. Pointless, in fact. This was supposed to be Churchill's finest hour, as he himself said. We are over England, 80 aircraft strong. This must make an impression. The Russians are said to be 'grinding us to powder'. We shall see about that.

I outline the entire situation at the Ministerial Conference and reveal our hand. Great astonishment in all quarters. Our tactics will aim at underlining English–Russian complicity. Churchill's speech provides excellent ammunition. Opinion in the USA very much divided. As a result of our assumption of the battle against Bolshevism. In Europe itself there is something like a united front forming. Very useful from our point of view. We are slowly beginning to bang the loud anti-Bolshevist drum. Gradually, so as not to make the transition too difficult. The public is still undecided. The volte-face came too suddenly. The public will have to get used to the idea. This will not take long. Just let us have the first concrete victories. Things in East Prussia have got a little out of hand, with air-raid precautions, evacuation, etc. I have this stopped immediately. They will have to get used to the situation first.

To the Führer with Pavolini. The Führer receives him with great warmth. Explains the Russian campaign for Italian domestic consumption. The Führer sees operations as continuing favourably for us. He makes it clear that the issue is unity against Bolshevism. This will be understood very well in Italy, where they only changed their traditional policy for our sake. Italy was always against Moscow.

I give the Führer an account of the results of our cultural co-operation with Italy. He is very taken with it. This will be very useful against the Foreign Ministry.

The Führer is about to set off for the front. I take my leave of him. He is very serious and solemn. Come back victorious! And keep safe! With God's help!

He is such a great man. One can only feel reverence in the face of his greatness.

Pavolini tells me about Ribbentrop's intrigues. That fellow pursues departmental advantage at the cost of our foreign policy. But I shall give him one where it hurts.

The latest film figures have been issued. Very good. Estimated profits of 40 million.

Pass new propaganda film against tobacco-abuse.

Martin wants permission for a big new Christian magazine aimed at the Wehrmacht. I turn the idea down. These milksop teachings are the very worst thing we can give our soldiers.

Work a little at Schwanenwerder. It is oppressively hot.

To the Ufa studios with Pavolini . . .

427

. . . Look at five hundred metres of Newsreel film of the beginning of our Russian campaign. Some of our new weapons are shown. Juggernauts that simply destroy everything in their path. Russian prisoners clamber out of their dugouts and trenches, shaking with terror. God's high court of history is now passing judgment on the Soviet state. Atrocity has been heaped on actrocity, and now the reckoning has come. Pavolini is totally thunderstruck at the monumental quality of the film material.

Alexandria bombed by our Luftwaffe. Final battle for Tobruk. 209 English tanks destroyed. 40,000 tons sunk. Just so that Churchill does not feel that he is being neglected. This devastating activity on all fronts has earned the unconfined admiration of the entire world. The European unity front against Russia is taking shape almost of its own accord. We are doing nothing to encourage it, so as to avoid arousing suspicion. I believe that the war against Moscow will be our greatest coup, from the psychological standpoint and perhaps also militarily.

Feeling against Moscow is on the upsurge all over Europe. Even *The Times* is expressing itself in very sceptical terms. But no clear opinion is discernible yet.

Newsreel in the evening. Simply magnificent. A masterly achievement of organisation, technique, and visual effectiveness.

Then a late dinner with Pavolini. A small party.

This visit has me dead on my feet.

25 June 1941 (Wednesday)

Yesterday: Accompany Pavolini to his plane. Friendly farewell. We shall meet again in Venice. We issue a detailed communiqué on the visit, which arouses the anger of the Foreign Ministry. Some minor intrigues by Ribbentrop, but they cannot alter the facts.

• War situation: middling English air raids on North-West Germany. Success slight. Serious damage only in Kiel. We attack towns at the mouth of the Thames. Kill ratio 22:5. In the East, 2585 Russian aircraft have been destroyed during the first two days, against fifty-one of ours. Operations on the ground are proceeding well. Significant successes, beyond our expectations. The enemy is fighting well. Attempted revolts in the Baltic countries. We have entered Kovno.* Parts of Leningrad are in flames. We have still issued no details in the High Command Bulletin. The enemy is to be kept in complete ignorance. He probably has no idea what is happening.

In Moscow, they are ranting and raving in the old Communist style. But it is beginning to sound hollow in the rumble of the guns. Plus wild atrocity propaganda against us, which we immediately take up and respond to with

* Kaunas in Lithuania.

counter-attacks. But their propaganda is better than London's. Here we find ourselves facing a more practised opponent.

Deomonstrations in our favour in Madrid. The European front against Moscow is becoming increasingly clearly defined, even without our direct intervention.

I have the press play down the multinational character of the Russian state, which has been over-emphasised. This will serve only to stiffen enemy resistance. I also order that we do not yet deal with the economic advantages of a victory over Moscow. Our press campaign is to be confined to the political sphere alone. I am also refraining from publishing big maps of Russia. The huge areas involved may frighten the public. I take a strong line against the imprudent tendency to set a time-limit on our victory, which is widespread in the Foreign Ministry. If we say four weeks and it turns into six, then our greatest victory will be transformed into a defeat in the end. The Foreign Ministry is also paying insufficient attention to military secrecy. I have the Gestapo take steps against one particular loudmouth.

A united front between Moscow, London and Washington is beginning to take clear shape. I ensure that it is given full attention. Here is our circumstantial evidence. Rosenberg has published a very instructive article on Eastern questions.

Glasmaier has had Anacker write a song for the Russian campaign. But as yet totally inadequate . . .

. . . Wide-ranging discussions with Funk in the course of a long visit from him. He is always glad to spend some time with us. He has a lot of worries. After all, these days he has the job of organising almost the entire European economy. The Italians are a thorn in his flesh. Always demanding more than they are entitled to, and indulging in state-sponsored black-market currency dealings. What a nation! Funk is involved in something of a row with Ley. Ley has too big an appetite, and is overstepping the mark.

I address the Reich propaganda speakers. I outline the present situation in the frankest possible way and show how it came about. Am rewarded with thunderous applause.

The heat is debilitating. I work on at Schwanenwerder, but I am so tired that I fall asleep at my desk and wake up two hours later in a totally dazed state. Straight back to the rough and tumble. Sick-making, but wonderful. I would have it no other way.

Sumner Welles has spoken on behalf of the USA. Totally subservient to Red Bolshevism.

The old, so-familiar alliance between capitalism and Bolshevism has been resurrected in the foreign-policy field. I write an article on the subject for the *Völkischer Beobachter* with the title, 'The Old Alliance.' Proof of the conspiracy against us.

We are publishing further documentary evidence on this score. But I give instructions that it should be evaluated rather than reprinted word-for-word at enormous length. This is too complicated. At the moment we need to get back to having a fighting press: tough, hard-hitting, aggressive. Just like in the good, old days.

The situation in Syria is very grave. Even Vichy admits it.

Finland is still pretending neutrality. For reasons of military tactics. But this will not last for much longer. The public there is going frantic. Hungary has broken off relations with Moscow. In Spain, the entire public is on our side. Japan is still holding back. USA totally divided. Our position there is very good. The first flush of joy has faded in England. Now opinion is very sceptical and fears a swift German victory, with all that this would entail.

Turkey is furious about the Straits question. We played a real trump there.

The London press is exaggerating the RAF's damage on German territory to a degree that is nothing short of grotesque. We deal with this easily.

This is how things stand by late evening.

I am totally drained by the oppressive heat.

These are difficult days for our soldiers.

26 June 1941 (Thursday)

Yesterday: The weather is oppressive and close, so that one can scarcely breathe. Nevertheless, I work at full stretch, telegrams pour in, and the telephone rings continually.

We have penetrated deep into Russian territory. Kovno, Vilna, Slonim and Brest-Litovsk are in our hands. Heavy fighting in the south. The Russians are resisting bravely. No moves to withdraw. A good thing. We shall have them all the more securely later. They are losing countless tanks and aircraft. This is the precondition of victory. We stand on the threshold of enormous successes. Our Wehrmacht High Command's Bulletin will say no more for the moment. The Russians are being left in the dark so far as our tactics are concerned. In the USA, they are now giving us ten days to victory. I take vigorous measures against such predictions. A great triumph can look like a defeat if we fail to live up to a date set in the USA.

English raids. With some success on Boulogne, Lille. We attack Liverpool with 80 aircraft. Tilsit,* Memel** and Königsberg† bombed by the Russians. Little fleabites.

The Russian military communiqués are putrid with lies. We are still holding our fire in that quarter. Our triumph will be all the greater when we really get going. Russian transmitters are trying to undermine our troops' morale. Ludicrous! Our transmitters are being jammed by Moscow. But now I shall be able to put the Kovno station into action. I have high expectations of it.

* Now Sovetsk in the Soviet Union.
** Now Klaipeda in the Soviet Union.
† Now Kaliningrad in the Soviet Union.

My article, 'The Old Alliance', has worked very well. It will appear in the *V.B.* Schwarz van Berk has written a brilliant foreword to my new book.

The European united front against Moscow is taking clearer shape. We are giving it every support.

Discuss cultural and troop entertainment questions with Hinkel. We are hard at work recruiting new talent. Tiessler raises some Party personnel issues. Fischer has a new propaganda plan for the Party. But it is too ambitious. No one will go to meetings in this heat. Bibrach reports from Cremona. Diewerge proposes a new method for making our broadcasting work more effective. He is very hardworking and thoughtful.

I receive the provincial leaders of the Red Cross and give the ladies an outline of their duties.

Discuss the revised plans for the Rembrandt film. Still a few blemishes.

Bruvers reports on a year's work in Belgium. Morale there is improving. If we crush Moscow now, we shall have permanent benefits.

A host of press issues with Fritzsche. Dietrich rings up from Headquarters and lets me know the most important news. The Führer is as optimistic as he could be.

More demonstrations in Spain. Our attack on Moscow has driven a wedge into the plutocratic camp. From a psychological point of view, our situation is superb at the moment.

To Schwanenwerder in the evening. I am completely exhausted. Berlin is stinkingly hot.

Finland has now officially declared war on Russia.

Then the newsreel, late in the evening. War material. Has turned out magnificently.

Then some film problems with Hippler. I cannot sleep in this broiling heat.

27 June 1941 (Friday)

Yesterday: Another hot day, in every respect. The air war between us and England continues. But for a long time now the RAF has not been attacking in the kind of force that we had feared. One skirmish after another. No one can explain it. A few sinkings. But all eyes are focused on the East. No decisive moves in the southern section of the front. Our forces are still keeping the enemy busy there. Thank God, he is showing no sign of retreating. Minsk is in our hands. The first big pocket is beginning to close. We are capturing masses of prisoners and matériel. The Russians are suffering huge losses in tanks and aircraft. But they are fighting well and have learned a great deal even since Sunday. Our success so far is more than satisfactory. So far as the northern sector is concerned, it could even be described as magnificent. Finland has officially attacked. Sweden has allowed a German division to pass through her territory. Denmark has declared strongly for us, there are demonstrations in Madrid against Mos-

431

cow, and Italy intends to send an expeditionary force – so long as it is not more trouble than it is worth. The anti-Bolshevik front in Europe is on the ascendant.

We are adding no more than sparse commentaries to the High Command's Bulletins. World tension is reaching a peak. The Bolshiviks are issuing military communiqués that contain more propaganda than facts. Totally crude and importunate. And quite ineffective. Everyone is waiting for our reports, because they know that they alone will show the true state of things.

Moscow Radio is mass-producing atrocity stories. Appeals to our troops to desert. Stupid and clumsy, but nevertheless we shall have to watch out there. The Bolsheviks are not Englishmen. They know a thing or two about subversive propaganda. We now have the Kovno transmitter in operation. Others will follow. We are now working on large-scale defeatist propaganda aimed at the population. It is true that the broadcasting situation is not brilliant from our point of view – Moscow's transmitters are much more powerful than ours – but it is improving daily. Our task now is to get through this difficult time. In any event, we shall not be short of an answer so far as Moscow is concerned.

Big dilemma in London. Likewise, public opinion in the USA divided. People are slowly beginning to feel uncomfortable about an alliance with Bolshevism. In contrast, our psychological position is unambiguous, clear and firm. Turkey is beginning to take our part increasingly strongly, largely because of the Straits question. London and Washington are suffering considerable loss of sympathy. Our stock is rising in the occupied territories as well. I am receiving reports from Paris, Brussels, the Hague, Oslo, Prague and Cracow. All say the same. Our position is very favourable at the moment.

A mass of current problems to be dealt with. Glasmaier plays some new songs for the Russian campaign for my approval. But none of them are good enough.

Schmidt-Decker reports on the work of the AO abroad. Very wide-ranging. A lot of useful work is being done there.

Discuss the new propaganda plans of the Party with Fischer and Wächter. No big meetings, more emphasis on clarifying matters to Party comrades and word-of-mouth propaganda. And extension of the 'slogan of the week' programme. Wächter is settling in well . . .

. . . Receive 60 members of the Party's old guard in Berlin. I am sending them on a holiday trip to the Upper Danube Gau, and I give them a short farewell speech. They are all very pleased to see me again. They remain the best, most loyal men imaginable.

Spend a long time arguing with Alfieri. Still to do with Pavolini's visit and the communiqué. I am now sick of the whole business, and I tell him so, without mincing my words. He has fallen victim to the Foreign Ministry's unspeakable, disloyal intrigues. But even Pavolini is a mere cipher. The faithful servant of his master, Ciano. It is impossible to work or get anywhere with such weaklings. I shall therefore have to make my own way and not allow these soulless diplomats to queer my pitch.

Personnel matters with Gutterer. A moving letter from Bömer in prison. His punishment has been too harsh. It is true that he talked stupidly, but not much more so than many others. When the Russian campaign is over, I shall intervene on his behalf.

The city is like an oven. Particularly on the Wilhelmplatz. I drive out to Schwanenwerder to work there. But it is not much of an improvement.

Spend the entire afternoon reading telegrams and reports. News from the front is very sparse. Everything is still in flux there. But it will soon be raining victories.

Wodarg comes to report in the evening. On the Luftwaffe's contribution in the East, which is absolutely magnificent. The only thing that worries us is that the Russians may pull back too soon and avoid the decisive battle. So far they have shown only isolated tendencies to do this. If they do not, however, then they will soon be lost.

Statements from Russian prisoners reveal a horrifying lack of awareness. The result of Bolshevik education. No question of proper military training. Many of them shoot themselves rather than be taken prisoner, because they have been told appalling stories about our soldiers. We shall have to deal with that problem by leaflets, since the radio is being jammed.

Wodarg spends the entire evening telling us about the work of the Luftwaffe High Command, which is extraordinarily complex and wide-ranging. Fascinating insights into how such a great military machine is directed.

We sit out on the terrace until long after midnight, discussing things. Wodarg is an intelligent boy, and above all he is totally decent.

I cannot sleep in this baking heat.

28 June 1941 (Saturday)

Yesterday: Broiling heat. Can work only with difficulty.

Middling air activity. We do not undertake much over England. The RAF is nowhere near exploiting the situation. More big sinkings. The battle of the oceans continues.

Eastern Front: very tough resistance in the southern sector. The enemy is defending desperately and is also very well led. The situation presents no threat, but we have our hands full.

Central section: very good progress. The first pocket has been closed. All sorts trapped inside. Signs of demoralisation among the enemy already apparent. Growing quantities of captured matériel. The tank battle has been decided completely in our favour. We are also advancing well in the north.

The Luftwaffe has destroyed 4000 enemy aircraft so far. Our losses are minimal. Finland's President Ryti has issued a moving appeal to his nation. A clear exposé of the evils of Bolshevism. We release it in unshortened form for all news media.

The entire front is screaming for propaganda material. Faced with the Russians, they have need of it. Particularly leaflets that guarantee the safety of prisoners and can be used as identity documents. The Russian military communiqués are very crude propaganda vehicles and scarcely of any value. We do not intend to follow Moscow along that path. We are still confining ourselves to vague statements. But our reticence is gradually having a deleterious effect on our overall propaganda effort. Nevertheless, we shall be all the better off when we finally let rip. The Russians are slowly withdrawing in the central sector. This does not accord with our intentions.

The Russian radio stations are putting out bad Bolshevik propaganda. We shall have no trouble dealing with it. Our own stations are not yet getting through, since they are being jammed even on the new frequencies. But things will, of course, improve when we capture more transmitters.

No calls for enemy soldiers to desert. Only statements by prisoners on the radio and in leaflets, which give a true description of the behaviour of the German Wehrmacht. The rest will follow.

Stalin gave a speech as early as the 6 May, in which he predicted war against Germany. So International Newspaper Service reports. This suits us very well. I am still working at proving the Anglo-Russian conspiracy.

Reports on the air war from London are completely absurd. According to them, half of Germany is in ruins. We are unable to deny much, since the Herr Englishmen are mostly hitting dummy installations. For the rest London is cobbling together the most improbable tissues of lies: the government is on the point of collapse, Ley has already been dismissed, I am on the point of going, and so on. We pay no attention.

I take measures to ensure that the newsreel and the newspapers do not keep issuing the same pictures from the front. This is due to bad organisation on the part of the Propaganda Companies. I am having trouble with the Wehrmacht High Command, which is hand in glove with the Foreign Ministry. At the moment they are refusing to allow the radio people from the occupied territories to come here and report to me. And Dominik is not being allowed to travel to Kovno to sort out the broadcasting problems. I am not taking all this lying down. One seems to be dealing with minor aggravations all the livelong day.

The food supply situation in Berlin is very bad. No potatoes, very few vegetables. But Backe tells me that it will improve in a week. It is due to the weather and the transport situation. But the people have to eat. I am keeping an eye on things. The position in the occupied territories is much worse. In some areas there is real starvation. In other respects, the position is not yet clear. Terboven reports complete confusion in Norway. Pro-

English groups are in conflict with Bolsheviks. The split in the enemy camp is deepening all the time. At the moment we must try to exploit is as much as possible. With time we may be able to deepen the rift to such an extent that the enemy front crumbles.

Still no new song for Russia. I keep up the pressure, but our writers cannot come up with anything.

Farewell from Greiner, who is off to his military service. He is to take over the management of the film-theatre company after the war. The ministry's three administrative departments will then be separate.

[. . .] is going to Italy as representative of the German cinema industry. His task: to get what he can for us. To smile and be a villain. Not to let the Italian film industry get too big. Germany must remain the leading film-making power in Europe and must constantly shore up her dominant position.

Some petit-bourgeois who happens to own the Philharmonia wants to rent it out as a grain warehouse. I stop this and issue a regulation to the effect that no part of our cultural heritage, including buildings, may be sold or disposed of without my permission.

It is killingly hot on the Wilhelmplatz. I drive out to Lanke, to work there in peace and quiet. It is fine outside, sunny but slightly cool.

Hungary has declared a state of war with Russia. Not much use to us from the military point of view, but psychologically beneficial. The united European front is growing. In the end, Churchill will be completely alone with his Bolsheviks.

All sorts to be done in the afternoon. By the evening it is cooler. Refreshing. Inspect our new log cabin, which will soon be ready and has turned out beautifully. Situated in the midst of the forest, but really meant for peacetime. That time will soon be coming.

Europe is closing ranks under our leadership. The entire continent is undergoing an awakening. Small and great nations alike are joining us. It is impossible to know yet where it will lead.

In any event, we shall go forward, forward, forward, until the great hour comes.

29 June 1941 (Sunday)

Yesterday: Situation in the East: stalemate in the south on the Rumanian front, small-scale Russian salients, some on Rumanian soil. No serious danger. In the central sector, everything is proceeding according to plan. We are already driving beyond Minsk. The enemy is losing huge numbers of tanks and aircraft. The first great cauldron is almost closed. On the northern front, everything is also going to plan. Except in the south, the situation is excellent. The Russians are fighting bravely. Their chain of command is functioning more efficiently than during the first few days. Moscow is spreading the most outrageous lies and atrocity reports. But world opinion refuses to believe a word the Bolsheviks say. In the USA, Stalin's position is reckoned to be hopeless. At home, our people are already indulging in illusions. There is talk of 600,000 prisoners, an entry into Leningrad, etc. This is the result of our long silence. Nevertheless, the Führer refuses to break it. Even though there is a danger that the public will be disappointed when it hears the first hard news. At the moment, military considerations must come first. We are all pressing for more detailed news to be released to the public. But the Führer intends to wait until Sunday – today – before opening the gates to a flood of special announcements. We are all busy preparing the ground for it. The SD report also complains of over-optimism in the country at large. This is fed by reports from abroad. The first shock has passed. A certain over-confidence has taken its place. We shall deal with that, too.

Our fleet is doing good work. The Red fleet has been given a bloody nose. I order the press and radio to exercise the greatest restraint in all these matters. And the over-optimistic reports from the USA must no longer be published. I have foreign journalists warned again about dressing mutton up as lamb. Otherwise, there may be Gestapo action.

Raids on Bremen and Hamburg. With some success. Russian air force ominously silent. We lay mines near English ports.

The Russian radio network is working totally in the old Bolshevik style. We shall counteract it without difficulty. And we are now getting our broadcasts through. The split in the enemy ranks is deepening. The movement for European unity against Moscow is growing.

The new song for Russia is ready: a co-operative work by Anacker, Tiessler and Kolbe, which I put together and revise. By the time I have finished, it is unrecognisable. A magnificent song. Niel and Norbert Schulze have each written a tune to go with it. Just in time, since we want to use it as an accompaniment to the first big news bulletins. I shall use the best.

Give approval to a new propaganda film by Fischer and Wächter. The minor skirmish with the Wehrmacht High Command continues. Always the same thing: spheres of authority. And now Rosenberg is joining in. He already sees himself as Czar of Russia.

If we go down, then it will be as a result of these disputes.

Look in briefly at the Göringstrasse to see all is well. The bunker is taking shape.

Work in peace and quiet at Lanke. It is raining. The cool is refreshing. One can get back to work again.

A European solidarity front is taking clearer shape all the time. Denmark, Spain, Portugal, etc. are part of it. 'Russia has no friends,' the US press says sadly. Quite right!

English journalist in Moscow claims that London and Moscow have been co-operating on the military level for some time. This is the kind of thing that we can use.

I write a leader-article, *News Policy*, in which I explain the reasons for our withholding of war reports. Such an explanation to the public is now urgently necessary. Turned out well.

New song for Russia set to music by Herms Niel and Norbert Schulze. Each plays me his composition. Schulze's is better. I make a few improvements. It must be ready by this morning, since today is the big day for announcements.

A total of 150,000 tons sunk in a single day. Aircraft losses against England 36:1. For this reason, little air activity over Germany. Vigorous demonstrations against the British Embassy in Madrid. Things are slowly starting to move.

Dr Dietrich rings up from the Führer's Headquarters: all is well. Führer in the best of form, very pleased with our work. The silence will now be broken. Ribbentrop was there and had been intending to complain. But he got nowhere.

Magda comes out to Lanke in the evening. We are able to chat for an hour.

The rain is falling. Blessed streams of water. The harvest will be a good one. In all respects.

30 June 1941 (Monday)

Yesterday: Day of special announcements. Twelve in all, and we begin broadcasting them on the radio at 11 a.m. The entire world is glued to its radio sets. We have won complete dominance in the air, have taken Grodno, Brest-Litovsk, Kovno and [. . .]. Two Red armies trapped east of Bialystok. No chance of a breakout. Minsk in our hands. The Russians have lost 2233 tanks and 5107 aircraft. This is what we tell the public. It is too much all at once. By the end, one can sense a slight numbness in the way they receive the news. The effect is not what we had hoped for. The listeners can see through our manipulation of the news too clearly. It is all laid on too thickly, in their opinion. I had warned of this at the time, but in vain. Nevertheless, the effect is still tremendous. Particularly abroad. In the USA, the sole reaction is boundless astonishment. We are back at the pinnacle of triumph.

Military position: no change on the Rumanian front. Russian thrusts towards Jassy beaten back. Neighbouring Army Group to the north moves towards Lvov. Strong enemy counter-attacks under good leadership. Huge quantities of equipment captured. Almost endless stream of prisoners. Armies near Bialystok completely surrounded. Minsk secured by Panzer units. To the north, Russians retreating. The whole front in flux again. So far everything has gone excellently for us.

No English raids during the night. We attack Hull.

We are now operating three clandestine transmitters aimed at Russia.

437

Tendencies: first Trotskyist, the second separatist, and the third nationalist-Russian. All hard against the Stalin régime. We are pulling out all the stops and working with the techniques we perfected during the Western campaign. In official broadcasts we are taking a hard line against Moscow, using techniques totally suited to the Bolshevik mentality. The Russian military communiqués are becoming more stupid by the day. They must be drafted by Jews. Trivial, moronic and simple-minded, like an editorial in *Rote Fahne*.* We can deal with them easily.

Some fifty million leaflets addressed to the Red Army printed, packed and sent off to be dropped from aeroplanes. Moscow is confiscating radio receivers, a sure sign that our propaganda is having an effect. But we shall carry on regardless. Many people will have managed to keep their sets, and in such uncertain times rumour ensures that every report spreads like wildfire. Moscow is accusing us of wanting to restore Czarism. We very quickly knock that lie on the head.

Growing crisis in the USA. Roosevelt is between two stools. The enemy front is also showing signs of cracking in London. Anti-Bolshevism is too deeply-rooted. We are reaping the benefits of our earlier propaganda. The whole of Europe is in motion. 50,000 volunteers have already reported for duty in Spain. This is a crusade, they are saying abroad. We are using this expression so far as the rest of the world is concerned. It is not so suitable for use at home. If anything, our military situation is being judged rather too optimistically, even by our enemies. They think our Wehrmacht capable of the most fantastic achievements. I am constantly careful to play these reports down.

The new song for Russia is ready. The musical arrangement by Schulze is better than Niel's. And so we choose the former. Anacker and Tiessler are arguing about the authorship of the text. I enforce a compromise. At 2.30 p.m. it is broadcast for the first time on the radio and arouses the greatest enthusiasm all over the country. The nation spends the entire Sunday in a state of huge excitement. Within a few hours, we have succeeded in making good the slight damage to morale caused by the unwise scheduling of the special announcements, and then resentment is replaced by pride and enthusiasm. The press completes the job by some well-rounded editorials. A wonderful Sunday, a rainy day brightened by the light of victory.

I put the finishing touches to my article on news policy. It is more necessary than ever.

Inspect plans for the rebuilding of Lanke with Magda and Bartels. Magda leaves in the evening. To Munich, to buy some pictures at the big art exhibition there, and then to Vienna, to look at a house that we want to use there. Then she intends to visit the children at Aussee. How glad I would be if I could go with her, just for a day. But now is no time for holidays. The

* 'Red Flag'. The newspaper of the German Communist Party 1919–33.

breathtaking pace of life in Berlin scarcely allows me time to fill my lungs. I have to commit robbery to find the time to write these lines. But this is the way I wanted my life to be, and it is wonderful.

Newsreel in the evening. Magnificent film from the East. A breathtaking collection of impressions, There is still a lot of correcting and cutting for me to do. But afterwards it is gripping.

Riga in our hands. A huge tank battle near Lutsk. The Moscow communiqés have become very low-key.

Our new song has pleased everyone. It will be a big hit.

Work goes on deep into the night. But it is a pleasure once more.

1 July 1941 (Tuesday)

Yesterday: Raids on Hamburg, Bremen, Kiel. With some success this time. We do not do much in England.

Eastern Front: No activity on the Rumanian border. On the Hungarian front, the enemy is falling back to his second line of defence. Our motorised corps has occupied his intended position. Part of Army Group South drives on Lvov. The city falls. Second Army thrusts on towards Ostrog and crosses the Goryn river. The Russians defend desperately. One Russian tank Division breaks through our Panzer lines. Army Group Centre: a Panzer Division has crossed the Beresina river near Bobruisk. The Bialystok cauldron has been cut in two and narrowed. Army Group North takes Jakobstadt.* Some resistance west of Dünaburg.** Libau† and Mitau‡ taken.

England has suggested to Moscow that the Russian Navy transfer to the Atlantic. Mannerheim Group in Finland ready to march. Dietl's Group massing to attack Murmansk.

General Russian intentions: probably a retreat behind the river Dnieper, on a line running Kiev – Vitebsk – Pskov. Expected pivot of the Russian army groups around Novgorod – Sieversk, on the river Desna, 200 kilometres to the north-east of Kiev.

Army Group South under Rundstedt, Centre under Bock, North under Leeb. Finnish army under Mannerheim and the Mountain Corps under Dietl. In general, things are going well, though the Russians are putting up more of a fight than we had expected. Our losses in men and equipment are not completely insignificant. It is only now that we can see how necessary the attack was. If we had waited for longer, what would have happened? Once again, the Führer's instincts have been proved right.

Moscow is lying its heart out. The academics and the churches are being

---

* Jekabpils in Latvia.
** Dougavpils in Latvia.
† Liepāja in Latvia.
‡ Jelgava in Latvia.

mobilised. The Bolsheviks have turned to prayer. We shall box their ears with that one. Moscow has been issuing lame denials of our bulletins. London seems to think that our victories are not all that great. Moscow pictures our troops as drunken rampagers, invents deserters who turn up on Russian radio to call on our soldiers to join them. Rather stupid and primitive. Our three clandestine transmitters are now in operation and doing good work. We are back on top form. Just like the offensive in the West. Particularly satisfying against the East. This war work by our broadcasters takes priority over all other commitments (England/USA).

Widespread criticism of our twelve special announcements on Sunday, both here and abroad. Justified! The operation was a complete failure. We tried to pour enthusiasm out of a bottle. The public caught a glimpse of what really goes on in the propaganda war. This is always a bad thing. I shall ensure that it never happens again. Our new battle-song for the campaign in the East meets with general approval.

In Spain, the Falangists are hurrying to the enlistment offices. An Italian corps is to go into active service in Russia with the Führer's permission. The Swedish Foreign Minister is openly supporting us. Terboven is raising a legion of volunteers in Norway. Europe is beginning to move. The press in England and the USA can only stutter lame excuses for their co-operation with Moscow. The process of disintegration in the enemy camp continues.

At my request, the Führer orders a ban on all Russian writers and composers. No exceptions for the moment. Likewise, he rejects the idea of a church magazine for soldiers, which the Wehrmacht High Command is pressing for. The soldiers have better things to do at the moment than reading religious tracts. I explain this to Martin and in the process give him a little lecture about the mindless lack of logic in Christian teachings, which impresses him deeply.

Haushofer and his son have been forced out of public life. They are both responsible for peddling mystic rubbish and have the Hess Affair on their consciences. For the rest, however, Hess has now been completely forgotten, at home and abroad.

Continuing to pursue the Jewish problem in Berlin. We still have so much to do, and so much to watch out for. No matter how strict the laws may be, the Jews are constantly finding loopholes. It is a matter of keeping a sharp eye and not letting them get away with anything.

I am looking for a new production chief for Prague, and also one for the private firms that are to be taken into state ownership. A few names have been suggested, but I have no time to check them and am leaving it to Gutterer.

Martin delivers a lengthy report, in which he outlines the whole military situation in the East. It shows how great the danger was, and from what perils the Führer has preserved Europe and the Reich in particular. Vichy has broken off relations with Moscow. A good thing! But a section of the

French press in the Unoccupied Zone is still very insolent.

Work at Lanke during the afternoon. I always take whole piles of undealt-with work home with me. Out here, in the tranquillity of the forest, is the best place to sort out such problems. And I must have my desk cleared every day, so that my mind too is clear.

The world response to our victories is enormous. Our Wehrmacht has earned the highest admiration in all countries. The only criticism, and severe at that, is saved for our technique of issuing the reports piecemeal, and I, though innocent, am singled out as the one to blame. This is also evident in the reports from the Reich Propaganda Offices.*

Public opinion increasingly divided in the USA. Hoover and the Isolationists are conducting a loud campaign against the war, as are church circles.

Similar developments, if covert, are discernible in London. Beaverbrook has been appointed Minister of Supply. So it seems that Churchill has found another home for this thorn in his flesh.

I put the finishing touches to my leader-article on news policy. Turned out very well.

The Soviets are now issuing their military communiqués twice a day; they bristle with lies and contain no military information, little, in fact, but Bolshevik propaganda. This is too much even for Reuter. No one is reprinting them. We are treating them with contempt and derision. They are not worth the paper they are written on.

Newsreel in the evening. A lot of work still to be done on it, mainly the editing and the music. But afterwards it flows beautifully, a cinematic masterpiece.

Still a thin trickle of news. And then finish for today.

2 July 1941 (Wednesday)

Yesterday: Eastern Campaign: fighting continues. Enemy's resistance stiffening; he is defending desperately. Troops massing on the Rumanian front. Hungarian army moving in the direction of [. . .] Army Group South beats back an enemy attempt at a breakthrough. Centre: the Bialystok cauldron has now divided into three smaller cauldrons. 20 divisions trapped. Desperate attempts at a breakout near Bialystok. Enemy suffering many fatal casualties, few wounded or taken prisoner. One Red regiment has succeeded in breaking out. North: Riga completely in our hands. Russians seem to be preparing to evacuate [. . .] Bock has gained some space. Fighting here dirty and vicious.

---

* Apart from the SD reports, Goebbels also received reports on popular morale from the *Reichspropagandaämter* (Reich Propaganda Offices) of his ministry. These local offices – of which there was one in each of the 42 Gaus – employed 1400 officials by 1941.

Luftwaffe is doing a fantastic job. 1000 German aircraft are being used in support of ground forces. Nine German losses against 220 for the enemy. Mölders has made his eighty-second kill. Unfortunately, the weather in the north has deteriorated.

In general, the fighting is very hard and bitter. There can be no question of a picnic. The Red régime has mobilised the people. Plus there is the proverbial stubbornness of the Russians. Our soldiers have their hands full. But so far everything is going according to plan. The situation is not serious, but it is tough, and we shall need all the strength we can summon.

The Russians are crowing in their communiqués. Rather too loudly and rather prematurely. We are launching powerful counter-blasts. London is helping them by issuing grandiose battle reports. But we have seen that before during the campaign in France. The collapse comes later. The torrent of abuse is on the increase again in the USA. Knox has made an insolent speech demanding an immediate entry into the war. Roosevelt apparently wants to make another attempt to sound out the public's reaction.

We are using every means possible. Particularly the three clandestine transmitters beamed at Russia. Our long wave transmitters are also at full stretch. In general, short wave is being jammed. Moscow is being forced to take strong defensive measures against our propaganda. Bolshevism has been forced on to the defensive. Its propaganda is totally primitive. Like the old stuff from Karl Liebknecht. It will cause us no problems.

Fink wants a transfer from the Hague to the East. He cannot work with Schmidt and Seyss-Inquart any more. And the Foreign Ministry is giving him problems, too. Are there any exceptions? I refuse to allow him to be taken away from Holland. And now Rosenberg, too, wants to start up his own propaganda outfit. Gutterer is taking appropriate measures to head this off. Everyone wants to make propaganda, and the less they know about it, the keener they are . . .

. . . We are working well with Bormann. He is tackling the problem of relations between the Party and the state with far more determination than Hess ever showed. And he has always behaved very loyally towards me personally.

Tough circular to the Gauleiters against listening to foreign radio stations. Has become necessary again. Particularly as our own announcements have been held back for so long.

Bohle tells me about events in the Foreign Ministry. He has not seen Ribbentrop for six months. Quite a situation. Also, he is frightened that the Führer may subordinate the AO to the Foreign Ministry. This is out of the question. The state cannot rule the Party. This would be a blow to the foundations of our Party. We shall prevent it. Bohle is looking for a protector after Hess's departure. I shall take him under my wing to some extent.

It is raining. It has turned cold. We are having to put on some heating. In

July. The world has gone completely mad. But one has to come to terms with it . . .

. . . Ley is screaming for the Seventh Chamber. We shall soon be announcing its creation. Besides which, he has become a happy father yet again.

Together with Italy, Spain, Rumania, we recognise the Nanking government under Wang-Ching-Wei. Japan must be given the freest possible hand in China so that she can be included in our calculations. Up to now, she has been too severely handicapped to be able to act resolutely.

The English attack Kiel by day, with some success but also with enormous losses. A middling raid on Cologne during the night. 24 English planes shot down. But they are cheeky, all right. Kick up a great fuss about their so-called command of the air over Western Europe. Conceited blabbermouths!

In return, we hit Cardiff and in North Africa Tobruk, very hard. The fighting there is still ebbing and flowing.

The Times has published a very pessimistic article about the position of the Soviet Union. And it probably hits the nail on the head. Our position is improving by the hour. If things continue this way for a few days, we shall be over the worst.

London is shouting from the rooftops about some peace offer that it claims was made by von Papen, which in fact can be traced back to an innocuous conversation. We pour the cold water of a denial over it.

Increasingly pessimistic voices from London. Moscow's position is viewed as increasingly hopeless.

Similar expressions of opinion from the USA. Grist to the mills of the Isolationists. Suits us very well.

Yet again, we have destroyed 235 Russian aircraft in a single day. Once the Russians lose their air force, then they too are lost.

May God grant it!

3 July 1941 (Thursday)

Yesterday: No air activity on either side. Bad weather! 40,000 tons sunk by U-boats.

The situation in the East is better again. The cauldron near Bialystok has been firmly closed. Twenty divisions, 100,000 men and incalculable quantities of equipment captured. Tank battle in Galicia has ended in our victory. Onwards to the East. Hard fighting. But the Russians are gradually beginning to weaken. The situation in the north is good. Twenty-one ships taken intact in Libau and Windau. In the south, the fighting is bitter and at present has provided no concrete successes. In Rumania, the front is stable. Moscow has already become very subdued. London continues to brag about the victories to come, but already there is an admixture of pessimism. Wavell transferred to India. The Napoleon of the desert. One less hope for England.

Our clandestine transmitters are now hard to work. Torgler, Kaspar and Albrecht are involved. Big noise about Stalin's planned flight from Moscow. Demand for the formation of workers' and soldiers' councils. But I forbid any calls for street demonstrations. If such were not to occur, then we would lose face. The official transmitters are also getting through now. They have moderated their approach slightly. Rosenberg has stopped causing trouble. He is leaving all the propaganda to us alone. Amann is already busy organising the establishment of four big newspapers for the occupied area. The *Völkischer Beobachter* in Moscow; now that would be a novelty.

There has been no relaxation of our propaganda aimed at England. We must destroy the last hopes that they place in Russia. The battle is especially fierce with regard to the war in the air. The English are issuing the craziest statistics. But then our Luftwaffe are probably doing the same thing. Even our people do not view figures with too much respect for truth.

Moscow's plans to attack Germany and Central Europe have now been established beyond all doubt. The Führer acted at the last possible moment. A Europe united under our leadership is anathema to London. The slogan there now is: 'Europe against Germany!' And England and the USA are claimed to be, as democracies, socialistic states. We shall soon deal with that canard.

Opinions still very strongly divided in the USA. The Isolationists have taken the offensive to such an extent that Roosevelt has been forced to say a few non-committal words about his love of peace.

Something close to starvation is widespread in France and Belgium. For this reason, feelings there are very mixed. What would the Bolshevik infection have been able to achieve if the Soviet Union had really attacked? It does not bear thinking about. Thank God, we have every prospect of a better harvest this time. So long as the weather does not play a dirty trick on us at the last moment.

The 'bomb hoboes',* idlers of both sexes who have cleared out of the areas threatened by bombing and are living in the open during this summer, are causing a great deal of concern. They are wrecking havoc with public morals and ruining the good name of North and North-West Germany. I shall set the police on them. If it were up to me, they would be forced to work.

The SD report gives evidence of good morale and huge excitement, but also a lot of illusions. The way the announcements were spaced out on Sunday caused general displeasure. In the occupied territories as well. It was not a good thing and must never be repeated.

Discuss the great exhibition in Munich with Bibrach. What I can see from the photographs is pretty mediocre.

* *Bombenfrischler.*

444

Discuss plans for the newsreel with Hippler. Boese is too stupid for artistic work and so will have to be put on ice. He is good at slave-driving, but he cannot take decisions.

I address radio officials from the occupied territories. On our jurisdiction in the face of claims by other departments, including the Foreign Ministry. Then to people from the entire broadcasting service. On the tasks of the present moment. With great success. The meeting acts as a fillip to the whole service at this crucial time.

Deal with a mass of day-to-day matters. They are always cropping up, are part of one's work, but remain deeply unimportant. They take up my time well into the evening, yet again.

Lanke! blessed tranquillity deep in the forest.

Things have started up on the Rumanian front. Now there will be fireworks there, too.

Our Luftwaffe chalks up some big sinkings. Particularly off Tobruk. Massive air raid on Alexandria. Things are going so badly for the English that they have promised the Jews Palestine again, with complete disregard for the Arabs. The recall of Wavell is turning into a big sensation. Churchill's scapegoat for the lost battle at Sollum. Profound depression on this score in the USA. Roosevelt is having a bad time altogether. Lindbergh and Wheeler are attacking him in tough speeches, with particular emphasis on Knox's statements. For tactical reasons, we make no reference to them. But the intellectual schism in the USA goes deep. Cross, the former English Minister for Shipping, has given a dramatic report on England's tonnage losses. Things are on the move once more in the enemy camp.

The Norwegian Legion is recruiting well. Terboven has handled the matter very skilfully.

The Soviet government of the Ukraine has moved its seat from Kiev to Kharkov. This is the grim reality behind the noisy slogans. Another special announcement in the evening: 160,000 prisoners taken so far at Bialystok, plus an enormous haul of matériel. In this place, History has given a decisive judgment.

The Jews in Moldavia are shooting at German soldiers. But Antonescu is dealing with the situation. His behaviour in this war as a whole has been magnificent.

Late in the evening, speak to Magda on the telephone. She is still in Vienna and is now travelling on to Aussee. To the children. How glad I would be to go with her.

Late to bed. Outside, the moon is rising. Over the mist-enshrouded forest.

4 July 1941 (Friday)

Yesterday: Heavy English air raids on North and West Germany. Considerable damage. On the Eastern Front: encirclement at Novgrodok completed.

We can expect a huge haul there. One dare not mention the probable figures yet. The advance continues apace in all other sections of the front. The situation is now good in the north as well. But the Russians are fighting a hard, bitter battle. We are renewing our attempts to break down their resistance by appropriate leaflet and radio propaganda. We shall see whether it will be successful. G. W. Müller* has been seriously wounded in the advance on Murmansk. Otherwise, however, our casualties so far have been very slight when one considers the scale of the fighting.

The situation on the central front is excellent. There the enemy is beginning to wilt. I ban any special emphasis on Moscow from German propaganda. We must beware of fixing the public gaze on this one, fascinating goal. The situation is good on the southern front, and the Rumanians are holding their own against enemy attacks. The Russians have lost a lot of aircraft. They are no longer prepared to risk any night attacks on our eastern cities. For the moment, their main ally is Slavic stubbornness. But one day even that will break.

Early today, Stalin made a speech. A bad conscience talking, and shot through with profound pessimism. The speech illustrates the gravity of the situation, calls for sabotage of our advance and warns against panic-mongers and rumours spread by the enemy. He means our work. I gather from other reports from and concerning Russia that our radio and transmission work is beginning to have an effect. It will now be pursued with all vigour. We respond to Stalin's speech quite differently, depending on whether it is for domestic or foreign consumption. So far as Russia is concerned, we portray it is a symptom of collapse. Here we are beginning to use the methods that were tried and tested during the Western campaign, e.g. panic-mongering and so on. Their success is already clearly discernible. The hinterland of Russia is beginning to disintegrate. The signs are quite unmistakable. We are now working on this open wound. In particular, we must defend ourselves against Stalin's accusation that we intend to restore Czarism. For the rest, we have a stock of effective arguments up our sleeves, which we intend to play out gradually. Our clandestine transmitters are operating at peak effectiveness.

Abroad, particularly in the USA and even in London, they see Moscow's position as very black. They believe that they are seeing the initial stages of one of the greatest wars of annihilation in history. And doubtless they are not wrong.

Our soldiers at the front are now completely convinced of the necessity of this war. Bolshevism is no longer a danger so far as they are concerned. However, they are astonished at the big Party buildings that the Soviets have built even in the villages. Ley, so they say, ought to do the same here some time. Well, that time will come!

Dispose of routine work with Gutterer. State Secretary Reinhardt has

* Also referred to as Müller-Oslo (*see* biographical note in Index).

446

made a speech in Passau which borders on treason. I shall have to tell the Führer about it.

Stephan reports on Dr Dietrich's worries: the Foreign Ministry is again sticking too big a finger into the pie of news policy. But I shall be well able to defend myself in that respect.

Discuss and deal with many film and theatre problems. A necessary, if marginal activity. But to some extent it is quite relaxing.

Draft and check propaganda material for the clandestine transmitters aimed at Russia. At the moment, magnificent work is being done in this field.

I take a great pile of work with me out to Lanke.

The weather has turned very fine again. Good for the harvest and for the war. We are unable to deny the pompous declarations of successes by the RAF, since most of them affected dummy installations. The statistics produced by the English are totally grotesque. But perhaps they even believe them themselves. They give us a certain breathing-space.

763,950 tons sunk during the month of June, 417,450 of it by the Luftwaffe alone. This must hit where it hurts. Great anxiety in London. The Wavell Affair is still the big talking-point in the world press. Churchill's position is not easy.

The Russians' losses in the Bialystok cauldron are enormous. The 160,000 taken prisoner are far exceeded by the numbers of dead and wounded. A disaster for Moscow Far worse than Tannenberg,* as the US press affirms. The Reds' resistance seems to be slowly crumbling along the entire front. Bolshevism is suffering its greatest crisis at the moment, both intellectual and organisational. We are doing all we can to exacerbate it and hasten the process. Stalin has called on his people to burn the harvest and corn stores. Our response is to declare quite publicly that after her defeat Russia will not be able to expect anything from us, and that we shall let her starve. This will probably cool a few of the hot-heads.

These days, the flood of news never lets up. New reports come in every half-hour. A crazy, exciting time.

In the evening, put the finishing touches to the newsreel. A really big hit. Thrilling from the point of view of film, music and text. Now I am completely satisfied with it. Then I sit outside on the terrace for half an hour and dream.

5 July 1941 (Saturday)

Yesterday: Military situation continues to develop favourably. The Hungarians are pushing forward over the Carpathians. Tarnopol occupied. Oil-

---

* At the Battle of Tannenberg in August 1914, a swift Russian advance into East Prussia was halted by a German army under Hindenburg. The Tsarist armies were routed so thoroughly that they never again threatened German territory, and Hindenburg became a national hero.

producing region in our hands, almost intact. Bitter fighting between motorised units near Dubno. Our Panzers are moving forward beyond Minsk. Things are very favourable in the Baltic states. The noose at Novogrodok is tightening. A big haul expected there. Our Luftwaffe is having to contend with bad weather. Ninety more Russians shot down. Dnieper crossed near Rogachev. Taking us through the Stalin Line. According to our estimates, Moscow has something like 2000 aircraft left. But the Bolsheviks are continuing to put up a tough, bitter resistance. Intend to hold on to Leningrad at all costs and are throwing forces into battle without regard for operational losses. This can only be to our advantage. The more forces engage us now, the better our position will be later.

No air incursions in the East, 120 aircraft in the West, with some success. The large-scale English attack that we had feared has not materialised so far. But then what they have managed is enough. Slight decline of morale in Cologne. A result of constant loss of sleep. I send Kolbe there to sort things out.

Our leaflets calling on the Russians to surrender are meeting with a big response on the other side. Entire battalions are ending up in prison camps as a result. Moscow has now ordered the death penalty for anyone who picks up one of our leaflets. In general, our propaganda seems to be greatly feared over there.

And we are launching a massive campaign. Our clandestine transmitters are models of deception and subtlety. Stalin has nothing to smile about. A large proportion of Russian domestic propaganda is aimed at countering ours. The famous and feared Bolshevik propaganda machine is completely on the defensive. Now our official broadcasts are getting through as well. They are deliberately objective, while the clandestine transmitters go for the jugular. Wonderfully effective, and it makes a great contribution to demoralising the enemy. Stalin's speech has been widely admired in the England and the USA. Evidence of where the fellow belongs. The split in public opinion in the USA is deepening. Roosevelt's canoodling with Bolshevism is making him a lot of enemies. He has made a speech which seems to consist entirely of platitudes. Now that he has jumped into bed with Moscow, there is no more talk of the loudly-proclaimed 'four freedoms' that he was willing to die for. We box his ears with that one.

In London they are really dancing on eggshells, trying to justify the *faux pas* of an alliance with Bolshevism. The statistical swindle regarding the air war is still in full swing. But we are hitting back vigorously. London is slowly coming to the realisation that the Russian campaign could bring us enormous advantages. We are working to reinforce this impression, without tying ourselves down to numbers, dates or specific goals. This is the best way at the moment.

Sunday's special announcements are still meeting with strong public criticism. I, who was always against such over-intrusive methods, am the scapegoat. But I have a broad back. And I can take a lot on my shoulders.

A few disagreements over the newsreel. The Führer wants more polemical material in the script. I would rather have the pictures speak for themselves and confine the script to explaining what the audience would not otherwise understand. I consider this to be more effective, because then the viewer does not see the art in it. But the Führer was very pleased with the last newsreel.

Raeder is making representations in favour of a Christian book about Narvik and has argued very strongly for it to me. He is a very pious Admiral. But the war at sea is being won not with prayers but with U-boats and torpedoes. The Führer must make the final decision on this contentious issue.

Cremer has submitted a plan for the intensification of cultural work in the countryside. Let him come back after the Eastern campaign. At the moment we have neither the time nor the staff for it.

The Munich Art Exhibition is to be opened by me in the middle of July. The Führer has told me to give his speech for him. I drive out to Lanke to start work on it straight away. Not a pleasant task at this time. Outside, it is raining buckets again. It gives one an appetite for this kind of desk work, even warms one to it. In the end, it turns out very well.

James Roosevelt has returned from his trip and given his father a very pessimistic view of England's situation. This is a big sensation. In general, England is in a very bad way at the moment, no matter how loudly her propagandists may crow. We issue an official statement on English atrocities against German naval crews during the Greek campaign and give notice that there will be retaliatory measures. We shall see how London reacts.

Magda is with the children on the Grundlsee. We talk on the telephone, and the dear little things are so delighted. Holde twitters into the telephone. Helga and Hilde wrote me a charming letter. I should so love to see the children again. But one cannot think of such things. So many fathers must live without their children these days.

A grey, misty and melancholy day of rain. Our troops are approaching Smolensk. The Russians are committing the most appalling atrocities. They will pay for them.

The Chunking régime* has broken off relations with us. For us, China is now Nanking.

The world is changing shape. Time is racing by. When will peace return? 20,000 Bolsheviks have surrendered near Minsk after shooting most of their political commissars. A sign of the storm to come? Perhaps it has already begun. Dr Dietrich rings me up late in the evening: the Führer wants us to start the great anti-Bolshevik campaign now. And it is high time. Let the hunt commence!

So, to work!

* The Chinese Nationalist government under Chiang-Kai-Shek.

6 July 1941 (Sunday)

Yesterday: the situation on all fronts is good. Unchanged in Rumania. The vice in the central sector is tightening. Our Panzers have turned north. For the moment, Moscow is staying put. And she is throwing in all her available reserves. An SS Division has shown itself lacking in the fighting on the Finnish border. Mannerheim's leadership is too inflexible, and he is not equal to the enemy's commanders. Elsewhere, everything is in motion. The Luftwaffe is doing excellent work. Our operations in general are working towards ambitious goals. It would take too long to describe everything in detail.

Raid on England with 100 aircraft. Birmingham successfully attacked. Middling English air raid on West Germany. The English are attacking the occupied territories during daylight hours at the moment. And suffering very serious losses in the process, some of which they admit. On the whole, however, they are making great play of their air war. But this will soon end after the Eastern campaign.

Morale in Cologne was not good. But is already better. All the people there need is a good night's sleep. There are also widespread shortages of vegetables and potatoes. Likewise here in Berlin. I shall try to exert some more pressure in that area.

As a temporary measure, I send Rommel a big plane full of material to entertain the troops.

Big propaganda campaign against Bolshevism introduced. Press, radio, film and propaganda. Our line: the veil has been swept away; here is Moscow unmasked. Plus we have all the atrocity material from Lvov, where I have now sent 20 journalists and radio people. Things there are totally horrific. Bolshevism is a scourge of humanity, a serious disease that must be eliminated. We must all be grateful to the Führer for having grasped this danger and destroyed it. The big campaign against Bolshevism is beginning immediately. All means of propaganda are being pressed into service. Within a few days, we shall see results both at home and abroad. Moscow is countering it with totally stupid and primitive propaganda. A pale imitation of the English lies. Even her army communiqués seem to have been copied from the English. We are taking a really hard-hitting approach in all our broadcasts to the East. Taubert and his people are doing magnificent work. These days, work is fun again.

SD reports show the mood of the country as good but tense. The ground lost on Sunday has been largely recovered. Our newsreel has been greeted with great approval. It is indeed a work of art. The Führer is quite delighted with it. He has invited me to visit him at Headquarters, and says that he has a lot to discuss with me. I shall be flying out there on Tuesday.

The 'bomb hoboes' continue to worry me. Now Esser, too, has taken their part. In his capacity as tourism chief. As for me, however, I start to kick over the traces. I tell Gutterer to consult the Gestapo about appropriate measures

450

to deal with the problem. These parasites are doing tremendous harm to morale. A pity that compulsory labour has not yet been introduced for these idle females.

Discuss the budget with Gutterer. Still a few staff that Krosigk will not let me have the money for. But we shall get our way soon enough.

Lanke. Weather improving slightly. I correct my Munich speech, which has turned out very well, and dictate a swingeing essay against Bolshevism. We are gradually getting back into well-loved, familiar territory here. The article turns out very well. The entire German press embarks on a massive offensive against Moscow in the afternoon editions. This is also very good from the point of view of people abroad, who are now totally transfixed by the fascination of this campaign.

Signs of unrest in France. They seem to believe that we no longer have sufficient troops in the West. They will get a shock. Vichy's situation in Syria is pretty hopeless. If the reinforcements at present in Salonica do not arrive soon, then France will have lost the battle.

Moscow's military communiqué continues to conceal the Bolshevik defeats and withdrawals with grandiose phrases. Proof that things are going very badly for them. *The Times* has published an article on the new order in Europe that could just as well have appeared in the *Völkischer Beobachter*. The aim is probably to undermine the force of our appeal for European solidarity. But we shall not let them get away with it. Eden has made a speech in which he has rejected any negotiations with us. But we have made no reference to any such talks. One day, however, they will come. Just wait!

The Turkish Prime Minister has made a speech that is very positive from our point of view. It seems that things down there are signed and sealed.

Otherwise, everything is in flux.

Great military developments are in prospect.

Perhaps the coming week will see decisive changes.

Our soldiers will do all they can.

We must act quickly, and the campaign in the East must not drag on for too long. But the Führer will ensure that.

7 July 1941 (Monday)

Yesterday: The situation on the Eastern Front is good. Large-scale operations are in progress. The Russians are bringing up huge reinforcements to the front. This is good and desirable. We shall not need to pursue them too far into the hinterland. 53,000 Bolsheviks have deserted near Minsk. Our haul there is still incalculable. The Reds are putting up a stiff resistance in places. But they are gradually realising the gravity of the military situation in Moscow. The Russian military communiqué proves it. All it can talk of are withdrawals.

The English launch heavy raids against Münster and other Westphalian cities, with some success. They are becoming cheeky and are even making attacks by daylight. Taking the pressure off Moscow. They are even boasting of an invasion of Western Europe. We do nothing to deny it. Let them come. Obviously they are making every attempt to exploit their stay of execution. But we can hope that it will not last for too long.

33,000 tons sunk by U-boats. It was getting to be high time.

We are giving a powerful blast against Moscow on all radio stations. The clandestine transmitters are working magnificently and causing the Bolsheviks a lot of trouble. We are issuing a warning against burning grain, using the same form of words over and over, so that it makes a deep impression.

Our big campaign against Bolshevism has got off to an excellent start. All the news and propaganda media are operating on top form. I order the campaign to be maintained and reinforced. The aim is not only to enlighten people at home but to take Europe with us, and also to deepen the rift in public opinion in the USA and even in England. In this respect, we have already had partial success. I am organising a big trip by journalists and Party speakers to Lvov and the former Russian territory. We must strike while the iron is hot. My article has appeared in the *V.B.* Very effective.

Esser and co. have now done something about the bomb-hoboes after all. My protest was not ineffective. From now on, vigorous steps will be taken.

It is now boiling hot again in Berlin and on the Wilhelmplatz. The city is enjoying Sunday. I drive out to Lanke in the afternoon.

Gentlemen from the radio visit me: Glasmaier, Diewerge, Winkelnkemper, plus Wächter and Studentkowski. We are able to discuss a host of issues and chat a little about the past and the future.

The newsreel arrives in the evening. The pictures are magnificent, but I still have a lot of work to do on it. The text and the editing are very heavy-handed this time. But we set it right.

The Russians are lying until they are blue in the face. It is impossible to find the time to deny everything. In particular, they are bragging about huge German losses – 700,000 men, they claim. It has been the same story during all of our offensives. In the final analysis, though, it is we who have 300,000 prisoners. The mood in Moscow is very gloomy. We shall do all we can to make it even worse.

In London they are fantasising about an invasion. Let them come.

It was such a long day. I am very tired.

8 July 1941 (Tuesday)

Yesterday: Situation very good on all fronts. Significant successes. Very hard fighting in the south. Roads almost impassable. Chernovtsy taken. Operations in flux. No operative command any more on the enemy side. Prisoners say that they only refuse to surrender for fear of being shot. Morale of our men at the front very good. The soldiers now realise that this campaign was necessary. Situation in the centre continues excellent. Very difficult in Finland. Finns not suited to offensive operations. Petsamo, with its nickel supplies, firmly secured. No air incursions in the East. Proof that the Red air force now longer has any offensive capacity. Our supply lines are functioning completely smoothly.

Quite heavy raids in West Germany again. With some success. We attack England in middling strength. London is boasting wildly about 'command of the air'. I have Haw-Haw issue a brief rebuttal. For reasons of security, we are unfortunately unable to give details.

The Bolsheviks are responding to our propaganda campaign with wild atrocity stories which are naturally eagerly supported by London. In the face of this response, we continue our offensive to unmask Bolshevism, and our slogans are being widely repeated abroad. The Reds are frightening their children with tales of German paratroops. We reinforce these, issue stories of our own, and succeed in causing widespread panic. According to unimpeachable sources, things in Moscow are looking very grim. We shall not rest until the Red bosses have been toppled. We succeeded here in 1933, and we shall succeed this time as well.

Since at the moment none of the territories that we have conquered are in Russia proper, world opinion has begun to waver slightly. We shall have to prove ourselves by concrete victories. Our leaflet propaganda against the Soviets is being stepped up. Surrender! is the slogan. I have had a snappy poster designed for use in the occupied territories. Schweitzer tried to design one, but it was unsuitable. We are on the offensive all along the line on the propaganda front. Moscow is being forced on to the defensive. And this already half the battle. We are doing all we can to ensure that there are no complications.

The enemy has made a 'V' (victoire) into his propaganda symbol in the occupied territories. Without any more ado, I have the symbol commandeered by us. Now we are using this 'V' ourselves and saying that it means a German victory. End of problem! I had given the matter a lot of thought, but I would never have dreamed that the solution would be so simple. In other respects, the position in the occupied territories remains very unclear. Our fight against Bolshevism has brought us many friends. But the effect of hunger is too strong. Even in the Balkans, where, as Prince Schaumburg has reported after his trip there, there is real starvation. Particularly in Greece. A lot of grumbling in Italy. Mussolini is not taking a firm enough line. Sympathy with us has also declined slightly in Rumania. Worries, wherever one looks.

Food situation in Berlin also bad. Delays in supplies of vegetables and potatoes. But things should supposedly improve at the end of next week. It is high time, too.

Visit to the Göringstrasse. Building work on the bunker in full swing. It will soon be ready. Broiling heat. To Lanke to work.

Give some thought to the question of television. The Post Office has too much power in this field. Will have to give it up. All the decisions regarding programming belong with my ministry. Television has a very great future after the war. Perhaps it will completely replace the cinema.

The great anti-Bolshevik campaign continues. The neutral press is co-operating. The Lvov case is our prime exhibit. The Russians are losing all sense of proportion in their atrocity propaganda, which is aimed at diverting attention from their problems. Our newspapers and radio stations are working very well. Opinion in the USA still divided. No one doubts any more that we shall be victorious in Russia. The Bolshevik military communiqué evaporates in a froth of Party slogans.

Smolensk bombed twice. We are getting closer to Moscow all the time.

The English have lost another 19 aircraft over the Channel. 8 during the night. 83 altogether during the past three days, against our 9. They are now admitting some of their losses. The preparations for the Second Front are costing them dear. What would an invasion bring?

In the USA, the talk is of peace. But it is empty gossip. Cudahy is concealing his attacks on Roosevelt behind a smokescreen of tough attacks on the Reich. Does this do us more harm than good? Over-subtle propaganda is no propaganda at all.

Someone should try telling the American people the pure and unvarnished truth for once.

Roosevelt has had Iceland occupied by American troops. In place of English forces. Plus appropriate protection for ships sailing to England. A brazen address to Congress on the subject. He is only trying to provoke us. But he will not succeed.

Work on the newsreel in the evening. Contains harrowing shots of the Bolshevik atrocities in Lvov. A real shocker! The Führer rings me up to say that it is the best newsreel we have ever made. I am very pleased.

Today I am flying to be with him at Headquarters.

Chronology of Goebbels' Life

1897	29 October. Born in Rheydt in the Rhineland to a lower middle-class Catholic family.
1917–21	Studies at the Universities of Freiburg, Bonn, Würzburg, Munich and Heidelberg. Awarded his doctorate for a dissertation on the German Romantic movement.
1922	After attempts to break into journalism and the literary world, joins the Nazi Party.
1924–5	Editor of the right-wing newspaper *Völkische Freiheit* (Folkish Freedom).
1925	Appointed Business Manager of the North Rhineland Gau of the Nazi Party. Edits Nazi publications, including the bulletin *NS-Briefe* (National Socialist Letters).
1926	Sides with Hitler against the Strasser brothers in the Nazi Party split.
1926	Appointed Gauleiter of Berlin by Hitler.
1927	Founds the newspaper *Der Angriff* (The Attack) in Berlin.
1928	Elected to the Reichstag as a deputy for Berlin.
1929	Appointed Reich Propaganda Leader of the Nazi Party.
1930	Nazi representation in the Reichstag rises from 12 seats to 107.
1931	Marries Magda Quandt, a wealthy divorcée.
1932	Organises Hitler's bid for the Presidency and two Reichstag elections.
1932	Daughter Helga Goebbels born.
1933	30 January. Hitler becomes Chancellor of Germany.
1933	5 March. Goebbels in charge of the Nazi campaign in the Reichstag elections.
1933	13 March. Appointed Reich Minister for Public Enlightenment and Propaganda. Begins the 'co-ordination' of cultural life, the press and communications under the control of the Nazi Party.
1934	Daughter Hilde Goebbels born.
1935	Son Helmut Goebbels born.
1936	Begins affair with Lida Baarova, a Czech film actress.
1937	Daughter Holde Goebbels born.
1938	Daughter Hedda Goebbels born.

1938	Summer. Magda Goebbels demands a divorce because of his affair with Baarova.
1938	Autumn. Goebbels is almost forced to resign. Hitler dictates a reconciliation with his wife. Goebbels retains his post. Baarova is deported from Germany.
1938	November. 'Crystal Night' outrages against Jews in Germany largely engineered by Goebbels.
1940	Heide Goebbels born.
1943	February. Goebbels makes a speech preaching 'total war'.
1944	July. Following the plot against Hitler, he is appointed 'General Plenipotentiary for the Mobilisation of Total War'.
1945	29 April. Appointed Chancellor of Germany in Hitler's Testament.
1945	1 May. After poisoning their children, Goebbels and Magda commit suicide in the garden of the Reich Chancellery, Berlin.

Chronology for the Goebbels Diaries 1938–41

1938

29–30 September	Munich Agreement. Hitler, Mussolini, Chamberlain and Daladier agree to Germany's acquisition of the Sudetenland. Czechoslovakia defenceless.
28 October	First deportation of Polish Jews from Germany.
7 November	Ernst von Rath, a German diplomat in Paris, assassinated by Herschel Grynszpan, a Polish Jew.
9 November	The 'Crystal Night'. Mobs goaded by Goebbels attack Jewish property and synagogues throughout Germany.
15 November	Expulsion of all Jewish pupils from German schools.
3 December	All Jewish enterprises and shops subjected to compulsory 'Aryanisation'.

1939

15 March	President Hácha of Czechoslovakia is forced to ask for German protection. German troops enter Prague. Neurath appointed 'Reich Protector of Bohemia and Moravia'.
23 March	Germany seizes Memel from Lithuania.
28 March	General Franco occupies Madrid.
31 March	Anglo-French guarantee of Poland's borders.
7 April	Italy occupies Albania.
14 April	President Roosevelt appeals to Hitler to respect the independence of nations.
28 April	Hitler's foreign policy speech to the Reichstag. He rejects Roosevelt's plea.
22 May	'Pact of Steel'. Italo-German military alliance.
23 May	Preparations begin for war with Poland. Goebbels' propaganda machine starts to accuse the Poles of 'atrocities' against their German-speaking minority.
23 August	German-Soviet pact signed in Moscow, including a secret protocol allowing for the division of Poland.
24 August	Pope Pius XII appeals for peace.

25 August	President Roosevelt appeals for peace.
	Anglo-Polish Treaty signed.
1 September	Germany invades Poland.
	Curfew for all German Jews.
3 September	Britain and France declare war on Germany.
	British liner *Athenia* sunk by a U-boat.
17 September	Soviet troops move into Eastern Poland.
24 September	Fall of Warsaw.
6 October	Peace offer by Hitler to Britain and France.
12 October	Hans Frank appointed Chief Civilian Officer in occupied Poland.
13 October	The British battleship *Royal Oak* sunk by a U-boat in Scapa Flow.
8 November	Attempted assassination of Hitler at the *Bürgerbräu* beer hall in Munich.
21 November	Beginning of British blockade of German exports.
30 November	The Soviet Union attacks Finland.
17 December	German cruiser *Graf Spee* scuttles herself off Montevideo after a battle with British warships.

1940

12 February	First deportation of German Jews.
1–6 March	Sumner Welles, American Under-Secretary of State, visits Germany.
12 March	Peace treaty signed between Finland and the Soviet Union.
18 March	Hitler and Mussolini meet at the Brenner.
9 April	Germany invades Denmark and Norway.
10 May	Germany invades France and the Low Countries.
	Chamberlain resigns as British Prime Minister.
	Winston Churchill succeeds him.
14 May	Rotterdam bombed. Dutch army capitulates.
17 May	Brussels occupied.
27 May–4 June	British Expeditionary Force evacuated from Dunkirk.
28 May	Belgium capitulates.
10 June	Italy declares war on Britian and France.
14 June	Paris occupied by German troops.
15–16 June	Soviet occupation of Lithuania, Latvia and Estonia.
16 June	Marshal Pétain becomes Prime Minister of France.
22 June	Armistice between Germany and France signed at Compiègne.
10 July	First German air attacks on Britain.
25 August	First British air raid on Berlin.

3 September	50 American destroyers exchanged for use of British bases in the Western Hemisphere.
6 September	Abdication of King Carol II of Rumania.
7 September	Beginning of massive German air raids on London.
27 September	Establishment of Rome-Tokyo-Berlin Axis (the Three-Power Pact).
7 October	German troops invade Rumania.
12 October	Official postponement of plans for the invasion of Britain (Operation Sea-Lion). End of the Battle of Britain.
23 October	Hitler meets Franco at Hendaye.
24 October	Hitler meets Pétain at Montoire.
28 October	Italy invades Greece.
6 November	Roosevelt elected for a third term as President of the USA.
11 November	British air attack on the Italian fleet at Taranto.
12 November	Soviet Foreign Minister Molotov visits Berlin.
14 November	German air raid on Coventry.
15 November	Warsaw Ghetto sealed.
20–25 November	Hungary, Rumania and Slovakia join the Three-Power Pact.
15 December	After their victory at Sidi Barani, the British invade Italian Libya.
17 December	'Lease-Lend' Bill announced in the USA. Massive aid for Britain.
18 December	First directive issued for 'Operation Barbarossa' – the German invasion of Russia.

1941

6 January	Roosevelt addresses Congress and calls for 'the Four Freedoms'.
10 January	Lease-Lend Bill placed before Congress.
22 January	Tobruk falls to British forces.
6 February	Fall of Benghazi.
12 February	General Rommel arrives in Tripoli to take command of the German Afrika Korps.
1 March	Bulgaria joins the Three-Power Pact.
2 March	German troops enter Bulgaria.
7 March	German Jews to be employed for compulsory labour.
11 March	Roosevelt signs the Lease-Lend Bill.
24 March	Rommel's troops take El Agheila in Libya.
26 March	Military coup d'état in Yugoslavia against the pro-German policies of Prince-Regent Paul. Simović becomes Prime Minister under King Peter II.

28 March	Naval battle of Cape Matapan in the eastern Mediterranean. British defeat the Italian fleet.
6 April	German invasion of Greece and Yugoslavia.
11 April	Rommel's siege of Tobruk begins.
17 April	Yugoslav army surrenders at Sarajevo.
19 April	British and Greek troops outflanked. Retreat towards Athens begins.
27 April	German forces occupy Athens.
1 May	British forces complete the evacuation of Greece.
10 May	Rudolf Hess flies to Scotland as 'peacemaker'.
14 May	Bormann appointed head of the Nazi Party Chancellery in Hess's place.
15 May	Pétain announces a policy of total French collaboration with Germany.
20 May	German parachute forces land on Crete.
27 May	Sinking of the German battleship *Bismarck* by the British Navy.
1 June	Crete falls to the Germans.
2 June	Hitler and Mussolini meet at the Brenner again.
8 June	British and Free French forces invade Vichy-held Syria.
14 June	Axis funds in the USA frozen.
18 June	Treaty of German-Turkish Friendship signed.
22 June	Germany attacks the Soviet Union.
8 July	Stalin announces the 'scorched earth' policy.
12 July	Soviet-British Mutual Assistance Pact signed.
17 July	Alfred Rosenberg appointed Minister for the Occupied Eastern Territories.
21 July	First extermination camp established at Maidenek.

Index

Biographical details introduce entries
for the leading characters

Aachen
  bombing of 349
Abetz, Otto (1903–58), German
    ambassador in occupied Paris
    1940–4. Sentenced to 20 years'
    imprisonment in 1949 for war
    crimes 148, 185–6, 198, 306, 353
Abyssinia 237, 241, 247
  campaign in: British advance 228–31
    passim, 233, 243, 244, 274, 277,
    280, 283, 284, 289, 291, 297, 299,
    302, 333; Addis Ababa taken 303;
    Italians surrender 373, 375
  French troops in 253
Admiral Hipper 233, 234, 241, 244
Air Defence League 376
Ajax, HMS 147
Albers, Hans, German actor 168, 269
Albrecht, Capt. 65
Alexander, A. V. (1885–1965), British
    First Lord of the Admiralty
    1940–5, 1945–6; Minister of
    Defence 1947–50 239, 258
Alexandria
  bombing of 398, 399, 403, 428, 445
Alfieri, Dino, Italian Minister of
    Popular Culture to 1939. Later
    Italian Ambassador in Berlin 37,
    37n, 39, 40, 54, 66, 88, 122, 124,
    127, 128, 198, 216, 217, 218, 247,
    285, 292, 332, 338, 346, 362, 369,
    401, 422, 423, 424, 425, 432
Alfonso XIII (1886–1941), King of
    Spain 1886–1930
  death 251
All Quiet On The Western Front 14
Amann, Max (1891–1957), Hitler's
    sergeant during World War I and
    publisher of *Mein Kampf*. Head of

the Reich Press Chamber and
    'Reich Press Leader' after 1933 40,
    49, 92, 110, 240, 346, 350, 379, 406,
    444
Anderson, Jane, pro-German
    American journalist 26, 257
Anderson, Sir John (1882–1958),
    British Home Secretary 1939–40
    118
Angriff, Der 306, 306n
Antonescu, Gen. Ion (1882–1946),
    Rumanian Prime Minister from
    1940 under German tutelage.
    Executed in 1946 in Bucharest
    135n, 139, 180, 181, 183, 186, 230,
    232, 235–9 *passim*, 249, 254, 255,
    256, 260, 262, 281–2, 327, 331, 387,
    397, 401, 415, 445
  meets Hitler 184
Antonescu, Mikail, Rumanian Deputy
    Prime Minister and Foreign
    Minister 1941–4. Executed 1946
    426
Aosta, Duke of, son of King Victor
    Emmanuel of Italy. Commander of
    Italian forces in East Africa 323,
    333, 373
Arent, Benno von, 'Reich Theatre
    Designer' and close associate of
    Goebbels 15, 337
Ark Royal, HMS 3
  'sinking' of 21, 21n
Athenia 47
  sinking of 25, 25n, 27–31 *passim*, 78,
    79
Athens 336
  taken by Germans 337, 338, 342
Attolico, Bernardo, Italian ambassador
    to Germany in 1940 18, 37n, 38

August Wilhelm von Preussen, Prince (1887–1949), fourth son of Kaiser Wilhelm II of Germany and member of the Nazi Party from 1929. Popularly known as 'Auwi'. A Gruppenführer in the SA, member of the Prussian State Council and Reichstag deputy 145, 145n

Auler, Prof. 234, 298, 424

Austria
as Ostmark 272, 272n, 275

Avonmouth
bombing of 299

Azaña, Manuel (1880–1940), President of the Spanish Republic 1936–9 9

Baarova, Lida 3

Backe, Herbert (1896–1947), Nazi agricultural expert. Food Minister 1944–5. Committed suicide in his cell at Nuremberg in 1947 343, 350, 434

Badoglio, Marshal Pietro (1871–1956), Chief-of-Staff of the Italian Army. Prime Minister of Italy 1943–4 177, 196, 200, 205, 208, 216, 217

Balkan League
conference in Belgrade 113, 115

Bardóssy, Lazlo, Hungarian Foreign Minister 1940–1. Prime Minister 1941–2 277, 297

Barnes, Peter 117n

Bartels, Hermann, architect and SS leader. Designer of Himmler's castle at Wewelsberg in Westphalia 99, 190, 233, 274, 438

Barth, Karl (1886–1968), Swiss-born Protestant theologian and opponent of Nazism. Stripped of his university posts in Germany because of his refusal to take an oath of allegiance to Hitler, he taught in Switzerland until his death 336

Basch, Dr 202

Beaverbrook, William Maxwell Aitken, Lord (1879–1964), British newspaper owner and Conservative politician. Minister of Information 1918, Minister of Aircraft Production 1940–1, Minister of Supply 1941–2, Lord Privy Seal 1943–5 346, 441

Belfast
bombing of 318, 350

Belfast, HMS 55

Belgium 95, 96
King's peace appeal 43, 45, 47, 51
near famine 1941 444
under German rule 138, 143, 232, 234, 263, 339, 383

Belgrade 308, 309, 334, 352, 396
air raids on 302, 303, 306
Germans enter 314

Berg, Bengt 48

Berlin 126
Adlon Hotel 127, 422
air-raid defences 161, 214, 219, 271, 366
air raids 126, 127, 128, 135, 142, 144, 149, 153, 161–2, 168, 174, 208, 215, 217, 267, 268, 279, 310, 321, 324, 335, 358, 394
child evacuation 125, 126, 127, 131, 281
Jews in armament factories 1941 277
problems in 1941 296, 306, 331, 434, 453
State Opera destroyed 310, 311
Ufapalast 40, 40n, 196, 235, 251, 299

Berlin Philharmonic Orchestra
forbidden to play for Paris public 263

Berliner Börsen-Zeitung 336, 336n, 359, 392, 396

Berliner Tageblatt 5

Berliner Zeitung 42

Berndt, Alfred-Ingemar. Former head of the German Press Division, from August 1939 head of the Radio Division of the Propaganda Ministry 22, 61, 71, 73, 91, 93, 105, 106, 109, 120, 129, 138, 139, 143, 146, 149, 150, 161, 177, 183, 209, 237, 341, 342, 347, 358, 374, 388, 399, 402, 419, 421, 424

Bertram, Hans, German film director specialising in war films 238, 259
his *Battle-Squadron Lützow* 234, 238, 251

Best, Capt. 52n

Bethlen, Count István (1874–1951), Former Prime Minister of Hungary and adviser to Regent Horthy 75, 76

Bethmann-Hollweg, Theobald von
(1856–1921), Chancellor of
Germany 1909–17 107, 273n
Bevin, Ernest (1881–1951), British
Labour politician. Minister of
Labour and National Service
1940–5, Foreign Secretary 1945–51
142, 368
Bibrach, official in the Fine Arts
Division of the Propaganda
Ministry 116, 146, 182, 244, 289,
431, 444
Biesterfeld, Prince 411
Birmingham
bombing of 158, 162, 180, 181, 183,
204, 311, 450
Bismarck 153, 160, 182
sinks HMS *Hood* 382–5 *passim*
sunk by British 384–9 *passim*
Bismarck, Prince Otto von (1815–98),
Minister-President of Prussia
1862–71, Chancellor of Germany
1871–90. Unifier of Germany 96,
99, 114
Blohm and Voss Co., Hamburg 206,
209
Blomberg, FM Werner von
(1878–1946), Minister of Defence
in the last pre-Nazi cabinet, a post
in which he was retained by Hitler.
Blomberg was forced to resign
when his young second wife was
accused of having been a prostitute
368
resignation of 11n
Blücher 187, 187n, 188
Bock, Gen. (later FM) Fedor von der
(1880–1945), Commander of an
Army Group during the French
campaign of 1940, for which he was
created FM. Later commanded the
Southern Front in Russia until his
dismissal in mid-1942. Killed in an
air raid on Berlin in May 1945 61,
274, 439, 441
Bodenschatz, Gen. Karl, Luftwaffe
commander and aide to Göring 53,
400, 419
Bohle, Ernst-Wilhelm, head of the
Foreign Organisation of the Nazi
Party (AO) 129n, 137, 145, 150,
174, 260, 281, 377, 442
Böhme, Gen. Franz (1885–1947),

Commander of Mountain Troops.
Army commander in Norway
1940–5 199
Bombing truce, Christmas 1940 219,
219n, 220
Bömer, Karl, Propaganda Ministry
official. Later head of the Foreign
Press Department until disgraced
and imprisoned in 1941 22, 34, 54,
102, 103, 105, 115, 151, 181, 229,
252, 263, 289, 395, 363, 367, 379,
410; drunken indiscretion 380–5
passim, 388; to face People's Court
390, 407; sent on leave 392;
imprisoned 433
Borghese, Prince 328
Boris II (1894–1943), King of Bulgaria
1918–43 328
Bormann, Martin (1900–?45), Hitler's
private secretary. Reichsleiter.
From April 1941 head of the Party
Chancellery. Probably killed
escaping from Berlin in May 1945
70, 190, 248, 273, 277, 280, 281,
374, 375, 377, 378, 387, 398, 420,
442
Bottai, Giuseppe, Italian Minister of
Education 174
Bouhler, Philip (1899–1945), Business
manager of the Nazi Party and
Reichsleiter. Director of the
Official Party Examination
Committee for the Defence of
National Socialist Literature, one
of several censorship bodies 49, 55,
60, 204, 249, 300, 303, 418
Boulogne
bombing of 430
Bournemouth
bombing of 270
Brauchitsch, FM Walther von
(1881–1948), Commander-in-Chief
of the Wehrmacht 1938–41 208,
211, 240, 244, 248, 255, 256, 257,
263, 265, 269, 390
speech of Christmas 1940 suppressed
221
Braun, Otto, leading Social-Democratic
politician in the Weimar Republic.
Minister-President of Prussia
1925–32 13
Braune, *Landesgericht* President 212,
213

Brauweiler, Ernst, high-ranking official in the Propaganda Section of the ministry 24, 53, 54, 61, 67, 87, 88, 91, 115, 116, 122, 139, 181, 193, 199, 405, 410, 411

Breker, Arno, leading German sculptor 194, 341, 342

Bremen 270
bombing of 267, 274, 288, 320, 337, 361, 419, 436

Bremen 65
destroyed by fire 270, 271, 273

Brest-Litovsk
taken by Germans 426, 430, 437

Bristol
bombing of 185, 192, 195, 270, 287, 297, 306

Britain
heavy shipping losses of Feb. 1941 252
White Book on German concentration camps 37, 38

British Ministry of Information 18n, 19, 31
traduced by Goebbels 18

Brückner, Anton (1824–96), Austrian composer 265, 266

Brüning, Heinrich (1885–1970), Catholic politician and Chancellor of Germany 1930–2. Later exiled in the USA 19, 29

Bulgaria 191, 212, 231, 236, 242, 246, 281: anti-Jewish law of Dec. 1940 215–16; signs non-aggression pact with Turkey 238; joins Three-Power Pact 251, 252, 253; occupied by German troops 253, 254, 256, 257; moves into newly acquired Balkan territories 325

Bülow, Herr von 357

Bürckel, Josef (1895–1944), Gauleiter of Vienna 1938–40 and Reich Staatholder of Austria 41, 154, 190

Busch, Wilhelm (1832–1908), German humorous artist and poet 346

Campbell, Sir Ronald (1883–1953), later Ambassador in Lisbon 342

Canaris, Adm. Franz Wilhelm (1887–1945), head of German Military Intelligence (the *Abwehr*) 1935–44. Executed for suspected complicity in the July 1944 plot against Hitler 98, 102

Cardiff
bombing of 249, 256, 443

Carol II (1893–1953), King of Rumania 1930–40 139, 184n
flees to Portugal 257

Carstensen, P., Ministry official. Later killed in North Africa 419, 421

Caspar, Horst, German stage and film actor 210

Catte's *Conversations with Frederick the Great* 257, 258, 262

Cavallero, Marshal Count Ugo, Italian Chief-of-Staff December 1940 to January 1943. Committed suicide in 1943 339

Chamberlain, Neville (1869–1940), British Prime Minister 1937–40 11, 17–20 *passim*, 24, 25, 45, 47n, 55, 91, 97, 107, 118, 160, 160n, 171: gives up Government office 130; resigns leadership of Conservative Party 140; death 169

Chatfield, Adm. Lord (1873–1967), Minister for Co-ordination of Defence in the British War Cabinet September 1939 to May 1940 160

Chiang-Kai-Shek (1887–1975), President of China 1927–49, of Taiwan to 1975 121, 241, 272, 449n

Churchill, Winston Spencer (1874–1965), British First Lord of the Admiralty 1939–40, Prime Minister 1940–5, 1951–5 20–32 *passim*, 47, 47n, 71, 100, 101, 102, 107, 113, 125, 130, 136, 141, 150, 167, 169, 173, 182, 213, 229, 230, 268, 274, 283, 284, 310, 314, 327, 330, 338, 339, 344, 346, 349, 355: answers German charges about *Athenia* 27–8, 29; becomes leader of Conservative Party 140, 140n; on British victory over Italians in N. Africa 201; appeals to Italian people Dec. 1940 218, 219, 220; *Step by Step* (book) 354; on Hess defection 368; speaks about Crete June 1941 404

Ciano, Count Galeazzo (1904–44), Mussolini's son-in-law and Italian Foreign Minister 1937–43. Shot for his complicity in the coup that

464

overthrew the Duce in July 1943
26, 54, 66, 68, 69, 88, 90, 173, 196,
198, 200, 205, 208, 231, 233, 252,
275, 281, 290, 422
visits Hitler 178
Clemenceau, Georges (1841–1929),
Prime Minister of France 1917–20
89, 107
Codreanu, Cornelius Zelia
(1899–1939), founder of the
Rumanian Legion. Executed by
the authorities in 1939 139n, 184
Cologne
bombing of 187, 236, 253, 264, 349,
372, 443
Comintern 43
Concordia radio transmitter 111, 111n
Condor Legion 13, 13n
Congress of Vienna 155
Conti, Leonard (1900–45), Reich
Minister of Health. State Secretary
in the Prussian Ministry of the
Interior, SS Grüppenfuhrer.
Committed suicide while awaiting
trial at Nuremberg 232, 248
Corriere della Sera 343
Coughlin, Father 6
Coventry
bombing of 175–9 *passim*, 195, 307,
314
Cremer, Hannes 332, 354, 449
Crete 330, 345, 376, 396, 397, 400, 415,
416: sea battles off 286, 287, 288,
381, 383, 386; German invasion
375, 377–85 *passim*, 387, 388, 389,
391, 392, 393: German victory 393,
394; prisoners taken 395
Cripps, Sir Richard Stafford
(1889–1952), British Ambassador
to Moscow 1940–2, Minister of
Aircraft Production 1942–5,
President of the Board of Trade
1945–7, Chancellor of the
Exchequer 1947–50 409, 412, 414
Cross, R. H., British Minister of
Economic Warfare 1939–40,
Minister for Shipping 1940–1, 346,
445
Csáky, Count Stephan, Hungarian
Foreign Minister 1940 88, 90
Cudahy, John (1887–1943), American
diplomat. Minister in Dublin
1936–9, Ambassador to Belgium

1939–40 331, 334–5, 381, 398, 400,
454
Cvetcović, Dragiša (1893–1969),
Yugoslav Prime Minister 1940–1
283, 285
Cyrenaica
German raids on 234
Czechoslovak Republic 29, 29n, 63
film industry 61, 71
national day 31–2, 34, 35
situation under German rule 46,
50–1, 52, 53, 54, 61, 69, 78, 114,
123–4, 128, 131, 134, 356

Daheim magazine
attacks Hitler's strategic abilities 257
Daily Herald 399
Daily Sketch
ridicules German leaders 50
Daily Telegraph 35
Daladier, Eduard (1884–1970), Prime
Minister of France 1938–40 17, 18,
19, 31, 59, 75, 88, 107, 120
D'Alquen, Gunther, SS
Standartenführer. Editor of the SS
newspaper *Das Schwarze Korps*
(The Black Corps) 4, 375, 377
Daluege, Kurt (1897–1946), Chief of
Security Police in the SD. From
1942 Deputy Reich Protector of
Bohemia and Moravia. Executed
in Prague 1946 157
D'Annunzio, Gabriele (1863–1938),
Italian poet and nationalist
politician 349
Danzig 8, 153, 154
position in 1939 8n
Darlan, Adm. Jean-Louis (1881–1942),
French Navy Minister and Deputy
Premier 1941. Declared against
Pétain in 1942 and murdered in
Algiers Dec. 1942 306, 393, 405
meets Hitler 364
Darré, Walter (1895–1953), Reich
Agriculture Leader and Food
Minister 23, 33, 41, 53, 59, 206, 361
De Gaulle, Gen. Charles (1890–1970),
leader of the Free French 1940–4,
Prime Minister of France 1944–6,
President of the Fifth Republic
1958–69 123, 278, 377, 401
Degrelle, Léon (1906–   ), Belgian
fascist and collaborator. Leader of

Degrelle, Léon – *contd*
the Rexist movement.
Commanded a Legion of Walloon
volunteers on the Eastern Front
1941–4. In exile in Spain since 1945
202, 234, 242, 339
Dekanosov, Vladimir, Soviet Deputy
Foreign Minister and Ambassador
in Berlin 1940–1, 185, 423
Delmer, Sefton, former British
newspaper correspondent in Berlin
295, 334
Demandowski, official in the Film
Division of the Propaganda
Ministry 4, 6, 26, 63, 87, 230, 269,
282, 351, 393, 412, 421
Denmark
under German rule 135
Dentz, Gen., Commander of the Vichy
forces in Syria 371, 401, 417
Deutsche Allgemeine Zeitung 228, 228n,
396
Deutsche Rundschau 66
De Valera, Eamonn (1882–1975), Irish
Republican politician. Prime
Minister during the Second World
War, later President of the
Republic of Eire 168, 169n
Diemen, Ursula van 260
Dietl, Gen. Edouard (1900–44),
Commander of Mountain Troops.
Hero of the seizure of Narvik in
April 1940. Killed in a car crash in
1944 185, 189, 192, 439
Dietrich, Dr Otto (1897–1952), Press
chief and State Secretary in the
Propaganda Ministry. Technically
Goebbels' junior, Dietrich
reported direct to Hitler, an
anomaly which led to constant
conflicts 5, 8, 12, 40, 54, 92, 96,
101, 116, 127, 136, 142, 159, 163,
176, 229–33 *passim*, 242, 271, 292,
301, 303, 312, 337, 379, 383, 392,
410, 422, 431, 437, 447, 449
visits France 198
Dietrich, Joseph 'Sepp' (1892–1966), a
former butcher and commander of
Hitler's SS bodyguard
(*Leibstandarte*). Later a
commander in the Waffen-SS on
active service. Sentenced to 25
years' imprisonment after the war
for complicity in the massacre of
American soldiers during the
Ardennes offensive of December
1944 but released in 1956 32, 46,
158, 313n, 375
Diewerge, Wolfgang, head of the Reich
Propaganda Office in Danzig to
1940. Later employed at the
Ministry of Propaganda in Berlin,
from 1941 as Director of Reich
Broadcasting 21, 232, 237, 294,
324, 325, 374, 422, 431, 452
Dittmar, Walther Wilhelm, head of the
News Division of the Broadcasting
Service 91, 169, 170, 175, 339, 357
Dolfuss, Engelbert (1892–1934),
Chancellor of Austria 1932–4.
Murdered during an attempted
Nazi coup d'état in Austria in July
1934 155
Dominik, an engineer employed in the
Propaganda Ministry (note of
personal recollection by Otte) 434
Dorpmüller, Julius Heinrich
(1869–1945), Minister of Transport
in Hitler's government 1937–45 72,
114
Dorsch, Kathë, leading film actress during
the Third Reich 75, 79, 98, 179
Draeger, Hans, official of the
Propaganda Ministry. Later head
of the Foreign Press Department
48, 264
Drewes, Dr 78, 150, 181, 182, 184, 193,
199, 295
Dublin
bombing of 393
Duff Cooper, A. (1890–1954), British
Secretary of State for War 1935–7,
First Lord of the Admiralty
1937–8. Resigned over
Appeasement in September 1938.
Minister of Information in
Churchill's government 1940–1 11,
125, 329, 364, 369
Duisburg
bombing of 235
Dürer, Albrecht (1471–1528), German
artist 287
Düsseldorf
bombing of 235, 236, 284, 349, 371

Eden, Sir Anthony (later Lord Avon)

(1897–1977), British Foreign Secretary 1937–8, 1940–5, 1951–5. Prime Minister 1955–7 191, 217, 252, 253, 276, 323, 327, 344, 352, 353, 355, 368, 451: visits Ankara 1941 248, 249; visits Athens 255, 291; visits Belgrade 1941 292, 293

Egk, Werner, German composer 250

Eichstätt, Bishop of 112

Eigruber, August, Gauleiter of the Upper Danube 203, 265, 266, 293, 370

Elser, Johann Georg 49n, 50

Emden
bombing of 329

Engel, Capt. Gerhard, adjutant to Hitler 32

Engelbrecht, Gen. Erwin von, Commander of the 163rd Division during the invasion of Norway 187

Epp, Franz Xavier Ritter von (1868–1947), Nazi governor in Bavaria in 1933 and Reichsleiter. From 1936 Reich Leader for the Colonies taken from Germany by the Treaty of Versailles in 1919 145, 164

Essen
bombing of 236

Esser, Herman (1900–), a co-founder of the Nazi Party while still in his teens. Dismissed as Bavarian Minister of Economics in 1935 because of financial irregularities and a sordid private life; appointed Secretary of State for Tourism in Goebbels' ministry in 1939 as a gesture of partial rehabilitation 8, 110, 139, 146, 150, 152, 351, 450, 452

Fabrizius, Prof. 27

Falange, the 162, 162n, 164, 281

Falckenhorst, Gen. Nikolaus von, Military Commander in Norway 1940–5 187

Farinacci, Roberto, former secretary of the Italian Fascist Party and one of Mussolini's chief lieutenants. Editor of the *Regime Fascistica* 7, 127–31 *passim*, 135, 217
attacks Badoglio 205, 216

Feder, Gottfried (1883–1941), economic theorist and co-founder of the Nazi Party in 1920. Feder was awarded a minor post in the Economics Ministry in 1933, quarrelled with Hitler, and was never reconciled with his former protégé 396

Feiler, Hertha 105

Female Labour Service 388

Fiehler, Karl, Burgomaster of Munich. Reichsleiter 179

Filov, Bogdan Dimitrov (1883–1945), Prime Minister of Bulgaria 1940–3. Executed 1945 252, 253

Finland 29, 37, 46, 430: German troops in 343; ready to attack Russia 1941 415, 420; declares war on Russia 1941 430; moves against Russia 1941 450, 453. *See also* Russo-Finnish War

Fischer, Dr 16, 25, 377

Fischer, Hugo, Staff Director of the Reich Propaganda Leadership 232, 271, 375, 397, 399, 420, 431, 432, 436

Flandin, Pierre Etienne (1889–1958), French Prime Minister 1934–5, Foreign Minister 1940–1. Acquitted of treason in 1945 207

Florian, Friedrich Karl, Gauleiter of Cologne 103, 104, 105

Foch, Marshal Ferdinand (1851–1929), Allied Commander-in-Chief in 1918 107

Foreign Organisation of Nazi Party (AO) 129, 129n, 137, 164, 260, 281, 373, 377, 432, 442

Forschungsamt (Research Office) 116, 116n

Forster, Albert (1902–), Nazi leader in the Free State of Danzig 1936–9. From December 1939 Gauleiter of Danzig and West Prussia. He was sentenced to life imprisonment by a Polish court in 1946 8, 57, 153, 154, 165, 237, 255, 273

France
actions before defeat: withdraws from German soil, 23, 24, 25: searches for German transmitters 84, 85, 89, 99, 101, 118; final resistance to German invasion 122–3; signs truce with Italy 124

France – *contd*
attacks Churchill over Dunkirk evacuation 342
German plunder from 251
near famine 1941 444
pro-Yugoslav demonstrations in Marseilles 287, 291
under German rule 130, 132, 151, 237, 306, 332
Franco y Bahamonde, Francisco (1892–1975), Commander of the nationalist forces during the Spanish Civil War 1936–9. Spanish Head of State 1939–75 8, 9, 85, 152, 159, 160, 162, 164, 210, 231, 232, 257, 292, 293, 323, 324, 355, 356, 373: advances on Barcelona Jan. 1939 6; takes Barcelona 7; meets Hitler 153; meets Mussolini Feb. 1941 233; meets Pétain Feb. 1941 233
François-Poncet, André, French Ambassador to Germany to 1939, to Italy 1939–40 17
Frank, Hans (1900–46), 'Chief Civilian Officer' and later Governor of German-occupied Poland. Executed at Nuremberg in 1946 19, 36, 50, 53, 105, 106, 107, 183, 272, 420
addresses foreign press 120
Frank, Karl-Hermann, deputy leader of the Sudeten-German Party to 1938. Chief of police in the Czech Protectorate. Executed in Prague in 1946 165, 166, 167
Franz-Josef II (1830–1916), Emperor of Austria 1848–1916. In 1899 his heir, Crown Prince Rudolf, committed suicide with his mistress at the hunting lodge at Mayerling 23
Frederick the Great (Frederick II) 1712–86), King of Prussia 1740–86 96, 99
Frederike, Princess, of Brunswick 74, 74n
Frick, Wilhelm (1877–1946), Reich Minister of the Interior from 1933. Hanged at Nuremberg in 1946 5, 39, 110, 177, 341, 370, 387, 390
report on Jewish question in Poland 42–3

Friedrich Wilhelm IV (1795–1861), King of Prussia 1840–61 114
Fritzsche, Hans (1900–53), head of the Press Section of the Propaganda Ministry 1933–42. From 1942 Plenipotentiary for the Political Organisation of the Greater German Radio. Acquitted at Nuremberg of incitement to war crimes 13, 49, 54, 71, 84, 91, 116, 120, 142, 149, 156, 159, 172, 177, 227, 229, 230, 231, 242, 289, 351, 363, 368, 371, 390, 396, 405, 409, 411, 431
Frölich, Prof. Carl, President of the 'Reich Film Chamber' 13, 106, 135, 153, 184, 235
his *Gas-Man* 234, 235, 237, 239, 240, 282
receives film prize 12
Frowein, Karl, personal adviser to Goebbels and aide in the Minister's Office 251, 283
Funk, Walther (1890–1960), former press chief under Goebbels and Minister of Economics and President of the Reich Bank from 1938. Sentenced to life imprisonment at Nuremberg 4, 11, 84, 145, 157, 268, 420, 429
Fürtwangler, Wilhelm (1886–1954), conductor, director of the Wagner Festival at Bayreuth from 1937 54, 85, 90, 129, 131, 155, 161, 168, 205, 213

Galland, Adolf (1911–), German fighter ace and later Luftwaffe General of Fighters 423
Gamelin, Gen., Commander-in-Chief of the French Army 1939–40 108
Gandhi, Mahatma (1869–1948), Indian spiritual leader and opponent of British rule 273
Genoa
shelled by British 227, 228, 235
George II (1890–1947), King of Greece 1922–3, 1935–47 324, 327, 329, 330, 383
George VI (1895–1952), King of Great Britain and Emperor of India 1937–52 17, 182, 220
Christmas speech 1939 75

George, Heinrich, German actor and
manager of the Schiller-Theatre in
Berlin. Died in Russian hands in
1951 115
German Academy 181, 254
German-Italian Society 129
German News Agency 8, 319
German–Turkey Treaty of Friendship
June 1941 418, 419, 421
Gibraltar 146, 161, 183, 329
German plan to attack 190, 210
Gigli, Beniamino 333
Giornale d'Italia 164n
Giraudoux, Jean (1882–1944), French
novelist and dramatist. Appointed
Commissioner of Information by
Daladier in July 1939 26, 55
Glasgow
bombing of 268, 269, 306
Glasmaier, Heinrich, official in the
Broadcasting Service in the
Propaganda Ministry. Appointed
Reich Intendant of the Greater
German Radio in 1941 91, 93, 105,
135, 143, 170, 171, 177, 204, 229,
303, 319, 325, 355, 374, 405, 419,
429, 432, 452
Gneisenau
damaged in Brest bombing 312
hit by torpedo 304
Goebbels children. Numerous
mentions, but we have listed them
only where they have been
mentioned by name. Helmut was
the only boy
Hedda (1938–45) 94, 184, 205, 264,
268, 269, 270, 273, 370
Heide (1940–5) 83, 158, 232, 370
Helga (1932–45) 13, 47, 56, 94, 95,
96, 109, 111, 112, 135, 142, 207,
221, 230, 255, 370, 372, 449
Helmut (1935–45) 94, 129, 370, 371
Hilde (1934–45) 94, 95, 96, 109, 111,
112, 135, 142, 207, 221, 255, 314,
449
Holde (1937–45) 9, 10, 13, 94, 95,
109, 184, 205, 239, 370, 449
Goebbels,
affair with Lida Baarova 3
approval of vegetarianism 6
Bogensee house 21–2, 33, 40, 47, 59,
76, 79
control of German radio 7–8, 10

day-to-day activities: gives New Year
radio address 1939 4; writes to
Hitler 4; invited to Obersalzberg by
Hitler 5; meeting with Hitler Jan.
1939 5; dictates essay *The
Intellectual* 6; eats with Hitler 6;
discussions with Hitler, early 1939
8; works on reorganising German
News Agency 8; contributes article
on Nazi Anniversary to *Völkischer
Beobachter* 8; articles on practical
jokes and coffee queues 9;
discovers traitor in Ministry 10; has
trouble with UFA 10, 12; writes in
VB May 1939 13; considers
Lloyd-George's peace article Oct.
1939 14, 15; considers
Germanification of Polish press 15;
hears Hitler's verdict on Poles 16;
scornful of British rumour-
mongering Oct. 1939 17, 18, 20–1;
organises press attacks on London
Oct. 1939 19; has problems with
rationing 20; criticises railways and
post office 20; rounds up artists
Oct. 1939 22; attacks Churchill 22;
on air attacks on British fleet 23,
24; surprised at French withdrawal
from German soil 23, 24, 25; tests
leaflet projectile-thrower 24;
describes Berlin welcome for
U-boat crews 24–5; 'proves'
Athenia was scuttled 25n, 27–8;
attacks Churchill Oct. 1939 27, 28,
29; meets men from Propaganda
Companies 28; 'Jerry-Letter' affair
31, 31n, 32, 33, 35, 36, 38;
entertains German poets 32; muses
on film losses 33; celebrates 42nd
birthday 30 Oct. 1939 34; takes tea
with Hitler 35; on German
administration in Poland 36; visits
Poland Nov. 1939 36–7; attacks
Jews 38; work on anti-English
White Books 38, 39, 50; on sale of
decadent art 39; visits Berlin
Ufapalast 40; restricts import of
foreign films Nov. 1939 40–1; limits
broadcasting 41; institutes press
attacks on West 42; attends
Bürgerbräukeller meeting Nov.
1939 43; investigates Munich
assassination attempt on Hitler

Goebbels,   – *contd*

44–5, 46; orders investigation into astrology 47–8, 89; angry with London press Nov. 1939 50, 51; plans for collecting books for front 52; institutes book censorship 55; censors pastoral letters 56; visits Poland 57–8; tours W. German fortifications 61–3; organises anti-French radio stations Dec. 1939 64, 65; over-optimistic about Battle of River Plate 66–71 *passim*; gives Christmas speech 1939 73, 74; presses for religious censorship 77; makes New Year speech 1940 79, 84; plans for Czech film industry 87; expands foreign radio broadcasts Jan. 1940 89; speaks to heads of Propaganda Companies 91; concerned about Nazi Party Jan. 1940 94; visit and speech at Posen 99–100; visits Western Front 103–4; considers paper shortage Feb. 1940 115; speeches to his subordinates 116; on evacuating German children Oct. 1940 125, 126, 127, 130; speaks in Prague Oct. 1940 128, 131, 134; orders confiscation of musical scores in France 129; mentions dummy installations to draw air attacks 133, 172; impressed by Hess 145; visits Göring's HQ 146–9; visits Paris with Göring 147–8; visits Danzig and speaks there 153–4; visits Vienna and speaks 154–5; reaches 43rd birthday 157; visits Berlin air-raid warning centre Nov. 1940 161; visits Prague 165–8; speaks in Prague 166; speech to armament workers Nov. 1940 174; visits Nuremberg and Munich 178–80, 191; speaks at Nuremberg 178; visits Norway Nov–Dec. 1940 187–9; visits Vienna 196–8; receives neutral journalist 201; visits Hamburg and speaks there Dec. 1940 209, 210, 211; attacks Churchill in *Das Reich* 216, 222; censors painting of 'Mars and Venus' 218; Christmas activities 1940 218–19, 221; speaks at Berlin *Sportpalast* Feb. 1941 231; gives to cancer research 234; writes article on total war for *Das Reich* 238; host to Party stalwarts Feb. 1941 245; considers paper and printing industries 246; negotiates with composers 250; speech at Leipzig Fair 253; speaks at AO March 1941 260; speaks at Foreign Club 260, 263; drafts new fire-fighting guidelines 264; speaks at Linz on anniversary of *Anschluss* 266; visits Vienna and speaks 267; disposes of 'degenerate' art 271; visits Posen and speaks 273–5; meets Rommel March 1941 275–6; receives Japanese youth representatives 277; bans church press 278, 294; visits Wilhelmshaven and Hamburg 283; lunches with Matsuoka and Hitler April 1941 284; deposits diaries in Reichsbank 287; propaganda campaign against Yugoslavia 295, 297, 298, 302–3; propaganda campaign against London and Washington 297; attends première of *Ohm Krüger* April 1941 299; receives summary of situation from Hitler 301; reorganises radio service 308–9; buys Van Dycks from Holland 319; buys painting for Hitler's birthday 321; discovers German secrets are known in Moscow 324; worried about his taxes 325; inspects Berlin damage April 1941 326–7; orders Jews to wear badges 328; presents Hitler with painting and cartoons 343; arranges for broadcasting of Hitler's speech of 5 May 1941 348; attends Gauleiters' conference 350–1; argues for female conscription 362, 378; visits Obersalzberg over Hess defection 364–5; issues orders against occultism May 1941 367; propaganda silence on Hess affair 368; visits Linz and family at Aussee 370–2; discusses plans for take-over of Russia 380, 381–2; propaganda deception over Operation Barbarossa 390–1, 394, 398, 400; plans for anti-Bolshevik propaganda June 1941 396; works on *Between Yesterday and Tomorrow* (essays) 398; buys a Goya 401; tests leaflet-dropping machine 405; writes deceptive article for *VB* 408–11 *passim*, 413; briefed by Hitler on Russian invasion June 1941 413–15, 423–4; prints leaflets for soldiers in Russian invasion 417–18, 419; propaganda line on Russian invasion 429, 434; explains withholding of war reports June 1941 437; arranges broadcast of song for Russian campaign 438; institutes propaganda campaign against Bolshevism 450, 452, 453, 454

enjoyment of Bach 129
essay *The 'Encirclers'* 12
film supervision. Nearly every entry contains some reference to film or newsreel
leader article *The Stubborn English* 332, 333, 335, 336
Ministry's budget and staff 1941 233
New Society, The (book) 9
on Czechs 51
on dealing with Jews 125
on English propaganda 116, 121
on English stupidity 361
on film industry's success 259, 284, 331, 377, 427
on ideological dance 138
on intellectualism and propaganda 206
on international affairs, March and May 1939 11
on London–Paris–Ankara Pact 26
on phoney war 19
on problem of treason 102
on Russian Army 46
on school books 204
on 'sinking' of *Ark Royal* 21, 21n
on sinking of *Royal Oak*, 21, 22
on torpedoing of *Repulse* 22
on question of TV's future 454
on U-boat successes 55, 56
on value of repetition in propaganda 84
panegyric on Hitler 18–19
view on church reorganisation 97
wishes to abolish German Script 204
Goebbels, Magda (1901–45), née Ritschel. Married Günther Quandt, businessman 1921. Divorced 1929. Married Josef Goebbels in 1931 and bore him six children. Died by suicide with her husband in Berlin, May 1 1945, after poisoning all their children. As she is mentioned many times in the diaries, just a few important entries are given below
birthdays 46–7, 170, 171
dines with Hitler Feb. 1941 235
gives birth to Heide 158
heart trouble 314, 385–6, 391
wedding anniversaries 70, 211
Goebbels, Maria, sister of Josef Goebbels. Married to Max Kimmich, a film producer, in 1938 139, 383
Goebbels, Maria Katherina, née Odenhausen. Mother of Josef Goebbels 13, 22, 111, 139, 323, 371, 407
Goedecke, Heinz, master-of-ceremonies of the *Request Concert* radio programme 189, 229, 247, 249, 351
Goetz, Curt 14
Göring, Edda and Emmy 155, 155n
Göring, Hermann (1890–1946), Reich Marshal and Hitler's designated successor. Commander of the Luftwaffe and holder of numerous political and administrative posts. Committed suicide while under sentence of death at Nuremburg in 1946 41, 44, 50, 51, 70, 92, 110, 117, 141, 143, 161, 175, 176, 218, 240, 255, 285, 319, 360, 364, 365: takes over German economic leadership 87; invites Goebbels to his HQ 146; gives interview to US journalist 164; puts house at Obersalzberg at Goebbels' disposal 232; makes speech on Hitler's birthday 1941 326
Görlitzer, Arthur, Goebbels' deputy as Gauleiter of Berlin 84, 88, 93, 95, 124, 127, 157, 191, 263, 296, 306, 407
Gradl, Prof. 179
Graener, Paul (1872–1944), German composer 250

Graf Spee, 3, 66–71 *passim*

Grandi, Dino, Italian Minister of Justice 290

Grauert, Col.-Gen. 382

Grawitz, Dr Ernest, Reich Chief Medical Officer of the SS 137

Graz
bombing of 303, 304

Graziani, Marshal Rodolfo (1882–1955), Italian commander in North Africa 1940–1 217, 241, 281

Great Yarmouth
bombing of 291

Greece 211, 236: attacked by Italy 156; British troops in 163, 304, 307, 344; German plan of attack 285, 289, 294, 298, 301; German invasion 302–4, 306, 307, 308, 310, 311, 314–30 *passim*, 333, 335, 336, 337, 339, 342; British leave 316, 317–18, 329; German casualties 325; British prisoners 342; German victory 344, 345; German material losses 414

Greiser, Arthur (1897–1946), Gauleiter of the Posen-Lodz region of Poland, recently annexed by Germany. Executed by the Poles in 1946 30, 58, 99, 100, 106, 107, 140, 175, 273, 274, 275

Gröber, Archbishop, of Freiburg 108–9

Gross, Dr 174

Gründgens, Gustav, German actor. Committed suicide in 1963 75, 78, 84, 86, 92, 369

Gunnarsson, Gunnar, Icelandic poet and novelist 114

Gutterer, Leopold, Ministerial Director and assistant to Goebbels. Appointed State Secretary in 1941. Dismissed in 1943 for corruption 90, 113, 122, 127, 129, 131, 138, 143, 146, 154, 164, 178, 181, 185, 193, 194, 196, 199, 202, 211, 229, 230, 232, 233, 246, 254, 255, 256, 258, 259, 264, 267, 271, 284, 289, 292, 295, 296, 298, 310, 312, 313, 321, 322, 329, 334, 339, 348, 355, 357, 359, 374, 375, 381, 383, 385, 396, 400, 403, 405, 407, 408, 409, 412, 418, 419, 420, 433, 446, 450, 451
promoted 380

Haase, Gen. von 202

Hácha, Emil (1872–1945), Czech politician and jurist. President of Czechoslovakia from November 1938 to March 1939. Retained by the Germans as puppet President of the Protectorate until 1945. Hácha died while awaiting trial in Prague after the war 51, 123, 166–7, 168

Hacken, Oberst von
translation of Nostradamus 60

Hadamovsky, Eugen, Director of Reich Broadcasting to 1942 4, 105, 150, 156, 169, 170, 173, 175, 183, 206, 235, 238, 239, 242, 312, 370, 371, 390, 423
receives Iron Cross First Class 141

Haegert, Wilhelm, head of the Propaganda Section of the Propaganda Ministry 60

Hagelin, A. V., Minister of the Interior in Quisling's government in Norway 343

Haifa
bombing of 404, 410, 411

Haile Selassie (1892–1975), Emperor of Abyssinia 352

Halbicht, Theodor, Ministerial Counsellor at the Foreign Ministry responsible for liaison with the Propaganda Ministry. Later Under-Secretary at the Foreign Ministry 64, 67

Halder, Gen. Franz, Chief-of-Staff of the German Army 1938–42. Dismissed in 1942, he was arrested after the July 1944 plot against Hitler but survived the war in a concentration camp 73

Halifax, Edward, Lord (1880–1959), British Foreign Secretary 1938–40. Ambassador to the USA 1940–6 28, 100, 171, 217, 263, 282, 320

Hamburg 209–10, 283
bombing of 176, 177, 178, 185, 265, 267, 268, 344, 347, 357, 359, 361, 373, 419, 436

Hamilton, Duke of 364

Hamsun, Knut (1856–1952), Norwegian novelist and Nobel Prize laureate. A prominent if eccentric collaborator 121, 252, 257

Hamsun, Tore 252, 257
  My Father 257
Hanfstängel, Ernst Franz Sedgwick
  ('Putzi') (1887–1975), born of
  mixed German and American
  parentage. An early supporter of
  Hitler in Munich and Press Chief of
  the Nazi Party 1933–7, he fled to
  America in 1937 and later served as
  a White House expert on Nazi
  affairs 295
Hanke, Karl (1903–1945), State
  Secretary at the Propaganda
  Ministry, SS Oberführer, and
  Gauleiter of Lower Silesia 1941–5.
  Hanke had intrigued to bring about
  Goebbels' resignation at the time
  of his affair with Lida Baarova.
  Hanke was reported to have been
  shot by Czech partisans in June
  1945 4, 5, 6, 8, 11, 228
Hannover
  bombing of 230, 234, 369
  dances banned in 259
Hapsburg, Otto von (1912–   ),
  claimant to the Austro-Hungarian
  throne 108
Harlan, Veit, prominent film director,
  responsible for a number of
  notorious Nazi films, including the
  anti-Semitic *Jew Süss* and *I Accuse*,
  an apologia for Nazi euthanasia
  policies 6, 296
  Great King, The 393, 393n, 398, 412
  Jud Süss 60, 67, 78, 87, 98, 110, 259
Haushofer, Albrecht (1903–45), son of
  Karl Haushofer. Writer and
  teacher, employed by the Foreign
  Ministry from 1940. Executed for
  his part in the July 1944 plot against
  Hitler's life 440
Haushofer, Karl (1869–1946), World
  War I general. Professor of
  Geopolitics at Munich University,
  he was an important influence on
  Nazi theory and the young Hess,
  who was his student in the early
  1920s. Hess carried his visiting card
  on his flight to Scotland, under the
  impression that it would give him
  access to British academic circles.
  Haushofer committed suicide in
  1946 364, 440

Hearst, William Randolph
  (1863–1951), American newspaper
  owner 14, 347
Hedin, Sven Anders von (1865–1952),
  Swedish traveller and writer.
  Author of a book about Hitler 28,
  48
Heidelberg
  bombing of 342, 351
Heiduschke, Herbert, one of Goebbels'
  personal adjutants. Killed in Crete
  May 1941 127, 158, 220, 230, 239,
  325, 376, 400, 402, 407, 408, 411,
  412
  death 402, 403, 406, 409
Helldorff, Wolf Heinrich, Graf von
  (1896–1944), Police President of
  Berlin. Executed for his part in the
  July 1944 plot against Hitler's life
  271, 294, 368
Henlein, Konrad (1898–1945), Leader
  of the Sudeten-German Party in
  Czechoslovakia to 1938. Gauleiter
  of the Sudetenland and head of
  Civil Administration in the
  Protectorate. Committed suicide in
  American captivity in May 1945
  165
Henry the Lion (1139–95), Duke of
  Saxony and Bavaria, conqueror of
  North-East German from the Slavs
  16
Heroes' Commemoration Day 1941
  270, 270n
Hertling, Georg Freiherr von
  (1843–1919), Chancellor of
  Germany 1917–18 107
Hess, Rudolf (1894–   ), Hitler's
  private secretary from 1925. After
  Nazi seizure of power Deputy
  Führer with the rank of minister
  and special powers over Party
  appointments. After his flight to
  Scotland in April 1941, Hess was
  imprisoned by the British and then
  sentenced to life imprisonment at
  Nuremberg 7, 39, 52, 55, 74, 136,
  143, 145, 174, 176, 185, 186, 219,
  228, 237, 239, 264, 276, 298, 319,
  374, 420, 442: on Munich
  assassination attempt 48; speech on
  Hitler's birthday 1941 326: defects
  to Scotland and repercussions

Hess, Rudolf – *contd*
363–75 *passim*, 377, 399, 424
Hesse, Col., Wehrmacht propaganda
chief 212, 234, 240, 250, 254, 255,
257, 259, 263, 264, 270, 273, 282,
285
Hettlage, Karl Maria, an aide of Albert
Speer 132
Hewel, Walter, Ambassador. The
Foreign Ministry's official
representative to the Reich
Chancellery 109
Heydrich, Reinhard (1904–42), Chief
of the Reich Main Security Office
(*Reichssicherheitshauptamt*).
Appointed Deputy Protector of
Bohemia and Moravia 1941.
Assassinated by Czech partisans
1942 21, 22, 25–6, 86
Himmler, Heinrich (1900–45), Head of
the SS since 1929. Chief of Police in
Munich 1933–6, and from 1936 in
charge of the Reich Security Police
and the Gestapo. Himmler
committed suicide when captured
by British forces in May 1945 45,
52, 98, 99, 101, 108, 125, 176, 189,
294, 340, 343–4
bans sale of contraceptives 312
discovers perpetrator of Munich
explosion 49
Hindenburg, FM Paul Ludwig von
Beckendorff (1847–1934).
German military commander in
World War I and President of the
Weimar Republic 1925–34 11,
114n
Hinkel, Hans, SS Gruppenführer and
close associate of both Goebbels
and Himmler. Head of the
'Cultural Personalities' Office,
responsible for ensuring the
political and racial 'reliability' of
cultural figures. Later manager of
the Reich Chamber of Culture and
Reich Film Intendant 49, 127, 134,
138, 144, 149, 150, 156, 164, 171,
174, 175, 190, 196, 242, 246, 258,
259, 263, 271, 283, 292, 339, 345,
357, 359, 366, 380, 383, 390, 431
Hippler, Fritz, Director of the Film
Department of the Propaganda
Ministry 22, 29, 41, 46, 48, 63, 92,
93, 106, 112, 113, 115, 122, 127,
129, 135, 137, 149, 151, 159, 161,
172, 175, 176, 189, 194, 196, 199,
222, 224, 237, 252, 254, 259, 278,
279, 316, 320, 321, 322, 334, 348,
351, 355, 373, 374, 384, 393, 398,
399, 403, 408, 412, 421, 431, 445
Hitler, Adolf 4, 5, 26, 35, 53, 69, 97,
103, 106, 126, 140, 159, 165, 186,
240, 309, 427
anniversary of assumption of power
7n
approval of vegetarianism 6, 77, 171
attitude to half-Jews 69–70
contempt for England 143
crisis of 1932 and 144n
day-by-day actions: orders Goebbels
to break off affair with Lida
Baarova 3; peace proposals after
fall of Poland 1939 14n; plans for
the Poles 16, 60; criticism of
Hungary Oct. 1939 20; speaks to
his gauleiters 27, 30; outburst
against England 28–9; plan to
attack West 41; escapes
assassination attempt at Munich
44, 45, 49, 50, 54; attacks Churchill
Dec. 1939 64; spends Christmas
1939 at West Wall 74, 76; ridicules
German Foreign Ministry 76;
annoyed at British blockade on
coffee 90; speaks at *Sportpalast*
Jan. 1940 108; complains about
cold 111; excited about victory over
France 122, 123; peace terms for
Britain 1940 123; receives farmers'
delegation Oct. 1940 145; receives
Laval 152; meets Franco 153;
receives Pétain 154, 156; speech of
16 Nov. 1940 169; visits Japanese
embassy 175; visits Munich 177;
housing programme published 178;
receives Süner and Ciano 178;
visits Vienna Nov. 1940 184;
criticises Italy 203, 214; on British
resistance Dec. 1940 202–3;
complains about Italy to Alfieri
198; addresses armament workers
200; speech of 12 Dec. 1940 202;
Party Foundation Day speech Feb.
1941 245, 247; brings Bulgaria into
Three-Power Pact 252; speaks at
Linz on anniversary of *Anschluss*

474

266; speaks on Heroes'
Commemoration Day March 1941
270, 271; on British stubbornness
272–3; decorates Rommel 275;
reaches accommodation with
Yugoslavia 281; entertains
Matsuoka March 1941 284–5; lays
down policy for Yugoslavia 290;
criticises Italy April 1941 290, 307;
plans for attacking Yugoslavia and
Greece 301; birthday celebrations
April 1941 326; meets Horthy 333,
334; returns from Balkan battle
zone 340; on treatment of Greeks
341; speaks to Reichstag May 1941
349–50, 352; analyses world
situation May 1941 355–6; unable
to bring Franco into war 356;
furious at Hess's defection 363,
365; elaborates plans and reasons
for attacking Russia 413–15
hatred of Christianity 304–5, 340
knowledge of Balkan history 305
on Bismarck and Frederick the Great
96
on Cardinal Pacelli's elevation to
Pope 10
on concept of authority 272
on Czechs 272
on espionage 91
on foreign opponents 107
on German history 114–15
on Hapsburg empire 23
on his anti-Semitism 23
on Jews in the arts 214
on life and bravery 95–6
on need for death sentences 214
on resettlement of S. Tyroleans 39
on Russian Army 48
on sex and morality 200–1
on Spanish question 8
on Styria and Carinthia 341
on war aims 51
opinion of France and Pétain 159–60,
171
opinion of Spain and Franco 159, 161,
290
plan for Jews 1941 272
plans for the theatre 78
plans for European conquest 100–1
scorn for teachers 76
talks with Mussolini 130, 131, 132,
134, 156, 394

view of Italian 'art' 138
views on churches and religion 76, 77
views on Russia 76, 77
visits to Goebbels family 95, 109, 171
Hitler Youth 23, 33, 95, 110
film festival 40
Hoffman, Major 170
Hohenlohe, Princess, a pre-war admirer
of Hitler 49, 215
Holland 95, 96, 104, 117, 205, 211, 251,
347
anti-German demonstrations 1941
246, 248, 249, 250
collaborators in 191
death sentences in 258–9, 273
German fines on cities 1941 252
loses *Simon Bolivar* 53
martial law in Amsterdam 247
Queen's peace appeal 43, 45, 47, 51
Holy Roman Empire 29n, 114
church under 115
Holz, Karl, Deputy Gauleiter of
Franconia. Appointed Gauleiter
after Streicher's dismissal 176
Hommels, the. Professor Hommel, a
prominent German portrait
painter, and his wife were
neighbours of the Goebbelses and
frequent visitors 228, 239, 241, 242,
253, 317, 380, 383, 394
Hood, HMS
sunk by *Bismarck* 382–5 *passim*
Hoover, Herbert (1874–1964),
President of the USA 1928–32 441
Hore-Belisha, Leslie (1893–1957),
British Secretary of State for War
1937–40. His Jewish descent made
him a favourite target for
Goebbels' propaganda 22, 399
resignation 1940 88–91 *passim*, 93,
97–8
Horthy, Adm. Nikolaus (1868–1957),
Regent of Hungary 1920–44, 20,
182, 312, 322
visits Hitler 333
Hull
bombing of 243, 268, 274, 291, 358,
395, 437
Hull, Cordell (1871–1955), US
Secretary of State 297
Hungary 20, 46, 69, 151, 182, 202:
victimises Rumanian subjects 139;
takes Transylvania from Rumania

Hungary – *contd*
139n; joins Three-Power Pact 180,
181; moves against Yugoslavia 312,
314; persecutes Germans in 333,
348; declares war on Russia 435;
moves into Russia 441, 447

Iceland
occupied by USA 454
Illustrated Cracow Courier 15
Inonü, Ismet (1884–1973), President of
Turkey 162, 421
International Film Chamber 265
Ipsen, Birgel, 115
Iraq 345, 359, 372
British take over 326
Iraqis revolt against British 345–52
passim, 355, 360, 368, 369, 376,
384, 391
revolt put down 392, 394, 403
Irish Free State
wartime neutrality 169n
Irish Republican Army (IRA)
bomb attacks in England 1939 56, 56n
execution of IRA men 1940 117n
Iron Guard, Rumanian 139, 139n, 187
Ironside, FM Lord (1880–1959), British
Chief of Imperial General Staff
1939, Commander-in-Chief Home
Forces 1940 300
Italo-Greek campaign
Italy attacks Greece 156, 157
progress 159, 161, 162, 165, 168, 170,
171, 173, 175, 176, 177, 18?, 182,
183, 185, 189, 190, 192, 194, 195,
198, 200–6 *passim*, 208, 212, 213,
215, 220, 222, 228, 230, 231, 236,
241, 257, 280, 332
Italy
German minority in *Alto Adige*
province 39n, 98
government changes 1939 37, 38–9
Grand Fascist Council 63
situation Dec. 1939 66
situation Dec. 1940 216
situation Feb. 1941 230–1
war comes to: on Germany's side 122;
defeated in Western Desert 201–8
passim, 211, 215, 222, 228, 231;
defeated at sea April 1941 291;
demands share of Balkans 346,
347; sets up King of Croatia 370,
370n; lands regiment on Crete 388;

declares war on Russia 425. *See
also* Abyssinia, Italo-Greek
campaign, Somaliland and Taranto
Izvestia
anti-Allies article Oct. 1939 15, 16
approves Axis pact 128
attacks London-Paris-Ankara Pact 27

Jagow, Dietrich von, SA leader. Reich
Police Commissar in Württemberg
in 1933. Later Ambassador to
Hungary 92, 120, 380
Jannings, Emil, German actor/director
of international repute. Jannings,
who starred in a number of films in
Hollywood in the 1920s, also
played in *The Blue Angel* opposite
the then unknown Marlene
Dietrich. He was an active
supporter of the Nazi regime 56,
87, 209, 228, 255, 269, 276, 293,
299, 360, 412, 416
receives 'Film Ring of Honour' 300
Japan 292
aggressive line with Vichy France 251
anniversary of Empire 175n
problem in China 272, 322
signatory of Three-Power Pact 125n
signs Treaty of Friendship with
Russia 314–17 *pasim*
threatens America 1940 202
Jeschonnek, Col.-Gen. Hans,
Luftwaffe Chief-of-Staff 147
Jodl, Col.-Gen. Alfred (1890–1946),
Chief of the Operations Staff of the
Wehrmacht 1939–45. Hanged at
Nuremberg for war crimes 93, 192,
200, 213, 270, 298, 312, 329, 340,
410
Johst, Hanns (1890–   ), Nazi writer
and dramatist. President of the
Reich Theatre Chamber from 1935
110, 255
Jordan, Rudolf, Gauleiter of
Magdeburg-Anhalt 317
Joyce, William, 'Lord Haw-Haw'
(1906–46). Born in the USA and
brought up in Ireland, Joyce was a
member of the British Union of
Fascists. He fled to Germany in
1939 and was made chief
English-language announcer. In his
broadcasts he affected a

pseudo-aristocratic, mocking tone that led to his nickname. He was hanged in London in 1946 87, 90, 113, 285

Jugos, the. Jenny Jugo, a well-known German film actress, and her husband, friends of the Goebbelses 105, 228, 285

Karajan, Herbert von (1907–), German conductor 161, 189. 205, 213

Kaufmann, Hitler Youth Leader and later in charge of Reich Propaganda Office in Vienna 23, 130, 155, 196, 352, 379

Kaufmann, Karl, Gauleiter of Hamburg 361, 209

Keitel, Gen. (later FM) Wilhelm (1882–1946), Chief of the Wehrmacht High Command. Executed at Nuremberg for war crimes 54, 77, 78, 93, 177, 255, 256, 257, 273, 283

Kennedy, Joseph (1888–1969), US Ambassador to London 1937–40. Father of John Fitzgerald Kennedy 175

Kerrl, Hans (1887–1941), Reich Minister without Portfolio in Hitler's government, with special responsibilities for religious affairs 97, 110, 119, 176, 270

Kiel 309, 320
    aid to 322, 332, 323
    bombing of 265, 274, 306, 307, 318, 319, 333, 335, 337, 353
    Canal 210, 210n

Kiev
    air attacks on 425

Kimmich, Max, German film director. Married to Goebbels' sister Maria 139n, 282, 383

Klagenfurt
    bombing of 303, 304

Klatteradatsch 114, 114n

Klimsch, Fritz, German sculptor 114, 194, 347

Klitsch, Ludwig, Managing Director of Ufa 110

Klöpfer, Eugen, German actor/manager 116, 137

Knappertbusch, Hans, German conductor 197, 299

Knittel, John, Indian-born Swiss novelist, who wrote in both German and English 421

Knox, Frank (1874–1944), American Secretary for the Navy 1940–4 334, 335, 371, 442, 445

Koch, Erich, Gauleiter of East Prussia. From 1941 Reich Commissar in the Ukraine 118, 164, 343, 378, 379, 379n

Köhler, Minister-President 65

Konoye, Prince (1891–1945), Japanese Prime Minister 309

Koryzis, Alexandros, Greek Prime Minister after the death of Metaxas 324

Kotzias, K., Greek politician. Minister-Governor of Athens 1938–41 10, 324, 325, 326, 349

Kraus, Herbert
    The Victors – Afterwards 88, 89

Krauss, Werner, German actor. Played several caricatured Jewish parts in the anti-Semitic hate film Jew Süss 56

Kretschmer, Otto (1912–), highly successful U-boat commander. Later in British POW camp 208 captured by British 308, 335

Kriebel, Hermann (died 1941), leader of the Bund Overland nationalist group in Bavaria during the early 1920s and one of Hitler's chief associates in the attempted Nazi coup in Munich in 1923 238, 239, 240

Kriegk, Otto, Nazi journalist close to Goebbels 264

Krosigk, Lutz Graf Schwerin von (1887–1977), German Finance Minister in 1932 and under Hitler 1933–45. Sentenced to 10 years' imprisonment at Nuremberg but released in 1951 451

Krüger, Arnold 96

Krupps 34, 102, 272

Kube, Wilhelm, Gauleiter of the Ostmark. Later Reich Commissar for Byelorussia. Assassinated by partisans in 1943 256

Kümmel, Geheimrat 150

Kuusinnen, Aino, Finnish Communist leader and Prime Minister of the puppet government installed by the Russians during the 'Winter War' of 1939–40 against Finland 101

Lammers, Hans Heinrich (1879–1962), State Secretary at the Reich Chancellery 44, 118, 119, 125, 176, 256, 292, 303, 372, 380, 412, 418
Langsdorff, Captain of the *Graf Spee* 71
funeral 73
Lauterbacher, Hartmann, Hitler Youth leader. Later Gauleiter of Hannover 95, 199, 211, 259
Laval, Pierre (1883–1945), French politician and collaborator. A former socialist, he joined Pétain's government as Vice-Premier and Foreign Minister in June 1940, but was dismissed in December 1940 because of extreme pro-German activities. Laval was made Prime Minister in 1942 under pressure from the Germans. He was executed in Paris in 1945 after being extradited from Spain, where he had fled on the collapse of the Third Reich 151, 210, 228, 251, 306
meets Hitler 152
resigns Dec. 1940 207, 209
Lawrence, Col. T. E. (Lawrence of Arabia) 319, 348
League of German Girls (BdM) 16, 16n, 33, 64, 205
League of Nations 325
Leander, Zara, Swedish-born star of German light-entertainment films during the Third Reich 92, 106, 135, 153, 184, 189, 297, 321, 337, 422
Leeb, FM Wilhelm Ritter von (1876–1956), Commander of an Army Group on the Western Front in 1940. From June 1941 to January 1942 Commander of the Northern Front in Russia 285, 439
Leibstandarte Division of SS 313, 313n, 328–9, 337, 343–4
Leipzig
Fair 253
Reichwehr Trial 1930 212, 212n

Leonding
Hitler's parents' grave and house 265
Leopold, King of the Belgians 339
Ley, Robert (1890–1945), from 1933 head of the German Labour Front, which controlled trade union activity, industrial relations and mass leisure facilities. Ley committed suicide while awaiting trial at Nuremberg 7, 13, 23, 41, 50, 91, 92, 110, 118, 119, 129, 131, 166, 174, 178, 184, 185, 186, 190, 196, 229, 237, 258, 264, 270, 306, 309, 319, 351, 375, 385, 396, 407, 410, 413, 429, 434, 443, 446
tours West Wall 28
visits Italy Dec. 1939 66
Liebel, Willy, Burgomaster of Nuremberg 91, 178, 179
Liebeneiner, Wolfgang, German film director 117, 176, 233
Bismarck film 163, 174, 176, 196–9 *passim*
Liebknecht, Karl (1871–1919), German socialist leader. Founder of the German Communist Party in January 1919. Murdered after the 'Spartacist' coup in Berlin 442
Life magazine
publishes interview with Hitler 398, 400
Lille
bombing of 430
Lindbergh, Col. Charles Augustus (1902–74), American aviator and opponent of American engagement in the war 322, 332, 335, 341, 381, 390, 400, 445
resigns from US Air Force 340
Lingen, Theo 5
Linz 265, 266, 267, 272, 370
celebrations of *Anschluss* anniversary 1941 265
Göring Works 265, 265n
plans for cultural expansion at 301–2, 321, 370
Lippert, Dr Julius, High Burgomaster of Berlin 4, 7, 17, 84, 93, 95, 124
Lippert, Propaganda Ministry official 339, 396
Lipski, Josef, Polish Ambassador in Berlin to 1939 16

478

Lithuania 122
Liverpool
  bombing of 156, 215, 216, 268, 306,
    337, 347, 349, 350, 354, 393
Lloyd-George, David 29, 107, 299, 354,
    355
  article on Hitler's peace proposals
    1939 14, 16
  attacks British government 22
  fears Russo-German alliance 14n
Lofoten Islands
  British attack on 256, 258, 260, 277
  German punitive court 260, 277
Lohse, Heinrich, Gauleiter of
    Schleswig-Holstein. Later Reich
    Commissar for the *Ostland* (the
    occupied Baltic States) 319, 320,
    379, 379n
London
  bombing of 126, 127, 128, 130, 132–5
    passim, 137, 139–47 *passim*,
    149–60 *passim*, 162, 163, 166, 168,
    169, 170, 172, 173, 175, 180, 185,
    188, 189, 198, 208, 218, 221, 222,
    240, 241, 243, 244, 249, 256, 261,
    265, 275, 276, 320, 326, 361, 362
'Lord Haw-Haw', *see* Joyce, William
Lothian, Philip Kerr, Lord
    (1882–1940), British Ambassador
    to the USA 1939–40 205
Ludwigshafen
  raids on 210, 211
Lueger, Karl (1844–1910), demagogic
    anti-Semitic mayor of Vienna
    1897–1910 23
Luetjens, Adm. Günther (1889–1941),
    Fleet Commander of the German
    Navy from 1940. Went down with
    the *Bismarck* 386
Luftwaffe 109, 113, 120, 128, 130, 135,
    137, 160, 182, 209, 282, 445; losses
    Sept. 1940 136; moves into Winter
    Quarters 1940 140; destroys convoy
    1941 249; in Russian campaign 433,
    442
Lunde, Gulbrand, Norwegian scientist
    and prominent collaborator. A
    member of Quisling's government
    until 1945 277
Lutze, Viktor (1890–1943), Chief of the
    SA 1934–43. Killed in a car crash
    in 1943 216, 221, 248, 269, 270,
    325, 365

Lützow 103
  torpedoed 409
Lvov
  used for German atrocity propaganda
    450, 452, 454

McDonnell, A. G. 217, 217n
MacMillan, Hugh (1873–1952), British
    jurist and politician. Minister of
    Information 1939–40 88
Maček (Matschek), Dr Vladimir, leader
    of the Croat Peasant Party in
    Yugoslavia 296, 297, 300, 309
Maginot Line 122
Mahler, Gustav (1860–1911), composer
    of Austrian-Jewish descent 214
Maisky, Ivan, Soviet Ambassador to
    London 1932–43 28
Malta
  bombing of 227, 230, 231, 233, 234,
    242, 253, 254, 256, 257, 258, 262,
    264, 274, 280, 342, 344, 349, 366,
    368
Manchester
  bombing of 217, 218, 219, 394
Mann, Thomas (1875–1955), German
    novelist and democrat. In exile in
    the USA to 1954 277
Mannerheim, Carl-Gustav Freiherr von
    (1867–1951), French military
    leader. President of Finland
    1944–6 439
Mannheim
  bombing of 204, 209, 212, 342, 351,
    358
Marian, Ferdinand, German actor who
    was to play the lead role Süss
    Oppenheimer in *Jud Süss* 87, 98
Marrenbach, Otto, senior aide to Reich
    Organisation Leader, SS
    Brigadeführer 319, 320
Martin, Major Hans-Leo, Group
    Director in the Propaganda Section
    of the Wehrmacht High Command,
    seconded by Keitel to liaise with
    Goebbels 85, 112, 114, 150, 178,
    211, 242, 254, 264, 265, 289, 294,
    312, 316, 375, 385, 390, 394, 405,
    409, 410, 422, 427, 440
  loses secret documents 141, 143
Matsuoka, Yosuke (1880–1946),
    Japanese Foreign Minister in the
    military government 235, 309, 315,

Matsuoka, Yosuke – *contd*
317, 319, 322, 332, 352, 400: visits
Berlin 261, 264, 276, 282–6 *passim*,
288; visits Moscow 280, 281; visits
Rome 292; meets Stalin 28, 331
Maul 175, 273, 274
Menzel, Gerhard 199
Messerschmitt, Willy (1898–   ),
German aircraft designer and
builder 346
Metaxas, Gen. Ioannis (1871–1941),
Prime Minister of Greece 1936–41
156, 157
Metternich, Prince Klemens von
(1773–1859), Chancellor of the
Austrian Empire 1809–48 155
Meyer, Alfred, Gauleiter of North
Westphalia 203, 380
Michaelis, Hubert von (1857–1936),
Chancellor of Germany 1917 107
Milch, FM Erhard (1892–1972),
Deputy Commander of the
German Luftwaffe. Sentenced to
life imprisonment in 1947 but
released in 1954 176, 180
Minsk 435, 449, 451
captured by Germans 431, 437
Mirković, Gen. 334
Mitford, Unity Valkyrie (1914–48),
English friend and admirer of
Hitler, sister-in-law to Sir Oswald
Mosley. Attempted suicide in
Munich on the outbreak of war,
but recovered and was sent back to
England by Hitler 115
Mölders, Major Werner (1913–41),
German air ace 152
Molotov, Vyacheslav Mikhailovich
(1890–   ), Soviet Foreign Minister
1939–49, 1953–6. Responsible for
negotiating the Nazi-Soviet Pact of
August 1939 28, 169, 170, 171, 315,
353, 354, 420, 425
support for Germany 1939 37, 38, 42
visits Germany Nov. 1940 171–4
passim
Morrison, Herbert (1888–1965), British
Home Secretary 1940–5, Lord
President 1945–51, Foreign
Secretary 1951 204
Moscow Radio 432
Mosley, Sir Oswald (1896–1980),
British politician. Conservative MP

1918–24, Labour MP and Minister
1924, 1929–31. Mosley founded
the 'New Party' in 1931 and in 1932
the British Union of Fascists. He
was finally interned in May 1940
under British war regulations 90,
103
Motta, Giuseppe (1871–1940), Swiss
Foreign Minister 1920–40 and
several times President of the Swiss
Confederation 102
Muir, Phyllis
book on Churchill 416–17
Müller, Georg Wilhelm, personal aide
to Goebbels 1939–40, from 1940
the Propaganda Ministry's
representative in Norway 271, 277,
284, 446
Müller, Ludwig (1883–1945), a former
army chaplain and exponent of
'Aryan Christianity' who was
appointed Hitler's Plenipotentiary
for the Evangelical Church in 1933
and elected 'Reich Bishop' in July
1933 97
Mündler, Eugen, former editor on the
Berliner Tageblatt, a quality daily
with Liberal credentials. Editor of
Das Reich 1940–3 355
Munich 179, 180
air-raids on 168, 170
Art Exhibition 1941 449
Bürgerbräukeller 43, 43n
explosion at Bürgerbräu hall 44, 45,
48, 307
Feldherrnhalle 240, 240n
'German Greatness' exhibition 180,
181
Münster
bombing of 451
Mussert, Anton (1894–1946), Dutch
Nazi leader and collaborator.
Named 'Leader of the Dutch
People' by the Germans in 1942.
Executed in The Hague in 1946
191, 236, 347
Mussolini, Benito (1883–1945), leader
of the Italian Fascist Party and
Duce of Italy 26, 35, 38, 42, 46, 53,
54, 59, 66, 85, 105, 111, 127, 129,
165, 171, 178, 196, 198, 205, 216,
217, 231, 242, 281, 294, 332, 364,
404, 405, 412: tours N. Africa 11;

attacks Greece 156; meets Franco 233; speech of 24 Feb. 1941 243, 244; claims victory in Greece 339. *See also* Hitler, talks with Mussolini

Muti, Ettore, Secretary of the Italian Fascist Party to 1943 37, 99

Mutschmann, Martin, Gauleiter of Saxony. Killed by the Russians in Dresden 1945 65, 252

Naples
  bombing of 207

Napoleon I (1769–1821), Emperor of France 1804–15 207, 286, 415

National Socialist People's Welfare 125, 125n, 126

Naumann, Werner, Director of the Reich Propaganda Office in Breslau to 1940. From 1941 Goebbels' chief aide at the Propaganda Ministry. Designated Goebbels' successor in Hitler's Testament of April 1945 98, 127, 137, 149, 158, 178, 180, 182, 205, 206, 209, 223, 340, 366, 370, 375, 390, 405, 418

Nazi-Soviet Pact 16n

Neue Baseler Zeitung 34, 34n, 35, 56

Neue Zürcher Zeitung 392, 392n

Neurath, Konstantin Freiherr von (1873–1956), diplomat. Ambassador to London and Foreign Minister under the Weimar Republic. Foreign Minister in Hitler's government to 1938. Neurath was appointed 'Reich Protector' of Bohemia and Moravia in March 1939. Sentenced to 15 years' imprisonment at Nuremberg but released in 1954 32, 33, 35, 50, 165–8 *passim*

News Chronicle 28, 378

Nicholas I (1841–1921), Prince of Montenegro from 1862. King from 1910. Deposed 1918 when Montenegro became part of the Yugoslav state 305

Niemöller, Martin (1892–   ), Protestant clergyman and opponent of Nazism. His imprisonment from 1938 was an international scandal 133, 215

Nordic Affiliation Bureau 264

North African campaign 247, 250, 253, 259, 277
  defence of Tobruk 317, 320, 322, 326, 329, 332, 335–6, 339, 345, 349, 351, 383, 389, 394, 399, 402, 413, 428
  progress: Italian defeat 201, 202, 203, 206, 207, 208, 211, 215, 222, 228, 231; German forces in Libya 146, 150, 173; first Anglo-German clashes 249, 264; German supplies to Libya 265, 280; German advance 1941 282, 283, 291, 293, 295, 297–8, 299, 306, 308, 309, 310, 313, 314, 316–20 *passim*, 322, 323, 326, 329; German advance halted 334–7 *passim*, 339, 341, 342, 344; inconclusive fighting 354, 358, 361, 366, 368, 370, 371, 376, 397, 409, 417–22 *passim*, 443

Norway
  German invasion 121
  Norwegian Legion 445
  under German rule 135, 175, 176, 187–9, 191, 216, 271–2, 277, 284, 343, 434–5

Nostradamus (1503–66), French mystic and soothsayer. His enigmatic pronouncements were carefully doctored by a team in the Propaganda Ministry to give them the appearance of predicting a Nazi victory in the war 60, 60n, 89, 95

November Democrats 114, 114n

Nuremberg 178

Obernitz, Gen. 104

Obersalzberg 4, 88, 146, 149, 191, 204, 221, 234, 239, 270, 362
  Berghof 4n, 363

Ohnesorge, Wilhelm, Minister of Posts in Hitler's government 1933–45 20, 41, 346, 378

Oldenburg
  bombing of 273

Oldenburg and Januschau, Graf Elard von. A Prussian landowner and leader of the ultra-reactionary wing of the German Conservative Party before 1918. Neighbour and confidant of President Hindenburg 107

Ondra, Anny, German film actress.
Wife of Max Schmeling 389
Operation Barbarossa 390. *See also*
Russo-German campaign
Oshima, Gen., Japanese Ambassador
to Berlin to 1940. Reappointed
shortly afterwards and remained
ambassador to 1945 101, 218, 285,
306
Ott, Karl, head of the Budget
Department of the Propaganda
Ministry 134, 179, 193

Pacelli, Cardinal (1876–1958), Papal
Nuncio for Bavaria 1917–25, for
the German Reich 1920–9. Elected
as Pope Pius XII in 1938 10
See also Pius XII
Padua, Paul, German sculptor and
painter
Leda with the Swan 343
'Mars and Venus' 218
Papen, Franz von (1879–1969),
Chancellor of Germany
June–December 1932,
Vice-Chancellor under Hitler
1933–4. Minister and Ambassador
in Austria 1934–8, Ambassador to
Turkey 1939–44. Acquitted at
Nuremberg 129, 144n, 204, 256
Paris 148–9, 222, 232, 263
film industry 196
under Germans 313
Paul, Prince Regent, of Yugoslavia
(1893–1976). Regent of Yugoslavia
in the minority of King Peter II,
1930–40 96, 278, 334
deposed 1941 283, 284, 285
Pavelić, Ante (1889–1959), 'Pglavnik'
(Führer) of the Croatian fascist
movement *Ustashi*. Later puppet
ruler of Croatia 309, 391
visits Hitler 401
Pavolini, Alessandro, Alfieri's
successor as Minister of Popular
Culture. Executed with Mussolini
in April 1945 37, 38, 105, 111, 174,
401, 412, 418, 424, 425, 432, 433
visits Hitler in Berlin 1941 422–3,
426, 427, 428
Peace of Westphalia 41, 41n, 51, 116
Pester Lloyd 69, 69n
Pétain, Marshal Philippe (1856–1951),

Marshal of France and hero of
Verdun in World War I.
Vice-Premier of France May 1940
Prime Minister June 1940. French
head of state 1940–4. Sentenced to
death by a French court in 1945 but
sentence commuted to life
imprisonment 107, 154, 155, 159,
160, 207, 220, 223, 231, 232, 278,
346, 355, 369, 371–5 *passim*, 402,
407
meets Franco 233
meets Hitler 154, 156
Peter the Great (1672–1725), Czar of
Russia 1682–75 121
Peters, Carl (1856–1918), German
explorer and colonialist
campaigner 168
Philipp, Prince, of Hesse. Aristocratic
sympathiser with Nazism and
son-in-law of the King of Italy 93,
343, 343n
Piel, Harry
Humans, Animals, Sensations 7
Pilsudski, Marshal Josef (1867–1935),
Military dictator of Poland
1925–35, 37, 37n
Pinelli, Col. 153
Pius XII, Pope 77, 122, 258
Christmas speech 1939 75
Ploesti, Rumania 231, 231n
Plymouth
bombing of 189, 276, 278, 280, 328,
330, 332, 341, 342, 344
Poland
ethnic Germans in 57, 58, 84, 84n
falls to Germany 1939 14, 15
film of battle from 34
German administration 36, 38, 42,
257
German plans for 20, 21, 25, 26
persecution of Jews 420
prisoners collect for German poor
112
Russian behaviour in 94
situation under Germans 51, 57–8,
61, 107, 118, 140, 165, 272
Polverelli, Gaetano, Italian Deputy
Minister of Popular Culture 290
Popolo d'Italia 253, 345
Portsmouth
bombing of 222, 262, 264, 307,
321–2, 330, 333, 339

Prague 165, 166, 173
  Czerny Palace 166
  defenestration of 166, 166n
  Hradschin Castle 165n
  St Vitus' Cathedral 166
Pravda 125
  waves olive branch at Germany 328
Prien, Günther (1909–), highly
  publicised U-boat commander. His
  U-47 sank the British battleship
  Royal Oak in a daring raid on
  Scapa Flow in October 1939 25n,
  57, 74, 149, 159, 164, 308, 380
Priestley, J. B. (1894–), British writer
  and broadcaster 254, 371
Prinz Eugen 386, 386n
Propaganda Companies 28, 28n, 32, 64,
  65, 67, 77, 78, 85, 87, 91, 92, 151,
  186, 187, 190, 240, 242, 256, 258,
  317, 347, 355, 357, 395, 420
  for use in Russia 380, 382

Quandt, Elenore (Ello) 79, 79n, 109,
  135, 192, 213, 219, 220, 228, 375,
  383
Quandt, Harald (1922–67), son of
  Magda Goebbels and Günther
  Quandt, her first husband. Died in
  a car crash in 1967 9, 14, 33, 34, 38,
  75, 76, 92, 99, 142, 165, 170, 230,
  232, 239, 325, 327, 376, 407, 413,
  415
  becomes a paratrooper 141
  decorated 410
  takes part in Crete invasion 381, 399,
  401, 409
Quandt, Ursel 165, 169, 170, 172, 186,
  189, 193, 197, 199, 205, 206, 220,
  232, 239, 241, 242, 253, 270, 279,
  285, 311, 312, 344, 345, 370, 371,
  372, 377, 383, 394, 396, 413
Quisling, Vidkun (1887–1945),
  Norwegian collaborator.
  Norwegian Foreign Minister
  1931–3. Installed by the Germans
  as head of a 'State Council' in 1940,
  as Prime Minister 1942–5.
  Executed in Oslo October 1945
  173, 199, 236, 277
  meets Goebbels 188

Radio Union 293
Raeder, Grand Adm. Erich
  (1876–1960), Commander-in-Chief
of the German Navy 1936–43.
  Sentenced to life imprisonment at
  Nuremberg but released on health
  grounds in 1955 92, 222, 230, 285,
  332, 384, 449
Rainer, Friedrich, Gauleiter of
  Carinthia 193
Rashid Ali, pro-Axis Prime Minister of
  Iraq in 1941 391
Raskin, H., Propaganda Ministry
  official. With Gutterer, originator
  of much of the 'black' propaganda
  disseminated abroad during the
  winter of 1939–40 169, 170, 171,
  175, 177, 183, 234
Rauschning, Hermann, former Nazi
  leader in Danzig. After 1936 an
  active opponent of Hitler from
  exile in Switzerland and Britain 29
Reich Chamber of Culture 6, 7n, 31,
  131, 185, 246, 258, 259, 271, 292,
  359, 390
Reich Circle for National Socialist
  Enlightenment 409
Reich, Das 175, 175n, 194, 208, 210,
  215, 216, 222, 233, 238, 248, 256,
  258, 276, 308, 355, 357, 375, 398
  circulation 194, 246
  prints Goebbels' *The Stubborn
  English* 336
Reich Defence Council 23
Reich Film Chamber 235
Reich Labour Service 296
Reich Propaganda Leadership 180,
  180n, 232, 271, 284, 332, 354
Reich Propaganda Offices 58, 61, 116,
  130, 137, 150, 153, 274, 334, 441
  reports on morale from 441n
Reichenau, Gen. (later FM) Walther
  von (1884–1942), Commander of
  an Army Group in France. Killed
  in an air crash in Russia in 1942 62,
  104, 285
Reichstadt, Duke of (Napoleon II)
  (1811–32), only son of Napoleon I
  and the Empress Marie-Louise 207
Reinecke, Gen. Hermann, Chief of the
  General Wehrmacht Office 103
Reinhardt, Max (1873–1943), theatrical
  director of Austrian-Jewish
  descent, famous in Berlin in the
  1920s. Exiled in the USA after
  1933 214

Reinhardt, Rolf, Amann's personal
adjutant 40, 49, 66, 94, 175, 194,
246, 256, 294, 379, 406, 446
Reith, Sir John (later Lord)
(1889–1971), former
Director-General of the BBC 89,
116
Renzetti, Giuseppe, former Italian
consul in Leipzig and
representative of Italian Chambers
of Trade in Germany. Mussolini's
unofficial emissary to the German
Right since the 1920s 275, 288
Repulse, HMS
torpedoed 22
Request Concerts for Wehrmacht 183n,
245–6, 249
Reynaud, Paul (1878–1966), French
Prime Minister March-June 1940.
Replaced on 16 June 1940 by
Pétain 123
Rheinmetall arms works 272
Rheydt 104
Ribbentropp, Joachim von
(1893–1946), a former wine
salesman who married the heiress
to the Henkel champagne fortune.
Hitler's foreign-policy adviser
1933–6, Ambassador in London
1936–8, Foreign Minister 1938 45.
Hanged at Nuremberg in 1946 3,
12, 30, 31, 32, 67, 76, 88, 96, 105,
109, 129, 136, 137, 145, 149, 150,
151, 166, 168, 170, 175, 176, 177,
189, 190, 194, 198, 236, 264, 267,
290, 291, 364, 410, 418, 422, 423,
425, 426, 427, 437, 442
attacks Goebbels Feb. 1940 115, 116
cold-shouldered 276, 281
Riccardi, Rafaello, Italian Minister of
Commerce 145
Richards, James 117n
Richthofen, Gen. Wolfgang Freiherr
von (1895–1945), Luftwaffe
commander. Committed suicide in
1945 104
Riefenstahl, Leni (1902–   ), German
film actress and producer/director
Lowlands film 194, 250, 259
reports to Goebbels on American trip
9
Riga
captured by Germans 439, 441

Ritter, Prof. Carl, prominent German
film director and producer 4, 12,
137, 144, 277, 278
River Plate, Battle of 66–71 *passim*, 86
Robin More
sinking of 404, 410, 413, 421
Rommel, Gen. (later FM) Erwin
(1891–1944), German Commander
in North Africa and 'Germany's
most popular general'.
Commander in Italy 1943.
Inspector of Western Defences
1943–4. Forced to commit suicide
in October 1944 because of his
complicity in July 1944 plot against
Hitler 295, 306, 308, 316, 334, 336,
337, 339, 358, 399, 450: given
command in Africa 241; decorated
by Hitler 275; promoted June 1941
419
Roosevelt, Eleanor (1884–1962), wife
of Franklin D. Roosevelt 241
Roosevelt, Franklin Delano
(1882–1945), President of the USA
1933–45 9, 14n, 15, 87, 123, 128,
142, 144, 160, 161, 172, 210, 211,
215, 249, 250, 261, 267, 269, 271,
279, 288, 310, 314, 321, 326, 327,
328, 334, 355, 371, 379, 380, 386,
400, 412: lifts arms embargo 1939
33, 40; peace offensive Feb. 1940
119; re-elected 1940 167; attacks
Germany Dec. 1940 222, 223
Roosevelt, James 310, 449
Rosay, François, French broadcaster 78
Rosenberg, Alfred (1893–1946), Nazi
theorist. Author of *The Myth of the
Twentieth Century* (1930), head of
the Foreign Political Office of the
Nazi Party from 1933, and from
1941 Minister for the Eastern
Territories. Executed at
Nuremberg in 1946 7, 55, 60, 63,
72, 110, 113, 181, 229, 237, 276,
356, 390, 407, 411, 436, 445
receives promotion Feb. 1940 118,
119
Ross, Colin (1885–1945), German
journalist and travel writer 121
Rothermere, Harold, Viscount
(1868–1940), British press baron,
owner of the *Daily Mail* 49
Royal Oak, HMS

484

sinking of 21, 22, 24, 25n
Rühmann, Heinz, German character
    actor 105, 157
Ruhr, the
    bombing of 247, 409, 425
Rumania 117, 146, 184, 203, 230, 232,
    236, 239, 327, 397, 412
    approach to war: loses territory to
        Hungary and Russia 139, 139n;
        accedes to Three-Power Pact 184;
        ready to attack Russia 415; moves
        against Russians 445, 446, 450
    German invasion 135, 135n, 136, 142,
        220, 221
    situation Jan. 1940 85
Rundstedt, FM Gerd von (1875–1953),
    Commander of the Southern Front
    in Russia to December 1941.
    Commander-in-Chief in the West
    1942–4, in charge of Ardennes
    offensive of December 1944 439
Russia 191, 203
    German plan of attack 286, 368,
        413–15, 422, 423
    German plans to divide up 379n, 380,
        400
    progress of events: trade delegation
        in Berlin Oct. 1939 32; war with
        Finland, see Russo-Finnish War;
        occupies Baltic coast 122; takes
        Bessarabia from Rumania 139;
        reaction to German occupation of
        Bulgaria 255; signs Treaty of
        Friendship with Japan 314–17
        passim; German troops massed to
        attack 409; invaded by Germany
        424
Russo-Finnish War 56, 58, 59, 60, 64,
    66, 67–8, 72, 74, 75, 87, 98, 101,
    103, 119
Russo-German campaign
    German Army Organisation 439
    German transmitters aimed at 438–9,
        442, 444, 448, 452
    progress: Germans invade 424, 425,
        426; early Russian losses 426–7,
        428, 437, 443, 447, 448; German
        penetration July 1941 430, 431,
        433, 435, 436, 437, 439, 441, 443,
        445–6, 448, 449–52 passim, 454
    Russian bombing of Germany 430
    Russian news and propaganda 434,
        436, 439–40, 441

Rust, Bernard (1883–1945), Reich
    Minister for Science, Education
    and Culture 1933–45 and Gauleiter
    of Hannover to 1940. Committed
    suicide in May 1945 110, 119, 176,
    204, 211, 234, 249
Ryti, Risto, President of Finland
    1940–4 213

Sandler, Rickard Johannes, Swedish
    Foreign Minister to 1939 66
Sauer, Prof. 155, 156, 161
Scaroglu, Sükrü, Foreign Minister of
    Turkey in 1941. Prime Minister
    1942–6 276
Schaub, Julius, SS Obergruppenführer.
    Personal aide to Hitler 194
Schaffner, Jacob 56, 56n
Schaumberg-Lippe, Prince Friedrich
    Christian zu (1906–   ), from 1933
    Goebbels' chief adjutant 113, 117,
    124, 223, 251, 254, 257, 453
Scheinfuss, Dr 61
Schell, Col. von 114
Schepke, Capt. 308, 335
Schickedanz, Arno, Chief-of-Staff to
    Rosenberg in the Foreign
    Department of the Party 379
Schiller Foundation 61
Schirach, Baldur von (1907–74), Reich
    Leader of the Hitler Youth and
    later Gauleiter of Vienna.
    Sentenced to 20 years'
    imprisonment at Nuremberg 40,
    95, 130, 132, 154, 155, 156, 165,
    197, 244, 245, 267, 290, 379
Schirmeister, M. A. von, Goebbels'
    personal press aide until 1943 67,
    84, 124, 151, 239
Schlajapin, Marina 285, 311, 312, 314,
    325, 327
Schleicher, Kurt von (1882–1934),
    army officer and last Chancellor of
    the Weimar Republic December
    1932 to January 1933. Murdered by
    Hitler's agents during the purge of
    June 1934 19, 204
Schlösser, Rainer, 'Reich Dramaturge'
    from 1940 90, 101, 138, 150, 218,
    290
Schmalz, Rust's deputy as Gauleiter of
    Hannover to 1940. Later Deputy

Schmalz – *contd*
 Gauleiter of Hamburg 199, 211,
 275
Schmeling, Max (1905–), World
 Heavyweight boxing champion
 1930–2. Served with airborne
 forces in World War II. From 1957
 owner of a Coca-Cola franchise in
 Hamburg 388, 389, 395
 taken prisoner in Crete 400
Schmidt, Col. 352
Schmidt-Holland 347, 442
Schmitz, Ludwig 419
Schmundt, Col. Rudolf (1896–1944),
 Hitler's adjutant and Chief of
 Army Personnel 1942–4. Killed in
 the attempt on Hitler's life in July
 1944 77, 78, 79, 90, 92, 93, 212, 273
Schobert, Gen. Eugen Ritter von,
 Commander of Defence District
 VII (East Prussia) 1940–1.
 Commander of the 11th Army
 during the invasion of Russia 253
Scholtze-Klink, Gertrud (1902–),
 Reich Leader of National Socialist
 Womanhood 296, 409
Schopenhauer, Arthur (1788–1860),
 German philosopher 138, 304
Schulenburg, Count Friedrich von der
 (1895–), German Ambassador in
 Moscow 1934–41 28, 90
Schwarz, Franz-Xavier, Treasurer of the
 Nazi Party 1925–45. Reichsleiter
 203
Schwarz van Berk, Hans, Nazi
 journalist. Political editor of
 Goebbels' newspaper *Das Reich*
 from 1940 96, 139, 140, 151, 412,
 420
Schwartzev, Soviet Ambassador in
 Berlin 1939–40 185
Schweitzer, Hans, Nazi artist, best
 known for his biting political
 cartoons, published in Goebbels'
 Berlin newspaper *Der Angriff*
 under the pseudonym 'Mjölnir'
 181n, 218, 453
SD (*Sicherheitsdienst*) 42, 42n, 116, 236,
 255
 captures British agents 1939 52, 52n
 on German reaction to Hess
 defection 373
 report praising Goebbels' work 315

reports on German morale 132, 141,
 158, 170, 172, 239, 265, 287, 296–7,
 353, 359, 365, 392, 399, 406, 412,
 418, 436, 444, 450
Seldte, Franz (1992–1947), leader of
 the nationalist ex-servicemen's
 organisation the *Stahlhelm* to 1933.
 Minister of Labour 1932–3 and
 under Hitler 1933–45 178
Semler, Rudolf, Press Officer to the
 Propaganda Ministry 1940–5
 214
Serano, Rosita 204
Severing, Carl, Social-Democratic
 politician. Minister of the Interior
 in Prussia 1925–32 13
Seyss-Inquart, Arthur (1892–1946),
 Frank's deputy in Poland 1939–40.
 Reich Commissar for the Occupied
 Netherlands 1940–5. Executed at
 Nuremberg in 1946 19, 36, 107,
 246, 247, 248, 260, 284, 442
Shaw, George Bernard (1856–1951),
 Anglo-Irish dramatist, critic and
 commentator 17, 18, 23, 29, 68
 On the Peace Conference 119, 120
Sheffield
 bombing of 205, 206, 208, 269
Siebert, Ludwig, Prime Minister of
 Bavaria 1933–42, 181, 254
Sima, Horia, leader of the Rumanian
 fascists, the 'Legion of the
 Archangel Michael' (also known as
 the Iron Guard) 139n, 184, 235,
 282
Simon, Gustav, Gauleiter of Moselland
 Gau. Later head of Civil
 Administration in Luxembourg 61,
 70, 250, 354
Simon, Sir John (1873–1954),
 Chancellor of the Exchequer and
 senior member of Chamberlain's
 war cabinet 45
Simović, Gen. Dusan (1882–1962),
 appointed Prime Minister of
 Yugoslavia in March 1941. From
 April 1941 Prime Minister of
 government-in-exile in Palestine
 298, 309, 316, 332, 334
Simplicissimus 195–6
Skoda arms works 33–4, 272
Smuts, Gen. (later FM) Jan Christiaan
 (1870–1950), Prime Minister of

South Africa 1910–24, 1939–48, 349

Soldmann, Lt-Col. 366

Somaliland: Italian advance 124; British successes 249, 273; Italian retreat 251, 254

South Tyroleans 39, 39n, 208–9

Southampton
bombing of 179, 189, 190, 193, 195, 245

Spaak, Paul-Henri (1889–1972), Belgian Prime Minister 1939–9, 1946, 1947–9. Secretary-General of NATO 1957–61 34

Spain 431
situation Jan. 1940 85
situation Nov. 1940 160, 162, 164
situation March-April 1941 281, 292, 298
volunteers for Russian front 438

Speer, Albert (1905–81), Hitler's personal architect and Minister for War Production 1942–5. Sentenced to 20 years' imprisonment at Nuremberg 4, 97, 132, 333
job of providing Berlin AR shelters 132

Sperrle, FM Hugo (1885–1953), Luftwaffe commander in Paris 148

Spoletto, Duke of (Prince Aimone of Savoy) (1900–48), son of Victor Emmanuel II, King of Italy. Reigned as King Tomoslav of Croatia 1941–3 370, 370n, 372, 373

Stalin, Josef Vissarionovich (1879–1953), First Secretary of the Soviet Communist Party to 1953 15, 16, 27, 77, 90, 121, 159, 185, 315, 319, 328, 332, 348, 351, 353, 354, 356, 397, 400, 411, 414, 416, 434, 444, 446, 448
approves Axis Pact 125, 126
meets Matsuoka 281, 331
sixtieth birthday 1939 72
worried about German attack 361

Stanley, Edward, Lord, Secretary of State for the Dominions until his death 11

Stanley, Oliver F. G. (1896–1950), British Secretary of State for War 1940–2 113

Starace, Achille, Secretary of the

Italian Fascist Party to 1939 37, 39, 54, 66, 391

Stavanger
bombed by British 227

Stennes, Walther, former 'Supreme Leader' of the SA. Expelled from the Nazi Party with his dissident followers in 1931 273, 298

Stephan, Werner, Propaganda Ministry official responsible for co-ordinating the photographic work of the Propaganda Companies 258, 353, 447

Stevens, Major 52n

Stimson, Henry Lewis (1867–1950), American Secretary for War 1940–45 353

Stoddard, Lothrop (1883–1950), American writer on international affairs 91, 93

Stohrer, Everhard von, German Ambassador in Spain 373

Stojadinović, Milan (1888–1961), pro-German Prime Minister and Foreign Minister of Yugoslavia 1935–9. Exiled from 1940 9, 276, 279

Strasser, Otto (1897–1974), a leading member of the radical wing of the Nazi Party until his expulsion by Hitler in 1930, when he founded his own party, the Union of Revolutionary National Socialists or 'Black Front'. His brother, Gregor Strasser, who remained as Hitler's most powerful opponent within the Party, was murdered in the 1934 purge. Otto Strasser continued his anti-Hitler activities from exile after 1933 50, 91
and Munich assassination attempt on Hitler 50, 54, 307

Strauss, Richard (1864–1949), German composer. President of the Reich Music Chamber 250, 253, 258

Streicher, Julius (1885–1946), Gauleiter of Franconia from 1935 and editor of the notorious anti-Semitic weekly Der Stürmer. Dismissed as Gauleiter late in 1940, he continued to publish Der Stürmer and exercise considerable influence. Streicher was executed

Streicher, Julius – *contd*
    at Nuremberg in 1946 91, 176, 178
Strength through Joy (*Kraft durch Freude*) organisation 21, 21n
Stritzky espionage case 397, 399, 400
Studnicki, Prof. Wladislaw 118, 118n
Stumpff, Col.-Gen Hans-Jürgen, Officer commanding the Luftwaffe in Norway 188
Suez Canal
    damaged by Germans 233
    raids on 256, 268
Suisse, La 336
Sunderland
    bombing of 335
Sündermann, Helmut, Dietrich's chief-of-staff at the Reich Press Office 229
Suñer, Ramón Serrano (1901–   ), Foreign Minister of Spain 1939–42 162, 164, 177, 178, 356, 373
Swansea
    bombing of 240–3 *passim*
Symo, Margit 269, 339
Syria 368, 370, 372
    British move into 370–3 *passim*, 376, 377, 396, 398, 401–4 *passim*, 407, 417, 418, 419, 421, 430, 451

Tannenberg, Battle of 447, 447n
Taranto
    British naval attack on 172, 173, 175, 178
Taubert, Eberhard, Propaganda Ministry Official. Director of the 'Anti-Comintern' and chief racial specialist 380, 381, 382, 405, 408
Teleki, Count Paul (1879–1941), Prime Minister of Hungary 1920–2, 1939–41. Committed suicide in 1941 85, 193, 296, 297, 322
Terboven, Josef (1898–1945), Gauleiter of Essen, Senior President of the Rhine Province, and later Reich Commissar for Norway. Committed suicide on Germany's surrender in May 1945 61, 62, 96, 105, 173, 176, 187, 190, 192, 195, 199, 216, 258, 260, 277, 284, 397
Thomalla, Dr 10
Threepenny Opera, The 16
Three-Power (Tripartite) Pact 125, 125n, 180, 184, 191, 413
Thyssen, Fritz (1873–1951), German industrialist and financial supporter of Hitler before 1933. Thyssen later turned against the Nazis and fled to Switzerland, from where he sent an accusing letter to Hitler on 28 December 1939 86, 86n
I Paid Hitler 86n
Tiessler, Walter, Director of the Reich Circle for National Socialist Propaganda, responsible for co-ordinating propaganda at all levels of the Party 249, 325, 357, 375, 377, 378, 387, 397, 407, 419, 420, 431, 436, 438
Tietjen, Heinz (1881–1967), Director of the Prussian State Theatre 1930–44 and of the Bayreuth Festival 1933–44, and postwar director of the opera houses in Berlin and Hamburg 311
Times, The 105, 111, 193, 215, 288, 405, 428, 443, 451
    attacked by German press 112
    expects German attack on Russia 406
    on German propaganda 88
Todt, Fritz (1891–1942), engineer and leader of the 'Organisation Todt', responsible for major public works and military construction, including the building of the West Wall. Reich Minister for Armaments and Munitions until his death in the air accident in 1942 19, 350;
    Organisation Todt 12n
    works on French coast 290
Torgler, Ernst, Communist politician and a defendant at the Reichstag fire trial in 1933. Held in custody by the Nazis and later used by Goebbels to assist with propaganda against the Soviet Union 307, 444
Transozean agency 268, 268n, 269, 311, 324, 354, 399
Trenker, Luis, film director and actor, born in the South Tyrol when it was part of the Austrian Empire, and prominent in the German film scene at this time 98
Treviranus, Gottfried, German nationalist politician and opponent

of Hitler. Exiled from 1934 in Britain and Canada 29

Troost, Frau, wife of Prof. Paul Ludwig Troost (died 1934), Hitler's favourite architect. Frau Troost completed her husband's 'House of German Art' in Munich after his death 181

Tschammer, Hans von Osten, Reich Director of Sport, 300

Tschimmer, Propaganda Ministry Official, 59, 73, 151

Tsolokagliou, Gen. George, Commander of the Army of Epirus and first collaborationist Prime Minister of Greece. Executed in Athens in 1945 340

Turkey 56, 157, 158, 162, 184, 212, 250, 253, 254, 262, 276, 319
  earthquake 1939 79, 85
  pact with England and France 1940 26, 27
  signs non-aggression pact with Bulgaria 238
  signs Treaty of Friendship with Germany 418, 419
  situation in 1940 129

U-47
  sinks *Royal Oak* 25n

Ucicky, Gustav von, leading German film director 75, 79, 131

Ufa (Universal-Film-Aktiengesellschaft) 10, 10n, 12, 13, 93, 102, 110, 121, 172, 190, 196, 281, 334, 374, 427

Ukraine 284, 415

Ullrich, Frau 191

Uschla (Committee for Investigation and Adjustment) 257, 257n

'Venlo Incident' 52n

Vienna 154–6, 161, 197–8, 266, 272, 352
  Clock Museum 197

Volhynia Germans 84, 101
  film on 112
  resettlement 98, 106

Völkischer Beobachter 8, 13, 304, 306, 315, 319, 387, 444, 451, 452
  Goebbels attacks Churchill in 218, 221
  Goebbels' *Crete as an Example* in 404, 405, 406, 408–11 *passim*, 413

Goebbels' *The Old Alliance* in 429, 431
  seized in deception plot 408

Volksempfänger radios 22n

Von Heeren, German Minister in Belgrade 286, 287

Vreme 235

Wächter, Werner, Director of the Reich Propaganda Office in Berlin 59, 122, 181, 186, 222, 232, 374, 432, 436, 452
  presents Hitler with French cartoons of himself 325

Wagner, Adolf, Gauleiter of Munich-Upper Bavaria 93, 126, 176, 181, 298

Waldegg, Propaganda Ministry official. Later on active service 4, 84, 222

Wang-Ching-Wei (1883–1944), puppet Prime Minister of Japanese-occupied China 443

Ward Price, George (1886–1961), British journalist, granted an interview with Hitler before the war with Goebbels' help 71

Warsaw 37
  Belvedere Castle 37, 38n

Warschauer Zeitung 107

Wavell, FM Sir A.P. (later Earl) Wavell (1883–1950), British commander in North Africa to June 1941 317, 445, 447
  transferred to India 443–4

Wehrmacht 50, 118, 119, 127, 214
  anti-Nazi feeling in 70
  attitude in Poland 36, 53, 98, 103
  control of propaganda 261
  has home rations reduced 23
  listens to foreign radio 89
  promises attacks on British residential areas 321
  relations with churches 72

Weimar Republic 114n, 219n

Weise, Col.-Gen. 146, 161, 174, 219

Weizsäcker, Ernst Freiherr von (1882–1951), State Secretary at the Foreign Ministry. German Ambassador to the Vatican 1943–5 420

Welles, Sumner (1882–1961), US Under-Secretary of State 119, 413, 429

Wells, H. G. (1866–1946), British
writer 105
Werra, Franz von (1914–41), Luftwaffe
officer who escaped from a British
POW camp in Canada and
eventually returned to Germany
via the USA, the only German to
do so. Lost over the North Sea in
October 1941 320, 331, 352
West Wall (Siegfried Line) 12, 12n, 24,
28, 32, 63, 74, 98, 110
Westrick, Dr 171
Weygand, Gen. Maxime Louis
(1867–1965), Commander-in-Chief
of the French army in 1940.
Interned in Germany 1942–5 259,
278
Wheeler, Burton, US Senator and
leading opponent of intervention
331, 332, 381, 445
Wiedemann, Fritz, formerly Hitler's
personal adjutant and from 1939
German Consul-General in San
Francisco 49, 215
Wiegand, Karl H. von, American
journalist, senior correspondent of
the Hearst Press 134, 317, 328
Wiener Freie Presse 5
Wienfilm 155
Wild, Col. von 242, 244
Wilhelm I (1797–1888), King of Prussia
1861–71. Emperor of Germany to
1888 114
Wilhelm II, Kaiser (1858–1941),
Emperor of Germany 1888–1918.
Abdicated in November 1918 and
went into exile at Doorn in Holland
112, 126, 391, 392
death 396
Wilhelmine, Queen, of Netherlands 141
Wilhelmshaven 283
bombing of 273, 290, 344
Winter Aid Fund 17, 17n, 244, 248, 276,
291, 329
Willkie, Wendell Lewis (1882–1944),
Republican candidate in the 1940
American presidential election
127–8, 142, 144, 160, 161, 229, 234,
268
Wilson, Thomas Woodrow
(1856–1924), President of the USA
1913–21 208
Winant, John Gilbert, American

Ambassador to London 1941–6
408
Windsor, Edward, Duke of
(1894–1972), heir to the British
throne 1910–36. King Edward VIII
January–December 1936 17, 17n,
344, 345
Winkler, Dr Max, financial controller of
the German film industry and a
close confidant of Goebbels 8, 102,
143, 161, 165, 196, 259, 284, 355
Wir Fahren gegen England 108, 108n
Wirth, Josef (1879–1956), German
Catholic politician. Chancellor of
Germany 1920–2, exiled after 1933
29
Woche
interviews Goebbels 264, 270, 278
Wodarg, Col. Rudolf, Deputy Chief of
Luftwaffe Intelligence in charge of
propaganda 130, 156, 160, 170,
174, 215, 282, 285, 365, 394, 402,
433
Woolton, Lord, British Minister of
Food 1940–4 239, 247

Yonäi, Adm. Mitsumasa, Japanese
Prime Minister in 1940 97
York, HMS 389, 391
Yugoslavia 56, 92, 96, 212, 276, 278,
280: authorities have talks with
Hitler 234, 235; accommodation
with Germany 281; demonstrations
against German Pact 282, 283, 286,
289; coup d'état March 1941 283,
284, 285; German plan of attack
285–6, 288, 289, 294, 298, 301;
fears German attack 287, 293, 297;
mobilises against Germans 299,
300; German invasion 302–4, 306,
307, 308, 310, 311, 313–16 *passim*,
318, 319; asks for truce 317;
surrenders to Germany 321, 322,
334; aftermath of defeat in 326

Zabern Incident 273, 273n
Ziegler, Adolf, sculptor. President of
the Reich Chamber of Art 255
Zionist Protocols 38, 38n, 39
Zita, Empress (1892–), wife of Karl
II, last Emperor of
Austria-Hungary (1916–18) 108